Mr. Ellery Queen
West 87th St.
Criminology Applied

HERE'S WHAT THEY SAID THE FIRST TIME AROUND:

The Adventures of Ellery Queen
"A collection of . . . distinguished merit."

—Isaac Anderson
The New York Times Book Review
November 18, 1934

The New Adventures of Ellery Queen
"As good as they come."

—*The New Yorker*
January 6, 1940

"Clever no end."

—*Saturday Review*
December 30, 1939

"As puzzle makers, the two men who write under the name of Ellery Queen have few equals."

—Isaac Anderson
The New York Times Book Review
January 7, 1940

Books by Ellery Queen
Available in Library of Crime Classics® Editions:

Cat of Many Tails
The Ellery Queen Omnibus
one volume containing:
The Adventures of Ellery Queen
The New Adventures of Ellery Queen

The Drury Lane/Barnaby Ross Novels:
The Tragedy of X
The Tragedy of Y
The Tragedy of Z
Drury Lane's Last Case

THE ELLERY QUEEN OMNIBUS

INTERNATIONAL POLYGONICS, LTD.
NEW YORK CITY

THE ELLERY QUEEN OMNIBUS

The Adventures of Ellery Queen
Copyright © 1933, 1934 Ellery Queen. Ellery Queen
renewal copyright 1961.

The New Adventures of Ellery Queen
Copyright © 1940 Ellery Queen. Ellery Queen renewal
copyright 1967.
Reprinted with permission of the authors' estates and Scott
Meredith Literary Agency.

Cover: Copyright © 1988 by International Polygonics, Ltd.
Library of Congress Card Catalog No. 88-82352
ISBN 1-55882-001-9

Printed and manufactured in the United States of America.
First IPL printing November 1988.
10 9 8 7 6 5 4 3 2 1

ACKNOWLEDGEMENTS

The Adventures of Ellery Queen

The Author wishes to express his gratitude to *Red Book, Mystery, Great Detective* and *Mystery League* for permission to include certain stories which appeared in their publications.

The New Adventures of Ellery Queen

The author wishes to express his gratitude to *Detective Story, Red Book, American, Cavalcade* and *Blue Book* for permission to include certain copyrighted stories which appeared in their publications as listed below.

The Lamp of God, Treasure Hunt: 1935, Detective Story
The Hollow Dragon: 1936, Red Book
The House of Darkness: 1935, American
The Bleeding Portrait (under the title Beauty and the Beast): 1937, Cavalcade
Man Bites Dog, Mind Over Matter, Long Shot, Trojan Horse: 1939, Blue Book

CONTENTS

The Adventure of THE AFRICAN TRAVELER 3

The Adventure of THE HANGING ACROBAT 31

The Adventure of THE ONE-PENNY BLACK 65

The Adventure of THE BEARDED LADY 93

The Adventure of THE THREE LAME MEN 127

The Adventure of THE INVISIBLE LOVER 161

The Adventure of THE TEAKWOOD CASE 189

The Adventure of "THE TWO-HEADED DOG" 215

The Adventure of THE GLASS-DOMED CLOCK 251

The Adventure of THE SEVEN BLACK CATS 281

The Adventure of THE MAD TEA-PARTY 315

A Short Novel

THE LAMP OF GOD 359

CONTENTS

New Adventures

The Adventure of THE TREASURE HUNT 447

The Adventure of THE HOLLOW DRAGON 473

The Adventure of THE HOUSE OF DARKNESS 503

The Adventure of THE BLEEDING PORTRAIT 533

A Unique Group of Ellery Queen
Sports Mysteries

Baseball: MAN BITES DOG 563

Horse-Racing: LONG SHOT 589

Pugilism: MIND OVER MATTER 613

Football: TROJAN HORSE 641

FOREWORD

In the past your humble prefator has garnered a vicarious fame by acting as master of ceremonies, *entrepreneur*, and general buffer between Mr. Ellery Queen and his public; and has, indeed, been quite happy in the task. In serving in my customary capacity in this volume, however, I must confess that I stand in the shadow of my friend by courtesy only, drawn there by the old fascination and a certain irresistible tug of habit. For while in the past I have had my legitimate excuse—I was personally responsible, for instance, for the introduction of Ellery's cases to the reading public—I have no tittle of excuse for participation in the present. In fact, this whole thing has come as a surprise to me.

The first I knew about it Ellery called me up and said: "Look here, J.J., you've been perfectly splendid about these things in the past—"

"What things?" I said.

"Forewords and things. You see—"

"What *are* you talking about?"

"Well," said Ellery rather sheepishly, "I've been bitten by the bug, J.J. I'm afraid your job as official goad and prodder extraordinary has become outmoded. I was looking over some of my notes not long ago—"

"Don't tell me," I cried, "you've unearthed some case I'm ignorant of!"

"Oodles of them. Fact is, there were so many I couldn't resist them. A few of them you know about.

Remember Mason—Phineas Mason, of the Park Row law firm?"

"Of course . . . By George! I sent him to you in that Shaw matter."

"Exactly. Then you went out of town or something —I don't believe you ever found out what happened. Well, that's one of them. I've already done a good deal of work and they'll be out in volume form very soon. Er—would you write a foreword, as usual?"

The truth of the matter is that I couldn't refuse Ellery, and he said that for various reasons it was impossible to turn the manuscript over to me; so in my travail I went to Sergeant Velie.

"Sergeant," I said pleadingly, "do you know anything about this book Ellery Queen's getting up?"

"What book?" growled the good Sergeant. He seemed suspicious. "He's always writing a book."

I realized that I couldn't even tell Velie what book it was. "There's something in it," I said hopefully, "about Mason and the Shaw case."

"Mason and the Shaw case . . ." Velie rubbed his steel jaw. "Oh, that one!" And he began to chuckle. "What a case that was!"

"Ah, then you do know something about it," I said with a sigh of relief. "Well, Sergeant, how would you like to write a little foreword for the volume? You know—for friendship's sake, and all that sort of thing."

"*Me?*" gasped Sergeant Velie, and he began to back away. " 'Scuse me, Mr. McC—, I think the Inspector's waitin' for me."

The Inspector may have been waiting for Velie, but it was I who got there first. I found the old gentleman up to his ears in reports, and apparently in a high dudgeon about something appurtenant to his office.

The moment did not seem propitious for the request, but I confess I was a desperate man, and I blurted it out without ceremony.

Inspector Queen put down his pen and sucked some snuff into his nostrils and leaned back in his chair. "Sit down, McC—," he said, not unkindly. "I want to talk to you like a Dutch uncle. I know you're a good friend of El's, and all that; but did it ever occur to you you're a sucker for a left jab?"

"A su—" It rather took the wind out of my sails. "I'm afraid I don't understand, Inspector."

"That's the trouble with my son's friends," sighed the old gentleman. "He hypnotizes 'em, or something. Don't you realize that for five or six years he's been victimizing you?"

"Victimizing me!"

"Exactly. He should have been a ward leader. Makin' you do all that work!"

"But it's been a pleasure, an—an honor," I protested, aghast.

The Inspector's frosty blue eyes twinkled. "That's the beauty of his technique," he said dryly. "Makes you work and like it, too. You're determined to keep on writing pretty little forewords for his books?"

"I don't think you get the point, Inspector," I began. "I'm asking you if *you* wouldn't be kind enough, under the circumstances—"

"Well, I've been trying to tell you," chuckled the old gentleman. "The answer is: I wouldn't. Honor's all yours." Then he added, with what I found to be a maddening thoughtfulness, "But they *were* pips, some of 'em."

I bit my nails. "What on earth am I to do? Ellery says this is rather a rush job—"

"Now, now, don't be stampeded," said the Inspector with a sort of pitying look. "I know just how you feel. El's been jumping me through hoops so long I'm kind of dizzy myself. Why don't you just scribble down that I wouldn't help you? Might give El a laugh, and it will fill a couple of pages."

And so here I am, grateful even for that suggestion. Ellery knows nothing of what I am doing—he's off somewhere in Minnesota tracking down a murderer who persists in removing the left forefinger of his victims— and I daresay he will complain at my lack of resourcefulness.

If there is one redeeming feature of the affair it is that I find myself in the pleasant and unaccustomed position—at least insofar as Ellery Queen's memoirs are concerned—of looking forward to a few nights of exciting reading. I suggest we indulge our pleasure together!

J. J. McC.

New York

The Adventure of
THE AFRICAN TRAVELER

The Adventure of
THE AFRICAN TRAVELER

Mr. Ellery Queen, wrapped loosely in English tweeds and reflections, proceeded—in a manner of speaking—with effort along the eighth-floor corridor of the Arts Building, that sumptuous citadel of the University. The tweeds were pure Bond Street, for Ellery was ever the sartorial fellow; whereas the reflections were Americanese, Ellery's ears being filled with the peculiar patois of young male and female collegians, and he himself having been Harvard, 'Teen.

This, he observed severely to himself as he lanced his way with the ferrule of his stick through a brigade of yelling students, was higher education in New York! He sighed, his silver eyes tender behind the lenses of his *pince-nez;* for, possessing that acute faculty of observation so essential to his business of studying criminal phenomena, he could not help but note the tea-rose complexions, the saucy eyes, and the osier figures of various female students in his path. His own Alma Mater, he reflected gloomily, paragon of the educational virtues that it was, might have been better, far better off had it besprinkled its muscular classes with nice-smelling co-eds like these—yes, indeed!

Shaking off these unprofessorial thoughts, Mr. Ellery Queen edged gingerly through a battalion of giggling girls and approached Room 824, his destination, with dignity.

He halted. A tall and handsome and fawn-eyed young woman was leaning against the closed door, so obviously

3

lying in wait for him that he began, under the buckling tweeds, to experience a—good lord!—a trepidation. Leaning, in fact, on the little placard which read:

CRIMINOLOGY, APPLIED
MR. QUEEN

This was, of course, sacrilege. . . . The fawn-eyes looked up at him soulfully, with admiration, almost with reverence. What did a member of the faculty do in such a predicament? Ellery wondered with a muted groan. Ignore the female person, speak to her firmly—?

The decision was wrested from his hands and, so to speak, placed on his arm. The brigand grasped his left biceps with devotional vigor and said in fluty tones: "You're Mr. Ellery Queen, himself, aren't you?"

"I—"

"I *knew* you were. You've the nicest eyes. Such a queer color. Oh, it's going to be *thrilling,* Mr. Queen!"

"I beg your pardon."

"Oh, I didn't say, did I?" The hand, which he observed with some astonishment was preposterously small, released his tingling biceps. She said sternly, as if in some way he had fallen in her estimation: "And you're the famous detective. Hmm. Another illusion blasted. . . . Old Icky sent me, of course."

"Old *Icky?*"

"You don't know even that. Heavens! Old Icky is Professor Ickthorpe, B.A., M.A., Ph.D., and goodness knows what else."

"Ah!" said Ellery. "I begin to understand."

"And high time, too," said the young woman severely. "Furthermore, Old Icky is my father, do you see. . . ." She became all at once very shy, or so Ellery reasoned, for the black lashes with their impossible sweep dropped suddenly to veil eyes of the ultimate brownness.

"I do see, Miss Ickthorpe." Ickthorpe! "I see all too clearly. Because Professor Ickthorpe—ah—inveigled me into giving this fantastic course, because you are Professor Ickthorpe's daughter, you think you may wheedle your way into my group. Fallacious reasoning," said Ellery, and planted his stick like a standard on the floor. "I think not. No."

Her slipper-toe joggled his stick unexpectedly, and he flailed wildly to keep from falling. "Do come off your perch, Mr. Queen. . . . There! That's settled. Shall we go in, Mr. Queen? Such a nice name."

"But—"

"Icky has arranged things, bless him."

"I refuse abso—"

"The Bursar has been paid his filthy lucre. I have my B.A., and I'm just dawdling about here working for my Master's. I'm really very intelligent. Oh, come on —don't be so professorish. You're much too nice a young man, and your *devastating* silv'ry eyes—"

"Oh, very well," said Ellery, suddenly pleased with himself. "Come along."

It was a small seminar room, containing a long table flanked with chairs. Two young men rose, rather respectfully, Ellery thought. They seemed surprised but not too depressed at the vision of Miss Ickthorpe, who was evidently a notorious character. One of them bounded forward and pumped Ellery's hand.

"Mr. Queen! I'm Burrows, John Burrows. Decent of you to pick me and Crane out of that terrific bunch of would-be manhunters." He was a nice young fellow, Ellery decided, with bright eyes and a thin intelligent face.

"Decent of your instructors and record, Burrows, I'd say. . . . And you're Walter Crane, of course?"

The second young man shook Ellery's hand decorously, as if it were a rite; he was tall, broad, and studious-looking in a pleasant way. "I am, sir. Degree in chemistry. I'm really interested in what you and the Professor are attempting to do."

"Splendid. Miss Ickthorpe—rather unexpectedly—is to be the fourth member of our little group," said Ellery. "Rather unexpectedly! Well, let's sit down and talk this over."

Crane and Burrows flung themselves into chairs, and the young woman seated herself demurely. Ellery threw hat and stick into a corner, clasped his hands on the bare table, and looked at the white ceiling. One must begin. . . . "This is all rather nonsensical, you know, and yet there's something solid in it. Professor Ickthorpe came to me some time ago with an idea. He had heard of my modest achievements in solving crimes by pure analysis, and he thought it might be interesting to develop the faculty of detection by deduction in young university students. I wasn't so sure, having been a university student myself."

"We're rather on the brainy side these days," said Miss Ickthorpe.

"Hmm. That remains to be seen," said Ellery dryly. "I suppose it's against the rules, but I can't think without tobacco. You may smoke, gentlemen. A cigarette, Miss Ickthorpe?"

She accepted one absently, furnished her own match, and kept looking at Ellery's eyes. "Field work, of course?" asked Crane, the chemist.

"Precisely." Ellery sprang to his feet. "Miss Ick-thorpe, *please* pay attention. . . . If we're to do this at all, we must do it right. . . . Very well. We shall study crimes out of the current news—crimes, it goes without saying, which lend themselves to our particular brand of detection. We start from scratch, all of us—no preconceptions, understand. . . . You will work under my direction, and we shall see what happens."

Burrows' keen face glowed. "Theory? I mean—won't you give us any principles of attack first—class-room lectures?"

"To hell with principles. I beg your pardon, Miss Ickthorpe. . . . The only way to learn to swim, Bur-rows, is to get into the water. . . . There were sixty-three applicants for this confounded course. I wanted only two or three—too many would defeat my pur-pose; unwieldy, you know. I selected you, Crane, be-cause you seem to have the analytical mind to a reason-able degree, and your scientific training has developed your sense of observation. You, Burrows, have a sound academic background and, evidently, an excellent top-piece." The two young men blushed. "As for you, Miss Ickthorpe," continued Ellery stiffly, "you selected yourself, so you'll have to take the consequences. Old Icky or no Old Icky, at the first sign of stupidity out you go."

"An Ickthorpe, sir, is never stupid."

"I hope—I sincerely hope—not. . . . Now, to cases. An hour ago, before I set out for the University, a flash came in over the Police Headquarters' wire. Most for-tuitously, I thought, and we must be properly grateful. . . . Murder in the theatrical district—chap by the name of Spargo is the victim. A queer enough affair, I gathered, from the sketchy facts given over the tape.

I've asked my father—Inspector Queen, you know—to leave the scene of the crime exactly as found. We go there at once."

"Bully!" cried Burrows. "To grips with crime! This is going to be great. Shan't we have any trouble getting in, Mr. Queen?"

"None at all. I've arranged for each of you gentlemen to carry a special police pass, like my own; I'll get one for you later, Miss Ickthorpe. . . . Let me caution all of you to refrain from taking anything away from the scene of the crime—at least without consulting me first. And on no account allow yourselves to be pumped by reporters."

"A murder," said Miss Ickthorpe thoughtfully, with a sudden dampening of spirits.

"Aha! Squeamish already. Well, this affair will be a test-case for all of you. I want to see how your minds work in contact with the real thing. . . . Miss Ickthorpe, have you a hat or something?"

"Sir?"

"Duds, duds! You can't traipse in there this way, you know!"

"Oh!" she murmured, blushing. "Isn't a sport dress *au fait* at murders?" Ellery glared, and she added sweetly: "In my locker down the hall, Mr. Queen. I shan't be a moment."

Ellery jammed his hat on his head. "I shall meet the three of you in front of the Arts Building in five minutes. Five minutes, Miss Ickthorpe!" And, retrieving his stick, he stalked like any professor from the seminar room. All the way down the elevator, through the main corridor, on the marble steps outside, he breathed deeply. A remarkable day! he observed to the campus. A really remarkable day.

The Fenwick Hotel lay a few hundred yards from Times Square. Its lobby was boiling with policemen, detectives, reporters and, from their universal appearance of apprehension, guests. Mountainous Sergeant Velie, Inspector Queen's right-hand man, was planted at the door, a cement barrier against curiosity-seekers. By his side stood a tall, worried-looking man dressed somberly in a blue serge suit, white linen, and black bow-tie.

"Mr. Williams, the hotel manager," said the Sergeant.

Williams shook hands. "Can't understand it. Terrible mess. You're with the police?"

Ellery nodded. His charges surrounded him like a royal guard—a rather timid royal guard, to be sure, for they pressed close to him as if for protection. There was something sinister in the atmosphere. Even the hotel clerks and attendants, uniformly dressed in gray—suits, ties, shirts—wore strained expressions, like stewards on a foundering ship.

"Nobody in or out, Mr. Queen," growled Sergeant Velie. "Inspector's orders. You're the first since the body was found. These people okay?"

"Yes. Dad's on the scene?"

"Upstairs, third floor, Room 317. Mostly quiet now."

Ellery leveled his stick. "Come along, young 'uns. And don't—" he added gently, "don't be so nervous. You'll become accustomed to this sort of thing. Keep your heads up."

They bobbed in unison, their eyes a little glassy. As they ascended in a policed elevator, Ellery observed that Miss Ickthorpe was trying very hard to appear professionally *blasée*. Ickthorpe indeed! This should take the starch out of her. . . . They walked down a hushed corridor to an open door. Inspector Queen, a small birdlike gray little man with sharp eyes remarkably like his son's, met them in the doorway.

Ellery, suppressing a snicker at the convulsive start of Miss Ickthorpe, who had darted one fearful glance into the death-room and then gasped for dear life, introduced the young people to the Inspector, shut the door behind his somewhat reluctant charges, and looked about the bedroom.

Lying on the drab carpet, arms outflung before him like a diver, lay a dead man. His head presented a curious appearance: as if some one had upset a bucket of thick red paint over him, clotting the brown hair and gushing over his shoulders. Miss Ickthorpe gave vent to a faint gurgle which certainly was not appreciation. Ellery observed with morbid satisfaction that her tiny hands were clenched and that her elfin face was whiter than the bed near which the dead man lay sprawled. Crane and Burrows were breathing hard.

"Miss Ickthorpe, Mr. Crane, Mr. Burrows—your first corpse," said Ellery briskly. "Now, dad, to work. How does it stand?"

Inspector Queen sighed. "Name is Oliver Spargo. Forty-two, separated from his wife two years ago. Mercantile traveler for a big drygoods exporting house. Returned from South Africa after a year's stay. Bad reputation with the natives in the outlying settlements —thrashed them, cheated them; in fact, was driven out of British Africa by a scandal. It was in the New York papers not long ago. . . . Registered at the Fenwick here for three days—same floor, by the way—then checked out to go to Chicago. Visiting relatives." The Inspector grunted, as if this were something justifiably punished by homicide. "Returned to New York this morning by 'plane. Checked in at 9:30. Didn't leave this room. At 11:30 he was found dead, just as you see him, by the colored maid on this floor, Agatha Robins."

"Leads?"

The old man shrugged. "Maybe—maybe not. We've looked this bird up. Pretty hard guy, from the reports, but sociable. No enemies, apparently; all his movements since his boat docked innocent and accounted for. *And* a lady-killer. Chucked his wife over before his last trip across, and took to his bosom a nice blonde gal. Fussed with her for a couple of months, and then skipped out—and *didn't* take her with him. We've had both women on the pan."

"Suspects?"

Inspector Queen stared moodily at the dead traveler. "Well, take your pick. He had one visitor this morning—the blonde lady I just mentioned. Name of Jane Terrill—no sign of occupation. Huh! She evidently read in the ship news of Spargo's arrival two weeks ago; hunted him up, and a week ago, while Spargo was in Chicago, called at the desk downstairs inquiring for him. She was told he was expected back this morning—he'd left word. She came in at 11:05 this a.m., was given his room-number, was taken up by the elevator-boy. Nobody remembers her leaving. But she says she knocked and there was no answer, so she went away and hasn't been back since. Never saw him—according to her story."

Miss Ickthorpe skirted the corpse with painful care, perched herself on the edge of the bed, opened her bag and began to powder her nose. "And the wife, Inspector Queen?" she murmured. Something sparkled in the depths of her fawn-brown eyes. Miss Ickthorpe, it was evident, had an idea and was taking heroic measures to suppress it.

"The wife?" snorted the Inspector. "God knows. She and Spargo separated, as I said, and she claims she didn't even know he'd come back from Africa. Says she was window-shopping this morning."

It was a small featureless hotel room, containing a bed, a wardrobe closet, a bureau, a night-table, a desk, and a chair. A dummy fireplace with a gas-log; an open door which led to a bathroom—nothing more.

Ellery dropped to his knees beside the body, Crane and Burrows trooping after with set faces. The Inspector sat down and watched with a humorless grin. Ellery turned the body over; his hands explored the rigid members, stiff in *rigor mortis*.

"Crane, Burrows, Miss Ickthorpe," he said sharply. "Might as well begin now. Tell me what you see.—Miss Ickthorpe, you first." She jumped from the bed and ran around the dead man; he felt her hot unsteady breath on the back of his neck. "Well, well? Don't you see *anything*? Good lord, there's enough here, I should think."

Miss Ickthorpe licked her red lips and said in a strangled voice: "He—he's dressed in lounging-robe, carpet-slippers and—yes, silk underwear beneath."

"Yes. And black silk socks and garters. And the robe and underwear bear the dealer's label: *Johnson's, Johannesburg, U.S.Afr.* What else?"

"A wrist-watch on his left wrist. I think"—she leaned over and with the shrinking tip of a finger nudged the dead arm—"yes, the watch crystal is cracked. Why, it's set at 10:20!"

"Good," said Ellery in a soft voice. "Dad, did Prouty examine the cadaver?"

"Yes," said the Inspector in a resigned voice. "Spargo died some time between 11:00 and 11:30, Doc says. I figure—"

Miss Ickthorpe's eyes were shining. "Doesn't that mean—?"

"Now, now, Miss Ickthorpe, if you have an idea keep it to yourself. Don't leap at conclusions. That's enough for you. Well, Crane?"

The young chemist's brow was ridged. He pointed to the watch, a large gaudy affair with a leather wrist-strap. "Man's watch. Concussion of fall stopped the works. Crease in leather strap at the second hole, where the prong now fits; but there's also a crease, a deeper one, at the third hole."

"That's really excellent, Crane. And?"

"Left hand splattered and splashed with dried blood. Left palm also shows stain, but fainter, as if he had grabbed something with his bloody hand and wiped most of the blood off. There ought to be something around here showing a red smudge from his clutching hand. . . ."

"Crane, I'm proud of you. Was anything found with a blood-smear on it, dad?"

The Inspector looked interested. "Good work, youngster. No, El, nothing at all. Not even a smear on the rug. Must be something the murderer took away."

"Now, Inspector," chuckled Ellery, "this isn't *your* examination. Burrows, can you add anything?"

Young Burrows swallowed rapidly: "Wounds on the head show he was struck with a heavy instrument many times. Disarranged rug probably indicates a struggle. And the face—"

"Ah! So you've noticed the face, eh? What about the face?"

"Freshly shaved. Talcum powder still on cheeks and chin. Don't you think we ought to examine the bathroom, Mr. Queen?"

Miss Ickthorpe said peevishly: "I noticed that, too, but you didn't give me a chance. . . . The powder *is* smoothly applied, isn't it? No streaks, no heavy spots."

Ellery sprang to his feet. "You'll be Sherlock Holmeses yet. . . . The weapon, dad?"

"A heavy stone hammer, crudely made—some kind of African curio, our expert says. Spargo must have had it in his bag—his trunk hasn't arrived yet from Chicago."

Ellery nodded; on the bed lay an open pigskin traveling-bag. Beside it, neatly laid out, was an evening outfit: tuxedo coat, trousers, and vest; stiff-bosomed shirt; studs and cuff-links; a clean wing-collar; black suspenders; a white silk handkerchief. Under the bed were two pairs of black shoes, one pair brogues, the other patent-leather. Ellery looked around; something, it seemed, disturbed him. On the chair near the bed lay a soiled shirt, a soiled pair of socks, and a soiled suit of underwear. None exhibited bloodstains. He paused thoughtfully.

"We took the hammer away. It was full of blood and hair," continued the Inspector. "No fingerprints anywhere. Handle anything you want—everything's been photographed and tested for prints."

Ellery began to puff at a cigarette. He noticed that Burrows and Crane were crouched over the dead man, occupied with the watch. He sauntered over, Miss Ickthorpe at his heels.

Burrows' thin face was shining as he looked up.

"Here's something!" He had carefully removed the timepiece from Spargo's wrist and had pried open the back of the case. Ellery saw a roughly circular patch of fuzzy white paper glued to the inside of the case, as if something had been rather unsuccessfully torn away. Burrows leaped to his feet. "That gives *me* an idea," he announced. "Yes, sir." He studied the dead man's face intently.

"And you, Crane?" asked Ellery with interest. The young chemist had produced a small magnifying-glass from his pocket and was scrutinizing the watchworks.

Crane rose. "I'd rather not say now," he mumbled. "Mr. Queen, I'd like permission to take this watch to my laboratory."

Ellery looked at his father; the old man nodded. "Certainly, Crane. But be sure you return it. . . . Dad, you searched this room thoroughly, fireplace and all?"

The Inspector cackled suddenly. "I was wondering when you'd get to that. There's something almighty interesting in that fireplace." His face fell and rather grumpily he produced a snuff-box and pinched some crumbs into his nostrils. "Although I'll be hanged if I know what it means."

Ellery squinted at the fireplace, his lean shoulders squaring; the others crowded around. He squinted again, and knelt; behind the manufactured gas-log, in a tiny grate, there was a heap of ashes. Curious ashes indeed, patently not of wood, coal, or paper. Ellery poked about in the débris—and sucked in his breath. In a moment he had dug out of the ashes ten peculiar objects: eight flat pearl buttons and two metal things, one triangular in outline, eye-like, the other hook-like—both small and made of some cheap alloy. Two of the eight buttons were slightly larger than the rest. The buttons were ridged, and in the depression in each center were four thread-holes. All ten objects were charred by fire.

"And what do you make of that?" demanded the Inspector.

Ellery juggled the buttons thoughtfully. He did not reply directly. Instead, he said to his three pupils, in a grim voice: "You might think about these. . . . Dad, when was this fireplace last cleaned?"

"Early this morning by Agatha Robins, the mulatto maid. Some one checked out of this room at seven o'clock, and she cleaned up the place before Spargo got here. Fireplace was clean this morning, she says."

Ellery dropped buttons and metal objects on the night-table and went to the bed. He looked into the open traveling-bag; its interior was in a state of confusion. The bag contained three four-in-hand neckties, two clean white shirts, socks, underwear, and handkerchiefs. All the haberdashery, he noted, bore the same dealer's tab—*Johnson's, Johannesburg, U.S.Afr.* He seemed pleased, and proceeded to the wardrobe closet. It contained merely a tweed traveling suit, a brown topcoat, and a felt hat.

He closed the door with a satisfied bang. "You've observed everything?" he asked the two young men and the girl.

Crane and Burrows nodded, rather doubtfully. Miss Ickthorpe was barely listening; from the rapt expression on her face, she might have been listening to the music of the spheres.

"Miss Ickthorpe!"

Miss Ickthorpe smiled dreamily. "Yes, Mr. Queen,"

she said in a submissive little voice. Her brown brown eyes began to rove.

Ellery grunted and strode to the bureau. Its top was bare. He went through the drawers; they were empty. He started for the desk, but the Inspector said: "Nothing there, son. He hadn't time to stow anything away. Except for the bathroom, you've seen everything."

As if she had been awaiting the signal, Miss Ickthorpe dashed for the bathroom. She seemed very anxious indeed to explore its interior. Crane and Burrows hurried after her.

Ellery permitted them to examine the bathroom before him. Miss Ickthorpe's hands flew over the objects on the rim of the washbowl. There was a pigskin toilet-kit, open, draped over the marble; an uncleansed razor; a still damp shaving-brush; a tube of shaving cream; a small can of talcum and a tube of tooth-paste. To one side lay a celluloid shaving-brush container, its cap on the open kit.

"Can't see a thing of interest here," said Burrows frankly. "You, Walter?"

Crane shook his head. "Except that he must have just finished shaving before he was murdered, not a thing."

Miss Ickthorpe wore a stern and faintly exultant look. "That's because, like all men, you're blinder'n bats. . . . *I've* seen enough."

They trooped by Ellery, rejoining the Inspector, who was talking with some one in the bedroom. Ellery chuckled to himself. He lifted the lid of a clothes-hamper; it was empty. Then he picked up the cap of the shaving-brush container. The cap came apart in his fingers, and he saw that a small circular pad fitted snugly inside. He chuckled again, cast a derisive glance

at the triumphant back of the heroic Miss Ickthorpe
outside, replaced cap and tube, and went back into the
bedroom.

He found Williams, the hotel manager, accompanied
by a policeman, talking heatedly to the Inspector. "We
can't keep this up forever, Inspector Queen," Williams
was saying. "Our guests are beginning to complain.
The night-shift is due to go on soon, I've got to go home
myself, and you're making us stay here all night, by
George. After all—"

The old man said: "Pish!" and cocked an inquiring
eye at his son. Ellery nodded. "Can't see any reason
for not lifting the ban, dad. We've learned as much as
we can. . . . You young people!" Three pairs of eager
eyes focused on him; they were like three puppies on a
leash. "Have you seen enough?" They nodded solemnly. "Anything else you want to know?"

Burrows said quickly: "I want a certain address."

Miss Ickthorpe paled. "Why, so do I! John, you
mean thing!"

And Crane muttered, clutching Spargo's watch in his
fist: "I want something, too—but I'll find it out right
in this hotel!"

Ellery smoothed away a smile, shrugged, and said:
"See Sergeant Velie downstairs—that Colossus we met
at the door. He'll tell you anything you may want to
know.

"Now, follow instructions. It's evident that the
three of you have definite theories. I'll give you two
hours in which to formulate them and pursue any in-
vestigations you may have in mind." He consulted his
watch. "At 6:30, meet me at my apartment on West
Eighty-seventh Street, and I'll try to rip your theories
apart. . . . Happy hunting!"

He grinned dismissal. They scrambled for the door, Miss Ickthorpe's turban slightly awry, her elbows working vigorously to clear the way.

"And now," said Ellery in a totally different voice when they had disappeared down the corridor, "come here a moment, dad. I want to talk to you alone."

At 6:30 that evening Mr. Ellery Queen presided at his own table, watching three young faces bursting with sternly repressed news. The remains of a dinner, barely touched, strewed the cloth.

Miss Ickthorpe had somehow contrived, in the interval between her dismissal and her appearance at the Queens' apartment, to change her gown; she was now attired in something lacy and soft, which set off—as she obviously was aware—the whiteness of her throat, the brownness of her eyes, and the pinkness of her cheeks. The young men were preoccupied with their coffee-cups.

"Now, class," chuckled Ellery, "recitations." They brightened, sat straighter and moistened their lips. "You've had, each of you, about two hours in which to crystallize the results of your first investigation. Whatever happens, I can't take credit, since so far I've taught you nothing. But by the end of this little confabulation, I'll have a rough idea of just what material I'm working with."

"Yes, sir," said Miss Ickthorpe.

"John—we may as well discard formality—what's *your* theory?"

Burrows said slowly: "I've more than a theory, Mr. Queen. I've the solution!"

"*A* solution, John. Don't be too cocky. And what," said Ellery, "is this solution of yours?"

Burrows drew a breath from the depths of his boots.
"The clue that led to my solution was Spargo's wrist-
watch." Crane and the girl started. Ellery blew smoke
and said, encouragingly: "Go on."

"The two creases on the leather strap," replied Burrows, "were significant. As Spargo wore the watch, the
prong was caught in the second hole, so that there was a
crease *across* the second hole. Yet a deeper crease appeared across the *third* hole. Conclusion: the watch was
habitually worn by a person with a smaller wrist. In
other words, the watch was not Spargo's!"

"Bravo," said Ellery softly. "Bravo."

"Why, then, was Spargo wearing some one else's
watch? For a very good reason, I maintain. The doctor had said Spargo died between 11:00 and 11:30. Yet
the watch-hands had apparently stopped at 10:20. The
answer to this discrepancy? That the murderer, finding
no watch on Spargo, took her own watch, cracked the
crystal and stopped the works, then set the hands at
10:20 and strapped it about Spargo's dead wrist. This
would seem to establish the time of death as 10:20 and
would give the murderer an opportunity to provide an
alibi for that time, when all the while the murder actually occurred about 11:20. How's that?"

Miss Ickthorpe said tartly: "You say 'her.' But it's a
man's watch, John—you forget that."

Burrows grinned. "A woman can own a man's
watch, can't she? Now whose watch was it? Easy. In
the back of the case there was a circular patch of fuzzy
paper, as if something had been ripped out. What made
of paper is usually pasted in the back of a watch? A
photograph. Why was it taken out? Obviously, because the murderer's face was in that photograph. . . .
In the last two hours I followed this lead. I visited my

suspect on a reportorial pretext and managed to get a look at a photograph-album she has. There I found one photograph with a circular patch cut out. From the rest of the photo it was clear that the missing circle contained the heads of a man and a woman. My case was complete!"

"Perfectly amazing," murmured Ellery. "And this murderess of yours is—?"

"Spargo's wife! . . . Motive—hate, or revenge, or thwarted love, or something."

Miss Ickthorpe sniffed, and Crane shook his head. "Well," said Ellery, "we seem to be in disagreement. Nevertheless a very interesting analysis, John. . . . Walter, what's yours?"

Crane hunched his broad shoulders. "I agree with Johnny that the watch did not belong to Spargo, that the murderer set the hands at 10:20 to provide an alibi; but I disagree as to the identity of the criminal. I also worked on the watch as the main clue. But with a vastly different approach.

"Look here." He brought out the gaudy timepiece and tapped its cracked crystal deliberately. "Here's something you people may not know. Watches, so to speak, breathe. That is, contact with warm flesh causes the air inside to expand and force its way out through the minute cracks and holes of the case and crystal. When the watch is laid aside, the air cools and contracts, and dust-bearing air is sucked into the interior."

"I always said I should have studied science," said Ellery. "That's a new trick, Walter. Continue."

"To put it specifically, a baker's watch will be found to contain flour-dust. A bricklayer's watch will collect brick-dust." Crane's voice rose triumphantly. "D'you know what I found in this watch? Tiny particles of a woman's face-powder!"

Miss Ickthorpe frowned. Crane continued in a deep voice: "And a very special kind of face-powder it is, Mr. Queen. Kind used only by women of certain complexions. What complexions? Negro brown! The powder came from a mulatto woman's purse! I've questioned her, checked her vanity-case, and although she denies it, I say that Spargo's murderess is Agatha Robins, the mulatto maid who 'found' the body!"

Ellery whistled gently. "Good work, Walter, splendid work. And of course from your standpoint she would deny being the owner of the watch anyway. That clears something up for *me*. . . . But motive?"

Crane looked uncomfortable. "Well, I know it sounds fantastic, but a sort of voodoo vengeance—reversion to racial type—Spargo had been cruel to African natives . . . it was in the papers. . . ."

Ellery shaded his eyes to conceal their twinkle. Then he turned to Miss Ickthorpe, who was tapping her cup nervously, squirming in her chair, and exhibiting other signs of impatience. "And now," he said, "we come to the star recitation. What have you to offer, Miss Ickthorpe? You've been simply saturated with a theory all afternoon. Out with it."

She compressed her lips. "You boys think you're clever. You, too, Mr. Queen—you especially. . . . Oh, I'll admit John and Walter have shown superficial traces of intelligence. . . ."

"*Will* you be explicit, Miss Ickthorpe?"

She tossed her head. "Very well. The watch had nothing to do with the crime at all!"

The boys gaped, and Ellery tapped his palms gently together. "*Very* good. I agree with you. Explain, please."

Her brown eyes burned, and her cheeks were very
pink. "Simple!" she said with a sniff. "Spargo had arrived from Chicago only two hours before his murder.
He had been in Chicago for a week and a half. Then
for a week and a half he had been living *by Chicago
time*. And, since Chicago time is *one hour earlier* than
New York time, it merely means that *nobody* set the
hands back; that they were standing at 10:20 when he
fell dead, because he'd neglected to set his watch ahead
on arriving in New York this morning!"

Crane muttered something in his throat, and Burrows
flushed a deep crimson. Ellery looked sad. "I'm afraid
the laurels so far go to Miss Ickthorpe, gentlemen. That
happens to be correct. Anything else?"

"Naturally. *I* know the murderer, and it isn't Spargo's wife or that outlandish mulatto maid," she said ex-
asperatingly. "Follow me. . . . Oh, this is so easy!
. . . We all saw that the powder on Spargo's dead face
had been applied very smoothly. From the condition of
his cheeks and the shaving things in the bathroom it was
evident that he'd shaved just before being murdered.
But how does a man apply powder after shaving? How
do *you* powder your face, Mr. Queen?" she shot at him
rather tenderly.

Ellery looked startled. "With my fingers, of course."
Crane and Burrows nodded.

"Exactly!" chortled Miss Ickthorpe. "And what
happens? *I* know, because I'm a very observant person
and, besides, Old Icky shaves every morning and I can't
help noticing when he kisses me good-morning. Applied with the fingers on cheeks still slightly moist, the
powder goes on in streaks, smudgy, heavier in some spots
than others. But look at *my* face!" They looked, with
varying expressions of appreciation. "You don't see
powder streaks on *my* face, do you? Of course not!

And why? Because I'm a woman, and a woman uses a powder-puff, and there isn't a single powder-puff in Spargo's bedroom or bathroom!"

Ellery smiled—almost with relief. "Then you suggest, Miss Ickthorpe, that the last person with Spargo, presumably his murderess, was a woman who watched him shave and then, with endearment perhaps, took out her own powder-puff and dabbed it over his face—only to bash him over the head with the stone hammer a few minutes later?"

"Well—yes, although I didn't think of it *that* way. . . . But—yes! And psychology points to the specific woman, too, Mr. Queen. A man's wife would never think of such an—an amorous proceeding. But a man's mistress would, and I say that Spargo's lady-love, Jane Terrill, whom I visited only an hour ago and who denies having powdered Spargo's face—she would!—killed him."

Ellery sighed. He rose and twitched his cigarette-stub into the fireplace. They were watching him, and each other, with expectancy. "Aside," he began, "from complimenting you, Miss Ickthorpe, on the acuteness of your knowledge of mistresses"—she uttered an outraged little gasp—"I want to say this before going ahead. The three of you have proved very ingenious, very alert; I'm more pleased than I can say. I do think we're going to have a cracking good class. Good work, all of you!"

"But, Mr. Queen," protested Burrows, "which one of us is right? Each one of us has given a different solution."

Ellery waved his hand. "Right? A detail, theoretically. The point is you've done splendid work—sharp observation, a rudimentary but promising linking of

cause and effect. As for the case itself, I regret to say—
you're all wrong!"

Miss Ickthorpe clenched her tiny fist. "I *knew* you'd
say that! I think you're horrid. And I *still* think I'm
right."

"There, gentlemen, is an extraordinary example of
feminine psychology," grinned Ellery. "Now attend,
all of you.

"You're all wrong for the simple reason that each of
you has taken just one line of attack, one clue, one
chain of reasoning, and completely ignored the other
elements of the problem. You, John, say it's Spargo's
wife, merely because her photograph-album contains a
picture from which a circular patch with two heads has
been cut away. That this might have been sheer coincidence apparently never occurred to you.

"You, Walter, came nearer the truth when you satisfactorily established the ownership of the watch as the
mulatto maid's. But suppose Maid Robins had accidentally dropped the watch in Spargo's room at the
hotel during his first visit there, and he had found it and
taken it to Chicago with him? That's what probably
happened. The mere fact that he wore her watch
doesn't make her his murderess.

"You, Miss Ickthorpe, explained away the watch business with the difference-in-time element, but you overlooked an important item. Your entire solution depends on the presence in Spargo's room of a powder-
puff. Willing to believe that no puff remained on the
scene of the crime, because it suited your theory, you
made a cursory search and promptly concluded no puff
was there. But a puff *is* there! Had you investigated
the cap of the celluloid tube in which Spargo kept his
shaving-brush, you would have found a circular pad of

powder-puff which toilet-article manufacturers in this effeminate age provide for men's traveling-kits."

Miss Ickthorpe said nothing; she seemed actually embarrassed.

"Now for the proper solution," said Ellery, mercifully looking away. "All three of you, amazingly enough, postulate a woman as the criminal. Yet it was apparent to me, after my examination of the premises, that the murderer *must have been a man.*"

"A man!" they echoed in chorus.

"Exactly. Why did none of you consider the significance of those eight buttons and the two metal clips?" He smiled. "Probably because again they didn't fit your preconceived theories. But *everything* must fit in a solution. . . . Enough of scolding. You'll do better next time.

"Six small pearl buttons, flat, and two slightly larger ones, found in a heap of ashes distinctly not of wood, coal, or paper. There is only one common article which possesses these characteristics—a man's shirt. A man's shirt, the six buttons from the front, the two larger ones from the cuffs, the débris from the linen or broadcloth. Some one, then, had burned a man's shirt in the grate, forgetting that the buttons would not be consumed.

"The metal objects, like a large hook and eye? A shirt suggests haberdashery, the hook and eye suggest only one thing—one of the cheap bow-ties which are purchased ready-tied, so that you do not have to make the bow yourself."

They were watching his lips like kindergarten children. "You, Crane, observed that Spargo's bloody left hand had clutched something, most of the blood coming off the palm. But nothing smudged with blood had been found. . . . A man's shirt and tie had been burned. . . . Inference: In the struggle with the murderer, after he had already been hit on the head and was streaming blood, Spargo had clutched his assailant's collar and tie, staining them. Borne out too by the signs of struggle in the room.

"Spargo dead, his own collar and tie wet with blood, what could the murderer do? Let me attack it this way: The murderer must have been from one of three classes of people: a rank outsider, or a guest at the hotel, or an employee of the hotel. What had he done? He had burned his shirt and tie. But if he had been an outsider, he could have turned up his coat-collar, concealing the stains long enough to get out of the hotel—no necessity, then, to burn shirt and tie when time was precious. Were he one of the hotel guests, he could have done the same thing while he went to his own room. Then he must have been an employee.

"Confirmation? Yes. As an employee he would be forced to remain in the hotel, on duty, constantly being seen. What could he do? Well, he had to change his shirt and tie. Spargo's bag was open—shirt inside. He rummaged through—you saw the confusion in the bag —and changed. Leave his shirt? No, it might be traced to him. So, boys and girls, burning was inevitable. . . .

"The tie? You recall that, while Spargo had laid out his evening-clothes on the bed, there was no bow-tie there, in the bag, or anywhere else in the room. Obviously, then, the murderer took the bow-tie of the tuxedo outfit, and burned his own bow-tie with the shirt."

Miss Ickthorpe sighed, and Crane and Burrows shook their heads a little dazedly. "I knew, then, that the murderer was an employee of the hotel, a man, and that he was wearing Spargo's shirt and black or white bow-tie, probably black. But all the employees of the hotel wear gray shirts and gray ties, as we observed on entering the Fenwick. Except"—Ellery inhaled the smoke of his cigarette—"except one man. Surely you noticed the difference in his attire? . . . And so, when you left on your various errands, I suggested to my father that this man be examined—he seemed the best possibility. And, sure enough, we found on him a shirt and bow-tie bearing Johannesburg labels like those we had observed on Spargo's other haberdashery. I knew we should find this proof, for Spargo had spent a whole year in South Africa, and since most of his clothes had been purchased there, it was reasonable to expect that the stolen shirt and tie had been, too."

"Then the case was finished when we were just beginning," said Burrows ruefully.

"But—who?" demanded Crane in bewilderment.

Ellery blew a great cloud. "We got a confession out of him in three minutes. Spargo, that gentle creature, had years before stolen this man's wife, and then thrown her over. When Spargo registered at· the Fenwick two weeks ago, this man recognized him and decided to revenge himself. He's at the Tombs right now—Williams, the hotel manager!"

There was a little silence. Burrows bobbed his head back and forth. "We've got a lot to learn," he said. "I can see that."

"Check," muttered Crane. "I'm going to like this course."

Ellery pshaw-pshawed. Nevertheless, he turned to Miss Ickthorpe who by all precedent should be moved to contribute to the general spirit of approbation. But Miss Ickthorpe's thoughts were far away. "Do you know," she said, her brown eyes misty, "you've never asked me my first name, Mr. Queen?"

The Adventure of
THE HANGING ACROBAT

The Adventure of
THE HANGING ACROBAT

Long, long ago in the Incubation Period of Man—long before booking agents, five-a-days, theatrical boarding houses, subway circuits, and *Variety*—when Megatherium roamed the trees, when Broadway was going through its First Glacial Period, and when the first vaudeville show was planned by the first lop-eared, low-browed, hairy impresario, it was decreed: "The acrobat shall be first."

Why the acrobat should be first no one ever explained; but that this was a dubious honor every one on the bill —including the acrobat—realized only too well. For it was recognized even then, in the infancy of Show Business, that the first shall be last in the applause of the audience. And all through the ages, in courts and courtyards and feeble theatres, it was the acrobat—whether he was called buffoon, *farceur*, merry-andrew, tumbler, mountebank, Harlequin, or *punchinello*—who was thrown, first among his fellow-mimes, to the lions of entertainment to whet their appetites for the more luscious feasts to come. So that to this day their muscular miracles are performed hard on the overture's last wall-shaking blare, performed with a simple resignation that speaks well for the mildness and resilience of the whole acrobatic tribe.

Hugo Brinkerhof knew nothing of the whimsical background of his profession. All he knew was that his father and mother had been acrobats before him with a traveling show in Germany, that he possessed huge

31

smooth muscles with sap and spring and strength in them, and that nothing gave him more satisfaction than the sight of a glittering trapeze. With his trapeze and his Myra, and the indulgent applause of audiences from Seattle to Okeechobee, he was well content.

Now Hugo was very proud of Myra, a small wiry handsome woman with the agility of a cat and something of the cat's sleepy green eyes. He had met her in the office of Bregman, the booker, and the sluggish heart under his magnificent chest had told him that this was his fate and his woman. It was Myra who had renamed the act "Atlas & Co." when they had married between the third and fourth shows in Indianapolis. It was Myra who had fought tooth and nail for better billing. It was Myra who had conceived and perfected the dazzling pinwheel of their finale. It was Myra's shapely little body and Myra's lithe gyrations on the high trapeze and Myra's sleepy smile that had made Atlas & Co. an "acrobatic divertissement acclaimed from coast to coast," had earned them a pungent paragraph in *Variety*, and had brought them with other topnotchers on the Bregman string to the Big Circuit.

That every one loved his Myra mighty Brinkerhof, the Atlas, knew with a swelling of his chest. Who could resist her? There had been that baritone with the dancing act in Boston, the revue comedian in Newark, the tap-dancer in Buffalo, the *adagio* in Washington. Now there were others—Tex Crosby, the Crooning Cowboy (Songs & Patter); the Great Gordi (Successor to Houdini); Sailor Sam, the low comic. They had all been on the same bill together now for weeks, and they all loved sleepy-eyed Myra, and big Atlas smiled his indulgent smile and thrilled in his stupid, stolid way to their admiration. For was not his Myra the finest female acrobat in the world and the most lovely creature in creation?

And now Myra was dead.

It was Brinkerhof himself, with a gaunt suffering look about him that mild Spring night, who had given the alarm. It was five o'clock in the morning and his Myra had not come home to their theatrical boarding-house room on Forty-seventh Street. He had stayed behind with his wife after the last performance in the Metropole Theatre at Columbus Circle to try out a new trick. They had rehearsed and then he had dressed in haste, leaving her in their joint dressing-room. He had had an appointment with Bregman, the booker, to discuss terms of a new contract. He had promised to meet her back at their lodgings. But when he had returned—ach! no Myra. He had hurried back to the theatre; it was locked up for the night. And all the long night he had waited. . . .

"Prob'ly out bummin', buddy," the desk-lieutenant at the West Forty-seventh Street station had said with a yawn. "Go home and sleep it off."

But Brinkerhof had been vehement, with many gestures. "She never haf this done before. I haf telephoned it the theatre, too, but there iss no answer. Captain, find her, please!"

"These heinies," sighed the lieutenant to a lounging detective. "All right, Baldy, see what you can do. If she's piffed in a joint somewhere, give this big hunk a clout on the jaw."

So Baldy and the pale giant had gone to see what they could do, and they had found the Metropole Theatre locked, as Brinkerhof had said, and it was almost six in the morning and dawn was coming up across the

Park and Baldy had dragged Brinkerhof into an all-night restaurant for a mug of coffee. And they had waited around the theatre until seven, when old Perk the stagedoor man and timer had come in, and he had opened the theatre for them, and they had gone backstage to the dressing-room of Atlas & Co. and found Myra hanging from one of the sprinkler-pipes with a dirty old rope, thick as a hawser, around her pretty neck.

And Atlas had sat down like the dumb hunk he was and put his shaggy head between his hands and stared at the hanging body of his wife with the silent grief of some Norse god crushed to earth.

When Mr. Ellery Queen pushed through the chattering crowd of reporters and detectives backstage and convinced Sergeant Velie through the door of the dressing-room that he was indeed who he was, he found his father the Inspector holding court in the stuffy little room before a gang of nervous theatrical people. It was only nine o'clock and Ellery was grumbling through his teeth at the unconscionable inconsiderateness of murderers. But neither the burly Sergeant nor little Inspector Queen was impressed with his grumblings to the point of lending ear; and indeed the grumblings ceased after he had taken one swift look at what still hung from the sprinkler-pipe.

Brinkerhof sat red-eyed and huge and collapsed in the chair before his wife's dressing-table. "I haf told you everything," he muttered. "We rehearsed the new trick. It was then an appointment with Mr. Bregman. I went." A fat hard-eyed man, Bregman the broker, nodded curtly. "Undt that's all. Who—why—I do not know."

In a bass *sotto voce* Sergeant Velie recited the sparse facts. Ellery took another look at the dead woman. Her stiff muscles of thigh and leg bulged in *rigor mortis* beneath the tough thin silk of her flesh tights. Her green eyes were widely open. And she swayed a little in a faint dance of death. Ellery looked away and at the people.

Baldy the precinct man was there, flushed with his sudden popularity with the newspaper boys. A tall thin man who looked like Gary Cooper rolled a cigaret beside Bregman—Tex Crosby, the cowboy-crooner; and he leaned against the grime-smeared wall and eyed the Great Gordi—in person—with flinty dislike. Gordi had a hawk's beak and sleek black mustachios and long olive fingers and black eyes; and he said nothing. Little Sam, the comedian, had purple pouches under his tired eyes and he looked badly in need of a drink. But Joe Kelly, the house-manager, did not, for he smelled like a brewery and kept mumbling something drunken and obscene beneath his breath.

"How long you been married, Brinkerhof?" growled the Inspector.

"Two years. *Ja.* In Indianapolis that was, *Herr Inspektor.*"

"Was she ever married before?"

"*Nein.*"

"You?"

"*Nein.*"

"Did she or you have any enemies?"

"*Gott, nein!*"

"Happy, were you?"

"Like two doves we was," muttered Brinkerhof.

Ellery strolled over to the corpse and stared up. Her ropy-veined wrists were jammed behind her back, bound

with a filthy rouge-stained towel, as were her ankles.
Her feet dangled a yard from the floor. A battered
stepladder leaned against one of the walls, folded up;
a man standing upon it, he mused, could easily have
reached the sprinkler-pipe, flung the rope over it, and
hauled up the light body.

"The stepladder was found against the wall there?"
he murmured to the Sergeant, who had come up behind
him and was staring with interest at the dead woman.

"Yep. It's always kept out near the switchboard
light panel."

"No suicide, then," said Ellery. "At least that's
something."

"Nice figger, ain't she?" said the Sergeant admiringly.

"Velie, you're a ghoul. . . . This *is* a pretty problem."

The dirty rope seemed to fascinate him. It had been
wound tightly about the woman's throat twice, in parallel strands, and concealed her flesh like the iron necklace of a Ubangi woman. A huge knot had been fashioned beneath her right ear, and another knot held the
rope to the pipe above.

"Where does this rope come from?" he said abruptly.

"From around an old trunk we found backstage, Mr.
Queen. Trunk's been here for years. In the prop-
room. Nothin' in it; some trouper left it. Want to see
it?"

"I'll take your word for it, Sergeant. Property room,
eh?" He sauntered back to the door to look the people
over again.

Brinkerhof was mumbling something about how
happy he and Myra had been, and what he would do
to the *verdammte Teufel* who had wrung his pretty
Myra's neck. His huge hands opened and closed con-

vulsively. "Joost like a flower she was," he said. "Joost like a flower."

"Nuts," snapped Joe Kelly, the house-manager, weaving on his feet like a punch-drunk fighter. "She was a floozy, Inspector. You ask *me*," and he leered at Inspector Queen.

"Floo-zie?" said Brinkerhof with difficulty, getting to his feet. "What iss that?"

Sam, the comic, blinked his puffy little eyes rapidly and said in a hoarse voice: "You're crazy, Kelly, crazy. Wha'd'ye want to say that for? He's pickled, Chief."

"Pickled, am I?" screamed Kelly, livid. "Aw right, you as' *him*, then!" and he pointed a wavering finger at the tall thin man.

"What is this?" crooned the Inspector, his eyes bright. "Get together, gentlemen. You mean, Kelly, that Mrs. Brinkerhof was playing around with Crosby here?"

Brinkerhof made a sound like a baffled gorilla and lunged forward. His long arms were curved flails and he made for the cowboy's throat with the unswervable fury of an animal. Sergeant Velie grabbed his wrist and twisted it up behind the vast back, and Baldy jumped in and clung to the giant's other arm. He swayed there, struggling and never taking his eyes from the tall thin man, who had not stirred but who had gone very pale.

"Take him away," snapped the Inspector to Sergeant Velie. "Turn him over to a couple of the boys and keep him outside till he calms down." They hustled the hoarsely breathing acrobat out of the room. "Now, Crosby, spill it."

"Nothin' to spill," drawled the cowboy, but his drawl was a little breathless and his eyes were narrowed to wary slits. "I'm Texas an' I don't scare easy, Mister

Cop. He's just a squarehead. An' as for that pie-eyed sawback over there"—he stared malevolently at Kelly— "he better learn to keep his trap shut."

"He's been two-timin' the hunk!" screeched Kelly. "Don't b'lieve him, Chief! That sassy little tramp got what was comin' to her, I tell y'! She's been pullin' the wool over the hunk's eyes all the way from Chi to Beantown!"

"You've said enough," said the Great Gordi quietly. "Can't you see the man's drunk, Inspector, and not responsible? Myra was—companionable. She may have taken a drink or two with Crosby or myself on the sly once or twice—Brinkerhof didn't like her to, so she never drank in front of him—but that's all."

"Just friendly, hey?" murmured the Inspector. "Well, who's lying? If you know anything solid, Kelly, come out with it."

"I know what I know," sneered the manager. "An' when it comes to that, Chief, the Great Gordi could tell you somethin' about the little bum. Ought to be able to! He swiped her from Crosby only a couple o' weeks ago."

"Quiet, both of you," snapped the old gentleman as the Texan and the dark mustachioed man stirred. "And how could you know that, Kelly?"

The dead woman swayed faintly, dancing her noiseless dance.

"I heard Tex there bawl Gordi out only the other day," said Kelly thickly, "for makin' the snatch. An' I saw Gordi grapplin' with her in the wings on'y yest'-day. How's 'at? Reg'lar wrestler, Gordi. Can he clinch!"

Nobody said anything. The tall Texan's fingers whitened as he glared at the drunken man, and Gordi the

magician did nothing at all but breathe. Then the door
opened and two men came in—Dr. Prouty, Assistant
Medical Examiner, and a big shambling man with a seared face.

Everybody relaxed. The Inspector said: "High time,
Doc. Don't touch her, though, till Bradford can take
a look at that knot up there. Go on, Braddy; on the
pipe. Use the ladder."

The shambling man took the stepladder and set it up
and climbed beside the dangling body and looked at the
knot behind the woman's ear and the knot at the top of
the pipe. Dr. Prouty pinched the woman's legs.

Ellery sighed and began to prowl. Nobody paid any
attention to him; they were all pallidly intent upon the
two men near the body.

Something disturbed him; he did not know what,
could not put his finger precisely upon the root of the
disturbance. Perhaps it was a feeling in the air, an
aura of tension about the silent dangling woman in
tights. But it made him restless. He had the feeling . . .

He found the loaded revolver in the top drawer of
the woman's dressing-table—a shiny little pearl-handled
.22 with the initials MB on the butt. And his eyes narrowed and he glanced at his father, and his father nodded. So he prowled some more. And then he stopped
short, his gray eyes suspicious.

On the rickety wooden table in the center of the
room lay a long sharp nickel-plated letter-opener among
a clutter of odds and ends. He picked it up carefully
and squinted along its glittering length in the light.
But there was no sign of blood.

He put it down and continued to prowl.

And the very next thing he noticed was the cheap battered gas-burner on the floor at the other side of the room. Its pipe fitted snugly over a gas outlet in the wall, but the gas-tap had been turned off. He felt the little burner; it was stone-cold.

So he went to the closet with the oddest feeling of inevitability. And sure enough, just inside the open door of the closet lay a wooden box full of carpenter's tools, with a heavy steel hammer prominently on top. There was a mess of shavings on the floor near the box, and the edge of the closet-door was unpainted and virgin-fresh from a plane.

His eyes were very sharp now, and deeply concerned. He went quickly to the Inspector's side and murmured: "The revolver. The woman's?"

"Yes."

"Recent acquisition?"

"No. Brinkerhof bought it for her soon after they were married. For protection, he said."

"Poor protection, I should say," shrugged Ellery, glancing at the Headquarters men. The shambling red-faced man had just lumbered off the ladder with an expression of immense surprise. Sergeant Velie, who had returned, was mounting the ladder with a pen-knife clutched in his big fingers. Dr. Prouty waited expectantly below. The Sergeant began sawing at the rope tied to the sprinkler-pipe.

"What's that box of tools doing in the closet?" continued Ellery, without removing his gaze from the dead woman.

"Stage carpenter was in here yesterday fixing the door —it had warped or something. Union rules are strict, so he quit the job unfinished. What of it?"

"Everything," said Ellery, "of it." The Great Gordi

was quietly watching his mouth; Ellery seemed not to
notice. The little comedian, Sam, was shrunken in a
corner, eyes popping at the Sergeant. And the Texan
was smoking without enjoyment, not looking at any one
or anything. "Simply everything. It's one of the most
remarkable things I've ever run across."

The Inspector looked bewildered. "But, El, for cripe's
sake—remarkable? I don't see—"

"You should," said Ellery impatiently. "A child
should. And yet it's astounding, when you come to
think of it. Here's a room with four dandy weapons in
it—a loaded revolver, a letter-cutter, a gas-burner, and
a hammer. And yet the murderer deliberately trussed
the woman with the towels, deliberately left this room,
deliberately crossed the stage to the property room, un-
wound that rusty old rope from a worthless trunk discarded years ago by some nameless actor, carried the rope
and the ladder from beside the switchboard back to this
room, used the ladder to sling the rope over the pipe and
fasten the knot, and strung the woman up."

"Well, but—"

"Well, but why?" cried Ellery. "Why? Why did
the murderer ignore the four simple, easy, handy methods of murder here—shooting, stabbing, asphyxiation,
bludgeoning—and go to all that extra trouble to *hang*
her?"

Dr. Prouty was kneeling beside the dead woman,
whom the Sergeant had deposited with a thump on the
dirty floor.

The red-faced man shambled over and said: "It's got
me, Inspector."

"What's got you?" snapped Inspector Queen.

"This knot." His thick red fingers held a length of

knotted rope. "The one behind her ear is just ordinary; even clumsy for the job of breakin' her neck." He shook his head. "But this one, the one that was tied around the pipe—well, sir, it's got me."

"An unfamiliar knot?" said Ellery slowly, puzzling over its complicated convolutions.

"New to me, Mr. Queen. All the years I been expertin' on knots for the Department I never seen one like that. Ain't a sailor's knot, I can tell you that; and it ain't Western."

"Might be the work of an amateur," muttered the Inspector, pulling the rope through his fingers. "A knot that just happened."

The expert shook his head. "No, sir, I wouldn't say that at all. It's some kind of variation. Not an accident. Whoever tied that knew his knots."

Bradford shambled off and Dr. Prouty looked up from his work. "Hell, I can't do anything here," he snapped. "I'll have to take this body over to the Morgue and work on it there. The boys are waiting outside."

"When'd she kick off, Doc?" demanded the Inspector, frowning.

"About midnight last night. Can't tell closer than that. She died, of course, of suffocation."

"Well, give us a report. Probably nothing, but it never hurts. Thomas, get that doorman in here."

When Dr. Prouty and the Morgue men had gone with the body and Sergeant Velie had hauled in old Perk, the stagedoor man and watchman, the Inspector growled: "What time'd you lock up last night, Mister?"

Old Perk was hoarse with nervousness. "Honest t' Gawd, Inspector, I didn't mean nothin' by it. On'y

Mr. Kelly here'd fire me if he knew. I was that sleepy—"

"What's this?" said the Inspector softly.

"Myra told me after the last show last night she an' Atlas were gonna rehearse a new stunt. I didn't wanna wait aroun', y'see," the old man whined, "so seein' as nob'dy else was in the house that late, the cleanin' women gone an' all, I locked up everything but the stage door an' I says to Myra an' Atlas, I says: 'When ye leave, folks,' I says, 'jest slam the stage door.' An' I went home."

"Rats," said the Inspector irritably. "Now we'll never know who could have come in and who didn't. Anybody could have sneaked back without being seen or waited around in hiding until—" He bit his lip. "You men there, where'd you all go after the show last night?"

The three actors started simultaneously. It was the Great Gordi who spoke first, in his soft smooth voice that was now uneasy. "I went directly to my rooming-house and to bed."

"Anybody see you come in? You live in the same hole as Brinkerhof?"

The magician shrugged. "No one saw me. Yes, I do."

"You, Texas?"

The cowboy drawled: "I moseyed round to a speak somewhere an' got drunk."

"What speak?"

"Dunno. I was primed. Woke up in my room this mornin' with a head."

"You boys sure are in a tough spot," said the Inspector sarcastically. "Can't even fix good alibis for yourself. Well, how about you, Mr. Comedian?"

The comic said eagerly: "Oh, I can prove where I was, Inspector. I went around to a joint I know an' can get twenny people to swear to it."

"What time?"

"Round midnight."

The Inspector snorted and said: "Beat it. But hang around. I'll be wanting you boys, maybe. Take 'em away, Thomas, before I lose my temper."

Long, long ago—when, it will be recalled, Megatherium roamed the trees—the same lop-eared impresario who said: "The acrobat shall be first," also laid down the dictum that: "The show must go on," and for as little reason. Accidents might happen, the juvenile might run off with the female lion-tamer, the ingénue might be howling drunk, the lady in the fifth row, right, might have chosen the theatre to be the scene of her monthly attack of epilepsy, fire might break out in Dressing Room A, but the show must go on. Not even a rare juicy homicide may annul the sacred dictum. The show must go on despite hell, high water, drunken managers named Kelly, and The Fantastic Affair of the Hanging Acrobat.

So it was not strange that when the Metropole began to fill with its dribble of early patrons there was no sign that a woman had been slain the night before within its gaudy walls and that police and detectives roved its backstage with suspicious, if baffled, eyes.

The murder was just an incident to Show Business. It would rate two columns in *Variety*.

Inspector Richard Queen chafed in the hard seat in the fifteenth row while Ellery sat beside him sunk in thought. Stranger than everything had been Ellery's insistence that they remain to witness the performance.

There was a motion picture to sit through—a film which, bitterly, the Inspector pointed out he had seen— a newsreel, an animated cartoon. . . .

It was while "Coming Attractions" were flitting over the screen that Ellery rose and said: "Let's go backstage. There's something—" He did not finish.

They passed behind the dusty boxes on the right and went backstage through the iron door guarded by a uniformed officer. The vast bare reaches of the stage and wings were oppressed with an unusual silence. Manager Kelly, rather the worse for wear, sat on a broken chair near the light panel and gnawed his unsteady fingers. None of the vaudeville actors was in evidence.

"Kelly," said Ellery abruptly, "is there anything like a pair of field glasses in the house?"

The Irishman gaped. "What the hell would you be wantin' *them* for?"

"Please."

Kelly fingered a passing stagehand, who vanished and reappeared shortly with the desired binoculars. The Inspector grunted: "So what?"

Ellery adjusted them to his eyes. "I don't know," he said, shrugging. "It's just a hunch."

There was a burst of music from the pit: the Overture.

"*Poet and Peasant*," snarled the Inspector. "Don't they ever get anything new?"

But Ellery said nothing. He merely waited, binoculars ready, eyes fixed on the now footlighted stage. And it was only when the last blare had died away, and grudging splatters of applause came from the orchestra, and the announcement cards read: "Atlas & Co.," that the Inspector lost something of his irritability and even became interested. For when the curtains slithered up there was Atlas himself, bowing and smiling, his immense body impressive in flesh tights; and there beside him stood a tall smiling woman with golden hair and at least one golden tooth which flashed in the footlights. And she too wore flesh tights. For Brinkerhof with the mildness and resilience of all acrobats had insisted on taking his regular turn, and Bregman the booker had sent him another partner, and the two strangers had spent an hour rehearsing their intimate embraces and clutches and swingings and nuzzlings before the first performance. The show must go on.

Atlas and the golden woman went through an intricate series of tumbles and equilibristic maneuvers. The orchestra played brassy music. Trapezes dived stageward. Simple swings. Somersaults in the air. The drummer rolled and smashed his cymbal.

Ellery made no move to use the binoculars. He and the Inspector and Kelly stood in the wings, and none of them said anything, although Kelly was breathing hard like a man who has just come out of deep water for air. A queer little figure materialized beside them; Ellery turned his head slowly. But it was only Sailor Sam, the low comic, rigged out in a naval uniform three sizes too large for his skinny little frame, his face daubed liberally with grease-paint. He kept watching Atlas & Co. without expression.

"Good, ain't he?" he said at last in a small voice.

No one replied. But Ellery turned to the manager and whispered: "Kelly, keep your eyes open for—" and his voice sank so low neither the comedian nor Inspector Queen could hear what he said. Kelly looked puzzled; his bloodshot eyes opened a little wider; but he nodded and swallowed, riveting his gaze upon the whirling figures on the stage.

And when it was all over and the orchestra was executing the usual *crescendo sustenuto* and Atlas was bowing and smiling and the woman was curtseying and showing her gold tooth and the curtain dropped swiftly, Ellery glanced at Kelly. But Kelly shook his head.

The announcement cards changed. "Sailor Sam." There was a burst of fresh fast music, and the little man in the oversize naval uniform grinned three times, as if trying it out, drew a deep breath, and scuttled out upon the stage to sprawl full-length with his gnomish face jutting over the footlights to the accompaniment of surprised laughter from the darkness below.

They watched from the wings, silent.

The comedian had a clever routine. Not only was he a travesty upon all sailormen, but he was a travesty upon all sailormen in their cups. He drooled and staggered and was silent and then chattered suddenly, and he described a mythical voyage and fell all over himself climbing an imaginary mast and fell silent again to go into a pantomime that rocked the house.

The Inspector said grudgingly: "Why, he's as good as Jimmy Barton any day, with that drunk routine of his."

"Just a slob," said Kelly out of the corner of his mouth.

Sailor Sam made his exit by the complicated expedient of swimming off the stage. He stood in the wings, panting, his face streaming perspiration. He ran out for a bow. They thundered for more. He vanished. He reappeared. He vanished again. There was a stubborn look on his pixie face.

"Sam!" hissed Kelly. "F'r cripe's sake, Sam, give 'em 'at encore rope number. F'r cripe's sake, Sam—"

"Rope number?" said Ellery quietly.

The comedian licked his lips. Then his shoulders drooped and he slithered out onto the stage again. There was a shout of laughter and the house quieted at once. Sam scrambled to his feet, weaving and blinking blearily.

" 'Hoy there!" he howled suddenly. "Gimme rope!"

A *papier-mâché* cigar three feet long dropped to the stage from the opposite wings. Laughter. "Naw! Rope! Rope!" the little man screamed, dancing up and down.

A blackish rope snaked down from the flies. Miraculously it coiled over his scrawny shoulders. He struggled with it. He scrambled after its tarred ends. He executed fantastic flying leaps. And always the tarred ends eluded him, and constantly he became more and more enmeshed in the black coils as he wrestled with the rope.

The gallery broke down. The man *was* funny; even Kelly's dour face lightened, and the Inspector was frankly grinning. Then it was over and two stagehands darted out of the wings and pulled the comedian off the stage, now a helpless bundle trussed in rope. His face under the paint was chalk-white. He extricated himself easily enough from the coils.

"Good boy," chuckled the Inspector. "That was fine!"

Sam muttered something and trudged away to his dressing-room. The black rope lay where it had fallen. Ellery glanced at it once, and then turned his attention back to the stage. The music had changed. A startling beautiful tenor voice rang through the theatre. The

orchestra was playing softly *Home on the Range*. The
curtain rose on Tex Crosby.

The tall thin man was dressed in gaudiest stage-cow-
boy costume. And yet he wore it with an air of authority. The pearl-butted six-shooters protruding from his
holsters did not seem out of place. His big white som-
brero shaded a gaunt Western face. His legs were a
little bowed. The man was real.

He sang Western songs, told a few funny stories in
his soft Texan drawl, and all the while his long-fingered
hands were busy with a lariat. He made the lariat live.
From the moment the curtain rose upon his lanky figure
the lariat was in motion, and it did not subside through
the jokes, the patter, even the final song, which was inevitably *The Last Round-Up*.

"Tinhorn Will Rogers," sneered Kelly, blinking his
bloodshot eyes.

For the first time Ellery raised the binoculars. When
the Texan had taken his last bow Ellery glanced inquiringly at the manager. Kelly shook his head.

The Great Gordi made his entrance in a clap of thunder, a flash of lightning, and a black Satanic cloak, faced
with red. There was something impressive about his
very charlatanism. His black eyes glittered and his
mustache-points quivered above his lips and his beak
jutted like an eagle's; and meanwhile neither his hands
nor his mouth kept still.

The magician had a smooth effortless patter which
kept his audience amused and diverted their attention
from the fluent mysteries of his hands. There was nothing startling in his routine, but it was a polished performance that fascinated. He performed seeming mir-

acles with cards. His sleight-of-hand with coins and handkerchiefs was, to the layman, amazing. His evening clothes apparently concealed scores of wonders.

They watched with a mounting tension while he went through his bag of tricks. For the first time Ellery noticed, with a faint start, that Brinkerhof, still in tights, was crouched in the opposite wings. The big man's eyes were fixed upon the magician's face. They ignored the flashing fingers, the swift movements of the black-clad body. Only the face . . . In Brinkerhof's eyes was neither rage nor venom; just watchfulness. What was the matter with the man? Ellery reflected that it was just as well that Gordi was unconscious of the acrobat's scrutiny; those subtle hands might not operate so fluidly.

Despite the tension the magician's act seemed interminable. There were tricks with odd-looking pieces of apparatus manipulated from backstage by assistants. The house was with him, completely in his grasp.

"Good show," said the Inspector in a surprised voice. "This is darned good vaudeville."

"It'll get by," muttered Kelly. There was something queer on his face. He too was watching intently.

And suddenly something went wrong on the stage. The orchestra seemed bewildered. Gordi had concluded a trick, bowed, and stepped into the wings near the watching men. Not even the curtain was prepared. The orchestra had swung into another piece. The conductor's head was jerking from side to side in a panicky, inquiring manner.

"What's the matter?" demanded the Inspector.

Kelly snarled: "He's left out his last trick. Good hunch, Mr. Queen. . . . Hey, ham!" he growled to the magician, "finish your act, damn you! While they're still clappin'!"

Gordi was very pale. He did not turn; they could see only his left cheek and the rigidity of his back. Nor did he reply. Instead, with all the reluctance of a tyro, he slowly stepped back onto the stage. From the other side Brinkerhof watched. And this time Gordi, with a convulsive start, saw him.

"What's coming off here?" said the Inspector softly, as alert as a wren.

Ellery swung the glasses to his eyes.

A trapeze hurtled stageward from the flies—a simple steel bar suspended from two slender strands. A smooth yellow rope, very new in appearance, accompanied it from above, falling to the stage.

The magician worked very, very, painfully slowly. The house was silent. Even the music had stopped.

Gordi grasped the rope and did something with it; his back concealed what he was doing; then he swung about and held up his left hand. Tied with an enormous and complicated knot to his left wrist was the end of the yellow rope. He picked up the other end and leaped a little, securing the trapeze. At the level of his chest he steadied it and turned again so that he concealed what he was doing, and when he swung about once more they saw that the rope's other end was now knotted in the same way about the steel bar of the trapeze. He raised his right hand in signal and the drummer began a long roll.

Instantly the trapeze began to rise, and they saw that the rope was only four feet long. As the bar rose, Gordi's lithe body rose with it, suspended from the bar by the full length of the rope attached to his wrist. The trapeze came to a stop when the magician's feet were two yards from the stage.

Ellery squinted carefully through the powerful lenses. Across the stage Brinkerhof crouched.

Gordi now began to squirm and kick and jump in the air, indicating in pantomime that he was securely tied to the trapeze and that not even the heavy weight of his suspended body could undo the knots; in fact, was tightening them.

"It's a good trick," muttered Kelly. "In a second a special drop'll come down, an' in eight seconds it'll go up again and there he'll be on the stage, with the rope on the floor."

Gordi cried in a muffled voice: "Ready!"

But at the same instant Ellery said to Kelly: "*Quick!* Drop the curtain! This instant. Signal those men in the flies, Kelly!"

Kelly leaped into action. He shouted something unintelligible and after a second of hesitation the main curtain dropped. The house was dumb with astonishment; they thought it was part of the trick. Gordi began to struggle frantically, reaching up the trapeze with his free hand.

"Lower that trapeze!" roared Ellery on the cut-off stage now, waving his arms at the staring men above. "Lower it! *Gordi, don't move!*"

The trapeze came down with a thud. Gordi sprawled on the stage, his mouth working. Ellery leaped upon him, an open blade in hand. He cut quickly, savagely, at the rope. It parted, its torn end dangling from the trapeze.

"You may get up now," said Ellery, panting a little. "It's the knot I wanted to see, *Signor* Gordi."

They crowded around Ellery and the fallen man, who

seemed incapable of rising. He sat on the stage, his mouth still working, naked fear in his eyes. Brinkerhof was there, his muscular biceps rigid. Crosby, Sailor Sam, Sergeant Velie, Kelly, Bregman. . . .

The Inspector stared at the knot on the trapeze. Then he slowly took from his pocket a short length of the dirty old rope which had hanged Myra Brinkerhof. The knot was there. He placed it beside the knot on the trapeze.

They were identical.

"Well, Gordi," said the Inspector wearily, "I guess it's all up with you. Get up, man. I'm holding you for murder, and anything you say—"

Without a sound Brinkerhof, the mighty Atlas, sprang upon the man on the floor, big hands on Gordi's throat. It took the combined efforts of the Texan, Sergeant Velie, and Manager Kelly to tear the acrobat off.

Gordi gasped, holding his throat: "I didn't do it, I tell you! I'm innocent! Yes, we had—we lived together. I loved her. But why should I kill her? I didn't do it. For God's sake—"

"*Schwein*," growled Atlas, his chest heaving.

Sergeant Velie tugged at Gordi's collar. "Come on, come on there. . . ."

Ellery drawled: "Very pretty. My apologies, Mr. Gordi. Of course you didn't do it."

A shocked silence fell. From behind the heavy curtain voices—loud voices—came. The feature picture had been flashed on the screen.

"Didn't—do—it?" muttered Brinkerhof.

"But the knots, El," began the Inspector in a bewildered voice.

"Precisely. The knots." In defiance of fire regula-
tions Ellery lit a cigaret and puffed throughtfully.
"The hanging of Myra Brinkerhof has bothered me
from the beginning. Why was she *hanged?* In preference to one of four other methods of committing murder which were simpler, more expedient, easier of ac-
complishment, and offered no extra work, as hanging
did? The point is that if the murderer chose the hard
way, the complicated way, the roundabout way of killing her, then he chose that way *deliberately.*"

Gordi was staring with his mouth open. Kelly was
ashen pale.

"But why," murmured Ellery, "did he choose hanging
deliberately? Obviously, because hanging offered the
murderer some peculiar advantage not offered by any
of the other four methods. Well, what advantage could
hanging conceivably offer that shooting, stabbing, gas-
sing, or hammering to death could not? To put it another way, what is characteristic of hanging that is not
characteristic of shooting and the rest? Only one thing.
The use of a rope."

"Well, but I still don't see—" frowned the Inspector.

"Oh, it's clear enough, dad. There's something about
the rope that made the murderer use it in preference to
the other methods. But what's the outstanding significance of this particular rope—the rope used to hang
Myra Brinkerhof? *Its knot*—its peculiar knot, so peculiar that not even the Department's expert could identify it. In other words, the use of that knot was like the
leaving of a fingerprint. Whose knot is it? Gordi's,
the magician's—and, I suspect, his exclusively."

"I can't understand it," cried Gordi. "Nobody knew
my knot. It's one I developed myself—" Then he bit
his lip and fell silent.

"Exactly the point.   I realize that stage-magicians
have developed knot-making to a remarkable degree.
Wasn't it Houdini who—?"

"The Davenport brothers, too," muttered the magician.   "My knot is a variation on one of their creations."

"Quite so," drawled Ellery.   "So I say, had Mr. Gordi
wanted to kill Myra Brinkerhof, would he have deliberately chosen *the single method that incriminated him,*
and him alone?   Certainly not if he were reasonably intelligent.   Did he tie his distinctive knot, then, from
sheer habit, subconsciously?   Conceivable, but then why
had he chosen hanging in the first place, when those four
easier methods were nearer to his hand?"   Ellery slapped
the magician's back.   "So, I say—our apologies, Gordi.
The answer is very patently that you're being framed by
some one who deliberately chose the hanging-plus-knot
method to implicate you in a crime you're innocent of."

"But he says nobody else knew his confounded knot,"
growled the Inspector.   "If what you say is true, El,
somebody must have learned it on the sly."

"Very plausible," murmured Ellery.   "Any sugges-
tions, *Signor?*"

The magician got slowly to his feet, brushing his
dress-suit off.   Brinkerhof gaped stupidly at him, at
Ellery.

"I don't know," said Gordi, very pale.   "I thought
no one knew.   Not even my technical assistants.   But
then we've all been travelling on the same bill for weeks.
I suppose if some one wanted to . . ."

"I see," said Ellery thoughtfully.   "So there's a dead
end, eh?"

"Dead beginning," snapped his father.   "And thanks,
my son, for the assistance. *You're* a help!"

"I tell you very frankly," said Ellery the next day in his father's office, "*I* don't know what it's all about. The only thing I'm sure of is Gordi's innocence. The murderer knew very well that somebody would notice the unusual knot Gordi uses in his rope-escape illusion. As for motive—"

"Listen," snarled the Inspector, thoroughly out of temper, "I can see through glass the same way you can. They all had motive. Crosby kicked over by the dame, Gordi . . . Did you know that this little comedian was sniffin' around Myra's skirts the last couple of weeks? Trying his darnedest to make her. And Kelly's had monkey business with her, too, on a former appearance at the Metropole."

"Don't doubt it," said Ellery sombrely. "The call of the flesh. She was an alluring little trick, at that. Real old Boccaccio melodrama, with the stupid husband playing cuckold—"

The door opened and Dr. Prouty, Assistant Medical Examiner, stumped in looking annoyed. He dropped into a chair and clumped his feet on the Inspector's desk. "Guess what?" he said.

"I'm a rotten guesser," said the old gentleman sourly.

"Little surprise for you gentlemen. For me, too. The woman wasn't hanged."

"What!" cried the Queens, together.

"Fact. She was dead when she was swung up." Dr. Prouty squinted at his ragged cigar.

"Well, I'll be eternally damned," said Ellery softly. He sprang from his chair and shook the physician's shoulder. "Prouty, for heaven's sake, don't look so smug! What killed her? Gun, gas, knife, poison—"

"Fingers."

"Fingers?"

Dr. Prouty shrugged. "No question about it. When

I took that dirty hemp off her lovely neck I found the distinct marks of fingers on the skin. It was a tight rope, and all that, but there were the marks, gentlemen. She was choked to death by a man's hands and then strung up—why, *I* don't know."

"Well," said Ellery. "Well," he said again, and straightened. "*Very* interesting. I begin to scent the proverbial rodent. Tell us more, good leech."

"Certainly is queer," muttered the Inspector, sucking his mustache.

"Something even queerer," drawled Dr. Prouty. "You boys have seen choked stiffs plenty. What's the characteristic of the fingermarks?"

Ellery was watching him intently. "Characteristic?" He frowned. "Don't know what you mean— Oh!" His gray eyes glittered. "Don't tell me. . . . The usual marks point upward, thumbs toward the chin."

"Smart lad. Well, these marks don't. They all point *downward.*"

Ellery stared for a long moment. Then he seized Dr. Prouty's limp hand and shook it violently. "Eureka! Prouty, old sock, you're the answer to a logician's prayer! Dad, come on!"

"What is this?" scowled the Inspector. "You're too fast for me. Come where?"

"To the Metropole. Urgent affairs. If my watch is honest," Ellery said quickly, "we're just in time to witness another performance. And I'll show you why our friend the murderer not only didn't shoot, stab, asphyxiate, or hammer little Myra into Kingdom Come, but didn't hang her either!"

Ellery's watch, however, was dishonest. When they reached the Metropole it was noon, and the feature picture was still showing. They hurried backstage in search of Kelly.

"Kelly or this old man they call Perk, the caretaker," Ellery murmured, hurrying his father down the dark side-aisle. "Just one question. . . ."

A patrolman let them through. They found backstage deserted except for Brinkerhof and his new partner, who were stolidly rehearsing what was apparently a new trick. The trapeze was down and the big man was hanging from it by his powerful legs, a rubber bit in his mouth. Below him, twirling like a top, spun the tall blonde, the other end of the bit in her mouth.

Kelly appeared from somewhere and Ellery said: "Oh, Kelly. Are all the others in?"

Kelly was drunk again. He wobbled and said vaguely: "Oh, sure. Sure."

"Gather the clans in Myra's dressing-room. We've still a little time. Question's unnecessary, dad. I should have known without—"

The Inspector threw up his hands.

Kelly scratched his chin and staggered off. "Hey, Atlash," he called wearily. "Stop Atlash-ing an' come on." He swayed off toward the dressing-rooms.

"But, El," groaned the Inspector, "I don't understand—"

"It's perfectly childish in its simplicity," said Ellery, "now that I've seen what I suspected was the case. Come along, sire; don't crab the act."

When they were assembled in the dead woman's cubbyhole Ellery leaned against the dressing-table, looked at the sprinkler-pipe, and said: "One of you might as well own up . . . you see, I know who killed the little —er—lady."

"You know that?" said Brinkerhof hoarsely. "Who is—" He stopped and glared at the others, his stupid eyes roving.

But no one else said anything.

Ellery sighed. "Very well, then, you force me to wax eloquent, even reminiscent. Yesterday I posed the question: Why should Myra Brinkerhof have been hanged in preference to one of four handier methods? And I said, in demonstrating Mr. Gordi's innocence, that the reason was that hanging permitted the use of a rope and consequently of Gordi's identifiable knot." He brandished his forefinger. "But I forgot an additional possibility. If you find a woman with a rope around her neck who has died of strangulation, you assume it was the rope that strangled her. I completely overlooked the fact that hanging, in permitting use of a rope, also accomplishes the important objective of *concealing the neck*. But why should Myra's neck have been concealed? By a rope? Because a rope is not the only way of strangling a victim, because a victim can be *choked* to death by fingers, because choking to death leaves marks on the neck, and because the choker didn't want the police to know there *were* fingermarks on Myra's neck. He thought that the tight strands of the rope would not only conceal the fingermarks but would obliterate them as well—sheer ignorance, of course, since in death such marks are ineradicable. But that is what he thought, and that *primarily* is why he chose hanging for Myra when she was already dead. The leaving of Gordi's knot to implicate him was only a secondary reason for the selection of rope."

"But, El," cried the Inspector, "that's nutty. Suppose he did choke the woman to death. I can't see that he'd be incriminating himself by leaving fingermarks on her neck. You can't match fingermarks—"

"Quite true," drawled Ellery, "but you *can* observe that fingermarks are on the neck *the wrong way*. For these point, not upward, but downward."

And still no one said anything, and there was silence for a space in the room with the heavily breathing men.

"For you see, gentlemen," continued Ellery sharply, "when Myra was choked she was choked *upside down*. But how is this possible? Only if one of two conditions existed. Either at the time she was choked she was hanging head down above her murderer, or—"

Brinkerhof said stupidly: "*Ja*. I did it. *Ja*. I did it." He said it over and over, like a phonograph with its needle grooved.

A woman's voice from the amplifier said: "But I love you, darling, love you, love you, love you . . ."

Brinkerhof's eyes flamed and he took a short step toward the Great Gordi. "Yesterday I say to Myra: 'Myra, tonight we rehearse the new trick.' After the second show I see Myra undt that *schweinhund* kissing undt kissing behind the scenery. I hear them talk. They haf been fooling me. I plan. I will kill her. When we rehearse. So I kill her." He buried his face in his hands and began to sob without sound. It was horrible; and Gordi seemed transfixed with its horror.

And Brinkerhof muttered: "Then I see the marks on her throat. They are upside down. I know that iss bad. So I take the rope undt I cover up the marks. Then I hang her, with the *schwein's* knot, that she had once told me he had shown to her—"

He stopped. Gordi said hoarsely, "Good God. I didn't remember—"

"Take him away," said the Inspector in a small dry voice to the policeman at the door.

"It was all so clear," explained Ellery a little later, over coffee. "Either the woman was hanging head down above her murderer, or her murderer was hanging head down above the woman. One squeeze of those powerful paws . . ." He shivered. "It had to be an acrobat, you see. And when I remembered that Brinkerhof himself had said they had been rehearsing a new trick—" He stopped and smoked thoughtfully.

"Poor guy," muttered the Inspector. "He's not a bad sort, just dumb. Well, she got what was coming to her."

"Dear, dear," drawled Ellery. "Philosophy, Inspector? I'm really not interested in the moral aspects of crime. I'm more annoyed at this case than anything."

"Annoyed?" said the Inspector with a sniff. "You look mighty smug to me."

"Do I? But I really am. I'm annoyed at the shocking unimaginativeness of our newspaper friends."

"Well, well," said the Inspector with a sigh of resignation. "I'll bite. What's the gag?"

Ellery grinned. "Not one of the reporters who covered this case saw the perfectly obvious headline. You see, they forgot that one of the cast is named—of all things, dear God!—Gordi."

"Headline?" frowned the Inspector.

"Oh, lord. How could they have escaped casting me in the rôle of Alexander and calling this The Affair of the Gordian Knot?"

The Adventure of
THE ONE-PENNY BLACK

The Adventure of
THE ONE-PENNY BLACK

"Ach!" 'said old Uneker. "It iss a terrible t'ing, Mr. Quveen, a terrible t'ing, like I vass saying. Vat iss New York coming to? Dey come into my store—*polizei*, undt bleedings, undt whackings on de headt. . . . Diss iss vun uff my oldest customers, Mr. Quveen. He too hass hadt exberiences. . . . Mr. Hazlitt, Mr. Quveen. . . . Mr. Quveen iss dot famous detectiff feller you read aboudt in de papers, Mr. Hazlitt. Inspector Richardt Quveen's son."

Ellery Queen laughed, uncoiled his length from old Uneker's counter, and shook the man's hand. "Another victim of our crime wave, Mr. Hazlitt? Unky's been regaling me with a feast of a whopping bloody tale."

"So you're Ellery Queen," said the frail little fellow; he wore a pair of thick-lensed goggles and there was a smell of suburbs about him. "This *is* luck! Yes, I've been robbed."

Ellery looked incredulously about old Uneker's bookshop. "Not *here?*" Uneker was tucked away on a side street in mid-Manhattan, squeezed between the British Bootery and Mme. Carolyne's, and it was just about the last place in the world you would have expected thieves to choose as the scene of a crime.

"Nah," said Hazlitt. "Might have saved the price of a book if it had. No, it happened last night about ten o'clock. I'd just left my office on Forty-fifth Street— I'd worked late—and I was walking crosstown. Chap

65

stopped me on the street and asked for a light. The street was pretty dark and deserted, and I didn't like the fellow's manner, but I saw no harm in lending him a packet of matches. While I was digging it out, though, I noticed he was eyeing the book under my arm. Sort of trying to read the title."

"What book was it?" asked Ellery eagerly. Books were his private passion.

Hazlitt shrugged. "Nothing remarkable. That best-selling non-fiction thing, *Europe in Chaos;* I'm in the export line and I like to keep up to date on international conditions. Anyway, this chap lit his cigarette, returned the matches, mumbled his thanks, and I began to walk on. Next thing I knew something walloped me on the back of my head and everything went black. I seem to remember falling. When I came to, I was lying in the gutter, my hat and glasses were on the stones, and my head felt like a baked potato. Naturally thought I'd been robbed; I had a lot of cash about me, and I was wearing a pair of diamond cuff-links. But—"

"But, of course," said Ellery with a grin, "the only thing that was taken was *Europe in Chaos.* Perfect, Mr. Hazlitt! A fascinating little problem. Can you describe your assailant?"

"He had a heavy mustache and dark-tinted glasses of some kind. That's all. I—"

"He? He can describe not'ing," said old Uneker sourly. "He iss like all you Americans—blindt, a *dummkopf.* But de book, Mr. Quveen—de book! Vhy should any von vant to steal a book like dot?"

"And that isn't all," said Hazlitt. "When I got home last night—I live in East Orange, New Jersey—I found my house broken into! And what do you think had been stolen, Mr. Queen?"

Ellery's lean face beamed. "I'm no crystal-gazer; but if there's any consistency in crime, I should imagine another book had been stolen."

"Right! And it was my second copy of *Europe in Chaos!*"

"Now you do interest me," said Ellery, in quite a different tone. "How did you come to have two, Mr. Hazlitt?"

"I bought another copy from Uneker two days ago to give to a friend of mine. I'd left it on top of my bookcase. It was gone. Window was open—it had been forced; and there were smudges of hands on the sill. Plain case of house-breaking. And although there's plenty of valuable stuff in my place—silver and things —nothing else had been taken. I reported it at once to the East Orange police, but they just tramped about the place, gave me funny looks, and finally went away. I suppose they thought I was crazy."

"Were any other books missing?"

"No, just that one."

"I really don't see . . ." Ellery took off his *pince-nez* eyeglasses and began to polish the lenses thoughtfully. "Could it have been the same man? Would he have had time to get out to East Orange and burglarize your house before you got there last night?"

"Yes. When I picked myself out of the gutter I reported the assault to a cop, and he took me down to a nearby station-house, and they asked me a lot of questions. He would have had plenty of time—I didn't get home until one o'clock in the morning."

"I think, Unky," said Ellery, "that the story *you* told me begins to have point. If you'll excuse me, Mr. Hazlitt, I'll be on my way. *Auf wiedersehen!*"

Ellery left old Uneker's little shop and went downtown to Center Street. He climbed the steps of Police Headquarters, nodded amiably to a desk lieutenant, and made for his father's office. The Inspector was out. Ellery twiddled with an ebony figurine of Bertillon on his father's desk, mused deeply, then went out and began to hunt for Sergeant Velie, the Inspector's chief-of-operations. He found the mammoth in the Press Room, bawling curses at a reporter.

"Velie," said Ellery, "stop playing bad man and get me some information. Two days ago there was an unsuccessful man-hunt on Forty-ninth Street, between Fifth and Sixth Avenues. The chase ended in a little bookshop owned by a friend of mine named Uneker. Local officer was in on it. Uneker told me the story, but I want less colored details. Get me the precinct report like a good fellow, will you?"

Sergeant Velie waggled his big black jaws, glared at the reporter, and thundered off. Ten minutes later he came back with a sheet of paper, and Ellery read it with absorption.

The facts seemed bald enough. Two days before, at the noon hour, a hatless, coatless man with a bloody face had rushed out of the office-building three doors from old Uneker's bookshop, shouting: "Help! Police!" Patrolman McCallum had run up, and the man yelled that he had been robbed of a valuable postage-stamp—"My one-penny black!" he kept shouting. "My one-penny black!"—and that the thief, black-mustached and wearing heavy blue-tinted spectacles, had just escaped. McCallum had noticed a man of this description a few minutes before, acting peculiarly, enter the nearby bookshop. Followed by the screaming stamp-dealer, he dashed into old Uneker's place with drawn revolver. Had a man with black mustaches and blue-tinted spectacles come into the shop within the past few minutes? "*Ja*—he?" said old Uneker. "Sure, he iss still here." Where? In the back-room looking at some books. McCallum and the bleeding man rushed into Uneker's back-room; it was empty. A door leading to the alley from the back-room was open; the man had escaped, apparently having been scared off by the noisy entrance of the policeman and the victim a moment before. McCallum had immediately searched the neighborhood; the thief had vanished.

The officer then took the complainant's statement. He was, he said, Friederich Ulm, dealer in rare postage stamps. His office was in a tenth-floor room in the building three doors away—the office of his brother Albert, his partner, and himself. He had been exhibiting some valuable items to an invited group of three stamp-collectors. Two of them had gone away. Ulm happened to turn his back; and the third, the man with the black mustache and blue-tinted glasses, who had introduced himself as Avery Beninson, had swooped on him swiftly from behind and struck at his head with a short iron bar as Ulm twisted back. The blow had cut open Ulm's cheekbone and felled him, half-stunned; and then with the utmost coolness the thief had used the same iron bar (which, said the report, from its description was probably a "jimmy") to pry open the lid of a glass-topped cabinet in which a choice collection of stamps was kept. He had snatched from a leather box in the cabinet an extremely high-priced item—"the Queen Victoria one-penny black"—and had then dashed out, locking the door behind him. It had taken the assaulted dealer several minutes to open the door and follow. McCallum went with Ulm to the office, examined the rifled cabinet, took the names and addresses

of the three collectors who had been present that morn‚
ing—with particular note of "Avery Beninson"—scribbled his report, and departed.

The names of the other two collectors were John
Hinchman and J. S. Peters. A detective attached to the
precinct had visited each in turn, and had then gone
to the address of Beninson. Beninson, who presumably
had been the man with black mustaches and blue-tinted
spectacles, was ignorant of the entire affair; and his
physical appearance did not tally with the description of
Ulm's assailant. He had received no invitation from the
Ulm brothers, he said, to attend the private sale. Yes,
he had had an employee, a man with black mustaches
and tinted glasses, for two weeks—this man had answered Beninson's advertisement for an assistant to take
charge of the collector's private stamp-albums, had
proved satisfactory, and had suddenly, without explanation or notice, disappeared after two weeks' service. He
had disappeared, the detective noted, on the morning of
the Ulms' sale.

All attempts to trace this mysterious assistant, who
had called himself William Planck, were unsuccessful.
The man had vanished among New York City's millions.

Nor was this the end of the story. For the day after
the theft old Uneker himself had reported to the precinct detective a queer tale. The previous night—the
night of the Ulm theft—said Uneker, he had left his
shop for a late dinner; his night-clerk had remained on
duty. A man had entered the shop, had asked to see
Europe in Chaos, and had then to the night-clerk's astonishment purchased all copies of the book in stock—
seven. The man who had made this extraordinary purchase wore black mustaches and blue-tinted spectacles!

"Sort of nuts, ain't it?" growled Sergeant Velie.

"Not at all," smiled Ellery. "In fact, I believe it has a very simple explanation."

"And that ain't the half of it. One of the boys told me just now of a new angle on the case. Two minor robberies were reported from local precincts last night. One was uptown in the Bronx; a man named Hornell said his apartment was broken into during the night, and what do you think? Copy of *Europe in Chaos* which Hornell had bought in this guy Uneker's store was stolen! Nothin' else. Bought it two days ago. Then a dame named Janet Meakins from Greenwich Village had *her* flat robbed the same night. Thief had taken her copy of *Europe in Chaos*—she'd bought it from Uneker the afternoon before. Screwy, hey?"

"Not at all, Velie. Use your wits." Ellery clapped his hat on his head. "Come along, you Colossus; I want to speak to old Unky again."

They left Headquarters and went uptown.

"Unky," said Ellery, patting the little old bookseller's bald pate affectionately, "how many copies of *Europe in Chaos* did you have in stock at the time the thief escaped from your back-room?"

"Eleffen."

"Yet only seven were in stock that same evening when the thief returned to buy them," murmured Ellery. "Therefore, four copies had been sold between the noon-hour two days ago and the dinner-hour. So! Unky, do you keep a record of your customers?"

"*Ach*, yes! De few who buy," said old Uneker sadly. "I addt to my mailing-lisdt. You vant to see?"

"There is nothing I crave more ardently at the moment."

Uneker led them to the rear of the shop and through a door into the musty back-room from whose alley-door

the thief had escaped two days before. Off this room
there was a partitioned cubicle littered with papers, files
and old books. The old bookseller opened a ponderous
ledger and, wetting his ancient forefinger, began to slap
pages over. "You vant to know de four who boughdt
Europe in Chaos dot afternoon?"

"*Ja.*"

Uneker hooked a pair of greenish-silver spectacies
over his ears and began to read in a singsong voice.
"Mr. Hazlitt—dot's the gentleman you met, Mr.
Quveen. *He* boughdt his second copy, de vun dot vass
robbed from his house. . . . Den dere vass Mr. Hornell,
an oldt customer. Den a Miss Janet Meakins—*ach!*
dese Anglo-Saxon names. *Schrecklich!* Undt de fourt'
vun vass Mr. Chester Singermann, uff t'ree-tvelf East
Siggsty-fift' Street. Und dot's all."

"Bless your orderly old Teutonic soul," said Ellery.
"Velie, cast those Cyclopean peepers of yours this way."
There was a door from the cubicle which, from its location, led out into the alley at the rear, like the door in the
back-room. Ellery bent over the lock; it was splintered
away from the wood. He opened the door; the outer
piece was scratched and mutilated. Velie nodded.
"Forced," he growled. "This guy's a regular Houdini."

Old Uneker was goggle-eyed. "Broken!" he shrilled.
"Budt dot door iss neffer used! I didn't notice not'ing,
undt de detectiff—"

"Shocking work, Velie, on the part of the local man,"
said Ellery. "Unky, has anything been stolen?" Old
Uneker flew to an antiquated bookcase; it was neatly
tiered with volumes. He unlocked the case with anguished fingers, rummaging like an aged terrier. Then
he heaved a vast sigh. "*Nein,*" he said. "Dose rare
vons . . . Not'ing stole."

"I congratulate you. One thing more," said Ellery briskly. "Your mailing-list—does it have the business as well as private addresses of your customers?" Uneker nodded. "Better and better. Ta-ta, Unky. You may have a finished story to relate to your other customers after all. Come along, Velie; we're going to visit Mr. Chester Singermann."

They left the bookshop, walked over to Fifth Avenue and turned north, heading uptown. "Plain as the nose on your face," said Ellery, stretching his long stride to match Velie's. "And that's pretty plain, Sergeant."

"Still looks nutty to me, Mr. Queen."

"On the contrary, we are faced with a strictly logical set of facts. Our thief stole a valuable stamp. He dodged into Uneker's bookshop, contrived to get into the back-room. He heard the officer and Friederich Ulm enter, and got busy thinking. If he were caught with the stamp on his person . . . You see, Velie, the only explanation that will make consistent the business of the subsequent thefts of the same book—a book not valuable in itself—is that the thief, Planck, slipped the stamp between the pages of one of the volumes on a shelf while he was in the back-room—it happened by accident to be a copy of *Europe in Chaos*, one of a number kept in stock on the shelf—and made his escape immediately thereafter. But he still had the problem of regaining possession of the stamp—what did Ulm call it?—the 'one-penny black,' whatever *that* may be. So that night he came back, watched for old Uneker to leave the shop, then went in and bought from the clerk all copies of *Europe in Chaos* in the place. He got seven. The stamp was not in any one of the seven he purchased, otherwise why did he later steal others which had been bought that afternoon? So far, so good. Not finding the stamp in any of the seven, then, he returned, broke into Unky's little office during the night—witness the shattered lock—from the alley, and looked up in Unky's Dickensian ledger the names and addresses of those who had bought copies of the book during that afternoon. The next night he robbed Hazlitt; Planck evidently followed him from his office. Planck saw at once that he had made a mistake; the condition of the weeks-old book would have told him that this wasn't a book purchased only the day before. So he hurried out to East Orange, knowing Hazlitt's private as well as business address, and stole Hazlitt's recently purchased copy. No luck there either, so he feloniously visited Hornell and Janet Meakins, stealing their copies. Now, there is still one purchaser unaccounted for, which is why we are calling upon Singermann. For if Planck was unsuccessful in his theft of Hornell's and Miss Meakins' books, he will inevitably visit Singermann, and· we want to beat our wily thief to it if possible."

Chester Singermann, they found, was a young student living with his parents in a battered old apartment-house flat. Yes, he still had his copy of *Europe in Chaos* —needed it for supplementary reading in political economy—and he produced it. Ellery went through it carefully, page for page; there was no trace of the missing stamp.

"Mr. Singermann, did you find an old postage-stamp between the leaves of this volume?" asked Ellery.

The student shook his head. "I haven't even opened it, sir. Stamp? What issue? I've got a little collection of my own, you know."

"It doesn't matter," said Ellery hastily, who had heard of the maniacal enthusiasm of stamp-collectors, and he and Velie beat a precipitate retreat.

"It's quite evident," explained Ellery to the Sergeant, "that our slippery Planck found the stamp in either Hornell's copy or Miss Meakins'. Which robbery was first in point of time, Velie?"

"Seem to remember that this Meakins woman was robbed second."

"Then the one-penny black was in her copy. . . . Here's that office-building. Let's pay a little visit to Mr. Friederich Ulm."

Number 1026 on the tenth floor of the building bore a black legend on its frosted-glass door:

ULM

Dealers in

Old & Rare Stamps

Ellery and Sergeant Velie went in and found themselves in a large office. The walls were covered with glass cases in which, separately mounted, could be seen hundreds of canceled and uncanceled postage stamps. Several special cabinets on tables contained, evidently, more valuable items. The place was cluttered; it had a musty air astonishingly like that of old Uneker's bookshop.

Three men looked up. One, from a crisscrossed plaster on his cheekbone, was apparently Friederich Ulm himself, a tall gaunt old German with sparse hair and the fanatic look of the confirmed collector. The second man was just as tall and gaunt and old; he wore a green eye-shade and bore a striking resemblance to Ulm, although from his nervous movements and shaky hands he must have been much older. The third man was a little fellow, quite stout, with an expressionless face.

Ellery introduced himself and Sergeant Velie; and the

third man pricked up his ears. "Not *the* Ellery Queen?" he said, waddling forward. "I'm Heffley, investigator for the insurance people. Glad to meet you." He pumped Ellery's hand with vigor. "These gentlemen are the Ulm brothers, who own this place. Friederich and Albert. Mr. Albert Ulm was out of the office at the time of the sale and robbery. Too bad; might have nabbed the thief."

Friederich Ulm broke into an excited gabble of German. Ellery listened with a smile, nodding at every fourth word. "I see, Mr. Ulm. The situation, then, was this: you sent invitations by mail to three well-known collectors to attend a special exhibition of rare stamps—object, sale. Three men called on you two mornings ago, purporting to be Messrs. Hinchman, Peters, and Beninson. Hinchman and Peters you knew by sight, but Beninson you did not. Very well. Several items were purchased by the first two collectors. The man you thought was Beninson lingered behind, struck you—yes, yes, I know all that. Let me see the rifled cabinet, please."

The brothers led him to a table in the center of the office. On it there was a flat cabinet, with a lid of ordinary thin glass framed by a narrow rectangle of wood. Under the glass reposed a number of mounted stamps, lying nakedly on a field of black satin. In the center of the satin lay a leather case, open; its white lining had been denuded of its stamp. Where the lid of the cabinet had been wrenched open there were the unmistakable marks of a "jimmy," four in number. The catch was snapped and broken.

"Amatchoor," said Sergeant Velie with a snort. "You could damn' near force that locked lid up with your fingers."

Ellery's sharp eyes were absorbed in what lay before him. "Mr. Ulm," he said, turning to the wounded dealer, "the stamp you call 'the one-penny black' was in this open leather box?"

"Yes, Mr. Queen. But the leather box was closed when the thief forced open the cabinet."

"Then how did he know so unerringly what to steal?"

Friederich Ulm touched his cheek tenderly. "The stamps in this cabinet were not for sale; they're the cream of our collection; every stamp in this case is worth hundreds. But when the three men were here we naturally talked about the rarer items, and I opened this cabinet to show them our very valuable stamps. So the thief saw the one-penny black. He was a collector, Mr. Queen, or he wouldn't have chosen that particular stamp to steal. It has a funny history."

"Heavens!" said Ellery. "Do these things have histories?"

Heffley, the man from the insurance company, laughed. "And how! Mr. Friederich and Mr. Albert Ulm are well known to the trade for owning two of the most unique stamps ever issued, both identical. The one-penny black, as it is called by collectors, is a British stamp first issued in 1840; there are lots of them around, and even an uncanceled one is worth only seventeen and a half dollars in American money. But the two in the possession of these gentlemen are worth thirty thousand dollars a piece, Mr. Queen—that's what makes the theft so dog-gone serious. In fact, my company is heavily involved, since the stamps are both insured for their full value."

"Thirty thousand dollars!" groaned Ellery. "That's a lot of money for a little piece of dirty paper. Why are they so valuable?"

Albert Ulm nervously pulled his green shade lower over his eyes. "Because both of ours were actually initialed by Queen Victoria, that's why. Sir Rowland Hill, the man who created and founded the standard penny-postage system in England in 1839, was responsible for the issue of the one-penny black. Her Majesty was so delighted—England, like other countries, had had a great deal of trouble working out a successful postage system—that she autographed the first two stamps off the press and gave them to the designer—I don't recall his name. Her autograph made them immensely valuable. My brother and I were lucky to get our hands on the only two in existence."

"Where's the twin? I'd like to take a peep at a stamp worth a queen's ransom."

The brothers bustled to a large safe looming in a corner of the office. They came back, Albert carrying a leather case as if it were a consignment of gold bullion, and Friederich anxiously holding his elbow, as if he were a squad of armed guards detailed to protect the consignment. Ellery turned the thing over in his fingers; it felt thick and stiff. It was an average-sized stamp rectangle, imperforate, bordered with a black design, and containing an engraving in profile view of Queen Victoria's head—all done in tones of black. On the lighter portion of the face appeared two tiny initials in faded black ink—V. R.

"They're both exactly alike," said Friederich Ulm. "Even to the initials."

"Very interesting," said Ellery, returning the case. The brothers scurried back, placed the stamp in a drawer of the safe, and locked the safe with painful care. "You closed the cabinet, of course, after your three visitors looked over the stamps inside?"

"Oh, yes," said Friederich Ulm. "I closed the case of the one-penny black itself, and then I locked the cabinet."

"And did you send the three invitations yourself? I noticed you have no typewriter here."

"We use a public stenographer in Room 1102 for all our correspondence, Mr. Queen."

Ellery thanked the dealers gravely, waved to the insurance man, nudged Sergeant Velie's meaty ribs, and the two men left the office. In Room 1102 they found a sharp-featured young woman. Sergeant Velie flashed his badge, and Ellery was soon reading carbon copies of the three Ulm invitations. He took note of the names and addresses, and the two men left.

They visited the collector named John Hinchman first. Hinchman was a thick-set old man with white hair and gimlet eyes. He was brusque and uncommunicative. Yes, he had been present in the Ulms' office two mornings before. Yes, he knew Peters. No, he'd never met Beninson before. The one-penny black? Of course. Every collector knew of the valuable twin stamps owned by the Ulm brothers; those little scraps of paper bearing the initials of a queen were famous in stampdom. The theft? Bosh! He, Hinchman, knew nothing of Beninson, or whoever it was that impersonated Beninson. He, Hinchman, had left before the thief. He, Hinchman, furthermore didn't care two raps in Hades who stole the stamp; all he wanted was to be let strictly alone.

Sergeant Velie exhibited certain animal signs of hostility; but Ellery grinned, sank his strong fingers into the muscle of the Sergeant's arm, and herded him out of Hinchman's house. They took the subway uptown.

J. S. Peters, they found, was a middle-aged man, tall and thin and yellow as Chinese sealing-wax. He seemed anxious to be of assistance. Yes, he and Hinchman had left the Ulms' office together, before the third man. He had never seen the third man before, although he had heard of Beninson from other collectors. Yes, he knew all about the one-penny blacks, had even tried to buy one of them from Friederich Ulm two years before; but the Ulms had refused to sell.

"Philately," said Ellery outside to Sergeant Velie, whose honest face looked pained at the word, "is a curious hobby. It seems to afflict its victims with a species of mania. I don't doubt these stamp-collecting fellows would murder each other for one of the things."

The Sergeant was wrinkling his nose. "How's she look now?" he asked rather anxiously.

"Velie," replied Ellery, "she looks swell—and different."

They found Avery Beninson in an old brownstone house near the River; he was a mild-mannered and courteous host.

"No, I never did see that invitation," Beninson said. "You see, I hired this man who called himself William Planck, and he took care of my collection and the bulky mail all serious collectors have. The man knew stamps, all right. For two weeks he was invaluable to me. He must have intercepted the Ulms' invitation. He saw his chance to get into their office, went there, said he was Avery Beninson . . ." The collector shrugged. "It was quite simple, I suppose, for an unscrupulous man."

"Of course, you haven't had word from him since the morning of the theft?"

"Naturally not. He made his haul and lit out."

"Just what did he do for you, Mr. Beninson?"

"The ordinary routine of the philatelic assistant—assorting, cataloguing, mounting, answering correspondence. He lived here with me for the two weeks he was in my employ." Beninson grinned deprecatingly. "You see, I'm a bachelor—live in this big shack all alone. I was really glad of his company, although he *was* a queer one."

"A queer one?"

"Well," said Beninson, "he was a retiring sort of creature. Had very few personal belongings, and I found those gone two days ago. He didn't seem to like people, either. He always went to his own room when friends of mine or collectors called, as if he didn't want to mix with company."

"Then there isn't any one else who might be able to supplement description of him?"

"Unfortunately, no. He was a fairly tall man, well advanced in age, I should say. But then his dark glasses and heavy black mustache would make him stand out anywhere."

Ellery sprawled his long figure over the chair, slumping on his spine. "I'm most interested in the man's habits, Mr. Beninson. Individual idiosyncrasies are often the innocent means by which criminals are apprehended, as the good Sergeant here will tell you. Please think hard. Didn't the man exhibit any oddities of habit?"

Beninson pursed his lips with anxious concentration. His face brightened. "By George, yes! He was a snuff-taker."

Ellery and Sergeant Velie looked at each other. "That's interesting," said Ellery with a smile. "So is my father—Inspector Queen, you know—and I've had the dubious pleasure of watching a snuff-taker's gyrations ever since my childhood. Planck inhaled snuff regularly?"

"I shouldn't say that exactly, Mr. Queen," replied Beninson with a frown. "In fact, in the two weeks he was with me I saw him take snuff only once, and I invariably spent all day with him working in this room. It was last week; I happened to go out for a few moments, and when I returned I saw him holding a carved little box, sniffing from a pinch of something between his fingers. He put the box away quickly, as if he didn't want me to see it—although *I* didn't care, lord knows, so long as he didn't smoke in here. I've had one fire from a careless assistant's cigaret, and I don't want another."

Ellery's face had come alive. He sat up straight and began to finger his *pince-nez* eyeglasses studiously. "You didn't know the man's address, I suppose?" he asked slowly.

"No, I did not. I'm afraid I took him on without the proper precautions." The collector sighed. "I'm fortunate that he didn't steal anything from me. My collection is worth a lot of money."

"No doubt," said Ellery in a pleasant voice. He rose. "May I use your telephone, Mr. Beninson?"

"Surely."

Ellery consulted a telephone directory and made several calls, speaking in tones so low that neither Beninson nor Sergeant Velie could hear what he was saying. When he put down the instrument he said: "If you can spare a half-hour, Mr. Beninson, I'd like to have you take a little jaunt with us downtown."

Beninson seemed astonished; but he smiled, said: "I'd be delighted," and reached for his coat.

Ellery commandeered a taxicab outside, and the three

men were driven to Forty-ninth Street. He excused himself when they got out before the little bookshop, hurried inside, and came out after a moment with old Uneker, who locked his door with shaking fingers.

In the Ulm brothers' office they found Heffley, the insurance man, and Hazlitt, Uneker's customer, waiting for them. "Glad you could come," said Ellery cheerfully to both men. "Good afternoon, Mr. Ulm. A little conference, and I think we'll have this business cleared up to the Queen's taste. Ha, ha!"

Friederich Ulm scratched his head; Albert Ulm, sitting in a corner with his hatchet-knees jack-knifed, his green shade over his eyes, nodded.

"We'll have to wait," said Ellery. "I've asked Mr. Peters and Mr. Hinchman to come, too. Suppose we sit down?"

They were silent for the most part, and not a little uneasy. No one spoke as Ellery strolled about the office, examining the rare stamps in their wall-cases with open curiosity, whistling softly to himself. Sergeant Velie eyed him doubtfully. Then the door opened, and Hinchman and Peters appeared together. They stopped short at the threshold, looked at each other, shrugged, and walked in. Hinchman was scowling.

"What's the idea, Mr. Queen?" he said. "I'm a busy man."

"A not unique condition," smiled Ellery. "Ah, Mr. Peters, good day. Introductions, I think, are not entirely called for . . . Sit down, gentlemen!" he said in a sharper voice, and they sat down.

The door opened and a small, gray, birdlike little man peered in at them. Sergeant Velie looked astounded, and Ellery nodded gaily. "Come in, dad, come in! You're just in time for the first act."

Inspector Richard Queen cocked his little squirrel's head, looked at the assembled company shrewdly, and closed the door behind him. "What the devil is the idea of the call, son?"

"Nothing very exciting. Not a murder, or anything in your line. But it may interest you. Gentlemen, Inspector Queen."

The Inspector grunted, sat down, took out his old brown snuff-box, and inhaled with the voluptuous gasp of long practise.

Ellery stood serenely in the hub of the circle of chairs, looking down at curious faces. "The theft of the one-penny black, as you inveterate stamp-fiends call it," he began, "presented a not uninteresting problem. I say 'presented' advisedly. For the case is solved."

"Is this that business of the stamp robbery I was hearing about down at Headquarters?" asked the Inspector.

"Yes."

"Solved?" asked Beninson. "I don't think I understand, Mr. Queen. Have you found Planck?"

Ellery waved his arm negligently. "I was never too sanguine of catching Mr. William Planck, as such. You see, he wore tinted spectacles and black mustachios. Now, any one familiar with the science of crime-detection will tell you that the average person identifies faces by superficial details. A black mustache catches the eye. Tinted glasses impress the memory. In fact, Mr. Hazlitt here, who from Uneker's description is a man of poor observational powers, recalled even after seeing his assailant in dim street-light that the man wore a black mustache and tinted glasses. But this is all fundamental and not even particularly smart. It was reasonable to assume that Planck wanted these special facial characteristics to be remembered. I was convinced that he had disguised himself, that the mustache was probably a false one, and that ordinarily he does not wear tinted glasses."

They all nodded.

"This was the first and simplest of the three psychological sign-posts to the culprit." Ellery smiled and turned suddenly to the Inspector. "Dad, you're an old snuff-addict. How many times a day do you stuff that unholy brown dust up your nostrils?"

The Inspector blinked. "Oh, every half-hour or so. Sometimes as often as you smoke cigarets."

"Precisely. Now, Mr. Beninson told me that in the two weeks during which Planck stayed at his house, and despite the fact that Mr. Beninson worked side by side with the man every day, he saw Planck take snuff only *once*. Please observe that here we have a most enlightening and suggestive fact."

From the blankness of their faces it was apparent that, far from seeing light, their minds on this point were in total darkness. There was one exception—the Inspector; he nodded, shifted in his chair, and coolly began to study the faces about him.

Ellery lit a cigaret. "Very well," he said, expelling little puffs of smoke, "there you have the second psychological factor. The third was this: Planck, in a fairly public place, bashes Mr. Friederich Ulm over the face with the robust intention of stealing a valuable stamp. Any thief under the circumstances would desire speed above all things. Mr. Ulm was only half-stunned —he might come to and make an outcry; a customer might walk in; Mr. Albert Ulm might return unexpectedly—"

"Just a moment, son," said the Inspector. "I under-

stand there are two of the stamp thingamajigs in existence. I'd like to see the one that's still here."

Ellery nodded. "Would one of you gentlemen please
get the stamp?"

Friederich Ulm rose, pottered over to the safe, tinkered with the dials, opened the steel door, fussed about
the interior a moment, and came back with the leather
case containing the second one-penny black. The Inspector examined the thick little scrap curiously; a
thirty-thousand-dollar bit of old paper was as awesome
to him as to Ellery.

He almost dropped it when he heard Ellery say to
Sergeant Velie: "Sergeant, may I borrow your revolver?"

Velie's massive jaw see-sawed as he fumbled in his hip
pocket and produced a long-barreled police revolver.
Ellery took it and hefted it thoughtfully. Then his
fingers closed about the butt and he walked over to the
rifled cabinet in the middle of the room.

"Please observe, gentlemen—to expand my third
point—that in order to open this cabinet Planck used
an iron bar; and that in prying up the lid he found it
necessary to insert the bar between the lid and the front
wall four times, as the four marks under the lid indicate.

"Now, as you can see, the cabinet is covered with thin
glass. Moreover, it was locked, and the one-penny black
was in this closed leather case inside. Planck stood
about here, I should judge, and mark that the iron bar
was in his hand. What would you gentlemen expect a
thief, working against time, to do under these circumstances?"

They stared. The Inspector's mouth tightened, and
a grin began to spread over the expanse of Sergeant
Velie's face.

"But it's so clear," said Ellery. "Visualize it. I'm Planck. The revolver in my hand is an iron 'jimmy.' I'm standing over the cabinet . . ." His eyes gleamed behind the *pince-nez,* and he raised the revolver high over his head. And then, deliberately, he began to bring the steel barrel down on the thin sheating of glass atop the cabinet. There was a scream from Albert Ulm, and Friederich Ulm half-rose, glaring. Ellery's hand stopped a half-inch from the glass.

"Don't break that glass, you fool!" shouted the green-shaded dealer. "You'll only—"

He leaped forward and stood before the cabinet, trembling arms outspread as if to protect the case and its contents. Ellery grinned and prodded the man's palpitating belly with the muzzle of the revolver. "I'm glad you stopped me, Mr. Ulm. Put your hands up. Quickly!"

"Why—why, what do you mean?" gasped Albert Ulm, raising his arms with frantic rapidity.

"I mean," said Ellery gently, "that you're William Planck, and that brother Friederich is your accomplice!"

The brothers Ulm sat trembling in their chairs, and Sergeant Velie stood over them with a nasty smile. Albert Ulm had gone to pieces; he was quivering like an aspen-leaf in high wind.

"A very simple, almost an elementary, series of deductions," Ellery was saying. "Point three first. Why did the thief, instead of taking the most logical course of smashing the glass with the iron bar, choose to waste precious minutes using a 'jimmy' four times to force open the lid? *Obviously to protect the other stamps in the cabinet which lay open to possible injury,* as Mr. Albert Ulm has just graphically pointed out. And who had the greatest concern in protecting these other stamps—Hinchman, Peters, Beninson, even the mythical Planck himself? Of course not. Only the Ulm brothers, owners of the stamps."

Old Uneker began to chuckle; he nudged the Inspector. "See? Didn't I say he vass smardt? Now me —me, I'd neffer t'ink of dot."

"And why didn't Planck steal these other stamps in the cabinet? You would expect a thief to do that. Planck did not. But if the *Herren* Ulm were the thieves, the theft of the other stamps became pointless."

"How about that snuff business, Mr. Queen?" asked Peters.

"Yes. The conclusion is plain from the fact that Planck apparently indulged only once during the days he worked with Mr. Beninson. Since snuff-addicts partake freely and often, Planck wasn't a snuff-addict. Then it wasn't snuff he inhaled that day. What else is sniffed in a similar manner? Well—drugs in powder form—heroin! What are the characteristics of a heroin-addict? Nervous drawn appearance; gauntness, almost emaciation; and most important, tell-tale eyes, the pupils of which contract under influence of the drug. Then here was another explanation for the tinted glasses Planck wore. They served a double purpose—as an easily recognizable disguise, and also to conceal his eyes, which would give his vice-addiction away! But when I observed that Mr. Albert Ulm—" Ellery went over to the cowering man and ripped the green eye-shade away, revealing two stark, pin-point pupils—"wore this shade, it was a psychological confirmation of his identity as Planck."

"Yes, but that business of stealing all those books," said Hazlitt.

"Part of a very pretty and rather far-fetched plot," said Ellery. "With Albert Ulm the disguised thief, Friederich Ulm, who exhibited the wound on his cheek, must have been an accomplice. Then with the Ulm brothers the thieves, the entire business of the books was a blind. The attack on Friederich the ruse of the bookstore-escape, the trail of the minor robberies of copies of *Europe in Chaos*—a cleverly planned series of incidents to authenticate the fact that there was an outside thief, to convince the police and the insurance company that the stamp actually was stolen when it was not. Object, of course, to collect the insurance without parting with the stamp. These men are fanatical collectors."

Heffley wriggled his fat little body uncomfortably. "That's all very nice, Mr. Queen, but where the deuce is that stamp they stole from themselves? Where'd they hide it?"

"I thought long and earnestly about that, Heffley. For while my trio of deductions were psychological indications of guilt, the discovery of the stolen stamp in the Ulms' possession would be evidential proof." The Inspector was turning the second stamp over mechanically. "I said to myself," Ellery went on, "in a reconsideration of the problem: what would be the most likely hiding-place for the stamp? And then I remembered that the two stamps were identical, even the initials of the good Queen being in the same place. So I said to myself: if I were Messrs. Ulm, I should hide that stamp—like the character in Edgar Allan Poe's famous tale—in the most obvious place. And what is the most obvious place?"

Ellery sighed and returned the unused revolver to Sergeant Velie. "Dad," he remarked to the Inspector, who started guiltily, "I think that if you allow one of the philatelists in our company to examine the second one-penny black in your fingers, you'll find that the *first* has been pasted with non-injurious rubber cement precisely over the second!"

The Adventure of
THE BEARDED LADY

The Adventure of
THE BEARDED LADY

Mr. Phineas Mason, attorney-at-law—of the richly, almost indigestibly respectable firm of *Dowling, Mason & Coolidge,* 40 Park Row—was a very un-Phineaslike gentleman with a chunky nose and wrinkle-bedded eyes which had seen thirty years of harassing American litigation and looked as if they had seen a hundred. He sat stiffly in the lap of a chauffeur-driven limousine, his mouth making interesting sounds.

"And now," he said in an angry voice, "there's actually been murder done. I can't imagine what the world is coming to."

Mr. Ellery Queen, watching the world rush by in a glaring Long Island sunlight, mused that life was like a Spanish wench: full of surprises, none of them delicate and all of them stimulating. Since he was a monastic who led a riotous mental existence, he liked life that way; and since he was also a detective—an appellation he cordially detested—he got life that way. Nevertheless, he did not vocalize his reflections: Mr. Phineas Mason did not appear the sort who would appreciate fleshly metaphor.

He drawled: "The world's all right; the trouble is the people in it. Suppose you tell me what you can about these curious Shaws. After all, you know, I shan't be too heartily received by your local Long Island constabulary; and since I foresee difficulties, I should like to be forearmed as well."

Mason frowned. "But McC. assured me—"

"Oh, bother J. J.! He has vicarious delusions of grandeur. Let me warn you now, Mr. Mason, that I shall probably be a dismal flop. I don't go about pulling murderers out of my hat. And with your Cossacks trampling the evidence—"

"I warned them," said Mason fretfully. "I spoke to Captain Murch myself when he telephoned this morning to inform me of the crime." He made a sour face. "They won't even move the body, Mr. Queen. I wield—ah—a little local influence, you see."

"Indeed," said Ellery, adjusting his *pince-nez*; and he sighed. "Very well, Mr. Mason. Proceed with the dreary details."

"It was my partner, Coolidge," began the attorney in a pained voice, "who originally handled Shaw's affairs. John A. Shaw, the millionaire. Before your time, I daresay. Shaw's first wife died in childbirth in 1895. The child—Agatha; she's a divorcee now, with a son of eight—of course survived her mother; and there was one previous child, named after his father. John's forty-five now. . . . At any rate, old John Shaw remarried soon after his first wife's death, and then shortly after his second marriage died himself. This second wife, Maria Paine Shaw, survived her husband by a little more than thirty years. She died only a month ago."

"A plethora of mortalities," murmured Ellery, lighting a cigaret. "So far, Mr. Mason, a prosaic tale. And what has the Shaw history to do—"

"Patience," sighed Mason. "Now old John Shaw bequeathed his entire fortune to this second wife, Maria. The two children, John and Agatha, got nothing, not even trusts; I suppose old Shaw trusted Maria to take care of them."

"I scent the usual story," yawned Ellery. "She didn't? No go between stepmother and acquired progeny?"

The lawyer wiped his brow. "It was horrible. They fought for thirty years like—like savages. I will say, in extenuation of Mrs. Shaw's conduct, that she had provocation. John's always been a shiftless, unreliable beggar: disrespectful, profligate, quite vicious. Nevertheless she's treated him well in money matters. As I said, he's forty-five now; and he hasn't done a lick of work in his life. He's a drunkard, too."

"Sounds charming. And Sister Agatha, the divorcee?"

"A feminine edition of her brother. She married a fortune-hunter as worthless as herself; when he found out she was penniless he deserted her and Mrs. Shaw managed to get her a quiet divorce. She took Agatha and her boy, Peter, into her house and they've been living there ever since, at daggers' points. Please forgive the—ah—brutality of the characterizations; I want you to know these people as they are."

"We're almost intimate already," chuckled Ellery.

"John and Agatha," continued Mason, biting the head of his cane, "have been living for only one event— their stepmother's death. So that they might inherit, of course. Until a certain occurrence a few months ago Mrs. Shaw's will provided generously for them. But when that happened—"

Mr. Ellery Queen narrowed his gray eyes. "You mean—?"

"It's complicated," sighed the lawyer. "Three months ago there was an attempt on the part of some one in the household to poison the old lady!"

"Ah!"

"The attempt was unsuccessful only because Dr. Arlen—Dr. Terence Arlen is the full name—had suspected such a possibility for years and had kept his eyes open. The cyanide—it was put in her tea—didn't reach Mrs. Shaw, but killed a house-cat. None of us, of course, knew who had made the poisoning attempt. But after that Mrs. Shaw changed her will."

"Now," muttered Ellery, "I *am* enthralled. Arlen, eh? That creates a fascinating mess. Tell me about Arlen, please."

"Rather mysterious old man with two passions: devotion to Mrs. Shaw and a hobby of painting. Quite an artist, too, though I know little about such things. He lived in the Shaw house about twenty years. Medico Mrs. Shaw picked up somewhere; I think only she knew his story, and he's always been silent about his past. She put him on a generous salary to live in the house and act as the family physician; I suspect it was rather because she anticipated what her stepchildren might attempt. And then too it's always seemed to me that Arlen accepted this unusual arrangement so tractably in order to pass out of—ah—circulation."

They were silent for some time. The chauffeur swung the car off the main artery into a narrow macadam road. Mason breathed heavily.

"I suppose you're satisfied," murmured Ellery at last through a fat smoke-ring, "that Mrs. Shaw died a month ago of natural causes?"

"Heavens, yes!" cried Mason. "Dr. Arlen wouldn't trust his own judgment, we were so careful; he had several specialists in, before and after her death. But she died of the last of a series of heart-attacks; she was an old woman, you know. Something-thrombosis, they called it." Mason looked gloomy. "Well, you can understand Mrs. Shaw's natural reaction to the poisoning episode. 'If they're so depraved,' she told me shortly after, 'that they'd attempt my *life,* they don't deserve any consideration at my *hands.*' And she had me draw up a new will, cutting both of them off without a cent."

"There's an epigram," chuckled Ellery, "worthy of a better cause."

Mason tapped on the glass. "Faster, Burroughs." The car jolted ahead. "In looking about for a beneficiary, Mrs. Shaw finally remembered that there was some one to whom she could leave the Shaw fortune without feeling that she was casting it to the winds. Old John Shaw had had an elder brother, Morton, a widower with two grown children. The brothers quarrelled violently and Morton moved to England. He lost most of his money there; his two children, Edith and Percy, were left to shift for themselves when he committed suicide."

"These Shaws seem to have a penchant for violence."

"I suppose it's in the blood. Well, Edith and Percy both had talent of a sort, I understand, and they went on the London stage in a brother-and-sister music-hall act, managing well enough. Mrs. Shaw decided to leave her money to this Edith, her niece. I made inquiries by correspondence and discovered that Edith Shaw was now Mrs. Edythe Royce, a childless widow of many years' standing. On Mrs. Shaw's decease I cabled her and she crossed by the next boat. According to Mrs. Royce, Percy—her brother—was killed in an automobile accident on the Continent a few months before; so she had no ties whatever."

"And the will—specifically?"

"It's rather queer," sighed Mason. "The Shaw estate was enormous at one time, but the depression whittled it down to about three hundred thousand dollars. Mrs. Shaw left her niece two hundred thousand outright. The remainder, to his astonishment," and Mason paused and eyed his tall young companion with a curious fixity, "was put in trust for Dr. Arlen."

"Arlen!"

"He was not to touch the principal, but was to receive the income from it for the remainder of his life. Interesting, eh?"

"That's putting it mildly. By the way, Mr. Mason, I'm a suspicious bird. This Mrs. Royce—you're satisfied she *is* a Shaw?"

The lawyer started; then he shook his head. "No, no, Queen, that's the wrong tack. There can be absolutely no question about it. In the first place she possesses the marked facial characteristics of the Shaws; you'll see for yourself; although I will say that she's rather—well, rather a character, rather a character! She came armed with intimate possessions of her father, Morton Shaw; and I myself, in company with Coolidge, questioned her closely on her arrival. She convinced us utterly, from her knowledge of *minutiæ* about her father's life and Edith Shaw's childhood in America—knowledge impossible for an outsider to have acquired—that she *is* Edith Shaw. We were more than cautious, I assure you; especially since neither John nor Agatha had seen her since childhood."

"Just a thought." Ellery leaned forward. "And what was to be the disposition of Arlen's hundred-thousand-dollar trust on Arlen's death?"

The lawyer gazed grimly at the two rows of prim poplars flanking a manicured driveway on which the limousine was now noiselessly treading. "It was to be equally divided between John and Agatha," he said in a

careful voice. The car rolled to a stop under a coldly
white *porte-cochère*.

"I see," said Ellery. For it was Dr. Terence Arlen
who had been murdered.

A county trooper escorted them through high Colonial halls into a remote and silent wing of the ample
old house, up a staircase to a dim cool corridor patrolled
by a nervous man with a bull neck.

"Oh, Mr. Mason," he said eagerly, coming forward.
"We've been waiting for you. This is Mr. Queen?"
His tone changed from unguent haste to abrasive sus-
picion.

"Yes, yes. Murch of the county detectives, Mr.
Queen. You've left everything intact, Murch?"

The detective grunted and stepped aside. Ellery
found himself in the study of what appeared to be a
two-room suite; beyond an open door he could see the
white counterpane of a bird's-eye-maple four-poster. A
hole at some remote period had been hacked through the
ceiling and covered with glass, admitting sunlight and
converting the room into a sky-light studio. The trivia
of a painter's paraphernalia lay in cofusion about the
room, overpowering the few medical implements.
There were easels, paint-boxes, a small dais, carelessly
draped smocks, a profusion of daubs in oils and water-
colors on the walls.

A little man was kneeling beside the outstretched
figure of the dead doctor—a long brittle figure frozen
in death, capped with curiously lambent silver hair.
The wound was frank and deep: the delicately chased
haft of a stiletto protruded from the man's heart.
There was very little blood.

Murch snapped: "Well, Doc, anything else?"

The little man rose and put his instruments away. "Died instantly from the stab-wound. Frontal blow, as you see. He tried to dodge at the last instant, I should say, but wasn't quick enough." He nodded and reached for his hat and quietly went out.

Ellery shivered a little. The studio was silent, and the corridor was silent, and the wing was silent; the whole house was crushed under the weight of a terrific silence that was almost uncanny. There was something indescribably evil in the air. . . . He shook his shoulders impatiently. "The stiletto, Captain Murch. Have you identified it?"

"Belonged to Arlen. Always right here on this table."

"No possibility of suicide, I suppose."

"Not a chance, Doc said."

Mr. Phineas Mason made a retching sound. "If you want me, Queen—" He stumbled from the room, awakening dismal echoes.

The corpse was swathed in a paint-smudged smock above pajamas; in the stiff right hand a paint-brush, its hairs stained jet-black, was still clutched. A color-splashed palette had fallen face down on the floor near him. . . . Ellery did not raise his eyes from the stiletto. "Florentine, I suppose. Tell me what you've learned so far, Captain," he said absently. "I mean about the crime itself."

"Damned little," growled the detective. "Doc says he was killed about two in the morning—about eight hours ago. His body was found at seven this a.m. by a woman named Krutch, a nurse in the house here for a couple of years. Nice wench, by God! Nobody's got an alibi for the time of the murder, because according to their yarns they were all sleeping, and they all sleep separately. That's about the size of it."

"Precious little, to be sure," murmured Ellery. "By the way, Captain, was it Dr. Arlen's custom to paint in the wee hours?"

"Seems so. I thought of that, too. But he was a queer old cuss and when he was hot on something he'd work for twenty-four hours at a clip."

"Do the others sleep in this wing?"

"Nope. Not even the servants. Seems Arlen liked privacy, and whatever he liked the old dame—Mrs. Shaw, who kicked off a month ago—said 'jake' to." Murch went to the doorway and snapped: "Miss Krutch."

She came slowly out of Dr. Arlen's bedroom—a tall fair young woman who had been weeping. She was in nurse's uniform and there was nothing in common between her name and her appearance. In fact, as Ellery observed with appreciation, she was a distinctly attractive young woman with curves in precisely the right places. Miss Krutch, despite her tears, was the first ray of sunshine he had encountered in the big old house.

"Tell Mr. Queen what you told me," directed Murch curtly.

"But there's so little," she quavered. "I was up before seven, as usual. My room's in the main wing, but there's a storeroom here for linen and things. . . . As I passed I—I saw Dr. Arlen lying on the floor, with the knife sticking up— The door was open and the light was on. I screamed. No one heard me. This is so far away. . . . I screamed and screamed and then Mr. Shaw came running, and Miss Shaw. Th-that's all."

"Did any of you touch the body, Miss Krutch?"

"Oh, no, sir!" She shivered.

"I see," said Ellery, and raised his eyes from the dead man to the easel above, casually, and looked away. And then instantly he looked back, his nerves tingling. Murch watched him with a sneer.

"How," jeered Murch, "d'ye like that, *Mr*. Queen?"

Ellery sprang forward. A smaller easel near the large one supported a picture. It was a cheap "processed" oil painting, a commercial copy of Rembrandt's famous self-portrait group, *The Artist and His Wife*. Rembrandt himself sat in the foreground, and his wife stood in the background. The canvas on the large easel was a half-finished replica of this painting. Both figures had been completely sketched in by Dr. Arlen and brushwork begun: the lusty smiling mustached artist in his gayly plumed hat, his left arm about the waist of his Dutch-garbed wife.

And on the woman's chin there was painted a beard.

Ellery gaped from the processed picture to Dr. Arlen's copy. But the one showed a woman's smooth chin, and the other—the doctor's—a squarish, expertly stroked black beard. And yet it had been daubed in hastily, as if the old painter had been working against time.

"Good heavens!" exclaimed Ellery, glaring. "That's insane!"

"Think so?" said Murch blandly. "Me, I don't know. I've got a notion about it." He growled at Miss Krutch: "Beat it," and she fled from the studio, her long legs twinkling.

Ellery shook his head dazedly and sank into a chair, fumbling for a cigaret. "That's a new wrinkle to me, Captain. First time I've ever encountered in a homicide

an example of the beard-and-mustache school of art—
you've seen the pencilled hair on the faces of men and
women in billboard advertisements? It's—" And then
his eyes narrowed as something leaped into them and he
said abruptly: "Is Miss Agatha Shaw's boy—that Peter
—in the house?"

Murch, smiling secretly as if he were enjoying a huge
jest, went to the hallway door and roared something.
Ellery got out of the chair and ran across the room and
returned with one of the smocks, which he flung over
the dead man's body.

A small boy with frightened yet inquisitive eyes came
slowly into the room, followed by one of the most remarkable creatures Ellery had ever seen. This apparition was a large stout woman of perhaps sixty, with
lined rugged features—so heavy they were almost wat-
tled—painted, bedaubed, and varnished with an astounding cosmetic technique. Her lips, gross as they were,
were shaped by rouge into a perfect and obscene
Cupid's-bow; her eyebrows had been tweezed to incredible thinness; round rosy spots punctuated her sagging cheeks; and the whole rough heavy skin was floury
with white powder.

But her costume was even more amazing than her
face. For she was rigged out in Victorian style—a
tight-waisted garment, almost bustle-hipped, full wide
skirts that reached to her thick ankles, a deep and
shiny bosom, and an elaborate boned lace choker-collar.
. . . And then Ellery remembered that, since this must
be Edythe Shaw Royce, there was at least a partial explanation for her eccentric appearance: she was an old
woman, she came from England, and she was no doubt
still basking in the vanished glow of her girlhood theatrical days.

"Mrs. Royce," said Murch mockingly, *"and* Peter."

"How d'ye do," muttered Ellery, tearing his eyes away. "Uh—Peter."

The boy, a sharp-featured and skinny little creature, sucked his dirty forefinger and stared.

"Peter!" said Mrs. Royce severely. Her voice was quite in tune with her appearance: deep and husky and slightly cracked. Even her hair, Ellery noted with a wince, was nostalgic—a precise deep brown, frankly dyed. Here was one female, at least, who did not mean to yield to old age without a determined struggle, he thought. "He's frightened. Peter!"

"Ma'am," mumbled Peter, still staring.

"Peter," said Ellery, "look at that picture." Peter did so, reluctantly. "Did you put that beard on the face of the lady in the picture, Peter?"

Peter shrank against Mrs. Royce's voluminous skirts. "N-no!"

"Curious, isn't it?" said Mrs. Royce cheerfully. "I was remarking about that to Captain Burch—Murch only this morning. I'm sure Peter wouldn't have drawn the beard on *that* one. He'd learned his lesson, hadn't you, Peter?" Ellery remarked with alarm that the extraordinary woman kept screwing her right eyebrow up and drawing it deeply down, as if there were something in her eye that bothered her.

"Ah," said Ellery. "Lesson?"

"You see," went on Mrs. Royce, continuing her ocular gymnastics with unconscious vigor, "it was only yesterday that Peter's mother caught him drawing a beard with chalk on one of Dr. Arlen's paintings in Peter's bedroom. Dr. Arlen gave him a round hiding, I'm afraid, and himself removed the chalk-marks. Dear

Agatha was *so* angry with poor Dr. Arlen. So you didn't do it, did you, Peter?"

"Naw," said Peter, who had become fascinated by the bulging smock on the floor.

"Dr. Arlen, eh?" muttered Ellery. "Thank you," and he began to pace up and down as Mrs. Royce took Peter by the arm and firmly removed him from the studio. A formidable lady, he thought, with her vigorous room-shaking tread. And he recalled that she wore flat-heeled shoes and had, from the ugly swelling of the leather, great bunions.

"Come on," said Murch suddenly, going to the door.

"Where?"

"Downstairs." The detective signalled a trooper to guard the studio and led the way. "I want to show you," he said as they made for the main part of the house, "the reason for the beard on that dame-in-the-picture's jaw."

"Indeed?" murmured Ellery, and said nothing more. Murch paused in the doorway of a pale Colonial living-room and jerked his head.

Ellery looked in. A hollow-chested, cadaverous man in baggy tweeds sat slumped in a Cogswell chair staring at an empty glass in his hand, which was shaking. His eyes were yellow-balled and shot with blood, and his loose skin was a web of red veins.

"That," said Murch contemptuously and yet with a certain triumph, "is Mr. John Shaw."

Ellery noted that Shaw possessed the same heavy features, the same fat lips and rock-hewn nose, as the wonderful Mrs. Royce, his cousin; and for that matter, as the dour and annoyed-looking old pirate in the portrait over the fireplace who was presumably his father.

And Ellery also noted that on Mr. John Shaw's unsteady chin there was a bedraggled, pointed beard.

Mr. Mason, a bit greenish about the jowls, was waiting for them in a sombre reception-room. "Well?" he asked in a whisper, like a supplicant before the Cumæan Sibyl.

"Captain Murch," murmured Ellery, "has a theory."

The detective scowled. "Plain as day. It's John Shaw. It's my hunch Dr. Arlen painted that beard as a clue to his killer. The only one around here with a beard is Shaw. It ain't evidence, I admit, but it's something to work on. And believe you me," he said with a snap of his brown teeth, "I'm going to work on it!"

"John," said Mason slowly. "He certainly had motive. And yet I find it difficult to . . ." His shrewd eyes flickered. "Beard? What beard?"

"There's a beard painted on the chin of a female face upstairs," drawled Ellery, "the face being on a Rembrandt Arlen was copying at the time he was murdered. That the good doctor painted the beard himself is quite evident. It's expertly stroked, done in black oils, and in his dead hand there's still the brush tipped with black oils. There isn't any one else in the house who paints, is there?"

"No," said Mason uncomfortably.

"*Voilà.*"

'But even if Arlen did such a—a mad thing," objected the lawyer, "how do you know it was just before he was attacked?"

"Aw," growled Murch, "when the hell else would it be?"

"Now, now, Captain," murmured Ellery, "let's be scientific. There's a perfectly good answer to your question, Mr. Mason. First, we all agree that Dr. Arlen couldn't have painted the beard *after* he was attacked; he died instantly. Therefore he must have painted it before he was attacked. The question is: How long before? Well, why did Arlen paint the beard at all?"

"Murch says as a clue to his murderer," muttered Mason. "But such a—a fantastic legacy to the police! It looks deucedly odd."

"What's odd about it?"

"Well, for heaven's sake," exploded Mason, "if he wanted to leave a clue to his murderer, why didn't he write the murderer's name on the canvas? He had the brush in his hand . . ."

"Precisely," murmured Ellery. "A very good question, Mr. Mason. Well, why didn't he? If he was alone—that is, if he was *anticipating* his murder—he certainly would have left us a written record of his concrete suspicions. The fact that he left no such record shows that he didn't anticipate his murder before the appearance of his murderer. Therefore he painted the beard *while his murderer was present*. But now we find an explanation for the painted beard as a clue. With his murderer present, he *couldn't* paint the name; the murderer would have noticed it and destroyed it. Arlen was forced, then, to adopt a subtle means: leave a clue that would escape his killer's attention. Since he was painting at the time, he used a painter's means. Even if his murderer noticed it, he probably ascribed it to Arlen's nervousness; although the chances are he didn't notice it."

Murch stirred. "Say, listen—"

"But a beard on a woman's face," groaned the lawyer. "I tell you—"

"Oh," said Ellery dreamily, "Dr. Arlen had a precedent."

"Precedent?"

"Yes; we've found, Captain Murch and I, that young Peter in his divine innocence had chalked a beard and mustache on one of Dr. Arlen's daubs which hangs in Peter's bedroom. This was only yesterday. Dr. Arlen whaled the tar out of him for this horrible crime *vers l'art,* no doubt justifiably. But Peter's beard-scrawl must have stuck in the doctor's mind; threshing about wildly in his mind while his murderer talked to him, or threatened him, the beard business popped out at him. Apparently he felt that it told a story, because he used it. And there, of course, is the rub."

"I still say it's all perfectly asinine," grunted Mason.

"Not asinine," said Ellery. "Interesting. He painted a beard on the chin of Rembrandt's wife. Why Rembrandt's wife, in the name of all that's wonderful?—a woman dead more than two centuries! These Shaws aren't remote descendants . . ."

"Nuts," said Murch distinctly.

"Nuts," said Ellery, "is a satisfactory word under the circumstances, Captain. Then a grim jest? Hardly. But if it wasn't Dr. Arlen's grisly notion of a joke, what under heaven was it? What did Arlen mean to convey?"

"If it wasn't so ridiculous," muttered the lawyer, "I'd say he was pointing to—Peter."

"Nuts and double-nuts," said Murch, "begging your pardon, Mr. Mason. The kid's the only one, I guess, that's got a real alibi. It seems his mother's nervous about him and she always keeps his door locked from the outside. I found it that way myself this morning. And he couldn't have got out through the window."

"Well, well," sighed Mason, "I'm sure I'm all at sea. John, eh. . . . What do *you* think, Mr. Queen?"

"Much as I loathe argument," said Ellery, "I can't agree with Brother Murch."

"Oh, yeah?" jeered Murch. "I suppose you've got reasons?"

"I suppose," said Ellery, "I have; not the least impressive of which is the dissimilar shapes of the real and painted beards."

The detective glowered. "Well, if he didn't mean John Shaw by it, what the hell did he mean?"

Ellery shrugged. "If we knew that, my dear Captain, we should know everything."

"Well," snarled Murch, "I think it's spinach, and I'm going to haul Mr. John Shaw down to county headquarters and pump the old bastard till I *find* it's spinach."

"I shouldn't do that, Murch," said Ellery quickly. "If only for—"

"I know my duty," said the detective with a black look, and he stamped out of the reception-room.

John Shaw, who was quietly drunk, did not even protest when Murch shoved him into the squad car. Followed by the county morgue-truck bearing Dr. Arlen's body, Murch vanished with his prey.

Ellery took a hungry turn about the room, frowning. The lawyer sat in a crouch, gnawing his fingernails. And again the room, and the house, and the very air were charged with silence, an ominous silence.

"Look here," said Ellery sharply, "there's something in this business you haven't told me yet, Mr. Mason."

The lawyer jumped, and then sank back biting his lips. "He's such a worrisome creature," said a cheerful voice from the doorway and they both turned, startled, to find Mrs. Royce beaming in at them. She came in with the stride of a grenadier, her bosom joggling. And she sat down by Mason's side and with daintiness lifted her capacious skirts with both hands a bit above each fat knee. "I know what's troubling you, Mr. Mason!"

The lawyer cleared his throat hastily. "I assure you—"

"Nonsense! I've excellent eyes. Mason, you haven't introduced this nice young man." Mason mumbled something placative. "Queen, is it? Charmed, Mr. Queen. First sample of reasonably attractive American I've seen since my arrival. I can appreciate a handsome man; I was on the London stage for many years. And really," she thundered in her formidable baritone, "I wasn't so ill-looking myself!"

"I'm sure of that," murmured Ellery. "But what—"

"Mason's afraid for me," said Mrs. Royce with a girlish simper. "A most conscientious barrister! He's simply petrified with fear that whoever did for poor Dr. Arlen will select me as his next victim. And I tell him now, as I told him a few moments ago when you were upstairs with that dreadful Murch person, that for one thing I shan't be such an easy victim—" Ellery could well believe that—"and for another I don't believe either John or Agatha, which is what's in Mason's mind—don't deny it, Mason!—was responsible for Dr. Arlen's death."

"I never—" began the lawyer feebly.

"Hmm," said Ellery. "What's your theory, Mrs. Royce?"

"Some one out of Arlen's past," boomed the lady with a click of her jaws as a punctuation mark. "I understand he came here twenty years ago under most mysterious circumstances. He may have murdered somebody, and that somebody's brother or some one has returned to avenge—"

"Ingenious," grinned Ellery. "As tenable as Murch's, Mr. Mason."

The lady sniffed. "He'll release Cousin John soon enough," she said complacently. "John's stupid enough under ordinary circumstances, you know, but when he's drunk—! There's no evidence, is there? A cigaret, if you please, Mr. Queen."

Ellery hastened to offer his case. Mrs. Royce selected a cigaret with a vast paw, smiled roguishly as Ellery held a match, and then withdrew the cigaret and blew smoke, crossing her legs as she did so. She smoked almost in the Russian fashion, cupping her hand about the cigaret instead of holding it between two fingers. A remarkable woman! "Why are you so afraid for Mrs. Royce?" he drawled.

"Well—" Mason hesitated, torn between discretion and desire. "There may have been a double motive for killing Dr. Arlen, you see. That is," he added hurriedly, "*if* Agatha or John had anything to do—"

"Double motive?"

"One, of course, is the conversion of the hundred thousand to Mrs. Shaw's stepchildren, as I told you. The other . . . Well, there is a proviso in connection with the bequest to Dr. Arlen. In return for offering him a home and income for the rest of his life, he was to continue to attend to the medical needs of the family, you see, with *special* attention to Mrs. Royce."

"Poor Aunt Maria," said Mrs. Royce with a tidal sigh. "She must have been a dear, dear person."

"I'm afraid I don't quite follow, Mr. Mason."

"I've a copy of the will in my pocket." The lawyer

fished for a crackling document. "Here it is. 'And in particular to conduct monthly medical examinations of my niece, Edith Shaw—or more frequently if Dr. Arlen should deem it necessary—to insure her continued good health; a provision' (mark this, Queen!) *'a provision I am sure my stepchildren will appreciate.'* "

"A cynical addendum," nodded Ellery, blinking a little. "Mrs. Shaw placed on her trusted leech the responsibility for keeping you healthy, Mrs. Royce, suspecting that her dearly beloved stepchildren might be tempted to—er—tamper with your life. But why should they?"

For the first time something like terror invaded Mrs. Royce's massive face She set her jaw and said, a trifle tremulously: "N-nonsense. I can't believe— Do you think it's possible they've already tr—"

"You don't feel ill, Mrs. Royce?" cried Mason, alarmed.

Under the heavy coating of powder her coarse skin was muddily pale. "No, I— Dr. Arlen was supposed to examine me for the first time tomorrow. Oh, if it's . . . The food—"

"Poison was tried three months ago," quavered the lawyer. "On Mrs. Shaw, Queen, as I told you. Good God, Mrs. Royce, you'll have to be careful!"

"Come, come," snapped Ellery. "What's the point? Why should the Shaws want to poison Mrs. Royce, Mason?"

"Because," said Mason in a trembling voice, "in the event of Mrs. Royce's demise her estate is to revert to the original estate; which would automatically mean to John and Agatha." He mopped his brow.

Ellery heaved himself out of the chair and took another hungry turn about the sombre room. Mrs.

Royce's right eyebrow suddenly began to go up and down with nervousness.

"This needs thinking over," he said abruptly; and there was something queer in his eyes that made both of them stare at him with uneasiness. "I'll stay the night, Mr. Mason, if Mrs. Royce has no objection."

"Do," whispered Mrs. Royce in a tremble; and this time she was afraid, very plainly afraid. And over the room settled an impalpable dust, like a distant sign of approaching villainy. "Do you think they'll actually try . . . ?"

"It is entirely," said Ellery dryly, "within the realm of possibility."

The day passed in a timeless haze. Unaccountably, no one came; the telephone was silent; and there was no word from Murch, so that John Shaw's fate remained obscure. Mason sat in a miserable heap on the front porch, a cigar cold in his mouth, rocking himself like a weazened old doll. Mrs. Royce retired, subdued, to her quarters. Peter was off somewhere in the gardens tormenting a dog; occasionally Miss Krutch's tearful voice reprimanded him ineffectually.

To Mr. Ellery Queen it was a painful, puzzling, and irritatingly evil time. He prowled the rambling mansion, a lost soul, smoking tasteless cigarets and thinking. . . . That a blanket of menace hung over this house his nerves convinced him. It took all his will-power to keep his body from springing about at unheard sounds; moreover, his mind was distracted and he could not think clearly. A murderer was abroad; and this was a house of violent people.

He shivered and darted a look over his shoulder and shrugged and bent his mind fiercely to the problem at

hand. . . . And after hours his thoughts grew calmer
and began to range themselves in orderly rows, until it
was evident that there was a beginning and an end.
He grew quiet.

He smiled a little as he stopped a tiptoeing maid and
inquired the location of Miss Agatha Shaw's room.
Miss Shaw had wrapped herself thus far in a mantle of
invisibility. It was most curious. A sense of rising
drama excited him a little. . . .

A tinny female voice responded to his knock, and
he opened the door to find a feminine Shaw as bony
and unlovely as the masculine edition curled in a hard
knot on a *chaise-longue*, staring balefully out the window. Her *négligé* was adorned with boa feathers and
there were varicose veins on her swollen naked legs.

"Well," she said acidly, without turning. "What do
you want?"

"My name," murmured Ellery, "is Queen, and Mr.
Mason has called me in to help settle your—ah—difficulties."

She twisted her skinny neck slowly. "I've heard all
about you. What do you want me to do, kiss you? I
suppose it was you who instigated John's arrest. You're
fools, the pack of you!"

"To the contrary, it was your worthy Captain
Murch's exclusive idea to take your brother in custody,
Miss Shaw. He's not formally arrested, you know.
Even so, I advised strongly against it."

She sniffed, but she uncoiled the knot and drew her
shapeless legs beneath her wrapper in a sudden consciousness of femininity. "Then sit down, Mr. Queen. I'll
help all I can."

"On the other hand," smiled Ellery, seating himself
in a gilt and Gallic atrocity, "don't blame Murch overly,

Miss Shaw. There's a powerful case against your brother, you know."

"And me!"

"And," said Ellery regretfully, "you."

She raised her thin arms and cried: "Oh, how I hate this damned, damned house, that damned woman! She's the cause of all our trouble. Some day she's likely to get—"

"I suppose you're referring to Mrs. Royce. But aren't you being unfair? From Mason's story it's quite evident that there was no ghost of coercion when your step-mother willed your father's fortune to Mrs. Royce. They had never met, never corresponded, and your cousin was three thousand miles away. It's awkward for you, no doubt, but scarcely Mrs. Royce's fault."

"Fair! Who cares about fairness? She's taken our money away from us. And now we've got to stay here and—and be *fed* by her. It's intolerable, I tell you! She'll be here at least two years—trust her for that, the painted old hussy!—and all that time . . ."

"I'm afraid I don't understand. Two years?"

"That *woman's* will," snarled Miss Shaw, "provided that this precious cousin of ours come to live here and preside as mistress for a minimum of two years. That was her revenge, the despicable old witch! Whatever father saw in her . . . To 'provide a home for John and Agatha,' she said in the will, 'until they find a per-manent solution of their problems.' How d'ye like that? I'll never forget those words. Our 'problems'! Oh, every time I think—" She bit her lip, eyeing him sidewise with a sudden caution.

Ellery sighed and went to the door. "Indeed? And if something should—er—drive Mrs. Royce from the house before the expiration of the required period?"

"We'd get the money, of course," she flashed with bitter triumph; her thin dark skin was greenish. "If something should happen—"

"I trust," said Ellery dryly, "that nothing will." He closed the door and stood for a moment gnawing his fingers, and then he smiled rather grimly and went downstairs to a telephone.

John Shaw returned with his escort at ten that night. His chest was hollower, his fingers shakier, his eyes bloodier; and he was sober. Murch looked like a thundercloud. The cadaverous man went into the living-room and made for a full decanter. He drank alone, with steady mechanical determination. No one disturbed him.

"Nothing," growled Murch to Ellery and Mason.

At twelve the house was asleep.

The first alarm was sounded by Miss Krutch. It was almost one when she ran down the upper corridor screaming at the top of her voice: "Fire! Fire! Fire!" Thick smoke was curling about her slender ankles and the moonlight shining through the corridor-window behind her silhouetted her long plump trembling shanks through the thin nightgown.

The corridor erupted, boiled over. Doors crashed open, dishevelled heads protruded, questions were shrieked, dry throats choked over the bitter smoke. Mr. Phineas Mason, looking a thousand years old without his teeth, fled in a cotton nightshirt toward the staircase. Murch came pounding up the stairs, followed by a bleary, bewildered John Shaw. Scrawny Agatha in silk pajamas staggered down the hall with Peter, howling at the top of his lusty voice, in her arms. Two servants scuttled downstairs like frantic rats.

But Mr. Ellery Queen stood still outside the door of his room and looked quietly about, as if searching for some one.

"Murch," he said in a calm, penetrating voice.

The detective ran up. "The fire!" he cried wildly. "Where the hell's the fire?"

"Have you seen Mrs. Royce?"

"Mrs. Royce? Hell, no!" He ran back up the hall, and Ellery followed on his heels, thoughtfully. Murch tried the knob of a door; the door was locked. "God, she may be asleep, or overcome by—"

"Well, then," said Ellery through his teeth as he stepped back, "stop yowling and help me break this door down. We don't want her frying in her own lard, you know."

In the darkness, in the evil smoke, they hurled themselves at the door. . . . At the fourth assault it splintered off its hinges and Ellery sprang through. An electric torch in his hand flung its powerful beam about the room, wavered. . . . Something struck it from Ellery's hand, and it splintered on the floor. The next moment Ellery was fighting for his life.

His adversary was a brawny, panting demon with muscular fingers that sought his throat. He wriggled about, coolly, seeking an armhold. Behind him Murch was yelling: "Mrs. Royce! It's only us!"

Something sharp and cold flicked over Ellery's cheek and left a burning line. Ellery found a naked arm. He twisted, hard, and there was a clatter as steel fell to the floor. Then Murch came to his senses and jumped in. A county trooper blundered in, fumbling with his electric torch. . . . Ellery's fist drove in, hard, to a fat stomach. Fingers relaxed from his throat. The trooper found the electric switch. . . .

Mrs. Royce, trembling violently, lay on the floor beneath the two men. On a chair nearby lay, in a mountain of Victorian clothing, a very odd and solid-looking contraption that might have been a rubber *brassière*. And something was wrong with her hair; she seemed to have been partially scalped.

Ellery cursed softly and yanked. Her scalp came away in a piece, revealing a pink gray-fringed skull.

"She's a man!" screamed Murch.

"Thus," said Ellery grimly, holding Mrs. Royce's throat firmly with one hand and with the other dabbing at his bloody cheek, "vindicating the powers of thought."

"I still don't understand," complained Mason the next morning, as his chauffeur drove him and Ellery back to the city, "how you guessed, Queen."

Ellery raised his eyebrows. "Guessed? My dear Mason, that's considered an insult at the Queen hearth. There was no guesswork whatever involved. Matter of pure reasoning. And a neat job, too," he added reflectively, touching the thin scar on his cheek.

"Come, come, Queen," smiled the lawyer, "I've never really believed McC.'s panegyrics on what he calls your uncanny ability to put two and two together; and though I'm not unintelligent and my legal training gives me a mental advantage over the layman and I've just been treated presumably to a demonstration of your —er—powers, I'll be blessed if I yet believe."

"A skeptic, eh?" said Ellery, wincing at the pain in his cheek. "Well, then, let's start where I started— with the beard Dr. Arlen painted on the face of Rem-

brandt's wife just before he was attacked. We've
agreed that he deliberately painted in the beard to leave
a clue to his murderer. What could he have meant?
He was not pointing to a *specific* woman, using the
beard just as an attention-getter; for the woman in the
painting was the wife of Rembrandt, a historical figure
and as far as our *personæ* went an utter unknown.
Nor could Arlen have meant to point to a woman with
a beard *literally;* for this would have meant a freak,
and there were no freaks involved. Nor was he pointing to a bearded man, for there was *a man's face* on the
painting which he left untouched; had he meant to
point to a bearded man as his murderer—that is, to
John Shaw—he would have painted the beard on Rembrandt's beardless face. Besides, Shaw's is a vandyke, a
pointed beard; and the beard Arlen painted was squarish in shape. . . . You see how exhaustive it is possible
to be, Mason."

"Go on," said the lawyer intently.

"The only possible conclusion, then, all others having
been eliminated, was that Arlen meant the beard *merely
to indicate masculinity,* since facial hair is one of the
few exclusively masculine characteristics left to our sex
by dear, dear Woman. In other words, by painting
a beard on a woman's face—any woman's face, mark—
Dr. Arlen was virtually saying: 'My murderer is a person who seems to be a woman but is really a man.' "

"Well, I'll be damned!" gasped Mason.

"No doubt," nodded Ellery. "Now, 'a person who
seems to be a woman but is really a man' suggests, surely,
impersonation. The only actual stranger at the house
was Mrs. Royce. Neither John nor Agatha could be
impersonators, since they were both well-known to Dr.
Arlen as well as to you; Arlen had examined them

periodically, in fact, for years as the personal physician of the household. As for Miss Krutch, aside from her unquestionable femininity—a ravishing young woman, my dear Mason—she could not possibly have had motive to be an impersonator.

"Now, since Mrs. Royce seemed the likeliest possibility, I thought over the infinitesimal phenomena I had observed connected with her person—that is, appearance and movements. I was amazed to find a vast number of remarkable confirmations!"

"Confirmations?" echoed Mason, frowning.

"Ah, Mason, that's the trouble with skeptics: they're so easily confounded. Of course! Lips constitute a strong difference between the sexes: Mrs. Royce's were shaped meticulously into a perfect Cupid's-bow with lipstick. Suspicious in an old woman. The general overuse of cosmetics, particularly the heavy application of face powder: *very* suspicious, when you consider that overpowdering is not common among genteel old ladies and also that a man's skin, no matter how closely and frequently shaved, is undisguisably coarser.

"Clothes? Really potent confirmation. Why on earth that outlandish Victorian get-up? Here was presumably a woman who had been on the stage, presumably a woman of the world, a sophisticate. And yet she wore those horrible doodads of the '90s. Why? Obviously, to swathe and disguise a padded figure—impossible with women's thin, scanty, and clinging modern garments. And the collar—ah, the collar! That was his inspiration. A choker, you'll recall, concealing the entire neck? But since a prominent Adam's-apple is an inescapable heritage of the male, a choker-collar becomes virtually a necessity in a female impersonation. Then the baritone voice, the vigorous movements, the

mannish stride, the flat shoes. . . . The shoes were especially illuminating. Not only were they flat, but they
showed signs of great bunions—and a man wearing
woman's shoes, no matter how large, might well be
expected to grow those painful excrescences."

"Even if I grant all that," objected Mason, "still
they're generalities at best, might even be coincidences
when you're arguing from a conclusion. Is that all?"
He seemed disappointed.

"By no means," drawled Ellery. "These were, as you
say, the generalities. But your cunning Mrs. Royce was
addicted to three habits which are exclusively masculine,
without argument. For one thing, when she sat down
on my second sight of her she elevated her skirts at the
knees with both hands; that is, one to each knee. Now
that's precisely what a man does when he sits down:
raises his trousers; to prevent, I suppose, their bagging
at the knees."

"But—"

"Wait. Did you notice the way she screwed up her
right eyebrow constantly, raising it far up and then
drawing it far down? What could this have been motivated by except the lifelong use of a monocle? And
a monocle is masculine. . . . And finally, her peculiar
habit, in removing a cigaret from her lips, of cupping
her hand about it rather than withdrawing it between
the forefinger and middle finger, as most cigaret-smok-
ers do. But the cupping gesture is precisely the result
of *pipe-smoking,* for a man cups his hands about the
bowl of a pipe in taking it out of his mouth. Man
again. When I balanced these three specific factors on
the same side of the scale as those generalities, I felt
certain Mrs. Royce was a male.

"What male? Well, that was simplest of all. You

had told me, for one thing, that when you and your partner Coolidge quizzed her she had shown a minute knowledge of Shaw history and specifically of Edith Shaw's history. On top of that, it took histrionic ability to carry off this female impersonation. Then there was the monocle deduction—England, surely? And the strong family resemblance. So I knew that 'Mrs. Royce,' being a Shaw undoubtedly, and an English Shaw to boot, was the other Shaw of the Morton side of the family—that is, Edith Shaw's brother Percy!"

"But she—he, I mean," cried Mason, "had told me Percy Shaw died a few months ago in Europe in an automobile accident!"

"Dear, dear," said Ellery sadly, "and a lawyer, too. She lied, that's all!—I mean 'he,' confound it. Your legal letter was addressed to Edith Shaw, and Percy received it, since they probably shared the same establishment. If he received it, it was rather obvious, wasn't it, that it was Edith Shaw who must have died shortly before; and that Percy had seized the opportunity to gain a fortune for himself by impersonating her?"

"But why," demanded Mason, puzzled, "did he kill Dr. Arlen? He had nothing to gain—Arlen's money was destined for Shaw's cousins, not for Percy Shaw. Do you mean there was some past connection—"

"Not at all," murmured Ellery. "Why look for past connections when the motive's slick and shiny at hand? If Mrs. Royce was a man, the motive was at once apparent. Under the terms of Mrs. Shaw's will Arlen was periodically to examine the family, with particular attention to Mrs. Royce. And Agatha Shaw told me yesterday that Mrs. Royce was constrained by will to remain in the house for two years. Obviously, then, the only way Percy Shaw could avert the cataclysm of being examined by Dr. Arlen and his disguise penetrated—for a doctor would have seen the truth instantly on examination, of course—was to kill Arlen. Simple, *nein?*"

"But the beard Arlen drew—that meant he *had* seen through it?"

"Not unaided. What probably happened was that the impostor, knowing the first physical examination impended, went to Dr. Arlen the other night to strike a bargain, revealing himself as a man. Arlen, an honest man, refused to be bribed. He must have been painting at the time and, thinking fast, unable to rouse the house because he was so far away from the others, unable to paint his assailant's name because 'Mrs. Royce' would see it and destroy it, thought of Peter's beard, made the lightning connection, and calmly painted it while 'Mrs. Royce' talked to him. Then he was stabbed."

"And the previous poisoning attempt on Mrs. Shaw?"

"That," said Ellery, "undoubtedly lies between John and Agatha."

Mason was silent, and for some time they rode in peace. Then the lawyer stirred, and sighed, and said: "Well, all things considered, I suppose you should thank Providence. Without concrete evidence—your reasoning was unsupported by legal evidence, you realize that, of course, Queen—you could scarcely have accused Mrs. Royce of being a man, could you? Had you been wrong, what a beautiful suit she could have brought against you! That fire last night was an act of God."

"I am," said Ellery calmly, "above all, my dear Mason, a man of free will. I appreciate acts of God when they occur, but I don't sit around waiting for them. Consequently . . ."

"You mean—" gasped Mason, opening his mouth wide.

"A telephone call, a hurried trip by Sergeant Velie, and smoke-bombs were the *materia* for breaking into Mrs. Royce's room in the dead of night," said Ellery comfortably. "By the way, you don't by any chance know the permanent address of—ah—Miss Krutch?"

The Adventure of
THE THREE LAME MEN

The Adventure of
THE THREE LAME MEN

When Ellery Queen walked into the bedroom, with its low ash-gray bed and its tinted walls and angular furniture and chromium gewgaws, he found his father the Inspector yammering at a frightened colored girl whose face looked like liverwurst with two red-brown marbles stuck into it.

Sergeant Velie leaned his impossible shoulders against the delicate gray door and said: "Look out for that rug, Mr. Queen."

It was a pastel-gray rug, unbordered; all around it lay a gleaming frame of polished hardwood floor. The rug was tracked with muddy footprints and on the waxed hardwood between the rug and an open window across the room there was a straight scratchy bruise tapering from a wide scab to a thin vanishing line, like a furrow on ice.

He clucked and shook his head. "Shocking, Velie, really revolting. Tramping mud and snow all over this feminine fairyland!"

"Who, me? Listen, Mr. Queen, we found those prints here."

"Ah," said Ellery. "And the scratch?"

"That, too."

He shivered in his ulster; the room was chilly with a snowy cold that swept through the open window from the white night outside. A velvet-and-steel chair beside the bed was draped with the cobwebs of a woman's chemise and *brassière*.

The Inspector said peevishly: " 'Lo, son. This is something in your line. Fancy. . . . All right, Thomas. Take her away, but keep her on ice."

Sergeant Velie steered the Negress clear of the evidence on the rug and pushed her past the gray door into the living-room, which was filled with smoke and laughing men. Then he closed the door.

Ellery sat down on the furry zibeline bedspread and pulled out a cigaret, and the Inspector sneezed three times over his snuff. "Queer set-up," he said thoughtfully, wiping his nose. "The legmen outside'll tell it in headlines. Park Avenue love-nest, beautiful ex-chorine —they're always beautiful—prominent clubman, a snatch. . . . The old bellywash, made to order for the tabs. And yet—"

"You know," said Ellery plaintively, "sometimes I think you give me credit for a sort of psychomancy. What is this, a *séance*? Murder, you say? Who was murdered? Who's been snatched? Whose love-nest? What's it all about? All I know is that some one from Headquarters 'phoned me a few minutes ago to hurry down here."

"I left word for you with the Lieutenant at the desk." The Inspector skirted the rug and pattered across the glistening floor. He slithered and teetered, and regained his balance. "Damn these slippery floors! . . . Have a look for yourself." He flung open the door of a wall-closet.

Something quiet was sitting on the floor of the closet, head hidden by hanging garments, slim long naked legs drawn up, tied at the ankles with a pair of silk stockings.

Ellery stared down with sharp impersonal eyes. It was a dead woman sitting there so quietly, on the floor of the closet, dressed in a shimmering kimono and stark naked underneath. He stooped and held aside the concealing garments. Her head hung on her breast and ash-blonde hair was tumbled over her face. Beneath the hair he saw a cloth which covered her mouth, nose, and eyes tightly. Her hands were out of sight behind her.

He straightened, raising his eyebrows.

"Smothered by the gag," said the Inspector in a matter-of-fact voice. "Looks as if whoever pulled this snatch tied her up and gagged her to get her out of the way."

"Forgetting," murmured Ellery, craning about, "that in order to continue living in this sorry world one must breathe. Quite so. . . . Her name?"

"Lily Divine," said Inspector Queen grimly.

"No! The Divine Lily?" His gray eyes glittered. "I thought she was out of circulation."

"She was. Left Jaffee's *Scandals* a few years ago, or was kicked out—I never did get it straight. Some man involved—they were hitched. It lasted three months. Then he divorced her. Since then she's been the belle of Park Avenue—traveled up and down the big street till there isn't a doorman or elevator-boy who doesn't know her. *Or* a renting agent."

"God's gift to the realtors. *Demi-mondaine,* eh?"

"That's one name for it."

Ellery's eyes for the third time strayed to the open window, one of three in the bedroom; the other two were shut. It was the only window in the room which gave on a fire-escape. "And who's the wealthy incumbent?"

"Come again?"

"Who's been paying for *this* playground?"

"Oh! Now that's interesting." The old gentleman kicked the closet-door shut and went to the fire-escape window. "Guess."

"Come, come, dad! I'm the world's poorest guesser."

"Joseph E. Sherman!"

"Ah. The banking chap?"

"That's the one." The Inspector sighed and continued with some bitterness: "That's the hell of having money. You begin to crave expensive toys. Who'd have thought it of the great J. E.? Straitlaced as they come, got a nice wife and a grown daughter, everything in the world money can buy; goes to church regularly— and means it. . . ." He stared out the window onto the snow-covered fire-escape. The snow was silver in the moonlight. "And here he is in this mess."

Sergeant Velie's back heaved and he whirled in some surprise. A chatter of men's pleading voices burst into the bedroom. A woman was backing in, saying: "No. Please, I—I can't say anything, really. I don't know—"

Velie leaped, thrust her aside, growled: "Lay off, you eggs," and slammed the door in the newspapermen's faces.

The woman faced about and said: "Hello?" in a surprised voice.

She was very young, no more than eighteen; but there was maturity in her full figure and something tired and wise in her pretty little face. She wore a mink coat and a mink toque.

"And who might you be?" asked the Inspector softly, coming forward.

Her lashes swept down and up. The surprise showed on her face. She was looking for some one, something.

Then she said rapidly: "I'm Rosanne Sherman. Where's my father, please?"

The Inspector grimaced. "This isn't the place for you, Miss Sherman. There's a dead woman in the closet—"

"Oh. So that's where—" She caught her breath a little, her liquid eyes pouncing upon the closet-door. "But where's my father?"

"Sit down, please," said Ellery. The girl obeyed quickly.

"He's gone, Miss Sherman," said the Inspector in a soothing voice. "I'm afraid we've bad news for you and your mother. Kidnaped—"

"Kidnaped!" She looked about in a sick daze. "Kidnaped? But this—this apartment, this woman . . ."

"You'll have to know," said Ellery. "Or perhaps you know already?"

She said with difficulty: "He's been living with her."

"Your mother knew?" snapped the Inspector.

"I—I don't know."

"How do *you* know?"

"You just know those—those things," she said dully.

There was a breath of silence. The Inspector looked at her with veiled keenness and went back to the window. "Your mother's coming?"

"Yes. I—I couldn't wait. She's coming with Bill— I mean with Mr. Kittering, father's . . . one of the vice-presidents at the bank."

There was another silence. Ellery ground his cigaret out in a writhing ashtray and, apologetically, went to the rug and stooped for a sharp look. Without raising his eyes he said: "What's the story, dad? Miss Sherman may as well know. Perhaps she can be of assistance."

"Yes, yes," she said eagerly. "Perhaps I can."

The Inspector rocked on his heels, eyeing the dim ceiling. "About two hours ago—around 7:30—Sherman came into the lobby downstairs. Doorman saw him. Seemed as usual. Elevator-boy took him up here to the sixth floor, saw him—" he hesitated—"fish out his key and open the front door to this apartment. That's the last of him. Nobody else came; at least not through the front way."

"There's another entrance into the building?"

"More'n one. Tradesmen's entrance in the basement, from the rear. Also the emergency stairway. *And* the fire-escape here." He thumbed the window behind him. "Anyway, about a half-hour ago this colored girl I was talking to when you came in—she's the Divine woman's maid—came back and . . ."

They ignored the girl. She sat very still, listening. From time to time her eyes went to the closet-door. Ellery frowned. "Came back from where?"

"Lily had given her a couple of hours off. Always did, the shine said, when she expected—uh—Sherman. Anyway, she came back. Front door was locked. She used her key but couldn't get in. It had not only been locked but bolted from the inside with one of those bolt-and-chain thimgamajigs. She called out but couldn't get any answer. So she called the super—"

"I know, I know," said Ellery impatiently. "Dilly-dallied, and finally they broke the door down. I saw it when I came in. They found the Divine woman in the closet?"

"Hold your horses, will you? Didn't find any such thing—*they* didn't. They forced the bedroom door—"

"Oh," said Ellery in a strange voice. "This door was locked, too?"

"Yes. They looked in. Room seemed kind of upset.

And they saw these muddy tracks on the rug." Rosanne Sherman looked at the rug. Then she closed her
eyes and leaned back, her pale lips quivering. "The
super's a smart Swede and called a cop without touching anything. The cop found the body and here we
are. . . . The note was pinned on the bed."

"Note?"

"Note?" murmured Miss Sherman, opening her eyes.

Ellery took a sheet of dainty paper from the Inspector's fingers. He read aloud: "J. E. Sherman is in our
hands and will be released on payment of fifty grand
according to instructions to come. Police, lay off. You
will find the woman, unharmed, in the closet." The
message had been scrawled in block letters and was un-
signed.

"They used her own paper and pencil," grunted the
Inspector. "Nice refined note."

"Restrained. There's a sort of grim elegance about
it," murmured Ellery. He returned the note and again
his eyes lingered upon the window overlooking the fire-
escape. "Unharmed, eh?"

The girl said quietly: "There was a note before this,
too. About a week ago. I found father reading it one
night. He tried to hide it but I—I made him let me
see it. A threatening note. Demanded twenty-five
thousand dollars at once for 'protection.' It said if he
didn't pay it they would—would . . ."

"Kill him?"

"Kidnap him. And ask for fifty." Then all at once
her reserve vanished and she sprang from the chair,
eyes blazing. "Why don't you *do* something?" she
cried. "They may be torturing him, murdering
him. . . ." She sank back, sobbing.

"Now, now," said the Inspector. "Keep cool, Miss Sherman. You've got your mother to think of."

"It will kill mother," she sobbed. "You should have seen her face—"

"Miss Sherman," murmured Ellery, "where is this first note?"

She raised her head. "He burned it. He said not to tell mother. He said it was from some crank, and didn't mean anything. He laughed it off."

Ellery shook his head dolefully and looked at the open window again. "If the bedroom door—" he mumbled. He stopped and went to the door. Sergeant Velie silently stepped aside. The door had no keyhole. On the bedroom side there was a knob which, on being turned, operated a hidden bolt which locked the door. He nodded absently. "Bolted from the bedroom side. Hmm. . . . So they got out through the window."

"That's right."

It was a small window, the lower pane raised as far as it would go. On the sill perched a window-box filled with churned, loose earth and the desiccated stalks of dead geraniums. The box covered the entire sill and was a foot high, leaving little more than two feet of open space above it. And it was immovable, built into the sill of the narrow window. Ellery blinked and leaned out, scrutinizing the iron-slatted floor of the fire-escape. Its snow-covered surface was pitted with clean crisp footprints, and only footprints; elsewhere the snow was virgin smooth. Mingled footprints, he saw, pattered downward and upward on the iron steps leading toward the alley below. He glanced down; as far as he could see the steps bore the same crisp prints. Beneath the ledge outside, coming to the edge of the sill, the snow had piled up in a drift, which was undisturbed.

"Now," said the Inspector imperturbably, "take another look at the rug."

Ellery drew back his tingling head. He knew very well what story the rug told. Three different pairs of men's shoes had desecrated the rich grayness of the rug with wet muddy prints. All three pairs were of large shoes, but the first had acutely pointed tips, the second blunter tips, and the third square bulldog tips. The prints pointed in all directions, and the rug was scuffed and wrinkled, as if there had been a struggle.

Ellery's thin nostrils began to oscillate. "You mean," he said slowly, "that there's something peculiar about these footprints, of course."

"Smart lad," chuckled the Inspector. "That's why I said there was something fancy about this case. The experts have been looking at these prints and the ones outside. What's your diagnosis?"

"The right shoes show lighter impressions uniformly," muttered Ellery, "especially the right heels. In most cases the right heelprints don't show at all."

"Right. *All three of the birds who pulled this job were lame.*"

Ellery puffed at another cigaret. "Nonsense."

"Hey?"

"I don't believe it. It's—it's impossible."

"And that from you," grinned the old gentleman. "Not only lame, but all three of 'em lame on the right foot."

"Impossible, I tell you!" snapped Ellery.

The girl gaped. The Inspector raised his bushy brows. "The best print men in the Department say it's not only not impossible, but it happened."

"I don't care what they say. Three limping men." Ellery scowled. "I—"

Sergeant Velie opened the door swiftly. There was a commotion outside. Thick cigaret smoke drifted into the bedroom out of a bedlam of shouting voices. A small woman and a tall athletic man were struggling in the center of a group of reporters, like honeypots attacked by flies. The Sergeant scattered the men with a rush, roaring at the top of his voice.

"Come in, come in," said the Inspector gently, closing the door. The woman looked at the girl, who had risen; then they fell into each other's arms, crying as if their hearts were breaking.

"Hello, Kittering," said Ellery awkwardly.

The tall man, lines of worry incised in his hard cheeks, muttered: "Hullo, Queen. Rough, eh? Poor old J. E. And this damned woman—"

"You know each other?" said the Inspector with glittering eyes.

"We've met at a club or two," drawled Ellery.

Kittering was still a young man, still well-conditioned. Bachelor, wealthy man-about-town, he was a familiar New York figure. His photograph was constantly turning up in rotogravure sections; he was a polo player, he bred pedigreed dogs, he owned a racing yawl. He paced up and down with the restless vitality of a caged animal, avoiding the sobbing women.

All at once the room was full of voices—the Inspector's, Rosanne's, Mrs. Sherman's. Ellery, at the open window, heard them through a haze of thought, while the Inspector in a sympathetic voice explained the situation. Kittering continued to patrol the polished floor; his feet were sure as a cat's.

Mrs. Sherman sank into the velvet-and-steel chair. Tears streaked her soft face, but she was no longer crying. She was perhaps forty, although she seemed younger. There was something gracious, even queenly, in her manner; a dignity and tempered beauty not even pain could destroy. "I've known about Joe's affair with this woman," she said in a low voice, "for some time." She pressed her daughter's hand. "Yes, Ro, I have. I—I never said anything. Bill—" she glanced at the tall man. "Bill knew, too. Didn't you, Bill?" A spasm of pain crossed her face.

Kittering looked uncomfortable. "Well, I suppose so," he said in a savage tone. "But Joe didn't mean anything by it, Enid. You know that—"

"No," said Mrs. Sherman gravely, "he never did. He's been good to me, to Rosanne, to all of us. It's just that he—he's weak."

"There have been others, Mrs. Sherman?" asked the Inspector.

"Yes. . . . I always knew. A woman can tell. Once—" her gloved hands clenched— "once he knew I knew. He was ashamed of himself, prostrate, h-humble." She paused. "He promised it would never happen again. But it did. I knew it would. He just couldn't help himself. But he always came back to me, you see. He always loved just me, you see." She spoke as if she were trying to explain things, not to them, but to herself.

The girl shook her head angrily; she took one of her mother's hands. Kittering said in a low voice: "Now, Enid. Now. It— Well, it doesn't help. It's all beside the point, anyway." He leveled his cool eyes at the Inspector. "How about the kidnaping, Inspector? That's the vital thing. Do you think they mean business?"

"What do you think?" said the Inspector grimly.

Mrs. Sherman rose suddenly. "Oh, Bill, we *must* get

Joe back!" she cried. "Pay what they ask. Anything—"

The Inspector shrugged. "You'll have to talk to the Commissioner, Mrs. Sherman. I personally can't—"

"Nonsense, man. You can't put any bars in our way," snarled Kittering. "These men are criminals. They won't stop at anything. Joe's life means more—"

"Now, now," said Ellery mildly, coming forward. "This discussion is getting us precisely nowhere. Kittering, what's the state of Mr. Sherman's finances?"

"Finances?" Kittering glared. "Sound as a dollar."

"No troubles of any kind?"

"No. See here, Queen, what are you hinting at?" The man's eyes flamed.

"*Tch, tch,*" said Ellery. "Keep your shirt on, old fellow. You say you knew about Mr. Sherman's relationship with Lily Divine. Did he know you knew?"

Kittering's eyes fell. "Yes," he muttered. "I told him he was playing with fire. I knew no good would come of it, that he'd get into some sort of scrape over her. She had underworld connections at one time—" He stopped, jaw dropping. "By George!" he bellowed. "Queen! Inspector! That's it!"

"What's it?" said the Inspector. For some reason he seemed amused.

"Bill! What's struck you?" cried Rosanne, springing to his side.

"Just came over me, Ro," said Kittering swiftly. He paced up and down. "Yes, that must be it. Underworld—of course. Inspector, d'ye know who used to be that woman's lover?"

"Certainly," smiled the Inspector. "Mac McKee."

"The gangster!" whispered Mrs. Sherman, horror in her eyes.

"Then you knew." Kittering flushed. "Well, why don't you do something? Don't you see? McKee must have engineered this job!"

"Dad," said Ellery coldly. "Why didn't you tell me? McKee's got a finger in this pie?"

"Didn't get the chance. I've got the boys out rounding him up now." The old man shook his head. "I'm not promising anything, Mrs. Sherman. He may be perfectly innocent. Or if he's guilty he'll have a good alibi. He's a slick article. We'll have to feel our way. Now why don't you good people go home and leave these things to us?" He continued quickly: "Kittering, take the ladies home. We'll keep you informed from this end. There's time, you know. We still have to hear from them about how to send the ransommoney. It isn't as bad as it might be. I—"

"I think we'll stay here," said Mrs. Sherman quietly.

"Enid—" said Kittering.

The door banged against Velie's back and two uniformed men came in with a covered basket. The women paled and crept into a corner. Kittering went with them, pleading. They all kept their eyes averted from the closet.

"How about this man McKee?" said Ellery in a low voice to his father, as the Morgue men tugged at something in the closet. "How hot is that angle?"

"Hot enough, son. I've known all along, of course, about the fact that Lily'd lived with Mac a couple of years ago. But tonight when I questioned the telephone operator on duty downstairs before you came I found out something."

"He called her this evening?" said Ellery sharply.

"She called him. A little before eight. Asked the operator to get her a number—a number which we know leads to McKee's mob headquarters. The 'phone girl's nosy and she listened in. Heard Lily speak to a man she called 'Mac,' asked him to come to her apartment here on the double-quick. Seemed upset about something, the operator says."

"Did McKee come?"

"Doorman says no. But then there are those other entrances."

Ellery's brow wriggled. "Yes, yes, but if Lily Divine called him at eight, how could he have—"

The Inspector chuckled. "I've got my own ideas about that."

The Morgue men dumped something in the basket that landed with a thud. Mrs. Sherman looked faint, and Kittering was supporting her, speaking in a low urgent voice. Ellery flashed a glance at them and whispered: "Those prints in the snow on the fire-escape and iron steps; are they of the same shoes that made the prints on the rug here?"

"What's eating you?" demanded the Inspector. "Sure."

"Did Sherman keep clothes here?"

"My dear son," said the Inspector plaintively. "Do I have to tell you the facts of life all over again? Of course he did!"

"Shoes?"

"We've checked all that. All his shoes are here, and they're all the same size, and none of 'em matches any of the prints on the rug or in the snow. That's how we know three men pulled this job. None of these prints belonged to Sherman; his shoes were dry."

"How do you know?"

"We found his wet rubbers in the foyer."

"Does Sherman limp?"

The Inspector said reproachfully: "Now how the hell should I know?" The Morgue men stooped, grasped the handles attached to the basket fore and aft, and stolidly trudged from the room. "Mrs. Sherman, does your husband limp?"

The woman, in a tremble, sat down again. "Limp? No."

"He's never limped?"

"No."

"Any one of your or his acquaintance limp?"

"Of course not!" growled Kittering. "What sort of hocus-pocus are you up to this time? How about getting after this cowardly thug McKee?"

"I think you'd better go now," said the Inspector evenly. "All of you. This has gone far enough."

"Just a moment," said Ellery. "I must get these facts straight. Do the prints on the fire-escape show the characteristic lameness, too?"

"Sure. Say, what are you driving at?"

"I'm sure I don't know," said Ellery irritably. "I'm just annoyed. Three lame men . . . Mrs. Sherman, isn't your husband rather a big man?"

"Big?" She seemed dazed. "Very. Six feet three. He weighs two-fifty."

Ellery nodded with a sort of restless satisfaction. He whispered to his father: "Aren't any of Sherman's prints in the snow?"

"No. He must have been carried. Probably knocked on the head."

"The scratch," said a deep voice over the Inspector's shoulder.

"Oh, it's you, Thomas. What d'ye mean, the scratch?"

"Well, sir," rumbled Sergeant Velie, eyes agleam with

the vastness of his inspiration, "he was dragged, see? Scratch there on the waxed floor goes from the rug to the window. So he was dragged to the window, then they h'isted him and slung him through and carried him down. That's an areaway down there. Must 'a' got up that way, too. Surprised these two tootsies billin' and cooin', tied up the frail and gagged her, socked Sherman on the head, dragged him to—"

"Heard you the first time," growled the Inspector. "That scratch has been pretty well fixed. Made by a shoe-heel, the boys say. Well, what are we wasting time for? Oh, yes, there's one thing more."

Kittering broke in stiffly: "Inspector. We're going. We rely upon you to—"

"Yes, yes," snapped Ellery. "Hold on a moment like a good chap, Kittering. What's that you were saying, dad? I have a notion—"

A hoarse yell hurled them at the bedroom door. Velie tore it open. In the living-room filled with men two detectives were grappling with a huge man in a camel's-hair overcoat. Smoky lights flashed all over the room as cameras clicked and photographers, delirious over their good fortune, worked madly. Two other men, snarling but cautious, were pinned against the wall by other detectives.

"What's this?" said the Inspector pleasantly from the doorway. The noise ceased and the huge man stopped fighting. Sanity flooded back into his eyes. "McKee!" drawled the old gentleman. "Well, well. This isn't like you, Mac. Fighting! I'm ashamed of you. All right, boys. Let go. He'll be good now."

The man twitched his immense shoulders viciously and the detectives fell back, panting. "This a plant?" he growled.

"We'll go now," said Rosanne in a small voice.

"Not yet, my dear," smiled the Inspector, without turning. "Come in, Mac. Thomas, close that door. You men there," he barked, "keep McKee's boy-friends company."

They all returned to the bedroom. The big man was watchful. He had heavy batrachian lids, and his mouth was loose and fat. But his jaw was vast, and there was cunning in his eyes. The Sherman women shrank back against Kittering, who was pale. For a moment naked animal cruelty had glittered in the gunman's eyes. But he was uneasy, too.

"Know what you were picked up for, Mac?" said the Inspector, stepping close to the giant and staring up into the cruel eyes.

"You're off your nut, Inspector," rumbled McKee. Then his eyes swept over the Shermans, Kittering, Ellery, the rug, the open window, the open door of the closet. "I wasn't picked up. I came here myself and those flatfeet of yours just ganged me."

"Oh, I see," said the old man softly. "Just walked in for a friendly call, hey? To see Lily?"

Velie hovered expectantly behind the man; they were of a height and breadth. But McKee was very quiet. "Suppose I was? What of it? Where is she? What's happened here?"

"Don't you know?"

"What the hell! Would I ask you if I knew?"

"Good boy," chuckled the Inspector. "Still the slickest hood in the big time. Ever see these people before, Mac?"

McKee's eyes flickered over Kittering and the two women. "No."

"Know who they are?"

"Ain't had the pleasure."

"That's Mrs. Sherman, and her daughter, and Mr. Kittering, a business associate of Joseph E. Sherman's."

"So what?"

"So what, he asks," murmured the Inspector. "Listen, you lunk!" he snarled suddenly, glaring up. "Lily's been given the works, and J. E. Sherman's been snatched. That mean anything to you?"

A faint pallor crept under the top skin of the big man's swarthy face. His tongue wet his lips, once. "Lily got it?" he muttered. "Here?" He looked around, as if for her body.

"Yes, here. Smothered to death. I admit it's not your usual technique, Mac; a little refined for you. But the snatch is right up your alley—"

The big man drew himself in, like a Galápagos turtle. His shoulders hunched in ridges of fat and muscle, and his eyes almost vanished. "If you think I had anything to do with this job, Inspector, you're nuts. Why, my alibi—"

"You dirty killer," said Kittering dully. McKee whirled, snatching at something beneath his coat under the armpit. Then he caught himself and relaxed. "Where's Joe Sherman?" Kittering sprang and, so suddenly that neither Sergeant Velie nor Ellery could intervene, lashed out at McKee's jaw. It was a solid smack, like wet meat slapping a sidewalk; and McKee staggered, blinking. But he made no move to retaliate. Only his eyes burned; burned at Kittering like a fuse. Rosanne and Enid Sherman grasped Kittering's arms, crying. Ellery swore beneath his breath, and Sergeant Velie stepped between the two men.

"That'll be just about enough," said Inspector Queen curtly. "Off with you, Kittering. You, too,

Mrs. Sherman; and the girl." And in an almost inaudible voice he said to Kittering: "That sock was a mistake, young man. Beat it!"

Kittering dropped his arms, sighing. The two women led him, speechless, from the bedroom. They were swallowed up in the deluge of clamoring men outside.

McKee's arms quivered and his eyes burned at the gray door. He said something very softly to himself, his lips barely moving.

"Lily 'phoned you tonight, didn't she?" rapped the Inspector.

The gunman licked his lips cautiously. "Oh. Yeah. That's right."

"Why? What'd she want?"

"I don't know."

"She asked you to come over?"

"Yeah."

"You once lived with Lily, didn't you?"

"You tell me. You know all the answers."

"She 'phoned you at eight tonight?"

"Yeah."

The Inspector said craftily: "And here it is about ten. Take you two hours to come down from the Bronx?"

"Somethin' held me up."

"You knew Sherman?"

"Heard of him."

"Did you know Lily was living with him?"

McKee shrugged. "Oh, hell, Inspector, you've got nothin' on me. Sure I knew, but what of it? I was washed up with that broad years ago. When she 'phoned tonight I thought she might 'a' been in some kind of trouble, so for old times' sake I thought I'd ankle down here and see what was up. That's all."

"I think," said Ellery mildly, "that you had better take your shoes off, McKee."

The gunman gaped. *"What?"*

"Off with your shoes," said Ellery in a patient voice. "In another age it would have been a different part of your anatomy. Velie, please get the shoes of the two—er—gentlemen who accompanied Mr. McKee."

Velie went out. McKee, like a blind bull, looked at the rug, and the muddy tracks, and then he cursed and snatched a guilty glance at his own gargantuan feet. Without a word he sat down in the velvet-and-steel chair and unlaced his oxfords, which were streaked with damp mud.

"That's a good idea, El," said the Inspector approvingly, stepping back.

Velie returned bearing two pairs of wet shoes to the accompaniment of a burst of derisive laughter from the men in the living-room. Ellery went to work in silence. After a time he looked up, handed the big shoes back to McKee and the others to Velie, who left the room again.

"No dice, hey?" sneered McKee, lacing up his shoes. "I told you you birds were cockeyed."

"Does either of the two men outside limp, Velie?" asked Ellery when the Sergeant returned.

"No, sir."

Ellery stepped back, tapping a cigaret on his thumb-nail; and McKee, with an ugly laugh, rose to go. "Just a second, Mac," said the Inspector. "I'm holding you."

"You're *what?*"

"Holding you on suspicion," said the old man evenly. "You and Lily Divine were working a game on Sher-

man. You put the woman up to playing Sherman on
his weak side, getting him under her thumb." McKee
glared, his face livid. "Tonight you came over, with
the trap set; double-crossed Lily, putting her away to
shut her up; left the note and beat it with Sherman.
What d'ye say to that?"

"I say to hell with it! How about the tracks on the
rug there? You saw yourself they didn't fit!"

"Clever," said the Inspector. "You wore different
shoes."

"Nuts. How about Lily's call to me at eight? I
heard somebody outside say she kicked off around that
time. If she called me up—"

"That was smart, too. You were here all the time.
You made her put in that call while you stood over
her, just to establish an alibi."

McKee grinned. "Go ahead and prove it," he said
shortly. He turned on his heel and walked out. Velie
followed him.

"And how about the limping tracks?" murmured
Ellery, when the door was shut. "Eh, gentle sire? Did
he and his minions fake the limp, too?"

"Why not?" The Inspector tugged his mustache irritably.

"An unanswerable question, I admit." Ellery
shrugged. "Look here. You were going to tell me
before that there was something else. What?"

"Oh, that! Something's missing from this room."

Ellery glared. "Missing? Why in thunder didn't
you say so before?"

"But—"

"Too much," muttered Ellery feverishly. "That
would be too much. Don't tell me it was a valise? A
suitcase? Something of the sort?"

The Inspector looked faintly astonished. "For the lord's sake, El! How did you guess? The colored wench says an alligator handbag, empty, belonging to the Divine woman, is gone. She saw it in the closet only an hour before Lily sent her out. There's nothing else missing."

"Sweet, sweet. Tra, la! We're going somewhere. The colored lady . . . Ah, Velie, there you are. Be a good chap and haul her in here, will you?"

Velie brought the Negress in. She looked sick. Ellery pounced upon her. "When was this floor waxed last?"

"Huh?" Her eyes grew enormous, and the Inspector started. "W-why, jest t'day."

"When today?"

" 'Safternoon, suh. I did it myse'f."

"Good enough, I suppose," he muttered impatiently. "All right, all right. That's all, young woman. Take her away, Sergeant."

"But, El—" protested the Inspector.

"Very pretty," Ellery continued to mutter, "very pretty indeed. But, damn it all, there's a piece missing. Without it . . ." He bit his lip.

"Say, listen," said the Inspector slowly, "what have you got, son?"

"Everything—and nothing."

"Bah! How about Sherman?"

"Follow Mrs. Sherman's wishes in the matter absolutely. Sherman's safety is the prime consideration. After that—we'll see."

"All right," said the Inspector with drooping resignation. "But I can't understand—"

"Three lame men," sighed Ellery. "Very interesting. *Very* interesting."

Joseph E. Sherman sat in an armchair in Inspector
Richard Queen's office in Centre Street and told his
story in a cracked voice. A police radio car had picked
him up—dirty, disheveled, dazed—in Pelham an hour
before. For a time he was incoherent, kept asking brokenly for his wife and daughter. He seemed half-starved,
and his eyes were red and staring, as if for days he had
gone without sleep. It was three days after the discovery of Lily Divine's body and the kidnapers' note. The
police had not interfered. A third note had come in
the post to Mrs. Sherman the day after the murder—an
untraceable note in the same disguised block capitals,
reiterating the demand for $50,000 and assigning a
clever rendezvous for the delivery of the ransom. Kittering had raised the cash and acted as intermediary.
The money had been paid the day before. And today
here was Sherman, his immense bulk shaking with nerves
and fatigue.

"What happened, Mr. Sherman? Who were they?
Tell us the whole story," the Inspector urged gently.
The man had been fortified with food and whisky, but
he continued to shiver as if he had a chill.

"My wife—" he mumbled.

"Yes, yes, Mr. Sherman. She's all right. We've sent
for her."

Sergeant Velie opened the door. Sherman tottered to
his feet, cried out vaguely, and fell into his wife's arms.
Rosanne wept and clung to his hand. Kittering was
with them; he retreated to the background, stonily
watching. No one said anything.

"That woman—" Sherman muttered at last.

Enid Sherman put her fingers on his lips. "Not another word, Joe. I—I understand. Thank God you're
back." She turned on the Inspector, eyes brimming

with tears. "Can't we take my husband home now, Inspector? He's so—so . . ."

"We must know what happened, Mrs. Sherman."

The banker glanced nervously at Kittering. "Bill, old man . . ." He sank back into the armchair, clutching his wife's hand. His tremendous body filled the chair. "I'll tell you what I know, Inspector," he said in a low voice. "I'm tired. I don't know much." A police stenographer was scribbling beside the desk. Ellery stood by the window, frowning and gnawing his lips. "I—went to—her apartment that night. As usual. She was acting funny—"

"Yes," said the Inspector encouragingly. "By the way, did you know she was an old flame of Mac Mc-Kee's, the gangster?"

"Not at first." Sherman's shoulders sagged. "When I found out, I was already hopelessly—embroiled. I would never have ventured into . . ." Mrs. Sherman pressed his hand, and he gave her a slow queer grateful look. "While we were—together," he went on very softly, "the front doorbell rang. She went out to answer it. I waited. Perhaps I was a little afraid—of being—well, caught. Then . . . I don't know what happened. A hand clamped over my eyes—"

"Man's or woman's?" snapped Ellery.

His bloodshot eyes shifted. "I—I don't know. Then a rag of some kind was jammed against my nose—it smelled sweet, sickening. I struggled, but it did no good. That's all I know. Everything went blank. I must have been chloroformed."

"Chloroformed!" They all turned, startled, upon Ellery. He was staring at Sherman with a wild light in his eyes. "Mr. Sherman," he said slowly, coming forward, "do you mean to say you were *hors de combat* through the rest of it? Unconscious?"

"Yes," said Sherman, blinking.

Ellery straightened. "Indeed," he said in a strange voice. "The missing piece at last." And he went back to the window to stare out.

"The missing piece?" faltered the banker.

"Let's get this over with," said Kittering harshly. "Joe's in no condition—"

Sherman passed a trembling hand over his mouth. "When I woke up I was sick. My eyes were bound. I was tied up. I didn't know where I was. No one came near me. Once, though, some one fed me. Then— God knows how much later—I was carried out somewhere and later I knew I was in a car. They pushed me out on a road somewhere. When I came to I realized I had been untied. I took the rag from my eyes. . . . You know the rest."

There was a silence. The Inspector clicked his teeth together and said pettishly: "Do you mean to say, then, you can't identify any of your kidnapers, Mr. Sherman? How about their voices? Anything, man, to give us a lead!"

The banker's shoulders sagged lower. "Nothing," he muttered. "Can't I go now?"

"Hold on," said Ellery. "There's no other information you can give us?"

"Eh? No."

Ellery scowled. "There's nothing about this you're concealing, Mr. Sherman? You'd rather drop the whole matter, I take it?"

"Nothing. . . . Yes, drop it," mumbled Sherman. "Drop it entirely."

"I'm afraid," murmured Ellery, "that that's impossible. Because, you see, Mr. Sherman, I know who kidnaped you and murdered Lily Divine."

"You *know?*" whispered Rosanne. The banker sat like stone, and Kittering took a short step forward and stopped.

"Knowledge is a tricky thing," said Ellery, "but within human limitations—I know." He thrust a cigaret into his mouth and his eyebrows twitched. Sergeant Velie, at the door, took his hands out of his pockets and looked about expectantly. "A very odd affair, you see. This won't take long, and it may prove—interesting."

"But, Ellery—" frowned the Inspector.

"Please, dad. Consider that gash on the waxed floor. Your experts maintained that it was made by the heel of a shoe. The good Sergeant here pointed out that since it was made by a shoe-heel, then clearly it denoted Mr. Sherman's being dragged toward the window by his assailants."

"Well, what of it?" said the Inspector sharply. The Shermans sat dumb and fascinated; and Kittering did not stir.

Ellery drawled: "Everything of it. It occurred to me then and there that our good Sergeant had been in error." Velie's face fell. "If a body is being dragged, with sufficient force to cause shoe-marks on a freshly waxed floor, then there should be *two* scratches, you see; because even a child knows that the usual complement of feet in bipeds is two, not one. So I said to my-self: 'Whatever this mark on the floor means, it was certainly not caused by dragging.' "

"What then?" growled the old gentleman.

"Well," smiled Ellery, "if the mark was made by a shoe-heel, and yet not by the shoe-heel of a man being dragged, then the only sensible alternative is that *some one slipped on the floor*, you see. You yourself, dad, slipped and almost fell the other night. Have we any confirmation?"

"What's this, a lesson in logic?" said Kittering gruffly. "You take an odd time, Queen, to go oratorical."

"Quiet, Kittering," said the Inspector. "Confirmation?"

"The three lame men," said Ellery gently.

"The three lame men!"

"Precisely. We had definite evidences of lameness, of limping, in the footprints. Considerably bolstering the slip-on-the-floor theory. The person who slipped either sprained an ankle or suffered some leg injury, not necessarily serious but painful enough to cause a temporary lameness. You see that?"

"I'm going home," said Rosanne suddenly. Her cheeks were scarlet.

Ellery said quickly: "Sit down, Miss Sherman. Now we have three sets of limping prints, all of different pairs of shoes. That this fact was utterly incredible, dad, I tried to point out to you. Did three men, or even two, slip and fall and go lame in that bedroom? Ridiculous. For one thing, there was only one scratch on the floor; for another, the exact triplication of a phenomenon— three limping right feet—shows falsity, not truth."

"You mean," said Mrs. Sherman with a puzzled frown, "that there weren't three men who kidnaped my husband, Mr. Queen?"

"Exactly," drawled Ellery. "I say that the argument shows that one man, the one who slipped on the floor, was responsible for all three different sets of limping footprints. How? Obviously, by using three different pairs of shoes."

"But what happened to the shoes, El?"

"They weren't found. So the limper must have taken them away with him. Any corroboration? Yes; *one of Lily Divine's bags was missing.*" Ellery's gray eyes hardened. "The crux of the matter is, of course, the answer to the question: Why did the limper go to the trouble of falsifying the trail, of planting three sets of apparently different footprints? The answer again must be apparent: to make the kidnaping look like the work of more than one person—specifically, of three. This suggests a gang, surely? Inversely, then, the limper is probably not a gangster at all. But aside from that we have now reached the point where we may say that our limper, a lone wolf, was the murderer of Lily Divine and the kidnaper of Mr. Sherman!"

No one said anything. Sergeant Velie's hands opened and closed tentatively.

Ellery sighed. "The window and the fire-escape tell most of the rest of the story. With the bedroom door found bolted from the inside, then the kidnaper got away through the only window in the room giving upon the fire-escape. The window is small, and on its sill there is an immovable window-box. The window-box reduces the size of the window opening by at least one-third, leaving about two feet of space vertically for possible exit.

"Now Mr. Sherman here is a giant of a man—well over six feet tall and weighing two hundred and fifty pounds. How would the limper get Mr. Sherman's unconscious body through that small window-space? Sling it over his shoulder and climb through? A palpable absurdity, under the circumstances; certainly the most difficult method, and it probably would not even occur to him. But even if it had, he would have found the method unsuccessful. There are only two other ways to get out with the body: one would be to climb out first, leaving the body hanging over the window-box to be accessible from outside, and then pull the body out onto the fire-escape. But he didn't use this method; nowhere did the snow on the fire-escape or directly below the window-sill show a sign of disturbance such as would have been made by a heavy body resting even partly in it. The remaining method would be to push the body out first, and then climb out after it. But here the same objection holds: there was no impression of a body in the snow; only footprints."

The Inspector blinked. "But I don't see—"

"I didn't either, for some time," said Ellery. His face was like stone now. "The immediate conclusion was unquestionably that *an unconscious body was not taken out of the window!*"

Joseph E. Sherman got to his feet with a hoarse cry. His splotched cheeks were furrowed with tears. "All right!" he shouted. "I did it! I planned the whole thing. I wrote the first note to myself and all the others. I brought the three pairs of shoes into the apartment at odd times in the past two weeks, under cover, and hid them there. The night—the other night when I'd—I'd done it I used the earth in the window-box to muddy the bottoms of the shoes. I killed her to make it look like a kidnaping of myself, killed her because she was bleeding me, the slut! She's been hammering at me to divorce Enid and marry her. *Marry* her! I couldn't stand it. I was trapped. My position . . ."

Mrs. Sherman was staring at her husband with the

glazed dullness of a dying animal. "But I knew—" she whispered.

He grew calmer. He said quietly: "I knew you knew, Enid darling. But I went crazy."

The Inspector said, with pity in his eyes: "Take him away, Thomas."

"But you must have known the whole story right there on the scene," complained the Inspector with some asperity an hour later, when the sordid business of Sherman's commitment had been finished.

Ellery shook his head sombrely. "No. The apex of my argument couldn't be arrived at until I knew definitely whether Sherman had been unconscious or not. That's why I recommended paying the ransom and getting the man to come back. I wanted to hear his story. When he said he'd been chloroformed in the apartment, my case was complete. Because I knew that no unconscious body was carried or dragged through the window. Sherman was lying, then, when he said that he had been chloroformed. In other words, there was no kidnaping. If there was no kidnaping, then obviously it was Sherman who had slipped on the floor, who limped, who had faked a kidnaping of himself to cover up the fact that he had murdered Lily Divine, concocting a plot by which he hoped to foster the illusion that a gang had kidnaped him and killed the woman incidentally. His slip on the floor was pure accident; he probably didn't realize that the tracks he was leaving would show the limping characteristics."

They sat in silence for a while, Ellery smoking and the Inspector staring out his iron-barred window. Then the old gentleman sighed. "I feel sorry for her."

"For whom?" said Ellery absently.

"Mrs. Sherman."

Ellery shrugged. "You always were a sentimentalist. But perhaps the most extraordinary thing about this case is its moral."

"Moral?"

"The moral that even a hardened criminal tells the truth sometimes. Lily called McKee, probably to get McKee to apply the well-known pressure to Sherman after Sherman refused to marry her. McKee was delayed, and he walked into the arms of the police. But he told the truth throughout. . . . So suppose," drawled Ellery, "you call up the Tombs—a detail you've forgotten in the excitement—and get poor old Mac his well-earned release."

The Adventure of
THE INVISIBLE LOVER

The Adventure of
THE INVISIBLE LOVER

Roger Bowen was thirty, blue-eyed, and white. He was taller than most, laughed a little more readily, spoke English with an apologetic Harvard accent, drank an occasional cocktail, smoked more cigarets than were good for him, was very thoughtful of his only living relative—an elderly aunt living, chiefly upon his bounty, in San Francisco—and balanced his reading between Sabatini and Shaw. And he practised what law there was to practise in the town of Corsica, N. Y. (population 745), where he had been born, stolen apples from old man Carter's orchard, swum raw in Major's Creek, and sparked with Iris Scott of Saturday nights on the veranda of the Corsica Pavilion (two bands, continuous dancing).

To listen to his acquaintances, who comprised one hundred percent of the population of Corsica, he was a "prince," a "real good boy," "no darned highbrow," and a "reg'lar guy." To listen to his friends—who for the most part shared the same residence, Michael Scott's boarding house on Jasmine Street off Main—there was no jollier, kindlier, gentler, more inoffensive young man in the length and breadth of the land.

Within a half-hour of his arrival in Corsica from New York, Mr. Ellery Queen was able to gauge the temper of the Corsican populace concerning its most talked-of citizen. He learned something from a Mr. Klaus, the grocer on Main Street, a juicy morsel from a nameless urchin playing marbles in the road near the

161

County Courthouse, and a good deal from one Mrs. Parkins, wife of the Corsican postmaster. He learned least of all from Mr. Roger Bowen himself, who seemed a decent enough sort, and quite plainly hurt and bewildered.

And as he left the county jail and headed for the boarding house and Roger Bowen's inner circle of friends, who were responsible for his hurried journey from Manhattan, it struck Mr. Ellery Queen that it was uncommonly curious such a paragon of all the virtues should be lying disconsolately on a cot in a dingy iron-barred cell awaiting trial on a charge of murder in the first degree.

"Now, now," said Mr. Ellery Queen after a space, rocking gently back and forth on the rose-curtained porch, "surely it can't be as black as all that? From all I've heard about young Bowen—"

Father Anthony clasped his bony hands tightly. "I baptized Roger myself," he said in a trembling voice. "It isn't possible, Mr. Queen. I baptized him! And he has told me he did not shoot McGovern. I believe him; he wouldn't lie to me. And yet . . . John Graham, the biggest lawyer in the county, who is defending Roger, Mr. Queen, says it's one of the worst circumstantial cases he has ever seen."

"For that matter," growled towering Michael Scott, snapping his suspenders over his burly breast, "the boy says so himself. Hell, I wouldn't believe it even if Roger confessed! Beggin' your pardon, Father."

"All I say," snapped Mrs. Gandy from her wheelchair, "any one says Roger Bowen shot that sneaky, black-haired devil from New York is a fool. Suppose Roger was in his room, alone, the night it happened?

A person has the right to go to sleep, hasn't he? And how on earth would there be a witness to *that*, hey, Mr. Queen? The poor child's no flibbertigibbet, like some I know!"

"No alibi," sighed Ellery.

"Makes it bad," grumbled Pringle, chief of police of Corsica, a very fat and brawny old man. "Makes it downright bad. Better if he'd *had* some one with him that night. Not," he added hastily at Mrs. Gandy's outraged glare, "that Roger would, ye understand. But when I heard about that there, now, fight he'd had with McGovern—"

"Oh," said Ellery softly. "They came to blows? There were threats?"

"Not exactly blows, Mr. Queen," said Father Anthony, wincing. "But they did quarrel. It was the same evening: McGovern was shot about midnight, and Roger had words with him only an hour or so before. As a matter of fact, sir, it wasn't the first time. They had quarreled violently on several previous occasions. Enough to establish motive to the District Attorney's satisfaction."

"But the slug," growled Michael Scott. "The slug!"

"Yes," said Dr. Dodd, a short mousy intelligent-looking man; he spoke unhappily. "I'm county coroner as well as local undertaker, you see, Mr. Queen, and it was my duty to examine that bullet when I dug it out of McGovern's body on autopsy. When Pringle held Roger on suspicion and got hold of the boy's gun, we naturally compared the bore-marks. . . ."

"Bore-marks?" drawled Ellery. "Really!" He inspected Chief Pringle and Coroner Dodd with rather grudging admiration.

"Oh, we didn't trust our own judgment in the matter," said the coroner hastily, "although under my microscope it did look . . . It was all very nasty, Mr. Queen, but duty's duty, and an officer of the law has his oath to uphold. We sent it to New York, with the gun, for examination by a ballistics expert. His report came back confirming our findings. What were we to do? Pringle arrested Roger."

"Sometimes," said Father Anthony quietly, "there is a higher duty, Samuel."

The coroner looked miserable. Ellery said: "Does Bowen have a license to carry firearms?"

"Yep," muttered the fat policeman. "Lot of folks up this way do. Good huntin' in the hills yonder. It's a .38 did the job, all right—Roger's .38. Colt automatic, and a dandy, too."

"Is he a good shot?"

"I'll say he is!" exclaimed Scott. "That boy can shoot." His hard face lengthened. "I ought to know. I've got six pieces of shrapnel in my left leg right now where a Heinie shell came after me in Belleau."

"Excellent shot," faltered the coroner. "We've often gone rabbit-hunting together, and I've seen him pot a running target at fifty yards with his Colt. He won't use a rifle; too tame for real sport, he says."

"But what does Mr. Bowen say to all this?" demanded Ellery, squinting at the smoke of his cigaret. "He wouldn't talk to me at all."

"Roger," murmured Father Anthony, "says no. He did not kill McGovern, he says. That's enough for me."

"But scarcely for the District Attorney, eh?" Ellery sighed again. "Then, since his automatic was used, it logically follows that—granted he's telling the truth—some one stole it from him and replaced it secretly after the murder?"

The men looked at one another uncomfortably, and
Father Anthony smiled a faint proud smile. Then Scott
growled: "Damnedest thing. Graham—that's our lawyer—Graham he says to Roger: 'Listen, young man.
It's absolutely necessary for you to testify that the gun
could have been stolen from you. Your life may de-
pend on it,' and all that. And what do you think that
young fool says? 'No,' he says, 'that's not the truth,
Mr. Graham. Nobody did steal my gun. I'm a light
sleeper,' he says, 'and the bureau with the gun in it is
right next my bed. And I'd bolted my door that night.
Nobody could have got in and taken it. So,' he says,
'I'm not going to testify to any such thing!'"

Ellery expelled smoke in a whistle. "Our hero, eh?
That's—" He shrugged. "Now, this—ah—series of
quarrels. If I understand correctly, it concerned—"

"Iris Scott," said a cool voice from the screen-door.
"No, don't get up, Mr. Queen! Oh, it's quite all right,
father. I'm of age, and there's no point in keeping from
Mr. Queen what the whole town knows anyway." Her
voice stopped and caught on something. "What do you
want to know, Mr. Queen?"

Mr. Queen, it was to be feared, was temporarily incapable of coherent speech. He was on his feet, gaping
like a lout in a museum. If he had found a perfect diamond winking in the dust of Corsica's Main Street he
could not have been more flabbergasted. Beauty anywhere is a rarity; in Corsica it was a miracle. So this
is Iris Scott, he thought. Well named, O Michael! She
was fresh and soft and handsomely made, and dewy and
delicate as the flower itself. Strange soil to spring from!
Her queerly wide black eyes held him fascinated, and
he lost himself in her loveliness. In the gloom of the
doorway she stood alone, a thing of beauty. It was joy

just to look at her.   If there was seductiveness in her, it was the unconscious lure of perfection—the swoop of an eyebrow, the curve of lips, the poise of a sculptured breast.

And so Mr. Ellery Queen understood why it was possible for such a paragon as Roger Bowen to be facing the electric chair.   Even if he himself had been blind to her beauty, the men on the porch would have made him see. Dodd was regarding her quietly, with remote and humble worship.   Pringle stared at her with vast thirst—yes, even Pringle, that enormous fat old man.   And Father Anthony's aged eyes were proud, and a little sad.   But in Michael Scott's eyes there was only the fierce jubilance of possession.   This was Circe and Vesta in one, and she might move a man to murder as easily as a poet to lyric ecstasy.

"Well!" he said at last, drawing a deep breath.   "Pleasant surprise.   Sit down, Miss Scott, while I collect my wits.   McGovern was an admirer of yours?"

Her heels made little clackings on the porch.   "Yes," she said in a subdued voice, staring at the ivory hands in her lap.   "You might call it that.   And I—I liked him. He was different.   An artist from New York.   He'd come up to Corsica about six months ago to paint our famous hills.   He knew so much, he'd travelled in France and Germany and England, so many celebrities were his friends. . . . We're almost peasants here, Mr. Queen.   I never m-met any one like him."

"Sneaky devil," hissed Mrs. Gandy, her thin features contorted.

"Forgive me," smiled Ellery.   "Did you love him?"

A bee buzzed about Pringle's hairy ears, and he angrily slapped at it.   She said: "I— It's— Now that he's dead, no. Death—somehow—makes a difference. Perhaps I—saw him in his true colors."

"But you spent a lot of time with him—alive?"

"Yes, Mr. Queen."

There was a small silence, and then Michael Scott said heavily: "I don't interfere in my daughter's affairs; see? She's got her own life to live. But I never cottoned to McGovern myself. He was a fourflusher with a smooth line, and plenty tough. I wouldn't trust him from here to there. I told Iris, but she wouldn't listen. Like a girl, she sort of went off her nut. He hung around longer than he'd expected—owed me," grimly, "five weeks' rent. Why the hell wouldn't he hang around? Why wouldn't anything in pants?"

"There," drawled Ellery, "is the perfect rhetorical question. And Roger Bowen, Miss Scott?"

"We—we've grown up together," said Iris in the same low voice. And she tossed her head suddenly. "It's always been so *settled*. I suppose I've resented that. And then his interference. He was simply furious about Mr. McGovern. Once, several weeks ago, Roger threatened to kill him. We all heard him; they—they were arguing in the parlor there, and we were sitting on the porch here. . . ."

There was another silence, and then Ellery said gently: "And do you think young Roger shot this city-slicker, Miss Scott?"

She raised her devastating eyes to his. "No! I'll never believe that. Not Roger. He was angry, that's all. He didn't mean what he said." And then she choked and to their horror began to sob. Michael Scott grew brick-red, and Father Anthony looked distressed. The others winced. "I-I'm sorry," she said.

"And who do you think did?" asked Ellery softly.

"Mr. Queen, I don't know."

"Any one?" They shook their heads. "Well, I believe, Pringle, you mentioned something about McGovern's room having been left precisely as you found it the night of the murder. . . . By the way, what happened to his body?"

"Well," said the coroner, "we held it after the autopsy for inquest, of course, and tried to find some relative to claim the body. But McGovern apparently was alone in the world, and not even a friend stepped forward. He left nothing except a few possessions in his New York studio. I fixed him up myself, and we buried him in the New Corsican Cemetery with the proceeds."

"Here's the key," wheezed the policeman, struggling to his feet. "I got to go on down to Lower Village. Dodd'll tell you everything you want to know. I hope—" He stopped helplessly, and then waddled off the porch. "Comin', padre?" he muttered without turning.

"Yes," said Father Anthony. "Mr. Queen . . . Anything at all, you understand—" His thin shoulders drooped as he slowly followed Pringle down the cement walk.

"If you'll excuse us, Mrs. Gandy?" murmured Ellery.

"Who found the body?" he demanded as they trudged upstairs in the cool semi-darkness of the house.

"I did," sighed the coroner. "I've been boarding with Michael for twelve years. Ever since Mrs. Scott died. Just a couple of old bachelors, eh, Michael?" They both sighed. "It was on that terribly stormy night three weeks ago—thundered and rained, remember? I'd been

reading in my room—it was about midnight—and I
started for the bathroom down the hall upstairs before
going to bed. I passed McGovern's room; the door was
open and the light was on. He was sitting in the chair,
facing the door." The coroner shrugged. "I saw at
once he was dead. Shot through the heart. The blood
on his pajamas . . . I roused Michael at once. Iris
heard us and came, too." They paused at the head of
the stairs. Ellery heard the girl catch her breath, and
Scott was panting.

"Had he been dead long?" he asked, making for a
closed door indicated by the coroner's forefinger.

"Just a few minutes; his body was still warm. He
died instantly."

"I presume the storm prevented any one from hearing
the shot—there was only one wound, I suppose?" Dr.
Dodd nodded. "Well, here we are." Ellery fitted the
key Pringle had given him into the lock, and twisted
it. Then he pushed open the door. No one said anything.

The room was flooded with sunlight; it looked as innocent of violence as a newborn baby. It was a very
large room, shaped exactly like Ellery's own. And it
was furnished exactly like Ellery's. The bed was identical, and it stood in a similar position between two windows; the table and rush-bottomed, cane-backed chair
in the middle of the room might have come from Ellery's room; the rug, the bureau, the highboy . . .
Hmm! There *was* a difference.

He murmured: "Are all your rooms furnished exactly
alike?"

Scott raised his tufted brows. "Sure. When I went
into this busines and changed the shack into a rooming
house, I bought up a lot of stuff from a bankrupt place

in Albany. All the same stuff. All these rooms up here are the same. Why?"

"No special reason. It's interesting, that's all." Ellery leaned against the jamb and took out a cigaret, searching the scene meanwhile with his restless gray eyes. There was no faintest sign of a struggle. Directly before the doorway were the table and cane-backed chair, and the chair faced the door. In a straight line with the door and chair on the far side of the room stood an old-fashioned highboy against the wall. His eyes narrowed again. Without turning, he said: "That highboy. In my room it's between the two windows."

He heard the girl's soft breathing behind him. "Why . . . father! The highboy wasn't there when—when Mr. McGovern was alive!"

"That's funny," muttered Scott in astonishment.

"But on the night of the murder was the highboy where it is now?"

"Why—yes, it was," said Iris in a puzzled way.

"Certainly. I remember now," said the coroner, frowning.

"Good," drawled Ellery, pushing away from the door. "Something to work on." He strode over to the highboy, stooped and tugged at it until he had pulled it back from the wall. He knelt behind it and went over the wall, inch by inch, intently. And then he stopped. He had found a peculiar dent in the plaster about a foot from the wainscoting. It was no more than a quarter of an inch in diameter, was roughly circular, and was impressed perhaps a sixteenth of an inch into the wall. A fragment of plaster had fallen away; he found it on the floor.

When he rose he wore an air of disappointment. He returned to the doorway. "Nothing much. You're sure nothing's been disturbed since the night of the murder?"

"I'll vouch for that," said Scott.

"Hmm. By the way, I see some of McGovern's personal belongings are still here. Did Pringle search this room thoroughly on the night of the murder, Dr. Dodd?"

"Oh, yes."

"But he didn't find anything," growled Scott.

"You're positive? Nothing at all?"

"Why, we were all here when he was looking, Mr. Queen!"

Ellery smiled, examining the room with a peculiar zest. "No offense, Mr. Scott. Well! I think I'll go to my own room and mull over this baffling business for a bit. I'll keep this key, Doctor."

"Of course. Anything you want, you know—"

"Not now, at any rate. Where will you be if something comes up?"

"At my undertaking parlors on Main Street."

"Good." And rather vaguely and wearily Ellery smiled again and turned the key in the lock and trudged down the hall.

He found his room cool and soothing, and he lay back on the bed with his hands crossed beneath his aching head, thinking. The house was quiet enough. Outside one of his windows a robin chirped and a bee zoomed; that was all. Past the fluttering curtains came the sweet-scented wind from the hills.

Once he heard Iris's light step in the hall outside; and again the rumble of Michael Scott's voice downstairs.

He lay smoking for perhaps twenty minutes; and then all at once he sprang from the bed and darted to the door. Opening it to a crack, he listened. . . . All clear. So he quietly stepped out into the hall and tiptoed to the locked door of the dead man's room, and unlocked it, and went in, and turned the key again behind him.

"If there's any sense in this misbegotten world—" he muttered, stopped, and hurried to the cane-chair in which McGovern had been sitting when he died. He knelt and closely examined the solid crisscrossing mesh of cane making up the back of the chair. But there was nothing wrong with it.

Frowning, he got to his feet and began to prowl. He prowled the length and breadth of the room, stooped over like an old hunchback, his underlip thrust forward and his eyes straining. He even sprawled full length on the floor to grope beneath pieces of furniture; and he made a tour under the bed like a sapper in No Man's Land. But when his inspection of the floor was completed, he was empty-handed. He brushed the dust from his clothes with a grimace.

It was as he was replacing the contents of the wastebasket, disconsolately, that his face lit up. "Lord! If it's possible that—" He left the room, locking the door again, and made a quick and cautious reconnaissance up and down the hall, listening. Apparently he was alone. So, noiselessly and quite without a feeling of guilt, he began room by room to search the sleeping quarters.

It was in the cane-chair of the fourth room he investigated that he found what his deductions had led him to believe he might find. And the room belonged to the person to whom he had even beforehand vaguely glimpsed it as belonging.

Very careful to leave the room precisely as he had found it, Mr. Ellery Queen returned to his own quarters, bathed his face and hands, adjusted his necktie, brushed his clothes again, and with a dreamy smile went downstairs.

Finding Mrs. Gandy and Michael Scott occupied on the porch playing a desultory game of two-handed whist, Ellery chuckled silently and made his way to the rear of the lower floor. He discovered Iris in a vast cavern of a kitchen, busy stirring something pungently savory over a huge stove. The heat had carmined her cheeks, she wore a crisp white apron, and altogether she looked delectable.

"Well, Mr. Queen?" she asked anxiously, dropping her ladle and facing him with grave, begging eyes.

"Do you love him as much as that?" sighed Ellery, drinking in her loveliness. "Lucky Roger! Iris, my child—you see, I'm being very fatherly, although I assure you my soul is in the proverbial torment—we progress. Yes, indeed. I think I may tell you that young Lothario faces a rosier prospect than he faced this morning. Yes, yes, we have made strides."

"You mean you—he— Oh, Mr. Queen!"

Ellery sat down in a gleaming kitchen chair, filched a sugared cookie from a platter on the porcelain table, munched it, swallowed, looked critical, smiled, and took another. "Yours? Delicious. A veritable Lucrece, b'gad! Or is it Penelope I'm thinking of? Yes, I mean just that, honey. If this is a sample of your cooking—"

"Baking." She rushed forward suddenly and to his stupefaction clutched at his hand and pulled it to her breast. "Oh, Mr. Queen, if you only could—would—I never knew I—I loved him so much until just—just now. . . . In jail!" She shuddered. "I'll do anything —anything—"

Ellery blinked, loosened his collar, tried to look nonchalant, and then gently disengaged his hand. "Now, now, my dear, I know you would. But don't ever do that to me again. It makes me feel like God. Whew!" He swabbed his brow. "Now, listen, beautiful. Listen hard. There *is* something you can do."

"Anything!" Her face glowed into his.

He rose and began to stride around the spotless floor. "Am I right in supposing that your Samuel Dodd's very faithful to his office?"

She stared. "Sam Dodd? What on earth— He takes his job seriously, if that's what you mean."

"I thought so. It complicates matters." He smiled grimly. "However, we must face reality, mustn't we? My dear young goddess, than whom no lovelier creature ever graced the sour earth, you're going to vamp your Dr. Sam Dodd to within an inch of his officious life tonight. Or didn't you know that?"

Anger flashed from her black eyes. "Mr. Queen!"

"Tut-tut, although it's most becoming. I'm not suggesting anything—er—drastic, my child. Another cookie is called for." He helped himself to two. "Can you get him to take you to the movies tonight? His being in the house here makes matters difficult, and I've got to have him out of the way or he's liable to call out the State Militia to stop me."

"I can make Sam Dodd do anything I want," said the goddess very coolly, the blush leaving her cheeks, "but I don't understand why."

"Because," mumbled Ellery over another cake, "I say so, dear heart. I'm going to trample over his authority tonight, you see. There's something I must get done, and without the proper hocus-pocus of papers and things it's distinctly illegal, if not criminal. Dodd could help, but if I'm any judge of character he won't; and so if he doesn't know anything about it neither he nor I will have anything on the well-known conscience."

She measured him impersonally, and he felt uncomfortable under those level eyes. "Will it help Roger?"

"And," said Ellery fervently, "how!"

"Then I'll do it." And she lowered her eyes suddenly and began to fuss with her apron. "And now if you'll please get out of my kitchen, Mr. Ellery Queen, I've some dinner to make. And I think"—she fled to the stove and took up the ladle—"you're very wonderful."

Mr. Ellery Queen gulped, flushed, and beat a hasty retreat.

When he pushed open the screen-door he found Mrs. Gandy gone, and Scott sitting silent with Father Anthony on the porch. "The very men," he said cheerily. "Where's the afflicted Mrs. Gandy? By the way, how does she negotiate those stairs in that wheel-chair?"

"Doesn't. She's got a room on the lower floor," said Scott. "Well, Mr. Queen?" His eyes were haggard.

Father Anthony was regarding him with steadfast gravity.

Ellery's face turned bleak of a sudden. He sat down and drew his rocker close to theirs. "Father," he said quietly, "something informs me that you serve—honestly serve—a higher law than man's."

The old priest studied him for a moment. "I know little of law, Mr. Queen. I serve two masters—Christ and the souls He died for."

Ellery considered this in silence. Then he said: "Mr. Scott, you mentioned before that you had gone through Belleau Wood. Death then holds no terrors for you."

The burly man's hard eyes bored into Ellery's. "Listen, Mr. Queen, I saw my best friend torn in half before me. I had to pick his guts off my hands. No, I'm not scared of all hell; I've been there."

"Very good," said Ellery softly. "Very good indeed. Aramis, Porthos, and—if I may presume—D'Artagnan. A little cockeyed, but it will serve. Father, Mr. Scott," and the priest and the burly father of Iris stared at his lips, "will you help me open a grave tonight?"

The eve of St. Walpurga was months dead, but the witches danced that night nevertheless. They danced in the shadows flung by the dark moon over the crazy hillside; they squealed and screeched in the wind over the mute, waiting graves.

Mr. Ellery Queen felt uncommonly glad that he was one of three that night. The cemetery lay on the outskirts of Corsica, ringed in iron and bordered with capering trees. An icy breeze blew death over their heads. The gravestones glimmered on the breast of the hillside like dead men's bones polished clean and white by the winds. An angry, furry black cloud hid half the moon, and the trees wept restlessly. No, it was not difficult to imagine that witches danced.

They walked in silence, instinctively keeping together. It was Father Anthony who braved the spirits, breasting the agitated air like a tall ship in the van, his vestments flapping and snapping. His face was dark and grave, but unruffled. Ellery and Michael Scott struggled behind under the weight of spades, picks, ropes, and a large bulky bundle. On all the moving, whispering, shadow-infested hillside they were the only living beings.

They found McGovern's grave in virgin soil, a little

away from the main colony of headstones. It was a
lonely spot high on the hill, a vulture's roost. Earth
still raw made a mound above the dead man, and there
was only a scrawny stick to mark the clay that lay there.
Still in silence, and with drawn faces, the two men set
to work with their picks while Father Anthony kept the
vigil above them. The moon swam in and out mad-
deningly.

When the hard earth had been loosened, they cast
aside the picks and attacked the soil with their spades.
Both wore old overalls over their clothes.

"Now I know," muttered Ellery, resting a moment
by the mounting pile of earth beside the grave, "what it
feels like to be a ghoul. Father, I'm thankful you're
along. I'm cursed with too much imagination."

"There is nothing to be afraid of, my son," said the
old priest in a little bitter murmur. "These are only
dead men."

Ellery shivered. Scott growled: "Let's get goin'!"

And so at last their spades struck hollowly upon
wood.

How they managed it Ellery never clearly remembered. It was titans' work, and long before it was finished he was drenched with perspiration which stung
like icicles under the cold fingers of the wind. He felt
disembodied, a phantom in a nightmare. Scott labored
in isolated silence, performing prodigies, while Ellery
panted beside him and Father Anthony looked somberly
on. And then Ellery realized that he was hauling upon
two ropes on one side of the pit, and that old Scott was
pulling on their other ends opposite him. Something
long and black-clotted and heavy came precariously up
from the depths, swaying as if it had life. One last
heave, and it thumped over the side, to Ellery's horror

overturning. He sank to the ground, squatting on his hams and fumbling for a cigaret.

"I—need—a—breather," he muttered, and puffed desperately. Scott leaned calmly on his spade. Only Father Anthony went to the pine box, and tugged until it righted itself, and with slow tender hands began to pry off the lid.

Ellery watched the old man, fascinated; and then he sprang to his feet, hurled his cigaret away, cursed himself beneath his breath, and snatched the pick from the priest's hands. A single powerful wrench, the lid screeched up. . . .

Scott set his muscular mouth and stepped forward. He pulled canvas gloves on his hands. Then he bent over the dead man. Father Anthony stepped back, closing his tired eyes. And Ellery feverishly unwrapped the bulky bundle he had carried all the way from Jasmine Street, disclosing a huge tripod-camera borrowed surreptitiously from the editor of the *Corsica Call*. He fumbled with something.

"Is it there?" he croaked. "Mr. Scott, is it there?"

The burly man said clearly: "Mr. Queen, it's there."

"Only one?"

"Only one."

"Turn him over." And, after a while, Ellery said: "Is it there?"

And Scott said: "Yes."

"Only one?"

"Yes."

"Where I said it would be?"

"Yes."

And Ellery raised something high above his head, directing the eye of the camera with his other hand upon what lay in the mud-coated coffin and made a convulsive fist, and something blue as witchfire flashed to the accompaniment of a reverberating boom, lighting up the hillside momentarily like a flare in purgatory.

And Ellery paused in his labors and leaned on his spade and said: "Let me tell you a story." Michael Scott worked on relentlessly, his broad back writhing with his exertions. Father Anthony sat on the re-wrapped camera-bundle and cupped his old face in his hands.

"Let me tell you," said Ellery tonelessly, "a story of remarkable cleverness that was thwarted by . . . There is a God, Father.

"When I discovered that the highboy in McGovern's room was out of its customary position, apparently moved to its new place some time within the general period of the murder, I saw that it was possible the murderer himself had so moved it. If he had, there must have been a reason for the action. I pushed aside the highboy and found on the wall behind it a foot or so from the wainscoting a small circular impression in the plaster. This dent and the highboy before it were in a direct line with two objects: the cane-chair facing the door in which McGovern had presumably been sitting when he was shot, and the doorway where the murderer must have been standing when he squeezed the trigger. Coincidence? It did not seem likely.

"I saw at once that the dent was just such a dent as might have been made by a bullet—a spent bullet, since the depression was so shallow. It was also evident that since the murderer must have been standing, and the victim sitting—being shot through the heart besides— then the dent on the wall several yards behind the chair would appear, if it was caused by a bullet fired by the murderer, just about where I found it, the line of fire being generally downward."

The clods thumped and bumped on the box.

"Now it was also evident," said Ellery in a strange voice, gripping the spade, "that had the spent bullet been one which had passed through McGovern's body there should be a hole in the cane-meshed back of McGovern's chair. I examined the chair; there was no bullet-hole. Then it was possible the bullet which had made the dent in the wall had not passed through McGovern's body but had gone wild; in other words, that two shots had been fired that stormy, noisy night, the one which lodged in the body and the one which caused the dent. But no mention had been made of a second bullet having been found in the room, despite unanimous testimony that the room had been thoroughly searched. I myself inspected every inch of that floor without success. But if a second bullet was not there, then it must have been taken away by the murderer at the same time he moved the highboy over to conceal the dent the bullet had made." He paused and gloomily eyed the filling grave. "But why should the murderer take away one bullet and leave the vital one to be found —the one in the victim's body? It did not make sense. On the other hand, its alternative did make sense. That there never had been two bullets at all; *that only one bullet had been fired.*"

The hillside quivered in shadow as the witches danced.

"I worked," continued Ellery wearily, "on this theory. If only one bullet had been fired, then it was that bullet which had killed McGovern, piercing his heart and emerging from his back, penetrating the cane of the chair-back, and winging on across the room to strike the wall where I found the dent; falling, spent, to the floor below. Then why didn't McGovern's chair show a bullet-hole? It could only be because it was *not* Mc-Govern's chair. The murderer had done one thing to conceal the fact that the bullet had emerged from the body: he had moved the highboy. Why not another? So he must have exchanged chairs. All your rooms, Mr. Scott, are identically furnished; he dragged McGovern's chair to his own room and brought his own chair to replace McGovern's. All my deductions up to this point would be demonstrated correct if I could find a cane-backed chair with a hole in its back—a hole where a hole should be, just at the place where a bullet would penetrate if it had gone through the heart of some one sitting in the chair. And find it I did—in the room of some one in your house, Mr. Scott."

The ugly raw earth was level with the hillside now; only a little heap was left. Father Anthony watched his friend with veiled and anguished eyes; and for an instant the black cloud draped the moon and they were in darkness.

"Why," muttered Ellery, "should the murderer want to conceal the fact that a spent bullet existed? There could be only one reason: he did not wish the bullet found and examined. But a bullet *was* found and examined." The cloud edged off angrily, and the moon glowered at them again. "Then the bullet which *was* found must have been *the wrong one!*"

At last it was done: the mound loomed, round and dark and smooth, in the moonlight. Father Anthony absently reached for the small wooden grave-marker and thrust it into the mound. Michael Scott rose to his full height, wiping his brow.

"The wrong bullet?" he said hoarsely.

"The wrong bullet. For what did that bullet's being

found accomplish? It directly involved Roger Bowen as the murderer; it was a bullet demonstrably from Bowen's .38 automatic. But if it was the wrong bullet, then Bowen was being framed by some one who, unable by reason of Bowen's nightly vigilance to get hold of Bowen's automatic, but possessing *a spent bullet which had already been fired* from Bowen's automatic, was able after the murder to switch Bowen's—as it were—innocent bullet for the one actually used to kill McGovern!" Ellery's voice rose stridently. "The bullet from the murderer's gun wouldn't show the telltale bore-markings of Bowen's gun, naturally. Had the murderer left his own bullet to be found, tests would have shown that it didn't come from Bowen's .38 and would have instantly defeated the frame-up. So the murderer had to take away the real, the lethal, bullet, conceal the dent in the wall, change cane-back chairs."

"But why," demanded Scott in a strangled growl, "didn't the damn' fool leave the chair there and let the dent be found? Why didn't he just take away his own bullet and drop Bowen's on the floor in its place? That would have been the easiest thing to do. And then he wouldn't have had to cover up the fact that the slug had gone clear through the body."

"A good question," said Ellery softly. "Why, indeed? If he didn't do it that way, then it must have been that he couldn't do it that way. He didn't have on him at the time of the murder the spent bullet he had stolen from Bowen; he'd left it somewhere where he couldn't get it on the spur of the moment."

"Then he didn't expect the bullet would go clear through the body," cried Scott, waving his huge arms so that their shadows slashed across McGovern's ugly grave. "And he must have expected to be able to substitute Bowen's bullet for the real slug *afterwards,* after the killing, after the police examination, after . . ."

"That's it," murmured Ellery, "exactly. That—" He stopped. A ghost in diaphanous white garments was floating up the hillside toward them, skimming the dark earth. Father Anthony rose, and he looked taller than a man should look. Ellery gripped his spade.

But Michael Scott called harshly: "Iris! What—"

She flung herself wildly at Ellery. "Mr. Queen!" she gasped. "They're—they're coming! They found out— some one saw you and father and Father Anthony come this way with the spades. . . . Pringle came for Sam Dodd. . . . I ran—"

"Thank you, Iris," said Ellery gently. "Among your other virtues you number courage, too." But he made no move to go.

"Let's roll," muttered Michael Scott. "I don't want—"

"Is it a crime," murmured Ellery, "to seek communion with the blessed dead? No, I wait."

Two dots appeared, became dancing dolls, loomed larger, scrambled frantically up the slope. The first was large and fat, and something winked dully in his hand. Behind him struggled a small white-faced man.

"Michael!" snarled Chief Pringle, waving his revolver. "Father! You, there, Queen! What the hell d'ye call this? Are ye all out of your minds? Diggin' up graves!"

"Thank God," panted the coroner. "We're not too late. They haven't dug—" He eyed the mound, the tools gratefully. "Mr. Queen, you know it's against the law to—"

"Chief Pringle," said Ellery regretfully, stepping forward and fixing the coroner with his gray eyes, "you

will arrest this man for the deliberate murder of Mc-
Govern and the frame-up of Roger Bowen."

The porch was in purple shadow; the moon had long
since set and Corsica was asleep; only Iris's white gown
glimmered a little, and Michael Scott's pipe glowed fretfully.

"Sam Dodd," he mumbled. "Why, I've known Sam
Dodd—"

"Oh, Father!" moaned Iris, and groped for the hand
of Father Anthony in the rocker beside her.

"It had to be Dodd, you know," said Ellery wearily;
his feet were on the railing. "You put your finger on
the precise point, Mr. Scott, when you said that the
murderer must have expected to be able to make the
substitution later, and that he hadn't expected that the
bullet he fired would pass clear through McGovern's
body. For who could have switched bullets had the bullet remained in McGovern's body, as the murderer expected it to remain before he fired? Only Dodd, the
coroner, who makes the autopsy which is mandatory in
a murder. Who could have continued to keep unknown
the fact that the bullet had passed through McGovern's
body? Only Dodd, the undertaker, who prepared the
body for burial. Who actually stated that the bullet
was *in* the body? Only Dodd, who performed the autopsy; if he were innocent why should he have lied?
Who introduced Bowen's bullet in evidence? Only
Dodd, who claimed to have recovered it from the heart
of the dead man." Iris sobbed a little. "Were there
confirmations? Plenty. Dodd lived in this house, and
therefore he had access to McGovern's room that night.
Dodd 'found' the body; therefore he could have done
everything that was necessary without interference.

Dodd as coroner set the time of death; he could have said it was a little later than it actually was to cover up the time he consumed in moving the highboy and switching chairs. Dodd by his own admission had often gone out rabbit-hunting with Roger Bowen; therefore he could easily have secured a spent bullet from Bowen's automatic, a bullet which Bowen had fired but which had missed its target. Dodd, being a coroner, was professionally minded; it took a professional mind to think of bore-marks. Dodd, being a coroner, was ballistically minded and had a microscope to check bore-marks. . . . Then I had proofs. It was in Dodd's room I found the cane-chair with the hole in its back. And, most important, I knew that if McGovern's body on exhumation showed one bullet-wound in the chest and one exit-hole in the back, then I had complete proof that Dodd had lied in his official report and that my whole chain of reasoning was correct. We dug up the body and there was the exit-hole. My photographs will send Dodd to the chair."

"And God, my son?" said Father Anthony quietly from the darkness.

Ellery sighed. "I prefer to think that it was some such Agency that made the bullet Dodd fired completely pierce McGovern's body. Had it lodged in McGovern's heart, as Dodd had every reason to expect it would, there would have been no dent in the wall, no hole in the chair, and therefore no reason to exhume the body. Dodd would have produced Bowen's bullet after autopsy, claiming it was the one he 'dug out,' as he did claim, and Bowen would have been a very unlucky young man."

"But Sam Dodd!" cried Iris, hiding her face in her hands. "I've known him so long, since I was a little girl. He's always been so quiet, so gentle, so—so . . ."

Ellery rose and his shoes creaked on the black porch. He bent over the glimmer of her and cupped her chin in his hand and stared down with the most whimsical yearning into her all-but-invisible face. "Beauty like yours, my dear, is a dangerous gift. Your gentle Sam Dodd killed McGovern to rid himself of one rival and framed Roger Bowen for the murder to rid himself of the other, you see."

"Rival?" gasped Iris.

"Rival, hell!" growled Scott.

"Your eyes, my son," whispered Father Anthony, "are good."

"Hope springs not only eternal but lethal," said Ellery softly. "Sam Dodd loves you."

The Adventure of
THE TEAKWOOD CASE

The Adventure of
THE TEAKWOOD CASE

The woody, leathery, homely living room of the Queens' apartment on West Eighty-seventh Street in New York City had seen queerer visitors than Mr. Seaman Carter, but surely none quite so ill at ease.

"Really, Mr. Carter," said Ellery Queen with amusement, stretching his long legs nearer the fireplace, "you've been wretchedly misinformed. I'm not a detective at all, you know. My father is the sleuth of this family! Officially I've no more right to investigate a crime than you have."

"But that's exactly the point, Mr. Queen!" wheezed Carter with a vast rolling of his porphyry eyes. "We don't *want* the police. We want *unofficial* advice. We want *you*, Mr. Queen, to clear up these devilish robberies, *sub rosa*—ahem!—so to speak; or I shouldn't have come. The Gothic Arms can't afford the notoriety, my dear, dear Mr. Queen. We're an exclusive development catering to the best people—"

"Pshaw, Mr. Carter," said Ellery between lazy puffs of the inevitable cigaret, "go to the police. You've had five robberies in as many months. All of jewels, all filched from different tenants on different floors. And now this latest theft two days ago—a diamond necklace from the bedroom wall-safe of a Mrs. Mallorie, an invalid and one of your oldest tenants. . . ."

"Mrs. Mallorie!" Carter shuddered with the sinuous ripplings of an octopus in motion. "She's an old woman. She went into hysterics—a terrible person, Mr. Queen.

189

Insists on calling in the police, informing the insurance company. . . . We're at our wits' end."

"It seems to me," said Ellery, fixing his sharp eyes on the man's lumpy cheeks, which were quivering, "that you'll be in the devil of a sweet mess, Mr. Carter, if you don't get official help at once. You're making an extraordinary fuss about very small potatoes."

The telephone-bell rang and Djuna, the Queens' boy-of-all-work, slipped into the bedroom to answer it. He popped his small gypsy head out of the doorway almost at once. "For you, Mr. Ellery. Dad Queen is on the wire and he's hopping."

"Excuse me," said Ellery, abruptly, and went into the bedroom.

When he came out all amusement had fled from his lean features. He had divested his tall body of the battered old dressing-gown and was fully attired for the street.

"You'll be interested to learn, no doubt," he said in a flat voice, "that once more fact has outdone fiction, Mr. Carter. I've been treated to the spectacle of an amazing coincidence. On which floor did you say Mrs. Mallorie's apartment lies?"

Mr. Seaman Carter shook like the damp flanks of a grumbling volcano; his little eyes became glassy. "My God!" he screeched, dragging himself to his feet. "What's happened now? Mrs. Mallorie occupies Apartment F on the sixteenth floor!"

"I'm delighted to hear it. Well, Mr. Carter, your laudable effort to smother legitimate news has failed, and you have enlisted my poor services. Except that we are *en route* to the scene of a crime more serious than theft. My father, Inspector Queen, informs me that a man in Apartment H on the sixteenth floor of the Gothic Arms has been found foully done in. In a word, he's been murdered."

An express elevator took Ellery and the Superintendent to the sixteenth floor. They emerged on the west corridor of the building. A central corridor bisected the hall in which they found themselves, and at its end could be seen the bronze doors of the elevator on the east corridor. Carter, his globular carcass trembling like gelatinous ooze, led the way toward the right. They came to a door before which stood a whistling detective. The door, marked with a gilded *H*, was closed. Carter opened it and they went in.

They were in a small foyer, through the open door of which they could see into a large room filled with men. Ellery brushed by a uniformed officer, nodded to his father—a small bird-like creature with gray plumage and bright little eyes—and stared down at a still figure in an armchair beside a small table in the center of the room.

"Strangled?"

"Yes," said Inspector Queen. "And who's this with you, Ellery?"

"Mr. Seaman Carter, Superintendent of the building." Ellery idly explained the purpose of Carter's visit; his eyes were roving.

"Carter, who's this dead man?" demanded the Inspector. "No one here seems to know."

Carter shifted from one elephantine foot to the other. "Who?" he babbled. "Who? Why, isn't it Mr. Lubbock?"

A foppish young man in morning coat dotted with a *boutonnière* coughed hesitantly. They turned to stare at him. "It's not Lubbock, Mr. Carter," he lisped.

"Though it does look like him from the back." His simpering lips were pale with fear.

"Who's *that?*" asked Ellery.

"Fullis, my assistant," muttered the Superintendent. "Heavens, Fullis, you're right at that." He pushed around the armchair for a better view of the body.

A trim tall man with a ruddy complexion came briskly into the room. He was carrying a black bag. Carter addressed him as Dr. Eustace. The physician set his bag down by the chair and proceeded to examine the dead man. Dr. Eustace was the house physician.

Ellery drew the Inspector aside. "Anything?" he asked in low tones.

The Inspector gasped over a generous noseful of snuff. "Nothing. A complete mystery. Body was found by accident about an hour or so ago. A woman from Apartment C across the central corridor came in here to see John Lubbock, who lives alone in this two-room suite. At least, that's what *she* says." He moved his head slightly in the direction of a platinum-haired young woman, whose tears had played havoc with the careful lacquer on her face; she was sitting forlornly across the room guarded by a policeman. "She's Billy Harms, the ingénue of that punk comedy at the Roman Theater. Managed to squeeze out of her the information that she's been Lubbock's playmate for a couple of months; her maid tells me—thank God for maids!— that she and Lubbock had a lovers' battle a few weeks ago. Seems he won't pay her rent any more, and I guess the market on sugar-daddies has gone 'way down."

"Lovely people," said Ellery. "And?"

"She walked herself plump in here—seems it was sort of dim; only a small light in the lamp on the table— thought this chap was asleep, shook him, saw he wasn't

Lubbock and that he was dead. . . . The old story. She screamed and a lot of people ran in—neighbors. Over there." Ellery saw five people huddled near Billy Harms's chair. "They all live on this floor. That elderly couple—Mr. and Mrs. Orkins, Apartment A across the hall. The sour-faced mutt next to the Orkinses is a jeweler, Benjamin Schley—Apartment B. Those other two people are Mr. and Mrs. Forrester—he's got some kind of soft job with the city; they're in Apartment D, next to Billy Harms."

"Get anything out of them?"

"Not a lead." The Inspector bit off the end of a gray hair from his mustache. "Lubbock left here this morning and hasn't been seen since. He's a man-about-town, it seems, and he's been pretty gay with the ladies. Understand from one of the house-maids that he's been playing around with Mrs. Forrester, too—kind of pretty, isn't she? But there doesn't seem to be any connection with the others." He shrugged. "Had a few feelers out already—Lubbock has no business and nobody seems to know his source of income. Anyway, it's not Lubbock we're interested in right now, although we're trying to locate him. Got Hagstrom on the job. But none of the people employed here can say who this feller is that was choked. Never saw him before, they say; and there's nothing in his effects to show who he is."

Dr. Eustace signaled the Inspector; he had risen from his inspection of the corpse. The Queens moved back toward the chair. "What's the dope, Doctor?" asked the Inspector.

"Strangled to death from behind," replied the physician, "a little more than an hour ago. That's really all I can tell, sir."

"That's a help, that is."

Ellery strolled over to the little table by the dead man's chair. The contents of the man's clothes had been dumped there. A worn cheap wallet containing fifty-seven dollars; a few coins; a small automatic; a single Yale key; a New York evening newspaper; a crumpled program of the Roman Theater; the torn half of a Roman Theater ticket, dated that very day; two soiled handkerchiefs; a stiff new packet of matches, its flap bearing the imprint of the Gothic Arms; a glistening green cigaret package, half of the tin-foil and blue seal at the top torn away. The package contained four cigarets, although it was apparently a fresh one and retained its full shape.

A meagre enough grist on the surface.

Ellery picked up the small key. "Have you identified this?" he asked the Inspector.

"Yes. It's the key to this apartment."

"A duplicate?"

Mr. Seaman Carter took it from Ellery's hand with slippery fingers, fumbled with it, consulted with lisping Fullis, and returned it to Ellery. "That's the original, Mr. Queen," he quavered. "Not the duplicate."

Ellery flung the key on the table; his sharp eyes began to prowl. He spied a small metal waste-basket beneath the table, and dug it out. It was clean and empty except for a crumpled ball of tin-foil and blue paper, and a crushed cellophane wrapper. Ellery at once matched his finds to the package of cigarets; he smoothed out the silver-and-blue scrap and discovered that it exactly fitted the hole torn in the top of the package.

The Inspector smiled at his look of concentration. "Don't get excited, sonny boy. He walked in the lobby downstairs from the street about an hour and a half ago, and bought that pack of butts at the desk; got the matches there, too, of course. Then he came upstairs. Elevatorman let him off at this floor, and that's the last any one saw of him."

"Except his murderer," said Ellery with a frown. "And yet . . . Did you look into this package, dad?"

"No. Why?"

"If you had, you would have seen that there are only four cigarets here. And that, I believe, is significant."

He said nothing more and commenced a leisurely amble about the room. It was large, rich, and furnished with a dilettante's taste. But Ellery was not interested in John Lubbock's interior decorations at the moment; he was looking for ash-trays. He saw several scattered about, of different shapes and sizes; all of them were perfectly clean. His eyes lowered to the floor, and leveled again as if they had not found what they were seeking. "Does that lead to the bedroom?" he asked, pointing to a door at the southeast corner of the room. The Inspector nodded, and Ellery crossed the room and disappeared through the doorway.

A group of newcomers—a police-photographer, a fingerprint man, the Assistant Medical Examiner of New York County—invaded the living room as Ellery left; he could hear dull booms from flashlights and the crackling insistence of the Inspector as the old man began to requestion the tenants of the sixteenth floor.

Ellery looked about the bedroom. The bed was a canopied affair, ornate with silk and tassels; there was a lush Chinese rug on the floor; and the furniture and fripperies made his simple eyes ache. He looked for exits. There were three doors—the one he had just opened from the living room; one to his right, which on investigation he found opened out on the west corridor;

and one to his left. He tried the knob of this door; it was locked, but there was a key in the keyhole. He unlocked the door and found himself looking into a room devoid of furniture, architecturally the counterpart of Lubbock's bedroom. Further investigation revealed an empty living room and a bare foyer. This, as he could see, was Apartment G; obviously unoccupied. All doors leading into Apartment G, as he discovered at once, were unlocked.

Ellery sighed, returned to Lubbock's bedroom, and turned the key in the lock, leaving it there. On impulse he paused to take out his handkerchief and wipe the knob clean. Then he proceeded directly to a wardrobe and began to rummage through the pockets of the numerous men's garments hanging on a rack inside—there were coats, suits, hats in profusion. He went through a curious routine; he seemed to be interested in nothing but crumbs. He turned pockets inside out and examined the sediment in the crevices. "No tobacco grains," he murmured to himself. "Interesting—but where the deuce does it get me?"

Then he carefully restored all pockets and garments to their original condition, closed the wardrobe, and went to the west corridor door. He opened it, stepped out, and hurried down the corridor to the front door of Lubbock's suite. He caught sight of the photographer, the fingerprint man, Sergeant Velie, and the tall, lank, saturnine figure of Dr. Prouty, Assistant Medical Examiner, standing near the elevators engaged in amiable conversation.

Nodding to the detective on guard before Apartment H—the man was still whistling—Ellery entered the foyer and repeated his odd examination of pockets in all the garments hanging in the foyer-closet; a fruitless quest, to judge from his expression.

Raised voices from the living room made him close the closet-door with a little snap. He heard his father say: "You'd better pull yourself together, Mr. Lubbock."

Ellery hurried into the living room. The neighbors had left, or had been sent to their apartments under guard. Of the original cast of the drama, only Mr. Seaman Carter and Dr. Eustace remained. But there was a newcomer—a small, slender, sunken-cheeked dandy with sandy hair and blue eyes whose well-scraped jaws wabbled ludicrously as he stared down at the dead man.

"Who's this?" asked Ellery pleasantly.

The man turned, looked at him without intelligence and twisted his head back toward the corpse.

"Mr. John Lubbock," said the Inspector. "Tenant of this apartment. He's just been found—Hagstrom brought him in. *And* we've identified the lad in the chair."

Ellery studied John Lubbock's face. "Relative of yours, Mr. Lubbock? There's a distinct resemblance."

"Yes," said Lubbock hoarsely, coming to life. "He's —he was my brother. I—he got into town from Guatemala this morning; he was an engineer and we hadn't seen each other for three years. Looked me up at one of my clubs. I had an appointment, gave him the key to my apartment, and he said he'd take in a matinée and meet me here late this afternoon. And here I find him—" He squared his shoulders, sucked in his breath, and sanity crept back into his marbly blue eyes. "It's beyond my comprehension."

"Mr. Lubbock," said the Inspector, "did your brother have any enemies?"

The sandy-haired man gripped the edge of the table. "I don't know," he said helplessly. "Harry never wrote me anything—anything like that."

Ellery said: "Mr. Lubbock, I want you to examine these things on the table. They are the contents of your brother's pockets. Is anything missing that should be here?"

The dilettante looked at the table. He shook his head. "I really wouldn't know," he said.

Ellery touched his arm. "*Are you certain his cigaret-case isn't missing, Mr. Lubbock?*"

Lubbock started, and something like curiosity came into his dull eyes. As for the Inspector, he was petrified with astonishment.

"Cigaret-case? What's this about a cigaret-case, Ellery? We haven't found any such thing!"

"Precisely the point," said Ellery gently. "Well, Mr. Lubbock?"

Lubbock moistened his dry lips. "Now that you mention it—yes," he said with an effort. "Though how in God's name you knew is more than I can see. Why, I forgot it myself! Before Harry left the States for Central America three years ago he showed me two cigaret-cases, exactly alike." He fumbled in the inner breast-pocket of his jacket and brought out a shallow dull-black case, intricately inset with an Oriental design in silver, one tiny sliver of which was missing from its groove.

Ellery opened the case, which contained half a dozen cigarets, with shining eyes; a rabid worshiper of the weed himself, cigaret-cases were one of Ellery's cherished passions.

"A friend of Harry's," continued Lubbock wearily, "sent the two cases to him from Bangkok. Finest teakwood in the world comes from the East Indies, you know. Harry gave one of them to me, and I've had it ever since. But how did you know, Mr. Queen, that—"

Ellery snapped the lid down and returned the case to Lubbock. He was smiling. "It's our business to know things, although really my knowledge isn't the least bit mysterious."

Lubbock was stowing the case carefully away in his breast-pocket—quite as if it were a treasure—when there came a mutter of voices from the foyer and two white-clad internes marched in. The Inspector nodded; they unrolled their stretcher, hauled the dead man out of the armchair, dumped him unceremoniously upon the canvas, covered him with a blanket, and marched out toting their burden as if it were a side of fresh-killed beef. John Lubbock clutched the edge of the table again, his pale face grew paler, he gulped, retched, and began to slip to the floor.

"Here! You, Eustace! Doc Prouty, out there! Quick!" cried the Inspector as he and Ellery lunged forward and caught the fainting man. Dr. Eustace opened his bag as Dr. Prouty dashed in. Lubbock muttered thickly: "Guess it was—too much—for me—seeing them take— Poor Harry . . . Give me a sedative— something—brace me up."

Dr. Prouty snorted and went right out again. Dr. Eustace produced a bottle and thrust it beneath Lubbock's nostrils. They quivered and Lubbock grinned faintly. "Here," said Ellery, pulling out his own cigaret-case. "Have a smoke. Do your nerves good." But Lubbock shook his head and pushed the pellet away. "I'll—be all right," he gasped, struggling erect. "Sorry."

Ellery said to Superintendent Carter, who stood like a

blind rhinoceros near the table, perspiration pouring down his face: "Please send up the maid who cleans this suite, Mr. Carter. At once."

The fat man nodded eagerly and waddled out of the living room as fast as his jelly legs could carry him. Sergeant Velie, strolling in, scowled at Carter with disgust. Ellery glanced at his father, jerked his head toward the foyer, and the old man said: "You stay here and rest up a bit, Mr. Lubbock; we'll be back shortly."

Ellery and the Inspector went out into the foyer, and Ellery very softly closed the door to the living room.

"What the devil's up now?" growled the Inspector.

Ellery smiled and said: "Wait." He put his hands behind his back and began to stroll about.

A trim little colored girl in black regalia hurried up to the apartment door, her face an alarming violet.

"Ah," said Ellery. "Come in. You're the maid who cleans this suite regularly?"

"Yes, suh!"

"You cleaned it this morning as usual?"

"Yes, suh!"

"And were there any ashes in the ashtrays?"

"No, suh! Nevuh is in Mistuh Lubbock's apa'tment 'ceptin' when he's had comp'ny."

"You're positive of that?"

"Cross mah haht, suh!"

The girl retreated hastily. The Inspector said: "I'll be jiggered."

Ellery had dropped his cloak of insouciance; he drew his father's slender little body closer. "Listen. The maid's testimony was all we needed. Delicate situation, O venerable ancestor. Follow my reasoning.

"The package of cigarets from Harry Lubbock's pocket: a fresh package, observe, confirmed by the fact that he purchased it just before coming up here, by the scrap of perfectly fitting tin-foil and blue paper from the basket, by the cellophane wrapper, and by the uncrushed condition of the package itself. Harry Lubbock came up here to wait for his brother. He sat down in the armchair his back to the foyer door. He didn't smoke; no ashes anywhere; no cigaret-stubs. Yet despite the fact that this was a new package, we find only *four* cigarets inside. What happened to the other sixteen, since there are twenty to the pack? First possibility is that his murderer took them away, stealing them from the package. Psychologically rotten—can't visualize a murderer taking fresh cigarets from his victim's package. Second possibility: that Lubbock himself opened the package before the arrival of the murderer *in order to fill a cigaret-case.* This would explain the peculiar number of missing cigarets; many cigaret-cases hold sixteen. Yes, I was convinced that the sixteen missing cigarets had been placed by Harry Lubbock, the engineer, in his case. But where was the case? Obviously, since it's gone, the murderer took it away." The Inspector chewed upon that, then nodded. "Good! Now where are we? The cigarets themselves, being brand new, couldn't have been the object of the theft. Then the *case* must have been the object of the theft!"

Inspector Queen pursed his old lips. "Why? There certainly isn't a hidden spring or compartment in that case. It's not thick enough to conceal a Chinaman's breath in the wood itself."

"Don't know, sire, don't know. Haven't the faintest notion *why*. But it's so.

"Now as to John Lubbock. Three psychological indications. . . . But I'll give them to you more graphically. Maid's testimony: no ashes in this apartment, ever, *except* after guests. Sign of a non-smoker? *Oui, papa.* John Lubbock half faints, asks for a sedative, and *refuses* the cigaret I offer him! Sign of a non-smoker? Decidedly; in moments of emotional stress a smoker by habit falls back on the weed—it's the nicotine-addict's nerve soother. And third: there isn't a shred of tobacco in any pocket of any garment in John Lubbock's closets! Ever examine my coat-pocket? There's always tobacco in small grains lurking in the crevices. None in John Lubbock's clothes. Sign of a non-smoker? You answer."

"All right," said the Inspector softly. "He doesn't indulge. Then why in tunket does he carry a cigaret-case with cigarets in it?"

"Precisely!" cried Ellery. "We've deduced that a cigaret-case was probably stolen from the murdered man. Since John Lubbock isn't a smoker and carries a cigaret-case . . . you see? It's almost tenable—it *is* tenable, by thunder—to say that the case John showed us was his murdered brother's!"

"And that would make him Harry Lubbock's killer," muttered the Inspector. "But there weren't sixteen cigarets in it, El. And the six that *were* there are of a different brand."

"Pie. Naturally our friend the dilettante would ditch the ones his engineer-brother had bought and substitute not only a different number but a different kind. I don't say this is conclusive. But at the moment the wind blows his way quite stiffly. If he's the murderer of his own brother then his story of *two* teakwood cases is a fabrication, composed on the spur of the moment to explain his possession of the teakwood case should there be a search."

The Queens turned swiftly at a knock on the foyer-
door. But it was only Dr. Eustace. He came out, leaving the door to the living room ajar. "Sorry to disturb
you," he said in gruff apology. "But I've got to see my
other patients."

"You'd better be available, Doctor," said the Inspector in a clear grim voice. "We've just decided to take
John Lubbock down to Headquarters for a little talk,
and we'll need your routine testimony, too."

"Lubbock?" Dr. Eustace stared, then shrugged.
"Well, I suppose it's none of my business. I'll be either
in my office on the mezzanine floor or I'll leave word at
the desk. Ready when you are, Inspector." He nodded
and went out.

"Don't scare him," suggested Ellery, as the Inspector
made a move toward the living room. "My logic may
be wetter than Triton's beard."

When they opened the door to the living room they
found Sergeant Velie alone, sitting in the dead man's
chair, feet propped on the table. "Where's Lubbock?"
asked Ellery swiftly.

Velie yawned; his mouth was a red cavern fringed
with enamel. "Went into the bedroom a coupla minutes ago," he rumbled. "Didn't see any harm in it myself." He pointed to the bedroom door, which was
closed.

"Oh, you gigantic idiot!" cried Ellery, dashing across
the room. He tore open the bedroom door. The bedroom was empty.

The Inspector yelled to his men in the corridor, Sergeant Velie flushed a wine-red and leaped to his feet.
. . . The alarm was sounded; men began to comb the
halls; the elderly Orkinses poked their white heads out
of Apartment A; Billy Harms flew into the central cor-

ridor in a lacy chemise; an old witch of a woman in a wheel-chair propelled herself from the front door of Apartment F and sent two cursing detectives sprawling with her clumsy manipulation of the conveyance. The scene was like a farcically rapid motion-picture reel.

Ellery wasted no time bewailing Sergeant Velie's unexpected stupidity. From the detective in the west corridor, he discovered that John Lubbock had not emerged from the western door of his bedroom. Ellery ran back to the eastern door, the door which led into the vacant suite. The key which he had left sticking in the door was gone. Gently, without touching the head of the knob, he tried to twist the bolt-bar. It refused to budge; the door was locked.

"The east corridor!" he yelled. "Door's open there!" and led the pack out of Lubbock's apartment, around the corner through the central corridor, up the east corridor and through the unlocked door into the bedroom of empty Apartment G. They tumbled through the doorway—and stopped.

John Lubbock lay sprawled on the floor, without hat or overcoat, fixed in the unmistakable contortions of violent death. Lubbock had been strangled!

At the instant of discovery Ellery had opened his mouth and gasped like a drowning man; the suspect himself murdered! So he sidled toward Sergeant Velie near the bedroom door—the door which communicated with Lubbock's own bedroom—and effaced himself.

His eyes went to this door and quickly narrowed. The key which he had last seen sticking in the lock on the Apartment H side was now in the lock of Apartment G. He fingered it thoughtfully, then slipped out of the room.

He went into the central corridor, found the finger-print expert, and took him back through Lubbock's bedroom to the door between the two apartments. "See what you can get out of this doorknob," he said. The expert went to work. Ellery watched anxiously. Under the man's ministrations several clear fingerprints appeared in white powder on the black stone of the knob. A photographer came in and snapped a picture of the fingerprints.

They repaired to the vacant bedroom of Apartment G. The physicians had completed their task and were discussing something in low tones with Inspector Queen. Ellery pointed to John Lubbock's dead fingers.

When the expert rose from the dusty floor he flourished a white card with ten inked fingerprints. He went to the door, unlocked it, and compared the dead man's prints with those on the knob of Lubbock's bedroom. "Okay," he said. "The stiff's mitts were on this knob."

Ellery sighed.

He knelt beside John Lubbock's body, which looked as if it had turned to stone in the midst of a fierce struggle, and explored the inside breast-pocket of Lubbock's coat.

Ellery looked thoughtfully at the teakwood case. "I owe an abject apology to the shade of our man-about-town. There *are* two cases, as he said. . . . For this *isn't* the one he showed us a few moments ago!"

The Inspector gaped. Where they had formerly observed in the silverwork of the teakwood case a groove whose sliver of metal was missing, the ornamental design on the case in Ellery's hand was unbroken, perfect.

"The inferences are plain," said Ellery. "Whoever killed John Lubbock did it for the teakwood case in his breast pocket. Everything is clear now. When the murderer strangled John Lubbock in this room, he stole John's case from John's body. The murderer then put into the case he had stolen from *Harry's* body—the first brother—six cigarets of the same brand John's case contained, and then placed *Harry's* case with these six cigarets on John's body, where we found it—in order to make us believe it was still John's case. Clever, but defeated by the fact that John's case had a sliver missing from the design whereas the engineer's had not. The murderer probably didn't notice the difference."

Ellery turned to the others; he held up his hand and they fell silent. "Ladies and gentlemen, the murderer's exceeded himself. He's done. I ask you to be attentive while I go over the ground and point out . . . Mr. Carter, stop shaking. I have every reason to believe that your executive worries are over."

Ellery stood at the feet of the dead man, his lean face expressionless. They watched him with stupid eyes. The detectives at the door retreated in response to Ellery's signal; and the Orkinses, Billy Harms in a négligé, the acid-faced jeweler Schley, Mr. and Mrs. Forrester of Apartment D, and even Mrs. Mallorie in her wheel-chair, crowded into the room.

"Certain lines of reasoning are inevitable," said Ellery, in a dry lecture-voice; he looked at none of them, seeming to be addressing the congested veins in John Lubbock's dead neck. "The only object taken from the first victim's dead body was the teakwood case. This means that the teakwood case was the object of the first murder. Now John Lubbock, the second victim, has been murdered; *his* teakwood case has been taken, and the first one put on his body. Conclusion: The only one who could have switched cases is the one who stole the first victim's case—the murderer. Therefore, both Harry and John Lubbock were strangled by the same hand. Two crimes and one culprit. Fundamental reasoning.

"Why was Harry Lubbock murdered? Simply because the murderer *mistook* him for his brother John, and did not discover the error until after he strangled his victim and examined the first teakwood case. It was the wrong one!

"The murderer's error is understandable. The first victim was choked from behind; superficially the engineer bore a resemblance to his brother John; no doubt the murderer was unaware that there were two Lubbocks. In other words, the engineer's case, the case on the floor, had nothing intrinsically to do with the crimes."

He leaned forward. "But mark this. Neither teakwood case *in itself* could have concealed anything—a hidden compartment, for example; then the cases were sought by the murderer not for themselves but for *what they contained*. What do cigaret-cases contain? What did both cases contain? Only cigarets. But why should a man commit murder for cigarets? Obviously, not for the pellets themselves. But if something had been *hidden* in those cigarets—if they had been doctored, if tobacco had been removed from them and something secreted inside, and the ends tamped up with tobacco again . . . then we arrive at a concrete inference."

Ellery straightened and drew a deep breath. "You're Mrs. Mallorie, I take it?" he asked the invalid in the wheel-chair.

"I am!" she replied.

"Only two days ago you were parted from a diamond necklace. How large were the stones?"

"Like small peas," shrilled Mrs. Mallorie. "Worth twenty thousand dollars, the lot of 'em."

"Like small peas. Hmm. A housewifely description, Mrs. Mallorie." Ellery smiled. "We progress. I postulated John Lubbock's cigarets as the hiding-place of something valuable . . . Mrs. Mallorie's rather expensive peas, ladies and gentlemen!"

They buzzed and peep-peeped like fowls in a barnyard. Ellery silenced them: "Yes, we have arrived at the point where it is indicated that your neighbor John Lubbock was not only a dilettante but a jewel thief as well!"

"Mr. Lubbock!" wheezed Seaman Carter in a shocked voice.

"Exactly. Inspector Queen has not been able to discover our man-about-town's source of income. A gigolo? Gigolos do not pay for ladies' apartments; the shoe is rather on the other foot. Ah, but the jewels! Here, then, is a minor mystery solved." Billy Harms stretched her white neck like an ostrich and sniffed. "But note that John Lubbock was murdered for those diamond-concealing cigarettes," Ellery continued. "Who could have known that he had those diamonds—moreover, in such a fantastic hiding-place? Surely none but an accomplice. In other words, when we lay hands on the murderer of Harry and John Lubbock we shall have found John Lubbock's partner-in-thievery."

The vague relief they had all exhibited gave way again to fear. No one stirred. Mrs. Mallorie was glaring at John Lubbock's purple face with the utmost malevolence. Ellery smiled again—a very playful and annoying smile. "Now," he said softly, "for the last act of our little drama: the details of the second murder. Jimmy," he said to the Headquarters fingerprint expert, "what did you find in your search?"

"This dead man on the floor had his fingers on the other side of this door—the side where his bedroom is."

"Thank you. Now it happens, ladies and gentlemen, that just before John Lubbock was murdered I had myself wiped the knob of his bedroom door—the door that leads into this vacant apartment—clean of all fingerprints. This means that Lubbock himself, when he went into his bedroom a few moments ago, put his fingers on the knob. This means that he deliberately opened the door in order to enter this vacant apartment. Was John Lubbock trying to escape? No; he did not don hat or overcoat, for one thing; for another, he could not hope to get far; and even if he did, escape would certainly tar him with the brush of suspicion that he had murdered his brother—and he, of course, was innocent, since he himself has been murdered. Then why did he go into this vacant apartment?

"I was talking with the Inspector some minutes ago in the foyer of Lubbock's apartment next door. At that time we had reason to believe John guilty of his brother's murder. I had myself shut the door to the living room so that he should not overhear. But when Dr. Eustace came out to visit his other patients in the building, unfortunately he left the door ajar, and it was at that moment that the Inspector, no doubt unaware that the door was open, said distinctly that we were intending to take John Lubbock down to Headquarters 'for a talk'—obviously, to search him and put him on the grid. The harm was done. Sergeant Velie, you were in the living room with Lubbock at that time. Did *you* hear the Inspector make that remark?"

"I did that," muttered the Sergeant, digging his heels

into the floor. "I guess he did, too. Only a minute later he said he wanted to go into the bedroom for something."

"Q. E. D.," murmured Ellery. "Lubbock, hearing that he was about to be taken to Police Headquarters, thought rapidly. The stolen diamonds were imbedded in the cigarets in his teakwood case; a thorough search would certainly reveal them. He must rid himself of those cigarets! So now we know why he went into the vacant apartment—not to escape, but to hide the cigarets somewhere until he could regain possession of them later. Naturally, he intended to return.

"But how could the murderer possibly anticipate John Lubbock's instantaneous decision to dispose of the jewels in this vacant apartment, the only immediately available hiding-place? *Only if the murderer, too, had heard the Inspector's remark about taking Lubbock to Headquarters, had realized that Lubbock had also heard, had foreseen what Lubbock would instantly have to do.*"

Ellery smiled wickedly and leaned forward; his long fingers were curved in a predatory hook; his body was tense. "Only five people overheard the Inspector's remark," he snapped. "The Inspector himself, I, Sergeant Velie, the late John Lubbock, and—"

Billy Harms screamed, and old Mrs. Mallorie screeched like a wounded parrot. Some one had plunged toward the door to the east corridor, bellowing and scattering people aside like a maddened bull-elephant, like a Malay running amuck, like an ancient Norseman in a berserker rage. . . . Sergeant Velie flung his two hundred and fifty pounds of muscle forward; there was a wild mix-up, the thudding of the Sergeant's chunky fists, clouds of dust. . . . Ellery stood quietly waiting. The

Inspector, who had observed Sergeant Velie in action on many former occasions, merely sighed.

"A double-crossing villain as well as a twofold murderer," said Ellery at last when the Sergeant had hammered his adversary into red pulp. "He wanted not only to get rid of John Lubbock, his accomplice, the only human being who knew his guilt as a thief and suspected no doubt his guilt as a murderer, but also to have Mrs. Mallorie's jewels all for himself. Dad, you will find the diamonds either on his person, in his bag, or somewhere about his quarters. The problem," said Ellery, lighting a cigaret and inhaling gratefully under the stony stares of his audience, "was after all a simple one, one which admitted of a strictly logical attack. The facts themselves pointed to that man on the floor as the only possible culprit."

The man writhing in Sergeant Velie's inexorable grip was Dr. Eustace.

The Adventure of
""THE TWO-HEADED DOG""

The Adventure of

"THE TWO-HEADED DOG"

As the lowslung Duesenberg hummed along the murk-dusted road between rows of stripped and silent trees, something in the salty wind which moaned over the tall slender man at the wheel on its journey across Martha's Vineyard, Cape Cod's heel, and Buzzards Bay stirred him. Many a traveler on that modern road had quivered to the slap of the Atlantic winds, prickled with molecules of spray, responding uneasily to the dim wind-call of some ancestor's sea-poisoned blood. But it was neither blood nor nostalgia which stirred the man in the open car. The wind, which was ululating like a banshee, held no charm for him, and the tingling spray no pleasure. His skin was crawling, it was true, but only because his coat was thin, the October wind cold, the spray distinctly discomforting, and the bare night-fall outside New Bedford indefinably grim and peopled with shadows.

Shivering behind the big wheel, he switched on his headlights. An antiqued sign sprang whitely into view some yards ahead and he slowed down to read it. It swung creaking to and fro in the wind, hinged on scabrous iron, and it flaunted a fearsome monstrosity with two heads whose *genus* had apparently eluded even the obscure wielder of the paints. Below the monster rur the legend:

THE ADVENTURE OF
"THE TWO-HEADED DOG"
(Cap'n Hosey's Rest)
Rooms—$2 And Up
Permanent—Transient
Auto-Campers Accommodated
In Clean Modern Cabins
DRIVE IN

"Even Cerberus would make an acceptable host to-night," thought the traveler with a wry smile, and he swung the car into a gravelly driveway lined with trees, soon bringing the machine to rest before a high white house crisply painted, its green shutters clear as eye-shades. The inn sprawled over considerable territory, he saw, examining the angular structure in the glare of floodlights over the clearing. Around both sides ran car-lanes, and dimly toward the sides going rearwards he made out small cabins and a large outbuilding which was apparently a garage. There was a smack of old New England about the inn, disagreeably leavened with the modern cabins on its flanks. The huge old ship's lantern creaking and gleaming in battered brass above the front door somehow lost its savor.

"Might be worse, I suppose," he grumbled, leaning on his klaxon. "Hybrid!" The unearthly racket caused the heavy-timbered door to pop open almost instantly. A young woman in a reefer that contrived to look rakish appeared under the brass lantern.

"Ah," sighed the traveler, "the farmer's daughter. No, I'm in the wrong county. Could this be Cap'n Hosey? My dear skipper, is it possible for a sore and weary wayfarer to secure food and shelter this wretched night? That portrait of a misbegotten Cerberus painted on the sign yonder wasn't too alluring."

"We're in the business, if that's what you mean," said the young woman crisply, in a cultured voice. "And I'm *not* Cap'n Hosey; I'm his daughter. Jump out. I'll have your—" she regarded the dusty old Duesenberg with a sniff and grinned—"your equipage taken round to the garage."

The man crawled out onto the gravel, shivering, and from nowhere appeared a shambling oil-smeared creature in dungarees who silently climbed into the car.

"Take her around, Isaac," directed the young woman. "Luggage?"

"I lost it somewhere between here and Davy Jones's Locker," groaned the tall young man. "No, by St. Elmo, here it is!" He chuckled and plucked a battered suitcase out of the car. "Proceed, Charon, and treat my steed well. . . . Ah! Is that codfish polluting the vigorous air? I might have known."

"We're rather full up," said the young woman curtly. "Can't give you a room in the inn. You'll have to take a cabin. We've got just one left."

He halted under the flickering ship's lantern and said in a stern voice: "I can't say I care for your atmosphere, Miss Hosey. Do you keep ghosts for pets? I've felt clammy fingers groping about my neck all the way from Duxbury. Dinner?"

She was a very young and pretty miss, he saw, with russet hair and windblown lips. Also, she was angry. "Look here—"

"Tut, tut," he said mildly, "mustn't beshrew the guests, my dear. I should have said 'supper,' I suppose. It's always supper, isn't it?"

Her lips relaxed suddenly. "Oh, all right. You're erratic but—nice. I do resent that crack about our 'misbegotten Cerberus,' though. Didn't Cerberus have two heads? I'll admit the art is dubious—"

"Erudition in New Bedford? My dear, Cerberus has had three heads, and fifty heads, and a hundred heads on various literary excursions, but I've never heard of his having had two."

"Darn," said Cap'n Hosey's daughter. "I was minoring in Greek at the time and I did think it *was* two. Won't you come in?"

They entered a large smoky room filled with chattering people—tourists, he saw at once, wincing—and some very lovely old furniture decidedly the worse for irreverent wear. A desk in the brass-cuspidor-and-leaky-pen tradition graced one corner of the room, presided over by a tall gaunt red-cheeked old man with white hair, frosty blue eyes, and a mildly benevolent expression. He wore a faded blue coat with brass buttons.

"This," said the young woman demurely, as the traveler dropped his suitcase on the linoleum-covered floor, "is Cap'n Hosey, the ancient mariner."

"Delighted to meet you, Captain Hosey," murmured the tall young man. "That's familiar for Hosea, I take it?"

"Ye k'n have it," chuckled the proprietor, extending a large and horny hand. "Howdy-do. Ye've met my daughter Jenny? I heard ye two jawin' outside. Don't pay no 'tention to Jenny, sir; she's eddicated, she is, an' that makes her a mite sharp, like the feller said when he was honin' his jackknife. Radcliffe, ye betcha," he said proudly.

Jenny turned very red. The young man said: "How charming; I must look into the Greek curriculum there," and reached for the register. He signed his name with weary fingers. "And now, if I may have a facial and manual rinse and a ton of supper?"

Jenny consulted the register, and her eyes widened and she exclaimed: "Why, don't tell me you're the—"

"Such," sighed Mr. Ellery Queen, "is fame. Don't tell *me* there's a murder in the vicinity—although I will say the environment is peculiarly conducive to tragedy. Quite Hardyesque, in fact. I've been running away from murders. Just saddled my faithful Rosinante and galloped off into New England, hoping for surcease."

"You *are* the Ellery Queen, though, who goes about solving—"

"Silence," he whispered fiercely. "No. I'm young Davy, Prince of Wales, and Papa George has permitted me to go gallivantin' incognito. For heaven's sake, Jenny, use discretion. All those people are listening."

"Queen, hey?" boomed Cap'n Hosey, beaming. "Well, well. I've heard tell of ye, young man. Proud to have ye. Jenny, ye go tell Martha to scramble up some vittles fer Mr. Queen. We'll mess down in th' taproom. Meanwhile, if ye'll come with me—"

"We?" said Ellery weakly.

"Well," grinned Cap'n Hosey, "we don't git such folks as th' usual thing, Mr. Queen. Now what was that last case I was readin' about . . . ?"

In a brass-and-wooden room downstairs redolent of hops and fish Mr. Ellery Queen found himself the focus of numerous respectful and excited eyes. He blessed his gods privately that they possessed the delicacy to permit him to eat in comparative peace. There were oysters, and codfish cakes, and broiled mackerel, and foamy lager, and airy apple pie and coffee. He stuffed himself with a will and actually began to feel better.

Outside the winds might howl and the ghosts wander, but here it was warm and cheerful and even companionable.

They were a curious company. Cap'n Hosey had apparently gathered the cream of his cronies for the honor of staring at the famous visitor from New York. There was a man named Barker, a traveling salesman "in hardware"; as he said: "Mechanics' and building tools, Mr. Queen, cement, quicklime, household wares, *et cetera* and so forth." He was a tall needle-thin man with sharp eyes and the glib tongue of the professional itinerant. He smoked long cheroots as emaciated as himself.

Then there was a chubby man named Heiman, with heavy pitted glistening features and a cast in one eye that contrived to give him a droll expression. Heiman, it appeared, was "in drygoods," and he and Barker from their cheerful raillery were boon companions, their itineraries crossing each other every three months or so when they were—as Heiman put it—"on the road"; for both covered the southern New England territory for their respective establishments.

The third of Cap'n Hosey's intimates needed only the costume to be Long John Silver in the flesh. There was something piratical in the cut of his jib; he possessed besides the traditional cold blue eyes—Ellery gulped down a slithery Cotuit instinctively when he first saw it—a pegleg; and his speech was bristly with the argot of the sea.

"So ye're the great d'tective," rumbled the peglegged pirate, whose name was Captain Rye, when Ellery had washed down the last delectable morsel of pie with the last warm drop of coffee. "Can't say I ever heard o' ye."

"Shush, Bull," growled Cap'n Hosey.

"No, no," said Ellery comfortably, lighting a cigaret. "That's refreshing candor. Cap'n Hosey, I like your place."

Jenny said: "Mr. Queen's been wondering about the name of the inn, father. That work-of-art over the bar inspired it, Mr. Queen. Relic of father's past."

Ellery noticed for the first time that a faded, seamy, and weatherworn wood-carving was nailed over the bar. It was a three-dimensional projection of the painted monstrosity swinging over the road—a remotely canine bust with two remotely canine heads branching off a single hairy neck.

"Figgerhead of my granddaddy's three-master," boomed Cap'n Hosey from behind stupefying clouds of clay-pipe smoke. "The whaler *Cerb'rus*. When we opened this here place Jenny she thought that was too high-a-mighty a handle. So she named it *Th' Two-Headed Dog*. Pretty, ain't it?"

"Speakin' about dogs," said Heiman in his piping voice, "tell Mr. Queen about that business happened here three months ago, Cap'n Hosey."

"Hell, yes," cried Barker. "Tell Mr. Queen about that, Cap'n." His Adam's apple bobbed eagerly as he turned to Ellery. "One of the most interesting things ever happened to the old coot, I guess, Mr. Queen. Haw-haw! Near turned the place inside out."

"Dogs?" murmured Ellery.

"Jee-rusalem!" roared Cap'n Hosey. "Clean fergot 'bout it. Reg'lar crime, Mr. Queen. Took th' wind slap out o' *my* sails. Happened—let's see, now . . ."

"July," said Barker promptly. "I remember Heiman and I were both here then on our regular summer trip."

"God, what a night that was!" muttered chubby Heiman. "Makes my skin creep to think of it."

An odd silence fell over the company, and Ellery regarded them one by one with curiosity. There was a queer unease on the clean fresh face of Jenny, and even Captain Rye had become subdued.

"Well," said Cap'n Hosey at last in a low tone, " 'twas round 'bout this time o' month, I sh'd say. Ter'ble dirty weather, Mr. Queen, that night. Stormed all over this end o' th' coast. Rainin' an' thunderin' to beat hell. One o' th' worst summer squalls I rec'lect. Well, sir, we was all settin' upstairs nice an' cozy, when Isaac— that's th' swab does my odd jobs—Isaac, he hollers in from outside there's a customer jest hove in with a car wantin' vittles and lodgin' fer th' night."

"Will you ever forget that—that hideous little creature?" shuddered Jenny.

"Who's spinnin' this yarn, Jenny?" demanded Cap'n Hosey. "Anyways, we was full up, like t'night—jest one cabin empty. This man comes in shakin' off th' wet; he was rigged out in a cross 'tween a sou'wester an' a rubber tire; an' he takes th' vacant cabin fer th' night."

"But the dog," sighed Ellery.

"I'm comin' to that, Mr. Queen. Well, sir, he was a runt—sawed-off lubber with scared lamps on 'm ye c'd see a league off, *an'* he was nervous."

"Craps, he was nervous," muttered Heiman. "Couldn't look you in the eye. About fifty, I'd say; looked like some kind of clerk, I remember thinkin'."

"Except for the chin-whiskers," said Barker ominously. "Red, they were, and you didn't have to be a detective to see right off they were phony."

"Disguised, eh?" said Ellery, stifling a yawn.

"Yes, *sir*," said Cap'n Hosey. "Anyways, he reg'sters under th' name o' Morse—John Morse—gobbles up a mess o' slum downstairs, an' Jenny shows 'm to th' cabin, with Isaac convoyin' 'em. Tell Mr. Queen what happened, Jenny."

"He was horrible," said Jenny in a shaky voice. "He wouldn't let Isaac touch the car—insisted on driving it around to the garage himself. Then he made me point out the cabin; wouldn't let me take him there. I did, and he—he swore at me in a tired sort of way, b-but savagely, Mr. Queen. I felt he was dangerous. So I went off, and Isaac too. But I watched; and I saw him sneak back to the garage. He stayed there for some time. When he came out he went into the cabin and locked the door; I heard him lock it." She paused, and for the moment the most curious tension crackled in the smoky air. Ellery, unaccountably, no longer felt sleepy. "Then I—I went into the garage . . ."

"What sort of car was it?"

"An old Dodge, I think, with side-curtains tightly drawn. But he'd been so mysterious about it—" She gulped and smiled wanly. "I got into the garage and put my hand on the nearest curtain. Curiosity killed a cat, and it almost got me a very badly bitten hand."

"Ah, there was a dog in the car?"

"Yes." She shuddered suddenly. "I'd left the garage-door open. When lightning flashed I could . . . It flashed. Something bit into the rubber curtain and I jerked my hand away just in time. I almost screamed. I heard him—it growl; low, rumbling, animal." They were very quiet now. "In the lightning a black muzzle poked out of a hole in the curtain and I saw two savage eyes. It was a dog, a big dog. Then I heard a noise outside and there was the—the little man with the red beard. He glared at me and shouted something. I ran."

"Naturally," murmured Ellery. "Can't say I'm over-fond of the more brutal canines myself. A sign of the effete times, I daresay. And?"

"Ain't a hound been whelped," growled Captain Rye, "can't be mastered. Whippin' does it. I mind I had a big brute once, mastiff he was—"

"Stow it, Bull," said Cap'n Hosey testily. "Ye wa'n't here, so what d'ye know 'bout it? Takes more'n jest dog to scare my Jenny. I tell ye that there wa'n't no or'n'ry mutt!"

"Oh, Captain Rye wasn't stopping at the inn then?" said Ellery.

"Naw. Hove in 'bout two-three weeks after. Any-ways, that ain't th' real part o' the yarn. When Jenny come back we nat'rally talked 'bout this swab, an'— 'twas real funny—we all agreed we'd seen his ugly map some'eres b'fore."

"Indeed?" murmured Ellery. "All of you?"

"Well, I knew I'd seen his pan somewhere," muttered the drygoods salesman, "and so had Barker. Later. when the two—"

"Haul up!" roared Cap'n Hosey. " 'M I tellin' this yarn or ain't I? Well, we went t' bed. Jenny 'n' me, we bunk in our own quarters in th' little shack back o' th' garage; 'n' Barker 'n' Heiman, here, they had cabins that night; bunch o' schoolmarms 'd took up jest 'bout all th' room there was. Well, sir, we took a look at this Morse's cabin on th' way out, but it was darker'n a Chinee lazaret. Then round 'bout three-four in th' mornin' it happened."

"By the way," said Ellery, "had you investigated the car before you turned in?"

"Sure did," said Cap'n Hosey grimly. "Ain't no

hound this side o' hell *I'm* skeered on. But he wa'n't in
th' car. Dog-stink was, though. This Morse must 'a'
taken th' dog to his cabin after he caught Jenny pokin'
round where she had no bus'ness pokin'."

"The man was a criminal, I suppose," sighed Ellery.

"How'd you know?" cried Barker, opening his eyes.

"Tut, tut," said Ellery modestly, and inwardly
groaned.

"He were a crim'nal, all right," said Cap'n Hosey emphatically. "Wait till I tell ye. Early mornin'—'twas
still dark—Isaac comes a-poundin' on th' door an' when
I opens it there's Isaac, nekkid under a reefer, with two
hard-lookin' customers drippin' rain. Still squally,
'twas. Make a long story short, they was d'tectives
lookin' fer this here Morse. They showed me a picture,
an' o' course I reco'nized him right off even though in
th' snap he was clean-shaved. They knew he'd been
sportin' a fake red beard, an' that he was travelin' with
a dog—big police dog—that he'd owned b'fore he
skipped with th' jool. He'd lived in a suburb outside
Chicawgo some'eres an' neighbors'd said they'd see him
walkin' out with a dog every once in a while."

"Here, here," said Ellery, sitting up alertly. "Do you
mean to say that was John Gillette, the little lapidary
who stole the Cormorant diamond from Shapley's in
Chicago last May?"

"That's him!" shouted Heiman, blinking his lid rapidly over the eye with the cast. "Gillette!"

"I remember reading about the case when the theft
occurred," said Ellery thoughtfully, "although I never
followed it through. Go on."

"He'd worked in Shapley's for twenty years," sighed
Jenny, "always quiet and honest and efficient. A stone-

cutter. Then he was tempted and stole the **Cormorant**
and disappeared."

"Worth a hundred grand," muttered Barker.

"A. hund'ed grand!" exclaimed Captain Rye suddenly, stamping his pegleg on the stone floor. And he
sank back and shoved his pipe into his mouth.

"Heap o' money," nodded Cap'n Hosey. "These
d'tectives'd follered Gillette's trail all over creation,
al'ays jest missin' 'm. But th' dog give 'm away finally.
He'd been seen up Dedham way with th' dog. Lot o'
this we found out fr'm them fellers later. Anyways,
I shows 'em th' cabin an' they busts in. Nothin' doin'.
He'd heard 'em or kep' an eye open, most likely, an'
skipped."

"Hmm," said Ellery. "He didn't take the car?"

"Couldn't," said Cap'n Hosey grimly. "Skeered to
take th' chance. Th' garage is too near where I bunked
an' where th' d'tectives was jawin' with me. He must
of got away through th' woods back o' th' cabins.
Them fellers was wild. In th' rain there wa'n't no
tracks t' foller. Got away clean. Prob'ly stole a launch
or had one hid down in th' Harbor an' headed either fer
Narragansett Bay or ducked round to th' Vineyard.
Never did find 'm."

"Did he leave anything behind besides the car?" murmured Ellery. "Personal belongings? The diamond?"

"The hell he did," snorted Barker. "What do you
think he is—a fool? He skipped clean, like Cap'n
Hosey says."

"Except," said Jenny, "for the dog."

"Seems a persistent brute, at any rate," chuckled
Ellery. "You mean he left the police dog behind? You
found him?"

"Th' d'tectives found th' mutt," scowled Cap'n

Hosey. "When they busted into th' cabin there was a big heavy double chain attached to th' grate o' th' fireplace. Jest the double chain. No dog. They found th' dog fifty yards off in th' woods, dead."

"Dead? How? What do you mean?" asked Ellery swiftly.

"Bashed over th' skull. An' an ugly brute she was, too. Female. All blood an' mud. Th' d'tectives said Gillette'd done it th' last minute to git rid o' her. She was gittin' too dangerous t' tote around. They took th' carkiss away."

"Well," smiled Ellery, "it must have been a hectic time, Captain. I don't think poor Jenny's over it yet."

The young woman shivered. "I'll not forget that hideous little b-bug as long as I live. And then—"

"Oh, there's something else? By the way, what happened to the car and the chain?"

"D'tectives took 'em away," rumbled Cap'n Hosey.

"I suppose," said Ellery, "there's no doubt they *were* detectives?"

They were all startled at that. Barker exclaimed: "Sure they were, Mr. Queen! Why, reporters were here from as far as Boston, and those dicks posed for pictures and everything!"

"Just a vagrant thought," said Ellery mildly. "You said: 'And then—' Jenny. And then what?"

There was an awkward silence. Barker and Heiman looked puzzled, but the two old seamen and Jenny turned pale.

"What's the matter?" shrilled Heiman, rolling his eyes.

"Well," muttered Cap'n Hosey, "I s'pose it's all foolishness an' sech, but that cabin ain't been th' same since—since that night, ye see."

"Say," chuckled Barker, "I have to sleep in that cabin tonight, Cap'n. What d'ye mean—not the same?"

Jenny said uneasily: "Oh, it's ridiculous, as father says, but the most extraordinary things have been happening there, Mr. Queen, since that night in July. J-just as if a—a ghost were prowling around."

"Ghost!" Heiman went white and shrank back, visibly affected.

"Now, now," said Ellery with a smile. "Surely that's overheated imagination, Jenny? I thought ghosts are indigenous only to old English castles."

"Ye may scoff all ye want," said Captain Rye darkly, "but I once seen a ghost with me own eyes. 'Twas off Hatteras in th' winter o' '93—"

"Dry up, Bull," said Cap'n Hosey irritably. "I'm a God-fearin' man, Mr. Queen, an' I ain't skeered o' th' toughest spook ever walked a midnight sea. But—well, it's mighty queer." He shook his head as a gust of wind rattled down the chimney and stirred the ashes in the fireplace. "Mighty queer," he repeated slowly. "Had that cabin occupied a couple o' times since that night, an' everybody tells me they hear funny sounds there."

Barker guffawed. "G'on! You're kidding, Cap'n!"

"Ain't doin' no sech thing. You tell 'em, Jenny."

"I—I tried it one night myself," said Jenny in a low voice. "I think I'm reasonably intelligent, Mr. Queen. They're two-room cabins, and the complaints had said the sounds came from the—the living room while they were trying to sleep in the bedroom. The night I stayed in that cabin I—well, I heard it, too."

"Sounds?" frowned Ellery. "What kind of sounds?"

"Oh," she hesitated, shrugging helplessly, "cries. Moans, mutters, whimpers, slithery noises, patters, scrapings—I can't really describe them, but they," she shivered, "they didn't sound—human. There was such a variety of them! As—as if it was a congress of ghosts." She smiled at Ellery's cynical eyebrows. "I suppose you think I'm a fool. But I tell you—hearing those muffled, stealthy, inhuman sounds . . . Well, they get you, Mr. Queen."

"Did you investigate the—ah—scene of the visitation while these sounds were being produced?" asked Ellery dryly.

She gulped. "I took one peek. It was dark, though, and I couldn't see a thing. The sounds stopped the minute I opened the door."

"And did they continue afterward?"

"I didn't wait to see, Mr. Queen," she said with a tremulous grin. "I ducked out of the bedroom window and ran for dear life."

"Hmm," said Barker, narrowing his shrewd eyes. "I always did say this part of the country produced more imagination to the square inch than a trunkful of fiction. Well, no goldarned sounds are going to keep *me* up. And if they happen I'll find out what made 'em or know the reason why!"

"I'll exchange cabins with you, Mr. Barker," murmured Ellery. "I've always felt the most poignant fear of—and the most insatiable curiosity about—ghosts. Never met one, I suppose. What say? Shall we trade?"

"Hell, no," chuckled Barker, rising. "You see, I'm prob'ly the world's greatest disbeliever in spirits, Mr. Queen. I've got a sweet little .32 Colt"—he grinned in a mirthless way—"I'm in hardware, you see—and I never heard of a spook yet that liked the taste of bullets. I'm goin' to bed."

"Well," sighed Ellery, "if you insist. Too bad. I'd

love to have met a wraith—all clanky with chains and dripping foul seaweed. . . . Think I'll turn in myself. By the way, this cabin which had been occupied by Gillette is the only one in which your ghost has walked, Cap'n Hosey?"

"Only one, yep," said the innkeeper gloomily.

"And have sounds been heard while the cabin's been unoccupied?"

"Nope. We watched a couple o' nights, too, but nothin' happened."

"Curious." Ellery sucked a fingernail thoughtfully for a moment. "Well! If Miss Jenny and these gentlemen will excuse me?"

"Here," said Heiman hurriedly, bouncing out of the chair. "I'm not goin' to cross that backyard alone. . . . W-wait for baby!"

The rear of the inn was a desolate place. As they emerged from the backstairs leading from the taproom its cold desolation struck them like a physical blow. Ellery could hear Heiman breathing hoarsely, as if he had run far and fast. There was a livid moon, and it lit up his companions' faces: Heiman's was drawn, fearful; Barker's amused and a trifle wary. The cabins were for the most part black and silent; it was late.

They walked shoulder to shoulder across the sandy terrain, instinctively keeping together. The wind kept up an incessant angry hissing through the dark trees beyond the cabins.

" 'Night," muttered Heiman suddenly and darted across to one of the cabins. They heard him scuttle inside and lock the door. Then the rattles of windows came to their ears as the chubby salesman closed them hastily; and a square of yellow brilliance sprang up as he flooded his quarters with ghost-dispelling light.

"I guess it's got Heiman, all right," laughed Barker, shrugging his bony shoulders. "Well, Mr. Queen, here's where the spook hangs out. D'y'ever hear anything so nutty? These old sailors are all the same—superstitious as hell. I'm surprised at Jenny, though; she's an educated girl."

"Are you sure you shouldn't like me to—" began Ellery.

"Naw. I'll be all right. I've got a quart of rye in one of my sample trunks that's the best little ghost-chaser y'ever saw." Barker chuckled deep in his throat. "Well, nighty-night, Mr. Queen. Sleep tight and don't let the spooks bite!" He sauntered to his cabin, squared his shoulders, whistled a rather dreary tune, and disappeared. A moment later the light flashed on and his thin long figure appeared at the front window and pulled down the shade.

"Whistling," thought Ellery grimly, "in the dark. At that, the man has intestines." He shrugged and flicked his cigaret away. It was no corncern of his; some natural phenomenon, no doubt—wind sobbing down a chimney shaft, the scratchings of a mouse, the rattle of a loose window-pane; and there was a ghost. Tomorrow he would be well out of it, headed for Newport and the home of his friend. . . . He flattened against the door of his cabin.

Some one was standing in the shadow of the inn's back door, watching.

Ellery crouched and slipped along the walls of the cabins toward the inn—crept like a cat upon the motionless watcher before he realized how ridiculous his stealth was. When he caught himself up, swearing, it was too late. The watcher had spied him. It was Isaac, the man-of-all work.

"Out for a breath of air?" asked Ellery lightly, fumbling for another cigaret. The man did not reply. Ellery said: "Uh—by the way, Isaac, if I may use the familiar—when a cabin is unoccupied are the windows kept closed?"

The broad bowed shoulders twitched contemptuously. "Yep."

"Locked?"

"Nope." The man answered in a heavy rumble, like aged thunder. He stepped out of the shadow and gripped Ellery's arm so tightly that the cigaret fell out of his hand. "I harkened to yer scoffin' an' sneerin' in th' taproom. An' I says to ye: Scoff not an' sin not. There're more things in heav'n 'n' earth, Horaysheeo, th'n 're drempt of in yer philos'phy. Amen!" And Isaac turned and vanished.

Ellery stared at the empty shadows with puzzled, angry eyes. An innkeeper's daughter who had studied Greek; a shambling countryman who quoted Shakespeare! What the deuce was going on here, anyway? Then he cursed himself for a meddling, imaginative fool and strode back to his cabin. And yet, despite himself, he shivered at the slash of the wind; and his scalp prickled at a perfectly natural night-sound from the silent woods.

Something cried out in the distance—faintly, desperately, a lost soul. It cried again. And again. And again.

Mr. Ellery Queen found himself sitting up in bed, covered with perspiration, listening with all the power of his ears. The cabin bedroom, the black world outside, were profoundly quiet. Had it been a dream?

He sat listening for minutes that were hours. Then, in the dark, he fumbled for his watch. The luminous dials glowed at 1:25.

Something in the very silence made him get out of bed, slip into his clothes, and go to the door of the cabin. The clearing was a pit of darkness; the moon had long since set. The wind had died somewhere in the lost hours and the air, while cold, was still. Cries . . . A conviction grew within him that they had come from Barker's cabin.

His shoes crunched loudly on the stiff earth as he went to Barker's front door and knocked. There was no answer. He knocked again.

A man's deep, curiously strained voice said behind him: "So ye heard it, too, Mr. Queen?" He whirled to find old Cap'n Hosey, in pants and slippers and a huge sweater, at his shoulder.

"Then it wasn't my imagination," muttered Ellery. He knocked again, and there was still no answer. Trying the door, he found it locked. He looked at Cap'n Hosey, and Cap'n Hosey looked at him. Then, without speaking, the old man led the way around the cabin to the back, facing the woods. The rear window to Barker's living room stood open, although the shade was down. Cap'n Hosey poked it aside and directed a flashlight into the thick blackness of the room. They caught their breaths, sharply.

The lank figure of Barker, dressed in pajamas and bathrobe, slippers on his skinny naked feet, lay on the rug in the center of the room—contorted like an open jackknife in the ghastly, unmistakable attitude of violent death.

How the others knew no one thought of asking. Death wings its way swiftly into human consciousness. When Ellery rose from his knees beside the dead man he found Jenny, Isaac, and Heiman crowded in the doorway; Cap'n Hosey had opened the door. Behind them peered the vulturous face of Captain Rye. They were all in various stages of undress.

"Dead only a few minutes," murmured Ellery, looking down at the sprawled body. "Those cries we heard must have been his death-cries." He lit a cigaret and went to the window and leaned against the sill and stood there, drooping and watchful as he smoked. No one said anything, and no one moved. Barker was dead. A matter of hours before he had been alive, laughing and breathing and joking. And now he was dead. It was a curious thing.

It was a curious thing, too, that except for a very small area on the rug with the dead man as its nucleus, nothing in the room had been disturbed. In one corner stood two big trunks, both open, with various heavy drawers; they contained samples of Barker's wares. The furniture stood neatly and sedately about. Only the rug around Barker's body was scuffed and wrinkled, as if there had been a struggle at precisely that spot. One bit of wreckage not native to the room lay a few feet away: a flashlight, its glass and bulb shattered.

The dead man lay partly on his back. His eyes were wide open and staring with an unearthly intensity of horror and fear. His fingers clutched the loose collar of his pajama-coat, quite as if some one had been strangling him. But he had not been strangled; he had bled to death. For his throat, fully revealed by the painful backward stretching of his head, had been ripped and slashed raggedly, grotesquely, at the jugular vein, and his hands and coat and the rug were smeared with his still liquid blood.

"Good God," choked Heiman; he covered his face with his hands and began to sob. Captain Rye pulled him roughly outside, growling something at him; they heard the chubby man stumble off to his cabin.

Ellery flipped his cigaret out the window past the shade, which they had raised on climbing into the room, and went to Barker's sample trunks. He pulled out all the drawers. But nothing was there that should not have been there, and the hammers and saws and chisels and electrical supplies and samples of cement and lime and plaster were ranged in neat unviolated rows. Finding no evidence of disturbance in either trunk, he went quietly into the bedroom. He returned soon enough, looking thoughtful.

"What—what d'ye do in a case like this?" croaked Cap'n Hosey. His weatherbeaten face was the color of wet ashes.

"And what do you think about your ghost now, Mr. Queen?" giggled Jenny; her face was convulsed with horror. "G-ghosts . . . Oh, my God!"

"Now, now, pull yourself together," murmured Ellery. "Why, notify the local authorities, naturally, Captain. In fact, I advise very prompt action. The murder occurred only a matter of minutes ago. The murderer must still be in the vicinity—"

"Oh, he is, is he?" growled Captain Rye, stepping crookedly into the room on his pegleg. "Well, Hosey, what in time ye waitin' fer?"

"I—" The old man shook his head in a daze.

"The murderer got out through the back window," said Ellery softly. "Probably hard on my first knock at the front door. He took the weapon with him, dripping blood. There are a few bloodstains on the sill here pointing to that." There was the most curious note in his voice: a compound of mockery and uncertainty.

Cap'n Hosey departed, heavily. Captain Rye hesitated and then stumped off after his friend. Isaac stood dumbly staring at the corpse. But there was a freshet of color in Jenny's young cheeks and her eyes reflected a returning sanity.

"What sort of weapon, Mr. Queen," she demanded in a small but steady voice, "do you think capable of inflicting such a frightful wound?"

Ellery started. "Eh?" Then he smiled. "There," he said dryly, "is a question indeed. Sharp and yet jagged. A vicious, lethal instrument. It suggests certain *outré* possibilities." Her eyes went wide, and he shrugged. "This is a curious case. I'm half-disposed to believe—"

"But you know nothing whatever about Mr. Barker!"

"Knowledge, my dear," he remarked gravely, "is the antidote to fear, as Emerson has pointed out. Moreover, it needs no catalyst." He paused. "Miss Jenny. This isn't going to be pleasant. Why don't you return to your own quarters? Isaac can stay and help me."

"You're going to—?" Terror glittered in her eyes again.

"There's something I must see. Please go." She sighed rather strangely and turned and went away. Isaac, a motionless hulk, still stared at the corpse. "Now, Isaac," said Ellery briskly, "stop gaping and help me with him. I want him moved out of the way."

The man stirred. "I told ye—" he began harshly, and then clamped his lips shut. He looked almost surly as he shambled forward. They raised the fast-chilling body without words and carried it into the bedroom. When they returned Isaac pulled out a lump of stiff brown stuff and bit off a piece. He chewed slowly, without enjoyment.

"Nothing missing, nothing stolen, so far as I can tell," muttered Ellery, half to himself. "That's a good sign. A very good sign indeed." Isaac stared at him without expression. Ellery shook his head and went to the middle of the room. He got to his knees and examined the rug in the area on which Barker's body had rested. There was a fairly smooth piece where the body had lain, surrounded like an island by the ripples of the disturbed rug. His eyes narrowed. Was it possible . . . He bent forward in some excitement, studying the rug fiercely. By God, it was!

"Isaac!" The countryman lumbered over. "What the devil caused this?" Ellery pointed. The nap of the rug where the corpse had sprawled was quite worn away. On examination it had a curiously scratched appearance, as if it had been subjected to a long and persistent scraping process. It was the only part of the rug, as he could see plainly enough, which was rubbed in that manner.

"Dunno," said Isaac phlegmatically.

"Who cleans these cabins?" snapped Ellery.

"Me."

"Have you ever noticed that spot before—that worn spot?"

"Cal'late."

"When, man, when? When'd you first begin to notice it?"

"Wall—round 'bout th' middle o' summer, I guess."

Ellery sprang to his feet. "*Banzai!* Better than my fondest hopes. That clinches it!" Isaac stared at him as if Ellery had suddenly gone mad. "The others," mumbled Ellery, "were mere speculations, stabs in the dark. This—" He smacked his lips together. "Look

here, man. Is there a weapon on the premises somewhere? Revolver? Shotgun? Anything?"

Isaac grunted: "Wall, Cap'n Hosey's got an ol'
shooter some'eres."

"Get it. See that it's oiled, loaded, ready for business.
For God's sake, man, hurry! And—oh, yes, Isaac. Tell
everybody to keep away from here. *Keep away!* No
noise. No disturbance. Except the police. Do you
understand?"

"I cal'late," muttered Isaac, and was gone.

For the first time something like fear leaped into
Ellery's eyes. He twisted toward the window, took a
step, stopped, shook his head, and hurried to the fireplace. There he found a heavy iron poker. Gripping
it nervously, he ran into the bedroom and half-closed
the door. He remained completely quiet until he heard
Isaac's heavy step outside. Then he dashed through the
living-room, snatched a big old-fashioned revolver from
the man's hand, sent him packing, made sure the weapon
was loaded and cocked, and returned to the living room.
But now he acted with more assurance. He knelt by
the telltale spot on the rug, placed the revolver near his
foot, and swiftly hauled up the rug until the bare
wooden floor was revealed. He scanned this closely for
some time. Then he replaced the rug and took up the
revolver again.

He met them at the door fifteen minutes later with
his finger at his lips. They were three husky, hatchet-
faced New Englanders with drawn revolvers. Curious
heads were poking out of lighted cabins all about.

"Oh, the idiots!" groaned Ellery. "Reassure those
people, blast 'em. You're the law here?" he whispered
to the leading stranger.

"Yep. Benson's my name," growled the man. "I met your daddy once—"

"Never mind that now. Make those people put out their lights and keep absolutely quiet; d'ye understand?" One of the officers darted away. "Now come inside, and for the love of heaven don't make any noise."

"But where's the body of this drummer?" demanded the New Bedford man.

"In the bedroom. He'll keep," rasped Ellery. "Come on, man, for God's sake." He herded them into the living room, shut the door with caution, got them into an alcove, snapped off the light. . . . The room blinked out, vanished.

"Have your weapons ready," whispered Ellery. "How much do you know about this business?"

"Well, Cap'n Hosey told me over the 'phone about Barker, and those damn funny noises—" muttered Benson.

"Good." Ellery crouched a little, his eyes fixed on the exact center of the room, although he could see nothing. "In a few moments, if my deductions are correct, you'll meet—the murderer of Barker."

The two men drew in their breaths. "By God," breathed Benson, "I don't see— How—"

"Quiet, man!"

They waited for an eternity. There were no sounds whatever. Then Ellery felt one of the officers behind him stir uneasily and mutter something beneath his breath. After that the silence was ear-splitting. He realized suddenly that the palm of his hand around the butt of the big revolver was wet; he wiped it off noiselessly against his thigh. His eyes did not waver from the invisible center of the black room.

How long they huddled there none of them could say. But after eons they became conscious of . . . something in the room. They had not actually heard a physical sound. A negation of sound, and yet it was louder than thunder. Something, some one, in the center of the room . . .

They almost gasped. A weird, snivelling, moaning cry, barely audible, accompanied by mysterious scratchy sounds like the scraping of ice, came to their ears.

The nervous officer behind Ellery lost control of himself. He uttered a fearful squeal.

"You damned fool!" shouted Ellery, and instantly fired. He fired again, and again, trying to trace the intruder's invisible career in the room. The place became sulphurous with stink; they coughed in the smoke. Then there was one long gurgling shriek like nothing human. Ellery darted like lightning to the switch and snapped it on.

The room was empty. But a trail of fresh copious blood led raggedly to the open window, and the shade was still flapping. Benson cursed and vaulted through, followed by his man.

Simultaneously the door clattered open and staring eyes glared in. Cap'n Hosey, Jenny, Isaac. . . . "Come in, come in," said Ellery wearily. "There's a badly wounded murderer in the woods now, and it's only a question of time. He can't get away." He sank into the nearest chair and fumbled for a cigaret, his eyes shadowed with strain.

"But who— What—"

Ellery waved a listless hand. "It was simple enough. But queer; damnably queer. I can't recall a queerer case."

"You know *who*—" began Jenny in a breathless voice.

"Certainly. And what I don't know I can piece together. But there's something to be done before I . . ." He rose. "Jenny, do you think you can withstand another shock?"

She blanched. "What do you mean, Mr. Queen?"

"I daresay you can. Cap'n Hosey, lend a hand, please." He went to one of Barker's sample trunks and extracted a couple of chisels and an ax. Cap'n Hosey glared at the unknown. "Come, come, Captain, there's no danger now. Jerk that rug away. I'm going to show you something." Ellery handed him a chisel when the old man had complied. "Pry up the nails holding these floor-boards together. Might's well do a neat job; there's no sense in ruining your floor utterly." He went to work with the second chisel at the opposite end of the board. They labored in silence for some time with chisels and ax, and finally loosened the boards.

"Stand back," said Ellery quietly, and he stooped and began to remove them one by one. . . . Jenny uttered an involuntary shriek and buried her face against her father's broad chest.

Beneath the floor, on the stony earth supporting the cabin, lay a horrible, shapeless, vaguely human mass, whitish in hue. Bones protruded here and there.

"You see lying here," croaked Ellery, "the remains of John Gillette, the jewel-thief."

"G-Gillette!" stuttered Cap'n Hosey, glaring into the hole.

"Murdered," sighed Ellery, "by your friend Barker three months ago."

He took a long scarf from one of the tables and flung it over the gap in the floor. "You see," he murmured in the stupefied silence, "when Gillette came here that night in July and asked for a cabin, while you all thought he looked vaguely familiar, Barker actually recognized him from having seen his photograph in the papers, no doubt. Barker himself was occupying a cabin that night. He knew Gillette had the Cormorant diamond. When everything was quiet he managed to get into this place and murdered Gillette. Since he carried all the hardware his heart could desire, *plus quicklime,* he pried up the boards under this rug, deposited Gillette's body there, poured the lime over it to destroy the flesh quickly and prevent the discovery of the body from an odor of putrefaction, nailed down the boards again. . . . There's more to it, of course. It all fitted nicely once I had deduced the identity of the murderer. It had to be."

"But," gulped Cap'n Hosey in a sick voice, "how'd ye *know,* Mr. Queen? An' who—"

"There were several pointers. Then I found something which clinched my vaguely glimpsed theory. I'll start from the clincher to make it more easily digestible." Ellery reached for the back-flung rug and pulled it out so that the curiously worn area was visible. "You see that? Nowhere on the rug except at this precise spot does such a strangely worn area appear. And mark, too, that it was on this precise spot that Barker was attacked and killed, since nowhere except closely about this spot was the rug wrinkled and scuffed; indicating that this must have been the vortex of a short struggle. . . . Any idea what might have caused such a peculiar wearing away of your rug, Captain?"

"Well," mumbled the old man, "it looks kinda scratchy, like as if—"

Benson's voice came from beyond the open window.

It held a note of supreme disbelief. "We got him, Mr. Queen. He died out in the woods."

They flocked to the window. Below, on the cold earth, revealed in the harsh glare of Benson's flash, lay a huge male police dog. His coat was rough and dirty and matted with burrs, and on his head was the cicatrix of a terrible wound, as if he had long before been struck violently over the head. His body was punctured in two places by fresh bullet-holes from Ellery's revolver; but the blood on the snarling muzzle was already dry.

"You see," said Ellery wearily, a little later, "it struck me at once that the worn spot looked scratchy—that is, *as if it had been scratched at* and thus rubbed away. The scratchy nature of the erosion suggested an animal; probably a dog, for of all domesticated animals the dog is the most inveterate scratcher. In other words, a dog had visited this room at various times during the summer nights and scratched away on the rug at this spot."

"But how could you be sure?" protested Jenny.

"Not by that alone. But there were confirmations. The sounds, for example, of your 'ghost.' From the way you described them they might easily have been canine sounds; in fact, you yourself said they were 'inhuman.' I believe you said 'moans, mutters, whimpers, slithery noises, patters, scrapings.' Moans and mutters and whimpers—surely a dog in pain or grief, if you're on the track of a dog already? Slithery noises, patters—a dog prowling about. Scrapings—a dog scratching . . . in this case, at the rug. I felt it was significant." He sighed. "Then there was the matter of the *occasions* your ghost selected for his visitations to the cabin. As far as any one could tell, he never came when the cabin was unoccupied. And yet that is when you would ex-

pect a marauder to come. Why did he come only when
some one was in the cabin? Well, Isaac told me that in
empty cabins the windows are kept closed—not locked,
merely closed. But a *human* marauder wouldn't be
stopped by a closed window; wouldn't be stopped, when
it comes to that, even by a locked window. Again the
suggestion of an animal, you see. He was able to get
in only when one of the windows was *open;* he could
get in therefore only at such times as the cabin was
occupied and its occupants *left* the living-room window
open."

"By Godfrey!" muttered Cap'n Hosey.

"There were other confirmations, too. There had
been evidence of one police dog in this case, a female. It
had come here with Gillette. Yet when the Chicago
detectives burst into the cabin and found Gillette apparently gone (which was what Barker relied on), they
found indirect evidence—had they realized it—not of
one dog but of *two.* For there was the heavy *double*
chain. Why a double chain? Wouldn't one heavy
chain be enough for even the most powerful dog? So
there was another confirmation of an extra dog, a live
dog—confirmation that Gillette really had had two all
the time, although no one knew of the existence of the
second; that when Miss Jenny tried to peer into Gillette's car in the garage there was still another dog behind the one that tried to bite her hand; that Gillette,
fearing the dogs would betray him, then took them both
into his cabin and chained them there. They were helpless while Barker murdered the thief. He must have
battered the heads of the two dogs—perhaps with this
very iron poker—thinking he was killing them both.
Any barks or growls they may have uttered were quite
swallowed up in the noise of the rain and thunder that

night, as were the sounds of Barker's hammering down the boards afterward. Barker then must have dragged the two dogs' bodies out into the woods, reasoning that it would be assumed Gillette had killed them. But the male was not dead, only badly stunned—you saw the terrible scar on his head, which is what permitted me to reconstruct Barker's activity against the animals. The male recovered and slunk off. You see, the double chain, the storm that night, the wound—they tell a remarkably clear story."

"But why—" began Heiman, who had crept into the cabin a moment before.

Ellery shrugged. "There are lots of whys. Incidentally, the wound itself on Barker's throat confirmed my theory of a dog—a ragged slashing above the jugular. That's a dog's method of killing. But why, I asked myself, had the dog remained invisibly in the neighborhood, as he must have—prowling the woods, wild, wolfish, existing on small game or refuse? Why had he persisted in returning to this cabin and scratching on the rug—of all things? There could be only one answer. Something he loved was *below that rug*, at that exact spot. Not the female dog, probably his mate—she was dead and had been taken away. Then his master. But his master was Gillette. Was it possible, then, that Gillette had not made his escape, but was under the floor? It was the only answer; and if he was under the floor he was dead. After that it was easy. Barker wanted this cabin tonight badly. He went to the rug, stooped over to lift it. The dog was watching, sprang through the window. . . ."

"You mean to say," gasped Cap'n Hosey, "he reco'-nized Barker?"

Ellery smiled wanly. "Who knows? I don't give

dogs credit for human intelligence, although they do startling enough things at times. If he did, then he must have lain paralyzed from Barker's blow on the night of Gillette's murder, but still conscious enough to witness Barker's burial of the body under the floor of the cabin. Either that, or it was merely that an alien hand was desecrating his master's grave. In any event, I knew Barker must have murdered Gillette; the juxtaposition of his sample trunks with its contents and the use of quicklime on the body was too significant."

"But why did Barker come back, Mr. Queen?" whispered Jenny. "That was stupid—ghoulish." She shivered.

"The answer to that, I fancy," murmured Ellery, "is simplicity itself. I have a notion—" They were in the alcove. He went out into the living room where Benson and his men were squatting over the hole in the floor, raking in the mess below with hammers and chisels. "Well, Benson?"

"Got it, by Christopher!" roared Benson, leaping to his feet and dropping a hammer. "You were dead right, Mr. Queen!" In his hand there was an enormous raw diamond.

"I thought so," murmured Ellery. "If Barker deliberately came back it could only have been for one reason, since the body was well buried and Gillette was considered to be alive. That was—the loot. But he must have taken what he thought to be the loot when he murdered Gillette. Therefore he had been fooled—Gillette, the lapidary, had cleverly made a paste replica of the diamond before he skipped, and it was the replica that Barker had stolen. When he discovered his error after leaving here in July it was too late. So he had to wait until his next sales trip to New Bedford and dig back under the floor. That was why he was crouched over that spot on the rug when the dog jumped him."

There was a little silence. Then Jenny said softly: "I think y— it's perfectly wonderful, Mr. Queen." She patted her hair.

Ellery shuffled to the door. "Wonderful? There's only one wonderful thing about this case, aside from the unorthodox identity of the murderer, my dear. Some day I shall write a monograph on the phenomenon of coincidence."

"What's that?" demanded Jenny.

He opened the door and sniffed the crisp morning air, its invigorating fillip of salt, with grateful nostils. The first streaks of dawn were visible in the cold black sky. "The name," he chuckled, "of the inn."

The Adventure of
THE GLASS-DOMED CLOCK

The Adventure of
THE GLASS-DOMED CLOCK

Of all the hundreds of criminal cases in the solution of which Mr. Ellery Queen participated by virtue of his self-imposed authority as son of the famous Inspector Queen of the New York Detective Bureau, he has steadfastly maintained that none offered a simpler diagnosis than the case which he has designated as "The Adventure of the Glass-Domed Clock." "So simple," he likes to say—sincerely!—"that a sophomore student in high school with the most elementary knowledge of algebraic mathematics would find it as easy to solve as the merest equation." He has been asked, as a result of such remarks, what a poor untutored first-grade detective on the regular police force—whose training in algebra might be something less than elementary—could be expected to make of such a "simple" case. His invariably serious response has been: "Amendment accepted. The resolution now reads: Anybody with common sense could have solved that crime. It's as basic as five minus four leaves one."

This was a little cruel, when it is noted that among those who had opportunity—and certainly wishfulness —to solve the crime was Mr. Ellery Queen's own father, the Inspector, certainly not the most stupid of criminal investigators. But then Mr. Ellery Queen, for all his mental prowess, is sometimes prone to confuse his definitions: *viz.*, his uncanny capacity for strict logic is far from the average citizen's common sense. Certainly one would not be inclined to term elementary a problem in which such components as the following figured: a pure purple amethyst, a somewhat bedraggled expatriate from Czarist Russia, a silver loving-cup, a poker game, five birthday encomiums, and of course that peculiarly ugly relic of early Americana catalogued as "the glass-domed clock"—among others! On the surface the thing seems too utterly fantastic, a maniac's howling nightmare. Anybody with Ellery's cherished "common sense" would have said so. Yet when he arranged those weird elements in their proper order and pointed out the "obvious" answer to the riddle—with that almost monastic intellectual innocence of his, as if everybody possessed his genius for piercing the veil of complexities! —Inspector Queen, good Sergeant Velie, and the others figuratively rubbed their eyes, the thing was so clear.

It began, as murders do, with a corpse. From the first the eeriness of the whole business struck those who stood about in the faintly musked atmosphere of Martin Orr's curio shop and stared down at the shambles that had been Martin Orr. Inspector Queen, for one, refused to credit the evidence of his old senses; and it was not the gory nature of the crime that gave him pause, for he was as familiar with scenes of carnage as a butcher and blood no longer made him squeamish. That Martin Orr, the celebrated little Fifth Avenue curio dealer whose establishment was a treasure-house of authentic rarities, had had his shiny little bald head bashed to red ruin—this was an indifferent if practical detail; the bludgeon, a heavy paperweight spattered with blood but wiped clean of fingerprints, lay not far from the body; so *that* much was clear. No, it was not the assault on Orr that opened their eyes, but what Orr had apparently done, as he lay gasping out his life on the cold cement floor of his shop, *after* the assault.

The reconstruction of events after Orr's assailant had fled the shop, leaving the curio dealer for dead, seemed perfectly legible: having been struck down in the main chamber of his establishment, toward the rear, Martin Orr had dragged his broken body six feet along a counter—the red trail told the story plainly—had by superhuman effort raised himself to a case of precious and semi-precious stones, had smashed the thin glass with a feeble fist, had groped about among the gem-trays, grasped a large unset amethyst, fallen back to the floor with the stone tightly clutched in his left hand, had then crawled on a tangent five feet past a table of antique clocks to a stone pedestal, raised himself again, and deliberately dragged off the pedestal the object it supported—an old clock with a glass dome over it—so that the clock fell to the floor by his side, shattering its fragile case into a thousand pieces. And there Martin Orr had died, in his left fist the amethyst, his bleeding right hand resting on the clock as if in benediction. By some miracle the clock's machinery had not been injured by the fall; it had been one of Martin Orr's fetishes to keep all his magnificent timepieces running; and to the bewildered ears of the little knot of men surrounding Martin Orr's corpse that gray Sunday morning came the pleasant *tick-tick-tick* of the no longer glass-domed clock.

Weird? It was insane!

"There ought to be a law against it," growled Sergeant Velie.

Dr. Samuel Prouty, Assistant Medical Examiner of New York County, rose from his examination of the body and prodded Martin Orr's dead buttocks—the curio dealer was lying face down—with his foot.

"Now here's an old coot," he said grumpily, "sixty if he's a day, with more real stamina than many a youngster. Marvelous powers of resistance! He took a fearful beating about the head and shoulders, his assailant left him for dead, and the old monkey clung to life long enough to make a tour about the place! Many a younger man would have died in his tracks."

"Your professional admiration leaves me cold," said Ellery. He had been awakened out of a pleasantly warm bed not a half-hour before to find Djuna, the Queens' gypsy boy-of-all-work, shaking him. The Inspector had already gone, leaving word for Ellery, if he should be so minded, to follow. Ellery was always so minded when his nose sniffed crime, but he had not had breakfast and he was thoroughly out of temper. So his taxicab had rushed through Fifth Avenue to Martin Orr's shop, and he had found the Inspector and Sergeant Velie already on the cluttered scene interrogating a grief-stunned old woman—Martin Orr's aged widow —and a badly frightened Slavic giant who introduced himself in garbled English as the "ex-Duke Paul." The ex-Duke Paul, it developed, had been one of Nicholas Romanov's innumerable cousins caught in the whirlpool of the Russian revolution who had managed to flee the homeland and was eking out a none too fastidious living in New York as a sort of social curiosity. This was in 1926, when royal Russian expatriates were still something of a novelty in the land of democracy. As Ellery pointed out much later, this was not only 1926, but precisely Sunday, March the seventh, 1926, although at the time it seemed ridiculous to consider the specific date of any importance whatever.

"Who found the body?" demanded Ellery, puffing at his first cigaret of the day.

"His Nibs here," said Sergeant Velie, hunching his colossal shoulders. "*And* the lady. Seems like the Dook or whatever he is has been workin' a racket—been a kind of stooge for the old duck that was murdered. Orr used to give him commissions on the customers he brought in —and I understand he brought in plenty. Anyway, Mrs. Orr here got sort of worried when her hubby didn't come home last night from the poker game. . . ."

"Poker game?"

The Russian's dark face lighted up. "Yuss. Yuss. It is remarkable game. I have learned it since my sojourn in your so amazing country. Meester Orr, myself, and some others here play each week. Yuss." His face fell, and some of his fright returned. He looked fleetingly at the corpse and began to edge away.

"You played last night?" asked Ellery in a savage voice.

The Russian nodded. Inspector Queen said: "We're rounding 'em up. It seems that Orr, the Duke, and four other men had a sort of poker club, and met in Orr's back room there every Saturday night and played till all hours. Looked over that back room, but there's nothing there except the cards and chips. When Orr didn't come home Mrs. Orr got frightened and called up the Duke—he lives at some squirty little hotel in the Forties—the Duke called for her, they came down here this morning. . . . This is what they found." The Inspector eyed Martin Orr's corpse and the débris of glass surrounding him with gloom, almost with resentment. "Crazy, isn't it?"

Ellery glanced at Mrs. Orr; she was leaning against a counter, frozen-faced. tearless, staring down at her husband's body as if she could not believe her eyes. Actually, there was little to see: for Dr. Prouty had flung outspread sheets of a Sunday newspaper over the body, and only the left hand—still clutching the amethyst—was visible.

"Unbelievably so," said Ellery dryly. "I suppose there's a desk in the back room where Orr kept his accounts?"

"Sure."

"Any paper on Orr's body?"

"Paper?" repeated the Inspector in bewilderment. "Why, no."

"Pencil or pen?"

"No. Why, for heaven's sake?"

Before Ellery could reply, a little old man with a face like wrinkled brown papyrus pushed past a detective at the front door; he walked like a man in a dream. His gaze fixed on the shapeless bulk and the bloodstains. Then, incredibly, he blinked four times and began to cry. His weazened frame jerked with sobs. Mrs. Orr awoke from her trance; she cried: "Oh, Sam, Sam!" and, putting her arms around the newcomer's racked shoulders, began to weep with him.

Ellery and the Inspector looked at each other, and Sergeant Velie belched his disgust. Then the Inspector grasped the crying man's little arm and shook him. "Here, stop that!" he said gruffly. "Who are you?"

The man raised his tear-stained face from Mrs. Orr's shoulder; he blubbered: "S-Sam Mingo, S-Sam Mingo, Mr. Orr's assistant. Who—who— Oh, I can't believe it!" and he buried his face in Mrs. Orr's shoulder again.

"Got to let him cry himself out, I guess," said the Inspector, shrugging. "Ellery, what the deuce do you make of it? I'm stymied."

Ellery raised his eyebrows eloquently. A detective appeared in the street-door escorting a pale, trembling man. "Here's Arnold Pike, Chief. Dug him out of bed just now."

Pike was a man of powerful physique and jutting jaw; but he was thoroughly unnerved and, somehow, bewildered. He fastened his eyes on the heap which represented Martin Orr's mortal remains and kept mechanically buttoning and unbuttoning his overcoat. The Inspector said: "I understand you and a few others played poker in the back room here last night. With Orr. What time did you break up?"

"Twelve-thirty." Pike's voice wabbled drunkenly.

"What time did you start?"

"Around eleven."

"Cripes," said Inspector Queen, "that's not a poker game, that's a game of tiddledywinks. . . . Who killed Orr, Mr. Pike?"

Arnold Pike tore his eyes from the corpse. "God, sir, I don't know."

"You don't, hey? All friends, were you?"

"Yes. Oh, yes."

"What's your business, Mr. Pike?"

"I'm a stock-broker."

"Why—" began Ellery, and stopped. Under the urging of two detectives, three men advanced into the shop —all frightened, all exhibiting evidences of hasty awakening and hasty dressing, all fixing their eyes at once on the paper-covered bundle on the floor, the streaks of blood, the shattered glass. The three, like the incredible ex-Duke Paul, who was straight and stiff and somehow ridiculous, seemed petrified; men crushed by a sudden blow.

A small fat man with brilliant eyes muttered that he

was Stanley Oxman, jeweler. Martin Orr's oldest, closest friend. He could not believe it. It was frightful, unheard of. Martin murdered! No, he could offer no explanation. Martin had been a peculiar man, perhaps, but as far as he, Oxman, knew the curio dealer had not had an enemy in the world. And so on, and so on, as the other two stood by, frozen, waiting their turn.

One was a lean, debauched fellow with the mark of the ex-athlete about him. His slight paunch and yellowed eyeballs could not conceal the signs of a vigorous prime. This was, said Oxman, their mutual friend, Leo Gurney, the newspaper feature-writer. The other was J. D. Vincent, said Oxman—developing an unexpected streak of talkativeness which the Inspector fanned gently—who, like Arnold Pike, was in Wall Street—"a manipulator," whatever that was. Vincent, a stocky man with the gambler's tight face, seemed incapable of speech; as for Gurney, he seemed glad that Oxman had constituted himself spokesman and kept staring at the body on the cement floor.

Ellery sighed, thought of his warm bed, put down the rebellion in his breakfastless stomach, and went to work —keeping an ear cocked for the Inspector's sharp questions and the halting replies. Ellery followed the streaks of blood to the spot where Orr had ravished the case of gems. The case, its glass front smashed, little frazzled splinters framing the orifice, contained more than a dozen metal trays floored with black velvet, set in two rows. Each held scores of gems—a brilliant array of semi-precious and precious stones beautifully variegated in color. Two trays in the center of the front row attracted his eye particularly—one containing highly polished stones of red, brown, yellow, and green; the other a single variety, all of a subtranslucent quality, leek-green in color, and covered with small red spots. Ellery noted that both these trays were in direct line with the place where Orr's hand had smashed the glass case.

He went over to the trembling little assistant, Sam Mingo, who had quieted down and was standing by Mrs. Orr, clutching her hand like a child. "Mingo," he said, touching the man. Mingo started with a leap of his stringy muscles. "Don't be alarmed, Mingo. Just step over here with me for a moment." Ellery smiled reassuringly, took the man's arm, and led him to the shattered case.

And Ellery said: "How is it that Martin Orr bothered with such trifles as these? I see rubies here, and emeralds, but the others. . . . Was he a jeweler as well as a curio dealer?"

Orr's assistant mumbled: "No. N-no, he was not. But he always liked the baubles. The baubles, he called them. Kept them for love. Most of them are birthstones. He sold a few. This is a complete line."

"What are those green stones with the red spots?"

"Bloodstones."

"And this tray of red, brown, yellow, and green ones?"

"All jaspers. The common ones are red, brown, and yellow. The few green ones in the tray are more valuable. . . . The bloodstone is itself a variety of jasper. Beautiful! And . . ."

"Yes, yes," said Ellery hastily. "From which tray did the amethyst in Orr's hand come, Mingo?"

Mingo shivered and pointed a crinkled forefinger to a tray in the rear row, at the corner of the case.

"*All* the amethysts are kept in this one tray?"

"Yes. You can see for yourself—"

"Here!" growled the Inspector, approaching. "Mingo!

I want you to look over the stock. Check everything.
See if anything's been stolen."

"Yes, sir," said Orr's assistant timidly, and began to
potter about the shop with lagging steps. Ellery looked
about. The door to the back room was twenty-five feet
from the spot where Orr had been assaulted. No desk
in the shop itself, he observed, no paper about. . . .

"Well, son," said the Inspector in troubled tones, "it
looks as if we're on the trail of something. I don't like
it. . . . Finally dragged it out of these birds. I *thought*
it was funny, this business of breaking up a weekly Saturday night poker game at half-past twelve. They had
a fight!"

"Who engaged in fisticuffs with whom?"

"Oh, don't be funny. It's this Pike feller, the stock-
broker. Seems they all had something to drink during
the game. They played stud, and Orr, with an ace-
king-queen-jack showing, raised the roof off the play.
Everybody dropped out except Pike; he had three sixes.
Well, Orr gave it everything he had and when Pike
threw his cards away on a big over-raise, Orr cackled,
showed his hole-card—a deuce!—and raked in the pot.
Pike, who'd lost his pile on the hand, began to grumble;
he and Orr had words—you know how those things
start. They were all pie-eyed, anyway, says the Duke.
Almost a fist-fight. The others interfered, but it broke
up the game."

"They all left together?"

"Yes. Orr stayed behind to clean up the mess in the
backroom. The five others went out together and separated a few blocks away. Any one of 'em could have
come back and pulled off the job before Orr shut up
shop!"

"And what does Pike say?"

"What the deuce would you expect him to say? That he went right home and to bed, of course."

"The others?"

"They deny any knowledge of what happened after they left here last night. . . . Well, Mingo? Anything missing?"

Mingo said helplessly: "Everything seems all right."

"I thought so," said the Inspector with satisfaction. "This is a grudge kill, son. Well, I want to talk to these fellers some more. . . . What's eating you?"

Ellery lighted a cigaret. "A few random thoughts. Have you decided in your own mind why Orr dragged himself about the shop when he was three-quarters dead, broke the glass-domed clock, pulled an amethyst out of the gem-case?"

"That," said the Inspector, the troubled look returning, "is what I'm all foggy about. I can't— 'Scuse me." He returned hastily to the waiting group of men.

Ellery took Mingo's lax arm. "Get a grip on yourself, man. I want you to look at that smashed clock for a moment. Don't be afraid of Orr—dead men don't bite, Mingo." He pushed the little assistant toward the paper-covered corpse. "Now tell me something about that clock. Has it a history?"

"Not much of one. It's a h-hundred and sixty-nine years old. Not especially valuable. Curious piece because of the glass dome over it. Happens to be the only glass-domed clock we have. That's all."

Ellery polished the lenses of his *pince-nez*, set the glasses firmly on his nose, and bent over to examine the fallen clock. It had a black wooden base, circular, about nine inches deep, and scarified with age. On this the clock was set—ticking away cosily. The dome of glass had fitted into a groove around the top of the black base, sheathing the clock completely. With the dome unshattered, the entire piece must have stood about two feet high.

Ellery rose, and his lean face was thoughtful. Mingo looked at him in a sort of stupid anxiety. "Did Pike, Oxman, Vincent, Gurney, or Paul ever own this piece?"

Mingo shook his head. "No, sir. We've had it for many years. We couldn't get rid of it. Certainly *those* gentlemen didn't want it."

"Then none of the five ever tried to purchase the clock?"

"Of course not."

"Admirable," said Ellery. "Thank you." Mingo felt that he had been dismissed; he hesitated, shuffled his feet, and finally went over to the silent widow and stood by her side. Ellery knelt on the cement floor and with difficulty loosened the grip of the dead man's fingers about the amethyst. He saw that the stone was a clear glowing purple in color, shook his head as if in perplexity, and rose.

Vincent, the stocky Wall Street gambler with the tight face, was saying to the Inspector in a rusty voice: "—can't see why you suspect any of us. Pike particularly. What's in a little quarrel? We've always been good friends, all of us. Last night we were pickled—"

"Sure," said the Inspector gently. "Last night you were pickled. A drunk sort of forgets himself at times, Vincent. Liquor affects a man's morals as well as his head."

"Nuts!" said the yellow-eyeballed Gurney suddenly. "Stop sleuthing, Inspector. You're barking up the wrong tree. Vincent's right. We're all friends. It was Pike's birthday last week." Ellery stood very still. "We all sent him gifts. Had a celebration, and Orr was the cockiest of us all. Does that look like the preparation for a pay-off?"

Ellery stepped forward, and his eyes were shining. All his temper had fled by now, and his nostrils were quivering with the scent of the chase. "And when was this celebration held, gentlemen?" he asked softly.

Stanley Oxman puffed out his cheeks. "Now they're going to suspect a birthday blowout! Last Monday, mister. This past Monday. What of it?"

"This past Monday," said Ellery. "How nice. Mr. Pike, your gifts—"

"For God's sake. . . ." Pike's eyes were tortured.

"When did you receive them?"

"After the party, during the week. Boys sent them up to me. I didn't see any of them until last night, at the poker game."

The others nodded their heads in concert; the Inspector was looking at Ellery with puzzlement. Ellery grinned, adjusted his *pince-nez,* and spoke to his father aside. The weight of the Inspector's puzzlement, if his face was a scale, increased. But he said quietly to the white-haired broker: "Mr. Pike, you're going to take a little trip with Mr. Queen and Sergeant Velie. Just for a few moments. The others of you stay here with me. Mr. Pike, please remember not to try anything—foolish."

Pike was incapable of speech; his head twitched sidewise and he buttoned his coat for the twentieth time. Nobody said anything. Sergeant Velie took Pike's arm, and Ellery preceded them into the early-morning peace of Fifth Avenue. On the sidewalk he asked Pike his address, the broker dreamily gave him a street-and-number, Ellery hailed a taxicab, and the three men were driven in silence to an apartment-building a mile farther uptown. They took a self-service elevator to the seventh floor, marched a few steps to a door, Pike fumbled with a key, and they went into his apartment.

"Let me see your gifts, please," said Ellery without expression—the first words uttered since they had stepped into the taxicab. Pike led them to a den-like room. On a table stood four boxes of different shapes, and a handsome silver cup. "There," he said in a cracked voice.

Ellery went swiftly to the table. He picked up the silver cup. On it was engraved the sentimental legend:

> *To a True Friend*
> ARNOLD PIKE
> *March 1, 1876, to* ——
> *J. D. Vincent*

"Rather macabre humor, Mr. Pike," said Ellery, setting the cup down, "since Vincent has had space left for the date of your demise." Pike began to speak, then shivered and clamped his pale lips together.

Ellery removed the lid of a tiny black box. Inside, imbedded in a cleft between two pieces of purple velvet, there was a man's signet-ring, a magnificent and heavy circlet the signet of which revealed the coat-of-arms of royalist Russia. "The tattered old eagle," murmured Ellery. "Let's see what our friend the ex-Duke has to say." On a card in the box, inscribed in minute script, the following was written in French:

> To my good friend Arnold Pike on his 50th birthday. March the first ever makes me sad. I remember that day in 1917—two weeks before the Czar's abdication—the quiet, then the storm. . . . But be merry, Arnold!

Accept this signet-ring. given to me by my
royal Cousin, as a token of my esteem. Long
life!

Paul

Ellery did not comment. He restored ring and card
to the box, and picked up another, a large flat packet.
Inside there was a gold-tipped Morocco-leather wallet.
The card tucked into one of the pockets said:

"Twenty-one years of life's rattle
And men are no longer boys,
They gird their loins for the battle
And throw away their toys—

"But here's a cheerful plaything
For a white-haired old mooncalf,
Who may act like any May-thing
For nine years more and a half!"

"Charming verse," chuckled Ellery. "Another misbegotten poet. Only a newspaper man would indite
such nonsense. This is Gurney's?"

"Yes," muttered Pike. "It's nice, isn't it?"

"If you'll pardon me," said Ellery, "it's rotten." He
threw aside the wallet and seized a larger carton. Inside there was a glittering pair of patent-leather carpet
slippers; the card attached read:

Happy Birthday, Arnold! May We Be All
Together On as Pleasant a March First to
Celebrate Your 100th Anniversary!

Martin

"A poor prophet," said Ellery dryly. "And what's
this?" He laid the shoebox down and picked up a small

flat box. In it he saw a gold-plated cigaret-case, with the initials *A. P.* engraved on the lid. The accompanying card read:

> Good luck on your fiftieth birthday. I look forward to your sixtieth on March first, 1936, for another bout of whoopee!
>
> *Stanley Oxman*

"And Mr. Stanley Oxman," remarked Ellery, putting down the cigaret-case, "was a little less sanguine than Martin Orr. His imagination reached no farther than sixty, Mr. Pike. A significant point."

"I can't see—" began the broker in a stubborn little mutter, "why you have to bring my friends into it—"

Sergeant Velie gripped his elbow, and he winced. Ellery shook his head disapprovingly at the man-mountain. "And now, Mr. Pike, I think we may return to Martin Orr's shop. Or, as the Sergeant might fastidiously phrase it, the scene of the crime. . . . Very interesting. *Very* interesting. It almost compensates for an empty belly."

"You got something?" whispered Sergeant Velie hoarsely as Pike preceded them into a taxicab downstairs.

"Cyclops," said Ellery, "all God's chillun got something. But *I* got everything."

Sergeant Velie disappeared somewhere *en route* to the curio shop, and Arnold Pike's spirits lifted at once. Ellery eyed him quizzically. "One thing, Mr. Pike," he said as the taxicab turned into Fifth Avenue, "before we disembark. How long have you six men been acquainted?"

The broker sighed. "It's complicated. *My* only friend of considerable duration is Leo; Gurney, you know. Known each other for fifteen years. But then Orr and the Duke have been friends since 1918, I understand, and of course Stan Oxman and Orr have known each other—knew each other—for many years. I met Vincent about a year ago through my business affiliations and introduced him into our little clique."

"Had you yourself and the others—Oxman, Orr, Paul—been acquainted before this time two years ago?"

Pike looked puzzled. "I don't see . . . Why, no. I met Oxman and the Duke a year and a half ago through Orr."

"And that," murmured Ellery, "is so perfect that I don't care if I *never* have breakfast. Here we are, Mr. Pike."

They found a glum group awaiting their return— nothing had changed, except that Orr's body had disappeared, Dr. Prouty was gone, and some attempt at sweeping up the glass fragments of the domed clock had been made. The Inspector was in a fever of impatience, demanded to know where Sergeant Velie was, what Ellery had sought in Pike's apartment. . . . Ellery whispered something to him, and the old man looked startled. Then he dipped his fingers into his brown snuff-box and partook with grim relish.

The regal expatriate cleared his bull throat. "You have mystery re-solved?" he rumbled. "Yuss?"

"Your Highness," said Ellery gravely, "I have indeed mystery re-solved." He whirled and clapped his palms together; they jumped. "Attention, please! Piggott," he said to a detective, "stand at that door and don't let any one in but Sergeant Velie."

The detective nodded. Ellery studied the faces about

him. If one of them was apprehensive, he had ample control of his physiognomy. They all seemed merely interested, now that the first shock of the tragedy had passed them by. Mrs. Orr clung to Mingo's fragile hand; her eyes did not once leave Ellery's face. The fat little jeweler, the journalist, the two Wall Street men, the Russian ex-duke . . .

"An absorbing affair," grinned Ellery, "and quite elementary, despite its points of interest. Follow me closely." He went over to the counter and picked up the purple amethyst which had been clutched in the dead man's hand. He looked at it and smiled. Then he glanced at the other object on the counter—the round-based clock, with the fragments of its glass dome protruding from the circular groove.

"Consider the situation. Martin Orr, brutally beaten about the head, manages in a last desperate living action to crawl to the jewel-case on the counter, pick out this gem, then go to the stone pedestal and pull the glass-domed clock from it. Whereupon, his mysterious mission accomplished, he dies.

"Why should a dying man engage in such a baffling procedure? There can be only one general explanation. He knows his assailant and is endeavoring to leave clues to his assailant's identity." At this point the Inspector nodded, and Ellery grinned again behind the curling smoke of his cigaret. "But such clues! Why? Well, what would you expect a dying man to do if he wished to leave behind him the name of his murderer? The answer is obvious: he would write it. But on Orr's body we find no paper, pen, or pencil; and no paper in the immediate vicinity. Where else might he secure writing materials? Well, you will observe that Martin Orr was assaulted at a spot twenty-five feet from the door of the back room. The distance, Orr must have felt, was too great for his failing strength. Then Orr couldn't write the name of his murderer except by the somewhat fantastic method of dipping his finger into his own blood and using the floor as a slate. Such an expedient probably didn't occur to him.

"He must have reasoned with rapidity, life ebbing out of him at every breath. Then—he crawled to the case, broke the glass, took out the amethyst. Then—he crawled to the pedestal and dragged off the glass-domed clock. Then—he died. So the amethyst and the clock were Martin Orr's bequest to the police. You can almost hear him say: 'Don't fail me. This is clear, simple, easy. Punish my murderer.'"

Mrs. Orr gasped, but the expression on her wrinkled face did not alter. Mingo began to sniffle. The others waited in total silence.

"The clock first," said Ellery lazily. "The first thing one thinks of in connection with a timepiece is time. Was Orr trying, then, by dragging the clock off the pedestal, to smash the works and, stopping the clock, so fix the time of his murder? Offhand a possibility, it is true; but if this was his purpose, it failed, because the clock didn't stop running after all. While this circumstance does not invalidate the time-interpretation, further consideration of the whole problem does. For you five gentlemen had left Orr in a body. The time of the assault could not possibly be so checked against your return to your several residences as to point inescapably to one of you as the murderer. Orr must have realized this, if he thought of it at all; in other words, there wouldn't be any particular *point* to such a purpose on Orr's part.

"And there is still another—and more conclusive—

consideration that invalidates the time-interpretation; and that is, that Orr crawled *past* a table full of running clocks to get to this glass-domed one. If it had been time he was intending to indicate, he could have preserved his energies by stopping at this table and pulling down one of the many clocks upon it. But no—he deliberately passed that table to get to the *glass-domed* clock. So it wasn't time.

"Very well. Now, since the glass-domed clock is *the only one* of its kind in the shop, it must have been not time in the general sense but this particular timepiece in the specific sense by which Martin Orr was motivated. But what could this particular timepiece possibly indicate? In itself, as Mr. Mingo has informed me, it has no personal connotation with any one connected with Orr. The idea that Orr was leaving a clue to a clockmaker is unsound; none of you gentlemen follows that delightful craft, and certainly Mr. Oxman, the jeweler, could not have been indicated when so many things in the gem-case would have served."

Oxman began to perspire; he fixed his eyes on the jewel in Ellery's hand.

"Then it wasn't a professional meaning from the clock, as a clock," continued Ellery equably, "that Orr was trying to convey. But what is there about this particular clock which is different from the other clocks in the shop?" Ellery shot his forefinger forward. "This particular clock has a glass dome over it!" He straightened slowly. "Can any of you gentlemen think of a fairly common object almost perfectly suggested by a glass-domed clock?"

No one answered, but Vincent and Pike began to lick their lips. "I see signs of intelligence," said Ellery. "Let me be more specific. What is it—I feel like Sam

Lloyd!—that has a base, a glass dome, and ticking machinery inside the dome?" Still no answer. "Well," said Ellery, "I suppose I should have expected reticence. Of course, *it's a stock-ticker!*"

They stared at him, and then all eyes turned to examine the whitening faces of J. D. Vincent and Arnold Pike. "Yes," said Ellery, "you may well gaze upon the countenances of the *Messieurs* Vincent and Pike. For they are the only two of our little cast who are connected with stock-tickers: Mr. Vincent is a Wall Street operator, Mr. Pike is a broker." Quietly two detectives left a wall and approached the two men.

"Whereupon," said Ellery, "we lay aside the glass-domed clock and take up this very fascinating little bauble in my hand." He held up the amethyst. "A purple amethyst—there are bluish-violet ones, you know. What could this purple amethyst have signified to Martin Orr's frantic brain? The obvious thing is that it is a jewel. Mr. Oxman looked disturbed a moment ago; you needn't be, sir. The jewelry significance of this amethyst is eliminated on two counts. The first is that the tray on which the amethysts lie is in a corner at the rear of the shattered case. It was necessary for Orr to reach far into the case. If it was a jewel he sought, why didn't he pick any one of the stones nearer to his palsied hand? For any single one of them would connote 'jeweler.' But no; Orr went to the excruciating trouble of ignoring what was close at hand—as in the business of the clock—and deliberately selected something from an inconvenient place. Then the amethyst did not signify a jeweler, but something else.

"The second is this, Mr. Oxman: certainly Orr knew that the stock-ticker clue would not fix guilt on *one* person; for two of his cronies are connected with stocks.

On the other hand, did Orr have two assailants, rather
than one? Not likely. For if by the amethyst he
meant to connote you, Mr. Oxman, and by the glass-
domed clock he meant to connote either Mr. Pike or Mr.
Vincent, he was still leaving a wabbly trail; for we still
would not know whether Mr. Pike or Mr. Vincent was
meant. Did he have *three* assailants, then? You see, we
are already in the realm of fantasy. No, the major prob-
ability is that, since the glass-domed clock cut the possibilities down to two persons, the amethyst was meant to
single out one of those two.

"How does the amethyst pin one of these gentlemen
down? What significance besides the obvious one of
jewelry does the amethyst suggest? Well, it is a rich
purple in color. Ah, but one of your coterie fits here:
His Highness the ex-Duke is certainly one born to the
royal purple, even if it is an ex-ducal purple, as it
were. . . ."

The soldierly Russian growled: "I am *not* Highness.
You know nothing of royal address!" His dark face became suffused with blood, and he broke into a volley of
guttural Russian.

Ellery grinned. "Don't excite yourself—Your Grace,
is it? *You* weren't meant. For if we postulate you, we
again drag in a third person and leave unsettled the
question of which Wall Street man Orr meant to accuse;
we're no better off than before. Avaunt, royalty!

"Other possible significances? Yes. There is a species of humming-bird, for instance, known as the
amethyst. Out! We have no aviarists here. For another thing, the amethyst was connected with ancient
Hebrew ritual—an Orientalist told me this once—
breastplate decoration of the high-priest, or some such
thing. Obviously inapplicable here. No, there is only

one other possible application." Ellery turned to the stocky gambler. "Mr. Vincent, what is your birth-date?"

Vincent stammered: "November s-second."

"Splendid. That eliminates *you*." Ellery stopped abruptly. There was a stir at the door and Sergeant Velie barged in with a very grim face. Ellery smiled. "Well, Sergeant, was my hunch about motive correct?"

Velie said: "And how. He forged Orr's signature to a big check. Money-trouble, all right. Orr hushed the matter up, paid, and said he'd collect from the forger. The banker doesn't even know who the forger is."

"Congratulations are in order, Sergeant. Our murderer evidently wished to evade repayment. Murders have been committed for less vital reasons." Ellery flourished his *pince-nez*. "I said, Mr. Vincent, that you are eliminated. Eliminated because the only other significance of the amethyst left to us is that it is a *birth-stone*. But the November birth-stone is a topaz. On the other hand, Mr. Pike has just celebrated a birthday which . . ."

And with these words, as Pike gagged and the others broke into excited gabble, Ellery made a little sign to Sergeant Velie, and himself leaped forward. But it was not Arnold Pike who found himself in the crushing grip of Velie and staring into Ellery's amused eyes.

It was the newspaper man, Leo Gurney.

"As I said," explained Ellery later, in the privacy of the Queens' living-room and after his belly had been comfortably filled with food, "this has been a ridiculously elementary problem." The Inspector toasted his stockinged feet before the fire, and grunted. Sergeant Velie scratched his head. "You don't think so?

"But look. It was evident, when I decided what the clues of the clock and the amethyst were intended to convey, that Arnold Pike was the man meant to be indicated. For what is the month of which the amethyst is the birth-stone? *February*—in both the Polish and Jewish birth-stone systems, the two almost universally recognized. Of the two men indicated by the clock-clue, Vincent was eliminated because his birthstone is a topaz. Was Pike's birthday then in February? Seemingly not, for he celebrated it—this year, 1926—in March! March first, observe. What could this mean? Only one thing: since Pike was the sole remaining possibility, then his birthday *was* in February, but on the *twenty-ninth*, on Leap Day, as it's called, and 1926 not being a Leap Year, Pike chose to celebrate his birthday on the day on which it would ordinarily fall, March first.

"But this meant that Martin Orr, to have left the amethyst, must have known Pike's birthday to be in February, since he seemingly left the February birthstone as a clue. Yet what did I find on the card accompanying Orr's gift of carpet-slippers to Pike last week? 'May we all be together on as pleasant a *March first* to celebrate your hundredth anniversary.' But if Pike is fifty years old in 1926, he was born in 1876—a Leap Year—and his hundredth anniversary would be 1976, also a Leap Year. They *wouldn't* celebrate Pike's birthday on his hundredth anniversary on March first! Then Orr *didn't* know Pike's real birthday was February twenty-ninth, or he would have said so on the card. He thought it was March.

"But the person who left the amethyst sign *did* know Pike's birth-month was February, since he left February's birth-stone. We've just established that Martin

Orr didn't know Pike's birth-month was February, but thought it was March. Therefore Martin Orr was not the one who selected the amethyst.

"Any confirmation? Yes. The birth-stone for March in the Polish system is the bloodstone; in the Jewish it's the jasper. But both these stones were nearer a groping hand than the amethysts, which lay in a tray at the back of the case. In other words, whoever selected the amethyst deliberately ignored the March stones in favor of the February stone, and therefore knew that Pike was born in February, not in March. But had Orr selected a stone, it would have been bloodstone or jasper, since he believed Pike *was* born in March. Orr eliminated again.

"But if Orr did not select the amethyst, as I've shown, then what have we? Palpably, a frame-up. Some one arranged matters to make us believe that Orr himself had selected the amethyst and smashed the clock. You can see the murderer dragging poor old Orr's dead body around, leaving the blood-trail on purpose. . . ."

Ellery sighed. "I never did believe Orr left those signs. It was all too pat, too slick, too weirdly unreal. It is conceivable that a dying man will leave one clue to his murderer's identity, but *two*. . . ." Ellery shook his head.

"If Orr didn't leave the clues, who did? Obviously the murderer. But the clues deliberately led to Arnold Pike. Then Pike couldn't be the murderer, for certainly he would not leave a trail to himself had he killed Orr.

"Who else? Well, one thing stood out. Whoever killed Orr, framed Pike, and really selected that amethyst, knew Pike's birthday to be in February. Orr and Pike we have eliminated. Vincent didn't know

Pike's birthday was in February, as witness his inscription on the silver cup. Nor did our friend the ex-Duke, who also wrote 'March the first' on his card. Oxman didn't—he said they'd celebrate Pike's sixtieth birthday on March first, 1936—a Leap Year, observe, when Pike's birthday would be celebrated on February twentyninth. . . . Don't forget that we may accept these cards' evidence as valid; the cards were sent before the crime, and the crime would have no connection in the murderer's mind with Pike's five birthday-cards. The flaw in the murderer's plot was that he assumed—a natural error—that Orr and perhaps the others, too, knew Pike's birthday really fell on Leap Day. And he never did see the cards which proved the others didn't know, because Pike himself told us that after the party Monday night he did not see any of the others until last night, the night of the murder."

"I'll be fried in lard," muttered Sergeant Velie, shaking his head.

"No doubt," grinned Ellery. "But we've left some one out. How about Leo Gurney, the newspaper feature-writer? His stick o' doggerel said that Pike wouldn't reach the age of twenty-one for another nine and a half years. Interesting? Yes, and damning. For this means he considered facetiously that Pike was at the time of writing eleven and a half years old. But how is this possible, even in humorous verse? It's possible only if Gurney knew that Pike's birthday falls on February twenty-ninth, which occurs only once in four years! Fifty divided by four is twelve and a half. But since the year 1900 for some reason I've never been able to discover, was not a Leap Year, Gurney was right, and actually Pike had celebrated only 'eleven and a half' birthdays."

And Ellery drawled: "Being the only one who knew Pike's birthday to be in February, then Gurney was the only one who could have selected the amethyst. Then Gurney arranged matters to make it seem that Orr was accusing Pike. Then Gurney was the murderer of Orr. . . .

"Simple? As a child's sum!"

The Adventure of
THE SEVEN BLACK CATS

The Adventure of
THE SEVEN BLACK CATS

The tinkly bell quavered over the door of Miss Curleigh's Pet Shoppe on Amsterdam Avenue, and Mr. Ellery Queen wrinkled his nose and went in. The instant he crossed the threshold he was thankful it was not a large nose, and that he had taken the elementary precaution of wrinkling it. The extent and variety of the little shop's odors would not have shamed the New York Zoological Park itself. And yet it housed only creatures, he was amazed to find, of the puniest proportions; who, upon the micrometrically split second of his entrance, set up such a chorus of howls, yelps, snarls, yawps, grunts, squeaks, caterwauls, croaks, screeches, chirrups, hisses, and growls that it was a miracle the roof did not come down.

"Good afternoon," said a crisp voice. "I'm Miss Curleigh. What can I do for you, please?"

In the midst of raging bedlam Mr. Ellery Queen found himself gazing into a pair of mercurial eyes. There were other details—she was a trim young piece, for example, with masses of titian hair and curves and at least one dimple—but for the moment her eyes engaged his earnest attention. Miss Curleigh, blushing, repeated herself.

"I beg your pardon," said Ellery hastily, returning to the matter at hand, "Apparently in the animal kingdom there is no decent ratio between lung-power and—ah—aroma on the one hand and size on the other. We live and learn! Miss Curleigh, would it be possible to purchase a comparatively noiseless and sweet-smelling canine with frizzy brown hair, inquisitive ears at the half-cock, and crooked hind-legs?"

Miss Curleigh frowned. Unfortunately, she was out of Irish terriers. The last litter had been gobbled up. Perhaps a Scottie—?

Mr. Queen frowned. No, he had been specifically enjoined by Djuna, the martinet, to procure an Irish terrier; no doleful-looking, sawed-off substitute, he was sure, would do.

"I expect," said Miss Curleigh professionally, "to hear from our Long Island kennels tomorrow. If you'll leave your name and address?"

Mr. Queen, gazing into the young woman's eyes, would be delighted to. Mr. Queen, provided with pencil and pad, hastened to indulge his delight.

As Miss Curleigh read what he had written the mask of business fell away. "You're not Mr. *Ellery* Queen!" she exclaimed with animation. "Well, I declare. I've heard *so* much about you, Mr. Queen. And you live practically around the corner, on Eighty-seventh Street! This is really thrilling. I never expected to meet—"

"Nor I," murmured Mr. Queen. "Nor I."

Miss Curleigh blushed again and automatically prodded her hair. "One of my best customers lives right across the street from you, Mr. Queen. I should say one of my most *frequent* customers. Perhaps you know her? A Miss Tarkle—Euphemia Tarkle? She's in that large apartment house, you know."

"I've never had the pleasure," said Mr. Queen absently. "What extraordinary eyes you have! I mean— Euphemia Tarkle? Dear, dear, this is a world of sudden wonders. Is she as improbable as her name?"

"That's unkind," said Miss Curleigh severely, "although she *is* something of a character, the poor creature. A squirrely-faced old lady, *and* an invalid. Paralytic, you know. The queerest, frailest, tiniest little thing. Really, she's quite mad."

"Somebody's grandmother, no doubt," said Mr. Queen whimsically, picking up his stick from the counter. "Cats?"

"Why, Mr. Queen, however did you guess?"

"It always is," he said in a gloomy voice, "cats."

"*You'd* find her interesting, I'm sure," said Miss Curleigh with eagerness.

"And why I, Diana?"

"The name," said Miss Curleigh shyly, "is Marie. Well, she's *so* strange, Mr. Queen. And I've always understood that strange people interest you."

"At present," said Mr. Queen hurriedly, taking a firmer grip on his stick, "I am enjoying the fruits of idleness."

"But do you know what Miss Tarkle's been doing, the mad thing?"

"I haven't the ghost of a notion," said Mr. Queen with truth.

"She's been buying cats from me at the rate of about one a week for weeks now!"

Mr. Queen sighed. "I see no special cause for suspicion. An ancient and invalid lady, a passion for cats— oh, they go together, I assure you. I once had an aunt like that."

"That's what's so strange about it," said Miss Curleigh triumphantly. "She doesn't *like* cats!"

Mr. Queen blinked twice. He looked at Miss Curleigh's pleasant little nose. Then he rather absently set. his stick on the counter again. "And how do you know that, pray?"

Miss Curleigh beamed. "Her sister told me.—Hush, Ginger! You see, Miss Tarkle is absolutely helpless with her paralysis and all, and her sister Sarah-Ann keeps house for her; they're both of an age, I should say, and they look so much alike. Dried-up little apples of old ladies, with the same tiny features and faces like squirrels. Well, Mr. Queen, about a year ago Miss Sarah-Ann came into my shop and bought a black male cat— she hadn't much money, she said, couldn't buy a really expensive one; so I got just a—well, just a cat for her, you see."

"Did she ask for a black tomcat?" asked Mr. Queen intently.

"No. Any kind at all, she said; she liked them all. Then only a few days later she came back. She wanted to know if she could return him and get her money back. Because, she said, her sister Euphemia couldn't stand having a cat about her; Euphemia just *detested* cats, she said with a sigh, and since she was more or less living off Euphemia's bounty she couldn't very well cross her, you see. I felt a little sorry for her and told her I'd take the cat back; but I suppose she changed her mind, or else her sister changed *her* mind, because Sarah-Ann Tarkle never came back. Anyway, that's how I know Miss Euphemia doesn't like cats."

Mr. Queen gnawed a fingernail. "Odd," he muttered. "A veritable saga of oddness. You say this Euphemia creature has been buying 'em at the rate of one a week? What kind of cats, Miss Curleigh?"

Miss Curleigh sighed. "Not very good ones. Of course, since she has pots of money—that's what her sister Sarah-Ann said, anyway—I tried to sell her an Angora—I had a beauty—and a Maltese that took a ribbon at one of the shows. But she wanted just cats, she said, like the one I sold her sister. Black ones."

"Black. . . . It's possible that—"

"Oh, she's not at all superstitious, Mr. Queen. In some ways she's a very weird old lady. Black tomcats with green eyes, all the same size. I thought it very queer."

Mr. Ellery Queen's nostrils quivered a little, and not from the racy odor in Miss Curleigh's Pet Shoppe, either. An old invalid lady named Tarkle who bought a black tomcat with green eyes every week!

"Very queer indeed," he murmured; and his gray eyes narrowed. "And how long has this remarkable business been going on?"

"You *are* interested! Five weeks now, Mr. Queen. I delivered the sixth one myself only the other day."

"Yourself? Is she totally paralyzed?"

"Oh, yes. She never leaves her bed; can't walk a step. It's been that way, she told me, for ten years now. She and Sarah-Ann hadn't lived together up to the time she had her stroke. Now she's absolutely dependent on her sister for everything—meals, baths, bedp . . . all sorts of attention."

"Then why," demanded Ellery, "hasn't she sent her sister for the cats?"

Miss Curleigh's mercurial eyes wavered. "I don't know," she said slowly. "Sometimes I get the shivers. You see, she's always telephoned me—she has a 'phone by her bed and can use her arms sufficiently to reach for it—the day she wanted the cat. It would always be the same order—black, male, green eyes, the same size as before, and as cheap as possible." Miss Curleigh's pleasant features hardened. "She's something of a haggler, Miss Euphemia Tarkle is."

"Fantastic," said Ellery thoughtfully. "Utterly fantastic. There's something in the basic situation that smacks of lavenderish tragedy. Tell me: how has her sister acted on the occasions when you've delivered the cats?"

"*Hush*, Ginger! I can't tell you, Mr. Queen, because she hasn't been there."

Ellery started. "Hasn't been there! What do you mean? I thought you said the Euphemia woman is help-less—"

"She is, but Sarah-Ann goes out every afternoon for some air, I suppose, or to a movie, and her sister is left alone for a few hours. It's been at such times, I think, that she's called me. Then, too, she always warned me to come at a certain time, and since I've never seen Sarah-Ann when I made the delivery I imagine she's planned to keep her purchases a secret from her sister. I've been able to get in because Sarah-Ann leaves the door unlocked when she goes out. Euphemia has told me time and time again not to breathe a word about the cats to any one."

Ellery took his *pince-nez* off his nose and began to polish the shining lenses—an unfailing sign of emotion. "More and more muddled," he muttered. "Miss Curleigh, you've stumbled on something—well, morbid."

Miss Curleigh blanched. "You don't think—"

"Insults already? I *do* think; and that's why I'm disturbed. For instance, how on earth could she have hoped to keep knowledge of the cats she's bought from her sister? Sarah-Ann isn't blind, is she?"

"Blind? Why, of course not. And Euphemia's sight is all right, too."

"I was only joking. It doesn't make sense, Miss Curleigh."

"Well," said Miss Curleigh brightly, "at least I've given the great Mr. Queen something to think about. . . . I'll call you the moment an Ir—"

Mr. Ellery Queen replaced the glasses on his nose, threw back his square shoulders, and picked up the stick again. "Miss Curleigh, I'm an incurable meddler in the affairs of others. How would you like to help me meddle in the affairs of the mysterious Tarkle sisters?"

Scarlet spots appeared in Miss Curleigh's cheeks. "You're not serious?" she cried.

"Quite."

"I'd love to! What am I to do?"

"Suppose you take me up to the Tarkle apartment and introduce me as a customer. Let's say that the cat you sold Miss Tarkle the other day had really been promised to me, that as a stubborn fancier of felines I won't take any other, and that you'll have to have hers back and give her another. Anything to permit me to see and talk to her. It's mid-afternoon, so Sarah-Ann is probably in a movie theatre somewhere languishing after Clark Gable. What do you say?"

Miss Curleigh flung him a ravishing smile. "I say it's —it's too magnificent for words. One minute while I powder my nose and get some one to tend the shop, Mr. Queen. I wouldn't miss this for *anything!*"

Ten minutes later they stood before the front door to Apartment 5-C of the *Amsterdam Arms,* a rather faded building, gazing in silence at two full quart-bottles of milk on the corridor floor. Miss Curleigh looked troubled, and Mr. Queen stooped. When he straightened he looked troubled, too.

"Yesterday's and today's," he muttered, and he put his hand on the doorknob and turned. The door was locked. "I thought you said her sister leaves the door unlocked when she goes out?"

"Perhaps she's in," said Miss Curleigh uncertainly. "Or, if she's out, that she's forgotten to take the latch off."

Ellery pressed the bell-button. There was no reply. He rang again. Then he called loudly: "Miss Tarkle, are you there?"

"I can't understand it," said Miss Curleigh with a nervous laugh. "She really should hear you. It's only a three-room apartment, and both the bedroom and the living room are directly off the sides of a little foyer on the other side of the door. The kitchen's straight ahead."

Ellery called again, shouting. After a while he put his ear to the door. The rather dilapidated hall, the ill-painted door . . .

Miss Curleigh's extraordinary eyes were frightened silver lamps. She said in the queerest voice: "Oh, Mr. Queen. Something dreadful's happened."

"Let's hunt up the superintendent," said Ellery quietly.

They found *Potter, Sup't* in a metal frame before a door on the ground floor. Miss Curleigh was breathing in little gusts. Ellery rang the bell.

A short fat woman with enormous forearms flecked with suds opened the door. She wiped her red hands on a dirty apron and brushed a strand of bedraggled gray hair from her sagging face. "Well?" she demanded stolidly.

"Mrs. Potter?"

"That's right. We ain't got no empty apartments. The doorman could 'a' told you—"

Miss Curleigh reddened. Ellery said hastily: "Oh,

we're not apartment-hunting, Mrs. Potter. Is the superintendent in?"

"No, he's not," she said suspiciously. "He's got a part-time job at the chemical works in Long Island City and he never gets home till ha'-past three. What you want?"

"I'm sure you'll do nicely, Mrs. Potter. This young lady and I can't seem to get an answer from Apartment 5-C. We're calling on Miss Tarkle, you see."

The fat woman scowled. "Ain't the door open? Generally is this time o' day. The spry one's out, but the paralyzed one—"

"It's locked, Mrs. Potter, and there's no answer to the bell or to our cries."

"Now ain't that funny," shrilled the fat woman, staring at Miss Curleigh. "I can't see— Miss Euphemia's a cripple; she *never* goes out. Maybe the poor thing's threw a fit!"

"I trust not. When did you see Miss Sarah-Ann last?"

"The spry one? Let's see, now. Why, two days ago. And, come to think of it, I ain't seen the cripple for two days, neither."

"Heavens," whispered Miss Curleigh, thinking of the two milk-bottles. "Two days!"

"Oh, you do see Miss Euphemia occasionally?" asked Ellery grimly.

"Yes, sir." Mrs. Potter began to wring her red hands as if she were still over the tub. "Every once in a while she calls me up by 'phone in the afternoon if her sister's out to take somethin' out to the incinerator, or do somethin' for her. The other day it was to mail a letter for her. She—she gives me somethin' once in a while. But it's been two days now. . . ."

Ellery pulled something out of his pocket and cupped it in his palm before the fat woman's tired eyes. "Mrs. Potter," he said sternly, "I want to get into that apartment. There's something wrong. Give me your master-key."

"P-p-police!" she stammered, staring at the shield. Then suddenly she fluttered off and returned to thrust a key into Ellery's hand. "Oh, I wish Mr. Potter was home!" she wailed. "You won't—"

"Not a word about this to any one, Mrs. Potter."

They left the woman gaping loose-tongued and frightened after them, and took the self-service elevator back to the fifth floor. Miss Curleigh was white to the lips; she looked a little sick.

"Perhaps," said Ellery kindly, inserting the key into the lock, "you had better not come in with me, Miss Curleigh. It might be unpleasant. I—" He stopped abruptly, his figure crouching.

Somebody was on the other side of the door.

There was the unmistakable sound of running feet, accompanied by an uneven scraping, as if something were being dragged. Ellery twisted the key and turned the knob in a flash, Miss Curleigh panting at his shoulder. The door moved a half-inch and stuck. The feet retreated.

"Barricaded the door," growled Ellery. "Stand back, Miss Curleigh." He flung himself sidewise at the door. There was a splintering crash and the door shot inward, a broken chair toppling over backward. "Too late—"

"The fire-escape!" screamed Miss Curleigh. "In the bedroom. To the left!"

He darted into a large narrow room with twin beds and an air of disorder and made for an open window. But there was no one to be seen on the fire-escape. He looked up: an iron ladder curved and vanished a few feet overhead.

"Whoever it is got away by the roof, I'm afraid," he muttered, pulling his head back and lighting a cigaret. "Smoke? Now, then, let's have a look about. No bloodshed, apparently. This may be a pig-in-the-poke after all. See anything interesting?"

Miss Curleigh pointed a shaking finger. "That's her —her bed. The messy one. But where is she?"

The other bed was neatly made up, its lace spread undisturbed. But Miss Euphemia Tarkle's was in a state of turmoil. The sheets had been ripped away and its mattress slashed open; some of the ticking was on the floor. The pillows had been torn to pieces. A depression in the center of the mattress indicated where the missing invalid had lain.

Ellery stood still, studying the bed. Then he made the rounds of the closets, opening doors, poking about, and closing them again. Followed closely by Miss Curleigh, who had developed an alarming habit of looking over her right shoulder, he glanced briefly into the living room, the kitchen, and the bathroom. But there was no one in the apartment. And, except for Miss Tarkle's bed, nothing apparently had been disturbed. The place was ghastly, somehow. It was as if violence had visited it in the midst of a cloistered silence; a tray full of dishes, cutlery, and half-finished food lay on the floor, almost under the bed.

Miss Curleigh shivered and edged closer to Ellery. "It's so—so deserted here," she said, moistening her lips. "Where's Miss Euphemia? And her sister? And who was that—that creature who barred the door?"

"What's more to the point," murmured Ellery, gazing at the tray of food, "where are the seven black cats?"

"Sev—"

"Sarah-Ann's lone beauty, and Euphemia's six. Where are they?"

"Perhaps," said Miss Curleigh hopefully, "they jumped out the window when that man—"

"Perhaps. And don't say 'man.' We just don't know." He looked irritably about. "If they did, it was a moment ago, because the catch on the window has been forced, indicating that the window has been closed and consequently that the cats might have—" He stopped short. "Who's there?" he called sharply, whirl-ing.

"It's me," said a timid voice, and Mrs. Potter appeared hesitantly in the foyer. Her tired eyes were luminous with fear and curiosity. "Where's—"

"Gone." He stared at the slovenly woman. "You're sure you didn't see Miss Euphemia or her sister today?"

"Nor yesterday. I—"

"There was no ambulance in this neighborhood within the past two days?"

Mrs. Potter went chalky. "Oh, no, sir! I can't understand how she got *out*. She couldn't walk a step. If she'd been carried, *some one* would have noticed. The doorman, sure. I just asked him. But nobody did. I know everythin' goes on—"

"Is it possible your husband may have seen one or both of them within the past two days?"

"Not Potter. He saw 'em night before last. Harry's been makin' a little side-money, sort of, see, sir. Miss Euphemia wanted the landlord to do some decoratin' and paperin', and a little carpentry, and they wouldn't do it. So, more'n a month ago, she asked Harry if he wouldn't do it on the sly, and she said she'd pay him, although less than if a reg'lar decorator did it. So he's been doin' it spare time, mostly late afternoons and nights—he's handy, Potter is. He's most done with the job. It's pretty paper, ain't it? So he saw Miss Euphemia night before last." A calamitous thought struck her, apparently, for her eyes rolled and she uttered a faint shriek. "I just thought if—if anythin's happened to the cripple, we won't get paid! All that work . . . And the landlord—"

"Yes, yes," said Ellery impatiently. "Mrs. Potter, are there mice or rats in this house?"

Both women looked blank. "Why, not a one of 'em," began Mrs. Potter slowly. "The exterminator comes—" when they all spun about at a sound from the foyer. Some one was opening the door.

"Come in," snapped Ellery, and strode forward; only to halt in his tracks as an anxious face poked timidly into the bedroom.

"Excuse me," said the newcomer nervously, starting at sight of Ellery and the two women. "I guess I must be in the wrong apartment. Does Miss Euphemia Tarkle live here?" He was a tall needle-thin young man with a scared, horsy face and stiff tan hair. He wore a rather rusty suit of old-fashioned cut and carried a small handbag.

"Yes, indeed," said Ellery with a friendly smile. "Come in, come in. May I ask who you are?"

The young man blinked. "But where's Aunt Euphemia? I'm Elias Morton, Junior. •Isn't she here?" His reddish little eyes blinked from Ellery to Miss Curleigh in a puzzled, worried way.

"Did you say 'Aunt' Euphemia, Mr. Morton?"

"I'm her nephew. I come from out of town—Albany. Where—"

Ellery murmured: "An unexpected visit, Mr. Morton?"

The young man blinked again; he was still holding his bag. Then he dumped it on the floor and eagerly fumbled in his pockets until he produced a much-soiled and wrinkled letter. "I—I got this only a few days ago," he faltered. "I'd have come sooner, only my father went off somewhere on a— I don't understand this."

Ellery snatched the letter from his lax fingers. It was scrawled painfully on a piece of ordinary brown wrapping paper; the envelope was a cheap one. The pencilled scribble, in the crabbed hand of age, said:

> Dear Elias:—You have not heard from your Auntie for so many years, but now I need you, Elias, for you are my only blood kin to whom I can turn in my Dire Distress! I am in great danger, my dear boy. You must help your poor Invalid Aunt who is so helpless. *Come at once.* Do not tell your Father or any one, Elias! When you get here make believe you have come just for a Visit. Remember. Please, please do not fail me. Help me, please! Your Loving Aunt—
>
> *Euphemia*

"Remarkable missive," frowned Ellery. "Written under stress, Miss Curleigh. Genuine enough. Don't tell any one, eh? Well, Mr. Morton, I'm afraid you're too late."

"Too— But—" The young man's horse-face whitened. "I tried to come right off, b-but my father had gone off somewhere on a—on one of his drunken spells and I couldn't find him. I didn't know what to do. Then I came. T-t-to think—" His buck teeth were chattering.

"This *is* your aunt's handwriting?"

"Oh, yes. Oh, yes."

"Your father, I gather, is not a brother of the Tarkle sisters?"

"No, sir. My dear mother w-was their sister, God rest her." Morton groped for a chair-back. "Is Aunt Euphemia—d-dead? And where's Aunt Sarah?"

"They're both gone." Ellery related tersely what he had found. The young visitor from Albany looked as if he might faint. "I'm—er—unofficially investigating this business, Mr. Morton. Tell me all you know about your two aunts."

"I don't know m-much," mumbled Morton. "Haven't seen them for about fifteen years, since I was a kid. I heard from my Aunt Sarah-Ann once in a while, and only twice from Aunt Euphemia. They never— I never expected— I do know that Aunt Euphemia since her stroke became . . . funny. Aunt Sarah wrote me that. She had some money—I don't know how much—left her by my grandfather, and Aunt Sarah said she was a real miser about it. Aunt Sarah didn't have anything; she had to live with Aunt Euphemia and take care of her. She wouldn't trust banks, Aunt Sarah said, and had hidden the money somewhere about her, Aunt Sarah didn't know where. She wouldn't even have doctors after her stroke, she was —is so stingy. They didn't get along; they were always fighting, Aunt Sarah wrote me, and Aunt Euphemia was always accusing her of trying to steal her money, and she didn't know how she stood it. That—that's about all I know, sir."

"The poor things," murmured Miss Curleigh with moist eyes. "What a wretched existence! Miss Tarkle can't be responsible for—"

"Tell me, Mr. Morton," drawled Ellery. "It's true that your Aunt Euphemia detested cats?"

The lantern-jaw dropped. "Why, how'd you know? She hates them. Aunt Sarah wrote me that many times. It hurt her a lot, because *she's* so crazy about them she treats her own like a child, you see, and that makes Aunt Euphemia jealous, or angry, or something. I guess they just didn't—don't get along."

"We seem to be having a pardonable difficulty with our tenses," said Ellery. "After all, Mr. Morton, there's no evidence to show that your aunts aren't merely off somewhere on a vacation, or a visit, perhaps." But the glint in his eyes remained. "Why don't you stop at a hotel somewhere nearby? I'll keep you informed." He scribbled the name and address of a hotel in the Seventies on the page of a notebook, and thrust it into Morton's damp palm. "Don't worry. You'll hear from me." And he hustled the bewildered young man out of the apartment. They heard the click of the elevator-door a moment later.

Ellery said slowly: "The country cousin in full panoply. Miss Curleigh, let me look at your refreshing loveliness. People with faces like that should be legislated against." He patted her cheek with a frown, hesitated, and then made for the bathroom. Miss Curleigh blushed once more and followed him quickly, casting another apprehensive glance over her shoulder.

"What's this?" she heard Ellery say sharply. "Mrs. Potter, come out of that— By George!"

"What's the matter now?" cried Miss Curleigh, dashing into the bathroom behind him.

Mrs. Potter, the flesh of her powerful forearms crawling with goose-pimples, her tired eyes stricken, was glaring with open mouth into the tub. The woman made a few inarticulate sounds, rolled her eyes alarmingly, and then fled from the apartment.

Miss Curleigh said: "Oh, my God," and put her hand to her breast. "Isn't that—isn't that *horrible!*"

"Horrible," said Ellery grimly and slowly, "and illuminating. I overlooked it when I glanced in here before. I think . . ." He stopped and bent over the tub. There was no humor in his eyes or voice now; only a sick watchfulness. They were both very quiet. Death lay over them.

A black tomcat, limp and stiff and boneless, lay in a welter and smear of blood in the tub. He was large, glossy black, green-eyed, and indubitably dead. His head was smashed in and his body seemed broken in several places. His blood had clotted in splashes on the porcelain sides of the tub. The weapon, hurled by a callous hand, lay beside him: a blood-splattered bathbrush with a heavy handle.

"That solves the mystery of the disappearance of at least one of the seven," murmured Ellery, straightening. "Battered to death with the brush. He hasn't been dead more than a day or so, either, from the looks of him. Miss Curleigh, we're engaged in a tragic business."

But Miss Curleigh, her first shock of horror swept away by rage, was crying: "Any one who would kill a puss so brutally is—is a monster!" Her silvery eyes were blazing. "That terrible old woman—"

"Don't forget," sighed Ellery, "she can't walk."

"Now this," said Mr. Ellery Queen some time later, putting away his cunning and compact little pocket-

kit, "is growing more and more curious, Miss Curleigh. Have you any notion what I've found here?"

They were back in the bedroom again, stooped over
the bedtray which he had picked up from the floor and
deposited on the night-table between the missing sisters' beds. Miss Curleigh had recalled that on all her
previous visits she had found the tray on Miss Tarkle's
bed or on the table, the invalid explaining with a tightening of her pale lips that she had taken to eating alone
of late, implying that she and the long-suffering Sarah-
Ann had reached a tragic parting of the ways.

"I saw you mess about with powder and things,
but—"

"Fingerprint test." Ellery stared enigmatically down
at the knife, fork, and spoon lying awry in the tray.
"My kit's a handy gadget at times. You saw me test
this cutlery Miss Curleigh. You would say that these
implements had been used by Euphemia in the process
of eating her last meal here?"

"Why, of course," frowned Miss Curleigh. "You can
still see the dried food clinging to the knife and fork."

"Exactly. The handles of knife, fork, and spoon are
not engraved, as you see—simple silver surfaces. They
should bear fingerprints." He shrugged. "But they
don't."

"What do you mean, Mr. Queen? How is that possible?"

"I mean that some one has wiped this cutlery free
of prints. Odd, eh?" Ellery lit a cigaret absently.
"Examine it, however. This is Euphemia Tarkle's bedtray, her food, her dishes her cutlery. She is known
to eat in bed, and alone. But if only Euphemia handled
the cutlery, who wiped off the prints? She? Why
should she? Some one else? But surely there would

be no sense in some one else's wiping off *Euphemia's* prints. Her fingerprints have a right to be there. Then, while Euphemia's prints were probably on these implements, some one else's prints were also on them, which accounts for their having been wiped off. Some one else, therefore, handled Euphemia's cutlery. Why? I begin," said Ellery in the grimmest of voices, "to see daylight. Miss Curleigh, would you like to serve as handmaiden to Justice?" Miss Curleigh, overwhelmed, could only nod. Ellery began to wrap the cold food leftovers from the invalid's tray. "Take this truck down to Dr. Samuel Prouty—here's his address—and ask him to analyze it for me. Wait there, get his report, and meet me back here. Try to get in here without being observed."

"The *food?*"

"The food."

"Then you think it's been—"

"The time for thinking," said Mr. Ellery Queen evenly, "is almost over."

When Miss Curleigh had gone, he took a final look around, even to the extent of examining some empty cupboards which had a look of newness about them, set his lips firmly, locked the front door behind him— pocketing the master-key which Mrs. Potter had given him—took the elevator to the ground floor, and rang the bell of the Potter apartment.

A short thickset man with heavy, coarse features opened the door; his hat was pushed back on his head. Ellery saw the agitated figure of Mrs. Potter hovering in the background.

"That's the policeman!" shrilled Mrs. Potter. "Harry, don't get mixed up in—"

"Oh, so you're the dick," growled the thickset man, ignoring the fat woman. "I'm the super here—Harry Potter. I just get home from the plant and my wife tells me there's somethin' wrong up in the Tarkle flat. What's up, for God's sake?"

"Now, now, there's no cause for panic, Potter," murmured Ellery. "Glad you're home, though; I'm in dire need of information which you can probably provide. Has either of you found anywhere on the premises recently—*any dead cats?*"

Potter's jaw dropped, and his wife gurgled with surprise. "Now that's damn' funny. We sure have. Mrs. Potter says one of 'em's dead up in 5-C now—I never thought *those* two old dames might be the ones—"

"Where did you find them, and how many?" snapped Ellery.

"Why, down in the incinerator. Basement."

Ellery smacked his thigh. "Of course! What a stupid idiot I am. I see it all now. The incinerator, eh? There were six, Potter, weren't there?"

Mrs. Potter gasped: "How'd you know that, for mercy's sake?"

"Incinerator," muttered Ellery, sucking his lower lip. "The bones, I suppose—the skulls?"

"That's right," exclaimed Potter; he seemed distressed. "I found 'em myself. Empty out the incinerator every mornin' for ash-removal. Six cats' skulls and a mess o' little bones. I raised hell around here with the tenants lookin' for the damn' fool who threw 'em down the chute but they all played dumb. Didn't all come down the same time. It's been goin' on now maybe four-five weeks. One a week, almost. The damn' fools. I'd like to get my paws on—"

"You're certain you found six?"

"Sure."

"And nothing else of a suspicious nature?"

"No, *sir*."

"Thanks. I don't believe there will be any more trouble. Just forget the whole business." And Ellery pressed a bill into the man's hand and strolled out of the lobby.

He did not stroll far. He strolled, in fact, only to the sidewalk steps leading down into the basement and cellar. Five minutes later he quietly let himself into Apartment 5-C again.

When Miss Curleigh stopped before the door to Apartment 5-C in late afternoon, she found it locked. She could hear Ellery's voice murmuring inside and a moment later the click of a telephone receiver. Reassured, she pressed the bell-button; he appeared instantly, pulled her inside, noiselessly shut the door again, and led her to the bedroom, where she slumped into a rosewood chair, an expression of bitter disappointment on her pleasant little face.

"Back from the wars, I see," he grinned. "Well, sister, what luck?"

"You'll be dreadfully put out," said Miss Curleigh with a scowl. "I'm sorry I haven't been more helpful—"

"What did good Dr. Prouty say?"

"Nothing encouraging. I like your Dr. Prouty, even if he *is* the Medical Examiner or something and wears a horrible little peaked hat in the presence of a lady; but I can't say I'm keen about his reports. He says there's not a thing wrong with that food you sent by me! It's a little putrefied from standing, but otherwise it's pure enough."

"Now isn't that too bad?" said Ellery cheerfully. "Come, come, Diana, perk up. It's the best news you could have brought me."

"Best n—" began Miss Curleigh with a gasp.

"It substitutes fact for theory very nicely. Fits, lassie, like a *brassière* on Mae West. We have," and he pulled over a chair and sat down facing her, "arrived. By the way, did any one see you enter this apartment?"

"I slipped in by the basement and took the elevator from there. No one saw me, I'm sure. But I don't underst—"

"Commendable efficiency. I believe we have some time for expatiation. I've had an hour or so here alone for thought, and it's been a satisfactory if morbid business." Ellery lit a cigaret and crossed his legs lazily. "Miss Curleigh, you have sense, plus the advantage of an innate feminine shrewdness, I'm sure. Tell me: Why should a wealthy old lady who is almost completely paralyzed stealthily purchase six cats within a period of five weeks?"

Miss Curleigh shrugged. "I told you I couldn't make it out. It's a deep, dark mystery to me." Her eyes were fixed on his lips.

"Pshaw, it can't be as completely baffling as all that. Very well, I'll give you a rough idea. For example, so many cats purchased by an eccentric in so short a period suggests—vivisection. But neither of the Tarkle ladies is anything like a scientist. So that's out. You see?"

"Oh, yes," said Miss Curleigh breathlessly. "I see now what you mean. Euphemia couldn't have wanted them for companionship, either, because she hates cats!"

"Precisely. Let's wander. For extermination of mice? No, this is from Mrs. Potter's report a pest-free building. For mating? Scarcely; Sarah-Ann's cat was a male, and Euphemia also bought only males. Besides, they were nondescript tabbies, and people don't play Cupid to nameless animals."

"She might have bought them for gifts," said Miss Curleigh with a frown. "That's possible."

"Possible, but I think not," said Ellery dryly. "Not when you know the facts. The superintendent found the skeletal remains of six cats in the ashes of the incinerator downstairs, and the other one lies, a very dead pussy, in the bathtub yonder." Miss Curleigh stared at him, speechless. "We seem to have covered the more plausible theories. Can you think of some wilder ones?"

Miss Curleigh paled. "Not—not for their *fur?*"

"*Brava,*" said Ellery with a laugh. "There's a wild one among wild ones. No, not for their fur; I haven't found any fur in the apartment. And besides, no matter who killed Master Tom in the tub, he remains bloody but unskinned. I think, too, that we can discard the even wilder food theory; to civilized people killing cats for food smacks of cannibalism. To frighten Sister Sarah-Ann? Hardly; Sarah is used to cats and loves them. To scratch Sister-Ann to death? That suggests poisoned claws. But in that case there would be as much danger to Euphemia as to Sarah-Ann; and why *six* cats? As—er—guides in eternal dark? But Euphemia is not blind, and besides she never leaves her bed. Can you think of any others?"

"But those things are *ridiculous!*"

"Don't call my logical meanderings names. Ridiculous, perhaps, but you can't ignore even apparent nonsense in an elimination."

"Well, I've got one that isn't nonsense," said Miss Curleigh suddenly. "Pure hatred. Euphemia loathed cats. So, since she's cracked, I suppose, she's bought them just for the pleasure of exterminating them."

"All black tomcats with green eyes and identical dimensions?" Ellery shook his head. "Her mania could scarcely have been so exclusive. Besides, she loathed cats even before Sarah-Ann bought her distinctive tom from you. No, there's only one left that I can think of, Miss Curleigh." He sprang from the chair and began to pace the floor. "It's not only the sole remaining possibility, but it's confirmed by several things . . . *Protection*."

"Protection!" Miss Curleigh's devastating eyes widened. "Why, Mr. Queen. How could that be? People buy dogs for protection, not cats."

"I don't mean that kind of protection," said Ellery impatiently. "I'm referring to a compound of desire to remain alive and an incidental hatred for felines that makes them the ideal instrument toward that end. This is a truly horrifying business, Marie. From every angle. Euphemia Tarkle was afraid. Of what? Of being murdered for her money. That's borne out amply by the letter she wrote to Morton, her nephew; and it's bolstered by her reputed miserliness, her distrust of banks, and her dislike for her own sister. How would a cat be protection against intended murder?"

"Poison!" cried Miss Curleigh.

"Exactly. *As a food-taster*. There's a reversion to mediævalism for you! Are there confirming data? A-plenty. Euphemia had taken to eating alone of late; that suggests some secret activity. Then she reordered cats five times within a short period. Why? Obviously, because each time her cat, purchased from you, had acted in his official capacity, tasted her food, and gone the way of all enslaved flesh. The cats were poi-

soned, poisoned by food intended for Euphemia. So she
had to re-order. Final confirmation: the six feline skel-
etons in the incinerator."

"But she can't walk," protested Miss Curleigh. "So
how could she dispose of the bodies?"

"I fancy Mrs. Potter innocently disposed of them for
her. You'll recall that Mrs. Potter said she was often
called here to take garbage to the incinerator for Euphemia when Sarah-Ann was out. The 'garbage,'
wrapped up, I suppose, was a cat's dead body."

"But why all the black, green-eyed tomcats of the
same size?"

"Self-evident. Why? Obviously, again, *to fool
Sarah-Ann*. Because Sarah-Ann had a black tomcat
of a certain size with green eyes, Euphemia purchased
from you identical animals. Her only reason for this
could have been, then, to fool Sarah-Ann into believing
that the black tom she saw about the apartment at any
given time was her own, the original one. That suggests, of course, that Euphemia used Sarah-Ann's cat
to foil the first attempt, and Sarah-Ann's cat was the
first poison-victim. When he died, Euphemia bought
another from you—without her sister's knowledge.

"How Euphemia suspected she was slated to be poisoned, of course, at the very time in which the poisoner
got busy, we'll never know. It was probably the merest
coincidence, something psychic—you never know about
slightly mad old ladies."

"But if she was trying to fool Sarah-Ann about the
cats," whispered Miss Curleigh, aghast, "then she suspected—"

"Precisely. She suspected her sister of trying to
poison her."

Miss Curleigh bit her lip. "Would you mind giving

me a—a cigaret? I'm—" Ellery silently complied.
"It's the most terrible thing I've ever heard of. Two
old women, sisters, practically alone in the world, one
dependent on the other for attention, the other for sub-
sistence, living at cross-purposes—the invalid helpless to
defend herself against attacks. . . ." She shuddered.
"What's *happened* to those poor creatures, Mr. Queen?"

"Well, let's see. Euphemia is missing. We know that
there were at least six attempts to poison her, all unsuccessful. It's logical to assume that there was a seventh
attempt, then, and that—since Euphemia is gone under
mysterious circumstances—*the seventh attempt was
successful.*"

"But how can you *know* she's—she's dead?"

"Where is she?" asked Ellery dryly. "The only other
possibility is that she fled. But she's helpless, can't
walk, can't stir from bed without assistance. Who can
assist her? Only Sarah-Ann, the very one she suspects
of trying to poison her. The letter to her nephew
shows that she wouldn't turn to Sarah-Ann. So flight
is out and, since she's missing, she must be dead. Now,
follow. Euphemia knew she was the target of poisoning
attacks via her food, and took precautions against them;
then how did the poisoner finally penetrate her defenses
—the seventh cat? Well, we may assume that Euphemia made the seventh cat taste the food we found
on the tray. We know that food was not poisoned,
from Dr. Prouty's report. The cat, then, didn't die of
poisoning from the food itself—confirmed by the fact
that he was beaten to death. But if the cat didn't die
of poisoned *food*, neither did Euphemia. Yet all the
indications are that she must have died of poisoning.
Then there's only one answer: she died of poisoning not
in eating but *in the process of* eating."

"I don't understand," said Miss Curleigh intently.

"The cutlery!" cried Ellery. "I showed you earlier this afternoon that some one other than Euphemia had handled her knife, spoon, and fork. Doesn't this suggest that the poisoner had *poisoned the cutlery* on his seventh attempt? If, for example, the fork had been coated with a colorless odorless poison which dried, Euphemia would have been fooled. The cat, flung bits of food by hand—for no one feeds an animal with cutlery—would live; Euphemia, eating the food with the poisoned cutlery, would die. Psychologically, too, it rings true. It stood to reason that the poisoner, after six unsuccessful attempts one way, should in desperation try a seventh with a variation. The variation worked and Euphemia, my dear, is dead."

"But her body— Where—"

Ellery's face changed as he whirled noiselessly toward the door. He stood in an attitude of tense attention for an instant and then, without a word, laid violent hands upon the petrified figure of Miss Curleigh and thrust her rudely into one of the bedroom closets, shutting the door behind her. Miss Curleigh, half-smothered by a soft sea of musty-smelling feminine garments, held her breath. She had heard that faint scratching of metal upon metal at the front door. It must be—if Mr. Queen acted so quickly—the poisoner. Why had he come back? she thought wildly. The key he was using —easy—a duplicate. Earlier when they had surprised him and he had barricaded the door, he must have entered the apartment by the roof and fire-escape window because he couldn't use the key . . . some one may have been standing in the hall. . . .

She choked back a scream, her thoughts snapping off as if a switch had been turned. A hoarse, harsh voice

—the sounds of a struggle—a crash . . . they were fighting!

Miss Curleigh saw red. She flung open the door of the closet and plunged out. Ellery was on the floor in a tangle of threshing arms and legs. A hand came up with a knife. . . . Miss Curleigh sprang and kicked in an instantaneous reflex action. Something snapped sharply, and she fell back, sickened, as the knife dropped from a broken hand.

"Miss Curleigh—the door!" panted Ellery, pressing his knee viciously downward. Through a dim roaring in her ears Miss Curleigh heard pounding on the door, and tottered toward it. The last thing she remembered before she fainted was a weird boiling of blue-clad bodies as police poured past her to fall upon the struggling figures.

"It's all right now," said a faraway voice, and Miss Curleigh opened her eyes to find Mr. Ellery Queen, cool and immaculate, stooping over her. She moved her head dazedly. The fireplace, the crossed swords on the wall . . . Don't be alarmed, Marie," grinned Ellery; "this isn't an abduction. You have achieved Valhalla. It's all over, and you're reclining on the divan in my apartment."

"Oh," said Miss Curleigh, and she swung her feet unsteadily to the floor. "I—I must look a sight. What happened?"

"We caught the bogey very satisfactorily. Now you rest, young lady, while I rustle a dish of tea—"

"Nonsense!" said Miss Curleigh with asperity. "I want to know how you performed that miracle. Come on, now, don't be irritating!"

"Yours to command. Just what do you want to know?"

"Did you *know* that awful creature was coming back?"

Ellery shrugged. "It was a likely possibility. Euphemia had been poisoned, patently, for her hidden money. She must have been murdered at the very latest yesterday—you recall yesterday's milk-bottle—perhaps the night before last. Had the murderer found the money after killing her? Then who was the prowler whom we surprised this afternoon and who made his escape out the window after barricading the door? It must have been the murderer. But if he came back *after* the crime, then he had not found the money when he committed the crime. Perhaps he had so much to do immediately after the commission of the crime that he had no time to search. At any rate, on his return we surprised him—probably just after he had made a mess of the bed. It was quite possible that he had still not found the money. If he had not, I knew he would come back—after all, he had committed the crime for it. So I took the chance that he would return when he thought the coast was clear, and he did. I 'phoned for police assistance while you were out seeing Dr. Prouty."

"Did you *know* who it was?"

"Oh, yes. It was demonstrable. The first qualification of the poisoner was availability; that is, in order to make those repeated poisoning attempts, the poisoner had to be near Euphemia or near her food at least since the attempts began, which was presumably five weeks ago. The obvious suspect was her sister. Sarah-Ann had motive—hatred and possibly cupidity; and certainly opportunity, since she prepared the food herself. But

Sarah-Ann I eliminated on the soundest basis in the world.

"For who had brutally beaten to death the seventh black tomcat? Palpably, either the victim or the murderer in a general sense. But it couldn't have been Euphemia, since the cat was killed in the bathroom and Euphemia lay paralyzed in the bedroom, unable to walk. Then it must have been the murderer who killed the cat. But if Sarah-Ann were the murderer, would she have clubbed to death a cat—she, who loved cats? Utterly inconceivable. Therefore Sarah-Ann was not the murderer."

"Then what—"

"I know. What happened to Sarah-Ann?" Ellery grimaced. "Sarah-Ann, it is to be feared, went the way of the cat and her sister. It must have been the poisoner's plan to kill Euphemia and have it appear that Sarah-Ann had killed her—the obvious suspect. Sarah-Ann, then, should be on the scene. But she isn't. Well, her disappearance tends to show—I think the confession will bear me out—that she was accidentally a witness to the murder and was killed by the poisoner on the spot to eliminate a witness to the crime. He wouldn't have killed her under any other circumstances."

"Did you find the money?"

"Yes. Lying quite loosely," shrugged Ellery, "between the pages of a Bible Euphemia always kept in her bed. The Poe touch, no doubt."

"And," quavered Miss Curleigh, "the bodies. . . ."

"Surely," drawled Ellery, "the incinerator? It would have been the most logical means of disposal. Fire is virtually all-consuming. What bones there were could have been disposed of more easily than . . . Well, there's no point in being literal. You know what I mean."

"But that means— Who was that fiend on the floor? I never saw him before. It couldn't have been Mr. Morton's f-father . . . ?"

"No, indeed. Fiend, Miss Curleigh?" Ellery raised his eyebrows. "There's only a thin wall between sanity and—"

"You called me," said Miss Curleigh, "Marie before."

Ellery said hastily: "No one but Sarah-Ann and Euphemia lived in the apartment, yet the poisoner had access to the invalid's food for over a month—apparently without suspicion. Who could have had such access? Only one person: the man who had been decorating the apartment in late afternoons and evenings—around dinner-time—for over a month; the man who worked in a chemical plant and therefore, better than any one, had knowledge of and access to poisons; the man who tended the incinerator and therefore could dispose of the bones of his human victims without danger to himself. In a word," said Ellery, "the super-intendent of the building, Harry Potter."

The Adventure of
THE MAD TEA-PARTY

The Adventure of
THE MAD TEA-PARTY

The tall young man in the dun raincoat thought that he had never seen such a downpour. It gushed out of the black sky in a roaring flood, gray-gleaming in the feeble yellow of the station lamps. The red tails of the local from Jamaica had just been drowned out in the west. It was very dark beyond the ragged blur of light surrounding the little railroad station, and unquestionably very wet. The tall young man shivered under the eaves of the platform roof and wondered what insanity had moved him to venture into the Long Island hinterland in such wretched weather. And where, damn it all, was Owen?

He had just miserably made up his mind to seek out a booth, telephone his regrets, and take the next train back to the City, when a lowslung coupé came splashing and snuffling out of the darkness, squealed to a stop, and a man in chauffeur's livery leaped out and dashed across the gravel for the protection of the eaves.

"Mr. Ellery Queen?" he panted, shaking out his cap. He was a blond young man with a ruddy face and sunsquinted eyes.

"Yes," said Ellery with a sigh. Too late now.

"I'm Millan, Mr. Owen's chauffeur, sir," said the man. "Mr. Owen's sorry he couldn't come down to meet you himself. Some guests— This way, Mr. Queen."

He picked up Ellery's bag and the two of them ran for the coupé. Ellery collapsed against the mohair in an indigo mood. Damn Owen and his invitations!

315

Should have known better. Mere acquaintance, when
it came to that. One of J.J.'s questionable friends.
People were always pushing so. Put him up on exhibition, like a trained seal. Come, come, Rollo; here's a
juicy little fish for you! . . . Got vicarious thrills out
of listening to crime yarns. Made a man feel like a curiosity. Well, he'd be drawn and quartered if they got
him to mention crime once! But then Owen had said
Emmy Willowes would be there, and he'd always
wanted to meet Emmy. Curious woman, Emmy, from
all the reports. Daughter of some blueblood diplomat
who had gone to the dogs—in this case, the stage.
Stuffed shirts, her tribe, probably. Atavi! There
were some people who still lived in mediæval . . .
Hmm. Owen wanted him to see "the house." Just
taken a month ago. Ducky, he'd said. "Ducky!" The
big brute . . .

The coupé splashed along in the darkness, its headlights revealing only remorseless sheets of speckled water
and occasionally a tree, a house, a hedge.

Millan cleared his throat. "Rotten weather, isn't it,
sir. Worst this spring. The rain, I mean."

Ah, the conversational chauffeur! thought Ellery with
an inward groan. "Pity the poor sailor on a night like
this," he said piously.

"Ha, ha," said Millan. "Isn't it the truth, though.
You're a little late, aren't you, sir? That was the
eleven-fifty. Mr. Owen told me this morning you were
expected tonight on the nine-twenty."

"Detained," murmured Ellery, wishing he were dead.

"A case, Mr. Queen?" asked Millan eagerly, rolling his
squinty eyes.

Even he, O Lord. . . . "No, no. My father had his

annual attack of elephantiasis. Poor dad! We thought
for a bad hour there that it was the end."

The chauffeur gaped. Then, looking puzzled, he returned his attention to the soggy pelted road. Ellery
closed his eyes with a sigh of relief.

But Millan's was a persevering soul, for after a moment of silence he grinned—true, a trifle dubiously—
and said: "Lots of excitement at Mr. Owen's tonight,
sir. You see, Master Jonathan—"

"Ah," said Ellery, starting a little. Master Jonathan,
eh? Ellery recalled him as a stringy, hot-eyed brat in
the indeterminate years between seven and ten who possessed a perfectly fiendish ingenuity for making a nui-
sance of himself. Master Jonathan. . . . He shivered
again, this time from apprehension. He had quite forgotten Master Jonathan.

"Yes, sir, Jonathan's having a birthday party tomorrow, sir—ninth, I think—and Mr. and Mrs. Owen've
rigged up something special." Millan grinned again,
mysteriously. "Something very special, sir. It's a secret, y'see. The kid— Master Jonathan doesn't know
about it yet. Will he be surprised!"

"I doubt it, Millan," groaned Ellery, and lapsed into
a dismal silence which not even the chauffeur's companionable blandishments were able to shatter.

Richard Owen's "ducky" house was a large rambling
affair of gables and ells and colored stones and bright
shutters, set at the terminal of a winding driveway
flanked by soldierly trees. It blazed with light and
the front door stood ajar.

"Here we are, Mr. Queen!" cried Millan cheerfully,
jumping out and holding the door open. "It's only a
hop to the porch; you won't get wet, sir."

Ellery descended and obediently hopped to the porch. Millan fished his bag out of the car and bounded up the steps. "Door open 'n' everything," he grinned. "Guess the help are all watchin' the show."

"Show?" gasped Ellery with a sick feeling at the pit of his stomach.

Millan pushed the door wide open. "Step in, step in, Mr. Queen. I'll go get Mr. Owen. . . . They're rehearsing, y'see. Couldn't do it while Jonathan was up, so they had to wait till he'd gone to bed. It's for tomorrow, y'see. And he was very suspicious; they had an awful time with him—"

"I can well believe that," mumbled Ellery. Damn Jonathan and all his tribe! He stood in a small foyer looking upon a wide brisk living room, warm and attractive. "So they're putting on a play. Hmm. . . . Don't bother, Millan; I'll just wander in and wait until they've finished. Who am I to clog the wheels of Drama?"

"Yes, sir," said Millan with a vague disappointment; and he set down the bag and touched his cap and vanished in the darkness outside. The door closed with a click curiously final, shutting out both rain and night.

Ellery reluctantly divested himself of his drenched hat and raincoat, hung them dutifully in the foyer-closet, kicked his bag into a corner, and sauntered into the living room to warm his chilled hands at the good fire. He stood before the flames soaking in heat, only half-conscious of the voices which floated through one of the two open doorways beyond the fireplace.

A woman's voice was saying in odd childish tones: "No, please go on! I won't interrupt you again. I dare say there may be *one*."

"Emmy," thought Ellery, becoming conscious very

abruptly. "What's going on here?" He went to the first doorway and leaned against the jamb.

An astonishing sight met him. They were all—as far as he could determine—there. It was apparently a library, a large bookish room done in the modern manner. The farther side had been cleared and a home-made curtain, manufactured out of starchy sheets and a pulley, stretched across the room. The curtain was open, and in the cleared space there was a long table covered with a white cloth and with cups and saucers and things on it. In an armchair at the head of the table sat Emmy Willowes, whimsically girlish in a pinafore, her gold-brown hair streaming down her back, her slim legs sheathed in white stockings, and black pumps with low heels on her feet. Beside her sat an apparition, no less: a rabbity creature the size of a man, his huge ears stiffly up, an enormous bow-tie at his furry neck, his mouth clacking open and shut as human sounds came from his throat. Beside the hare there was another apparition: a creature with an amiably rodent little face and slow sleepy movements. And beyond the little one, who looked unaccountably like a dormouse, sat the most remarkable of the quartet—a curious creature with shaggy eyebrows and features reminiscent of George Arliss's, at his throat a dotted bow-tie, dressed Victorianishly in a quaint waistcoat, on his head an extraordinary tall cloth hat in the band of which was stuck a placard reading: "For This Style 10/6."

The audience was composed of two women: an old lady with pure white hair and the stubbornly sweet facial expression which more often than not conceals a chronic acerbity; and a very beautiful young woman with full breasts, red hair, and green eyes. Then Ellery noticed that two domestic heads were stuck in another doorway, gaping and giggling decorously.

"The mad tea-party," thought Ellery, grinning. "I might have known, with Emmy in the house. Too good for that merciless brat!"

"They were learning to draw," said the little dormouse in a high-pitched voice, yawning and rubbing its eyes, "and they drew all manner of things—everything that begins with an M—"

"Why with an M?" demanded the woman-child.

"Why not?" snapped the hare, flapping his ears indignantly.

The dormouse began to doze and was instantly beset by the top-hatted gentleman, who pinched him so roundly that he awoke with a shriek and said: "—that begins with an M, such as mousetraps, and the moon, and memory, and muchness—you know you say things are 'much of a muchness'—did you ever see such a thing as a drawing of a muchness?"

"Really, now you ask me," said the girl, quite confused, "I don't think—"

"Then you shouldn't talk," said the Hatter tartly.

The girl rose in open disgust and began to walk away, her white legs twinkling. The dormouse fell asleep and the hare and the Hatter stood up and grasped the dormouse's little head and tried very earnestly to push it into the mouth of a monstrous teapot on the table.

And the little girl cried, stamping her right foot: "At any rate I'll never go *there* again. It's the stupidest tea-party I was ever at in all my life!"

And she vanished behind the curtain; an instant later it swayed and came together as she operated the rope of the pulley.

"Superb," drawled Ellery, clapping his hands.

"*Brava,* Alice. And a couple of *bravi* for the zoological characters, Messrs. Dormouse and March Hare, not to speak of my good friend the Mad Hatter."

The Mad Hatter goggled at him, tore off his hat, and came running across the room. His vulturine features under the make-up were both good-humored and crafty; he was a stoutish man in his prime, a faintly cynical and ruthless prime. "Queen! When on earth did you come? Darned if I hadn't completely forgotten about you. What held you up?"

"Family matter. Millan did the honors. Owen, that's your natural costume, I'll swear. I don't know what ever possessed you to go into Wall Street. You were born to be the Hatter."

"Think so?" chuckled Owen, pleased. "I guess I always did have a yen for the stage; that's why I backed Emmy Willowes's *Alice* show. Here, I want you to meet the gang. Mother," he said to the white-haired old lady, "may I present Mr. Ellery Queen. Laura's mother, Queen—Mrs. Mansfield." The old lady smiled a sweet, sweet smile; but Ellery noticed that her eyes were very sharp. "Mrs. Gardner," continued Owen, indicating the buxom young woman with the red hair and green eyes. "Believe it or not, she's the wife of that hairy Hare over there. Ho, ho, ho!"

There was something a little brutal in Owen's laughter. Ellery bowed to the beautiful woman and said quickly: "Gardner? You're not the wife of Paul Gardner, the architect?"

"Guilty," said the March Hare in a cavernous voice; and he removed his head and disclosed a lean face with twinkling eyes. "How are you, Queen? I haven't seen you since I testified for your father in that Schultz murder case in the Village."

They shook hands. "Surprise," said Ellery. "This *is* nice. Mrs. Gardner, you have a clever husband. He set the defense by their respective ears with his expert testimony in that case."

"Oh, I've always said Paul is a genius," smiled the red-haired woman. She had a queer husky voice. "But he won't believe me. He thinks I'm the only one in the world who doesn't appreciate him."

"Now, Carolyn," protested Gardner with a laugh; but the twinkle had gone out of his eyes and for some odd reason he glanced at Richard Owen.

"Of course you remember Laura," boomed Owen, taking Ellery forcibly by the arm. "That's the Dormouse. Charming little rat, isn't she?"

Mrs. Mansfield lost her sweet expression for a fleeting instant; very fleeting indeed. What the Dormouse thought about being publicly characterized as a rodent, however charming, by her husband was concealed by the furry little head; when she took it off she was smiling. She was a wan little woman with tired eyes and cheeks that had already begun to sag.

"And this," continued Owen with the pride of a stock-raiser exhibiting a prize milch-cow, "is the one and only Emmy. Emmy, meet Mr. Queen, that murder-smelling chap I've been telling you about. Miss Willowes."

"You see us, Mr. Queen," murmured the actress, "in character. I hope you aren't here on a professional visit? Because if you are, we'll get into mufti at once and let you go to work. I know *I've* a vicariously guilty conscience. If I were to be convicted of every mental murder I've committed, I'd need the nine lives of the Cheshire Cat. Those damn' critics—"

"The costume," said Ellery, not looking at her legs,

"is most fetching. And I think I like you better as
Alice." She made a charming Alice; she was curved in
her slimness, half-boy, half-girl. "Whose idea was this,
anyway?"

"I suppose you think we're fools or nuts," chuckled
Owen. "Here, sit down, Queen. Maud!" he roared.
"A cocktail for Mr. Queen. Bring some more fixin's."
A frightened domestic head vanished. "We're having a
dress-rehearsal for Johnny's birthday party tomorrow;
we've invited all the kids of the neighborhood. Emmy's
brilliant idea; she brought the costumes down from the
theatre. You know we closed Saturday night."

"I hadn't heard. I thought *Alice* was playing to
S.R.O."

"So it was. But our lease at the *Odeon* ran out and
we've our engagements on the road to keep. We open
in Boston next Wednesday."

Slim-legged Maud set a pinkish liquid concoction before Ellery. He sipped slowly, succeeding in not making a face.

"Sorry to have to break this up," said Paul Gardner,
beginning to take off his costume. "But Carolyn and I
have a bad trip before us. And then tomorrow . . .
The road must be an absolute washout."

"Pretty bad," said Ellery politely, setting down his
three-quarters'-full glass.

"I won't hear of it," said Laura Owen. Her pudgy
little Dormouse's stomach gave her a peculiar appearance, tiny and fat and sexless. "Driving home in this
storm! Carolyn, you and Paul must stay over."

"It's only four miles, Laura," murmured Mrs. Gardner.

"Nonsense, Carolyn! More like forty on a night like
this," boomed Owen. His cheeks were curiously pale

and damp under the make-up. "That's settled! We've got more room than we know what to do with. Paul saw to that when he designed this development."

"That's the insidious part of knowing architects socially," said Emmy Willowes with a grimace. She flung herself in a chair and tucked her long legs under her. "You can't fool 'em about the number of available guest-rooms."

"Don't mind Emmy," grinned Owen. "She's the Peck's Bad Girl of show business: no manners at all. Well, well! This is great. How's about a drink, Paul?"

"No, thanks."

"You'll have one, won't you, Carolyn? Only good sport in the crowd." Ellery realized with a furious embarrassment that his host was, under the red jovial glaze of the exterior, vilely drunk.

She raised her heavily-lidded green eyes to his. "I'd love it, Dick." They stared with peculiar hunger at each other. Mrs. Owen suddenly smiled and turned her back, struggling with her cumbersome costume.

And, just as suddenly, Mrs. Mansfield rose and smiled her unconvincing sweet smile and said in her sugary voice to no one in particular: "*Will* you all excuse me? It's been a trying day, and I'm an old woman. . . . Laura, my darling." She went to her daughter and kissed the lined, averted forehead.

Everybody murmured something; including Ellery, who had a headache, a slow pinkish fire in his vitals, and a consuming wishfulness to be far, far away.

Mr. Ellery Queen came to with a start and a groan. He turned over in bed, feeling very poorly. He had dozed in fits since one o'clock, annoyed rather than

soothed by the splash of the rain against the bedroom
windows. And now he was miserably awake, inexplicably sleepless, attacked by a rather surprising in-
somnia. He sat up and reached for his wrist-watch,
which was ticking thunderously away on the night-table
beside his bed. By the radium hands he saw that it was
five past two.

He lay back, crossing his palms behind his head, and
stared into the half-darkness. The mattress was deep
and downy, as one had a right to expect of the mattress
of a plutocrat, but it did not rest his tired bones. The
house was cosy, but it did not comfort him. His hostess
was thoughtful, but uncomfortably woebegone. His
host was a disturbing force, like the storm. His fellow-
guests; Master Jonathan snuffling away in his junior
bed—Ellery was positive that Master Jonathan snuf-
fled. . . .

At two-fifteen he gave up the battle and, rising,
turned on the light and got into his dressing-gown and
slippers. That there was no book or magazine on or in
the night-table he had ascertained before retiring.
Shocking hospitality! Sighing, he went to the door and
opened it and peered out. A small night-light glimmered at the landing down the hall. Everything was
quiet.

And suddenly he was attacked by the strangest diffi-
dence. He definitely did not want to leave the bedroom.

Analyzing the fugitive fear, and arriving nowhere,
Ellery sternly reproached himself for an imaginative
fool and stepped out into the hall. He was not habitually a creature of nerves, nor was he psychic; he laid
the blame to lowered physical resistance due to fatigue,
lack of sleep. This was a nice house with nice people in

it. It was like a man, he thought, saying: "Nice doggie, nice doggie," to a particularly fearsome beast with slavering jaws. That woman with the sea-green eyes. Put to sea in a sea-green boat. Or was it pea-green. . . . "No room! No room!" . . . "There's *plenty* of room," said Alice indignantly. . . . And Mrs. Mansfield's smile did make you shiver.

Berating himself bitterly for the ferment his imagination was in, he went down the carpeted stairs to the living room.

It was pitch-dark and he did not know where the light-switch was. He stumbled over a hassock and stubbed his toe and cursed silently. The library should be across from the stairs, next to the fireplace. He strained his eyes toward the fireplace, but the last embers had died. Stepping warily, he finally reached the fireplace-wall. He groped about in the rain-splattered silence, searching for the library door. His hand met a cold knob, and he turned the knob rather noisily and swung the door open. His eyes were oriented to the darkness now and he had already begun to make out in the mistiest black haze the unrecognizable outlines of still objects.

The darkness from beyond the door however struck him like a blow. It was darker darkness. . . . He was about to step across the sill when he stopped. It was the wrong room. Not the library at all. How he knew he could not say, but he was sure he had pushed open the door of the wrong room. Must have wandered orbitally to the right. Lost men in the dark forest. . . . He stared intently straight before him into the absolute, unrelieved blackness, sighed, and retreated. The door shut noisily again.

He groped along the wall to the left. A few feet.

. . . There it was! The very next door. He paused to test his psychic faculties. No, all's well. Grinning, he pushed open the door, entered boldly, fumbled on the nearest wall for the switch, found it, pressed. The light flooded on to reveal, triumphantly, the library.

The curtain was closed, the room in disorder as he had last seen it before being conducted upstairs by his host.

He went to the built-in bookcases, scanned several shelves, hesitated between two volumes, finally selected *Huckleberry Finn* as good reading on a dour night, put out the light, and felt his way back across the living room to the stairway. Book tucked under his arm, he began to climb the stairs. There was a footfall from the landing above. He looked up. A man's dark form was silhouetted below the tiny landing light.

"Owen?" whispered a dubious male voice.

Ellery laughed. "It's Queen, Gardner. Can't you sleep, either?"

He heard the man sigh with relief. "Lord, no! I was just coming downstairs for something to read. Carolyn —my wife's asleep, I guess, in the room adjoining mine. How she can sleep—! There's something in the air to-night."

"Or else you drank too much," said Ellery cheerfully, mounting the stairs.

Gardner was in pajamas and dressing-gown, his hair mussed. "Didn't drink at all to speak of. Must be this confounded rain. My nerves are all shot."

"Something in that. Hardy believed, anyway, in the Greek unities. . . . If you can't sleep, you might join me for a smoke in my room, Gardner."

"You're sure I won't be—"

"Keeping me up? Nonsense. The only reason I

fished about downstairs for a book was to occupy my mind with something. Talk's infinitely better than Huck Finn, though he does help at times. Come on."

They went to Ellery's room and Ellery produced cigarets and they relaxed in chairs and chatted and smoked until the early dawn began struggling to emerge from behind the fine gray wet bars of the rain outside. Then Gardner went yawning back to his room and Ellery fell into a heavy, uneasy slumber.

He was on the rack in a tall room of the Inquisition and his left arm was being torn out of his shoulder-socket. The pain was almost pleasant. Then he awoke to find Millan's ruddy face in broad daylight above him, his blond hair tragically dishevelled. He was jerking at Ellery's arm for all he was worth.

"Mr. Queen!" he was crying. "Mr. Queen! For God's sake, wake up!"

Ellery sat up quickly, startled. "What's the matter, Millan?"

"Mr. Owen, sir. He's—he's gone!"

Ellery sprang out of bed. "What d'ye mean, man?"

"Disappeared, Mr. Queen. We—we can't find him. Just gone. Mrs. Owen is all—"

"You go downstairs, Millan," said Ellery calmly, stripping off his pajama-coat, "and pour yourself a drink. Please tell Mrs. Owen not to do anything until I come down. And nobody's to leave or telephone. You understand?"

"Yes, sir," said Millan in a low voice, and blundered off.

Ellery dressed like a fireman, splashed his face, spat water, adjusted his necktie, and ran downstairs. He found Laura Owen in a crumpled négligé on the sofa, sobbing. Mrs. Mansfield was patting her daughter's shoulder. Master Jonathan Owen was scowling at his grandmother, Emmy Willowes silently smoked a cigaret, and the Gardners were pale and quiet by the graywashed windows.

"Mr. Queen," said the actress quickly. "It's a drama, hot off the script. At least Laura Owen thinks so. Won't you assure her that it's all probably nothing?"

"I can't do that," smiled Ellery, "until I learn the facts. Owen's gone? How? When?"

"Oh, Mr. Queen," choked Mrs. Owen, raising a tear-stained face. "I know something—something dreadful's happened. I had a feeling— You remember last night, after Richard showed you to your room?"

"Yes."

"Then he came back downstairs and said he had some work to do in his den for Monday, and told me to go to bed. Everybody else had gone upstairs. The servants, too. I warned him not to stay up too late and I went up to bed. I—I was exhausted, and I fell right asleep—"

"You occupy one bedroom, Mrs. Owen?"

"Yes. Twin beds. I fell asleep and didn't wake up until a half-hour ago. Then I saw—" She shuddered and began to sob again. Her mother looked helpless and angry. "His bed hadn't been slept in. His clothes —the ones he'd taken off when he got into the costume —were still where he had left them on the chair by his bed. I was shocked, and ran downstairs; but he was gone. . . ."

"Ah," said Ellery queerly. "Then, as far as you know, he's still in that Mad Hatter's rig? Have you looked over his wardrobe? Are any of his regular clothes missing?"

"No, no; they're all there. Oh, he's dead. I know he's dead."

"Laura, dear, please," said Mrs. Mansfield in a tight quavery voice.

"Oh, mother, it's too horrible—"

"Here, here," said Ellery. "No hysterics. Was he worried about anything? Business, for instance?"

"No, I'm sure he wasn't. In fact, he said only yesterday things were picking up beautifully. And he isn't—isn't the type to worry, anyway."

"Then it probably isn't amnesia. He hasn't had a shock of some sort recently?"

"No, no."

"No possibility, despite the costume, that he went to his office?"

"No. He never goes down Saturdays."

Master Jonathan jammed his fists into the pockets of his Eton jacket and said bitterly: "I bet he's drunk again. Makin' mamma cry. I hope he *never* comes back."

"Jonathan!" screamed Mrs. Mansfield. "You go up to your room this very minute, do you hear, you nasty boy? This minute!"

No one said anything; Mrs. Owen continued to sob; so Master Jonathan thrust out his lower lip, scowled at his grandmother with unashamed dislike, and stamped upstairs.

"Where," said Ellery with a frown, "was your husband when you last saw him, Mrs. Owen? In this room?"

"In his den," she said with difficulty. "He went in just as I went upstairs. I saw him go in. That door, there." She pointed to the door at the right of the library door. Ellery started; it **was** the door to the room he had almost blundered into during the night in his hunt for the library.

"Do you think—" began Carolyn Gardner in her husky voice, and stopped. Her lips were dry, and in the gray morning light her hair did not seem so red and her eyes did not seem so green. There was, in fact, a washed-out look about her, as if all the fierce vitality within her had been quenched by what had happened.

"Keep out of this, Carolyn," said Paul Gardner harshly. His eyes were red-rimmed from lack of sleep.

"Come, come," murmured Ellery, "we may be, as Miss Willowes has said, making a fuss over nothing at all. If you'll excuse me . . . I'll have a peep at the den."

He went into the den, closing the door behind him, and stood with his back squarely against the door. It was a small room, so narrow that it looked long by contrast; it was sparsely furnished and seemed a business-like place. There was a simple neatness about its desk, a modern severity about its furnishings that were reflections of the direct, brutal character of Richard Owen. The room was as trim as a pin; it was almost ludicrous to conceive of its having served as the scene of a crime.

Ellery gazed long and thoughtfully. Nothing out of place, so far as he could see; and nothing, at least perceptible to a stranger, added. Then his eyes wavered and fixed themselves upon what stood straight before him. That *was* odd. . . . Facing him as he leaned against the door there was a bold naked mirror set flush into the opposite wall and reaching from floor to ceiling—a startling feature of the room's decorations. Ellery's lean figure, and the door behind him, were perfectly reflected in the sparkling glass. And there, above . . . In the mirror he saw, above the reflection of the door against which he was leaning, the reflection of the face of a modern electric clock. In the dingy grayness of the light there was a curious lambent quality about its dial. . . . He pushed away from the door and turned and stared up. It was a chromium-and-onyx clock, about a foot in diameter, round and simple and startling.

He opened the door and beckoned Millan, who had joined the silent group in the living room. "Have you a step-ladder?"

Millan brought one. Ellery smiled, shut the door firmly, mounted the ladder, and examined the clock. Its electric outlet was behind, concealed from view. The plug was in the socket, as he saw at once. The clock was going; the time—he consulted his wrist-watch —was reasonably accurate. But then he cupped his hands as best he could to shut out what light there was and stared hard and saw that the numerals and the hands, as he had suspected, were radium-painted. They glowed faintly.

He descended, opened the door, gave the ladder into Millan's keeping, and sauntered into the living room. They looked up at him trustfully.

"Well," said Emmy Willowes with a light shrug, "has the Master Mind discovered the all-important clue? Don't tell us that Dickie Owen is out playing golf at the Meadowbrook links in that Mad Hatter's get-up!"

"Well, Mr. Queen?" asked Mrs. Owen anxiously.

Ellery sank into an armchair and lighted a cigaret. "There's something curious in there. Mrs. Owen, did you get this house furnished?"

She was puzzled. "Furnished? Oh, no. We bought it, you know; brought all our own things."

"Then the electric clock above the door in the den is yours?"

"The clock?" They all stared at him. "Why, of course. What has that—"

"Hmm," said Ellery. "That clock has a disappearing quality, like the Cheshire Cat—since we may as well continue being Carrollish, Miss Willowes."

"But what can the clock possibly have to do with Richard's—being gone?" asked Mrs. Mansfield with asperity.

Ellery shrugged. "*Je n'sais.* The point is that a little after two this morning, being unable to sleep, I ambled downstairs to look for a book. In the dark I blundered to the door of the den, mistaking it for the library door. I opened it and looked in. But I saw nothing, you see."

"But how could you, Mr. Queen?" said Mrs. Gardner in a small voice; her breasts heaved. "If it was dark—"

"That's the curious part of it," drawled Ellery. "I *should* have seen something *because* it was so dark, Mrs. Gardner."

"But—"

"The clock over the door."

"Did you go in?" murmured Emmy Willowes, frowning. "I can't say I understand. The clock's above the door, isn't it?"

"There is a mirror facing the door," explained Ellery absently, "and the fact that it was so dark makes my seeing nothing quite remarkable. Because that clock has luminous hands and numerals. Consequently I should have seen their reflected glow very clearly indeed in that pitch-darkness. But I didn't, you see. I saw literally nothing at all."

They were silent, bewildered. Then Gardner muttered: "I still don't see— You mean something, somebody was standing in front of the mirror, obscuring the reflection of the clock?"

"Oh, no. The clock's above the door—a good seven feet or more from the floor. The mirror reaches to the ceiling. There's isn't a piece of furniture in that room seven feet high, and certainly we may dismiss the possibility of an intruder seven feet or more tall. No, no, Gardner. It does seem as if the clock wasn't above the door at all when I looked in."

"Are you sure, young man," snapped Mrs. Mansfield, "that you know what you're talking about? I thought we were concerned with my son-in-law's absence. And how on earth could the clock not have been there?"

Ellery closed his eyes. "Fundamental. *It was moved from its position.* Wasn't above the door when I looked in. After I left, it was returned."

"But why on earth," murmured the actress, "should any one want to move a mere clock from a wall, Mr. Queen? That's almost as nonsensical as some of the things in *Alice*."

"That," said Ellery, "is the question I'm propounding to myself. Frankly I don't know." Then he opened his eyes. "By the way, has any one seen the Mad Hatter's hat?"

Mrs. Owen shivered. "No, that—that's gone, too."

"You've looked for it?"

"Yes. Would you like to look yours—"

"No, no, I'll take your word for it, Mrs. Owen. Oh, yes. Your husband has no enemies?" He smiled. "That's the routine question, Miss Willowes. I'm afraid I can't offer you anything startling in the way of technique."

"Enemies? Oh, I'm sure not," quavered Mrs. Owen. "Richard was—is strong and—and sometimes rather curt and contemptuous, but I'm sure no one would hate him enough to—to kill him." She shivered again and drew the silk of her négligé closer about her plump shoulders.

"Don't say that, Laura," said Mrs. Mansfield sharply. "I do declare, you people are like children! It probably has the simplest explanation."

"Quite possible," said Ellery in a cheerful voice. "It's the depressing weather, I suppose. . . . There! I believe the rain's stopped." They dully looked out the windows. The rain had perversely ceased, and the sky was growing brighter. "Of course," continued Ellery, "there are certain possibilities. It's conceivable—I say conceivable, Mrs. Owen—that your husband has been . . . well, kidnaped. Now, now, don't look so frightened. It's a theory only. The fact that he has disappeared in the costume does seem to point to a very abrupt—and therefore possibly enforced—departure. You haven't found a note of some kind? Nothing in your letter-box? The morning mail—"

"Kidnaped," whispered Mrs. Owen feebly.

"Kidnaped?" breathed Mrs. Gardner, and bit her lip. But there was a brightness in her eye, like the brightness of the sky outdoors.

"No note, no mail," snapped Mrs. Mansfield. "Personally, I think this is ridiculous. Laura, this is your house, but I think I have a duty. . . . You should do one of two things. Either take this seriously and telephone the *regular* police, or forget all about it. *I'm* inclined to believe Richard got befuddled—he *had* a lot to drink last night, dear—and wandered off drunk somewhere. He's probably sleeping it off in a field somewhere and won't come back with anything worse than a bad cold."

"Excellent suggestion," drawled Ellery. "All except for the summoning of the *regular* police, Mrs. Mansfield. I assure you I possess—er—*ex officio* qualifications. Let's not call the police and say we did. If there's any explaining to do—afterward—I'll do it. Meanwhile, I suggest we try to forget all this unpleasantness and wait. If Mr. Owen hasn't returned by nightfall, we can go into conference and decide what measures to take. Agreed?"

"Sounds reasonable," said Gardner disconsolately. "May I—" he smiled and shrugged—"this *is* exciting!—telephone my office, Queen?"

"Lord, yes."

Mrs. Owen shrieked suddenly, rising and tottering toward the stairs. "Jonathan's birthday party! I forgot all about it! And all those children invited— What *will* I say?"

"I suggest," said Ellery in a sad voice, "that Master Jonathan is indisposed, Mrs. Owen. Harsh, but necessary. You might 'phone all the potential spectators of the mad tea-party and voice your regrets." And Ellery rose and wandered into the library.

It was a depressing day for all the lightening skies and the crisp sun. The morning wore on and nothing whatever happened. Mrs. Mansfield firmly tucked her daughter into bed, made her swallow a small dose of luminol from a big bottle in the medicine-chest, and remained with her until she dropped off to exhausted sleep. Then the old lady telephoned to all and sundry the collective Owen regrets over the unfortunate turn of events. Jonathan *would* have to run a fever when . . . Master Jonathan, apprised later by his grandmother of the *débâcle*, sent up an ululating howl of surprisingly healthy anguish that caused Ellery, poking about downstairs in the library, to feel prickles slither up and down his spine. It took the combined labors of Mrs. Mansfield, Millan, the maid, and the cook to pacify the Owen hope. A five-dollar bill ultimately restored a rather strained *entente*. . . . Emmy Willowes spent the day serenely reading. The Gardners listlessly played two-handed bridge.

Luncheon was a dismal affair. No one spoke in more than monosyllables, and the strained atmosphere grew positively taut.

During the afternoon they wandered about, restless ghosts. Even the actress began to show signs of tension: she consumed innumerable cigarets and cocktails and lapsed into almost sullen silence. No word came; the telephone rang only once, and then it was merely the local confectioner protesting the cancellation of the ice-cream order. Ellery spent most of the afternoon in mysterious activity in the library and den. What he was looking for remained his secret. At five o'clock he emerged from the den, rather gray of face. There was a deep crease between his brows. He went out onto the porch and leaned against a pillar, sunk in thought. The gravel was dry; the sun had quickly sopped up the rain. When he went back into the house it was already dusk and growing darker each moment with the swiftness of the country nightfall.

There was no one about; the house was quiet, its miserable occupants having retired to their rooms. Ellery sought a chair. He buried his face in his hands and thought for long minutes, completely still.

And then at last something happened to his face and he went to the foot of the stairs and listened. No sound. He tiptoed back, reached for the telephone, and spent the next fifteen minutes in low-voiced, earnest conversation with some one in New York. When he had finished, he went upstairs to his room.

An hour later, while the others were downstairs gathering for dinner, he slipped down the rear stairway and out of the house unobserved even by the cook in the kitchen. He spent some time in the thick darkness of the grounds.

How it happened Ellery never knew. He felt its effects soon after dinner; and on retrospection he recalled that the others, too, had seemed drowsy at approximately the same time. It was a late dinner and a cold one, Owen's disappearance apparently having disrupted the culinary organization as well; so that it was not until a little after eight that the coffee—Ellery was certain later it had been the coffee—was served by the trim-legged maid. The drowsiness came on less than half an hour later. They were seated in the living room, chatting dully about nothing at all. Mrs. Owen, pale and silent, had gulped her coffee thirstily; had called for a second cup, in fact. Only Mrs. Mansfield had been belligerent. She had been definitely of a mind, it appeared, to telephone the police. She had great faith in the local constabulary of Long Island, particularly in one Chief Naughton, the local prefect; and she left no doubt in Ellery's mind of *his* incompetency. Gardner had been restless and a little rebellious; he had tinkered with the piano in the alcove. Emmy Willowes had drawn herself into a slant-eyed shell, no longer amused and very, very quiet. Mrs. Gardner had been nervous. Jonathan packed off screaming to bed. . . .

It came over their senses like a soft insidious blanket of snow. Just a pleasant sleepiness. The room was warm, too, and Ellery rather hazily felt beads of perspiration on his forehead. He was half-gone before his dulled brain sounded a warning note. And then, trying in panic to rise, to use his muscles, he felt himself slipping, slipping into unconsciousness, his body as leaden and remote as Vega. His last conscious thought, as the room whirled dizzily before his eyes and he saw blearily the expressions of his companions, was that they had all been drugged. . . .

The dizziness seemed merely to have taken up where it had left off, almost without hiatus. Specks danced before his closed eyes and somebody was hammering petulantly at his temples. Then he opened his eyes and saw glittering sun fixed upon the floor at his feet. Good God, all night. . . .

He sat up groaning and feeling his head. The others were sprawled in various attitudes of labored-breathing coma about him—without exception. Some one—his aching brain took it in dully; it was Emmy Willowes—stirred and sighed. He got to his feet and stumbled toward a portable bar and poured himself a stiff, nasty drink of Scotch. Then, with his throat burning, he felt unaccountably better; and he went to the actress and pummeled her gently until she opened her eyes and gave him a sick, dazed, troubled look.

"What—when—"

"Drugged," croaked Ellery. "The crew of us. Try to revive these people, Miss Willowes, while I scout about a bit. And see if any one's shamming."

He wove his way a little uncertainly, but with purpose, toward the rear of the house. Groping, he found the kitchen. And there were the trim-legged maid and Millan and the cook unconscious in chairs about the kitchen table over cold cups of coffee. He made his way back to the living room, nodded at Miss Willowes working over Gardner at the piano, and staggered upstairs. He discovered Master Jonathan's bedroom after a short search; the boy was still sleeping—a deep natural sleep punctuated by nasal snuffles. Lord, he *did* snuffle! Groaning, Ellery visited the lavatory adjoining the master-bedroom. After a little while he went downstairs and into the den. He came out almost at once, haggard and wild-eyed. He took his hat from the foyer-closet and hurried outdoors into the warm sunshine. He spent fifteen minutes poking about the grounds; the Owen house was shallowly surrounded by timber and seemed isolated as a Western ranch. . . . When he returned to the house, looking grim and disappointed, the others were all conscious, making mewing little sounds and holding their heads like scared children.

"Queen, for God's sake," began Gardner hoarsely.

"Whoever it was used that luminol in the lavatory upstairs," said Ellery, flinging his hat away and wincing at a sudden pain in his head. "The stuff Mrs. Mansfield gave Mrs. Owen yesterday to make her sleep. Except that almost the whole of that large bottle was used. Swell sleeping draught! Make yourselves comfortable while I conduct a little investigation in the kitchen. I think it was the java." But when he returned he was grimacing. "No luck. *Madame la Cuisinière*, it seems, had to visit the bathroom at one period; Millan was out in the garage looking at the cars; and the maid was off somewhere, doubtless primping. Result: our friend the luminolist had an opportunity to pour most of the powder from the bottle into the coffeepot. Damn!"

"I *am* going to call the police!" cried Mrs. Mansfield hysterically, striving to rise. "We'll be murdered in our beds, next thing we know! Laura, I positively insist—"

"Please, please, Mrs. Mansfield," said Ellery wearily. "No heroics. And you would be of greater service if you went into the kitchen and checked the insurrection that's brewing there. The two females are on the verge of packing, I'll swear."

Mrs. Mansfield bit her lip and flounced off. They heard her no longer sweet voice raised in remonstrance a moment later.

"But, Queen," protested Gardner, "we can't go unprotected—"

"What I want to know in my infantile way," drawled Emmy Willowes from pale lips, "is who did it, and why. That bottle upstairs . . . It looks unconscionably like one of us, doesn't it?"

Mrs. Gardner gave a little shriek. Mrs. Owen sank back into her chair.

"One of us?" whispered the red-haired woman.

Ellery smiled without humor. Then his smile faded and he cocked his head toward the foyer. "What was that?" he snapped suddenly.

They turned, terror-stricken, and looked. But there was nothing to see. Ellery strode toward the front door.

"What is it now, for heaven's sake?" faltered Mrs. Owen.

"I thought I heard a sound—" He flung the door open. The early morning sun streamed in. Then they saw him stoop and pick up something from the porch and rise and look swiftly about outside. But he shook his head and stepped back, closing the door.

"Package," he said with a frown. "I *thought* some one . . ."

They looked blankly at the brown-paper bundle in his hands. "Package?" asked Mrs. Owen. Her face lit up. "Oh, it may be from Richard!" And then the light went out, to be replaced by fearful pallor. "Oh, do you think——?"

"It's addressed," said Ellery slowly, "to you, Mrs. Owen. No stamp, no postmark, written in pencil in disguised block-letters. I think I'll take the liberty of opening this, Mrs. Owen." He broke the feeble twine and tore away the wrapping of the crude parcel. And then he frowned even more deeply. For the package contained only a pair of large men's shoes, worn at the heels and soles—sport oxfords in tan and white.

Mrs. Owen rolled her eyes, her nostrils quivering with nausea. "Richard's!" she gasped. And she sank back, half-fainting.

"Indeed?" murmured Ellery. "How interesting. Not, of course, the shoes he wore Friday night. You're positive they're his, Mrs. Owen?"

"Oh, he *has* been kidnaped!" quavered Mrs. Mansfield from the rear doorway. "Isn't there a note, b-blood . . ."

"Nothing but the shoes. I doubt the kidnap theory now, Mrs. Mansfield. These weren't the shoes Owen wore Friday night. When did you see these last, Mrs. Owen?"

She moaned: "In his wardrobe closet upstairs only yesterday afternoon. Oh—"

"There. You see?" said Ellery cheerfully. "Probably stolen from the closet while we were all unconscious last night. And now returned rather spectacularly. So far, you know, there's been no harm done. I'm afraid," he said with severity, "we're nursing a viper at our bosoms."

But they did not laugh. Miss Willowes said strangely:

"Very odd. In fact, insane, Mr. Queen. I can't see the slightest purpose in it."

"Nor I, at the moment. Somebody's either playing a monstrous prank, or there's a devilishly clever and warped mentality behind all this." He retrieved his hat and made for the door.

"Wherever are you going?" gasped Mrs. Gardner.

"Oh, out for a thinking spell under God's blue canopy. But remember," he added quietly, "that's a privilege reserved to detectives. No one is to set foot outside this house."

He returned an hour later without explanation.

At noon they found the second package. It was a squarish parcel wrapped in the same brown paper. Inside there was a cardboard carton, and in the carton, packed in crumpled tissue-paper, there were two magnificent toy sailing-boats such as children race on summer lakes. The package was addressed to Miss Willowes.

"This is getting dreadful," murmured Mrs. Gardner, her full lips trembling. "I'm all goose-pimples."

"I'd feel better," muttered Miss Willowes, "if it was a bloody dagger, or something. Toy boats!" She stepped back and her eyes narrowed. "Now, look here, good people, I'm as much a sport as anybody, but a joke's a joke and I'm just a bit fed up on this particular one. Who's manœuvring these monkeyshines?"

"Joke," snarled Gardner. He was white as death. "It's the work of a madman, I tell you!"

"Now, now," murmured Ellery, staring at the green-and-cream boats. "We shan't get anywhere this way. Mrs. Owen, have you ever seen these before?"

Mrs. Owen, on the verge of collapse, mumbled: "Oh,

my good dear God.   Mr. Queen, I don't— Why, they're—they're Jonathan's!"

Ellery blinked.   Then he went to the foot of the stairway and yelled: "Johnny!   Come down here a minute."

Master Jonathan descended sluggishly, sulkily. "What you want?" he asked in a cold voice.

"Come here, son."   Master Jonathan came with dragging feet.   "When did you see these boats of yours last?"

"Boats!" shrieked Master Jonathan, springing into life.   He pounced on them and snatched them away, glaring at Ellery.   "My boats!   Never seen such a place. My boats!   You stole 'em!"

"Come, come," said Ellery, flushing, "be a good little man.   When did you see them last?"

"Yest'day!   In my toy-chest!   My boats!   Scan'-lous," hissed Master Jonathan, and fled upstairs, hugging his boats to his scrawny breast.

"Stolen at the same time," said Ellery helplessly.   "By thunder, Miss Willowes, I'm almost inclined to agree with you.   By the way, who bought those boats for your son, Mrs. Owen?"

"H-his father."

"Damn," said Ellery for the second time that impious Sunday, and he sent them all on a search of the house to ascertain if anything else were missing.   But no one could find that anything had been taken.

It was when they came down from upstairs that they found Ellery regarding a small white envelope with puzzlement.

"Now what?" demanded Gardner wildly.

"Stuck in the door," he said thoughtfully. "Hadn't noticed it before. This *is* a queer one."

It was a rich piece of stationery, sealed with blue wax on the back and bearing the same pencilled scrawl, this time addressed to Mrs. Mansfield.

The old lady collapsed in the nearest chair, holding her hand to her heart. She was speechless with fear.

"Well," said Mrs. Gardner huskily, "open it."

Ellery tore open the envelope. His frown deepened.

"Why," he muttered, "there's nothing at all inside!"

Gardner gnawed his fingers and turned away, mumbling. Mrs. Gardner shook her head like a dazed pugilist and stumbled toward the bar for the fifth time that day. Emmy Willowes's brow was dark as thunder.

"You know," said Mrs. Owen almost quietly, "that's mother's stationery." And there was another silence.

Ellery muttered: "Queerer and queerer. I *must* get this organized. . . . The shoes are a puzzler. The toy boats might be construed as a gift; yesterday was Jonathan's birthday; the boats are his—a distorted practical joke. . . ." He shook his head. "Doesn't wash. And this third—an envelope without a letter in it. That would seem to point to the envelope as the important thing. But the envelope's the property of Mrs. Mansfield. The only other thing—ah, the wax!" He scanned the blue blob on the back narrowly, but it bore no seal-insignia of any kind.

"That," said Mrs. Owen again in the quiet unnatural voice, "looks like our wax, too, Mr. Queen, from the library."

Ellery dashed away, followed by a troubled company. Mrs. Owen went to the library desk and opened the top drawer.

"Was it here?" asked Ellery quickly.

"Yes," she said, and then her voice quivered. "I used it only Friday when I wrote a letter. Oh, good . . ."

There was no stick of wax in the drawer.

And while they stared at the drawer, the front door-bell rang.

It was a market-basket this time, lying innocently on the porch. In it, nestling crisp and green, were two large cabbages.

Ellery shouted for Gardner and Millan, and himself led the charge down the steps. They scattered, searching wildly through the brush and woods surrounding the house. But they found nothing. No sign of the bell-ringer, no sign of the ghost who had cheerfully left a basket of cabbages at the door as his fourth odd gift. It was as if he were made of smoke and materialized only for the instant he needed to press his impalpable finger to the bell.

They found the women huddled in a corner of the living room, shivering and white-lipped. Mrs. Mansfield, shaking like an aspen, was at the telephone ringing for the local police. Ellery started to protest, shrugged, set his lips, and stooped over the basket.

There was a slip of paper tied by string to the handle of the basket. The same crude pencil-scrawl. . . . "Mr. Paul Gardner."

"Looks," muttered Ellery, "as if you're elected, old fellow, this time."

Gardner stared as if he could not believe his eyes. "Cabbages!"

"Excuse me," said Ellery curtly. He went away. When he returned he was shrugging. "From the vege-table-bin in the outside pantry, says Cook. She hadn't

thought to look for missing *vegetables*, she told me with
scorn."

Mrs. Mansfield was babbling excitedly over the telephone to a sorely puzzled officer of the law. When she
hung up she was red as a newborn baby. "That will be
quite enough of this crazy nonsense, Mr. Queen!" she
snarled. And then she collapsed in a chair and laughed
hysterically and shrieked: "Oh, I knew you were making the mistake of your life when you married that
beast, Laura!" and laughed again like a madwoman.

The law arrived in fifteen minutes, accompanied by a
howling siren and personified by a stocky brick-faced
man in chief's stripes and a gangling young policeman.

"I'm Naughton," he said shortly. "What the devil's
goin' on here?"

Ellery said: "Ah, Chief Naughton. I'm Queen's son—
Inspector Richard Queen of Centre Street. How d'ye
do?"

"Oh!" said Naughton. He turned on Mrs. Mansfield sternly. "Why didn't you say Mr. Queen was
here, Mrs. Mansfield? You ought to know—"

"Oh, I'm sick of the lot of you!" screamed the old
lady. "Nonsense, nonsense, nonsense from the instant
this week-end began! First that awful actress-woman
there, in her short skirt and legs and things, and then
this—this—"

Naughton rubbed his chin. "Come over here, Mr.
Queen, where we can talk like human beings. What
the deuce happened?"

Ellery with a sigh told him. As he spoke, the Chief's
face grew redder and redder. "You mean you're serious
about this business?" he rumbled at last. "It sounds
plain crazy to me. Mr. Owen's gone off his nut and

he's playing jokes on you people. Good God, you can't take this thing serious!"

"I'm afraid," murmured Ellery, "we must. . . . What's that? By heaven, if that's another manifestation of our playful ghost—!" And he dashed toward the door while Naughton gaped and pulled it open, to be struck by a wave of dusk. On the porch lay the fifth parcel, a tiny one this time.

The two officers darted out of the house, flashlights blinking and probing. Ellery picked up the packet with eager fingers. It was addressed in the now familiar scrawl to Mrs. Paul Gardner. Inside were two identically shaped objects: chessmen, kings. One was white and the other was black.

"Who plays chess here?" he drawled.

"Richard," shrieked Mrs. Owen. "Oh, my God, I'm going mad!"

Investigation proved that the two kings from Richard Owen's chess-set were gone.

The local officers came back, rather pale and panting. They had found no one outside. Ellery was silently studying the two chessmen.

"Well?" said Naughton, drooping his shoulders.

"Well," said Ellery quietly. "I have the most brilliant notion, Naughton. Come here a moment." He drew Naughton aside and began to speak rapidly in a low voice. The others stood limply about, twitching with nervousness. There was no longer any pretense of self-control. If this was a joke, it was a ghastly one indeed. And Richard Owen looming in the background . . .

The Chief blinked and nodded. "You people," he said shortly, turning to them, "get into that library there." They gaped. "I mean it! The lot of you. This tomfoolery is going to stop right now."

"But, Naughton," gasped Mrs. Mansfield, "it couldn't be any of us who sent those things. Mr. Queen will tell you we weren't out of his sight today—"

"Do as I say, Mrs. Mansfield," snapped the officer.

They trooped, puzzled, into the library. The policeman rounded up Millan, the cook, the maid, and went with them. Nobody said anything; nobody looked at any one else. Minutes passed; a half-hour; an hour. There was the silence of the grave from beyond the door to the living room. They strained their ears. . . .

At seven-thirty the door was jerked open and Ellery and the Chief glowered in on them. "Everybody out," said Naughton shortly. "Come on, step on it."

"Out?" whispered Mrs. Owen. "Where? Where is Richard? What—"

The policeman herded them out. Ellery stepped to the door of the den and pushed it open and switched on the light and stood aside.

"Will you please come in here and take seats," he said dryly; there was a tense look on his face and he seemed exhausted.

Silently, slowly, they obeyed. The policeman dragged in extra chairs from the living room. They sat down. Naughton drew the shades. The policeman closed the door and set his back against it.

Ellery said tonelessly: "In a way this has been one of the most remarkable cases in my experience. It's been unorthodox from every angle. Utterly nonconforming. I think, Miss Willowes, the wish you expressed Friday night has come true. You're about to witness a slightly cock-eyed exercise in criminal ingenuity."

"Crim—" Mrs. Gardner's full lips quivered. "You mean—there's been a crime?"

"Quiet," said Naughton harshly.

"Yes," said Ellery in gentle tones, "there has been a crime. I might say—I'm sorry to say, Mrs. Owen—a major crime."

"Richard's d—"

"I'm sorry." There was a little silence. Mrs. Owen did not weep; she seemed dried out of tears. "Fantastic," said Ellery at last. "Look here." He sighed. "The crux of the problem was the clock. The Clock That Wasn't Where It Should Have Been, the clock with the invisible face. You remember I pointed out that, since I hadn't seen the reflection of the luminous hands in that mirror there, the clock must have been moved. That was a tenable theory. But it wasn't the *only* theory."

"Richard's dead," said Mrs. Owen, in a wondering voice.

"Mr. Gardner," continued Ellery quickly, "pointed out one possibility: that the clock may still have been over this door, but that something or some one may have been standing in front of the mirror. I told you why that was impossible. But," and he went suddenly to the tall mirror, "there was still another theory which accounted for the fact that I hadn't seen the luminous hands' reflection. And that was: that when I opened the door in the dark and peered in and saw nothing, the clock was still there but the *mirror* wasn't!"

Miss Willowes said with a curious dryness: "But how could that be, Mr. Queen? That—that's silly."

"Nothing is silly, dear lady, until it is proved so. I said to myself: How could it be that the mirror wasn't there at that instant? It's apparently a solid part of the wall, a built-in section in this modern room." Something glimmered in Miss Willowes's eyes. Mrs. Mansfield was staring straight before her, hands clasped tightly in her lap. Mrs. Owen was looking at Ellery with glazed eyes, blind and deaf. "Then," said Ellery with another sigh, "there was the very odd nature of the packages which have been descending upon us all day like manna from heaven. I said this was a fantastic affair. Of course it must have occurred to you that some one was trying desperately to call our attention to the secret of the crime."

"Call our at—" began Gardner, frowning.

"Precisely. Now, Mrs. Owen," murmured Ellery softly, "the first package was addressed to you. What did it contain?" She stared at him without expression. There was a dreadful silence. Mrs. Mansfield suddenly shook her, as if she had been a child. She started, smiled vaguely; Ellery repeated the question.

And she said, almost brightly: "A pair of Richard's sport oxfords."

He winced. "In a word, *shoes*. Miss Willowes," and despite her nonchalance she stiffened a little, "you were the recipient of the second package. And what did that contain?"

"Jonathan's toy boats," she murmured.

"In a word, again—*ships*. Mrs. Mansfield, the third package was sent to you. It contained what, precisely?"

"Nothing." She tossed her head. "I still think this is the purest drivel. Can't you see you're driving my daughter—all of us—insane? Naughton, are you going to permit this farce to continue? If you know what's happened to Richard, for goodness' sake tell us!"

"Answer the question," said Naughton with a scowl.

"Well," she said defiantly, "a silly envelope, empty, and sealed with our own wax."

"And again in a word," drawled Ellery, "*sealing-wax.* Now, Gardner, to you fell the really whimsical fourth bequest. It was—?"

"Cabbage," said Gardner with an uncertain grin.

"Cabba*ges,* my dear chap; there were two of them. And finally, Mrs. Gardner, you received what?"

"Two chessmen," she whispered.

"No, no. Not just two chessmen, Mrs. Gardner. Two *kings.*" Ellery's gray eyes glittered. "In other words, in the order named we were bombarded with gifts . . ." he paused and looked at them, and continued softly, " '*of shoes and ships and sealing-wax, of cabbages and kings.*' "

There was the most extraordinary silence. Then Emmy Willowes gasped: "The Walrus and the Carpenter. *Alice's Adventures in Wonderland!*"

"I'm ashamed of you, Miss Willowes. Where precisely does Tweedledee's Walrus speech come in Carroll's duology?"

A great light broke over her eager features. "*Through the Looking Glass!*"

"*Through the Looking Glass,*" murmured Ellery in the crackling silence that followed. "And do you know what the subtitle of *Through the Looking Glass* is?"

She said in an awed voice: "*And What Alice Found There.*"

"A perfect recitation, Miss Willowes. We were instructed, then, to go through the looking glass and, by inference, find something on the other side connected with the disappearance of Richard Owen. Quaint idea, eh?" He leaned forward and said brusquely: "Let me revert to my original chain of reasoning. I said that a likely theory was that the mirror didn't reflect the luminous hands because the mirror wasn't there. But since the wall at any rate is solid, the mirror itself must be movable to have been shifted out of place. How was this possible? Yesterday I sought for two hours to find the secret of that mirror—or should I say . . . looking glass?" Their eyes went with horror to the tall mirror set in the wall, winking back at them in the glitter of the bulbs. "And when I discovered the secret, I looked *through the looking glass* and what do you suppose I— a clumsy Alice, indeed!—found there?"

No one replied.

Ellery went swiftly to the mirror, stood on tiptoe, touched something, and something happened to the whole glass. It moved forward as if on hinges. He hooked his fingers in the crack and pulled. The mirror, like a door, swung out and away, revealing a shallow closet-like cavity.

The women with one breath screamed and covered their eyes.

The stiff figure of the Mad Hatter, with Richard Owen's unmistakable features, glared out at them—a dead, horrible, baleful glare.

Paul Gardner stumbled to his feet, choking and jerking at his collar. His eyes bugged out of his head. "O-O-Owen," he gasped. "Owen. He *can't* be here. I b-b-buried him myself under the big rock behind the house in the woods. Oh, my God." And he smiled a dreadful smile and his eyes turned over and he collapsed in a faint on the floor.

Ellery sighed. "It's all right now, De Vere," and the Mad Hatter moved and his features ceased to resemble Richard Owen's magically. "You may come out now.

Admirable bit of statuary histrionics. And it turned the trick, as I thought it would. There's your man, Mr. Naughton. And if you'll question Mrs. Gardner, I believe you'll find that she's been Owen's mistress for some time. Gardner obviously found it out and killed him. Look out—there *she* goes, too!"

"What I can't understand," murmured Emmy Willowes after a long silence late that night, as she and Mr. Ellery Queen sat side by side in the local bound for Jamaica and the express for Pennsylvania Station, "is—" She stopped helplessly. "I can't understand so many things, Mr. Queen."

"It was simple enough," said Ellery wearily, staring out the window at the rushing dark countryside.

"But who is that man—that De Vere?"

"Oh, he! A Thespian acquaintance of mine temporarily 'at liberty.' He's an actor—does character bits. You wouldn't know him, I suppose. You see, when my deductions had led me to the looking glass and I examined it and finally discovered its secret and opened it, I found Owen's body lying there in the Hatter costume—"

She shuddered. "Much too realistic drama to my taste. Why didn't you announce your discovery at once?"

"And gain what? There wasn't a shred of evidence against the murderer. I wanted time to think out a plan to make the murderer give himself away. I left the body there—"

"You mean to sit there and say you knew Gardner did it all the time?" she demanded, frankly skeptical.

He shrugged. "Of course. The Owens had lived in that house barely a month. The spring on that compartment is remarkably well concealed; it probably would never be discovered unless you knew it existed and were looking for it. But I recalled that Owen himself had remarked Friday night that Gardner had designed 'this development.' I had it then, naturally. Who more likely than the architect to know the secret of such a hidden closet? Why he designed and had built a secret panel I don't know; I suppose it fitted into some architectural whim of his. So it had to be Gardner, you see." He gazed thoughtfully at the dusty ceiling of the car. "I reconstructed the crime easily enough. After we retired Friday night Gardner came down to have it out with Owen about Mrs. Gardner—a lusty wench, if I ever saw one. They had words; Gardner killed him. It must have been an unpremeditated crime. His first impulse was to hide the body. He couldn't take it out Friday night in that awful rain without leaving traces on his night-clothes. Then he remembered the panel behind the mirror. The body would be safe enough there, he felt, until he could remove it when the rain stopped and the ground dried to a permanent hiding-place; dig a grave, or whatnot. . . . He was stowing the body away in the closet when I opened the door of the den; that was why I didn't see the reflection of the clock. Then, while I was in the library, he closed the mirror-door and dodged upstairs. I came out quickly, though, and he decided to brazen it out; even pretended he thought I might be 'Owen' coming up.

"At any rate, Saturday night he drugged us all, took the body out, buried it, and came back and dosed himself with the drug to make his part as natural as possible. He didn't know I had found the body behind the mirror Saturday afternoon. When, Sunday morning, I found the body gone, I knew of course the reason for the drugging. Gardner by burying the body in a place unknown to any one—without leaving, as far as he knew, even a clue to the fact that murder had been committed at all—was naturally doing away with the primary piece of evidence in any murder-case . . . the *corpus delicti*. . . . Well, I found the opportunity to telephone De Vere and instruct him in what he had to do. He dug up the Hatter's costume somewhere, managed to get a photo of Owen from a theatrical office, came down here. . . . We put him in the closet while Naughton's man was detaining you people in the library. You see, I had to build up suspense, make Gardner give himself away, break down his moral resistance. He had to be forced to disclose where he had buried the body; and he was the only one who could tell us. It worked."

The actress regarded him sidewise out of her clever eyes. Ellery sighed moodily, glancing away from her slim legs outstretched to the opposite seat. "But the most puzzling thing of all," she said with a pretty frown. "Those perfectly fiendish and fantastic packages. Who sent them, for heaven's sake?"

Ellery did not reply for a long time. Then he said drowsily, barely audible above the clatter of the train: "You did, really."

"*I?*" She was so startled that her mouth flew open.

"Only in a manner of speaking," murmured Ellery, closing his eyes. "Your idea about running a mad tea-party out of *Alice* for Master Jonathan's delectation— the whole pervading spirit of the Reverend Dodgson— started a chain of fantasy in my own brain, you see. Just opening the closet and saying that Owen's body had been there, or even getting De Vere to act as Owen, wasn't enough. I had to prepare Gardner's mind psychologically, fill him with puzzlement first, get him to realize after a while where the gifts with their implications were leading. . . . Had to torture him, I suppose. It's a weakness of mine. At any rate, it was an easy matter to telephone my father, the Inspector; and he sent Sergeant Velie down and I managed to smuggle all those things I'd filched from the house out into the woods behind and hand good Velie what I had. . . . He did the rest, packaging and all."

She sat up and measured him with a severe glance. "*Mr.* Queen! Is that cricket in the best detective circles?"

He grinned sleepily. "I had to do it, you see. Drama, Miss Willowes. You ought to be able to understand that. Surround a murderer with things he doesn't understand, bewilder him, get him mentally punch-drunk, and then spring the knock-out blow, the crusher. . . . Oh, it was devilish clever of me, I admit."

She regarded him for so long and in such silence and with such supple twisting of her boyish figure that he stirred uncomfortably, feeling an unwilling flush come to his cheeks. "And what, if I may ask," he said lightly, "brings that positively lewd expression to your Peter Pannish face, my dear? Feel all right? Anything wrong? By George, how *do* you feel?"

"As Alice would say," she said softly, leaning a little toward him, "curiouser and curiouser."

THE LAMP OF GOD
A Short Novel

THE LAMP OF GOD

A Short Novel

I

If a story began: "Once upon a time in a house cowering
in wilderness there lived an old and eremitical creature named
Mayhew, a crazy man who had buried two wives and lived
a life of death; and this house was known as *The Black
House*"—if a story began in this fashion, it would strike no
one as especially remarkable. There are people like that who
live in houses like that, and very often mysteries materialize
like ectoplasm about their wild-eyed heads.

Now however disorderly Mr. Ellery Queen may be by
habit, mentally he is an orderly person. His neckties and
shoes might be strewn about his bedroom helter-skelter, but
inside his skull hums a perfectly oiled machine, functioning
as neatly and inexorably as the planetary system. So if there
was a mystery about one Sylvester Mayhew, deceased, and his
buried wives and gloomy dwelling, you may be sure the
Queen brain would seize upon it and worry it and pick it
apart and get it all laid out in neat and shiny rows. Ration-
ality, that was it. No esoteric mumbo-jumbo could fool *that*
fellow. Lord, no! His two feet were planted solidly on
God's good earth, and one and one made two—always—and
that's all there was to that.

Of course, Macbeth had said that stones have been known
to move and trees to speak; but, pshaw! for these literary
fancies. In this day and age, with its *Cominterns*, its wars of
peace, its *fasces* and its rocketry experiments? Nonsense!
The truth is, Mr. Queen would have said, there is something
about the harsh, cruel world we live in that's very rough on
miracles. Miracles just don't happen any more, unless they

are miracles of stupidity or miracles of national avarice. Everyone with a grain of intelligence knows that.

"Oh, yes," Mr. Queen would have said; "there are yogis, voodoos, fakirs, shamans, and other tricksters from the effete East and primitive Africa, but nobody pays any attention to such pitiful monkeyshines—I mean, nobody with sense. This is a reasonable world and everything that happens in it must have a reasonable explanation."

You couldn't expect a sane person to believe, for example, that a three-dimensional, flesh-and-blood, veritable human being could suddenly stoop, grab his shoelaces, and fly away. Or that a water-buffalo could change into a golden-haired little boy before your eyes. Or that a man dead one hundred and thirty-seven years could push aside his tombstone, step out of his grave, yawn, and then sing three verses of *Mademoiselle from Armentières*. Or even, for that matter, that a stone could move or a tree speak—yea, though it were in the language of Atlantis or Mu.

Or . . . *could you?*

The tale of Sylvester Mayhew's house is a strange tale. When what happened happened, proper minds tottered on their foundations and porcelain beliefs threatened to shiver into shards. Before the whole fantastic and incomprehensible business was done, God Himself came into it. Yes, God came into the story of Sylvester Mayhew's house, and that is what makes it quite the most remarkable adventure in which Mr. Ellery Queen, that lean and indefatigable agnostic, has ever become involved.

The early mysteries in the Mayhew case were trivial—mysteries merely because certain pertinent facts were lacking; pleasantly provocative mysteries, but scarcely savorous of the supernatural.

Ellery was sprawled on the hearthrug before the hissing fire that raw January morning, debating with himself whether it was more desirable to brave the slippery streets and biting wind on a trip to Centre Street in quest of amusement, or to remain where he was in idleness but comfort, when the telephone rang.

It was Thorne on the wire. Ellery, who never thought of Thorne without perforce visualizing a human monolith—a long-limbed, gray-thatched male figure with marbled cheeks and agate eyes, the whole man coated with a veneer of ebony, was rather startled. Thorne was excited; every crack and blur in his voice spoke eloquently of emotion. It was the first time, to Ellery's recollection, that Thorne had betrayed the least evidence of human feeling.

"What's the matter?" Ellery demanded. "Nothing's wrong with Ann, I hope?" Ann was Thorne's wife.

"No, no." Thorne spoke hoarsely and rapidly, as if he had been running.

"Where the deuce have you been? I saw Ann only yesterday and she said she hadn't heard from you for almost a week. Of course, your wife's used to your preoccupation with those interminable legal affairs, but an absence of six days——"

"Listen to me, Queen, and don't hold me up. I must have your help. Can you meet me at Pier 54 in half an hour? That's North River."

"Of course."

Thorne mumbled something that sounded absurdly like: "Thank God!" and hurried on: "Pack a bag. For a couple of days. And a revolver. Especially a revolver, Queen."

"I see," said Ellery, not seeing at all.

"I'm meeting the Cunarder *Coronia*. Docking this morning. I'm with a man by the name of Reinach, Dr. Reinach. You're my colleague; get that? Act stern and omnipotent. Don't be friendly. Don't ask him—or me—questions. And don't allow yourself to be pumped. Understood?"

"Understood," said Ellery, "but not exactly clear. Anything else?"

"Call Ann for me. Give her my love and tell her I shan't be home for days yet, but that you're with me and that I'm all right. And ask her to telephone my office and explain matters to Crawford."

"Do you mean to say that not even your partner knows what you've been doing?"

But Thorne had hung up.

Ellery replaced the receiver, frowning. It was stranger than strange. Thorne had always been a solid citizen, a successful attorney who led an impeccable private life and whose legal practice was dry and unexciting. To find old Thorne entangled in a web of mystery. . . .

Ellery drew a happy breath, telephoned Mrs. Thorne, tried to sound reassuring, yelled for Djuna, hurled some clothes into a bag, loaded his .38 police revolver with a grimace, scribbled a note for Inspector Queen, dashed downstairs and jumped into the cab Djuna had summoned, and landed on Pier 54 with thirty seconds to spare.

There was something terribly wrong with Thorne, Ellery saw at once, even before he turned his attention to the vast fat man by the lawyer's side. Thorne was shrunken within his Scotch-plaid greatcoat like a pupa which has died prematurely in its cocoon. He had aged years in the few weeks since Ellery had last seen him. His ordinarily sleek cobalt cheeks were covered with a straggly stubble. Even his clothing looked tired and uncared-for. And there was a glitter of furtive relief in his bloodshot eyes as he pressed Ellery's hand that was, to one who knew Throne's self-sufficiency and aplomb, almost pathetic.

But he merely remarked: "Oh, hello, there, Queen. We've a longer wait than we anticipated, I'm afraid. Want you to shake hands with Dr. Herbert Reinach. Doctor, this is Ellery Queen."

" 'D'you do," said Ellery curtly, touching the man's immense gloved hand. If he was to be omnipotent, he thought, he might as well be rude, too.

"Surprise, Mr. Thorne?" said Dr. Reinach in the deepest

voice Ellery had ever heard; it rumbled up from the caverns of his chest like the echo of thunder. His little purplish eyes were very, very cold.

"A pleasant one, I hope," said Thorne.

Ellery snatched a glance at his friend's face as he cupped his hands about a cigaret, and he read approval there. If he had struck the right tone, he knew how to act thenceforth. He flipped the match away and turned abruptly to Thorne. Dr. Reinach was studying him in a half-puzzled, half-amused way.

"Where's the *Coronia*?"

"Held up in quarantine," said Thorne. "Somebody's seriously ill aboard with some disease or other and there's been difficulty in clearing her passengers. It will take hours, I understand. Suppose we settle down in the waiting-room for a bit."

They found places in the crowded room, and Ellery set his bag between his feet and disposed himself so that he was in a position to catch every expression on his companions' faces. There was something in Thorne's repressed excitement, an even more piquing aura enveloping the fat doctor, that violently whipped his curiosity.

"Alice," said Thorne in a casual tone, as if Ellery knew who Alice was, "is probably becoming impatient. But that's a family trait with the Mayhews, from the little I saw of old Sylvester. Eh, Doctor? It's trying, though, to come all the way from England only to be held up on the threshold."

So they were to meet an Alice Mayhew, thought Ellery, arriving from England on the *Coronia*. Good old Thorne! He almost chuckled aloud. "Sylvester" was obviously a senior Mayhew, some relative of Alice's.

Dr. Reinach fixed his little eyes on Ellery's bag and rumbled politely: "Are you going away somewhere, Mr. Queen?"

Then Reinach did not know Ellery was to accompany them—wherever they were bound for.

Thorne stirred in the depths of his greatcoat, rustling like a sack of desiccated bones. "Queen's coming back with me, Dr. Reinach." There was something brittle and hostile in his voice.

The fat man blinked, his eyes buried beneath half-moons of damp flesh. "Really?" he said, and by contrast his bass voice was tender.

"Perhaps I should have explained," said Thorne abruptly. "Queen is a colleague of mine, Doctor. This case has interested him."

"Case?" said the fat man.

"Legally speaking. I really hadn't the heart to deny him the pleasure of helping me—ah—protect Alice Mayhew's interests. I trust you won't mind?"

This was a deadly game, Ellery became certain. Something important was at stake, and Thorne in his stubborn way was determined to defend it by force or guile.

Reinach's puffy lids dropped over his eyes as he folded his paws on his stomach. "Naturally, naturally not," he said in a hearty tone. "Only too happy to have you, Mr. Queen. A little unexpected, perhaps, but delightful surprises are as essential to life as to poetry. Eh?" And he chuckled.

Samuel Johnson, thought Ellery, recognizing the source of the doctor's remark. The physical analogy struck him. There was iron beneath those layers of fat and a good brain under that dolichocephalic skull. The man sat there on the waiting-room bench like an octopus, lazy and inert and peculiarly indifferent to his surroundings. Indifference—that was it, thought Ellery; the man was a colossal remoteness, as vague and darkling as a storm cloud on an empty horizon.

Thorne said in a weary voice: "Suppose we have lunch. I'm famished."

By three in the afternoon Ellery felt old and worn. Several hours of nervous, cautious silence, threading his way smiling among treacherous shoals, had told him just enough to put him on guard. He often felt knotted-up and tight inside when a crisis loomed or danger threatened from an unknown quarter. Something extraordinary was going on.

As they stood on the pier watching the *Coronia's* bulk being nudged alongside, he chewed on the scraps he had managed to glean during the long, heavy, pregnant hours. He knew definitely now that the man called Sylvester Mayhew was dead, that he had been a pronounced paranoic, that his house was buried in an almost inaccessible wilderness on Long Island. Alice Mayhew, somewhere on the decks of the *Coronia* doubtless straining her eyes pierward, was the dead man's daughter, parted from her father since childhood.

And he had placed the remarkable figure of Dr. Reinach in the puzzle. The fat man was Sylvester Mayhew's half-brother. He had also acted as Mayhew's physician during the old man's last illness. This illness and death seemed to have been very recent, for there had been some talk of "the funeral" in terms of fresh if detached sorrow. There was also a Mrs. Reinach glimmering unsubstantially in the background, and a queer old lady who was the dead man's sister. But what the mystery was, or why Thorne was so perturbed, Ellery could not figure out.

The liner tied up to the pier at last. Officials scampered about, whistles blew, gang-planks appeared, passengers disembarked in droves to the accompaniment of the usual howls and embraces.

Interest crept into Dr. Reinach's little eyes, and Thorne was shaking.

"There she is!" croaked the lawyer. "I'd know her anywhere from her photographs. That slender girl in the brown turban!"

As Thorne hurried away Ellery studied the girl eagerly. She was anxiously scanning the crowd, a tall charming creature with an elasticity of movement more esthetic than athletic and a harmony of delicate feature that approached beauty. She was dressed so simply and inexpensively that he narrowed his eyes.

Thorne came back with her, patting her gloved hand and speaking quietly to her. Her face was alight and alive, and there was a natural gayety in it which convinced Ellery that whatever mystery or tragedy lay before her, it was still unknown to her. At the same time there were certain signs about her eyes and mouth—fatigue, strain, worry, he could not put his finger on the exact cause—which puzzled him.

"I'm so glad," she murmured in a cultured voice, strongly British in accent. Then her face grew grave and she looked from Ellery to Dr. Reinach.

"This is your uncle, Miss Mayhew," said Thorne. "Dr. Reinach. This other gentleman is not, I regret to say, a relative. Mr. Ellery Queen, a colleague of mine."

"Oh," said the girl; and she turned to the fat man and said tremulously: "Uncle Herbert. How terribly odd. I mean—I've felt so all alone. You've been just a legend to me, Uncle Herbert, you and Aunt Sarah and the rest, and now . . ." She choked a little as she put her arms about the fat man and kissed his pendulous cheek.

"My dear," said Dr. Reinach solemnly; and Ellery could have struck him for the Judas quality of his solemnity.

"But you must tell me everything! Father—how is father? It seems so strange to be . . . to be saying that."

"Don't you think, Miss Mayhew," said the lawyer quickly, "that we had better see you through the Customs? It's growing late and we have a long trip before us. Long Island, you know."

"Island?" Her candid eyes widened. "That sounds so exciting!"

"Well, it's not what you might think——"

"Forgive me. I'm acting the perfect gawk." She smiled. "I'm entirely in your hands, Mr. Thorne. Your letter was more than kind."

As they made their way toward the Customs, Ellery dropped a little behind and devoted himself to watching Dr.

Reinach. But that vast lunar countenance was as inscrutable as a gargoyle.

Dr. Reinach drove. It was not Thorne's car; Thorne had a regal new Lincoln limousine and this was a battered if serviceable old Buick sedan.

The girl's luggage was strapped to the back and sides; Ellery was puzzled by the scantness of it—three small suitcases and a tiny steamer-trunk. Did these four pitiful containers hold all of her worldly possessions?

Sitting beside the fat man, Ellery strained his ears. He paid little attention to the road Reinach was taking.

The two behind were silent for a long time. Then Thorne cleared his throat with an oddly ominous finality. Ellery saw what was coming; he had often heard that throat-clearing sound emanate from the mouths of judges pronouncing sentence of doom.

"We have something sad to tell you, Miss Mayhew. You may as well learn it now."

"Sad?" murmured the girl after a moment. "Sad? Oh, it's not——"

"Your father," said Thorne inaudibly. "He's dead."

She cried: "Oh!" in a small helpless voice; and then she grew quiet.

"I'm dreadfully sorry to have to greet you with such news," said Thorne in the silence. "We'd anticipated . . . And I realize how awkward it must be for you. After all, it's quite as if you had never known him at all. Love for a parent, I'm afraid, lies in direct ratio to the degree of childhood association. Without any association at all . . ."

"It's a shock, of course," Alice said in a muffled voice. "And yet, as you say, he was a stranger to me, a mere name. As I wrote you, I was only a toddler when mother got her divorce and took me off to England. I don't remember father at all. And I've not seen him since, or heard from him."

"Yes," muttered the attorney.

"I might have learned more about father if mother hadn't died when I was six; but she did, and my people—her people—in England. . . . Uncle John died last fall. He was the last one. And then I was left all alone. When your letter came I was—I was so glad, Mr. Thorne. I didn't feel lonely any more. I was really happy for the first time in years. And now—" She broke off to stare out the window.

Dr. Reinach swiveled his massive head and smiled benignly. "But you're not alone, my dear. There's my unworthy self, and your Aunt Sarah, and Milly—Milly's my wife, Alice; naturally you wouldn't know anything about her—and there's even a husky young fellow named Keith who works about the place—bright lad who's come down in the world." He chuckled. "So you see there won't be a dearth of companionship for you."

"Thank you, Uncle Herbert," she murmured. "I'm sure you're all terribly kind. Mr. Thorne, how did father . . . When you replied to my letter you wrote me he was ill, but——"

"He fell into a coma unexpectedly nine days ago. You hadn't left England yet and I cabled you at your antique-shop address. But somehow it missed you."

"I'd sold the shop by that time and was flying about, patching up things. When did he . . . die?"

"A week ago Thursday. The funeral . . . Well, we couldn't wait, you see. I might have caught you by cable or telephone on the *Coronia*, but I didn't have the heart to spoil your voyage."

"I don't know how to thank you for all the trouble you've taken." Without looking at her Ellery knew there were tears in her eyes. "It's good to know that someone——"

"It's been hard for all of us," rumbled Dr. Reinach.

"Of course, Uncle Herbert. I'm sorry." She fell silent. When she spoke again, it was as if there were a compulsion expelling the words. "When Uncle John died, I didn't know where to reach father. The only American address I had was yours, Mr. Thorne, which some patron or other had given me. It was the only thing I could think of. I was sure a solicitor could find father for me. That's why I wrote to you in such detail, with photographs and all."

"Naturally we did what we could." Thorne seemed to be having difficulty with his voice. "When I found your father and went out to see him the first time and showed him your letter and photographs, he . . . I'm sure this will please you, Miss Mayhew. He wanted you badly. He'd apparently been having a hard time of late years—ah, mentally, emotionally. And so I wrote you at his request. On my second visit, the last time I saw him alive, when the question of the estate came up——"

Ellery thought that Dr. Reinach's paws tightened on the wheel. But the fat man's face bore the same bland, remote smile.

"Please," said Alice wearily. "Do you greatly mind, Mr. Thorne? I—I don't feel up to discussing such matters now."

The car was fleeing along the deserted road as if it were trying to run away from the weather. The sky was gray lead; a frowning, gloomy sky under which the countryside lay cowering. It was growing colder, too, in the dark and draughty tonneau; the cold seeped in through the cracks and their overclothes.

Ellery stamped his feet a little and twisted about to glance at Alice Mayhew. Her oval face was a glimmer in the murk; she was sitting stiffly, her hands clenched into tight little fists in her lap. Thorne was slumped miserably by her side, staring out the window.

"By George, it's going to snow," announced Dr. Reinach with a cheerful puff of his cheeks.

No one answered.

The drive was interminable. There was a dreary sameness about the landscape that matched the weather's mood. They had long since left the main highway to turn into a frightful byroad, along which they jolted in an unsteady eastward curve between ranks of leafless woods. The road was pitted and frozen hard; the woods were tangles of dead trees and underbrush densely packed but looking as if they had been repeatedly seared by fire. The whole effect was one of widespread and oppressive desolation.

"Looks like No Man's Land," said Ellery at last from his bouncing seat beside Dr. Reinach. "And feels like it, too."

Dr. Reinach's cetaceous back heaved in a silent mirth. "Matter of fact, that's exactly what it's called by the natives. Land-God-forgot, eh? But then Sylvester always swore by the Greek unities."

The man seemed to live in a dark and silent cavern, out of which he maliciously emerged at intervals to poison the atmosphere.

"It isn't very inviting-looking, is it?" remarked Alice in a low voice. It was clear she was brooding over the strange old man who had lived in this wasteland, and of her mother who had fled from it so many years before.

"It wasn't always this way," said Dr. Reinach, swelling his cheeks like a bull-frog. "Once it was pleasant enough; I remember it as a boy. Then it seemed as if it might become the nucleus of a populous community. But progress has passed it by, and a couple of uncontrollable forest fires did the rest."

"It's horrible," murmured Alice, "simply horrible."

"My dear Alice, it's your innocence that speaks there. All life is a frantic struggle to paint a rosy veneer over the ugly realities. Why not be honest with yourself? Everything in this world is stinking rotten; worse than that, a bore. Hardly worth living, in any impartial analysis. But if you have to live, you may as well live in surroundings consistent with the rottenness of everything."

The old attorney stirred beside Alice, where he was buried in his greatcoat. "You're quite a philosopher, Doctor," he snarled.

"I'm an honest man."

"Do you know, Doctor," murmured Ellery, despite himself, "you're beginning to annoy me."

The fat man glanced at him. Then he said: "And do you agree with this mysterious friend of yours, Thorne?"

"I believe," snapped Thorne, "that there is a platitude extant which says that actions speak with considerably more volume than words. I haven't shaved for six days, and today has been the first time I left Sylvester Mayhew's house since his funeral."

"Mr. Thorne!" cried Alice, turning to him. "Why?"

The lawyer muttered: "I'm sorry, Miss Mayhew. All in good time, in good time."

"You wrong us all," smiled Dr. Reinach, deftly skirting a deep rut in the road. "And I'm afraid you're giving my niece quite the most erroneous impression of her family. We're odd, no doubt, and our blood is presumably turning sour after so many generations of cold storage; but then don't the finest vintages come from the deepest cellars? You've only to glance at Alice to see my point. Such vital loveliness could only have been produced by an old family."

"My mother," said Alice, with a faint loathing in her glance, "had something to do with that, Uncle Herbert."

"Your mother, my dear," replied the fat man, "was merely a contributory factor. You have the typical Mayhew features."

Alice did not reply. Her uncle, whom until today she had not seen, was an obscene enigma; the others, waiting for them at their destination, she had never seen at all, and she had no great hope that they would prove better. A livid streak ran through her father's family; he had been a paranoic with delusions of persecution. The Aunt Sarah in the dark distance, her father's surviving sister, was apparently something of a character. As for Aunt Milly, Dr. Reinach's wife, whatever she might have been in the past, one had only to glance at Dr. Reinach to see what she undoubtedly was in the present.

Ellery felt prickles at the nape of his neck. The farther they penetrated this wilderness the less he liked the whole adventure. It smacked vaguely of a fore-ordained theatricalism, as if some hand of monstrous power were setting the stage for the first act of a colossal tragedy. . . . He shrugged this sophomoric foolishness off, settling deeper into his coat. It was queer enough, though. Even the lifelines of the most indigent community were missing; there were no telephone poles and, so far as he could detect, no electric cables. That meant candles. He detested candles.

The sun was behind them, leaving them. It was a feeble sun, shivering in the pallid cold. Feeble as it was, Ellery wished it would stay.

They crashed on and on, endlessly, shaken like dolls. The road kept lurching toward the east in a stubborn curve. The sky grew more and more leaden. The cold seeped deeper and deeper into their bones.

When Dr. Reinach finally rumbled: "Here we are," and steered the jolting car leftward off the road into a narrow, wretchedly gravelled driveway, Ellery came to with a start of surprise and relief. So their journey was really over, he thought. Behind him he heard Thorne and Alice stirring; they must be thinking the same thing.

He roused himself, stamping his icy feet, looking about. The same desolate tangle of woods to either side of the by-road. He recalled now that they had not once left the main road nor crossed another road since turning off the highway. No chance, he thought grimly, to stray off this path to perdition.

Dr. Reinach twisted his fat neck and said: "Welcome home, Alice."

Alice murmured something incomprehensible; her face was

buried to the eyes in the moth-eaten laprobe Reinach had
flung over her. Ellery glanced sharply at the fat man; there
had been a note of mockery, of derision, in that heavy rasp-
ing voice. But the face was smooth and damp and bland,
as before.

Dr. Reinach ran the car up the driveway and brought it
to rest a little before, and between, two houses. These struc-
tures flanked the drive, standing side by side, separated by
only the width of the drive, which led straight ahead to a
ramshackle garage. Ellery caught a glimpse of Thorne's
glittering Lincoln within its crumbling walls.

The three buildings huddled in a ragged clearing, surrounded by the tangle of woods, like three desert islands in
an empty sea.

"That," said Dr. Reinach heartily, "is the ancestral mansion, Alice. To the left."

The house to the left was of stone; once gray, but now
so tarnished by the elements and perhaps the ravages of fire
that it was almost black. Its face was blotched and streaky,
as if it had succumbed to an insensate leprosy. Rising three
stories, elaborately ornamented with stone flora and gargoyles,
it was unmistakably Victorian in its architecture. The façade
had a neglected, granular look that only the art of great age
could have etched. The whole structure appeared to have
thrust its roots immovably into the forsaken landscape.

Ellery saw Alice Mayhew staring at it with a sort of speechless horror; it had nothing of the pleasant hoariness of old
English mansions. It was simply old, old with the dreadful
age of this seared and blasted countryside. He cursed Thorne
beneath his breath for subjecting the girl to such a shocking
experience.

"Sylvester called it The Black House," said Dr. Reinach
cheerfully as he turned off the ignition. "Not pretty, I admit, but as solid as the day it was built, seventy-five years
ago."

"Black House," grunted Thorne. "Rubbish."

"Do you mean to say," whispered Alice, "that father . . . mother lived *here*?"

"Yes, my dear. Quaint name, eh, Thorne? Another illustration of Sylvester's preoccupation with the morbidly colorful. Built by your grandfather, Alice. The old gentleman built this one, too, later; I believe you'll find it considerably more habitable. Where the devil is everyone?"

He descended heavily and held the rear door open for his niece. Mr. Ellery Queen slipped down to the driveway on the other side and glanced about with the sharp, uneasy sniff of a wild animal. The old mansion's companion-house was a much smaller and less pretentious dwelling, two stories high and built of an originally white stone which had turned gray. The front door was shut and the curtains at the lower windows were drawn. But there was a fire burning somewhere inside; he caught the tremulous glimmers. In the next moment they were blotted out by the head of an old woman, who pressed her face to one of the panes for a single instant and then vanished. But the door remained shut.

"You'll stop with us, of course," he heard the doctor say genially; and Ellery circled the car. His three companions were standing in the driveway, Alice pressed close to old Thorne as if for protection. "You won't want to sleep in the Black House, Alice. No one's there, it's in rather a mess; and a house of death, y'know. . . ."

"Stop it," growled Thorne. "Can't you see the poor child is half-dead from fright as it is? Are you trying to scare her away?"

"Scare me away?" repeated Alice, dazedly.

"Tut, tut," smiled the fat man. "Melodrama doesn't become you at all, Thorne. I'm a blunt old codger, Alice, but I mean well. It will really be more comfortable in the White House." He chuckled suddenly again. "White House. That's what *I* named it to preserve a sort of atmospheric balance."

"There's something frightfully wrong here," said Alice in a tight voice. "Mr. Thorne, what is it? There's been noth-

ing but innuendo and concealed hostility since we met at
the pier. And just why *did* you spend six days in father's
house after the funeral? I think I've a right to know."

Thorne licked his lips. "I shouldn't——"

"Come, come, my dear," said the fat man. "Are we to
freeze here all day?"

Alice drew her thin coat more closely about her. "You're
all being beastly. Would you mind, Uncle Herbert? I
should like to see the inside—where father and mother . . ."

"I don't think so, Miss Mayhew," said Thorne hastily.

"Why not?" said Dr. Reinach tenderly, and he glanced
once over his shoulder at the building he had called the
White House. "She may as well do it now and get it over
with. There's still light enough to see by. Then we'll go
over, wash up, have a hot dinner, and you'll feel worlds
better." He seized the girl's arm and marched her toward
the dark building, across the dead, twig-strewn ground. "I
believe," continued the doctor blandly, as they mounted the
steps of the stone porch, "that Mr. Thorne has the keys."

The girl stood quietly waiting, her dark eyes studying the
faces of the three men. The attorney was pale, but his lips
were set in a stubborn line. He did not reply. Taking a
bunch of large rusty keys out of a pocket, he fitted one into
the lock of the front door. It turned over with a creak.

Then Thorne pushed open the door and they stepped into
the house.

It was a tomb. It smelled of must and damp. The furniture, ponderous pieces which once no doubt had been regal,
was uniformly dilapidated and dusty. The walls were peel-
ing, showing broken, discolored laths beneath. There was
dirt and débris everywhere. It was inconceivable that a
human being could once have inhabited this grubby den.

The girl stumbled about, her eyes a blank horror, Dr.
Reinach steering her calmly. How long the tour of inspection lasted Ellery did not know; even to him, a stranger, the

effect was so oppressive as to be almost unendurable. They wandered about, silent, stepping over trash from room to room, impelled by something stronger than themselves.

Once Alice said in a strangled voice: "Uncle Herbert, didn't anyone . . . take care of father? Didn't anyone ever clean up this horrible place?"

The fat man shrugged. "Your father had notions in his old age, my dear. There wasn't much anyone could do with him. Perhaps we had better not go into that."

The sour stench filled their nostrils. They blundered on, Thorne in the rear, watchful as an old cobra. His eyes never left Dr. Reinach's face.

On the middle floor they came upon a bedroom in which, according to the fat man, Sylvester Mayhew had died. The bed was unmade; indeed, the impress of the dead man's body on the mattress and tumbled sheets could still be discerned.

It was a bare and mean room, not as filthy as the others, but infinitely more depressing. Alice began to cough.

She coughed and coughed, hopelessly, standing still in the center of the room and staring at the dirty bed in which she had been born.

Then suddenly she stopped coughing and ran over to a lopsided bureau with one foot missing. A large, faded chromo was propped on its top against the yellowed wall. She looked at it for a long time without touching it. Then she took it down.

"It's mother," she said slowly. "It's really mother. I'm glad now I came. He did love her, after all. He's kept it all these years."

"Yes, Miss Mayhew," muttered Thorne. "I thought you'd like to have it."

"I've only one portrait of mother, and that's a poor one. This—why, she was beautiful, wasn't she?"

She held the chromo up proudly, almost laughing in her hysteria. The time-dulled colors revealed a stately young woman with hair worn high. The features were piquant

and regular. There was little resemblance between Alice
and the woman in the picture.

"Your father," said Dr. Reinach with a sigh, "often spoke
of your mother toward the last, and of her beauty."

"If he had left me nothing but this, it would have been
worth the trip from England." Alice trembled a little. Then
she hurried back to them, the chromo pressed to her breast.
"Let's get out of here," she said in a shriller voice. "I—
I don't like it here. It's ghastly. I'm . . . afraid."

They left the house with half-running steps, as if someone
were after them. The old lawyer turned the key in the
lock of the front door with great care, glaring at Dr. Reinach's back as he did so. But the fat man had seized his
niece's arm and was leading her across the driveway to the
White House, whose windows were now flickeringly bright
with light and whose front door stood wide open.

As they crunched along behind, Ellery said sharply to
Thorne: "Thorne. Give me a clue. A hint. Anything.
I'm completely in the dark."

Thorne's unshaven face was haggard in the setting sun.
"Can't talk now," he muttered. "Suspect everything, everybody. I'll see you tonight, in your room. Or wherever they
put you, if you're alone . . . Queen, for God's sake, be
careful!"

"Careful?" frowned Ellery.

"As if your life depended on it." Thorne's lips made a
thin, grim line. "For all I know, it does."

Then they were crossing the threshold of the White House.

Ellery's impressions were curiously vague. Perhaps it was
the effect of the sudden smothering heat after the hours of
cramping cold outdoors; perhaps he thawed out too suddenly,
and the heat went to his brain.

He stood about for a while in a state almost of semi-con-
sciousness, basking in the waves of warmth that eddied from

a roaring fire in a fireplace black with age. He was only dimly aware of the two people who greeted them, and of the interior of the house. The room was old, like everything else he had seen, and its furniture might have come from an antique shop. They were standing in a large living-room, comfortable enough; strange to his senses only because it was so old-fashioned in its appointments. There were actually antimacassars on the overstuffed chairs! A wide staircase with worn brass treads wound from one corner to the sleeping quarters above.

One of the two persons awaiting them was Mrs. Reinach, the doctor's wife. The moment Ellery saw her, even as she embraced Alice, he knew that this was inevitably the sort of woman the fat man would choose for a mate. She was a pale and weazened midge, almost fragile in her delicacy of bone and skin; and she was plainly in a silent convulsion of fear. She wore a hunted look on her dry and bluish face; and over Alice's shoulder she glanced timidly, with the fascinated obedience of a whipped bitch, at her husband.

"So you're Aunt Milly," sighed Alice, pushing away. "You'll forgive me if I . . . It's all so very new to me."

"You must be exhausted, poor darling," said Mrs. Reinach in the chirping twitter of a bird; and Alice smiled wanly and looked grateful. "And I quite understand. After all, we're no more than strangers to you. Oh!" she said, and stopped. Her faded eyes were fixed on the chromo in the girl's hands. "Oh," she said again. "I see you've been over to the other house *already*."

"Of course she has," said the fat man; and his wife grew even paler at the sound of his bass voice. "Now, Alice, why don't you let Milly take you upstairs and get you comfortable?"

"I am rather done in," confessed Alice; and then she looked at her mother's picture and smiled again. "I suppose you think I'm very silly, dashing in this way with just—" She did not finish; instead, she went to the fireplace. There was a broad flame-darkened mantel above it, crowded with gewgaws of a vanished era. She set the chromo of the handsome Victorian-garbed woman among them. "There! Now I feel ever so much better."

"Gentlemen, gentlemen," said Dr. Reinach. "Please don't stand on ceremony. Nick! Make yourself useful. Miss Mayhew's bags are strapped to the car."

A gigantic young man, who had been leaning against the wall, nodded in a surly way. He was studying Alice Mayhew's face with a dark absorption. He went out.

"Who," murmured Alice, flushing, "is that?"

"Nick Keith." The fat man slipped off his coat and went to the fire to warm his flabby hands. "My morose protégé. You'll find him pleasant company, my dear, if you can pierce that thick defensive armor he wears. Does odd jobs about the place, as I believe I mentioned, but don't let that hold you back. This is a democratic country."

"I'm sure he's very nice. Would you excuse me? Aunt Milly, if you'd be kind enough to . . ."

The young man reappeared under a load of baggage, clumped across the living-room, and plodded up the stairs. And suddenly, as if at a signal, Mrs. Reinach broke out into a noisy twittering and took Alice's arm and led her to the staircase. They disappeared after Keith.

"As a medical man," chuckled the fat man, taking their wraps and depositing them in a hall-closet, "I prescribe a large dose of . . . this, gentlemen." He went to a sideboard and brought out a decanter of brandy. "Very good for chilled bellies." He tossed off his own glass with an amazing facility, and in the light of the fire the finely etched capillaries in his bulbous nose stood out clearly. "Ah-h! One of life's major compensations. Warming, eh? And now I suppose you feel the need of a little sprucing up yourselves. Come along, and I'll show you to your rooms."

Ellery shook his head in a dogged way, trying to clear it. "There's something about your house, Doctor, that's unusually soporific. Thank you, I think both Thorne and I would appreciate a brisk wash."

"You'll find it brisk enough," said the fat man, shaking with silent laughter. "This is the forest primeval, you know. Not only haven't we any electric light or gas or telephone, but we've no running water, either. Well behind the house keeps us supplied. The simple life, eh? Better for you than the pampering influences of modern civilization. Our ancestors may have died more easily of bacterial infections, but I'll wager they had a greater body immunity to coryza! . . . Well, well, enough of this prattle. Up you go."

The chilly corridor upstairs made them shiver, but the very shiver revived them; Ellery felt better at once. Dr. Reinach, carrying candles and matches, showed Thorne into a room overlooking the front of the house, and Ellery into one on the side. A fire burned crisply in the large fireplace in one corner, and the basin on the old-fashioned washstand was filled with icy-looking water.

"Hope you find it comfortable," drawled the fat man, lounging in the doorway. "We were expecting only Thorne and my niece, but one more can always be accommodated. Ah—colleague of Thorne's, I believe he said?"

"Twice," replied Ellery. "If you don't mind—"

"Not at all." Reinach lingered, eying Ellery with a smile. Ellery shrugged, stripped off his coat, and made his ablutions. The water *was* cold; it nipped his fingers like the mouths of little fishes. He scrubbed his face vigorously.

"That's better," he said, drying himself. "Much. I wonder why I felt so peaked downstairs."

"Sudden contrast of heat after cold, no doubt." Dr. Reinach made no move to go.

Ellery shrugged again. He opened his bag with pointed nonchalance. There, plainly revealed on his haberdashery, lay the .38 police revolver. He tossed it aside.

"Do you always carry a gun, Mr. Queen?" murmured Dr. Reinach.

"Always." Ellery picked up the revolver and slipped it into his hip pocket.

"Charming!" The fat man stroked his triple chin. "Charming. Well, Mr. Queen, if you'll excuse me I'll see how Thorne is getting on. Stubborn fellow, Thorne. He could have taken pot luck with us this past week, but he insisted on isolating himself in that filthy den next door."

"I wonder," murmured Ellery, "why."

Dr. Reinach eyed him. Then he said: "Come downstairs when you're ready. · Mrs. Reinach has an excellent dinner prepared and if you're as hungry as I am, you'll appreciate it." Still smiling, the fat man vanished.

Ellery stood still for a moment, listening. He heard the fat man pause at the end of the corridor; a moment later the heavy tread was audible again, this time descending the stairs.

Ellery went swiftly to the door on tiptoe. He had noticed that the instant he had come into the room.

There was no lock. Where a lock had been there was a splintery hole, and the splinters had a newish look about them. Frowning, he placed a rickety chair against the door-knob and began to prowl.

He raised the mattress from the heavy wooden bedstead and poked beneath it, searching for he knew not what. He opened closets and drawers; he felt the worn carpet for wires.

But after ten minutes, angry with himself, he gave up and went to the window. The prospect was so dismal that he scowled in sheer misery. Just brown stripped woods and the leaden sky; the old mansion picturesquely known as the Black House was on the other side, invisible from this window.

A veiled sun was setting; a bank of storm clouds slipped aside for an instant and the brilliant rim of the sun shone directly into his eyes, making him see colored, dancing balls.

Then other clouds, fat with snow, moved up and the sun slipped below the horizon. The room darkened rapidly.

Lock taken out, eh? Someone had worked fast. They could not have known he was coming, of course. Then someone must have seen him through the window as the car stopped in the drive. The old woman who had peered out for a moment? Ellery wondered where she was. At any rate, a few minutes' work by a skilled hand at the door . . . He wondered, too, if Thorne's door had been similarly mutilated. And Alice Mayhew's.

Thorne and Dr. Reinach were already seated before the fire when Ellery came down, and the fat man was rumbling: "Just as well. Give the poor girl a chance to return to normal. With the shock she's had today, it might be the finisher. I've told Mrs. Reinach to break it to Sarah gently . . . Ah, Queen. Come over here and join us. We'll have dinner as soon as Alice comes down."

"Dr. Reinach was just apologizing," said Thorne casually, "for this Aunt Sarah of Miss Mayhew's—Mrs. Fell, Sylvester Mayhew's sister. The excitement of anticipating her niece's arrival seems to have been a bit too much for her."

"Indeed," said Ellery, sitting down and planting his feet on the nearest firedog.

"Fact is," said the fat man, "my poor half-sister is cracked. The family paranoia. She's off-balance; not violent, you know, but it's wise to humor her. She isn't normal, and for Alice to see her——"

"Paranoia," said Ellery. "An unfortunate family, it seems. Your half-brother Sylvester's weakness seems to have expressed itself in rubbish and solitude. What's Mrs. Fell's delusion?"

"Common enough—she thinks her daughter is still alive. As a matter of fact, poor Olivia was killed in an automobile accident three years ago. It shocked Sarah's maternal instinct out of plumb. Sarah's been looking forward to seeing Alice, her brother's daughter, and it may prove awkward. Never can tell how a diseased mind will react to an unusual situation."

"For that matter," drawled Ellery, "I should have said the same remark might be made about any mind, diseased or not."

Dr. Reinach laughed silently. Thorne, hunched by the fire, said: "This Keith boy."

The fat man set his glass down slowly. "Drink, Queen?"

"No, thank you."

"This Keith boy," said Thorne again.

"Eh? Oh, Nick. Yes, Thorne? What about him?"

The lawyer shrugged. Dr. Reinach picked up his glass again. "Am I imagining things, or is there the vaguest hint of hostility in the circumambient ether?"

"Reinach—" began Thorne harshly.

"Don't worry about Keith, Thorne. We let him pretty much alone. He's sour on the world, which demonstrates his good sense; but I'm afraid he's unlike me in that he hasn't the emotional buoyancy to rise above his wisdom. You'll probably find him anti-social. . . . Ah, there you are, my dear! Lovely, lovely."

Alice was wearing a different gown, a simple unfrilled frock, and she had freshened up. There was color in her cheeks and her eyes were sparkling with a light and tinge they had not had before. Seeing her for the first time without her hat and coat, Ellery thought she looked different, as all women contrive to look different divested of their outer clothing and refurbished by the mysterious activities which go on behind the closed doors of feminine dressing-rooms. Apparently the ministrations of another woman, too, had cheered her; there were still rings under her eyes, but her smile was more cheerful.

"Thank you, Uncle Herbert." Her voice was slightly husky. "But I do think I've caught a nasty cold."

"Whisky and hot lemonade," said the fat man promptly. "Eat lightly and go to bed early."

"To tell the truth, I'm famished."

"Then eat as much as you like. I'm one hell of a physician, as no doubt you've already detected. Shall we go in to dinner?"

"Yes," said Mrs. Reinach in a frightened voice. "We shan't wait for Sarah, or Nicholas."

Alice's eyes dulled a little. Then she sighed and took the fat man's arm and they all trooped into the dining-room.

Dinner was a failure. Dr. Reinach divided his energies between gargantuan inroads on the viands and copious drinking. Mrs. Reinach donned an apron and served, scarcely touching her own food in her haste to prepare the next course and clear the plates; apparently the household employed no domestic. Alice gradually lost her color, the old strained look reappearing on her face; occasionally she cleared her throat. The oil lamp on the table flickered badly, and every mouthful Ellery swallowed was flavored with the taste of oil. Besides, the *pièce de résistance* was curried lamb: if there was one dish he detested, it was lamb; and if there was one culinary style that sickened him, it was curry. Thorne ate stolidly, not raising his eyes from his plate.

As they returned to the living-room the old lawyer managed to drop behind. He whispered to Alice: "Is everything all right? Are you?"

"I'm a little scarish, I think," she said quietly. "Mr Thorne, please don't think me a child, but there's something so strange about—everything. . . . I wish now I hadn't come."

"I know," muttered Thorne. "And yet it was necessary, quite necessary. If there was any way to spare you this, I should have taken it. But you obviously couldn't stay in that horrible hole next door——"

"Oh, no," she shuddered.

"And there isn't a hotel for miles and miles. Miss Mayhew, has any of these people———"

"No, no. It's just that they're so strange to me. I suppose it's my imagination and this cold. Would you greatly
mind if I went to bed? Tomorrow will be time enough to
talk."

Thorne patted her hand. She smiled gratefully, murmured an apology, kissed Dr. Reinach's cheek, and went upstairs with Mrs. Reinach again.

They had just settled themselves before the fire again and
were lighting cigarets when feet stamped somewhere at the
rear of the house.

"Must be Nick," wheezed the doctor. "Now where's *he*
been?"

The gigantic young man appeared in the living-room arch-
way, glowering. His boots were soggy with wet. He
growled: "Hello," in his surly manner and went to the fire
to toast his big reddened hands. He paid no attention whatever to Thorne, although he glanced once, swiftly, at Ellery
in passing.

"Where've you been, Nick? Go in and have your dinner."

"I ate before you came."

"What's been keeping you?"

"I've been hauling in firewood. Something you didn't
think of doing." Keith's tone was truculent, but Ellery
noticed that his hands were shaking. Damnably odd! His
manner was noticeably not that of a servant, and yet he was
apparently employed in a menial capacity. "It's snowing."

"Snowing?"

They crowded to the front windows. The night was
moonless and palpable, and big fat snowflakes were sliding
down the panes.

"Ah, snow," sighed Dr. Reinach; and for all the sigh
there was something in his tone that made the nape of Ellery's neck prickle. " 'The whited air hides hills and woods,

the river, and the heaven, and veils the farmhouse at the garden's end.' "

"You're quite the countryman, Doctor," said Ellery.

"I like Nature in her more turbulent moods. Spring is for milksops. Winter brings out the fundamental iron." The doctor slipped his arm about Keith's broad shoulders. "Smile, Nick. Isn't God in His heaven?"

Keith flung the arm off without replying.

"Oh, you haven't met Mr. Queen. Queen, this is Nick Keith. You know Mr. Thorne already." Keith nodded shortly. "Come, come, my boy, buck up. You're too emotional, that's the trouble with you. Let's all have a drink. The disease of nervousness is infectious."

Nerves! thought Ellery grimly. His nostrils were pinched, sniffing the little mysteries in the air. They tantalized him. Thorne was tied up in knots, as if he had cramps; the veins at his temples were pale blue swollen cords and there was sweat on his forehead. Above their heads the house was soundless.

Dr. Reinach went to the sideboard and began hauling out bottles—gin, bitters, rye, vermouth. He busied himself mixing drinks, talking incessantly. There was a purr in his hoarse undertones, a vibration of pure excitement. What in Satan's name, thought Ellery in a sort of agony, was going on here?

Keith passed the cocktails around, and Ellery's eyes warned Thorne. Thorne nodded slightly; they had two drinks apiece and refused more. Keith drank doggedly, as if he were anxious to forget something.

"Now that's better," said Dr. Reinach, settling his bulk into an easy-chair. "With the women out of the way and a fire and liquor, life becomes almost endurable."

"I'm afraid," said Thorne, "that I shall prove an unpleasant influence, Doctor. I'm going to make it unendurable."

Dr. Reinach blinked. "Well, now," he said. "Well, now." He pushed the brandy decanter carefully out of the way of his elbow and folded his pudgy paws on his stomach. His purple little eyes shone.

Thorne went to the fire and stood looking down at the flames, his back to them. "I'm here in Miss Mayhew's interests, Dr. Reinach," he said, without turning. "In her interests alone. Sylvester Mayhew died last week very suddenly. Died while waiting to see the daughter whom he hadn't seen since his divorce from her mother almost twenty years ago."

"Factually exact," rumbled the doctor, without stirring.

Thorne spun about. "Dr. Reinach, you acted as Mayhew's physician for over a year before his death. What was the matter with him?"

"A variety of things. Nothing extraordinary. He died of cerebral hemorrhage."

"So your certificate claimed." The lawyer leaned forward. "I'm not entirely convinced," he said slowly, "that your certificate told the truth."

The doctor stared at him for an instant, then he slapped his bulging thigh. "Splendid!" he roared. "Splendid! A man after my own heart. Thorne, for all your desiccated exterior you have juicy potentialities." He turned on Ellery, beaming. "You heard that, Mr. Queen? Your friend openly accuses me of murder. This is becoming quite exhilarating. So! Old Reinach's a fratricide. What do you think of that, Nick? Your patron accused of cold-blooded murder. Dear, dear."

"That's ridiculous, Mr. Thorne," growled Nick Keith. "You don't believe it yourself."

The lawyer's gaunt cheeks sucked in. "Whether I believe it or not is immaterial. The possibility exists. But I'm more concerned with Alice Mayhew's interests at the moment than with a possible homicide. Sylvester Mayhew is dead, no matter by what agency—divine or human; but Alice Mayhew is very much alive."

"And so?" asked Reinach softly.

"And so I say," muttered Thorne, "it's damnably queer her father should have died when he did. Damnably."

For a long moment there was silence. Keith put his elbows on his knees and stared into the flames, his shaggy boyish hair over his eyes. Dr. Reinach sipped a glass of brandy with enjoyment.

Then he set his glass down and said with a sigh: "Life is too short, gentlemen, to waste in cautious skirmishings. Let us proceed without feinting movements to the major engagement. Nick Keith is in my confidence and we may speak freely before him." The young man did not move. "Mr. Queen, you're very much in the dark, aren't you?" went on the fat man with a bland smile.

Ellery did not move, either. "And how," he murmured, "did you know that?"

Reinach kept smiling. "Pshaw. Thorne hadn't left the Black House since Sylvester's funeral. Nor did he receive or send any mail during his self-imposed vigil last week. This morning he left me on the pier to telephone someone. You showed up shortly after. Since he was gone only a minute or two, it was obvious that he hadn't had time to tell you much, if anything. Allow me to felicitate you, Mr. Queen, upon your conduct today. It's been exemplary. An air of omniscience covering a profound and desperate ignorance."

Ellery removed his *pince-nez* and began to polish their lenses. "You're a psychologist as well as a physician, I see."

Thorne said abruptly: "This is all beside the point."

"No, no, it's all very much *to* the point," replied the fat man in a sad bass. "Now the canker annoying your friend, Mr. Queen—since it seems a shame to keep you on tenterhooks any longer—is roughly this: My half-brother Sylvester, God rest his troubled soul, was a miser. If he'd been able to take his gold with him to the grave—with any assurance that it would remain there—I'm sure he would have done so."

"Gold?" asked Ellery, raising his brows.

"You may well titter, Mr. Queen. There was something mediaeval about Sylvester; you almost expected him to go about in a long black velvet gown muttering incantations in Latin. At any rate, unable to take his gold with him to the grave, he did the next best thing. He hid it."

"Oh, lord," said Ellery. "You'll be pulling clanking ghosts out of your hat next."

"Hid," beamed Dr. Reinach, "the filthy lucre in the Black House."

"And Miss Alice Mayhew?"

"Poor child, a victim of circumstances. Sylvester never thought of her until recently, when she wrote from London that her last maternal relative had died. Wrote to friend Thorne, he of the lean and hungry eye, who had been recommended by some friend as a trustworthy lawyer. As he is, as he is! You see, Alice didn't even know if her father was alive, let alone where he was. Thorne, good Samaritan, located us, gave Alice's exhaustive letters and photographs to Sylvester, and has acted as *liaison* officer ever since. And a downright circumspect one, too, by thunder!"

"This explanation is wholly unnecessary," said the lawyer stiffly. "Mr. Queen knows——"

"Nothing," smiled the fat man, "to judge by the attentiveness with which he's been following my little tale. Let's be intelligent about this, Thorne." He turned to Ellery again, nodding very amiably. "Now, Mr. Queen, Sylvester clutched at the thought of his new-found daughter with the pertinacity of a drowning man clutching a life-preserver. I betray no secret when I say that my half-brother, in his paranoic dotage, suspected his own family —imagine!—of having evil designs on his fortune."

"A monstrous slander, of course."

"Neatly put, neatly put! Well, Sylvester told Thorne in my presence that he had long since converted his fortune into specie, that he'd hidden this gold somewhere in the house next door, and that he wouldn't reveal the hiding-place to anyone but Alice, his daughter, who was to be his sole heir. You see?"

"I see," said Ellery.

"He died before Alice's arrival, unfortunately. Is it any wonder, Mr. Queen, that Thorne thinks dire things of us?"

"This is fantastic," snapped Thorne, coloring. "Naturally, in the interests of my client, I couldn't leave the premises unguarded with that mass of gold lying about loose somewhere——"

"Naturally not," nodded the doctor.

"If I may intrude my still, small voice," murmured Ellery, "isn't this a battle of giants over a mouse? The possession of gold is a clear violation of the law in this country, and has been for several years. Even if you found it, wouldn't the government confiscate it?"

"There's a complicated legal situation, Queen," said Thorne; "but one which cannot come into existence before the gold is found. Therefore my efforts to——"

"And successful efforts, too," grinned Dr. Reinach. "Do you know, Mr. Queen, your friend has slept behind locked, barred doors, with an old cutlass in his hand—one of Sylvester's prized mementoes of a grandfather who was in the Navy? It's terribly amusing."

"I don't find it so," said Thorne shortly. "If you insist on playing the buffoon——"

"And yet—to go back to this matter of your little suspicions, Thorne—have you analyzed the facts? Whom do you suspect, my dear fellow? Your humble servant? I assure you that I am spiritually an ascetic——"

"An almighty fat one!" snarled Thorne.

"—and that money, *per se*, means nothing to me," went on the doctor imperturbably. "My half-sister Sarah? An anile wreck living in a world of illusion, quite as antediluvian as Sylvester—they were twins, you know—who isn't very long for this world. Then that leaves my estimable Milly and our saturnine young friend Nick. Milly? Absurd; she hasn't had an idea, good or bad, for two decades. Nick? Ah, an outsider—we may have struck something there. Is it Nick you suspect, Thorne?" chuckled Dr. Reinach.

Keith got to his feet and glared down into the bland damp lunar countenance of the fat man. He seemed quite drunk. "You damned porker," he said thickly.

Dr. Reinach kept smiling, but his little porcine eyes were wary. "Now, now, Nick," he said in a soothing rumble.

It all happened very quickly. Keith lurched forward, snatched the heavy cut-glass brandy decanter, and swung it at the doctor's head. Thorne cried out and took an instinctive forward step; but he might have spared himself the exertion. Dr. Reinach jerked his head back like a fat snake and the blow missed. The violent effort pivoted Keith's body completely about; the decanter slipped from his fingers and flew into the fireplace, crashing to pieces. The fragments splattered all over the fireplace, strewing the hearth, too; the little brandy that remained in the bottle hissed into the fire, blazing with a blue flame.

"That decanter," said Dr. Reinach angrily, "was almost a hundred and fifty years old!"

Keith stood still, his broad back to them. They could see his shoulders heaving.

Ellery sighed with the queerest feeling. The room was shimmering as in a dream, and the whole incident seemed unreal, like a scene in a play on a stage. Were they acting? Had the scene been carefully planned? But, if so, why? What earthly purpose could they have hoped to achieve by pretending to quarrel and come to blows? The sole result had been the wanton destruction of a lovely old decanter. It didn't make sense.

"I think," said Ellery, struggling to his feet, "that I shall go to bed before the Evil One comes down the chimney. Thank you for an altogether extraordinary evening, gentlemen. Coming, Thorne?"

He stumbled up the stairs, followed by the lawyer, who seemed as weary as he. They separated in the cold corridor without a word to stumble to their respective bedrooms. From below came a heavy silence.

It was only as he was throwing his trousers over the footrail of his bed that Ellery recalled hazily Thorne's whispered intention hours before to visit him that night and explain the whole fantastic business. He struggled into his dressing-gown and slippers and shuffled down the hall to Thorne's room. But the lawyer was already in bed, snoring sterterously.

Ellery dragged himself back to his room and finished undressing. He knew he would have a head the next morning; he was a notoriously poor drinker. His brain spinning, he crawled between the blankets and fell asleep almost stertorously.

He opened his eyes after a tossing, tiring sleep with the uneasy conviction that something was wrong. For a moment he was aware only of the ache in his head and the fuzzy feel of his tongue; he did not remember where he was. Then, as his glance took in the faded wall-paper, the pallid patches of sunlight on the worn blue carpet, his trousers tumbled over the footrail where he had left them the night before, memory returned; and, shivering, he consulted his wrist-watch, which he had forgotten to take off on going to bed. It was five minutes to seven. He raised his head from the pillow in the frosty air of the bedroom; his nose was half-frozen. But he could detect nothing wrong; the sun looked brave if weak in his eyes; the room was quiet and exactly as he had seen it on retiring; the door was closed. He snuggled between the blankets again.

Then he heard it. It was Thorne's voice. It was Thorne's voice raised in a thin faint cry, almost a wail, coming from somewhere outside the house.

He was out of bed and at the window in his bare feet in

one leap. But Thorne was not visible at this side of the house, upon which the dead woods encroached directly; so he scrambled back to slip shoes on his feet and his gown over his pajamas, darted toward the footrail and snatched his revolver out of the hip pocket of his trousers, and ran out into the corridor, heading for the stairs, the revolver in his hand.

"What's the matter?" grumbled someone, and he turned to see Dr. Reinach's vast skull protruding nakedly from the room next to his.

"Don't know. I heard Thorne cry out," and Ellery pounded down the stairs and flung open the front door.

He stopped within the doorway, gaping.

Thorne, fully dressed, was standing ten yards in front of the house, facing Ellery obliquely, staring at something outside the range of Ellery's vision with the most acute expression of terror on his gaunt face Ellery had ever seen on a human countenance. Beside him crouched Nicholas Keith, only half-dressed; the young man's jaws gaped foolishly and his eyes were enormous glaring discs.

Dr. Reinach shoved Ellery roughly aside and growled: "What's the matter? What's wrong?" The fat man's feet were encased in carpet slippers and he had pulled a raccoon coat over his night-shirt, so that he looked like a particularly obese bear.

Thorne's Adam's-apple bobbed nervously. The ground, the trees, the world were blanketed with snow of a peculiarly unreal texture; and the air was saturated with warm woolen flakes, falling softly. Deep drifts curved upwards to clamp the boles of trees.

"Don't move," croaked Thorne as Ellery and the fat man stirred. "Don't move, for the love of God. Stay where you are." Ellery's grip tightened on the revolver and he tried perversely to get past the doctor; but he might have been trying to budge a stone wall. Thorne stumbled through the snow to the porch, paler than his background, leaving two deep ruts behind him. "Look at me," he shouted. "*Look at me.* Do I seem all right? Have I gone mad?"

"Pull yourself together, Thorne," said Ellery sharply. "What's the matter with you? I don't see anything wrong."

"Nick!" bellowed Dr. Reinach. "Have you gone crazy, too?"

The young man covered his sunburnt face suddenly with his hands; then he dropped his hands and looked again.

He said in a strangled voice: "Maybe we all have. This is the most—Take a look yourself."

Reinach moved then, and Ellery squirmed by him to land in the soft snow beside Thorne, who was trembling violently. Dr. Reinach came lurching after. They ploughed through the snow toward Keith, squinting, straining to see.

They need not have strained. What was to be seen was plain for any seeing eye to see. Ellery felt his scalp crawl as he looked; and at the same instant he was aware of the sharp conviction that this was inevitable, this was the only possible climax to the insane events of the previous day. The world had turned topsy-turvy. Nothing in it meant anything reasonable or sane.

Dr. Reinach gasped once; and then he stood blinking like a huge owl. A window rattled on the second floor of the White House. None of them looked up. It was Alice Mayhew in a wrapper, staring from the window of her bedroom, which was on the side of the house facing the driveway. She screamed once; and then she, too, fell silent.

There was the house from which they had just emerged, the house Dr. Reinach had dubbed the White House, with its front door quietly swinging open and Alice Mayhew at an upper side window. Substantial, solid, an edifice of stone and wood and plaster and glass and the patina of age. It was everything a house should be. That much was real, a thing to be grasped.

But beyond it, beyond the driveway and the garage, where the Black House had stood, the house in which Ellery himself had set foot only the afternoon before, the house of the filth and the stench, the house of the equally stone walls, wooden facings, glass windows, chimneys, gargoyles, porch; the house of the blackened look; the old Victorian house built during the Civil War where Sylvester Mayhew had died, where Thorne had barricaded himself with a cutlass for a week; the house which they had all seen, touched, smelled . . . there, *there stood nothing.*

No walls. No chimney. No roof. No ruins. No débris. No house. Nothing.

Nothing but empty space covered smoothly and warmly with snow.

The house had vanished during the night.

II

"There's even," thought Mr. Ellery Queen dully, "a character named Alice."

He looked again. The only reason he did not rub his eyes was that it would have made him feel ridiculous; besides, his sight, all his senses, had never been keener.

He simply stood there in the snow and looked and looked and looked at the empty space where a three-story stone house seventy-five years old had stood the night before.

"Why, it isn't there," said Alice feebly from the upper window. "It . . . isn't . . . there."

"Then I'm not insane." Thorne stumbled toward them. Ellery watched the old man's feet sloughing through the snow, leaving long tracks. A man's weight still counted for something in the universe, then. Yes, and there was his own shadow; so material objects still cast shadows. Absurdly, the discovery brought a certain faint relief.

"It *is* gone!" said Thorne in a cracked voice.

"Apparently." Ellery found his own voice thick and slow; he watched the words curl out on the air and become nothing. "Apparently, Thorne." It was all he could find to say.

Dr. Reinach arched his fat neck, his wattles quivering like a gobbler's. "Incredible. Incredible!"

"Incredible," said Thorne in a whisper.

"Unscientific. It can't be. I'm a man of sense. Of senses. My mind is clear. Things like this—damn it, they just don't happen!"

"As the man said who saw a giraffe for the first time," sighed Ellery. "And yet . . . there it was."

Thorne began wandering helplessly about in a circle. Alice stared, bewitched into stone, from the upper window. And Keith cursed and began to run across the snow-covered driveway toward the invisible house, his hands outstretched before him like a blind man's.

"Hold on," said Ellery. "Stop where you are."

The giant halted, scowling. "What d'ye want?"

Ellery slipped his revolver back into his pocket and sloshed through the snow to pause beside the young man in the driveway. "I don't know precisely. Something's wrong. Something's out of kilter either with us or with the world. It isn't the world as we know it. It's almost . . . almost a matter of transposed dimensions. Do you suppose the solar system has slipped out of its niche in the universe and gone stark crazy in the uncharted depths of space-time? I suppose I'm talking nonsense."

"You know best," shouted Keith. "I'm not going to let this screwy business stampede *me*. There was a solid house on that plot last night, by God, and nobody can convince me it still isn't there. Not even my own eyes. We've—we've been hypnotized! The hippo could do it here—he could do anything. Hypnotized. You hypnotized us, Reinach!"

The doctor mumbled: "What?" and kept glaring at the empty lot.

"I tell you it's there!" cried Keith angrily.

Ellery sighed and dropped to his knees in the snow; he began to brush aside the white, soft blanket with chilled palms. When he had laid the ground bare, he saw wet gravel and a rut.

"This *is* the driveway, isn't it?" he asked without looking up.

"The driveway," snarled Keith, "or the road to hell. You're as mixed up as we are. Sure it's the driveway! Can't you see the garage? Why shouldn't it be the driveway?"

"I don't know." Ellery got to his feet, frowning. "I don't know anything. I'm beginning to learn all over again. Maybe—maybe it's a matter of gravitation. Maybe we'll all fly into space any minute now."

Thorne groaned: "My God."

"All I can be sure of is that something very strange happened last night."

"I tell you," growled Keith, "it's an optical illusion!"

"Something strange." The fat man stirred. "Yes, decidedly. What an inadequate word! A house has disappeared. Something strange." He began to chuckle in a choking, mirthless way.

"Oh that," said Ellery impatiently. "Certainly. Certainly, Doctor. That's a *fact*. As for you, Keith, you don't really believe this mass-hypnosis bilge. The house is gone, right enough. . . . It's not the fact of its being gone that bothers me. It's the agency, the *means*. It smacks of—of—" He shook his head. "I've never believed in . . . this sort of thing, damn it all!"

Dr. Reinach threw back his vast shoulders and glared, red-eyed, at the empty snow-covered space. "It's a trick," he bellowed. "A rotten trick, that's what it is. That house is right there in front of our noses. Or— or— They can't fool *me*!"

Ellery looked at him. "Perhaps," he said, "Keith has it in his pocket?"

Alice clattered out on the porch in high-heeled shoes over bare feet, her hair streaming, a cloth coat flung over her night-clothes. Behind her crept little Mrs. Reinach. The women's eyes were wild.

"Talk to them," muttered Ellery to Thorne. "Anything; but keep their minds occupied. We'll all go balmy if we don't preserve at least an air of sanity. Keith, get me a broom."

He shuffled up the driveway, skirting the invisible house very carefully and not once taking his eyes off the empty space. The fat man hesitated; then he lumbered along in Ellery's tracks. Thorne stumbled back to the porch and Keith strode off, disappearing behind the White House.

There was no sun now. A pale and eerie light filtered down

through the cold clouds. The snow continued its soft, thick fall.

They looked like dots, small and helpless, on a sheet of blank paper.

Ellery pulled open the folding doors of the garage and peered. A healthy odor of raw gasoline and rubber assailed his nostrils. Thorne's car stood within, exactly as Ellery had seen it the afternoon before, a black monster with glittering chrome-work. Beside it, apparently parked by Keith after their arrival, stood the battered Buick in which Dr. Reinach had driven them from the city. Both cars were perfectly dry.

He shut the doors and turned back to the driveway. Aside from the catenated links of their footprints in the snow, made a moment before, the white covering on the driveway was virgin.

"Here's your broom," said the giant. "What are you going to do—ride it?"

"Hold your tongue, Nick," growled Dr. Reinach.

Ellery laughed. "Let him alone, Doctor. His angry sanity is infectious. Come along, you two. This may be the Judgment Day, but we may as well go through the motions."

"What do you want with a broom, Queen?"

"It's hard to decide whether the snow was an accident or part of the plan," murmured Ellery. "Anything may be true today. Literally anything."

"Rubbish," snorted the fat man. "Abracadabra. *Om mani padme hum.* How could a man have planned a snowfall? You're talking gibberish."

"I didn't say a human plan, Doctor."

"Rubbish, rubbish, rubbish!"

"You may as well save your breath. You're a badly scared little boy whistling in the dark—for all your bulk, Doctor."

Ellery gripped the broom tightly and stamped out across the driveway. He felt his own foot shrinking as he tried

to make it step upon the white rectangle. His muscles were
gathered in, as if in truth he expected to encounter the ada-
mantine bulk of a house which was still there but unaccountably impalpable. When he felt nothing but cold air, he
laughed a little self-consciously and began to wield the broom
on the snow in a peculiar manner. He used the most delicate
of sweeping motions, barely brushing the surface crystals
away; so that layer by layer he reduced the depth of the
snow. He scanned each layer with anxiety as it was
uncovered. And he continued to do this until the ground
itself lay revealed; and at no depth did he come across the
minutest trace of a human imprint.

"Elves," he complained. "Nothing less than elves. I confess it's beyond me."

"Even the foundation—" began Dr. Reinach heavily.

Ellery poked the tip of the broom at the earth. It was
hard as corundum.

The front door slammed as Thorne and the two women
crept into the White House. The three men outside stood
still, doing nothing.

"Well," said Ellery at last, "this is either a bad dream or
the end of the world." He made off diagonally across the
plot, dragging the broom behind him like a tired charwoman,
until he reached the snow-covered drive; and then he trudged
down the drive towards the invisible road, disappearing
around a bend under the stripped white-dripping trees.

It was a short walk to the road. Ellery remembered it
well. It had curved steadily in a long arc all the way from
the turn-off at the main highway. There had been no cross-
road in all the jolting journey.

He went out into the middle of the road, snow-covered
now but plainly distinguishable between the powdered
tangles of woods as a gleaming, empty strip. There was the
long curve exactly as he remembered it. Mechanically he
used the broom again, sweeping a small area clear. And there
were the pits and ruts of the old Buick's journeys.

"What are you looking for," said Nick Keith quietly, "gold?"

Ellery straightened up by degrees, turning about slowly until he was face to face with the giant. "So you thought it was necessary to follow me? Or—no, I beg your pardon. Undoubtedly it was Dr. Reinach's idea."

The sun-charred features did not change expression. "You're crazy as a bat. Follow you? I've got all I can do to follow myself."

"Of course," said Ellery. "But did I understand you to ask me if I was looking for gold, my dear young Prometheus?"

"You're a queer one," said Keith as they made their way back toward the house.

"Gold," repeated Ellery. "Hmm. There was gold in that house, and now the house is gone. In the shock of the discovery that houses fly away like birds, I'd quite forgotten that little item. Thank you, Mr. Keith," said Ellery grimly, "for reminding me."

"Mr. Queen," said Alice. She was crouched in a chair by the fire, white to the lips. "What's happened to us? What are we to do? Have we ... Was yesterday a dream? Didn't we walk into that house, go through it, touch things? ... I'm frightened."

"If yesterday *was* a dream," smiled Ellery, "then we may expect that tomorrow will bring a vision; for that's what holy Sanskrit says, and we may as well believe in parables as in miracles." He sat down, rubbing his hands briskly. "How about a fire, Keith? it's arctic in here."

"Sorry," said Keith with surprising amiability, and he went away.

"We could use a vision," shivered Thorne. "My brain is—sick. It just isn't possible. It's horrible." His hand slapped his side and something jangled in his pocket.

"Keys," said Ellery, "and no house. It *is* staggering."

Keith came back under a mountain of firewood. He grimaced at the litter in the fireplace, dropped the wood, and began sweeping together the fragments of glass, the remains of the brandy decanter he had smashed against the brick wall the night before. Alice glanced from his broad back to the chromo of her mother on the mantel. As for Mrs. Reinach, she was as silent as a scared bird; she stood in a corner like a weazened little gnome, her wrapper drawn about her, her stringy sparrow-colored hair hanging down her back, and her glassy eyes fixed on the face of her husband.

"Milly," said the fat man.

"Yes, Herbert, I'm going," said Mrs. Reinach instantly, and she crept up the stairs and out of sight.

"Well, Mr. Queen, what's the answer? Or is this riddle too esoteric for your taste?"

"No riddle is esoteric," muttered Ellery, "unless it's the riddle of God; and that's no riddle—it's a vast blackness. Doctor, is there any way of reaching assistance?"

"Not unless you can fly."

"No phone," said Keith without turning, "and you saw the condition of the road for yourself. You'd never get a car through those drifts."

"If you had a car," chuckled Dr. Reinach. Then he seemed to remember the disappearing house, and his chuckle died.

"What do you mean?" demanded Ellery. "In the garage are—"

"Two useless products of the machine age. Both cars are out of fuel."

"And mine," said old Thorne suddenly, with a resurrection of grim personal interest, "mine has something wrong with it besides. I left my chauffeur in the city, you know, Queen, when I drove down last time. Now I can't get the engine running on the little gasoline that's left in the tank."

Ellery's fingers drummed on the arm of his chair. "Bother! Now we can't even call on other eyes to test whether we've been bewitched or not. By the way, Doctor, how far is the nearest community? I'm afraid I didn't pay attention on the drive down."

"Over fifteen miles by road. If you're thinking of footing it, Mr. Queen, you're welcome to the thought."

"You'd never get through the drifts," muttered Keith. The drifts appeared to trouble him.

"And so we find ourselves snowbound," said Ellery, "in the middle of the fourth dimension—or perhaps it's the fifth. A pretty kettle! Ah there, Keith, that feels considerably better."

"You don't seem bowled over by what's happened," said Dr. Reinach, eying him curiously. "I'll confess it's given even me a shock."

Ellery was silent for a moment. Then he said lightly: "There wouldn't be any point to losing our heads, would there?"

"I fully expect dragons to come flying over the house," groaned Thorne. He eyed Ellery a bit bashfully. "Queen . . . perhaps we had better . . . try to get out of here."

"You heard Keith, Thorne."

Thorne bit his lip. "I'm frozen," said Alice, drawing nearer the fire. "That was well done, Mr. Keith. It—it— a fire like this makes me think of home, somehow." The young man got to his feet and turned around. Their eyes met for an instant.

"It's nothing," he said shortly. "Nothing at all."

"You seem to be the only one who—Oh!"

An enormous old woman with a black shawl over her shoulders was coming downstairs. She might have been years dead, she was so yellow and emaciated and mummified. And yet she gave the impression of being very much alive, with a sort of ancient, ageless life; her black eyes were young and bright and cunning, and her face was extraordinarily mobile. She was sidling down stiffly, feeling her way with one foot and clutching the banister with two dried claws, while her

lively eyes remained fixed on Alice's face. There was a curious
hunger in her expression, the flaring of a long-dead hope
suddenly, against all reason.

"Who— who—" began Alice, shrinking back.

"Don't be alarmed," said Dr. Reinach quickly. "It's
unfortunate that she got away from Milly. . . . Sarah!" In
a twinkling he was at the foot of the staircase, barring the
old woman's way. "What are you doing up at this hour?
You should take better care of yourself, Sarah."

She ignored him, continuing her snail's pace down the
stairs until she reached his pachyderm bulk. "Olivia," she
mumbled, with a vital eagerness. "It's Olivia come back to
me. Oh, my sweet, sweet darling. . . ."

"Now, Sarah," said the fat man, taking her hand gently.
"Don't excite yourself. This isn't Olivia, Sarah. It's Alice
—Alice Mayhew, Sylvester's girl, come from England. You
remember Alice, little Alice? Not Olivia, Sarah."

"Not Olivia?" The old woman peered across the banister,
her wrinkled lips moving. "Not Olivia?"

The girl jumped up. "I'm Alice, Aunt Sarah. Alice—"

Sarah Fell darted suddenly past the fat man and scurried
across the room to seize the girl's hand and glare into her
face. As she studied those shrinking features her expression
changed to one of despair. "Not Olivia. Olivia's beautiful
black hair. . . . Not Olivia's voice. Alice? Alice?" She
dropped into Alice's vacated chair, her skinny broad shoulders
sagging, and began to weep. They could see the yellow skin
of her scalp through the sparse gray hair.

Dr. Reinach roared: "Milly!" in an enraged voice. Mrs.
Reinach popped into sight like Jack-in-the-box. "Why did
you let her leave her room?"

"B-but I thought she was—" began Mrs. Reinach, stam-
mering.

"Take her upstairs at once!"

"Yes, Herbert," whispered the sparrow, and Mrs. Reinach
hurried downstairs in her wrapper and took the old woman's

hand and, unopposed, led her away. Mrs. Fell kept repeat-
ing, between sobs: "Why doesn't Olivia come back? Why
did they take her away from her mother?" until she was out
of sight.

"Sorry," panted the fat man, mopping himself. "One of
her spells. I knew it was coming on from the curiosity she
exhibited the moment she heard you were coming, Alice.
There *is* a resemblance; you can scarcely blame her."

"She's—she's horrible," said Alice faintly. "Mr. Queen
—Mr. Thorne, must we stay here? I'd feel so much easier in
the city. And then my cold, these frigid rooms——"

"By heaven," burst out Thorne, "I feel like chancing it
on foot!"

"And leave Sylvester's gold to our tender mercies?" smiled
Dr. Reinach. Then he scowled.

"I don't want father's legacy," said Alice desperately. "At
this moment I don't want anything but to get away. I—I
can manage to get along all right. I'll find work to do—I
can do so many things. I want to go away. Mr. Keith,
couldn't you possibly——"

"*I'm* not a magician," said Keith rudely; and he buttoned
his mackinaw and strode out of the house. They could see
his tall figure stalking off behind a veil of snowflakes.

Alice flushed, turning back to the fire.

"Nor are any of us," said Ellery. "Miss Mayhew, you'll
simply have to be a brave girl and stick it out until we can
find a means of getting out of here."

"Yes," murmured Alice, shivering; and stared into the
flames.

"Meanwhile, Thorne, tell me everything you know about
this case, especially as it concerns Sylvester Mayhew's house.
There may be a clue in your father's history, Miss Mayhew.
If the house has vanished, so has the gold *in* the house; and
whether you want it or not, it belongs to you. Consequently
we must make an effort to find it."

"I suggest," muttered Dr. Reinach, "that you find the

house first. House!" he exploded, waving his furred arms. And he made for the sideboard.

Alice nodded listlessly. Thorne mumbled: "Perhaps, Queen, you and I had better talk privately."

"We made a frank beginning last night; I see no reason why we shouldn't continue in the same candid vein. You needn't be reluctant to speak before Dr. Reinach. Our host is obviously a man of parts—unorthodox parts."

Dr. Reinach did not reply. His globular face was dark as he tossed off a water-goblet full of gin.

Through air metallic with defiance, Thorne talked in a hardening voice; not once did he take his eyes from Dr. Reinach.

His first suspicion that something was wrong had been germinated by Sylvester Mayhew himself.

Hearing by post from Alice, Thorne had investigated and located Mayhew. He had explained to the old invalid his daughter's desire to find her father, if he still lived. Old Mayhew, with a strange excitement, had acquiesced; he was eager to be reunited with his daughter; and he seemed to be living, explained Thorne defiantly, in mortal fear of his relatives in the neighboring house.

"Fear, Thorne?" The fat man sat down, raising his brows. "You know he was afraid, not of us, but of poverty. He was a miser."

Thorne ignored him. Mayhew had instructed Thorne to write Alice and bid her come to America at once; he meant to leave her his entire estate and wanted her to have it before he died. The repository of the gold he had cunningly refused to divulge, even to Thorne; it was "in the house," he had said, but he would not reveal its hiding-place to anyone but Alice herself. The "others," he had snarled, had been looking for it ever since their "arrival."

"By the way," drawled Ellery, "how long have you good people been living in this house, Dr. Reinach?"

"A year or so. You certainly don't put any credence in the paranoic ravings of a dying man? There's no mystery about our living here. I looked Sylvester up over a year ago after a long separation and found him still in the old homestead, and this house boarded up and empty. The White House, this house, incidentally, was built by my stepfather —Sylvester's father—on Sylvester's marriage to Alice's mother; Sylvester lived in it until my stepfather died, and then moved back to the Black House. I found Sylvester, a degenerated hulk of what he'd once been, living on crusts, absolutely alone and badly in need of medical attention."

"Alone—here, in this wilderness?" said Ellery incredulously.

"Yes. As a matter of fact, the only way I could get his permission to move back to this house, which belonged to him, was by dangling the bait of free medical treatment before his eyes. I'm sorry, Alice; he was quite unbalanced. . . . And so Milly and Sarah and I—Sarah had been living with us ever since Olivia's death—moved in here."

"Decent of you," remarked Ellery. "I suppose you had ·to give up your medical practice to do it, Doctor?"

Dr. Reinach grimaced. "I didn't have much of a practice to give up, Mr. Queen."

"But it was an almost pure brotherly impulse, eh?"

"Oh, I don't deny that the possibility of falling heir to some of Sylvester's fortune had crossed our minds. It was rightfully ours, we believed, not knowing anything about Alice. As it's turned out—" he shrugged his fat shoulders. "I'm a philosopher."

"And don't deny, either," shouted Thorne, "that when I came back here at the time Mayhew sank into that fatal coma you people watched me like a—like a band of spies! I was in your way!"

"Mr. Thorne," whispered Alice, paling.

"I'm sorry, Miss Mayhew, but you may as well know the truth. Oh, you didn't fool me, Reinach! You wanted that gold, Alice or no Alice. I shut myself up in that house just to keep you from getting your hands on it!"

Dr. Reinach shrugged again; his rubbery lips compressed.

"You want candor; here it is!" rasped Thorne. "I was in that house, Queen, for six days after Mayhew's funeral and before Miss Mayhew's arrival, *looking for the gold.* I turned that house upside down. And I didn't find the slightest trace of it. I tell you it isn't there." He glared at the fat man. "I tell you it was stolen before Mayhew died!"

"Now, now," sighed Ellery. "That makes less sense than the other. Why then has somebody intoned an incantation over the house and caused it to disappear?"

"I don't know," said the old lawyer fiercely. "I know only that the most dastardly thing's happened here, that everything is unnatural, veiled in that—that false creature's smile! Miss Mayhew, I'm sorry I must speak this way about your own family. But I feel it my duty to warn you that you've fallen among human wolves. Wolves!"

"I'm afraid," said Reinach sourly, "that I shouldn't come to you, my dear Thorne, for a reference."

"I wish," said Alice in a very low tone, "I truly wish I were dead."

But the lawyer was past control. "That man Keith," he cried. "Who is he? What's he doing here? He looks like a gangster. I suspect him, Queen——"

"Apparently," smiled Ellery, "you suspect everybody."

"Mr. Keith?" murmured Alice. "Oh, I'm sure not. I—I don't think he's that sort at all, Mr. Thorne. He looks as if he's had a hard life. As if he's suffered terribly from something."

Thorne threw up his hands, turning to the fire.

"Let us," said Ellery amiably, "confine ourselves to the problem at hand. We were, I believe, considering the problem of a disappearing house. Do any architect's plans of the so-called Black House exist?"

"Lord, no," said Dr. Reinach.

"Who has lived in it since your stepfather's death besides Sylvester Mayhew and his wife?"

"Wives," corrected the doctor, pouring himself another glassful of gin. "Sylvester married twice; I suppose you didn't know that, my dear." Alice shivered by the fire. "I dislike raking over old ashes, but since we're at confessional ... Sylvester treated Alice's mother abominably."

"I—guessed that," whispered Alice.

"She was a woman of spirit and she rebelled; but when she'd got her final decree and returned to England, the reaction set in and she died very shortly afterward, I understand. Her death was recorded in the New York papers."

"When I was a baby," whispered Alice.

"Sylvester, already unbalanced, although not so anchoretic in those days as he became later, then wooed and won a wealthy widow and brought her out here to live. She had a son, a child by her first husband, with her. Father'd died by this time, and Sylvester and his second wife lived in the Black House. It was soon evident that Sylvester had married the widow for her money; he persuaded her to sign it over to him—a considerable fortune for those days—and promptly proceeded to devil the life out of her. Result: the woman vanished one day, taking her child with her."

"Perhaps," said Ellery, seeing Alice's face, "we'd better abandon the subject, Doctor."

"We never did find out what actually happened—whether Sylvester drove her out or whether, unable to stand his brutal treatment any longer, she left voluntarily. At any rate, I discovered by accident, a few years later, through an obituary notice, that she died in the worst sort of poverty."

Alice was staring at him with a wrinkle-nosed nausea. "Father ... did that?"

"Oh, stop it," growled Thorne. "You'll have the poor child gibbering in another moment. What has all this to do with the house?"

"Mr. Queen asked," said the fat man mildly. Ellery was studying the flames as if they fascinated him.

"The real point," snapped the lawyer, "is that you've watched me from the instant I set foot here, Reinach. Afraid to leave me alone for a moment. Why, you even had Keith meet me in your car on both my visits—to 'escort' me here! And I didn't have five minutes alone with the old gentleman —you saw to that. And then he lapsed into the coma and was unable to speak again before he died. Why? Why all this surveillance? God knows I'm a forbearing man; but you've given me every ground for suspecting your motives."

"Apparently," chuckled Dr. Reinach, "you don't agree with Caesar."

"I beg your pardon?"

" 'Would,' " quoted the fat man, " 'he were fatter.' Well, good people, the end of the world may come, but that's no reason why we shouldn't have breakfast. Milly!" he bellowed.

Thorne awoke sluggishly, like a drowsing old hound dimly aware of danger. His bedroom was cold; a pale morning light was struggling in through the window. He groped under his pillow.

"Stop where you are!" he said harshly.

"So you have a revolver, too?" murmured Ellery. He was dressed and looked as if he had slept badly. "It's only I, Thorne, stealing in for a conference. It's not so hard to steal in here, by the way."

"What do you mean?" grumbled Thorne, sitting up and putting his old-fashioned revolver away.

"I see your lock has gone the way of mine, Alice's, the Black House, and Sylvester Mayhew's elusive gold."

Thorne drew the patchwork comforter about him, his old lips blue. "Well, Queen?"

Ellery lit a cigaret and for a moment stared out Thorne's window at the streamers of crêpy snow still dropping from the sky. The snow had fallen without a moment's let-up the entire previous day. "This is a curious business all round, Thorne. The queerest medley of spirit and matter. I've just reconnoitered. You'll be interested to learn that our young friend the Colossus is gone."

"Keith gone?"

"His bed hasn't been slept in at all. I looked."

"And he was away most of yesterday, too!"

"Precisely. Our surly Crichton, who seems afflicted by a particularly acute case of *Weltschmerz*, periodically vanishes. Where does he go? I'd give a good deal to know the answer to that question."

"He won't get far in those nasty drifts," mumbled the lawyer.

"It gives one, as the French say, to think. Comrade Reinach is gone, too." Thorne stiffened. "Oh, yes; his bed's been slept in, but briefly, I judge. Have they eloped together? Separately? Thorne," said Ellery thoughtfully, "this becomes an increasingly subtle devilment."

"It's beyond me," said Thorne with another shiver. "I'm just about ready to give up. I don't see that we're accomplishing a thing here. And then there's always that annoying, incredible fact . . . the house—vanished."

Ellery sighed and looked at his wristwatch. It was a minute past seven.

Thorne threw back the comforter and groped under the bed for his slippers. "Let's go downstairs," he snapped.

"Excellent bacon, Mrs. Reinach," said Ellery. "I suppose it must be a trial carting supplies up here."

"We've the blood of pioneers," said Dr. Reinach cheerfully, before his wife could reply. He was engulfing mounds of scrambled eggs and bacon. "Luckily, we've enough in the larder to last out a considerable siege. The winters are severe out here—we learned that last year."

Keith was not at the breakfast table. Old Mrs. Fell was.

She ate voraciously, with the unconcealed greed of the very old, to whom nothing is left of the sensual satisfactions of life but the filling of the belly. Nevertheless, although she did not speak, she contrived as she ate to keep her eyes on Alice, who wore a haunted look.

"I didn't sleep very well," said Alice, toying with her coffee-cup. Her voice was huskier. "This abominable snow! Can't we manage somehow to get away today?"

"Not so long as the snow keeps up, I'm afraid," said Ellery gently. "And you, Doctor? Did you sleep badly, too? Or hasn't the whisking away of a whole house from under your nose affected your nerves at all?"

The fat man's eyes were red-rimmed and his lids sagged. Nevertheless, he chuckled and said: "I? I always sleep well. Nothing on my conscience. Why?"

"Oh, no special reason. Where's friend Keith this morning? He's a seclusive sort of chap, isn't he?"

Mrs. Reinach swallowed a muffin whole. Her husband glanced at her and she rose and fled to the kitchen. "Lord knows," said the fat man. "He's as unpredictable as the ghost of Banquo. Don't bother yourself about the boy; he's harmless."

Ellery sighed and pushed back from the table. "The passage of twenty-four hours hasn't softened the wonder of the event. May I be excused? I'm going to have another peep at the house that isn't there any more." Thorne started to rise. "No, no, Thorne; I'd rather go alone."

He put on his warmest clothes and went outdoors. The drifts reached the lower windows now; and the trees had almost disappeared under the snow. A crude path had been hacked by someone from the front door for a few feet; already it was half-refilled with snow.

Ellery stood still in the path, breathing deeply of the raw air and staring off to the right at the empty rectangle where the Black House had once stood. Leading across that expanse to the edge of the woods beyond were barely discernible tracks. He turned up his coat-collar against the cutting wind and plunged into the snow waist-deep.

It was difficult going, but not unpleasant. After a while he began to feel quite warm. The world was white and silent—a new, strange world.

When he had left the open area and struggled into the woods, it was with a sensation that he was leaving even that new world behind. Everything was so still and white and beautiful, with a pure beauty not of the earth; the snow draping the trees gave them a fresh look, making queer patterns out of old forms.

Occasionally a clump of snow fell from a low branch, pelting him.

Here, where there was a roof between ground and sky, the snow had not filtered into the mysterious tracks so quickly. They were purposeful tracks, unwandering, striking straight as a dotted line for some distant goal. Ellery pushed on more rapidly, excited by a presentiment of discovery.

Then the world went black.

It was a curious thing. The snow grew gray, and grayer, and finally very dark gray, becoming jet black at the last instant, as if flooded from underneath by ink. And with some surprise he felt the cold wet kiss of the drift on his cheek.

He opened his eyes to find himself flat on his back in the snow and Thorne in the great-coat stooped over him, nose jutting from blued face like a winter thorn.

"Queen!" cried the old man, shaking him. "Are you all right?"

Ellery sat up, licking his lips. "As well as might be expected," he groaned. "What hit me? It felt like one of God's angrier thunderbolts." He caressed the back of his head, and staggered to his feet. "Well, Thorne, we seem to have reached the border of the enchanted land."

"You're not delirious?" asked the lawyer anxiously.

Ellery looked about for the tracks which should have been there. But except for the double line at the head of which Thorne stood, there were none. Apparently he had lain unconscious in the snow for a long time.

"Farther than this," he said with a grimace, "we may not go. Hands off. Nose out. Mind your own business. Beyond this invisible boundary-line lie Sheol and Domdaniel and Abaddon. *Lasciate ogni speranza voi ch'entrate.* . . . Forgive me, Thorne. Did you save my life?"

Thorne jerked about, searching the silent woods. "I don't know. I think not. At least I found you lying here, alone. Gave me quite a start—thought you were dead."

"As well," said Ellery with a shiver, "I might have been."

"When you left the house Alice went upstairs, Reinach said something about a cat-nap, and I wandered out of the house. I waded through the drifts on the road for a spell, and then I thought of you and made my way back. Your tracks were almost obliterated; but they were visible enough to take me across the clearing to the edge of the woods, and I finally blundered upon you. By now the tracks are gone."

"I don't like this at all," said Ellery, "and yet in another sense I like it very much."

"What do you mean?"

"I can't imagine," said Ellery, "a divine agency stooping to such a mean assault."

"Yes, it's open war now," muttered Thorne. "Whoever it is—he'll stop at nothing."

"A benevolent war, at any rate. I was quite at his mercy, and he might have killed me as easily as——"

He stopped. A sharp report, like a pine-knot snapping in a fire or an ice-stiffened twig breaking in two, but greatly magnified, had come to his ears. Then the echo came to them, softer but unmistakable.

It was the report of a gun.

"From the house!" yelled Ellery. "Come on!"

Thorne was pale as they scrambled through the drifts.

"Gun . . . I forgot. I left my revolver under the pillow in my bedroom. Do you think——?"

Ellery scrabbled at his own pocket. "Mine's still here. . . . No, by George, I've been scotched!" His cold fingers fumbled with the cylinder. "Bullets taken out. And I've no spare ammunition." He fell silent, his mouth hardening.

They found the women and Reinach running about like startled animals, searching for they knew not what.

"Did you hear it, too?" cried the fat man as they burst into the house. He seemed extraordinarily excited. "Some-one fired a shot!"

"Where?" asked Ellery, his eyes on the rove. "Keith?"

"Don't know where he is. Milly says it might have come from behind the house. I was napping and couldn't tell. Revolvers! At least he's come out in the open."

"Who has?" asked Ellery.

The fat man shrugged. Ellery went through to the kitchen and opened the back door. The snow outside was smooth, untrodden. When he returned to the living-room Alice was adjusting a scarf about her neck with fingers that shook.

"I don't know how long you people intend to stay in this ghastly place," she said in a passionate voice. "But I've had *quite* enough, thank you. Mr. Thorne, I insist you take me away at once. At once! I shan't stay another instant."

"Now, now, Miss Mayhew," said Thorne in a distressed way, taking her hands. "I should like nothing better. But can't you see——"

Ellery, on his way upstairs three steps at a time, heard no more. He made for Thorne's room and kicked the door open, sniffing. Then, with rather a grim smile, he went to the tumbled bed and pulled the pillow away. A long-barreled, old-fashioned revolver lay there. He examined the cylinder; it was empty. Then he put the muzzle to his nose.

"Well?" said Thorne from the doorway. The English girl was clinging to him.

"Well," said Ellery, tossing the gun aside, "we're facing

fact now, not fancy. It's war, Thorne, as you said. The shot was fired from your revolver. Barrel's still warm, muzzle still reeks, and you can smell the burnt gunpowder if you sniff this cold air hard enough. *And* the bullets are gone."

"But what does it mean?" moaned Alice.

"It means that somebody's being terribly cute. It was a harmless trick to get Thorne and me back to the house. Probably the shot was a warning as well as a decoy."

Alice sank onto Thorne's bed. "You mean we——"

"Yes," said Ellery, "from now on we're prisoners, Miss Mayhew. Prisoners who may not stray beyond the confines of the jail. I wonder," he added with a frown, "precisely why."

The day passed in a timeless haze. The world of outdoors became more and more choked in the folds of the snow. The air was a solid white sheet. It seemed as if the very heavens had opened to admit all the snow that ever was, or ever would be.

Young Keith appeared suddenly at noon, taciturn and leaden-eyed, gulped down some hot food, and without explanation retired to his bedroom. Dr. Reinach shambled about quietly for some time; then he disappeared, only to show up, wet, grimy, and silent, before dinner. As the day wore on, less and less was said. Thorne in desperation took to a bottle of whisky. Keith came down at eight o'clock, made himself some coffee, drank three cups, and went upstairs again. Dr. Reinach appeared to have lost his good nature; he was morose, almost sullen, opening his mouth only to snarl at his wife.

And the snow continued to fall.

They all retired early, without conversation.

At midnight the strain was more than even Ellery's iron nerves could bear. He had prowled about his bedroom for hours, poking at the brisk fire in the grate, his mind leaping from improbability to fantasy until his head throbbed with one great ache. Sleep was impossible.

Moved by an impulse which he did not attempt to analyze, he slipped into his coat and went out into the frosty corridor.

Thorne's door was closed; Ellery heard the old man's bed creaking and groaning. It was pitch-dark in the hall as he groped his way about. Suddenly Ellery's toe caught in a rent in the carpet and he staggered to regain his balance, coming up against the wall with a thud, his heels clattering on the bare planking at the bottom of the baseboard.

He had no sooner straightened up than he heard the stifled exclamation of a woman. It came from across the corridor; if he guessed right, from Alice Mayhew's bedroom. It was such a weak, terrified exclamation that he sprang across the hall, fumbling in his pockets for a match as he did so. He found match and door in the same instant; he struck one and opened the door and stood still, the tiny light flaring up before him.

Alice was sitting up in bed, quilt drawn about her shoulders, her eyes gleaming in the quarter-light. Before an open drawer of a tallboy across the room, one hand arrested in the act of scattering its contents about, loomed Dr. Reinach, fully dressed. His shoes were wet; his expression was blank; and his eyes were slits.

"Please stand still, Doctor," said Ellery softly as the match sputtered out. "My revolver is useless as a percussion weapon, but it still can inflict damage as a blunt instrument." He moved to a nearby table, where he had seen an oil-lamp before the match went out, struck another match, lighted the lamp, and stepped back again to stand against the door.

"Thank you," whispered Alice.

"What happened, Miss Mayhew?"

"I . . . don't know. I slept badly. I came awake a moment ago when I heard the floor creak. And then you dashed in." She cried suddenly: "Bless you!"

"You cried out."

"Did I?" She sighed like a tired child. "I . . . Uncle
Herbert!" he said suddenly, fiercely. "What's the meaning
of this? What are you doing in my room?"

The fat man's eyes came open, innocent and beaming; his
hand withdrew from the drawer and closed it; and he shifted
his elephantine bulk until he was standing erect. "Doing,
my dear?" he rumbled. "Why, I came in to see if you were
all right." His eyes were fixed on a patch of her white
shoulders visible above the quilt. "You were so over-
wrought today. Purely an avuncular impulse, my child.
Forgive me if I startled you."

"I think," sighed Ellery, "that I've misjudged you, Doctor.
That's not clever of you at all. Downright clumsy, in fact;
I can only attribute it to a certain understandable confusion
of the moment. Miss Mayhew isn't normally to be found
in the top drawer of a tallboy, no matter how capacious it
may be." He said sharply to Alice: "Did this fellow touch
you?"

"Touch me?" Her shoulders twitched with repugnance.
"No. If he had, in the dark, I—I think I should have died."

"What a charming compliment," said Dr. Reinach ruefully.

"Then what," demanded Ellery, "*were* you looking for,
Dr. Reinach?"

The fat man turned until his right side was toward the
door. "I'm notoriously hard of hearing," he chuckled, "in
my right ear. Good night, Alice; pleasant dreams. May
I pass, Sir Launcelot?"

Ellery kept his gaze on the fat man's bland face until the
door closed. For some time after the last echo of Dr.
Reinach's chuckle died away they were silent.

Then Alice slid down in the bed and clutched the edge
of the quilt. "Mr. Queen, please! Take me away tomorrow.
I mean it. I truly do. I—can't tell you how frightened I
am of . . . all this. Every time I think of that—that . . .
How can such things be? We're not in a place of sanity, Mr.

Queen. We'll all go mad if we remain here much longer.
Won't you take me away?"

Ellery sat down on the edge of her bed. "Are you really
so upset, Miss Mayhew?" he asked gently.

"I'm simply terrified," she whispered.

"Then Thorne and I will do what we can tomorrow." He
patted her arm through the quilt. "I'll have a look at his
car and see if something can't be done with it. He said
there's some gas left in the tank. We'll go as far as it will
take us and walk the rest of the way."

"But with so little petrol . . . Oh, I don't care!" She
stared up at him wide-eyed. "Do you think . . . he'll let
us?"

"He?"

"Whoever it is that . . ."

Ellery rose with a smile. "We'll cross that bridge when it
gets to us. Meanwhile, get some sleep; you'll have a strenu-
ous day tomorrow."

"Do you think I'm—he'll——"

"Leave the lamp burning and set a chair under the door-
knob when I leave." He took a quick look about. "By the
way, Miss Mayhew, is there anything in your possession
which Dr. Reinach might want to appropriate?"

"That's puzzled me, too. I can't imagine what I've got he
could possibly want. I'm so poor, Mr. Queen—quite the
Cinderella. There's nothing; just my clothes, the things I
came with."

"No old letters, records, mementoes?"

"Just one very old photograph of mother."

"Hmm, Dr. Reinach doesn't strike me as *that* sentimental.
Well, good night. Don't forget the chair. You'll be quite
safe, I assure you."

He waited in the frigid darkness of the corridor until he
heard her creep out of bed and set a chair against the door.
Then he went into his own room.

And there was Thorne in a shabby dressing-gown, looking like an ancient and dishevelled spectre of gloom.

"What ho! The ghost walks. Can't you sleep, either?"

"Sleep!" The old man shuddered. "How can an honest man sleep in this God-forsaken place? I notice you seem rather cheerful."

"Not cheerful. Alive." Ellery sat down and lit a cigaret. "I heard you tossing about your bed a few minutes ago. Anything happen to pull you out into this cold?"

"No. Just nerves." Thorne jumped up and began to pace the floor. "Where have you been?"

Ellery told him. "Remarkable chap, Reinach," he concluded. "But we mustn't allow our admiration to overpower us. We'll really have to give this thing up, Thorne, at least temporarily. I *had* been hoping . . . But there! I've promised the poor girl. We're leaving tomorrow as best we can."

"And be found frozen stiff next March by a rescue party," said Thorne miserably. "Pleasant prospect! And yet even death by freezing is preferable to this abominable place." He looked curiously at Ellery. "I must say I'm a trifle disappointed in you, Queen. From what I'd heard about your professional cunning . . ."

"I never claimed," shrugged Ellery, "to be a magician. Or even a theologian. What's happened here is either the blackest magic or palpable proof that miracles can happen."

"It would seem so," muttered Thorne. "And yet, when you put your mind to it . . . It goes against reason, by thunder!"

"I see," said Ellery dryly, "the man of law is recovering from the initial shock. Well, it's a shame to have to leave here now, in a way. I detest the thought of giving up—especially at the present time."

"At the present time? What do you mean?"

"I dare say, Thorne, you haven't emerged far enough from your condition of shock to have properly analyzed this little problem. I gave it a lot of thought today. The goal eludes me—but I'm near it," he said softly, "very near it."

"You mean," gasped the lawyer, "you mean you actually——"

"Remarkable case," said Ellery. "Oh, extraordinary—there isn't a word in the English language or any other, for that matter, that properly describes it. If I were religiously inclined . . ." He puffed away thoughtfully. "It gets down to very simple elements, as all truly great problems do. A fortune in gold exists. It is hidden in a house. The house disappears. To find the gold, then, you must first find the house. I believe . . ."

"Aside from that mumbo-jumbo with Keith's broom the other day," cried Thorne, "I can't recall that you've made a single effort in that direction. Find the house!—why, you've done nothing but sit around and wait."

"Exactly," murmured Ellery.

"What?"

"Wait. That's the prescription, my lean and angry friend. That's the sigil that will exorcise the spirit of the Black House."

"Sigil?" Thorne stared. "Spirit?"

"Wait. Precisely. Lord, how I'm waiting!"

Thorne looked puzzled and suspicious, as if he suspected Ellery of a contrary midnight humor. But Ellery sat soberly smoking. "Wait! For what, man? You're more exasperating than that fat monstrosity! What are you waiting for?"

Ellery looked at him. Then he rose and flung his butt into the dying fire and placed his hand on the old man's arm. "Go to bed, Thorne. You wouldn't believe me if I told you."

"Queen, you *must*. I'll go mad if I don't see daylight on this thing soon!"

Ellery looked shocked, for no reason that Thorne could see. And then, just as inexplicably, he slapped Thorne's shoulder and began to chuckle.

"Go to bed," he said, still chuckling.

"But you must tell me!"

Ellery sighed, losing his smile. "I can't. You'd laugh."

"I'm not in a laughing mood!"

"Nor is it a laughing matter. Thorne, I began to say a moment ago that if I, poor sinner that I am, possessed religious susceptibilities, I should have become permanently devout in the past three days. I suppose I'm a hopeless case. But even I see a power not of earth in this."

"Play-actor," growled the old lawyer. "Professing to see the hand of God in . . . Don't be sacrilegious, man. We're not all heathen."

Ellery looked out his window at the moonless night and the glimmering grayness of the snow-swathed world.

"Hand of God?" he murmured. "No, not hand, Thorne. If this case is ever solved, it will be by . . . a lamp."

"Lamp?" said Thorne faintly. "Lamp?"

"In a manner of speaking. *The lamp of God.*"

III

The next day dawned sullenly as ashen and hopeless a morning as ever was. Incredibly, it still snowed in the same thick fashion, as if the whole sky were crumbling bit by bit.

Ellery spent the better part of the day in the garage, tinkering at the big black car's vitals. He left the doors wide open, so that anyone who wished might see what he was about. He knew little enough of automotive mechanics, and he felt from the start that he was engaged in a futile business.

But in the late afternoon, after hours of vain experimentation, he suddenly came upon a tiny wire which seemed to him to be out of joint with its environment. It simply hung, a useless thing. Logic demanded a connection. He experimented. He found one.

As he stepped on the starter and heard the cold motor sputter into life, a shape darkened the entrance of the garage. He turned off the ignition quickly and looked up.

It was Keith, a black mass against the background of snow, standing with widespread legs, a large can hanging from each big hand.

"Hello, there," murmured Ellery. "You've assumed human shape again, I see. Back on one of your infrequent jaunts to the world of men, Keith?"

Keith said quietly: "Going somewhere, Mr. Queen?"

"Certainly. Why—do you intend to stop me?"

"Depends on where you're going."

"Ah, a threat. Well, suppose I tell *you* where to go?"

"Tell all you want. You don't get off these grounds until I know where you're bound for."

Ellery grinned. "There's a naive directness about you,

Keith, that draws me in spite of myself. Well, I'll relieve your mind. Thorne and I are taking Miss Mayhew back to the city."

"In that case it's all right." Ellery studied his face; it was worn deep with ruts of fatigue and worry. Keith dropped the cans to the cement floor of the garage. "You can use these, then. Gas."

"Gas! Where on earth did you get it?"

"Let's say," said Keith grimly, "I dug it up out of an old Indian tomb."

"Very well."

"You've fixed Thorne's car, I see. Needn't have. I could have done it."

"Then why didn't you?"

"Because nobody asked me to." The giant swung on his heel and vanished.

Ellery sat still, frowning. Then he got out of the car, picked up the cans, and poured their contents into the tank. He reached into the car again, got the engine running, and leaving it to purr away like a great cat he went back to the house.

He found Alice in her room, a coat over her shoulders, staring out her window. She sprang up at his knock.

"Mr. Queen, you've got Mr. Thorne's car going!"

"Success at last," smiled Ellery. "Are you ready?"

"Oh, yes! I feel so much better, now that we're actually to leave. Do you think we'll have a hard time? I saw Mr. Keith bring those cans in. Petrol, weren't they? Nice of him. I never did believe such a nice young man—" She flushed. There were hectic spots in her cheeks and her eyes were brighter than they had been for days. Her voice seemed less husky, too.

"It may be hard going through the drifts, but the car is equipped with chains. With luck we should make it. It's a powerful——"

Ellery stopped very suddenly indeed, his eyes fixed on the worn carpet at his feet, stony yet startled.

"Whatever is the matter, Mr. Queen?"

"Matter?" Ellery raised his eyes and drew a deep, deep breath. "Nothing at all. God's in His heaven and all's right with the world."

She looked down at the carpet. "Oh . . . the sun!" With a little squeal of delight she turned to the window. "Why, Mr. Queen, it's stopped snowing. There's the sun setting— at last!"

"And high time, too," said Ellery briskly. "Will you please get your things on? We leave at once." He picked up her bags and left her, walking with a springy vigor that shook the old boards. He crossed the corridor to his room opposite hers and began, whistling, to pack his bag.

The living-room was noisy with a babble of adieux. One would have said that this was a normal household, with normal people in a normal human situation. Alice was positively gay, quite as if she were not leaving a fortune in gold for what might turn out to be all time.

She set her purse down on the mantel next to her mother's chromo, fixed her hat, flung her arms about Mrs. Reinach, pecked gingerly at Mrs. Fell's withered cheek, and even smiled forgivingly at Dr. Reinach. Then she dashed back to the mantel, snatched up her purse, threw one long enigmatic glance at Keith's drawn face, and hurried outdoors as if the devil himself were after her.

Thorne was already in the car, his old face alight with incredible happiness, as if he had been reprieved at the very moment he was to set his foot beyond the little green door. He beamed at the dying sun.

Ellery followed Alice more slowly. The bags were in Thorne's car; there was nothing more to do. He climbed in, raced the motor, and then released the brake.

The fat man filled the doorway, shouting: "You know the

road, now, don't you? Turn to the right at the end of this drive. Then keep going in a straight line. You can't miss. You'll hit the main highway in about . . ."

His last words were drowned in the roar of the engine. Ellery waved his hand. Alice, in the tonneau beside Thorne, twisted about and laughed a little hysterically. Thorne sat beaming at the back of Ellery's head.

The car, under Ellery's guidance, trundled unsteadily out of the drive and made a right turn into the road.

It grew dark rapidly. They made slow progress. The big machine inched its way through the drifts, slipping and lurching despite its chains. As night fell, Ellery turned the powerful headlights on.

He drove with unswerving concentration.

None of them spoke.

It seemed hours before they reached the main highway. But when they did the car leaped to life on the road, which had been partly cleared by snowplows, and it was not long before they were entering the nearby town.

At the sight of the friendly electric lights, the paved streets, the solid blocks of houses, Alice gave a cry of sheer delight. Ellery stopped at a gasoline station and had the tank filled.

"It's not far from here, Miss Mayhew," said Thorne reassuringly. "We'll be in the city in no time. The Triborough Bridge . . ."

"Oh, it's wonderful to be alive!"

"Of course you'll stay at my house. My wife will be delighted to have you. After that . . ."

"You're so kind, Mr. Thorne. I don't know how I shall ever be able to thank you enough." She paused, startled. "Why, what's the matter, Mr. Queen?"

For Ellery had done a strange thing. He had stopped the car at a traffic intersection and asked the officer on duty something in a low tone. The officer stared at him and replied with gestures. Ellery swung the car off into another street. He drove slowly.

"What's the matter?" asked Alice again, leaning forward.

Thorne said, frowning: "You can't have lost your way. There's a sign which distinctly says . . ."

"No, it's not that," said Ellery in a preoccupied way. "I've just thought of something."

The girl and the old man looked at each other, puzzled. Ellery stopped the car at a large stone building with green lights outside and went in, remaining there for fifteen minutes. He came out whistling.

"Queen!" said Thorne abruptly, eyes on the green lights. "What's up?"

"Something that must be brought down." Ellery swung the car about and headed it for the traffic intersection. When he reached it he turned left.

"Why, you've taken the wrong turn," said Alice nervously. "This is the direction from which we've just come. I'm sure of that."

"And you're quite right, Miss Mayhew. It is." She sank back, pale, as if the very thought of returning terrified her. "We're going back, you see," said Ellery.

"Back!" exploded Thorne, sitting up straight.

"Oh, can't we just forget all those horrible people?" moaned Alice.

"I've a viciously stubborn memory. Besides, we have reinforcements. If you'll look back you'll see a car following us. It's a police car, and in it are the local Chief of Police and a squad of picked men."

"But why, Mr. Queen?" cried Alice. Thorne said nothing; his happiness had quite vanished, and he sat gloomily staring at the back of Ellery's neck.

"Because," said Ellery grimly, "I have my own professional pride. Because I've been on the receiving end of a damnably cute magician's trick."

"Trick?" she repeated dazedly.

"Now I shall turn magician myself. You saw a house disappear." He laughed softly. "I shall make it appear again!"

They could only stare at him, too bewildered to speak.

"And then," said Ellery, his voice hardening, "even if we chose to overlook such trivia as dematerialized houses, in all conscience we can't overlook . . . *murder*."

IV

And there was the Black House again. Not a wraith. A solid house, a strong dirty time-encrusted house, looking as if it would never dream of taking wing and flying off into space.

It stood on the other side of the driveway, where it had always stood.

They saw it even as they turned into the drive from the drift-covered road, its bulk looming black against the brilliant moon, as substantial a house as could be found in the world of sane things.

Thorne and the girl were incapable of speech; they could only gape, dumb witnesses of a miracle even greater than the disappearance of the house in the first place.

As for Ellery, he stopped the car, sprang to the ground, signalled to the car snuffling up behind, and darted across the snowy clearing to the White House, whose windows were bright with lamp- and fire-light. Out of the police car swarmed men, and they ran after Ellery like hounds. Thorne and Alice followed in a daze.

Ellery kicked open the White House door. There was a revolver in his hand and there was no doubt, from the way he gripped it, that its cylinder had been replenished.

"Hello again," he said, stalking into the living-room. "Not a ghost; Inspector Queen's little boy in the too, too solid flesh. Nemesis, perhaps. I bid you good evening. What—no welcoming smile, Dr. Reinach?"

The fat man had paused in the act of lifting a glass of Scotch to his lips. It was wonderful how the color seeped out of his pouchy cheeks, leaving them gray. Mrs. Reinach whimpered in a corner, and Mrs. Fell stared stupidly. Only Nick Keith showed no great astonishment. He was standing

by a window, muffled to the ears; and on his face there was
bitterness and admiration and, strangely, a sort of relief.

"Shut the door." The detectives behind Ellery spread out
silently. Alice stumbled to a chair, her eyes wild, studying
Dr. Reinach with a fierce intensity. . . . There was a sighing little sound and one of the detectives lunged toward the
window at which Keith had been standing. But Keith was
no longer there. He was bounding through the snow toward
the woods like a huge deer.

"Don't let him get away!" cried Ellery. Three men dived
through the window after the giant, their guns out. Shots
began to sputter. The night outside was streaked with
orange lightning.

Ellery went to the fire and warmed his hands. Dr. Reinach slowly, very slowly, sat down in the armchair. Thorne
sank into a chair, too, putting his hands to his head.

Ellery turned around and said: "I've told you, Captain,
enough of what's happened since our arrival to allow you an
intelligent understanding of what I'm about to say." A
stocky man in uniform nodded curtly.

"Thorne, last night for the first time in my career," continued Ellery whimsically, "I acknowledged the assistance
of . . . Well, I tell you, who are implicated in this extraordinary crime, that had it not been for the good God above
you would have succeeded in your plot against Alice Mayhew's inheritance."

"I'm disappointed in you," said the fat man from the
depths of the chair.

"A loss I keenly feel." Ellery looked at him, smiling.
"Let me show you, skeptic. When Mr. Thorne, Miss Mayhew and I arrived the other day, it was late afternoon. Upstairs, in the room you so thoughtfully provided, I looked
out the window and saw the sun setting. This was nothing
and meant nothing, surely: sunset. Mere sunset. A trivial
thing, interesting only to poets, meteorologists, and astrono-
mers. But this was one time when the sun was vital to a man

seeking truth . . . a veritable lamp of God shining in the darkness.

"For, see. Miss Mayhew's bedroom that first day was on the opposite side of the house from mine. If the sun *set* in my window, then I faced west and she faced east. So far, so good. We talked, we retired. The next morning I awoke at seven—shortly after sunrise in this winter month—and what did I see? *I saw the sun streaming into my window.*"

A knot hissed in the fire behind him. The stocky man in the blue uniform stirred uneasily.

"Don't you understand?" cried Ellery. "The sun had *set* in my window, and now it was *rising* in my window!"

Dr. Reinach was regarding him with a mild ruefulness. The color had come back to his fat cheeks. He raised the glass he was holding in a gesture curiously like a salute. Then he drank, deeply.

And Ellery said: "The significance of this unearthly reminder did not strike me at once. But much later it came back to me; and I dimly saw that chance, cosmos, God, whatever you may choose to call it, had given me the instrument for understanding the colossal, the mind-staggering phenomenon of a house which vanished overnight from the face of the earth."

"Good lord," muttered Thorne.

"But I was not sure; I did not trust my memory. I needed another demonstration from heaven, a bulwark to bolster my own suspicions. And so, as it snowed and snowed and snowed, the snow drawing a blanket across the face of the sun through which it could not shine, I waited. I waited for the snow to stop, and for the sun to shine again."

He sighed. "When it shone again, there could no longer be any doubt. It appeared first to me in Miss Mayhew's room, which had faced east the afternoon of our arrival. But what was it I saw in Miss Mayhew's room late this afternoon? I saw the sun *set.*"

"Good lord," said Thorne again; he seemed incapable of saying anything else.

"Then her room faced west today. How could her room face west today when it had faced east the day of our arrival? How could my room face west the day of our arrival and face east today? Had the sun stood still? Had the world gone mad? Or was there another explanation—one so extraordinarily simple that it staggered the imagination?"

Thorne muttered: "Queen, this is the most——"

"Please," said Ellery, "let me finish. The only logical conclusion, the only conclusion that did not fly in the face of natural law, of science itself, was that while the house we were in today, the rooms we occupied, *seemed* to be identical with the house and the rooms we had occupied on the day of our arrival, *they were not*. Unless this solid structure had been turned about on its foundation like a toy on a stick, which was palpably absurd, then *it was not the same house.* It looked the same inside and out, it had identical furniture, identical carpeting, identical decorations . . . but it was not the same house. It was another house. It was another house exactly like the first in every detail except one: and that was its terrestrial position in relation to the sun."

A detective outside shouted a message of failure, a shout carried away by the wind under the bright cold moon.

"See," said Ellery softly, "how everything fell into place. If this White House we were in was not the same White House in which we had slept that first night, but was a twin house in a different position in relation to the sun, then the Black House, which apparently had vanished, had not vanished at all. It was where it had always been. It was not the Black House which had vanished, but we who had vanished. It was not the Black House which had moved away, but we who had moved away. We had been transferred during that first night to a new location, where the surrounding woods looked similar, where there was a similar driveway with a similar garage at its terminus, where the road outside was similarly old and pitted, where everything was similar except that there was no Black House, only an empty clearing.

"So we must have been moved, body and baggage, to this twin White House during the time we retired the first night and the time we awoke the next morning. We, Miss Mayhew's chromo on the mantel, the holes in our doors where locks had been, even the fragments of a brandy decanter which had been shattered the night before in a cleverly staged scene against the brick wall of the fireplace at the original house . . . all, all transferred to the twin house to further the illusion that we were still in the original house the next morning."

"Drivel," said Dr. Reinach, smiling. "Such pure drivel that it smacks of fantasmagoria."

"It was beautiful," said Ellery. "A beautiful plan. It had symmetry, the polish of great art. And it made a beautiful chain of reasoning, too, once I was set properly at the right link. For what followed? Since we had been transferred without our knowledge during the night, it must have been while we were unconscious. I recalled the two drinks Thorne and I had had, and the fuzzy tongue and head that resulted the next morning. Mildly drugged, then; and the drinks had been mixed the night before by Dr. Reinach's own hand. Doctor—drugs; very simple." The fat man shrugged with amusement, glancing sidewise at the stocky man in blue. But the stocky man in blue wore a hard, unchanging mask.

"But Dr. Reinach alone?" murmured Ellery. "Oh, no, impossible. One man could never have accomplished all that was necessary in the scant few hours available . . . fix Thorne's car, carry us and our clothes and bags from the one White House to its duplicate—by machine—put Thorne's car out of commission again, put us to bed again, arrange our clothing identically, transfer the chromo, the fragments of the cut-glass decanter in the fireplace, perhaps even a few knickknacks and ornaments not duplicated in the second White House, and so on. A prodigious job, even if most of the preparatory work had been done before our arrival. Obviously the work of a whole group. Of accomplices. Who but everyone in the house? With the possible exception of Mrs. Fell, who in her condition could be swayed easily enough, with no clear perception of what was occurring."

Ellery's eyes gleamed. "And so I accuse you all—including young Mr. Keith, who has wisely taken himself off—of having aided in the plot whereby you would prevent the rightful heiress of Sylvester Mayhew's fortune from taking possession of the house in which it was hidden."

Dr. Reinach coughed politely, flapping his paws together like a great seal. "Terribly interesting, Queen, terribly. I don't know when I've been more captivated by sheer fiction. On the other hand, there are certain personal allusions in your story which, much as I admire their ingenuity, cannot fail to provoke me." He turned to the stocky man in blue. "Certainly, Captain," he chuckled, "you don't credit this incredible story? I believe Mr. Queen has gone a little mad from sheer shock."

"Unworthy of you, Doctor," sighed Ellery. "The proof of what I say lies in the very fact that we are here, at this moment."

"You'll have to explain that," said the police chief, who seemed out of his depth.

"I mean that we are now in the original White House. I led you back here, didn't I? And I can lead you back to the twin White House, for now I know the basis of the illusion. After our departure this evening, incidentally, all these people returned to this house. The other White House had served its purpose and they no longer needed it.

"As for the geographical trick involved, it struck me that this side-road we're on makes a steady curve for miles. Both driveways lead off this same road, one some six miles farther

up the road; although, because of the curve, which is like
a number 9, the road makes a wide sweep and virtually dou-
bles back on itself, so that as the crow flies the two settlements
are only a mile or so apart, although by the curving road
they are six miles apart.

"When Dr. Reinach drove Thorne and Miss Mayhew and
me out here the day the *Coronia* docked, he deliberately
passed the almost imperceptible drive leading to the substitute
house and went on until he reached this one, the original.
We didn't notice the first driveway.

"Thorne's car was put out of commission deliberately to
prevent his driving. The driver of a car will observe land-
marks when his passengers notice little or nothing. Keith
even met Thorne on both Thorne's previous visits to Mayhew
—ostensibly 'to lead the way,' actually to prevent Thorne
from familiarizing himself with the road. And it was Dr.
Reinach who drove the three of us here that first day. They
permitted me to drive away tonight for what they hoped was
a one-way trip because we started from the substitute house
—of the two, the one on the road nearer to town. We
couldn't possibly, then, pass the tell-tale second drive and
become suspicious. And they knew the relatively shorter
drive would not impress our consciousness."

"But even granting all that, Mr. Queen," said the policeman, "I don't see what these people expected to accomplish.
They couldn't hope to keep you folks fooled forever."

"True," cried Ellery, "but don't forget that by the time
we caught on to the various tricks involved they hoped to
have laid hands on Mayhew's fortune and disappeared with
it. Don't you see that the whole illusion was planned *to give
them time*? Time to dismantle the Black House without interference, raze it to the ground if necessary, to find that
hidden hoard of gold? I don't doubt that if you examine
the house next door you'll find it a shambles and a hollow
shell. That's why Reinach and Keith kept disappearing.
They were taking turns at the Black House, picking it apart,

stone by stone, in a frantic search for the cache, while we were occupied in the duplicate White House with an apparently supernatural phenomenon. That's why someone—probably the worthy doctor here—slipped out of the house behind your back, Thorne, and struck me over the head when I rashly attempted to follow Keith's tracks in the snow. I could not be permitted to reach the original settlement, for if I did the whole preposterous illusion would be revealed."

"How about that gold?" growled Thorne.

"For all I know," said Ellery with a shrug, "they've found it and salted it away again."

"Oh, but we didn't," whimpered Mrs. Reinach, squirming in her chair. "Herbert, I *told* you not to——"

"Idiot," said the fat man. "Stupid swine." She jerked as if he had struck her.

"If you hadn't found the loot," said the police chief to Dr. Reinach brusquely, "why did you let these people go tonight?"

Dr. Reinach compressed his blubbery lips; he raised his glass and drank quickly.

"I think I can answer that," said Ellery in a gloomy tone. "In many ways it's the most remarkable element of the whole puzzle. Certainly it's the grimmest and least excusable. The other illusion was child's play compared to it. For it involves two apparently irreconcilable elements—Alice Mayhew and a murder."

"A murder!" exclaimed the policeman, stiffening.

"Me?" said Alice in bewilderment.

Ellery lit a cigaret and flourished it at the policeman. "When Alice Mayhew came here that first afternoon, she went into the Black House with us. In her father's bedroom she ran across an old chromo—I see it's not here, so it's still in the other White House—portraying her long-dead mother as a girl. Alice Mayhew fell on the chromo like a Chinese refugee on a bowl of rice. She had only one picture of her mother, she explained, and that a poor one. She treasured this unexpected discovery so much that she took it with her, then and there, to the White House—this house. And she placed it on the mantel over the fireplace here in a prominent position."

The stocky man frowned; Alice sat very still; Thorne looked puzzled. And Ellery put the cigaret back to his lips and said: "Yet when Alice Mayhew fled from the White House in our company tonight for what seemed to be the last time, *she completely ignored her mother's chromo,* that treasured memento over which she had gone into such raptures the first day! She could not have failed to overlook it in, let us say, the excitement of the moment. She had placed her purse on the mantel, a moment before, next to the chromo. She returned to the mantel for her purse. And yet she passed the chromo up without a glance. Since its sentimental value to her was overwhelming, by her own admission, it's the one thing in all this property she would not have left. *If she had taken it in the beginning, she would have taken it on leaving.*"

Thorne cried: "What in the name of heaven are you saying, Queen?" His eyes glared at the girl, who sat glued to her chair, scarcely breathing.

"I am saying," said Ellery curtly, "that we were blind. I am saying that not only was a house impersonated, but a woman as well. *I am saying that this woman is not Alice Mayhew.*"

The girl raised her eyes after an infinite interval in which no one, not even the policemen present, so much as stirred a foot.

♦ "I thought of everything," she said with the queerest sigh, and quite without the husky tone, "but that. And it was going off so beautifully."

"Oh, you fooled me very neatly," drawled Ellery. "That pretty little bedroom scene last night. . . . I know now what happened. This precious Dr. Reinach of yours had

stolen into your room at midnight to report to you on the
progress of the search at the Black House, perhaps to urge
you to persuade Thorne and me to leave today—at any cost.
I happened to pass along the hall outside your room,
stumbled, and fell against the wall with a clatter; not knowing who it might be or what the intruder's purpose, you both
fell instantly into that cunning deception. . . . Actors!
Both of you missed a career on the stage."

The fat man closed his eyes; he seemed asleep. And the
girl murmured, with a sort of tired defiance: "Not missed,
Mr. Queen. I spent several years in the theatre."

"You were devils, you two. Psychologically this plot has
been the conception of evil genius. You knew that Alice
Mayhew was unknown to anyone in this country except by
her photographs. Moreover, there was a startling resemblance between the two of you, as Miss Mayhew's photographs showed. And you knew Miss Mayhew would be in
the company of Thorne and me for only a few hours, and
then chiefly in the murky light of a sedan."

"Good lord," groaned Thorne, staring at the girl in horror.

"Alice Mayhew," said Ellery grimly, "walked into this
house and was whisked upstairs by Mrs. Reinach. *And Alice*
Mayhew, the English girl, never appeared before us again.
It was you who came downstairs; you, who had been secreted
from Thorne's eyes during the past six days deliberately, so
that he would not even suspect your existence; you who
probably conceived the entire plot when Thorne brought the
photographs of Alice Mayhew here, and her gossipy, inform-
ative letters; you, who looked enough like the real Alice
Mayhew to get by with an impersonation in the eyes of two
men to whom Alice Mayhew was a total stranger. I did
think you looked different, somehow, when you appeared
for dinner that first night; but I put it down to the fact that
I was seeing you for the first time refreshed, brushed up,
and without your hat and coat. Naturally, after that, the
more I saw of you the less I remembered the details of the

real Alice Mayhew's appearance and so became more and
more convinced, unconsciously, that you were Alice Mayhew.
As for the husky voice and the excuse of having caught cold
on the long automobile ride from the pier, that was a clever
ruse to disguise the inevitable difference between your voices.
The only danger that existed lay in Mrs. Fell, who gave us
the answer to the whole riddle the first time we met her.
She thought you were her own daughter Olivia. Of course.
Because that's who you are!"

Dr. Reinach was sipping brandy now with a steady indifference to his surroundings. His little eyes were fixed on a
point miles away. Old Mrs. Fell sat gaping stupidly at the
girl.

"You even covered that danger by getting Dr. Reinach
to tell us beforehand that trumped-up story of Mrs. Fell's
'delusion' and Olivia Fell's 'death' in an automobile accident
several years ago. Oh, admirable! Yet even this poor creature, in the frailty of her anile faculties, was fooled by a
difference in voice and hair—two of the most easily distinguishable features. I suppose you fixed up your hair at the
time Mrs. Reinach brought the real Alice Mayhew upstairs
and you had a living model to go by. . . . I could find
myself moved to admiration if it were not for one thing."

"You're so clever," said Olivia Fell coolly. "Really a fascinating monster. What do you mean?"

Ellery went to her and put his hand on her shoulder.
"Alice Mayhew vanished and you took her place. Why did
you take her place? For two possible reasons. One—to get
Thorne and me away from the danger zone as quickly as
possible, and to keep us away by 'abandoning' the fortune
or dismissing us, which as Alice Mayhew would be your
privilege: in proof, your vociferous insistence that we take
you away. Two—of infinitely greater importance to the
scheme: if your confederates did not find the gold at once,
you were still Alice Mayhew in our eyes. You could then

dispose of the house when and as you saw fit. Whenever the gold was found, it would be yours and your accomplices'.

"But the real Alice Mayhew vanished. For you, her impersonator, to be in a position to go through the long process of taking over Alice Mayhew's inheritance, it was necessary that Alice Mayhew remain *permanently invisible*. For you to get possession of her rightful inheritance and live to enjoy its fruits, it was necessary that Alice Mayhew die. And that, Thorne," snapped Ellery, gripping the girl's shoulder hard, "is why I said that there was something besides a disappearing house to cope with tonight. Alice Mayhew was murdered."

There were three shouts from outside which rang with tones of great excitement. And then they ceased, abruptly.

"Murdered," went on Ellery, "by the only occupant of the house who was not *in* the house when this impostor came downstairs that first evening—Nicholas Keith. A hired killer. Although these people are all accessories to that murder."

A voice said from the window: "Not a hired *killer*."

They wheeled sharply, and fell silent. The three detectives who had sprung out of the window were there in the background, quietly watchful. Before them were two people.

"Not a killer," said one of them, a woman. "That's what he was supposed to be. Instead, and without their knowledge, he saved my life . . . dear Nick."

And now the pall of grayness settled over the faces of Mrs. Fell, and of Olivia Fell, and of Mrs. Reinach, and of the burly doctor. For by Keith's side stood Alice Mayhew. She was the same woman who sat near the fire only in general similitude of feature. Now that both women could be compared in proximity, there were obvious points of difference. She looked worn and grim, but happy withal; and she was holding to the arm of bitter-mouthed Nick Keith with a grip that was quite possessive.

ADDENDUM

Afterwards, when it was possible to look back on the whole amazing fabric of plot and event, Mr. Ellery Queen said: "The scheme would have been utterly impossible except for two things: the character of Olivia Fell and the—in itself—fantastic existence of that duplicate house in the woods."

He might have added that both of these would in turn have been impossible except for the aberrant strain in the Mayhew blood. The father of Sylvester Mayhew—Dr. Reinach's stepfather—had always been erratic, and he had communicated his unbalance to his children. Sylvester and Sarah, who became Mrs. Fell, were twins, and they had always been insanely jealous of each other's prerogatives. When they married in the same month, their father avoided trouble by presenting each of them with a specially-built house, the houses being identical in every detail. One he had erected next to his own house and presented to Mrs. Fell as a wedding gift; the other he built on a piece of property he owned some miles away and gave to Sylvester.

Mrs. Fell's husband died early in her married life; and she moved away to live with her half-brother Herbert. When old Mayhew died, Sylvester boarded up his own house and moved into the ancestral mansion. And there the twin houses stood for many years, separated by only a few miles by road, completely and identically furnished inside—fantastic monuments to the Mayhew eccentricity.

The duplicate White House lay boarded up, waiting, idle, requiring only the evil genius of an Olivia Fell to be put to use. Olivia was beautiful, intelligent, accomplished, and as unscrupulous as Lady Macbeth. It was she who had influenced the others to move back to the abandoned house next

443

to the Black House for the sole purpose of coercing or robbing Sylvester Mayhew. When Thorne appeared with the news of Sylvester's long-lost daughter, she recognized the peril to their scheme and, grasping her own resemblance to her English cousin from the photographs Thorne brought, conceived the whole extraordinary plot.

Then obviously the first step was to put Sylvester out of the way. With perfect logic, she bent Dr. Reinach to her will and caused him to murder his patient before the arrival of Sylvester's daughter. (A later exhumation and autopsy revealed traces of poison in the corpse.) Meanwhile, Olivia perfected the plans of the impersonation and illusion.

The house illusion was planned for the benefit of Thorne, to keep him sequestered and bewildered while the Black House was being torn down in the search for the gold. The illusion would perhaps not have been necessary had Olivia felt certain that her impersonation would succeed perfectly.

The illusion was simpler, of course, than appeared on the surface. The house was there, completely furnished, ready for use. All that was necessary was to take the boards down, air the place out, clean up, put fresh linen in. There was plenty of time before Alice's arrival for this preparatory work.

The one weakness of Olivia Fell's plot was objective, not personal. That woman would have succeeded in anything. But she made the mistake of selecting Nick Keith for the job of murdering Alice Mayhew. Keith had originally insinuated himself into the circle of plotters, posing as a desperado prepared to do anything for sufficient pay. Actually, he was the son of Sylvester Mayhew's second wife, who had been so brutally treated by Mayhew and driven off to die in poverty.

Before his mother expired she instilled in Keith's mind a hatred for Mayhew that waxed, rather than waned, with the ensuing years. Keith's sole motive in joining the conspirators was to find his stepfather's fortune and take that part of it which Mayhew had stolen from his mother. He had never intended to murder Alice—his ostensible rôle. When he carried her from the house that first evening under the noses of Ellery and Thorne, it was not to strangle and bury her, as Olivia had directed, but to secrete her in an ancient shack in the nearby woods known only to himself.

He had managed to smuggle provisions to her while he was ransacking the Black House. At first he had held her frankly prisoner, intending to keep her so until he found the money, took his share, and escaped. But as he came to know her he came to love her, and he soon confessed the whole story to her in the privacy of the shack. Her sympathy gave him new courage; concerned now with her safety above everything else, he prevailed upon her to remain in hiding until he could find the money and outwit his fellow-conspirators. Then they both intended to unmask Olivia.

The ironical part of the whole affair, as Mr. Ellery Queen was to point out, was that the goal of all this plotting and counterplotting—Sylvester Mayhew's gold—remained as invisible as the Black House apparently had been. Despite the most thorough search of the building and grounds no trace of it had been found.

"I've asked you to visit my poor diggings," smiled Ellery a few weeks later, "because something occurred to me that simply cried out for investigation."

Keith and Alice glanced at each other blankly; and Thorne, looking clean, rested, and complacent for the first time in weeks, sat up straighter in Ellery's most comfortable chair.

"I'm glad something occurred to somebody," said Nick Keith with a grin. "I'm a pauper; and Alice is only one jump ahead of me."

"You haven't the philosophic attitude towards wealth," said Ellery dryly, "that's so charming a part of Dr. Reinach's personality. Poor Colossus! I wonder how he likes our jails. . . ." He poked a log into the fire. "By this time, Miss

Mayhew, our common friend Thorne has had your father's house virtually annihilated. No gold. Eh, Thorne?"

"Nothing but dirt," said the lawyer sadly. "Why, we've taken that house apart stone by stone."

"Exactly. Now there are two possibilities, since I am incorrigibly categorical: either your father's fortune exists, Miss Mayhew, or it does not. If it does not and he was lying, there's an end to the business, of course, and you and your precious Keith will have to put your heads together and agree to live either in noble, ruggedly individualistic poverty or by the grace of the Relief Administration. But suppose there was a fortune, as your father claimed, and suppose he did secrete it somewhere in that house. What then?"

"Then," sighed Alice, "it's flown away."

Ellery laughed. "Not quite; I've had enough of vanishments for the present, anyway. Let's tackle the problem differently. Is there anything which was in Sylvester Mayhew's house before he died which is not there now?"

Thorne stared. "If you mean the—er—the body . . ."

"Don't be gruesome, Literal Lyman. Besides, there's been an exhumation. No, guess again."

Alice looked slowly down at the package in her lap. "So that's why you asked me to fetch this with me today!"

"You mean," cried Keith, "the old fellow was deliberately putting everyone off the track when he said his fortune was gold?"

Ellery chuckled and took the package from the girl. He unwrapped it and for a moment gazed appreciatively at the large old chromo of Alice's mother.

And then, with the self-assurance of the complete logician, he stripped away the back of the frame.

Gold-and-green documents cascaded into his lap.

"Converted into bonds," grinned Ellery. "Who said your father was cracked, Miss Mayhew? A very clever gentleman! Come, come, Thorne, stop rubber-necking and let's leave these children of fortune alone!"

The Adventure of
THE TREASURE HUNT

The Adventure of
THE TREASURE HUNT

"Dismount!" roared Major-General Barrett gaily, scrambling off his horse. "How's that for exercise before breakfast, Mr. Queen?"

"Oh, lovely," said Ellery, landing on *terra firma* somehow. The big bay tossed his head, visibly relieved. "I'm afraid my cavalry muscles are a little atrophied, General. We've been riding since six-thirty, remember." He limped to the cliff's edge and rested his racked body against the low stone parapet.

Harkness uncoiled himself from the roan and said: "You lead a life of armchair adventure, Queen? It must be embarrassing when you poke your nose out into the world of men." He laughed. Ellery eyed the man's yellow mane and nervy eyes with the unreasoning dislike of the chronic shut-in. That broad chest was untroubled after the gallop.

"Embarrassing to the horse," said Ellery. "Beautiful view, General. You couldn't have selected this site blindly. Must be a streak of poetry in your make-up."

"Poetry your foot, Mr. Queen! I'm a military man." The old gentleman waddled to Ellery's side and gazed down over the Hudson River, a blue-glass reflector under the young sun. The cliff was sheer; it fell cleanly to a splinter of beach far below, where Major-General Barrett had his boathouse. A zigzag of steep stone steps in the face of the cliff was the only means of descent.

An old man was seated on the edge of a little jetty below, fishing. He glanced up, and to Ellery's astonishment sprang to his feet and snapped his free hand up in a stiff salute. Then he very placidly sat down and resumed his fishing.

449

"Braun," said the General, beaming. "Old pensioner of mine. Served under me in Mexico. He and Magruder, the old chap at the caretaker's cottage. You see? Discipline, that's it. . . . Poetry?" He snorted. "Not for me, Mr. Queen. I like this ledge for its military value. Commands the river. Miniature West Point, b'gad!"

Ellery turned and looked upward. The shelf of rock on which the General had built his home was surrounded on its other three sides by precipitous cliffs, quite unscalable, which towered so high that their crests were swimming in mist. A steep road had been blasted in the living rock of the rearmost cliff; it spiralled down from the top of the mountain, and Ellery still remembered with vertigo the automobile descent the evening before.

"You command the river," he said dryly, "but an enemy could shoot the hell out of you by commanding that road up there. Or are my tactics infantile?"

The old gentleman spluttered: "Why, I could hold that gateway to the road against an army, man!"

"And the artillery," murmured Ellery. "Heavens, General, you *are* prepared." He glanced with amusement at a small sleek cannon beside the nearby flagpole, its muzzle gaping over the parapet.

"General's getting ready for the revolution," said Harkness with a lazy laugh. "We live in parlous times."

"You sportsmen," snapped the General, "have no respect whatever for tradition. You know very well this is a sunset gun—you don't sneer at the one on the Point, do you? That's the only way Old Glory," he concluded in a parade-ground voice, "will ever come down on *my* property, Harkness—to the boom of a cannon salute!"

"I suppose," smiled the big-game hunter, "my elephant-gun wouldn't serve the same purpose? On *safari* I——"

"Ignore the fellow, Mr. Queen," said the General testily. "We just tolerate him on these week-ends because he's a friend of Lieutenant Fiske's. . . . Too bad you arrived too

late last night to see the ceremony. Quite stirring! You'll
see it again at sunset today. Must keep up the old traditions.
Part of my life, Mr. Queen. . . . I guess I'm an old fool."

"Oh, indeed not," said Ellery hastily. "Traditions are the
backbone of the nation; anybody knows that." Harkness
chuckled, and the General looked pleased. Ellery knew the
type—retired army man, too old for service, pining for the
military life. From what Dick Fiske, the General's prospec-
tive son-in-law, had told him on the way down the night
before, Barrett had been a passionate and single-tracked sol-
dier; and he had taken over with him into civilian life as
many mementoes of the good old martial days as he could
carry. Even his servants were old soldiers; and the house,
which bristled with relics of three wars, was run like a regi-
mental barracks.

A groom led their horses away, and they strolled back
across the rolling lawns toward the house. Major-General
Barrett, Ellery was thinking, must be crawling with money;
he had already seen enough to convince him of that. There
was a tiled swimming-pool outdoors; a magnificent solarium;
a target-range; a gun-room with a variety of weapons
that . . .

"General," said an agitated voice; and he looked up to see
Lieutenant Fiske, his uniform unusually disordered, running
toward them. "May I see you a moment alone, sir?"

"Of course, Richard. Excuse me, gentlemen?"

Harkness and Ellery hung back. The Lieutenant said
something, his arms jerking nervously; and the old gentleman paled. Then, without another word, both men broke
into a run, the General waddling like a startled grandfather
gander toward the house.

"I wonder what's eating Dick," said Harkness, as he and
Ellery followed more decorously.

"Leonie," ventured Ellery. "I've known Fiske for a long
time. That ravishing daughter of the regiment is the only

unsettling influence the boy's ever encountered. I hope there's nothing wrong."

"Pity if there is," shrugged the big man. "It promised to be a restful week-end. I had my fill of excitement on my last expedition."

"Ran into trouble?"

"My boys deserted, and a flood on the Niger did the rest. Lost everything. Lucky to have escaped with my life. . . . Ah, there, Mrs. Nixon. Is anything wrong with Miss Barrett?"

A tall pale woman with red hair and amber eyes looked up from the magazine she was reading. "Leonie? I haven't seen her this morning. Why?" She seemed not too interested. "Oh, Mr. Queen! That dreadful game we played last night kept me awake half the night. How *can* you sleep with all those murdered people haunting you?"

"My difficulty," grinned Ellery, "is not in sleeping too little, Mrs. Nixon, but in sleeping too much. The original sluggard. No more imagination than an amoeba. Nightmare? You must have something on your conscience."

"But was it necessary to take our *fingerprints*, Mr. Queen? I mean, a game's a game. . . ."

Ellery chuckled. "I promise to destroy my impromptu little Bureau of Identification at the very first opportunity. No thanks, Harkness; don't care for any this early in the day."

"Queen," said Lieutenant Fiske from the doorway. His brown cheeks were muddy and mottled, and he held himself very stiffly. "Would you mind——?"

"What's wrong, Lieutenant?" demanded Harkness.

"Has something happened to Leonie?" asked Mrs. Nixon.

"Wrong? Why, nothing at all." The young officer smiled, took Ellery's arm, and steered him to the stairs. He was smiling no longer. "Something rotten's happened, Queen. We're—we don't quite know what to do. Lucky you're here. You might know. . . ."

"Now, now," said Ellery gently. "What's happened?"

"You remember that rope of pearls Leonie wore last night?"

"Oh," said Ellery.

"It was my engagement gift to her. Belonged to my mother." The Lieutenant bit his lip. "I'm not—well, a lieutenant in the United States Army can't buy pearls on his salary. I wanted to give Leonie something—expensive. Foolish of me, I suppose. Anyway, I treasured mother's pearls for sentimental reasons, too, and——"

"You're trying to tell me," said Ellery as they reached the head of the stairs, "that the pearls are gone."

"Damn it, yes!"

"How much are they worth?"

"Twenty-five thousand dollars. My father was wealthy— once."

Ellery sighed. In the workshop of the cosmos it had been decreed that he should stalk with open eyes among the lame, the halt, and the blind. He lit a cigaret and followed the officer into Leonie Barrett's bedroom.

There was nothing martial in Major-General Barrett's bearing now; he was simply a fat old man with sagging shoulders. As for Leonie, she had been crying; and Ellery thought irrelevantly that she had used the hem of her *peignoir* to stanch her tears. But there was also a set to her chin and a gleam in her eye; and she pounced upon Ellery so quickly that he almost threw his arm up to defend himself.

"Someone's stolen my necklace," she said fiercely. "Mr. Queen, you must get it back. You *must*, do you hear?"

"Leonie, my dear," began the General in a feeble voice.

"No, father! I don't care *who's* going to be hurt. That— that rope of pearls meant a lot to Dick, and it means a lot to me, and I don't propose to sit by and let some *thief* snatch it right from under my nose!"

"But darling," said the Lieutenant miserably. "After all, your guests . . ."

"Hang my guests, and yours, too," said the young woman with a toss of her head. "I don't think there's anything in Mrs. Post's book which says a thief gathers immunity simply because he's present on an invitation."

"But it's certainly more reasonable to suspect that one of the servants——"

The General's head came up like a shot. "My dear Richard," he snorted, "put that notion out of your head. There isn't a man in my employ who hasn't been with me for at least twenty years. I'd trust any one of 'em with anything I have. I've had proof of their honesty and loyalty a hundred times."

"Since I'm one of the guests," said Ellery cheerfully, "I think I'm qualified to pass an opinion. Murder will out, but it was never hindered by a bit of judicious investigation, Lieutenant. Your *fiancée's* quite right. When did you discover the theft, Miss Barrett?"

"A half-hour ago, when I awoke." Leonie pointed to the dressing-table beside her four-posted bed. "Even before I rubbed the sleep out of my eyes I saw that the pearls were gone. Because the lid of my jewel-box was up, as you see."

"And the box was closed when you retired last night?"

"Better than that. I awoke at six this morning feeling thirsty. I got out of bed for a glass of water, and I distinctly remember that the box was closed at that time. Then I went back to sleep."

Ellery strolled over and glanced down at the box. Then he blew smoke and said: "Happy chance. It's a little after eight now. You discovered the theft, then, at a quarter of eight or so. Therefore the pearls were stolen between six and seven-forty-five. Didn't you hear anything, Miss Barrett?"

Leonie smiled ruefully. "I'm a disgustingly sound sleeper, Mr. Queen. That's something you'll learn, Dick. And then for years I've suspected that I snore, but nobody ever——"

The Lieutenant blushed. The General said: "Leonie," not

very convincingly, and Leonie made a face and began to weep again, this time on the Lieutenant's shoulder.

"What the deuce are we to do?" snarled the General. "We can't—well, hang it all, you just can't *search* people. Nasty business! If the pearls weren't so valuable I'd say forget the whole ruddy thing."

"A body search is scarcely necessary, General," said Ellery. "No thief would be so stupid as to carry the loot about on his person. He'd expect the police to be called; and the police, at least, are notoriously callous to the social niceties."

"Police," said Leonie in a damp voice, raising her head. "Oh, goodness. Can't we——"

"I think," said Ellery, "we can struggle along without them for the proverbial nonce. On the other hand, a search of the premises. . . . Any objection to my prowling about?"

"None whatever," snapped Leonie. "Mr. Queen, you prowl!"

"I believe I shall. By the way, who besides the four of us—and the thief—knows about this?"

"Not another soul."

"Very good. Now, discretion is our shibboleth today. Please pretend nothing's happened. The thief will know we're acting, but he'll be constrained to act, too, and perhaps . . ." He smoked thoughtfully. "Suppose you dress and join your guests downstairs, Miss Barrett. Come, come, get that Wimpole Street expression off your face, my dear!"

"Yes, sir," said Leonie, trying out a smile.

"You gentlemen might co-operate. Keep everyone away from this floor while I go into my prowling act. I shouldn't like to have Mrs. Nixon, for example, catch me red-handed among her *brassières*."

"Oh," said Leonie suddenly. And she stopped smiling.

"What's the matter?" asked the Lieutenant in an anxious voice.

"Well, Dorothy Nixon is up against it. Horribly short of

funds. No, that's a—a rotten thing to say." Leonie flushed. "Goodness, I'm half-naked! Now, *please*, clear out."

"Nothing," said Ellery in an undertone to Lieutenant Fiske after breakfast. "It isn't anywhere in the house."

"Damnation," said the officer. "You're positive?"

"Quite. I've been through all the rooms. Kitchen. Solarium. Pantry. Armory. I've even visited the General's cellar."

Fiske gnawed his lower lip. Leonie called gaily: "Dorothy and Mr. Harkness and I are going into the pool for a plunge. Dick! Coming?"

"Please go," said Ellery softly; and he added: "And while you're plunging, Lieutenant, search that pool."

Fiske looked startled. Then he nodded rather grimly and followed the others.

"Nothing, eh?" said the General glumly. "I saw you talking to Richard."

"Not yet." Ellery glanced from the house, into which the others had gone to change into bathing costume, to the riverside. "Suppose we stroll down there, General. I want to ask your man Braun some questions."

They made their way cautiously down the stone steps in the cliff to the sliver of beach below, and found the old pensioner placidly engaged in polishing the brasswork of the General's launch.

"Mornin', sir," said Braun, snapping to attention.

"At ease," said the General moodily. "Braun, this gentleman wants to ask you some questions."

"Very simple ones," smiled Ellery. "I saw you fishing, Braun, at about eight this morning. How long had you been sitting on the jetty?"

"Well, sir," replied the old man, scratching his left arm, "on and off since ha'-past five. Bitin' early, they are. Got a fine mess."

"Did you have the stairs there in view all the time?"

"Sure thing, sir."

"Has anyone come down this morning?" Braun shook his gray thatch. "Has anyone approached from the river?"

"Not a one, sir."

"Did anyone drop or throw anything down here or into the water from the cliff up there?"

"If they'd had, I'd 'a' heard the splash, sir. No, sir."

"Thank you. Oh, by the way, Braun, you're here all day?"

"Well, only till early afternoon, unless someone's usin' the launch, sir."

"Keep your eyes open, then. General Barrett is especially anxious to know if anyone comes down this afternoon. If someone does, watch closely and report."

"General's orders, sir?" asked Braun, cocking a shrewd eye.

"That's right, Braun," sighed the General. "Dismissed."

"And now," said Ellery, as they climbed to the top of the cliff, "let's see what friend Magruder has to say."

Magruder was a gigantic old Irishman with leathery cheeks and the eyes of a top-sergeant. He occupied a rambling little cottage at the only gateway to the estate.

"No, sir," he said emphatically, "ain't been a soul near here all mornin'. Nob'dy, in or out."

"But how can you be sure, Magruder?"

The Irishman stiffened. "From a quarter to six till seventhirty I was a-settin' right there in full view o' the gate a-cleanin' some o' the Gin'ral's guns, sir. And afther I was trimmin' the privets."

"You may take Magruder's word as gospel," snapped the General.

"I do, I do," said Ellery soothingly. "This is the only vehicular exit from the estate, of course, sir?"

"As you see."

"Yes, yes. And the cliffside . . . Only a lizard could scale those rocky side-walls. Very interesting. Thanks, Magruder."

"Well, what now?" demanded the General, as they walked back toward the house.

Ellery frowned. "The essence of any investigation, General, is the question of how many possibilities you can eliminate. This little hunt grows enchanting on that score. You say you trust your servants implicitly?"

"With anything."

"Then round up as many as you can spare and have them go over every inch of the grounds with a finecomb. Fortunately your estate isn't extensive, and the job shouldn't take long."

"Hmm." The General's nostrils quivered. "B'gad, there's an idea! I see, I see. Splendid, Mr. Queen. You may trust my lads. Old soldiers, every one of 'em; they'll love it. And the trees?"

"I beg your pardon?"

"The trees, man, the trees! Crotches of 'em; good hiding-places."

"Oh," said Ellery gravely, "the trees. By all means search them."

"Leave that to me," said the General fiercely; and he trotted off breathing fire.

Ellery sauntered over to the pool, which churned with vigorous bodies, and sat down on a bench to watch. Mrs. Nixon waved a shapely arm and dived under, pursued by a bronzed giant who turned out to be Harkness when his dripping curls reappeared. A slim slick figure shot out of the water almost at Ellery's feet and in the same motion scaled the edge of the pool.

"I've done it," murmured Leonie, smiling and preening as if to invite Ellery's admiration.

"Done what?" mumbled Ellery, grinning back.

"Searched them."

"Searched—! I don't understand."

"Oh, are all men fundamentally stupid?" Leonie leaned back and shook out her hair. "Why d'ye think I suggested the pool? So that everyone would have to take his clothes off! All I did was slip into a bedroom or two before going down myself. I searched *all* our clothes. It was possible the —the thief had slipped the pearls into some unsuspecting pocket, you see. Well . . . nothing."

Ellery looked at her. "My dear young woman, *I'd* like to play Browning to your Ba, come to think of it. . . . But their bathing-suits——"

Leonie colored. Then she said firmly: "That was a long, six-stranded rope. If you think Dorothy Nixon has it on her person *now*, in *that* bathing-suit . . ." Ellery glanced at Mrs. Nixon.

"I can't say," he chuckled, "that any of you in your present costumes could conceal an object larger than a fly's wing. Ah, there, Leftenant! How's the water?"

"No good," said Fiske, thrusting his chin over the pool's edge.

"Why, Dick!" exclaimed Leonie. "I thought you liked——"

"Your *fiancé*," murmured Ellery, "has just informed me that your pearls are nowhere in the pool, Miss Barrett."

Mrs. Nixon slapped Harkness's face, brought up her naked leg, set her rosy heel against the man's wide chin, and shoved. Harkness laughed and went under.

"Swine," said Mrs. Nixon pleasantly, climbing out.

"It's your own fault," said Leonie. "I *told* you not to wear that bathing-suit."

"Look," said the Lieutenant darkly, "who's talking."

"If you *will* invite Tarzan for a week-end," began Mrs. Nixon, and she stopped. "What on earth are those men doing out there? They're crawling!"

Everybody looked. Ellery sighed. "I believe the General is tired of our company and is directing some sort of war-game with his veterans. Does he often get that way, Miss Barrett?"

"Infantry manœuvers," said the Lieutenant quickly.

"That's a silly game," said Mrs. Nixon with spirit, taking

off her cap. "What's on for this afternoon, Leonie? Let's do something exciting!"

"I think," grinned Harkness, clambering out of the pool like a great monkey, "I'd like to play an exciting game, Mrs. Nixon, if you're going to be in it." The sun gleamed on his wet torso.

"Animal," said Mrs. Nixon. "What shall it be? Suggest something, Mr. Queen."

"Lord," said Ellery. "*I* don't know. Treasure hunt? It's a little *passé*, but at least it isn't too taxing on the brain."

"That," said Leonie, "has all the earmarks of a nasty crack. But I think it's a glorious idea. You arrange things, Mr. Queen."

"Treasure hunt?" Mrs. Nixon considered it. "Mmm. Sounds nice. Make the treasure something worth while, won't you? I'm stony."

Ellery paused in the act of lighting a cigaret. Then he threw his match away. "If I'm elected . . . When shall it be—after luncheon?" He grinned. "May as well do it up brown. I'll fix the clues and things. Keep in the house, the lot of you. I don't want any spying. Agreed?"

"We're in your hands," said Mrs. Nixon gaily.

"Lucky dog," sighed Harkness.

"See you later, then." Ellery strolled off toward the river. He heard Leonie's fresh voice exhorting her guests to hurry into the house to dress for luncheon.

Major-General Barrett found him at noon standing by the parapet and gazing absently at the opposite shore, half a mile away. The old gentleman's cheeks were bursting with blood and perspiration, and he looked angry and tired.

"Damn all thieves for black-hearted scoundrels!" he exploded, mopping his bald spot. Then he said inconsistently: "I'm beginning to think Leonie simply mislaid it."

"You haven't found it?"

"No sign of it."

"Then where did she mislay it?"

"Oh, thunderation, I suppose you're right. I'm sick of the whole blasted business. To think that a guest under my roof——"

"Who said," sighed Ellery, "anything about a guest, General?"

The old gentleman glared. "Eh? What's that? What d'ye mean?"

"Nothing at all. You don't know. *I* don't know. Nobody but the thief knows. Shouldn't jump to conclusions, sir. Now, tell me. The search has been thorough?" Major-General Barrett groaned. "You've gone through Magruder's cottage, too?"

"Certainly, certainly."

"The stables?"

"My dear sir——"

"The trees?"

"*And* the trees," snapped the General. "Every last place."

"Good!"

"What's good about it?"

Ellery looked astonished. "My dear General, it's superb! I'm prepared for it. In fact, I anticipated it. Because we're dealing with a very clever person."

"You know——" gasped the General.

"Very little concretely. But I see a glimmer. Now will you go back to the house, sir, and freshen up? You're fatigued, and you'll need your energies for this afternoon. We're to play a game."

"Oh, heavens," said the General; and he trudged off toward the house, shaking his head. Ellery watched him until he disappeared.

Then he squatted on the parapet and gave himself over to thought.

"Now, ladies and gentlemen," began Ellery after they had assembled on the veranda at two o'clock, "I have spent the last two hours hard at work—a personal sacrifice which I gladly contribute to the gayety of nations, and in return for which I ask only your lusty co-operation."

"Hear," said the General gloomily.

"Come, come, General, don't be anti-social. Of course, you all understand the game?" Ellery lit a cigaret. "I have hidden the 'treasure' somewhere. I've left a trail to it—a winding trail, you understand, which you must follow step by step. At each step I've dropped a clue which, correctly interpreted, leads to the next step. The race is, naturally, to the mentally swift. This game puts a premium on brains."

"That," said Mrs. Nixon ruefully, "lets me out." She was dressed in tight sweater and tighter slacks, and she had bound her hair with a blue ribbon.

"Poor Dick," groaned Leonie. "I'm sure I shall have to pair up with him. He wouldn't get to first base by himself."

Fiske grinned, and Harkness drawled: "As long as we're splitting up, I choose Mrs. N. Looks as if you'll have to go it alone, General."

"Perhaps," said the General hopefully, "you young people would like to play by yourselves. . . ."

"By the way," said Ellery, "all the clues are in the form of quotations, you know."

"Oh, dear," said Mrs. Nixon. "You mean such things as 'first in war, first in peace'?"

"Ah—yes. Yes. Don't worry about the source; it's only the words themselves that concern you. Ready?"

"Wait a minute," said Harkness. "What's the treasure?"

Ellery threw his cigaret, which had gone out, into an ashtray. "Mustn't tell. Get set, now! Let me quote you the first clue. It comes from the barbed quill of our old friend, Dean Swift—but disregard that. The quotation is—" he paused, and they leaned forward eagerly—"'*first (a fish) should swim in the sea.*'"

The General said: "Hrrumph! Damned silly," and settled in his chair. But Mrs. Nixon's amber eyes shone and she jumped up.

"Is *that* all?" she cried. "Goodness, that isn't the least bit difficult, Mr. Queen. Come on, Tarzan," and she sped away over the lawns, followed by Harkness, who was grinning. They made for the parapet.

"Poor Dorothy," sighed Leonie. "She means well, but she isn't exactly blessed with brains. She's taking the wrong tack, of course."

"You'd put her hard a-port, I suppose?" murmured Ellery.

"*Mr.* Queen! You obviously didn't mean us to search the entire Hudson River. Consequently it's a more restricted body of water you had in mind." She sprang off the veranda.

"The pool!" cried Lieutenant Fiske, scrambling after her.

"Remarkable woman, your daughter, sir," said Ellery, following the pair with his eyes. "I'm beginning to think Dick Fiske is an extraordinarily fortunate young man."

"Mother's brain," said the General, beaming suddenly. "B'gad, I *am* interested." He waddled rapidly off the porch.

They found Leonie complacently deflating a large rubber fish which was still dripping from its immersion in the pool. "Here it is," she said. "Come on, Dick, pay attention. *Not* now, silly! Mr. Queen's looking. What's this? *'Then it should swim in butter.'* Butter, butter . . . Pantry, of course!" And she was off like the wind for the house, the Lieutenant sprinting after.

Ellery replaced the note in the rubber fish, inflated it, stoppered the hole, and tossed the thing back into the pool. "The others will be here soon enough. There they are! I think they've caught on already. Come along, General."

Leonie was on her knees in the pantry, before the huge refrigerator, digging a scrap of paper out of a butter-tub. "Goo," she said, wrinkling her nose. "Did you have to use butter? Read it, Dick. I'm filthy."

Lieutenant Fiske declaimed: " *'And at last, sirrah, it should swim in good claret.'* "

"Mr. Queen! I'm ashamed of you. This is too easy."

"It gets harder," said Ellery dryly, "as it goes along." He

watched the young couple dash through the doorway to the cellar, and then replaced the note in the tub. As he and the General closed the cellar-door behind them, they heard the clatter of Mrs. Nixon's feet in the pantry.

"Damned if Leonie hasn't forgotten all about that necklace of hers," muttered the General as they watched from the stairs. "Just like a woman!"

"I doubt very much if she has," murmured Ellery.

"Whee!" cried Leonie. "Here it is. . . . What's this, Mr. Queen—Shakespeare?" She had pried a note from between two dusty bottles in the wine-cellar and was frowning over it.

"What's it say, Leonie?" asked Lieutenant Fiske.

" '*Under the greenwood tree*'. . . . Greenwood tree." She replaced the note slowly. "It *is* getting harder. Have we any greenwood trees, father?"

The General said wearily: "Blessed if I know. Never heard of 'em. You, Richard?" The Lieutenant looked dubious.

"All I know about the greenwood tree," frowned Leonie, "is that it's something in *As You Like It* and a novel by Thomas Hardy. But——"

"Come *on*, Tarzan!" shrieked Mrs. Nixon from above them. "They're still here. Out of the way, you two men! No fair setting up hazards."

Leonie scowled. Mrs. Nixon came flying down the cellar stairs followed by Harkness, who was still grinning, and snatched the note from the shelf. Her face fell. "Greek to me."

"Let me see it." Harkness scanned the note, and laughed aloud. "Good boy, Queen," he chuckled. "*Chlorosplenium æruginosum*. You need a little botany in jungle work. I've seen that tree any number of times on the estate." He bounded up the stairs, grinned once more at Ellery and Major-General Barrett, and vanished.

"Damn!" said Leonie, and she led the charge after Harkness.

When they came up with him, the big man was leaning against the bark of an ancient and enormous shade-tree, reading a scrap of paper and scratching his handsome chin. The bole of the tree was a vivid green which looked fungoid in origin.

"Green wood!" exclaimed Mrs. Nixon. "That *was* clever, Mr. Queen."

Leonie looked chagrined. "A man would take the honors. I'd never have thought it of you, Mr. Harkness. What's in the note?"

Harkness read aloud: "'*And . . . seeks that which he lately threw away . . .*'"

"Which who lately threw away?" complained the Lieutenant. "That's ambiguous."

"Obviously," said Harkness, "the pronoun couldn't refer to the finder of the note. Queen couldn't possibly have known who would track it down. Consequently . . . Of course!" And he sped off in the direction of the house, thumbing his nose.

"I don't *like* that man," said Leonie. "Dickie, haven't you any brains at all? And now we have to follow him again. I think you're mean, Mr. Queen."

"I leave it to you, General," said Ellery. "Did *I* want to play games?" But they were all streaming after Harkness, and Mrs. Nixon was in the van, her red hair flowing behind her like a pennon.

Ellery reached the veranda, the General puffing behind him, to find Harkness holding something aloft out of reach of Mrs. Nixon's clutching fingers. "No, you don't. To the victor——"

"But how did you know, you nasty man?" cried Leonie.

Harkness lowered his arm; he was holding a half-consumed cigaret. "Stood to reason. The quotation had to refer to Queen himself. And the only thing I'd seen him 'lately' throw away was this cigaret-butt just before we started." He took the cigaret apart; imbedded in the tobacco near the tip there was a tiny twist of paper. He smoothed it out and read its scribbled message.

Then he read it again, slowly.

"Well, for pity's sake!" snapped Mrs. Nixon. "Don't be a *pig*, Tarzan. If you don't know the answer, give the rest of us a chance." She snatched the paper from him and read it. " '*Seeking . . . even in the cannon's mouth.*' "

"Cannon's mouth?" panted the General. "Why——"

"Why, that's *pie!*" giggled the red-haired woman, and ran.

She was seated defensively astride the sunset gun overlooking the river when they reached her. "This is a fine howd'ye-do," she complained. "Cannon's mouth! How the deuce can you look into the cannon's mouth when the cannon's mouth is situated in thin air seventy-five feet over the Hudson River? Pull this foul thing back a bit, Lieutenant!"

Leonie was helpless with laughter. "You *idiot!* How do you think Magruder loads this gun—through the muzzle? There's a chamber in the back."

Lieutenant Fiske did something expertly to the mechanism at the rear of the sunset gun, and in a twinkling had swung back the safe-like little door of the breech-block and revealed a round orifice. He thrust his hand in, and his jaw dropped. "It's the treasure!" he shouted. "By George, Dorothy, you've won!"

Mrs. Nixon slid off the cannon, gurgling: "Gimme, gimme!" like an excited *gamine*. She bumped him rudely aside and pulled out a wad of oily cotton batting.

"What is it?" cried Leonie, crowding in.

"I . . . Why, Leonie, you *darling!*" Mrs. Nixon's face fell. "I knew it was too good to be true. Treasure! I should say so."

"*My pearls!*" screamed Leonie. She snatched the rope of snowy gems from Mrs. Nixon, hugging them to her bosom; and then she turned to Ellery with the oddest look of inquiry.

"Well, I'll be—be blasted," said the General feebly. "Did *you* take 'em, Queen?"

"Not exactly," said Ellery. "Stand still, please. That means everybody. We have Mrs. Nixon and Mr. Harkness possibly at a disadvantage. You see, Miss Barrett's pearls were stolen this morning."

"Stolen?" Harkness lifted an eyebrow.

"Stolen!" gasped Mrs. Nixon. "So that's why——"

"Yes," said Ellery. "Now, perceive. Someone filches a valuable necklace. Problem: to get it away. Was the necklace still on the premises? It was; it had to be. There are only two physical means of egress from the estate: by the cliff-road yonder, at the entrance to which is Magruder's cottage; and by the river below. Everywhere else there are perpendicular cliffs impossible to climb. And their crests are so high that it was scarcely feasible for an accomplice, say, to let a rope down and haul the loot up. . . . Now, since before six Magruder had the land exit under observation and Braun the river exit. Neither had seen a soul; and Braun said that nothing had been thrown over the parapet to the beach or water, or he would have heard the impact or splash. Since the thief had made no attempt to dispose of the pearls by the only two possible routes, it was clear then that the pearls were still on the estate."

Leonie's face was pinched and pale now, and she kept her eyes steadfastly on Ellery. The General looked embarrassed.

"But the thief," said Ellery, "must have had a plan of disposal, a plan that would circumvent all normal contingencies. Knowing that the theft might be discovered at once, he would expect an early arrival of the police and plan accordingly; people don't take the loss of a twenty-five thousand dollar necklace without a fight. If he expected police, he expected a search; and if he expected a search, he could not have planned to hide his loot in an obvious place— such as on his person, in his luggage, in the house, or in the usual places on the estate. Of course, he might have meant to dig a hole somewhere and bury the pearls; but I didn't think so, because he would in that case still have the problem of disposal, with the estate guarded.

"As a matter of fact, I myself searched every inch of the house; and the General's servants searched every inch of the grounds and outbuildings . . . just to make sure. We called no police, but acted as police ourselves. And the pearls weren't found."

"But—" began Lieutenant Fiske in a puzzled way.

"Please, Lieutenant. It was plain, then, that the thief, whatever his plan, had discarded any *normal* use of either the land or water route. As a means of getting the pearls off the estate. Had he intended to walk off with them himself, or mail them to an accomplice? Hardly, if he anticipated a police investigation and surveillance. Besides, remember that he deliberately planned and committed his theft with the foreknowledge that a detective was in the house. And while I lay no claim to exceptional formidability, you must admit it took a daring, clever thief to concoct and carry out a theft under the circumstances. I felt justified in assuming that, whatever his plan was, it was itself daring and clever; not stupid and commonplace.

"But if he had discarded the *normal* means of disposal, he must have had in mind an extraordinary means, still using one of the only two possible routes. And then I recalled that there was one way the river route could be utilized to that end which was so innocent in appearance that it would probably be successful even if a whole regiment of infantry were on guard. And I knew that must be the answer."

"The sunset gun," said Leonie in a low voice.

"Precisely, Miss Barrett, the sunset gun. By preparing a package with the pearls inside, opening the breech-block of the gun and thrusting the package into the chamber and walking away, he disposed very simply of the bothersome problem of getting the pearls away. You see, anyone with a knowledge of ordnance and ballistics would know that this gun, like all guns which fire salutes, uses 'blank' ammunition. That is, there is no explosive shell; merely a charge of powder which goes off with a loud noise and a burst of smoke.

"Now, while this powder is a noise-maker purely, it still possesses a certain propulsive power—not much, but enough for the thief's purpose. Consequently Magruder would come along at sundown today, slip the blank into the breech, pull the firing-cord, and—boom! away go the pearls in a puff of concealing smoke, to be hurled the scant twenty feet or so necessary to make it clear the little beach below and fall into the water."

"But how—" spluttered the General, red as a cherry.

"Obviously, the container would have to float. Aluminum, probably, or something equally strong yet light. Then an accomplice must be in the scheme—someone to idle along in the Hudson below in a boat at sunset, pick up the container, and cheerfully sail away. At that time Braun is not on duty, as he told me; but even if he were, I doubt if he would have noticed anything in the noise and smoke of the gun."

"Accomplice, eh?" roared the General. "I'll 'phone——"

Ellery sighed. "Already done, General. I telephoned the local police at one o'clock to be on the lookout. Our man will be waiting at sundown, and if you stick to schedule with your salute to the dying sun, they'll nab him red-handed."

"But where's this container, or can?" asked the Lieutenant.

"Oh, safely hidden away," said Ellery dryly. "Very safely."

"You hid it? But why?"

Ellery smoked peacefully for a moment. "You know, there's a fat-bellied little god who watches over such as me. Last night we played a murder-game. To make it realistic, and to illustrate a point, I took everyone's fingerprints with the aid of that handy little kit I carry about. I neglected to destroy the exhibits. This afternoon, before our treasure hunt, I found the container in the gun here—naturally, having reasoned out the hiding-place, I went straight to it for confirmation. And what do you think I found on the can? Fingerprints!" Ellery grimaced. "Disappointing, isn't it? But then our clever thief was so sure of himself he never dreamed anyone would uncover his cache before the gun was fired. And so he was careless. It was child's-play, of course, to compare the prints on the can with the master sets from last night's game." He paused. *"Well?"* he said.

There was silence for as long as one can hold a breath; and in the silence they heard the flapping of the flag overhead.

Then, his hands unclenching, Harkness said lightly: "You've got me, pal."

"Ah," said Ellery. "So good of you, Mr. Harkness."

They stood about the gun at sunset, and old Magruder yanked the cord, and the gun roared as the flag came down, and Major-General Barrett and Lieutenant Fiske stood rigidly at attention. The report echoed and re-echoed, filling the air with hollow thunder.

"Look at the creature," gurgled Mrs. Nixon a moment later, leaning over the parapet and staring down. "He looks like a bug running around in circles."

They joined her silently. The Hudson below was a steel mirror reflecting the last copper rays of the sun. Except for a small boat with an outboard motor the river was free of craft; and the man was hurling his boat this way and that in puzzled parabolas, scanning the surface of the river anxiously. Suddenly he looked up and saw the faces watching him; and with ludicrous haste frantically swept his boat about and shot it for the opposite shore.

"I still don't understand," complained Mrs. Nixon, "why you called the law off that person, Mr. Queen. He's a criminal, isn't he?"

Ellery sighed. "Only in intent. And then it was Miss

Barrett's idea, not mine. I can't say I'm sorry. While I hold no brief for Harkness and his accomplice, who's probably some poor devil seduced by our dashing friend into doing the work of disposal, I'm rather relieved Miss Barrett hasn't been vindictive. Harkness has been touched and spoiled by the life he leads; it's really not his fault. When you spend half your life in jungles, the civilized moralities lose their edge. He needed the money, and so he took the pearls."

"He's punished enough," said Leonie gently. "Almost as much as if we'd turned him over to the police instead of sending him packing. He's through socially. And since I've my pearls back——"

"Interesting problem," said Ellery dreamily. "I suppose you all saw the significance of the treasure hunt?"

Lieutenant Fiske looked blank. "I guess I'm thick. *I* don't."

"Pshaw! At the time I suggested the game I had no ulterior motive. But when the reports came in, and I deduced that the pearls were in the sunset gun, I saw a way to use the game to trap the thief." He smiled at Leonie, who grinned back. "Miss Barrett was my accomplice. I asked her privately to start brilliantly—in order to lull suspicion—and slow up as she went along. The mere use of the gun had made me suspect Harkness, who knows guns; I wanted to test him.

"Well, Harkness came through. As Miss Barrett slowed up he forged ahead; and he displayed cleverness in detecting the clue of the 'greenwood' tree. He displayed acute observation in spotting the clue of the cigaret. Two rather difficult clues, mind you. Then, at the easiest of all, he becomes puzzled! He didn't 'know' what was meant by the cannon's mouth! Even Mrs. Nixon—forgive me—spotted that one. Why had Harkness been reluctant to go to the gun? It could only have been because he knew what was in it."

"But it all seems so unnecessary," objected the Lieutenant. "If you had the fingerprints, the case was solved. Why the rigmarole?"

Ellery flipped his butt over the parapet. "My boy," he said, "have you ever played poker?"

"Of course I have."

Leonie cried: "You fox! Don't tell me——"

"Bluff," said Ellery sadly. "Sheer bluff. There *weren't* any fingerprints on the can."

The Adventure of
THE HOLLOW DRAGON

The Adventure of
THE HOLLOW DRAGON

Miss Merrivel always said (she said) that the Lord took care of everything, and she affirmed it now with undiminished faith, although she was careful to add in her vigorous contralto that it didn't hurt to help Him out if you could.

"And can you?" asked Mr. Ellery Queen a trifle rebelliously, for he was a notorious heretic, besides having been excavated from his bed without ceremony by Djuna at an obscene hour to lend ear to Miss Merrivel's curiously inexplicable tale. Morpheus still beckoned plaintively, and if this robust and bountiful young woman—she was as healthy-looking and overflowing as a cornucopia—had come only to preach Ellery firmly intended to send her about her business and return to bed.

"Can I?" echoed Miss Merrivel grimly. "*Can* I!" and she took off her hat. Aside from a certain rakish improbability in the hat's design, which looked like a soup-plate, Ellery could see nothing remarkable in it; and he blinked wearily at her. "Look at this!"

She lowered her head, and for a horrified instant Ellery thought she was praying. But then her long brisk fingers came up and parted the reddish hair about her left temple, and he saw a lump beneath the titian strands that was the shape and size of a pigeon's egg and the color of spoiled meat.

"How on earth," he cried, sitting up straight, "did you acquire *that* awful thing?"

Miss Merrivel winced stoically as she patted her hair down and replaced the soup-plate. "I don't know."

"You don't know!"

"It's not so bad now," said Miss Merrivel, crossing her long

475

legs and lighting a cigaret. "The headache's almost gone.
Cold applications and pressure . . . you know the technique? I sat up half the night trying to bring the swelling
down. You should have seen it at one o'clock this morning!
It looked as if someone had put a bicycle pump in my mouth
and forgotten to stop pumping."

Ellery scratched his chin. "There's no error, I trust? I'm
—er—not a physician, you know. . . ."

"What I need," snapped Miss Merrivel, "is a detective."

"But how in mercy's name——"

The broad shoulders under the tweeds shrugged. "It's not
important, Mr. Queen. I mean my being struck on the head.
I'm a brawny wench, as you can see, and I haven't been a
trained nurse for six years without gathering a choice assort-
ment of scratches and bruises on my lily-white body. I once
had a patient who took the greatest delight in kicking my
shins." She sighed; a curious gleam came into her eye and
her lips compressed a little. "It's something else, you see.
Something—funny."

A little silence swept over the Queens' living room and out
the window, and Ellery was annoyed to feel his skin crawling. There was something in the depths of Miss Merrivel's
voice that suggested a hollow moaning out of a catacomb.

"Funny?" he repeated, reaching for the solace of his
cigaret-case.

"Queer. Prickly. You feel it in that house. I'm not a
nervous woman, Mr. Queen, but I declare if I weren't
ashamed of myself I'd have quit my job weeks ago." Looking into her calm eyes, Ellery fancied it would go hard with
any ordinary ghost who had the temerity to mix with her.

"You're not taking this circuitous method of informing
me," he said lightly, "that the house in which you're cur-
rently employed is haunted?"

She sniffed. "Haunted! I don't believe in that nonsense,
Mr. Queen. You're pulling my leg——"

"My dear Miss Merrivel, what a charming thought!"

"Besides, who ever heard of a ghost raising bumps on people's heads?"

"An excellent point."

"It's something different," continued Miss Merrivel thoughtfully. "I can't quite describe it. It's just as if something were going to happen, and you waited and waited without knowing where it would strike—or, for that matter, what it would be."

"Apparently the uncertainty has been removed," remarked Ellery dryly, glancing at the soup-plate. "Or do you mean that what you anticipated *wasn't* an assault on yourself?"

Miss Merrivel's calm eyes opened wide. "But, Mr. Queen, no one has assaulted me!"

"I beg your pardon?" Ellery said in a feeble voice.

"I mean to say I *was* assaulted, but I'm sure not intentionally. I just happened to get in the way."

"Of what?" asked Ellery wearily, closing his eyes.

"I don't know. That's the horrible part of it."

Ellery pressed his fingers delicately to his temples, groaning. "Now, now, Miss Merrivel, suppose we organize? I confess to a vast bewilderment. Just why are you here? Has a crime been committed——"

"Well, you see," cried Miss Merrivel with animation, "Mr. Kagiwa is such an odd little man, so helpless and everything. I do feel sorry for the poor old creature. And when they stole that fiendish little door-stop of his with the tangled-up animal on it . . . Well, it was enough to make anyone suspicious, don't you think?" And she paused to dab her lips with a handkerchief that smelled robustly of disinfectant, smiling triumphantly as she did so, as if her extraordinary speech explained everything.

Ellery puffed four times on his cigaret before trusting himself to speak. "Did I understand you to say *door-stop*?"

"Certainly. You know, one of those thingamabobs you put on the floor to keep a door open."

"Yes, yes. Stolen, you say?"

"Well, it's gone. And it was there before they hit me on the head last night; I saw it myself, right by the study door, as innocent as you please. Nobody ever paid much attention to it, and——"

"Incredible," sighed Ellery. "A door-stop. Pretty taste in petit larceny, I must say! Er—animal? I believe you mentioned something about its being 'tangled up'? I'm afraid I don't visualize the beast from your epithet, Miss Merrivel."

"Snaky sort of monster. They're all over the house. Dragons, I suppose you'd call them. Although *I've* never heard of anyone actually seeing them, except in *delirium tremens*."

"I begin," said Ellery with a reflective nod, "to see. This old gentleman, Kagiwa—I take it he's your present patient?"

"That's right," said Miss Merrivel brightly, nodding at this acute insight. "A chronic renal case. Dr. Sutter of Polyclinic took out one of Mr. Kagiwa's kidneys a couple of months ago, and the poor man is just convalescing. He's quite old, you see, and it's a marvel he's alive to tell the tale. Surgery was risky, but Dr. Sutter had to——"

"Spare the technical details, Miss Merrivel. I believe I understand. Of course, your uni-kidneyed convalescent is Japanese?"

"Yes. My first."

"You say that," remarked Ellery with a chuckle, "like a young female after her initial venture into maternity. . . . Well, Miss Merrivel, your Japanese and your unstable door-stop and that bump on your charming noddle interest me hugely. If you'll be kind enough to wait, I'll throw some clothes on and go a-questing with you. And on the way you can tell me all about it in something like sane sequence."

In Ellery's ugly but voracious Duesenberg Miss Merrivel watched the city miles devoured, drew a powerful breath, and plunged into her narrative. She had been recommended by

Dr. Sutter to nurse Mr. Jito Kagiwa, the aged Japanese gentleman, back to health on his Westchester estate. From the moment she had set foot in the house—which from Miss Merrivel's description was a lovely old non-Nipponese place that rambled over several acres and at the rear projected on stone piles into the waters of the Sound—she had been oppressed by the most annoying and tantalizing feeling of apprehension. She could not put her finger on the source. It might have come from the manner in which the outwardly Colonial house was furnished: inside it was like an Oriental museum, she said, full of queer alien furniture and pottery and pictures and things.

"It even smells foreign," she explained with a handsome frown. "That sticky-sweet smell. . . ."

"The effluvium of sheer age?" murmured Ellery; he was occupied between driving at his customary breakneck speed and listening intently. "We seem up to our respective ears in intangibles, Miss Merrivel. Or perhaps it's merely incense?"

Miss Merrivel did not know. She was slightly psychic, she explained; that might account for her sensitivity to impressions. Then again, she continued, it might have been merely the *people*. Although the Lord Himself knew, she said piously, they were nice enough on the surface; all but Letitia Gallant. Mr. Kagiwa was an extremely wealthy importer of Oriental curios; he had lived in the United States for over forty years and was quite Americanized. So much so that he had actually married an American divorcee who had subsequently died, bequeathing her Oriental widower a host of fragrant memories, a big blond footballish son, and a vinegary and hard-bitten spinster sister. Bill, Mr. Kagiwa's stepson, who retained his dead mother's maiden name of Gallant, was very fond of his ancient little Oriental stepfather and for the past several years, according to Miss Merrivel, had practically run the old Japanese's business for him.

As for Letitia Gallant, Bill's aunt, she made life miserable for everyone, openly bewailing the cruel fate which had thrown her on "the tender mercies of the heathen," as she expressed it, and treating her gentle benefactor with a contempt and sharp-tongued scorn which, said Miss Merrivel with a snap of her strong teeth, were "little short of scandalous."

"Heathen," said Ellery thoughtfully, sliding the Duesenberg into the Pelham highway. "Perhaps that's it, Miss Merrivel. Alien atmospheres generally affect us disagreeably. . . . By the way, was this door-stop valuable?" The theft of that commonplace object was nibbling away at his brain-cells.

"Oh, no. Just a few dollars; I once heard Mr. Kagiwa say so." And Miss Merrivel brushed the door-stop aside with a healthy swoop of her arm and sailed into the more dramatic portion of her story, glowing with its reflected vitality and investing it with an aura of suspense and horror.

On the previous night she had tucked her aged charge into his bed upstairs at the rear of the house, waited until he fell asleep, and then—her duties for the day over—had gone downstairs to the library, which adjoined the old gentleman's study, for a quiet hour of reading. She recalled how hushed the house had been and how loudly the little Japanese clock had ticked away on the mantel over the fireplace. She had been busy with her patient since after dinner and had no idea where the other members of the household were; she supposed they were sleeping, for it was past eleven o'clock. . . . Miss Merrivel's calm eyes were no longer calm; they reflected something unpleasant and yet exciting.

"It was so cozy in there," she said in a low troubled voice. "And so still. I had the lamp over my left shoulder and was reading *White Woman*—all about a beautiful young nurse who went on a case and fell in love with the secretary of . . . well, I was reading it," she went on quickly, with a faint flush, "and the house began to get creepy. Simply—creepy. It shouldn't have, from the book. It's an awfully nice book, Mr. Queen. And the clock went ticking away, and I could hear the water splashing against the piles down at the rear of the house, and suddenly I began to shiver. I don't know why. I felt cold all over. I looked around, but there was nothing; the door to the study was open but it was pitch-dark in there. I—I think I got to feeling a little silly. Me hearing things!"

"Just what do you think you heard?" asked Ellery patiently.

"I really don't know. I can't describe it. A slithery sound, like a—a—" She hesitated, and then burst out: "Oh, I know you'll laugh, Mr. Queen, but it was like a *snake!*"

Ellery did not laugh. Dragons danced on the macadam road. Then he sighed and said: "Or like a dragon, if you can imagine what a dragon would sound like; eh, Miss Merrivel? By the way, have you ever heard sounds like that over the radio? An aspirin dropped into a glass of water becomes a beautiful girl diving into the sea. Powerful thing, imagination. . . . And where did this remarkable sound come from?"

"From Mr. Kagiwa's study. From the dark." Miss Merrivel's pink skin was paler now, and her eyes were luminous with half-glimpsed terrors, impervious to such sane analogies. "I was annoyed with myself for making up things in my head and I got out of the chair to investigate. And—and the door of the study suddenly swung shut!"

"Oh," said Ellery in a vastly different tone. "And despite everything you opened the door and investigated?"

"It was silly of me," breathed Miss Merrivel. "Foolhardy, really. There was danger there. But I've always been a fool and I did open the door, and the moment I opened it and gawped like an idiot into the darkness something hit me on the head. I really saw stars, Mr. Queen." She laughed, but it was a mirthless, desperate sort of laugh; and her eyes looked sidewise at him, as if for comfort.

"Nevertheless," murmured Ellery, "that was very brave,

Miss Merrivel. And then?" They had swung into the Post Road and were heading north.

"I was unconscious for about an hour. When I came to I was still lying on the threshold, half in the library, half in the study. The study was still dark. Nothing had changed. . . . I put the light on in the study and looked around. It seemed the same, you know. All except the door-stop; that was gone, and I knew then why the door had swung shut so suddenly. Funny, isn't it? . . . I spent most of the rest of the night bringing the swelling down."

"Then you haven't told anyone about last night?"

"Well, no." She screwed up her features and peered through the windshield with a puckered concentration. "I didn't know that I should. If there's anyone in that house who's—who's homicidally inclined, let him think I don't know what it's all about. Matter of fact, I don't." Ellery said nothing. "They all looked the same to me this morning," continued Miss Merrivel after a pause. "It's my morning off, you see, and I was able to come to town without exciting comment. Not that anyone would care! It's all very silly, isn't it, Mr. Queen?"

"Precisely why it interests me. We turn here, I believe?"

Two things struck Mr. Ellery Queen as a maid with frightened eyes opened the front door for them and ushered them into a lofty reception hall. One was that this house was not like other houses in his experience, and the other that there was something queerly wrong in it. The first impression arose from the boldly Oriental character of the furnishings—a lush rug on the floor brilliant and soft with the vivid technique of the East, a mother-of-pearl-inlaid teak table, an overhead lamp that was a miniature pagoda, a profusion of exotic chrysanthemums, silk hangings embroided with colored dragons. . . . The second troubled him. Perhaps it arose from the scared pallor of the maid, or the penetrating aroma. A sticky-sweet odor, even as Miss Merrivel had described it, hung heavily in the air, cloying his senses and instantly making him wish for the open air.

"Miss Merrivel!" cried a man's voice, and Ellery turned quickly to find a tall young man with thin cheeks and intelligent eyes advancing upon them from a doorway which led, from what he could see beyond it, to the library Miss Merrivel had mentioned. He turned back to the young woman and was astonished to see that her cheeks were a flaming crimson.

"Good morning, Mr. Cooper," she said with a catch of her breath. "I want you to meet Mr. Ellery Queen, a friend of mine. I happened to run into him—" They had cooked up a story between them to account for Ellery's visit, but it was destined never to be served.

"Yes, yes," said the young man excitedly, scarcely glancing at Ellery. He pounced upon Miss Merrivel, seizing her hands; and her cheeks burned even more brightly. "Merry, where on earth is old Jito?"

"Mr. Kagiwa? Why, isn't he upstairs in his——"

"No, he isn't. He's gone!"

"Gone?" gasped the nurse, sinking into a chair. "Why, I put him to bed myself last night! When I looked into his room this morning, before I left the house, he was still sleeping. . . ."

"No, he wasn't. You only thought he was. He'd rigged up a crude dummy of sorts—I suppose it was he—and covered it with the bedclothes." Cooper paced up and down, worrying his fingernails. "I simply don't understand it."

"I beg your pardon," said Ellery mildly. "I have some experience in these matters." The tall young man stopped short, flinging him a startled glance. "I understand that your Mr. Kagiwa is an old man. He may have crossed the line. It's conceivable that he's playing a senile prank on all of you."

"Lord, no! He's keen as a whippet. And the Japanese don't indulge in childish tomfoolery. There's something up;

no question about it, Mr. Queen . . . Queen!" Cooper
glared at Ellery with sudden suspicion. "By George, I've
heard that name before——"

"Mr. Queen," said Miss Merrivel in a damp voice, "is a
detective."

"Of course! I remember now. You mean you—" The
young man became very still as he looked at Miss Merrivel.
Under his steady inspection she grew red again. "Merry, you
know something!"

"The merest tittle," murmured Ellery. "She's told me
what she knows, and it's just skimpy enough to whet my
curiosity. Were you aware, Mr. Cooper, that Mr. Kagiwa's
door-stop is missing?"

"Door-stop. . . . Oh, you mean that monstrosity he keeps
in his study. It can't be. I saw it myself only last
night——"

"Oh, it is!" wailed Miss Merrivel. "And—and somebody
hit me over the head, Mr. C-Cooper, and t-took it. . . ."

The young man paled. "Why, Merry. I mean—that's
perfectly barbarous! Are you hurt?"

"Oh, Mr. Cooper . . ."

"Now, now," said Ellery sternly, "let's not get maudlin.
By the way, Mr. Cooper, just what factor do you represent
in this bizarre equation? Miss Merrivel neglected to mention
your name in her statement of the problem."

Miss Merrivel blushed again, positively glowing, and this
time Ellery looked at her very sharply indeed. It occurred to
him suddenly that Miss Merrivel had been reading a romance
in which the beautiful young nurse fell in love with the secretary of her patient.

"I'm old Jito's secretary," said Cooper abstractedly. "Look
here, old man. What has that confounded door-stop to do
with Kagiwa's disappearance?"

"That," said Ellery, "is what I propose to find out." There
was a little silence, and Miss Merrivel sent a liquidly pleading

glance at Ellery, as if to beg him to keep her secret. "Is anything else missing?"

"I don't know what business it is of yours, young man," snapped a female from the library doorway, "but, praise be! the heathen is gone, bag and baggage, and good riddance, I say. I always said that slinky yellow devil would come to no good."

"Miss Letitia Gallant, I believe?" sighed Ellery, and from the stiffening backbones and freezing faces of Miss Merrivel and Mr. Cooper it was evident that truth had prevailed.

"Stow it, Aunt Letty, for heaven's sake," said a man worriedly from behind her, and she swept her long skirts aside with a sniff that had something Airedale-ish about it. Bill Gallant was a giant with a red face and bloodshot eyes in sacs. He looked as if he had not slept and his clothes were rumpled and droopy. His aunt in the flesh was all that Miss Merrivel had characterized her, and more. Thin to the point of emaciation, she seemed composed of whalebone, tough rubber, and acid—a tall she-devil of fifty, with slightly mad eyes, dressed in the height of pre-War fashion. Ellery fully expected to find that her tongue was forked; but she shut her lips tightly and, with a cunning perversity, persisted in keeping quiet thenceforward and glaring at him with a venomous intensity that made him uncomfortable inside.

"Baggage?" he said, after he had introduced himself and they had repaired to the library.

"Well, his suitcase is gone," said Gallant hoarsely, "and his clothes are missing—not all, but several suits and plenty of haberdashery. I've questioned all the servants and no one saw him leave the house. We've searched every nook and cranny in the house, and every foot of the grounds. He's just vanished into thin air. . . . Lord, what a mess! He must have gone crazy."

"Ducked out during the night?" Cooper passed his hand over his hair. "But he isn't crazy, Mr. Gallant; you know that. If he's gone, there was a thumping good reason for it."

"Have you looked for a note?" asked Ellery absently, glancing about. The heavy odor had followed them into the library and it bathed the Oriental furnishings with a peculiar fittingness. The door to what he assumed was the missing Japanese's study was closed, and he crossed the room and opened it. There was another door in the study; apparently it led to an extension of the main hall. Miss Merrivel's assailant of the night before, then, had probably entered the study through that door. But why had he stolen the door-stop?

"Of course," said Gallant; they had followed Ellery into the study and were watching him with puzzled absorption. "But there isn't any. He's left without a word."

Ellery nodded; he was kneeling on the thick Oriental rug a few feet behind the library door, scrutinizing a rectangular depression in the nap. Something heavy, about six inches wide and a foot long, had rested on that very spot for a long time; the nap was crushed to a uniform flatness as if from great and continuous pressure. The missing door-stop, obviously; and he rose and lit a cigaret and perched himself on the arm of a huge mahogany chair, carved tortuously in a lotus and dragon motif and inlaid with mother-of-pearl.

"Don't you think," suggested Miss Merrivel timidly, "that we ought to telephone the police?"

"No hurry," said Ellery with a cheerful wave of his hand. "Let's sit down and talk things over. There's nothing criminal in a man's quitting his own castle without explanation—even, Miss Gallant, a heathen. I'm not even sure anything's wrong. The little yellow people are a subtle race with thought-processes worlds removed from ours. This business of the pilfered door-stop, however, is provocative. Will someone please describe it to me?"

Miss Merrivel looked helpful; the others glanced at one another, however, with a sort of inert helplessness.

Then Bill Gallant hunched his thick shoulders and growled: "Now, look here, Queen, you're evading the issue." He looked worried and haggard, as if a secret maggot were nibbling at his conscience. "This is certainly a matter for old Jito's attorney, if not for the police. I must call——"

"You must follow the dictates of your own conscience, of course," said Ellery gently, "but if you will take my advice someone will describe the door-stop for my edification."

"I can tell you exactly," said young Cooper, brushing his thin hair back again with his white, musician's fingers, "because I've handled the thing a number of times and, in fact, signed the express-receipt when it was delivered. It's six inches wide, six inches high, and an even foot long. Perfectly regular in shape, you see, except for the decorative bas-reliefs—the dragons. Typical conventionalized Japanese craftsmanship, by the way. Nothing really remarkable."

"Heathen idolatry," said Miss Letitia distinctly; her ophidian eyes glared their chronic hate with a fanatical fire. "Devil!"

Ellery glanced at her. Then he said: "Miss Merrivel has told me that the door-stop isn't valuable." Cooper and Gallant nodded. "What's its composition?"

"Natural soapstone," said Gallant; his expression was still worried. "You know, that smooth and slippery mineral that's used so much in the Orient—steatite, technically. It's a talc. Jito imports hundred of gadgets made out of it."

"Oh, this door-stop was something from his curio establishment?"

"No. It was sent to the old man four or five months ago as a gift by some friend traveling in Japan."

"A white man?" asked Ellery suddenly.

They all looked blank. Then Cooper said with an uneasy smile: "I don't believe Mr. Kagiwa ever mentioned his name, or said anything about him, Mr. Queen."

"I see," said Ellery, and he smoked for a moment in silence. "Sent, eh? By express?" Cooper nodded. "You're a man of method, Mr. Cooper?"

The secretary looked surprised. "I beg your pardon?"

"Obviously, obviously. Secretaries have a deplorable habit

of saving things. May I see that express-receipt, please? Evidence is always better than testimony, as any lawyer will tell you. The receipt may provide us with a clue—sender's name may indicate . . ."

"Oh," said Cooper. "So that's your notion? I'm sorry, Mr. Queen. There was no sender's name on the receipt. I remember very clearly."

Ellery looked pained. He blew out a curtain of smoke, communing with his thoughts in its folds. When he spoke again it was with abruptness, as if he had decided to take a plunge. "How many dragons are there on this door-stop, Mr. Cooper?"

"Idolatry," repeated Miss Letitia venomously.

Miss Merrivel paled a little. "You think——"

"Five," said Cooper. "The bottom face, of course, is blank. Five dragons, Mr. Queen."

"Pity it isn't seven," said Ellery without smiling. "The mystic number." And he rose and took a turn about the room, smoking and frowning in the sweet heavy air at the coils of a golden monster embroidered on a silk wall-hanging. Miss Merrivel shivered suddenly and moved closer to the tall thin-faced young man. "Tell me," continued Ellery with a snap of his teeth, turning on his heel and squinting at them through the smoke-haze. "Is your little Jito Kagiwa a Christian?"

Only Miss Letitia was not startled; that woman would have outstared Beelzebub himself. "Lord preserve us!" she cried in a shrill voice. "That devil?"

"Now why," asked Ellery patiently, "do you persist in calling your brother-in-law a devil, Miss Gallant?"

She set her metallic lips and glared. Miss Merrivel said in a warm tone: "He is not. He's a nice kind old gentleman. He may not be a Christian, Mr. Queen, but he isn't a heathen, either. He doesn't believe in anything like that. He's often said so."

"Then he certainly isn't a heathen, strictly speaking," murmured Ellery. "A heathen, you know, is a person belonging to a nation or race neither Christian, Jewish, nor Mohammedan who has not abandoned the original creed of his people."

Miss Letitia looked baffled. But then she shrilled triumphantly: "He is, too! I've often heard him talk of some outlandish belief called—called . . ."

"Shinto," muttered Cooper. "It's not true, Merry, that Mr. Kagiwa doesn't believe in anything. He believes in the essential goodness of mankind, in each man's conscience being his best guide. That's the moral essence of Shinto, isn't it, Mr. Queen?"

"Is it?" murmured Ellery in an absent way. "I suppose so. Most interesting. He wasn't a cultist? Shinto is rather primitive, you know."

"Idolater," said Miss Letitia nastily, like a phonograph needle caught in one groove.

They looked uneasily about them. On the study desk there was a fat-bellied little idol of shiny black obsidian. In a corner stood a squat and powerful suit of Samurai armor. The silk of the dragon rippled a little on the wall under the push of the sea breeze coming in through the open window.

"He didn't belong to some ancient secret Japanese society?" persisted Ellery. "Has he had much correspondence from the East? Has he received slant-eyed visitors? Did he seem afraid of anything?"

His voice died away, and the dragon stirred again wickedly, and the Samurai looked on with his sightless, enigmatic, invisible face. The sickly-sweet odor seemed to grow stronger, filling their heads with dizzying, horrid fancies. They looked at Ellery mutely and helplessly, caught in the grip of vague primeval fears.

"And was this door-stop *solid* soapstone?" murmured Ellery, gazing out the window at the heaving Sound. Everything heaved and swayed; the house itself seemed afloat in an endless ocean, bobbing to the breathing of the sea. He waited for their reply, but none came. Big Bill Gallant shuffled his feet; he looked even more worried than before. "It couldn't have been, you know," continued Ellery thoughtfully, answering his own question. He wondered what they were thinking.

"What makes you say that, Mr. Queen?" asked Miss Merrivel in a subdued voice.

"Common-sense. The piece being valueless from a practical standpoint, why was it stolen last night? For sentimental reasons? The only one for whom it might have possessed such an attachment is Mr. Kagiwa, and I scarcely think he would have struck you over the head, Miss Merrivel, to retrieve his own property if he merely had a fondness for it." Aunt and nephew looked startled. "Oh, you didn't know that, of course. Yes, we had a case of simple but painful assault here last night. Gave Miss Merrivel quite a headache. The bump is, take my word for it, a thing of singular beauty. . . . Did the door-stop possess an esoteric meaning? Was it a symbol of something, a sign, a portent, a *warning*?" Again the breeze stirred the dragon, and they shuddered; the hatred had vanished from Miss Letitia's mad eyes, to be replaced by the naked fear of a small and malicious soul trapped in the filthy den of its own malice at last.

"It—" began Cooper, shaking his head. Then he licked his dry lips and said: "This is the Twentieth Century, Mr. Queen."

"So it is," said Ellery, nodding, "wherefore we shall confine ourselves to sane and demonstrable matters. The practical alternative is that, since the door-stop *was* taken, it was valuable to the taker. But not, obviously, for itself alone. Deduction: It *contained* something valuable. That's why I said it couldn't have been a solid chunk of soapstone."

"That's the most—" said Gallant; his shoulders hunched, and he stopped and stared at Ellery in a fascinated way.

"I beg your pardon?" said Ellery softly.

"Nothing. I was just thinking——"

"That I had shot straight to the mark, Mr. Gallant?"

The big young man dropped his gaze and flushed; and he began to pace up and down with his hands loosely behind his back, the worried expression more evident than ever. Miss Merrivel bit her lip and sank into the nearest chair. Cooper looked restive, and Letitia Gallant's stiff clothing made rustling little sounds, like furtive animals in underbrush at night. Then Gallant stopped pacing and said in a rush: "I suppose I may as well come out with it. Yes, you guessed it, Queen, you guessed it." Ellery looked pained. "The door-stop isn't solid. There's a hollow space inside."

"Ah! And what did it contain, Mr. Gallant?"

"Fifty thousand dollars in hundred-dollar bills."

It is proverbial that money works miracles. In Jito Kagiwa's study it lived up to its reputation.

The dragon died. The Samurai became an empty shell of crumbling leather and metal. The house ceased rocking and stood firmly on its foundation. The very air freshened and crept into its normal niche and was noticed no more. Money talked in familiar accents and before the logic of its speech the spectre of dread, creeping things vanished in a snuffed instant. They sighed with relief in unison and their eyes cleared again with that peculiar blankness which passes for sanity in the social world. There had been mere money in the door-stop! Miss Merrivel giggled a little.

"Fifty thousand dollars in hundred-dollar bills," nodded Mr. Ellery Queen, looking both envious and disappointed in the same instant. "That's an indecent number of hundred-dollar bills, Mr. Gallant. Elucidate."

Bill Gallant elucidated—rapidly, his expression vastly comforted, as if a great weight had been lifted from his mind. Old Kagiwa's business, there was no concealing it longer, was on the verge of bankruptcy. Tariffs on Japanese goods had risen steeply, the universal depression had made heavy inroads on the sales of the products of frivolous industries. Before the China "incident," a year or so before, it would still have been possible to retrench and lie low, weathering the economic storm. But against his stepson's advice old Kagiwa, with the serene, silent, and unconquerable will of his race, had refused to alter his lifelong business policies. Only when ruin stared him in the eyes did his resolution waver, and then it was too late to do more than salvage the battered wreck.

"He did it on the q.t.," said Gallant, shrugging, "and the first I knew about it was the other day when he called me into this room, locked the door, picked up the door-stop— he'd left it on the floor all the time!—unscrewed one of the dragons . . . Came out like a plug. He told me he'd found the secret cavity in the door-stop by accident right after he received it. Nothing in it, he said, and went into some long-winded explanation about the probable origin of the piece. It hadn't been a door-stop originally, of course—don't suppose the Japanese have such things. Well . . . There was the money, in a tight wad, which he'd stowed away in the hole. I told him he was a fool to leave it lying around that way, but he said no one knew except him and me. Naturally—" He flushed.

"I see now," said Ellery mildly, "why you were reluctant to tell me about it. It looks bad for you, obviously."

The big young man spread his hands in a helpless gesture. "I didn't steal the damned thing, but who'd believe me?" He sat down, fumbling for a cigaret.

"There's one thing in your favor," murmured Ellery. "Or at least I suppose there is. Are you his heir?"

Gallant looked up wildly. "Yes!"

"Yes, he is," said Cooper in a slow, almost reluctant, voice. "I witnessed the old man's will myself."

"Tut, tut. Much ado about nothing. You naturally wouldn't steal what belongs to you anyway. Buck up, Mr. Gallant; you're safe enough." Ellery sighed and began to button up his coat. "Well, ladies and gentlemen, my interest in the case, I fear, is dissipated. I had foreseen something *outré. . . . "* He smiled and picked up his hat. "This is a matter for the police, after all. Of course, I'll help if I can, but it's been my experience that local officers prefer to work alone. And really, there's nothing more that I can do."

"But what do you think happened?" asked Miss Merrivel in hushed tones. "Do you think poor Mr. Kagiwa——"

"I'm not a psychologist, Miss Merrivel. Even a psychologist, as a matter of fact, might be baffled by the inner workings of an Oriental's mind. Your policeman doesn't worry about such subtle matters, and I don't doubt the local men will clear this business up in short order. Good day."

Miss Letitia sniffed and swept by Ellery with a disdainful swish of her skirts. Miss Merrivel wearily followed, tugging at her hat. Cooper went to the telephone and Gallant frowned out of the window at the Sound.

"Headquarters?" said Cooper, clearing his throat. "I want to speak to the Chief."

A little of the old heavy-scented, alien silence crept back as they waited.

"One moment," said Ellery from the doorway. "One moment, please." The men turned, surprised. Ellery was smiling apologetically. "I've just discovered something. The human mind is a fearful thing. I've been criminally negligent, gentlemen. There's still another possibility."

"Hold the wire, hold the wire," said Cooper. "Possibility?"

Ellery waved an airy hand. "I may be wrong," he admitted handsomely. "Can either of you gentlemen direct me to an almanac?"

"Almanac?" repeated Gallant, bewildered. "Why, certainly. I don't—There's one on the library table, Queen. Here, I'll get it for you." He disappeared into the adjoining room and returned a moment later with a fat paper-backed volume.

Ellery seized it and riffled pages, humming. Cooper and Gallant exchanged glances; and then Cooper shrugged and hung up.

"Ah," said Ellery, dropping his aria like a hot coal. "Ah. Hmm. Well, well. Mind over matter. The pen is mightier . . . I may be wrong," he said quietly, closing the book and taking off his coat, "but the odds are now superbly against it. Useful things, almanacs. . . . Mr. Cooper," he said in a new voice, "let me see that express-receipt."

The metallic quality of the tone brought them both up, stiffening. The secretary got to his feet, his face suffused with blood. "Look here," he growled, "are you insinuating that I've lied to you?"

"Tut, tut," said Ellery. "The receipt, Mr. Cooper, quickly."

Bill Gallant said uneasily: "Of course, Cooper. Do as Mr. Queen says. But I don't see what possible value there can be . . ."

"Value is in the mind, Mr. Gallant. The hand may be quicker than the eye, but the brain is quicker than both of them."

Cooper glared, but he pulled open a drawer of the carved desk and began to rummage about. Finally he came up with a sheaf of motley papers and went through them with reluctance until he found a small yellow slip.

"Here," he said, scowling. "Damned impertinence, *I* think."

"It's not a question," said Ellery gently, "of what *you* think, Mr. Cooper." He picked up the slip and scanned the yellow paper with the painful scrupulosity of an archeologist. It was an ordinary express-receipt, describing the contents of the package delivered, the date, the sending point, charges, and similar information. The name of the sender was missing. The package had been shipped by a Nippon Yusen Kaisha steamer from Yokohama, Japan, had been picked up in San Francisco by the express company, and forwarded to its consignee, Jito Kagiwa, at his Westchester address. Shipping and expressage charges had been prepaid in Yokohama, it appeared, on the basis of the 44-pound weight of the door-stop, which was sketchily described as being of soap-stone, 6 by 6 by 12 inches in dimensions, and decorated with dragons in bas-relief.

"Well," said Cooper with a sneer. "I suppose that mess of statistics means something to you."

"This mess of statistics," said Ellery gravely, pocketing the receipt, "means everything to me. Pity if it had been lost. It's like the Rosetta Stone—it's the key to an otherwise mystifying set of facts." He looked pleased with himself, and at the same time his gray eyes were watchful. "The old adage was wrong. It isn't safety that you find in numbers, but enlightenment."

Gallant threw up his hands. "You're talking gibberish, Queen."

"I'm talking sense." Ellery stopped smiling. "You gentlemen are excused. By all means the Chief of Police must be called—but it's I who'll call him and, by your leave . . . alone."

"I was not to be cheated of my tidbit of *bizarrerie*," announced Mr. Ellery Queen that evening, "after all." He was serene and self-contained. He was perched on the edge of the study desk, and his hand played with the belly of the obsidian image.

Cooper, Miss Merrivel, the two Gallants stared at him. They were all in the last stages of nervousness. The house was rocking again, and the dragon quivered in all his coils in the wind coming through the open window; and the Samurai had magically taken watchful life unto himself once more. The sky through the window was dark and dappled with blacker clouds; the moon had not yet slipped from under the hem of the sea.

Ellery had departed from the Kagiwa mansion after his telephonic conversation with the Chief of Police, to be seen no more by interested mortal eyes until evening. When he had returned, there were men with him. These men, quiet and solid creatures, had not come into the house. No one had approached the Gallants, the secretary, the nurse, the servants. Instead the deputation had disappeared, swallowed up by the darkness. Now strange clankings and swishings were audible from the sea outside the study window, but no one dared rise and look.

And Ellery said: " 'What a world were this, how unendurable its weight, if they whom Death had sundered did not meet again.' A moving thought. And very apt on this occasion. We shall meet Death tonight, my friends; and even more strangely, the weight shall be lifted. As Southey predicted."

They gaped, utterly bewildered. From the night outside the clankings and swishings continued, and occasionally there was the far shout of a man.

Ellery lit a cigaret. "I find," he said, inhaling deeply, "that once more I have been in error. I demonstrated to you this morning that the most likely reason for the theft of the door-stop was that it was stolen for its contents. I was wrong. It was not stolen for its contents. It was never intended that the belly of the dragon should be ravished."

"But the fifty thousand dollars—" began Miss Merrivel weakly.

"Mr. Queen," cried Bill Gallant, "what's going on here? What are those policemen doing outside? What are those noises? You owe us——"

"Logic," murmured Ellery, "has a way of being slippery. Quite like soapstone, Mr. Gallant. It eluded my fingers today. I pointed out that the door-stop could *not* have been stolen for itself. I was wrong again. It could have been stolen for itself in one remote contingency. There was one value possible to the door-stop beyond its worth in dollars and cents, or in a sentiment attached to it, or in its significance as a symbol. And that was—*its utility*."

"Utility?" gasped Cooper. "You mean somebody stole it to use as a door-stop?"

"That's absurd, of course. But there is still another possible utility, Mr. Cooper. What are the characteristics of this piece of carved stone which might be made use of? Well, what are its chief points physically? Its substance and weight. It is stone, and it weighs 44 pounds."

Gallant made a queer brushing-aside gesture with one hand and rose as if under compulsion and went to the window. The others wavered, and then they too rose and went to the window, pressing eagerly toward the last, their pent-up fears and curiosity urging them on. Ellery watched them quietly.

The moon was rising now. The scene below was blue-black and sharp, a miniature etching in motion. A large rowboat was anchored a few yards from the rear of the Kagiwa house. There were men in it, and apparatus. Someone was leaning overside, gazing intently into the water. The surface suddenly quickened into concentric life, becoming violently agitated. A man's dripping head appeared, open mouth sucking in air. And then, half-nude, he climbed into the boat and said something, and the apparatus creaked, and a rope emerged from the blue-black water and began to wind about a small winch.

"But why," came Ellery's voice from behind them, "should an object be stolen because it is stone and weighs 44 pounds? Regarded in this light, the view became brilliantly clear. A man was mysteriously and inexplicably missing— a sick, defenseless, wealthy old man. A heavy stone was missing. And there was the sea at his back door. Put one, two, and three together and you have——"

Someone shouted hoarsely from the boat. In the full moon a dripping mass emerged from the water at the end of the rope. As it was pulled into the boat the silver light revealed it as a mass made up of three parts. One was a suitcase. Another was a small rectangular chunk of stone with carving on it. And the third was the stiff naked body of a little old man with yellow skin and slanted eyes.

"And you have," continued Ellery sharply, slipping from

the edge of the desk and poking the muzzle of an automatic into the small of Bill Gallant's rigid back, "the murderer of Jito Kagiwa!"

The shouts of the triumphant fishers made meaningless sound in the old Japanese's study, and Bill Gallant without turning or moving a muscle said in a dead voice: "You damned devil. How did you know?"

Miss Letitia's bitter mouth opened and closed without achieving the dignity of speech.

"I knew," said Ellery, holding the automatic quite still, "because I knew that the door-stop had no hollow at all, that it was a piece of solid stone."

"You couldn't have known that. You never saw it. You were guessing. Besides, you said——"

"That's the second time you have accused me of guessing," said Ellery in an aggrieved tone. "I assure you, my dear Mr. Gallant, that I did nothing of the sort. But knowing that the door-stop was solid, I knew that you had lied when you maintained that you had seen with your own eyes Kagiwa's withdrawal of the dragon 'plug,' that you had seen the 'cavity' and the 'money' in it. And so I asked myself why such an obviously distressed and charming gentleman had lied. And I saw that it could only have been because you had something to conceal and were sure the door-stop would never be found to give you the lie."

The waters were stilling under the moon.

"But to be sure that the door-stop would never be found, you had to know where the door-stop was. To know where it was, you had to be the person who had disposed of it after striking Miss Merrivel over the head and stealing it from this room, unconsciously making that slithery, dragonish sound in the process which was merely the scuffing of your shoes in the thick pile of this rug. But the person who disposed of the door-stop was the person who disposed of the carcass of gentle little Jito Kagiwa; which is to say, the murderer. No, no, my dear Gallant; be fair. It wasn't precisely guesswork."

Miss Merrivel said in a ghastly voice: "Mr. Gallant. I can't—But why did you do this awful—awful . . ."

"I think I can tell you that," sighed Ellery. "It was apparent to me, when I saw that his story of the cache in the door-stop was a lie, that he had probably planned to tell that ingenious story from the beginning. Why? One reason might have been to cover up the real motive for the theft of the carved piece; divert the trail from its use as a mere weight for a dead body to a fabricated use as the receptacle of a fortune, and its theft for that reason. But why the lie about the fifty thousand dollars? Why so detailed, so specific, so careful? Was it because you had embezzled fifty thousand dollars from your stepfather's business, Mr. Gallant, knew that the discovery of this shortage was imminent, and therefore created a figmentary thief who last night stole the money which you had stolen and dissipated possibly months ago?"

Bill Gallant was silent.

"And so you built up a series of events," murmured Ellery. "You arranged the old gentleman's bedclothes during the night to form a human figure, as if he had done it himself. You threw some clothes of his in one of his suitcases, as if he had planned to flee. In fact, you arranged the whole thing to give the impression that Mr. Kagiwa, whose business I have no doubt is shaky—largely due to your peculations—had cut loose from his Occidental surroundings once and for all time and vanished into the mysterious Orient from which he had come . . . with the remnants of his fortune. In this way there would be no body to look for, no murder, indeed, to suspect; and you yourself would escape the consequences of your original crime of grand larceny. For you knew that, like all honorable and gentle men, your stepfather, who had given you everything, would forgive everything except your crime against honor. Had Mr. Kagiwa discovered your larceny, all would have been lost."

But Bill Gallant said nothing to these inexorable words; he was still staring out the window where nothing more was to be seen except the quieting water. The rowboat, the stone, the suitcase, the dead body, the men had vanished.

And Ellery nodded at that paralyzed back with something like sad satisfaction.

"And the inheritance," muttered Cooper. "Of course, he was the heir. Clever, clever."

"Stupid," said Ellery gently, "stupid. All crime is stupid."

Gallant said in the same dead voice: "I still think you were guessing about the door-stop being solid," as if he were engaged in a polite difference of opinion. Ellery was not fooled. His grip tightened on the automatic. The window was open and the water might look inviting to a desperate man, for whom even death would be an escape.

"No, no," said Ellery, almost protesting. "Please give the devil his due. It was all obscure to me, you know, until on my way out I thought of the fact that the door-stop was made of soapstone. I knew soapstone to be fairly heavy. I knew the piece was almost perfectly regular in shape, and therefore admissible to elementary calculation. It was conceivable that I could test the accuracy of your statement that the door-stop was hollow. And so I came back and asked to consult an almanac. Once I had run across in such a reference book a list of the weights of common minerals. I looked up soapstone. And there it was."

"There what was?" asked Gallant, almost with curiosity.

"The almanac said that 1 cubic foot of soapstone weighs between 162 and 175 pounds. The door-stop was of soapstone; what were its dimensions? 6 by 6 by 12 inches, or 432 cubic inches. In other words, ¼ cubic foot. Or, by computing from the almanac's figures and allowing for the small additional weight of the shallow bas-relief dragons, the door-stop should weigh one-quarter of the cubic-foot pound-age, which is 44 pounds."

"But that's what the receipt said," muttered Cooper.

"Quite so. But what do those 44 pounds represent? They represent 44 pounds of *solid* soapstone! Mr. Gallant had said the door-stop was *not* solid, had a hollow inside large enough to hold fifty thousand dollars in hundred-dollar bills. That's five hundred bills. Any space large enough to contain five hundred bills, no matter how tightly rolled or compressed, would make the total weight of the door-stop considerably *less* than 44 pounds. And so I knew that the door-stop was solid and that Mr. Gallant had lied."

Heavy feet tramped outside. Suddenly the room was full of men. The corpse of Jito Kagiwa was deposited on a divan, naked and yellow as old marble, where it dripped quietly, almost apologetically. Bill Gallant was turned about, still frozen, and they saw that his eyes, too, were dead as they regarded the corpse . . . as if for the first time the enormity of what he had done had struck home.

Ellery took the heavy door-stop, glistening from the sea, from the hand of a policeman and turned it over in his fingers. And he looked up at the wall and smiled in friendly fashion at the dragon, which was now obviously a pretty thing of silk and golden threads and nothing more.

The Adventure of
THE HOUSE OF DARKNESS

The Adventure of
THE HOUSE OF DARKNESS

"And this," proclaimed Monsieur Dieudonné Duval with a deprecatory twirl of his mustache, "is of an ingenuity incomparable, my friend. It is not I that should say so, perhaps. But examine it. Is it not the—how do you say—the pip?"

Mr. Ellery Queen wiped his neck and sat down on a bench facing the little street of amusements. "It is indeed," he sighed, "the pip, my dear Duval. I quite share your creative enthusiasm. . . . Djuna, for the love of mercy! Sit still." The afternoon sun was tropical and his whites had long since begun to cling.

"Let's go on it," suggested Djuna hopefully.

"Let's not and say we did," groaned Mr. Queen, stretching his weary legs. He had promised Djuna this lark all summer, but he had failed to reckon with the Law of Diminishing Returns. He had already—under the solicitous wing of Monsieur Duval, that tireless demon of the scenic-designing art; one of the variegated hundreds of his amazing acquaintanceship—partaken of the hectic allurements of Joyland Amusement Park for two limb-rending hours, and they had taken severe toll of his energy. Djuna, of course, what with excitement, sheer pleasure, and indefatigable youth, was a law unto himself; he was still as fresh as the breeze blowing in from the sea.

"You will find it of the most amusing," said Monsieur Duval eagerly, showing his white teeth. "It is my *chef-d'oeuvre* in Joyland." Joyland was something new to the county, a model amusement park meticulously landscaped and offering a variety of ingenious entertainments and mechanical divertissements—planned chiefly by Duval—not to be duplicated anywhere along the Atlantic. "A house of darkness. . . . That, my friend, was an inspiration!"

"I think it's swell," said Djuna craftily, glancing at Ellery.

"A mild word, Djun'," said Mr. Queen, wiping his neck again. *The House of Darkness* which lay across the thoroughfare did not look too diverting to a gentleman of even catholic tastes. It was a composite of all the haunted houses of fact and fiction. A diabolic imagination had planned its crazy walls and tumbledown roofs. It reminded Ellery—although he was tactful enough not to mention it to Monsieur Duval—of a set out of a German motion picture he had once seen, *The Cabinet of Dr. Caligari.* It wound and leaned and stuck out fantastically and had broken false windows and doors and decrepit balconies. Nothing was normal or decent. Constructed in a huge rectangle, its three wings overlooked a court which had been fashioned into a nightmarish little street with broken cobbles and tired lampposts; and its fourth side was occupied by the ticket-booth and a railing. The street in the open court was atmosphere only; the real dirty work, thought Ellery disconsolately, went on behind those grim surrealistic walls.

"*Alors,*" said Monsieur Duval, rising, "if it is permitted that I excuse myself? For a moment only. I shall return. Then we shall visit . . . *Pardon!*" He bowed his trim little figure away and went quickly toward the booth, near which a young man in park uniform was haranguing a small group.

Mr. Queen sighed and closed his eyes. The park was never crowded; but on a hot summer's afternoon it was almost deserted, visitors preferring the adjoining bath-houses and beach. The camouflaged loudspeakers concealed all over the park played dance-music to almost empty aisles and walks.

"That's funny," remarked Djuna, crunching powerfully upon a pink, conic section of popcorn.

"Eh?" Ellery opened a bleary eye.

"I wonder where *he's* goin'. 'N awful hurry."

"Who?" Ellery opened the other eye and followed the direction of Djuna's absent nod. A man with a massive body and thick gray hair was striding purposefully along up the walk. He wore a slouch hat pulled down over his eyes and dark clothes, and his heavy face was raw with perspiration. There was something savagely decisive in his bearing.

"Ouch," murmured Ellery with a wince. "I sometimes wonder where people get the energy."

"Funny, all right," mumbled Djuna, munching.

"Most certainly is," said Ellery sleepily, closing his eyes again. "You've put your finger on a nice point, my lad. Never occurred to me before, but it's true that there's something unnatural in a man's hurrying in an amusement park of a hot afternoon. Chap might be the White Rabbit, eh, Djuna? Running about so. But the *genus* Joylandei is, like all such orders, a family of inveterate strollers. Well, well! A distressing problem." He yawned.

"He must be crazy," said Djuna.

"No, no, my son, that's the conclusion of a sloppy thinker. The proper deduction begins with the observation that Mr. Rabbit hasn't come to Joyland to dabble in the delights of Joyland *per se*, if you follow me. Joyland is, then, merely a means to an end. In a sense Mr. Rabbit—note the cut of his wrinkled clothes, Djuna; he's a distinguished bunny—is oblivious to Joyland. It doesn't exist for him. He barges past *Dante's Inferno* and the perilous *Dragon-Fly* and the popcorn and frozen custard as if he is blind or they're invisible. . . . The diagnosis? A date, I should say, with a lady. And the gentleman is late. *Quod erat demonstrandum.* . . . Now for heaven's sake, Djuna, eat your petrified shoddy and leave me in peace."

"It's all gone," said Djuna wistfully, looking at the empty bag.

"I am here!" cried a gay Gallic voice, and Ellery suppressed another groan at the vision of Monsieur Duval bouncing toward them. "Shall we go, my friends? I promise you entertainment of the most divine . . . *Ouf!*" Monsieur Duval expelled his breath violently and staggered backward. Ellery sat up in alarm. But it was only the massive man with the slouch hat, who had collided with the dapper little Frenchman, almost upsetting him, muttered something meant to be conciliatory, and hurried on. "*Cochon,*" said Monsieur Duval softly, his black eyes glittering. Then he shrugged his slim shoulders and looked after the man.

"Apparently," said Ellery dryly, "our White Rabbit can't resist the lure of your *chef-d'oeuvre,* Duval. I believe he's stopped to listen to the blandishments of your barker!"

"White Rabbit?" echoed the Frenchman, puzzled. "But yes, he is a customer. *Voilà!* One does not fight with such, *hein?* Come, my friends!"

The massive man had halted abruptly in his tracks and pushed into the thick of the group listening to the attendant. Ellery sighed, and rose, and they strolled across the walk.

The young man was saying confidentially: "Ladies and gentlemen, you haven't visited Joyland if you haven't visited *The House of Darkness.* There's never been a thrill like it! It's new, different. Nothing like it in any amusement park in the *world!* It's grim. It's shivery. It's terrifying. . . ."

A tall young woman in front of them laughed and said to the old gentleman leaning on her arm: "Oh, daddy, let's try it! It's sure to be loads of fun." Ellery saw the white head under its Leghorn nod with something like amusement, and the young woman edged forward through the crowd eagerly. The old man did not release her arm. There was a curious stiffness in his carriage, a slow shuffle in his walk, that puzzled Ellery. The young woman purchased two tickets at the booth and led the old man along a fenced lane inside.

"*The House of Darkness,*" the young orator was declaiming in a dramatic whisper, "is . . . just . . . that. There's not a light you can see by in the whole place! You have to

feel your way, and if you aren't *feeling* well . . . ha, ha!
Pitch-dark. Ab-so-lutely *black* . . . I see the gentleman in
the brown tweeds is a little frightened. Don't be afraid.
We've taken care of even the faintest-hearted——"

"Ain't no sech thing," boomed an indignant bass voice
from somewhere in the van of the crowd. There was a mild
titter. The faint-heart addressed by the attendant was a
powerful young Negro, attired immaculately in symphonic
brown, his straw skimmer dazzling against the sooty carbon
of his skin. A pretty colored girl giggled on his arm.
"C'mon, honey, we'll show 'em! Heah—two o' them theah
tickets, Mistuh!" The pair beamed as they hurried after the
tall young woman and her father.

"You could wander around in the dark inside," cried the
young man enthusiastically, "for *hours* looking for the way
out. But if you can't stand the suspense there's a little green
arrow, every so often along the route, that points to an invisible door, and you just go through that door and you'll
find yourself in a dark passage that runs *all* around the house
in the back and leads to the—uh—ghostly cellar, the assembly-room, downstairs there. Only *don't* go out any of those
green-arrow doors unless you want to *stay* out, because they
open only one way—into the hall, ha, ha! You can't get
back into *The House of Darkness* proper again, you see.
But nobody uses that *easy* way out. Everybody follows the
little *red* arrows. . . ."

A man with a full, rather untidy black beard, shabby
broad-brimmed hat, a soft limp tie, and carrying a flat case
which looked like an artist's box, purchased a ticket and
hastened down the lane. His cheek bones were flushed with
self-consciousness as he ran the gauntlet of curious eyes.

"Now what," demanded Ellery, "is the idea of *that*,
Duval?"

"The arrows?" Monsieur Duval smiled apologetically. "A
concession to the old, the infirm, and the apprehensive. It is
really of the most blood-curdling, my masterpiece, Mr.

Queen. So—" He shrugged. "I have planned a passage to permit of exit at any time. Without it one could, as the admirable young man so truly says, wander about for hours. The little green and red arrows are non-luminous; they do not disturb the blackness."

The young man asserted: "But if you follow the red arrows you are bound to come out. Some of them go the right way, others don't. But eventually . . . After exciting adventures on the way . . . Now, ladies and gentlemen, for the price of——"

"Come *on*," panted Djuna, overwhelmed by this salesmanship. "Boy, I bet that's *fun*."

"I bet," said Ellery gloomily as the crowd began to shuffle and mill about. Monsieur Duval smiled with delight and with a gallant bow presented two tickets.

"I shall await you, my friends, here," he announced. "I am most curious to hear of your reactions to my little *maison des ténèbres*. Go," he chuckled, "with God."

As Ellery grunted, Djuna led the way in prancing haste down the fenced lane to a door set at an insane angle. An attendant took the tickets and pointed a solemn thumb over his shoulder. The light of day struggled down a flight of tumbledown steps. "Into the crypt, eh?" muttered Ellery. "Ah, the young man's 'ghostly cellar.' Dieudonné, I could cheerfully strangle you!"

They found themselves in a long narrow cellar-like chamber dimly illuminated by bulbs festooned with spurious spider-webs. The chamber had a dank appearance and crumbly walls, and it was presided over by a courteous skeleton who took Ellery's Panama, gave him a brass disc, and deposited the hat in one of the partitions of a long wooden rack. Most of the racks were empty, although Ellery noticed the artist's box in one of the partitions and the white-haired old man's Leghorn in another. The rite was somehow ominous, and Djuna shivered with ecstatic anticipation. An iron grating divided the cellar in two, and Ellery reasoned that visitors to the place emerged after their adventures into the division beyond the grating, redeemed their checked belongings through the window in the grate, and climbed to blessed daylight through another stairway in the righthand wing.

"Come *on*," said Djuna again, impatiently. "Gosh, you're slow. Here's the way in." And he ran toward a crazy door on the left which announced *Entrance*. Suddenly he halted and waited for Ellery, who was ambling reluctantly along behind. "I saw him," he whispered.

"Eh? Whom?"

"*Him*.. The Rabbit!"

Ellery started. "Where?"

"He just went inside there." Djuna's passionate gamineyes narrowed. "Think he's got his date in *here*?"

"Pesky queer place to have one, I'll confess," murmured Ellery, eying the crazy door with misgivings. "And yet logic . . . Now, Djuna, it's no concern of ours. Let's take our punishment like men and get the devil out of here. I'll go first."

"I wanna go first!"

"Over my dead body. I promised Dad Queen I'd bring you back—er—alive. Hold on to my coat—tightly, now! Here we go."

What followed is history. The Queen clan, as Inspector Richard Queen has often pointed out, is made of the stuff of heroes. And yet while Ellery was of the unpolluted and authentic blood, it was not long before he was feeling his way with quivering desperation and wishing himself at least a thousand light-years away.

The place was fiendish. From the moment they stepped through the crazy doorway to fall down a flight of padded stairs and land with a gentle bump on something which squealed hideously and fled from beneath them, they knew the tortures of the damned. There was no conceivable way of orienting themselves; they were in the deepest, thickest, blackest darkness Ellery had ever had the misfortune to encounter. All they could do was grope their way, one shrink-ing foot at a time, and pray for the best. It was literally impossible to see their hands before their faces.

They collided with walls which retaliated ungratefully with an electric shock. They ran into things which were all rattling bones and squeaks. Once they followed a tiny arrow of red light which had no sheen and found a hole in a wall just large enough to admit a human form if its owner crawled like an animal. They were not quite prepared for what they encountered on the other side: a floor which tipped precariously under their weight and, to Ellery's horror, slid them gently downward toward the other side of the room—if it was a room—and through a gap to a padded floor three feet below. . . . Then there was the incident of the flight of steps which made you mount rapidly and get nowhere, since the steps were on a treadmill going the other way; the wall which fell on your head; the labyrinth where the passage was just wide enough for a broad man's shoulders and just high enough for a gnome walking erect; the grating which blew blasts of frigid air up your legs; the earthquake room; and such abodes of pleasantry. And, to frazzle already frayed nerves, the air was filled with rumbles, gratings, clank-ings, whistlings, crashes and explosions in a symphony of noises which would have done credit to the inmates of Bedlam.

"Some fun, eh, kid?" croaked Ellery feebly, landing on his tail after an unexpected slide. Then he said some unkind things about Monsieur Dieudonné Duval under his breath. "Where are we now?"

"Boy, is it *dark*," said Djuna with satisfaction, clutching Ellery's arm. "I can't see a thing, can you?"

Ellery grunted and began to grope. "This looks promis-ing." His knuckles had rapped on a glassy surface. He felt it all over; it was a narrow panel, but taller than he. There were cracks along the sides which suggested that the panel was a door or window. But search as he might he could find no knob or latch. He bared a blade of his penknife and began to scratch away at the glass, which reason told him must have been smeared with thick opaque paint. But after several minutes of hot work he had uncovered only a faint and miserable sliver of light.

"That's not it," he said wearily. "Glass door or window here, and that pinline of light suggests it opens onto a balcony or something, probably overlooking the court. We'll have to find——"

"*Ow!*" shrieked Djuna from somewhere behind him. There was a scraping sound, followed by a thud.

Ellery whirled. "For heaven's sake, Djuna, what's the matter?"

The boy's voice wailed from a point close at hand in the darkness. "I was lookin' for how to get out an'—an' I slipped on somethin' an' fell!"

"Oh." Ellery sighed with relief. "From the yell you unloosed I thought a banshee had attacked you. Well, pick yourself up. It's not the first fall you've taken in this confounded hole."

"B-but it's *wet*," blubbered Djuna.

"Wet?" Ellery groped toward the anguished voice and seized a quivering hand. "Where?"

"On the f-floor. I got some of it on my hand when I slipped. My other hand. It—it's wet an' sticky an'—an' warm."

"Wet and sticky and wa . . ." Ellery released the boy's hand and dug about in his clothes until he found his tiny pencil-flashlight. He pressed the button with the most curious feeling of drama. There was something tangibly unreal, and yet, final, in the darkness. Djuna panted by his side. . . .

It was a moderately sane door with only a suggestion of cubistic outline, a low lintel, and a small knob. The door was shut. Something semi-liquid and dark red in color stained the floor, emanating from the other side of the crack.

"Let me see your hand," said Ellery tonelessly. Djuna

staring, tendered a small thin fist. Ellery turned it over and gazed at the palm. It was scarlet. He raised it to his nostrils and sniffed. Then he took out his handkerchief almost absently and wiped the scarlet away. "Well! That hasn't the smell of paint, eh, Djuna? And I scarcely think Duval would have so far let enthusiasm run away with better sense as to pour anything else on the floor as atmosphere." He spoke soothingly, divided between the stained floor and the dawning horror on Djuna's face. "Now, now, son. Let's open this door."

He shoved. The door stirred a half-inch, stuck. He set his lips and rammed, pushing with all his strength. There was something obstructing the door, something large and heavy. It gave way stubbornly, an inch at a time. . . .

He blocked Djuna's view deliberately, sweeping the flashlight's thin finger about the room disclosed by the opening of the door. It was perfectly octagonal, devoid of fixtures. Just eight walls, a floor, and a ceiling. There were two other doors besides the one in which he stood. Over one there was a red arrow, over the other a green. Both doors were shut. . . . Then the light swept sidewise and down to the door he had pushed open, seeking the obstruction.

The finger of light touched something large and dark and shapeless on the floor, and quite still. It sat doubled up like a jackknife, rump to the door. The finger fixed itself on four blackish holes in the middle of the back, from which a ragged cascade of blood had gushed, soaking the coat on its way to the floor.

Ellery growled something to Djuna and knelt, raising the head of the figure. It was the massive White Rabbit, and he was dead.

When Mr. Queen rose he was pale and abstracted. He swept the flash slowly about the floor. A trail of red led to the dead man from across the room. Diagonally opposite lay a short-barreled revolver. The smell of powder still lay heavily over the room.

"Is he— is he—?" whispered Djuna.

Ellery grabbed the boy's arm and hustled him back into the room they had just left. His flashlight illuminated the glass door on whose surface he had scratched. He kicked high, and the glass shivered as the light of day rushed in. Hacking out an aperture large enough to permit passage of his body, he wriggled past the broken glass and found himself on one of the fantastic little balconies overlooking the open inner court of *The House of Darkness*. A crowd was collecting below, attracted by the crash of falling glass. He made out the dapper figure of Monsieur Duval by the ticket-booth, in agitated conversation with a khaki-clad special officer, one of the regular Joyland police.

"Duval!" he shouted. "Who's come out of the *House*?"

"Eh?" gulped the little Frenchman.

"Since I went in? Quick, man, don't stand there gaping!"

"Who has come out?" Monsieur Duval licked his lips, staring up with scared black eyes. "But no one has come out, Mr. Queen. . . . What is it that is the matter? Have you— your head—the sun——"

"Good!" yelled Ellery. "Then he's still in this confounded labyrinth. Officer, send in an alarm for the regular county police. See that nobody leaves. Arrest 'em as soon as they try to come out. A man has been murdered up here!"

The note, in a woman's spidery scrawl, said: "Darling Anse—I *must* see you. It's important. Meet me at the old place, Joyland, Sunday afternoon, three o'clock, in that House of Darkness. I'll be awfully careful not to be seen. Especially this time. *He suspects.* I don't know what to do. I love you, love you!!! —Madge."

Captain Ziegler of the county detectives cracked his knuckles and barked: "That's the payoff, Mr. Queen. Fished it out of his pocket. Now who's Madge, and who the hell's the guy that 'suspects'? Hubby, d'ye suppose?"

The room was slashed with a dozen beams. Police criss-crossed flashlights in a pattern as bizarre as the shape of the chamber, with the shedding lantern held high by a policeman over the dead man as their focal point. Six people were lined up against one of the eight walls; five of them glared, mesmerized, at the still heap in the center of the rays. The sixth —the white-haired old man, still leaning on the arm of the tall young woman—was looking directly before him.

"Hmm," said Ellery; he scanned the prisoners briefly. "You're sure there's no one else skulking in the *House*, Captain Ziegler?"

"That's the lot of 'em. Mr. Duval had the machinery shut off. He led us through himself, searched every nook and cranny. And, since nobody left this hellhole, the killer must be one o' these six." The detective eyed them coldly; they all flinched—except the old man.

"Duval," murmured Ellery. Monsieur Duval started; he was deadly pale. "There's no 'secret' method of getting out of here unseen?"

"Ah, no, no, Mr. Queen! Here, I shall at once secure a copy of the plans myself, show you . . ."

"Scarcely necessary."

"The—the assembly-chamber is the sole means of emerging," stammered Duval. "Eh, that this should happen to——"

Ellery said quietly to a dainty woman, somberly gowned, who hugged the wall: "*You're* Madge, aren't you?" He recalled now that she was the only one of the six prisoners he had not seen while listening with Djuna and Monsieur Duval to the oration of the barker outside. She must have preceded them all into the *House*. The five others were here—the tall young woman and her odd father, the bearded man with his artist's tie, and the burly young Negro and his pretty mulatto companion. "Your name, please—your last name?"

"I—I'm not Madge," she whispered, edging, shrinking away. There were half-moons of violet shadow under her tragic eyes. She was perhaps thirty-five, the wreck of a once beautiful woman. Ellery got the curious feeling that it was not age, but fear, which had ravaged her.

"That's Dr. Hardy," said the tall young woman suddenly in a choked voice. She gripped her father's arm as if she were already sorry she had spoken.

"Who?" asked Captain Ziegler quickly.

"The . . . dead man. Dr. Anselm Hardy, the eye-specialist. Of New York City."

"That's right," said the small quiet man kneeling by the corpse. He tossed something over to the detective. "Here's one of his cards."

"Thanks, Doc. What's *your* name, Miss?"

"Nora Reis." The tall young woman shivered. "This is my father, Matthew Reis. We don't know anything about this—this horrible thing. We've just come out to Joyland today for some fun. If we'd known——"

"Nora, my dear," said her father gently; but neither his eyes nor his head moved from their fixed position.

"So you know the dead man, hey?" Ziegler's disagreeable face expressed heavy suspicion.

"If I may," said Matthew Reis. There was a soft musical pitch to his voice. "We knew Dr. Hardy, my daughter and I, only in his professional capacity. That's a matter of record, Captain Ziegler. He treated me for over a year. Then he operated upon my eyes." A spasm of pain flickered over his waxy features. "Cataracts, he said . . ."

"Hmm," said Ziegler. "Was it——"

"I am totally blind."

There was a shocked silence. Ellery shook his head with impatience at his own blindness. He should have known. The old man's helplessness, the queer fixed stare, that vague smile, the shuffling walk. . . . "This Dr. Hardy was responsible for your blindness, Mr. Reis?" he demanded abruptly.

"I didn't say that," murmured the old man. "It was no doubt the hand of God. He did what he could. I have been blind for over two years."

"Did you know Dr. Hardy was here, in this place, today?"

"No. We haven't seen him for two years."

"Where were you people when the police found you?"

Matthew Reis shrugged. "Somewhere ahead. Near the exit, I believe."

"And you?" asked Ellery of the colored couple.

"M'name is—is," stuttered the Negro, "Juju Jones, suh. Ah'm a prizefighter. Light-heavy, suh. Ah don't know nothin' 'bout this doctuh man. Me an' Jessie we been havin' a high ol' time down yonduh in a room that bounced 'n' jounced all roun'. We been——"

"Lawd," moaned the pretty mulatto, hanging on to her escort's arm.

"And how about you?" demanded Ellery of the bearded man.

He raised his shoulders in an almost Gallic gesture. "How about me? This is all classical Greek to *me*. I've been out on the rocks at the Point most of the day doing a couple of sea-pictures and a landscape. I'm an artist—James Oliver Adams, at your service." There was something antagonistic, almost sneering, in his attitude. "You'll find my paint-box and sketches in the checkroom downstairs. Don't know this dead creature, and I wish to God I'd never been tempted by this atrocious gargoyle of a place."

"Garg—" gasped Monsieur Duval; he became furious. "Do you know of whom you speak?" he cried, advancing upon the bearded man. "I am Dieudonné Du——"

"There, there, Duval," said Ellery soothingly. "We don't want to become involved in an altercation between clashing artistic temperaments; not now, anyway. Where were you, Mr. Adams, when the machinery stopped?"

"Somewhere ahead." The man had a harsh cracked voice, as if there was something wrong with his vocal chords. "I was looking for a way out of the hellish place. *I'd* had a bellyful. I——"

"That's right," snapped Captain Ziegler. "I found this bird myself. He was swearin' to himself like a trooper, stumblin' around in the dark. He says to me: 'How the hell do you get out of here? That barker said you've got to follow the green lights, but they don't get you anywhere except in another silly hole of a monkeyshine room, or somethin' like that. Now why'd you want to get out so fast, Mr. Adams? What do you know? Come on, spill it!"

The artist snorted his disgust, disdaining to reply. He shrugged again and set his shoulders against the wall in an attitude of resignation.

"I should think, Captain," murmured Ellery, studying the faces of the six against the wall, "that you'd be much more concerned with finding the one who 'suspects' in Madge's note. Well, Madge, are you going to talk? It's perfectly silly to hold out. This is the sort of thing that can't be kept secret. Sooner or later——"

The dainty woman moistened her lips; she looked faint. "I suppose you're right. It's bound to come out," she said in a low empty voice. "I'll talk. Yes, my name *is* Madge— Madge Clarke. It's true. I wrote that note to—to Dr. Hardy." Then her voice flamed passionately. "But I didn't write it of my own free will! *He* made me. It was a trap. I knew it. But I couldn't——"

"*Who* made you?" growled Captain Ziegler.

"My husband. Dr. Hardy and I had been friends . . . well, friends, quietly. My husband didn't know at first. Then he—he did come to know. He must have followed us —many times. We—we've met here before. My husband is very jealous. He made me write the note. He threatened to—to kill me if I didn't write it. Now I don't care. Let him! He's a murderer!" And she buried her face in her hands and began to sob.

Captain Ziegler said gruffly: "Mrs. Clarke." She looked

up and then down at the snub-nosed revolver in his hand. "Is that your husband's gun?"

She shrank from it, shuddering. "No. He has a revolver, but it's got a long barrel. He's a—a good shot."

"Pawnshop," muttered Ziegler, putting the gun in his pocket; and he nodded gloomily to Ellery.

"You came here, Mrs. Clarke," said Ellery gently, "in the face of your husband's threats?"

"Yes. Yes. I—I couldn't stay away. I thought I'd warn——"

"That was very courageous. Your husband—did you see him in Joyland, in the crowd before this place?"

"No. I didn't. But it must have been Tom. He *told* me he'd kill Anse!"

"Did you meet Dr. Hardy in here, before he was dead?"

She shivered. "No. I couldn't find——"

"Did you meet your husband here?"

"No . . ."

"Then where is he?" asked Ellery dryly. "He couldn't have vanished in a puff of smoke. The age of miracles is past. . . . Do you think you can trace that revolver, Captain Ziegler?"

"Try." Ziegler shrugged. "Manufacturer's number has been filed off. It's an old gun, too. And no prints. Bad for the D.A."

Ellery clucked irritably and stared down at the quiet man by the corpse. Djuna held his breath a little behind him. Suddenly he said: "Duval, isn't there some way of illuminating this room?"

Monsieur Duval started, his pallor deeper than before in the sword-thrusts of light crossing his face. "There is not an electrical wire or fixture in the entire structure. Excepting for the assembly-room, Mr. Queen."

"How about the arrows pointing the way? They're visible."

"A chemical. I am desolated by this——"

"Naturally; murder's rarely an occasion for hilarity. But this Stygian pit of yours complicates matters. What do you think, Captain?"

"Looks open and shut to *me*. I don't know how he got away, but this Clarke's the killer. We'll find him and sweat it out of him. He shot the doctor from the spot where you found the gun layin'—" Ellery frowned—"and then dragged the body to the door of the preceding room and set it up against the door to give him time for his getaway. Blood-trail tells that. The shots were lost in the noise of this damn' place. He must have figured on that."

"Hmm. That's all very well, except for the manner of Clarke's disappearance . . . if it *was* Clarke." Ellery sucked his fingernail, revolving Ziegler's analysis in his mind. There was one thing wrong . . . "Ah, the coroner's finished. Well, Doctor?"

The small quiet man rose from his knees in the light of the lantern. The six against the wall were incredibly still. "Simple enough. Four bullets within an area of inches. Two of them pierced the heart from behind. Good shooting, Mr. Queen."

Ellery blinked. "Good shooting," he repeated. "Yes, very good shooting indeed, Doctor. How long has he been dead?"

"About an hour. He died instantly, by the way."

"That means," muttered Ellery, "that he must have been shot only a few minutes before I found him. His body was still warm." He looked intently at the empurpled dead face. "But you're wrong, Captain Ziegler, about the position of the killer when he fired the shots. He couldn't have stood so far away from Dr. Hardy. In fact, as I see it, he must have been very close to Hardy. There are powder-marks on the dead man's body, of course, Doctor?"

The county coroner looked puzzled. "Powder-marks? Why, no. Of course not. Not a trace of burnt powder. Captain Ziegler's right."

Ellery said in a strangled voice: "No powder-marks? Why,

that's impossible! You're positive? There *must* be powder-marks!"

The coroner and Captain Ziegler exchanged glances. "As something of an expert in these matters, Mr. Queen," said the little man icily, "let me assure you that the victim was shot from a distance of at least twelve feet, probably a foot or two more."

The most remarkable expression came over Ellery's face. He opened his mouth to speak, closed it again, blinked once more, and then took out a cigaret and lit it, puffing slowly. "Twelve feet. No powder-marks," he said in a hushed voice. "Well, well. Now, that's downright amazing. That's a lesson in the illogicalities that would interest Professor Dewey himself. I can't believe it. Simply can't."

The coroner eyed him hostilely. "I'm a reasonably intelligent man, Mr. Queen, but you're talking nonsense as far as I'm concerned."

"What's on your mind?" demanded Captain Ziegler.

"Don't *you* know, either?" Then Ellery said abstractedly: "Let's have a peep at the contents of his clothes, please."

The detective jerked his head toward a pile of miscellaneous articles on the floor. Ellery went down on his haunches, indifferent to his staring audience. When he rose he was mumbling to himself almost with petulance. He had not found what he was seeking, what logic told him should be there. There were not even smoking materials of any kind. And there was no watch; he even examined the dead man's wrists for marks.

He strode about the room, nose lowered, searching the floor with an absorption that was oblivious to the puzzled looks directed at him. The flashlight in his hand was a darting, probing finger.

"But we've searched this room!" exploded Captain Ziegler. "What in the name of heaven are you looking for, Mr. Queen?"

"Something," murmured Ellery grimly, "that must be here

if there's any sanity in this world. Let's see what your men have scraped together from the floors of all the rooms, Captain."

"But they didn't find anything!"

"I'm not talking of things that would strike a detective as possibly 'important.' I'm referring to trivia: a scrap of paper, a sliver of wood—anything."

A broad-shouldered man said respectfully: "I looked myself, Mr. Queen. There wasn't even dust."

"*S'il vous plaît*," said Monsieur Duval nervously. "Of that we have taken care with ingenuity. There is here both a ventilation system and another, a vacuum system, which sucks in the dust and keeps *la maison des ténèbres* of a cleanliness immaculate."

"Vacuum!" exclaimed Ellery. "A sucking process . . . It's possible! Is this vacuum machine in operation all the time, Duval?"

"But no, my friend. Only in the night, when *The House of Darkness* is empty and—how do you say?—inoperative. But that is why your *gendarmes* found nothing, not even the dust."

"Foiled," muttered Ellery whimsically, but his eyes were grave. "The machine doesn't operate in the daytime. So that's out. Captain, forgive my persistence. But *everything's* been searched? The assembly-room downstairs, too? · Someone here might have——"

Captain Ziegler's face was stormy. "I can't figure you out. How many times do I have to say it? The man on duty in the cellar says no one even popped in there and went back during the period of the murder. So what?"

"Well, then," sighed Ellery, "I'll have to ask you to search each of these people, Captain." There was a note of desperation in his voice.

Mr. Ellery Queen's frown was a thing of beauty when he put down the last personal possession of the six prisoners. He had picked them apart to the accompaniment of a chorus of protests, chiefly from the artist Adams and Miss Reis. But he had not found what should have been there. He rose from his squatting position on the floor and silently indicated that the articles might be returned to their owners.

"*Parbleu!*" cried Monsieur Duval suddenly. "I do not know what is it for which you seek, my friend; but it is possible that it has been secretly placed upon the person of one of us, *n'est-ce pas*? If it is of a nature damaging, that would be——"

Ellery looked up with a faint interest. "Good for you, Duval. I hadn't thought of that."

"We shall see," said Monsieur Duval excitedly, beginning to turn out his pockets, "if the brain of Dieudonné Duval is not capable . . . *Voici!* Will you please to examine, Mr. Queen?"

Ellery looked over the collection of odds and ends briefly. "No dice. That was generous, Duval." He began to poke about in his own pockets.

Djuna announced proudly: "I've got everything *I* ought to."

"Well, Mr. Queen?" asked Ziegler impatiently.

Ellery waved an absent hand. "I'm through, Captain . . . Wait!" He stood still, eyes lost in space. "Wait here. It's still possible——" Without explanation he plunged through the doorway marked with the green arrow, found himself in a narrow passageway as black as the rooms leading off from it, and flashed his light about. Then he ran back to the extreme end of the corridor and began a worm's progress, scrutinizing each inch of the corridor-floor as if his life depended upon his thoroughness. Twice he turned corners, and at last he found himself at a dead end confronted by a door marked "*Exit*: *Assembly-Room*." He pushed the door in and blinked at the lights of the cellar. A policeman touched his cap to him; the attendant skeleton looked scared.

"Not even a bit of wax, or a few crumbs of broken glass,

or a burnt matchstick," he muttered. A thought struck him. "Here, officer, open this door in the grating for me, will you?"

The policeman unlocked a small door in the grating and Ellery stepped through to the larger division of the room. He made at once for the rack on the wall, in the compartments of which were the things the prisoners—and he himself —had checked before plunging into the main body of the *House*. He inspected these minutely. When he came to the artist's box he opened it, glanced at the paints and brushes and palette and three small daubs—a landscape and two seascapes—which were quite orthodox and uninspired, closed it. . . . ..

He paced up and down under the dusty light of the bulbs, frowning fiercely. Minutes passed. *The House of Darkness* was silent, as if in tribute to its unexpected dead. The policeman gaped.

Suddenly he halted and the frown faded, to be replaced by a grim smile. "Yes, yes, that's it," he muttered. "Why didn't I think of it before? Officer! Take all this truck back to the scene of the crime. I'll carry this small table back with me. We've all the paraphernalia, and in the darkness we should be able to conduct a very thrilling *séance*!"

When he knocked on the door of the octagonal room from the corridor, it was opened by Captain Ziegler himself.

"You back?" growled the detective. "We're just ready to scram. Stiff's crated——"

"Not for a few moments yet, I trust," said Ellery smoothly, motioning the burdened policeman to precede him. "I've a little speech to make."

"Speech!"

"A speech fraught with subtleties and clevernesses, my dear Captain. Duval, this will delight your Gallic soul. Ladies and gentlemen, you will please remain in your places. That's right, officer; on the table. Now, gentlemen, if you will kindly focus the rays of your flashes upon me and the table, we can begin our demonstration."

The room was very still. The body of Dr. Anselm Hardy lay in a wickerwork basket, brown-covered, invisible. Ellery presided like a *Swami* in the center of the room, the nucleus of thin beams. Only the glitter of eyes was reflected back to him from the walls.

He rested one hand on the small table, cluttered with the belongings of the prisoners. "*Alors, mesdames et messieurs,* we begin. We begin with the extraordinary fact that the scene of this crime is significant for one thing above all: its darkness. Now, that's a little out of the usual run. It suggests certain disturbing nuances before you think it out. This is literally a house of darkness. A man has been murdered in one of its unholy chambers. In the house itself—excluding, of course, the victim, myself, and my panting young charge—we find six persons presumably devoting themselves to enjoyment of Monsieur Duval's satanic creation. No one during the period of the crime was observed to emerge from the only possible exit, if we are to take the word of the structure's own architect, Monsieur Duval. It is inevitable, then, that one of these six is the killer of Dr. Hardy."

There was a mass rustle, a rising sigh, which died almost as soon as it was born.

"Now observe," continued Ellery dreamily, "what pranks fate plays. In this tragedy of darkness, the cast includes at least three characters associated with darkness. I refer to Mr. Reis, who is blind; and to Mr. Juju Jones and his escort, who are Negroes. Isn't that significant? Doesn't it mean something to you?"

Juju Jones groaned: "Ah di'n't do it, Mistuh Queen."

Ellery said: "Moreover, Mr. Reis has a possible motive; the victim treated his eyes, and in the course of this treatment Mr. Reis became blind. And Mrs. Clarke offered us a jealous husband. Two motives, then. So far, so good. . . . But all this tells us nothing vital about the crime itself."

"Well," demanded Ziegler harshly, "what does?"

"The darkness, Captain, the darkness," replied Ellery in gentle accents. "I seem to have been the only one who was disturbed by that darkness." A brisk note sprang into his voice. "This room is totally black. There is no electricity, no lamp, no lantern, no gas, no candle, no window in its equipment. Its three doors open onto places as dark as itself. The green and red lights above the doors are nonluminous, radiate no light visible to the human eye beyond the arrows themselves. . . . *And yet, in this blackest of black rooms, someone was able at a distance of at least twelve feet to place four bullets within an area of inches in this invisible victim's back!*"

Someone gasped. Captain Ziegler muttered: "By damn . . ."

"How?" asked Ellery softly. "Those shots were accurate. They couldn't have been accidents—not four of them. I had assumed in the beginning that there must be powder-burns on the dead man's coat, that the killer must have stood directly behind Dr. Hardy, touching him, even holding him steady, jamming the muzzle of the revolver into his back and firing. But the coroner said no! It seemed impossible. In a totally dark room? At twelve feet? The killer couldn't have hit Hardy by ear alone, listening to movements, foot-steps; the shots were too accurately placed for that theory. Besides, the target must have been moving, however slowly. I couldn't understand it. The only possible answer was that *the murderer had light to see by.* And yet there was no light."

Matthew Reis said musically: "Very clever, sir."

"Elementary, rather, Mr. Reis. There was no light in the room itself. . . . Now, thanks to Monsieur Duval's vacuum-suction system, there is never any débris in this place. That meant that if we found something it might belong to one of the suspects. But the police had searched minutely and found literally nothing. I myself finecombed this room looking for a flashlight, a burnt match, a wax taper—anything that might have indicated the light by which the murderer shot Dr. Hardy. Since I had analyzed the facts, I knew what to look for, as would anyone who had analyzed them. When I found nothing in the nature of a light-giver, I was flabbergasted.

"I examined the contents of the pockets of our six suspects; still no clue to the source of the light. A single matchstick would have helped, although I realized that that would hardly have been the means employed; for this had been a trap laid in advance. The murderer had apparently enticed his victim to *The House of Darkness*. He had planned the murder to take place here. Undoubtedly he had visited it before, seen its complete lack of lighting facilities. He therefore would have planned in advance to provide means of illumination. He scarcely would have relied on matches; certainly he would have preferred a flashlight. But there was nothing, nothing, not even the improbable burnt match. If it was not on his person, had he thrown it away? But where? It has not been found. Nowhere in the rooms or corridor."

Ellery paused over a cigaret. "And so I came to the conclusion," he drawled, puffing smoke, "that *the light must have emanated from the victim himself.*"

"But no!" gasped Monsieur Duval. "No man would so foolish be——"

"Not consciously, of course. But he might have provided light unconsciously. I looked over the very dead Dr. Hardy. He wore dark clothing. There was no watch which might possess radial hands. He had no smoking implements on his person; a non-smoker, obviously. No matches or lighter, then. And no flashlight. Nothing of a luminous nature which might explain how the killer saw where to aim. That is," he murmured, "nothing but one last possibility."

"What——"

"Will you gentlemen please put the lantern and your flashes out?"

For a moment there was uncomprehending inaction; and then lights began to snap off, until finally the room was steeped in the same thick palpable darkness that had existed when Ellery had stumbled into it. "Keep your places, please," said Ellery curtly. "Don't move, anyone."

There was no sound at first except the quick breaths of rigid people. The glow of Ellery's cigaret died, snuffed out. Then there was a slight rustling and a sharp click. And before their astonished eyes a roughly rectangular blob of light no larger than a domino, misty and nacreous, began to move across the room. It sailed in a straight line, like a homing pigeon, and then another blob detached itself from the first and touched something, and lo! there was still a third blob of light.

"Demonstrating," came Ellery's cool voice, "the miracle of how Nature provides for her most wayward children. Phosphorus, of course. Phosphorus in the form of paint. If, for example, the murderer had contrived to daub the back of the victim's coat before the victim entered *The House of Darkness*—perhaps in the press of a crowd—he insured himself sufficient light for his crime. In a totally black place he had only to search for the phosphorescent patch. Then four shots in the thick of it from a distance of twelve feet—no great shakes to a good marksman—the bullet-holes obliterate most of the light-patch, any bit that remains is doused in gushing blood . . . and the murderer's safe all round. . . . Yes, yes, very clever. *No, you don't!*"

The third blob of light jerked into violent motion, lunging forward, disappearing, appearing, making progress toward the green-arrowed door. . . . There was a crash, and a clatter, the sounds of a furious struggle. Lights flicked madly on, whipping across one another. They illuminated an area on the floor in which Ellery lay entwined with a man who fought in desperate silence. Beside them lay the paint-box, open.

Captain Ziegler jumped in and rapped the man over the

head with his billy. He dropped back with a groan, unconscious. It was the artist, Adams.

"But how did you know it was Adams?" demanded Ziegler a few moments later, when some semblance of order had been restored. Adams lay on the floor, manacled; the others crowded around, relief on some faces, fright on others.

"By a curious fact," panted Ellery, brushing himself off. "Djuna, stop pawing me! I'm quite all right. . . . You yourself told me, Captain, that when you found Adams blundering around in the dark he was complaining that he wanted to get out but couldn't find the exit. (Naturally he would!) He said that he knew he should follow the green lights, but when he did he only got deeper into the labyrinth of rooms. But how could that have been if he *had* followed the green lights? Any one of them would have taken him directly into the straight, monkeyshineless corridor leading to the exit. Then he *hadn't* followed the green lights. Since he could have no reason to lie about it, it must simply have meant, I reasoned, that he *thought* he had been following the green lights but had been following the red lights instead, since he continued to blunder from room to room."

"But how——"

"Very simple. Color-blindness. He's afflicted with the common type of color-blindness in which the subject confuses red and green. Unquestionably he didn't know that he had such an affliction; many color-blind persons don't. He had expected to make his escape quickly, before the body was found, depending on the green light he had previously heard the barker mention to insure his getaway.

"But that's not the important point. The important point is that *he claimed to be an artist*. Now, it's almost impossible for an artist to work in color and still be color-blind. The fact that he had found himself trapped, misled by the red lights, proved that he was not conscious of his red-green affliction. But I examined his landscape and seascapes in the paint-box and found them quite orthodox. I knew, then, that they weren't his; that he was masquerading, that he was not an artist at all. But if he was masquerading, he became a vital suspect!

"Then, when I put that together with the final deduction about the source of light, I had the whole answer in a flash. Phosphorus paint—paint-box. And he had directly preceded Hardy into the *House*. . . . The rest was pure theatre. He felt that he wasn't running any risk with the phosphorus, for whoever would examine the paint-box would naturally open it *in the light*, where the luminous quality of the chemical would be invisible. And there you are."

"Then my husband—" began Mrs. Clarke in a strangled voice, staring down at the unconscious murderer.

"But the motive, my friend," protested Monsieur Duval, wiping his forehead. "The motive! A man does not kill for nothing. Why——"

"The motive?" Ellery shrugged. "You already know the motive, Duval. In fact, you know—" He stopped and knelt suddenly by the bearded man. His hand flashed out and came away—with the beard. Mrs. Clarke screamed and staggered back. "He even changed his voice. This, I'm afraid, is your vanishing Mr. Clarke!"

The Adventure of
THE BLEEDING PORTRAIT

The Adventure of
THE BLEEDING PORTRAIT

Natchitauk is the sort of place where the Gramatons and Eameses and Angerses of this world may be found when the barns are freshly red and the rambler roses begin to sprinkle the winding roadside fences. In summer its careless hills seethe with large children who paint vistas and rattle typewriters under trees and mumble unperfected lines to the rafters of a naked backstage. These colonials prefer rum to rye, and applejack to rum; and most of them are famous and charming and great talkers.

Mr. Ellery Queen, who was visiting Natchitauk at Pearl Angers's invitation to taste her scones and witness her *Candida*, had hardly more than shucked his coat and seated himself on the porch with an applejack highball when the great lady told him the story of how Mark Gramaton met his Mimi.

It seems that Gramaton had been splashing away at a water-color of the East River from a point high above Manhattan when a dark young woman appeared on a roof below him, spread a Navajo blanket, removed her clothes, and lay down to sun herself.

The East River fluttered fifteen stories to the street.

And after a while Gramaton bellowed down: "You! You woman, there!"

Mimi sat up, scared. There was Gramaton straining over the parapet, his thick blond hair in tufts and his ugly face the color of an infuriated persimmon.

"Turn over!" roared Gramaton in a terrible voice. "I'm finished with that side!"

Ellery laughed. "He sounds amusing."

"But that's not the point of the story," protested the

535

Angers. "For when Mimi spied the paintbrush in his hand she did meekly turn over. And when Gramaton saw her dark back under the sun—well, he divorced his wife, who was a sensible woman, and married the girl."

"Ah, impulsive, too."

"You don't know Mark! He's a frustrated Botticelli. To him Mimi is beauty incarnate." It appeared, too, that no Collatinus had a more faithful Lucretia. At least four unsuccessful Tarquins of the Natchitauk aristocracy were—if not publicly prepared—at least privately in a position to attest Mimi's probity. "Besides, they're essentially gentlemen," said the actress, "and Gramaton is such a large and muscular man."

"Gramaton," said Ellery. "That's an odd name."

"English. His father was a yachtsman who clung barnacle-like to the tail of a long line of lords, and his mother's epidermis was so incrusted with tradition that she considered Queen Anne's death without surviving issue a major calamity to the realm, inasmuch as it ended the Stuart succession. At least, that's what Mark says!" The Angers sighed emotionally.

"Wasn't he a little hard on his first wife?" asked Ellery, who was inclined to be strait-laced.

"Oh, not really! She knew she couldn't hold him, and besides she had her own career to think of. They're still friends."

The next evening, taking his seat in the Natchitauk Playhouse, Ellery found himself staring at the loveliest female back within his critical memory. No silkworm spun, nor oyster strained, that dared aspire to that perfect flesh. The nude dark glowing skin quite obliterated the stage and Miss Angers and Mr. Shaw's aged dialogue.

. When the lights came on Ellery awoke from his rhapsodizing to find that the seat in front of him had been vacated; and he rose with a purpose. Shoulders like that enter a man's life only once.

On the sidewalk he spied Emilie Eames, the novelist.

"Look," said Ellery. "I was introduced to you once at a party. How are you, and all that. Miss Eames, you know everybody in America, don't you?"

"All except a family named Radewicz," replied Miss Eames.

"I didn't see her face, curse it. But she has hazel shoulders, a tawny, toasty, nutty sort of back that . . . You *must* know her!"

"That," said Miss Eames reflectively, "would be Mimi."

"Mimi!" Ellery became glum.

"Well, come along. We'll find her where the cummerbunds are thickest."

And there was Mimi in the lounge, surrounded by seven speechless young men. Against the red plush of the chair, with her lacquered hair, child's eyes, and soft tight backless gown, she looked like a Polynesian queen. And she was altogether beautiful.

"Out of the way, you cads." Miss Eames dispersed the courtiers. "Mimi darling, here's somebody named Queen. Mrs. Gramaton."

"Gramaton," groaned Ellery. "My *bête blonde.*"

"And this," added Miss Eames through her teeth, "is the foul fiend. Its name is Borcca."

It seemed a curious introduction. Ellery shook hands with Mr. Borcca, wondering if a smile or a cough were called for. Mr. Borcca was a sallow swordblade of a man with an antique Venetian face, looking as if he needed only a pitchfork.

Mr. Borcca smiled, showing a row of sharp vulpine teeth. "Miss Eames is my indefatigable admirer."

Miss Eames turned her back on him. "Queen has fallen in love with you, darling."

"How nice." Mimi looked down modestly. "And do you know my husband, Mr. Queen?"

"Ouch," said Ellery.

"My dear sir, it is not of the slightest use," said Mr. Borcca, showing his teeth again. "Mrs. Gramaton is that *rara avis,* a beautiful lady who cannot be dissuaded from adoring her husband."

The beautiful lady's beautiful back arched.

"Go away," said Miss Eames coldly. "You annoy me." Mr. Borcca did not seem to mind; he bowed as if at a compliment and Mrs. Gramaton sat very still.

Candida was a success; the Angers was radiant; Ellery soaked in the sun and rambled over the countryside and consumed mountains of brook trout and scones; and several times he saw Mimi Gramaton, so the week passed .pleasantly.

The second time he saw her he was sprawled on the Angers jetty, fishing in the lake for dreams. One came, fortunately escaping his hook—she bobbed up under the line, wet and sealbrown and clad in something shimmery, scant, and adhesive.

Mimi laughed at him, twisted, coiled against the jetty, and shot off toward the large island in the middle of the lake. A fat hairy-chested man fishing from a rowboat she hailed joyously; he grinned back at her; and she streaked on, her bare back incandescent under the sun.

And then, as if she had swum into a net, she stopped. Ellery saw her jerk; tread water, blink through wet lashes at the island.

Mr. Borcca stood on the island's beach, leaning upon a curiously shaped walking-stick.

Mimi dived. When she reappeared she was swimming on a tangent, headed for the cove at the eastern tip of the island. Mr. Borcca started to walk toward the eastern tip of the island. Mimi stopped again. . . . After a moment, with a visible resignation, she swam slowly for the beach again. When she emerged dripping from the lake, Mr. Borcca was before her. He merely stood still, and she went by him as if he were invisible. He followed her eagerly up the path into the woods.

"Who," demanded Ellery that evening, "is this Borcca?"

"Oh, you've met him?" The Angers paused. "One of Mark Gramaton's pets. A political refugee—he's been vague about it. Gramaton collects such people the way old ladies collect cats. . . . Borcca is—rather terrifying. Let's not talk about him."

The next day, at Emilie Eames's place, Ellery saw Mimi again. She wore linen shorts and a gay halter, and she had just finished three sets of tennis with a wiry gray man, Dr. Varrow, the local leech. She sauntered off the court, laughing, waved to Ellery and Miss Eames, who were lying on the lawn, and began to stroll toward the lake swinging her racket.

Suddenly she began to run. Ellery sat up.

She ran desperately. She cut across a clover-field. She dropped her racket and did not stop to pick it up.

There was Mr. Borcca following her flight with rapid strides along the edge of the woods, his curiously-shaped stick under his arm.

"It strikes me," said Ellery slowly, "that *someone* ought to teach that fellow——"

"Please lie down again," said Miss Eames.

Dr. Varrow came off the court swabbing his neck, and stopped short. He saw Mimi running; he saw Mr. Borcca striding. Dr. Varrow's mouth tightened and he followed. Ellery got to his feet.

Miss Eames plucked a daisy. "Gramaton," she said softly, "doesn't know, you see. And Mimi is a brave child who is terribly in love with her husband."

"Bosh," said Ellery, watching the three figures. "If the man's a menace Gramaton should be told. How can he be so blind? Apparently everyone in Natchitauk——"

"Mark's peculiar. As many faults as virtues. When it is aroused he has the most jealous temper in the world."

"Will you excuse me?" said Ellery.

He strode toward the woods. Under the trees he stopped, listening. A man was crying out somewhere, thickly, helplessly, and yet defiantly. Ellery nodded, feeling his knuckles.

On his way back he saw Mr. Borcca stumble out of the woods. The man's medallion face was convulsed; he blundered into a rowboat and rowed off toward Gramaton's island with choppy strokes. And then Dr. Varrow and Mimi Gramaton strolled into view as if nothing had happened.

"I suppose every ablebodied man in Natchitauk," remarked Miss Eames calmly when Ellery rejoined her, "has had a crack at Borcca this summer."

"Why doesn't somebody run him out of town?"

"He's a queer animal. Complete physical coward, never defends himself, and yet undiscourageable. His seems to be an epic passion." Miss Eames shrugged. "If you noticed, Johnny Varrow didn't leave any marks on him. If his pet were mussed up Mark might ask inescapable questions."

"I don't understand it," muttered Ellery.

"Well, if he found out, you see," said Miss Eames in a light tone, "Mark would kill the beast."

Ellery met Gramaton and first encountered the phenomenon of the fourth Lord Gramaton's leaky breast at one of those carefully spontaneous entertainments with which the colonial *illuminati* periodically amuse themselves. There were charades, Guggenheim, Twenty Questions, and some sparkling pasquinade; and it all took place Sunday evening at Dr. Varrow's.

The doctor was gravely exhibiting a contraption. It was a tubular steel frame in which, suspended by invisible cords, hung a glistening cellophane heart filled with a fluid that looked like blood and was obviously tomato juice. Varrow announced in a sepulchral voice: "She is unfaithful," and squeezed a rubber ball. Whereupon the heart pursed itself and squirted a red stream that was caught uncannily by a brass cuspidor on the floor. Everyone folded up with laughter.

"Surrealism?" asked Ellery politely, wondering if he was mad.

The Angers collapsed. "It's Gramaton's bleeder," she gasped. "The *nerve* of Johnny! Of course, he's Gramaton's best friend."

"What has that to do with it?" asked Ellery, bewildered.

"You poor thing! Don't you know the story of the Bleeding Heart?"

She pulled him toward a very large and ugly blond man who was leaning helplessly on Mimi Gramaton's bare shoulders from behind, burying his face in her hair and laughing in gusts.

"Mark," said the Angers, "this is Ellery Queen. And he never heard the story of the Bleeding Heart!"

Gramaton released his wife, wiping his eyes with one hand and groping for Ellery with the other.

"Hullo there. That Johnny Varrow! He's the only man I know who can exhibit bad taste so charmingly it becomes good. . . . Queen? Don't believe I've seen you in Natchitauk before."

"Naturally not," said Mimi, poking her hair, "since Mr. Queen's only been staying with Pearl a few days and you've been shut up with that mural of yours."

"So you've met, you two," grinned Gramaton, but he placed his enormous arm about his wife's shoulders.

"Mark," pleaded the Angers, "tell him the story."

"Oh, he must see the portrait first. Artist?"

"Ellery writes murder stories," said Pearl. "Most people say 'How quaint' and he gets furious, so don't say it."

"Then you certainly must see the fourth Lord Gramaton. Murder stories? By George, this should be material for you." Gramaton chuckled. "Are you irrevocably committed to Pearl?"

"Certainly not," said the Angers. "He's eating me out of house and home. Do go, Ellery," she said. "He's going to ask you; he always does."

"Besides," said Gramaton, "I like your face."

"He means," murmured Mimi, "that he wants to use it on his mural."

"But—" began Ellery, rather helplessly.

"Of course you'll come," said Mimi Gramaton.

"Of course," beamed Ellery.

Mr. Queen found himself being borne across the lake under the stars to Gramaton's island, his suitcase under his feet, trying to recall exactly how he had got there as he watched the big man row. Mimi faced him bewitchingly from the stern, with Gramaton's huge shoulders spread between them, rising and falling like the flails of time; and Ellery shivered a little.

It was queer, because Gramaton seemed the friendliest fellow. He had stopped at Pearl's and fetched Ellery's bag himself; he chattered on, promising Ellery peace, rabbit-shooting, intelligent arguments about Communism, 16-milli-metre views of Tibet, Tanganyika, and the Australian bush, and all manner of pleasant diversions.

"Simple life," chuckled Gramaton. "We're primitive here, you know—no bridge to the island, no motorboats . . . a bridge would spoil our natural isolation and I've a horror of things that make noise. Interested in art?"

"I don't know much about it," admitted Ellery.

"Appreciation doesn't necessarily require knowledge, de-spite what the academicians say." They landed on the beach; a figure rose, dark and fat against the sands, and took the boat. "Jeff," explained Gramaton, as they entered the woods. "Professional hobo; like him hanging around. . . . Appreciation? You could appreciate Mimi's back without knowing the least thing about the geometric theory of esthetics."

"He makes me exhibit it," complained Mimi, not very convincingly, "like a freak. Why, he selects my clothes! I feel naked half the time."

They came to the house and stopped to let Ellery admire it.

Fat Jeff, the hairy man, came up from behind and took Ellery's bag and silently carried it off. The house was odd, all angles, ells, and wings, built of hewn logs on a rough stone foundation.

"It's just a house," said Gramaton. "Come along to my studio; I'll introduce you to Lord Gramaton."

The studio occupied the second story of a far wing. The north wall was completely glass, in small panes, and the other walls were covered with oils, water-colors, pastels, etchings, plasters, and carvings in wood.

"Good evening," bowed Mr. Borcca. He was standing before a large covered framework, and he had just turned around.

"Oh, there's Borcca," smiled Gramaton. "Inhaling art, you pagan? Queen, meet——"

"I've had the pleasure," said Ellery politely. He was wondering what the framework concealed; the cover was askew and it seemed to him that Mr. Borcca had been examining what lay under it with passionate absorption when they had surprised him.

"I think," said Mimi in a small voice, "I'll see about Mr. Queen's room."

"Nonsense. Jeff's doing that. Here's my mural," Gramaton said, ripping the cover off the framework. "Just the preliminary work on one corner—it's to go over the lobby entrance of the New Arts building. Of course you recognize Mimi."

And indeed Ellery did. The central motif of a throng of curious masculine faces was a gargantuan female back, dark and curved and womanly. He glanced at Mr. Borcca; but Mr. Borcca was looking at Mrs. Gramaton.

"And this is His Nibs."

The ancient portrait had been placed where the north light tactfully did not venture—a lifesize canvas the color of gloomy molasses, set flush with the floor. The fourth Lord Gramaton glared down out of the habiliments of the Seventeenth Century, remarkable only for the diameter of his belly and flare of his nose. Ellery thought he had never seen a more repulsive daub.

"Isn't he a beauty?" grinned Gramaton. "Shove an armful of those canvases off that chair. . . . Done by some earnest but, as you can see, horny-handed forerunner of Hogarth."

"But what's the connection between Lord Gramaton and Dr. Varrow's little pleasantry?" demanded Ellery.

"Come here, darling." Mimi went to her husband and sat down on his lap, resting her dark head against his shoulder. Mr. Borcca turned away, stumbling over a sharp-pointed palette-knife on the floor. "Borcca, pour Mr. Queen a drink.

"Well, my noble ancestor married a carefully preserved Lancashire lass who'd never been two miles from her father's hayrick. The old pirate was very proud of his wife, because of her beauty; and he exhibited her at Court much as he had exhibited his blacks in the African slave markets. Lady Gramaton quickly became the ambition of London's more buckety buckos."

"Scotch, Mr. Queen?" mumbled Mr. Borcca.

"No."

Gramaton kissed his wife's neck, and Mr. Borcca helped himself to two quick drinks. "It seems," continued Gramaton, "that, conscious of his responsibility to posterity, Lord Gramaton soon after his marriage commissioned some pot-slinger to paint his portrait, with the foul result you see.

"The old chap was terribly pleased with it, though, and hung it over the fireplace in the great hall of his castle, in the most conspicuous place. Well, the story says that one night —he was gouty, too,—unable to sleep, he hobbled downstairs for something and was horrified to see blood dripping from the waistcoat of his own portrait."

"Oh, no," protested Ellery. "Or was it some Restoration joke?"

"No, it was blood," chuckled the artist "—the old cut-throat knew blood when he saw it! Well, he hobbled upstairs to his wife's chamber to inform her of the miracle and caught the poor girl enjoying a bit of life with one of the young bucks I mentioned. Naturally, he skewered them both with his sword, and as I recall it lived to be ninety and remarried and had five children by his second wife."

"But—blood," said Ellery, staring at Lord Gramaton's immaculate waistcoat. "What did that have to do with his wife's infidelity?"

"Nobody understands that," said Mimi in a muffled voice. "That's why it's a story."

"And when he went downstairs again," said Gramaton, fondling his wife's ear, "wiping his sword, the blood on the portrait had vanished. Typical British symbolism, you know —mysteriously dull. Ever after the tradition has persisted that the fourth Lord Gramaton's heart would bleed every time a Gramaton wife strayed to greener pastures."

"Sort of domestic tattletale," remarked Ellery dryly.

Mimi jumped off her husband's lap. "Mark, I'm simply weary."

"Sorry." Gramaton stretched his long arms. "Rum sort of thing, eh? Use it if you like. . . . Shall I show you your room? Borcca, be a good chap and turn off the lights."

Mimi went out quickly, like a woman pursued. And indeed she was—by Mr. Borcca's eyes, as they left him standing by the sideboard with the decanter of Scotch in his hand.

"Awkward," said Gramaton at breakfast. "Will you forgive me? I've had a telegram from the architect and I must run into the city this afternoon."

"I'll go with you," suggested Ellery. "You've been so kind——"

"Won't hear of it. I'll be back tomorrow morning and we'll have some sport."

Ellery strolled into the woods for a tramping survey of Gramaton's island. It was, he found, shaped like a peanut;

a densely wooded place except in the middle, covering at least thirty acres. The sky was overcast and he felt chilled, despite his leather jacket. But whether it was from the natural elements or not he did not know. The place depressed him.

Finding himself following an old, almost obliterated path, he pursued it with curiosity. It led across a rocky neck and vanished near the eastern end of the island in an overgrown clearing in which stood a wooden hut, its roof half fallen in and its wall-timbers sticking out like broken bones.

"Some deserted squatter's shack," he thought; and it caught his fancy to explore it. One found things in old places.

But what Ellery found was a dilemma. Stepping upon the crumbly stone doorstep he heard voices from the gloom inside. And at the same instant, faintly from the wood behind, rose Gramaton's voice calling: "Mimi!"

Ellery stood still.

Mimi's voice came passionately from the shack. "Don't you dare. Don't touch me. I didn't ask you here for that."

Mr. Borcca's plaintive voice said: "Mimi. Mimi. Mimi," like a grooved phonograph record.

"Here's money. Take it and get out of here. Take it!" She seemed hysterical.

But Mr. Borcca merely repeated: "Mimi," and his feet scuffed across the rough floor.

"Borcca! You're a mad animal. Borcca! I'll scream! My husband——"

"I shall kill you," said Mr. Borcca in a tired voice. "I cannot stand this——"

"Gramaton!" shouted Ellery, as the big man came into view. The voices in the shack ceased. "Don't look so concerned. I've kidnaped Mrs. Gramaton and made her show me your forest."

"Oh," said Gramaton, wiping his head. "Mimi!"

Mimi appeared, smiling, and her arm, close to Ellery's

jacket, shook. "I've just been showing Mr. Queen the shack. Were you worried about me, darling?" She ran past Ellery and linked her arms about her husband's neck.

"But Mimi, you know I needed you to pose this morning." Gramaton seemed uneasy; his big blond head jerked from side to side. Then his head stopped jerking.

"I forgot, Mark. Don't look so grumpy!" She took his arm, turned him around and, laughing, walked him off.

"Lovely place," called Ellery fatuously, standing still. Gramaton smiled back at him, but the gray eyes were intent. Mimi drew him into the woods.

Ellery looked down. Mr. Borcca's curiously-shaped walking stick lay on the path. Gramaton had seen it.

He picked up the stick and went into the hut. But it was empty.

He came out, broke the stick over his knee, pitched the pieces into the lake, and slowly followed the Gramatons down the path.

When Mimi returned from the village after seeing Gramaton off she was accompanied by Emilie Eames and Dr. Varrow.

"I spend more time with a paintbrush than a stethoscope," explained the doctor to Ellery. "I find art catching. And people here are so depressingly healthy."

"We'll swim and things," announced Mimi, "and tonight we'll toast wieners and marshmallows outdoors. We do owe you something, Mr. Queen." But she did not look at him. It seemed to Ellery that she was unnaturally animated; her cheeks were dark red.

While they played in the lake Mr. Borcca appeared on the beach and quietly sat down. Mimi stopped being gay. Later, when they came out of the lake, Mr. Borcca rose and went away.

After dinner Jeff built a fire. Mimi sat very close to Miss Eames, snuggling as if she were cold. Dr. Varrow unex-

pectedly produced a guitar and sang some obscure sailors'
chanteys. It turned out that Mimi possessed a clear, sweet
soprano voice; she sang, too, until she caught sight of a pair
of iridescent eyes regarding her from the underbrush. Then
she abruptly stopped, and Ellery observed to himself that at
night Mr. Borcca might easily turn into a wolf. There was
such a feral glare in those orbs that his muscles tightened.

A light rain began to fall; they scampered for the house
gratefully, Jeff trampling out the fire.

"Do stay over," urged Mimi. "With Mark away——"

"You couldn't drive me home," said Dr. Varrow cheerfully.
"I like your beds."

"Do you want me to sleep with you, Mimi?" asked Miss
Eames.

"No," said Mimi slowly. "That won't be—necessary."

Ellery was just removing his jacket when someone tapped
on his door. "Mr. Queen," whispered a voice.

Ellery opened the door. Mimi stood there in the semi-
darkness clad in a gauzy backless negligée. She said nothing
more, but her large eyes begged.

"Perhaps," suggested Ellery, "it would be more discreet if
we talked in your husband's studio."

He retrieved his jacket and she led him in silence to the
studio, turning on a single bulb. Details sprang up—the
fourth Lord Gramaton glowering, the sheen of the unbroken
north wall windows, the palette-knife lying on the floor.

"I owe you an explanation," whispered Mimi, sinking into
a chair. "And such terribly important thanks that I can't
ever——"

"You owe me nothing," said Ellery gently. "But you owe
yourself a good deal. How long do you think you can keep
this up?"

"So you know, too!" She began to weep without sound
into her hands. "That animal has been here since May, and
. . . what am I to do?"

"Tell your husband."

"No, oh, no! You don't know Mark. It's not myself, but Mark . . . he'd strangle Borcca slowly. He'd—he'd break his arms and legs and . . . He'd kill the creature! Don't you see I've got to protect Mark from that?"

Ellery was silent, for the excellent reason that he could think of nothing to say. Short of killing Borcca himself, he was helpless. Mimi sat collapsed in the chair, crying again.

"Please go," she sobbed. "And I do thank you."

"Do you think it's wise to stay here alone?"

She did not reply. Feeling a perfect fool, Ellery left. Outside the house the rolypoly figure of Jeff separated itself from a tree.

"It's all right, Mr. Queen," said Jeff.

Ellery went to bed, reassured.

Gramaton was red-eyed and grayish the next morning, as if he had spent a sleepless night in the city. But he seemed cheerful enough.

"I promise you I shan't run off again," he said, over the eggs. "What's the matter, Mimi—are you cold?"

It was an absurd thing to suggest, because the morning was hot, with every sign of growing hotter. And yet Mimi wore a heavy gown of some unflattering stuff and a long camel's-hair coat. Her face was oddly drawn.

"I don't feel awfully well," she said with a pale smile. "Did you have a nice trip, Mark?"

He made a face. "There's been a change in the plans; the design must be altered. I'll have to pose your back all over again."

"Oh . . . Darling." Mimi put down her toast. "Would you be terribly cross if . . . if I didn't pose for you?"

"Bother! Well, all right, dear. We'll begin tomorrow."

"I mean," murmured Mimi, picking up her fork, "I—I'd rather not pose at all . . . any more."

Gramaton set his cup down very, very slowly, as if he had

suddenly developed a griping ache in his arm. No one said anything.

"Of course, Mimi."

Ellery felt the need of fresh air.

Emilie Eames said lightly: "You've done something to the man, Mimi. When he was my husband he'd have thrown something."

It was all very confusing to Ellery. Gramaton smiled, and Mimi pecked at her omelet, and Dr. Varrow folded his napkin with absorption. When Jeff lumbered in, scratching his stubble, Ellery could have embraced him.

"Can't find the skunk nowheres," Jeff growled. "He didn't sleep in his bed last night, Mr. Gramaton."

"Who?" said Gramaton absently. "What?"

"Borcca. Didn't you want him for paintin'? He's gone."

Gramaton drew his blond brows together, concentrating. Miss Eames exclaimed hopefully: "Do you suppose he fell into the lake and was drowned?"

"This seems to be my morning for disappointments," said Gramaton, rising. "Would you care to come up to my shop, Queen? I'd be grateful if you'd allow me to sketch your head into the group." He walked out without looking back.

"I think," said Mimi faintly, "I have a headache."

When Ellery reached the studio he found Gramaton standing wide-legged, hands clenched behind his back. The room was curiously disordered; two chairs were overturned, and canvases cluttered the floor. Gramaton was glaring at the portrait of his ancestor. A hot breeze ruffled his hair; one of the windows on the glass wall stood open.

"This," said Gramaton in a gravelly voice, "is simply intolerable." Then his voice swelled into a roar; he sounded like a lion in agony. "Varrow! Emilie! Jeff!"

Ellery went to the portrait and squinted into the shadow. He stared, unbelieving.

Some time during the night, the fourth Lord Gramaton's heart had bled.

There was a smear of brownish stuff directly over the painted left breast. Some of it, while in a liquid state, had trickled in drops an inch or two. More of it was splattered down Lord Gramaton's waistcoat and over his belly. Whatever it was, there had been a good deal of it.

Gramaton made a whimpering noise, ripped the portrait from the wall, and flung it to the floor in the full light.

"Who did this?" he asked huskily.

Mimi covered her mouth. Dr. Varrow smiled. "Little boys have a habit of smearing filth on convenient walls, Mark."

Gramaton looked at him, breathing heavily. "Don't act so tragic, Mark," said Miss Eames. "It's just some moron's idea of a practical joke. Goodness knows there's enough paint lying around here."

Ellery stooped over the prostrate, wounded nobleman and sniffed. Then he rose and said: "But it isn't paint."

"Not paint?" echoed Miss Eames feebly. Gramaton paled, and Mimi closed her eyes and felt for a chair.

"I'm rather familiar with the concomitants of violence, and this looks remarkably like dry blood to me."

"Blood!"

Gramaton laughed. He ground his heels very deliberately into Lord Gramaton's face. He jumped up and down on the frame, cracking it in a dozen places. He crumpled the canvas and kicked the remains into the fireplace. He ignited a whole packet of matches and carefully pushed it under the débris. Then he stumbled out.

Ellery smiled apologetically. He bent over and managed to rip away a sample of brown-stained canvas before Lord Gramaton suffered complete cremation. When he rose, only Dr. Varrow remained in the room.

"Borcca," said Dr. Varrow thickly. "Borcca."

"These English," mumbled Ellery. "Old saws are true saws. No sense of humor at all. Could you test this for me at once, Dr. Varrow?"

When the doctor had gone Ellery, finding himself alone and the house wonderfully quiet, sat down in Gramaton's studio to think. While he thought, he looked. It seemed to him that something which had been on the studio floor the day before was no longer there. And then he remembered. It had been Gramaton's sharp-pointed palette-knife.

He went over to the north wall and stuck his head out of the open section of the window.

"He ain't anywheres," said Jeff, from behind him.

"Still looking for Borcca? Very sensible, Jeff."

"Aw, he's just skipped. And good riddance, the dog."

"Nevertheless, would you show me his room, please?"

The fat man blinked his shrewd eyes and scratched his hairy breast. Then he led the way to a room on the first floor of the same wing. The silence hummed.

"No," decided Ellery after a while, "Mr. Borcca didn't just skip out, Jeff. Until the moment he vanished he had every intention of staying, to judge from the undisturbed condition of his belongings. Nervous, though—look at those cigaret butts."

Closing Mr. Borcca's door softly, he left the house and tramped around until he stood below the north window of Gramaton's studio. There were flower beds here, and the soft loam was gay with pansies.

But someone or something had been very brutal with the pansies. Below Gramaton's studio window they lay crushed and broken, and imbedded in the earth, as if a considerable weight had landed heavily on them. Where the devastated area began, near the wall, there were two deep trenches in the loam, parallel and narrow scoops, with the impressions of a man's shoe at the lowest depth of each scoop.

The toes pointed away from the wall and were queerly turned inwards toward each other.

"Borcca wore shoes like that," muttered Ellery. He sucked his lower lip, standing still. Beyond the pansy bed lay a gravel walk; snaking across the walk from the two trenches led a faint trail, rough and irregular, about the width of a human body.

Jeff flapped his arms suddenly, as if he wanted to fly away. But he merely clumped off, shoulders sagging.

Pearl Angers and Emilie Eames came hurrying around the house. The actress was very pale.

"I came over to be neighborly, and Emilie told me the frightful——"

"How," asked Ellery absently, "is Mrs. Gramaton?"

"How would you think!" cried Miss Eames. "Oh, Mark's still the big stupid fool I know! Prowling his room like a bear thrashing up his temper. You'd think that, since it's his pet story, he'd appreciate the joke, anyway."

"Blood," said the Angers damply. "Blood, Emilie."

"Mimi's simply prostrated," said Miss Eames furiously. "Oh, Mark's an idiot! That cock-and-bull story! Joke!"

"I'm afraid," said Ellery, "that it isn't as much a joke as you seem to think." He pointed at the pansy bed.

"What," faltered the Angers, shrinking against her friend and pointing to the dim trail, "is—that?"

Ellery did not reply. He turned and slowly began to follow the trail, bent over and peering.

Miss Eames moistened her lips and stared from the open window of Gramaton's studio two stories above to the crushed area in the pansy bed directly below.

The actress giggled hysterically, staring at the trail Ellery was pursuing. "Why, it looks," she said in a stricken voice, "as if—someone—dragged a . . . body. . . ."

The two women joined hands like children and stumbled along behind.

The erratic trail meandered across the garden in zigzags and arcs; in its course it revealed a narrower track of thin parallel scrapings, as if shoes had dragged. When it entered the woods it became harder to follow, for the ground here was a confusion of leaf-mold, roots and twigs.

The women followed Ellery like sleepwalkers, making no

sound. Somewhere along the route Mark Gramaton caught up with them; he stalked behind on stiff iron legs.

It was very hot in the woods. Sweat dripped off their noses. And after a while Mimi, bundled up as if she were cold, crept up to her husband. He paid no attention. She dropped behind, whimpering.

As the underbrush grew more tangled the trail became even more difficult to trace. Ellery, leading the voiceless procession, had to skirt several places and skip over rotting logs. At one point the trail led under a tangle of bramble so wide and thick and impenetrable that it was impossible to accompany it, even on hands and knees. For a time Ellery lost the scent altogether. His eyes were unnaturally bright. Then, after a detour by way of a broad grove, he picked up the trail again.

Not long after, he stopped; they all stopped. In the center of the trail lay a gold cufflink. Ellery examined it—it was initialed exquisitely *B*—and dropped it in his pocket.

Gramaton's island pinched up near the middle. The pinched area was extensive, completely rock—a dangerous, boulder-strewn ankle-trap. The lake hemmed it in on two sides.

Here Ellery lost the trail again. He searched among the boulders for a while, but only a bloodhound could have retained hope there. So he stepped thoughtfully, with a curious lack of interest.

"Oh, look," said Pearl Angers in a shocked voice.

Miss Eames had her arms about Mimi, holding her up. Gramaton stood alone, staring stonily. Ellery picked his way to the Angers, who was perched perilously on a jutting bone of the rocky neck, pointing with horror into the lake.

The water was shallow there. Gleaming on the sandy bottom, at arm's length, lay Gramaton's palette-knife, patently hurled away.

Ellery seated himself on a boulder and lit a cigaret. He made no attempt to retrieve the knife; the lake had long since washed away any clues it might last night have betrayed.

The Angers restlessly eyed the lake, repelled and yet eager, searching, searching for something larger than a knife.

"Queen!" shouted a faraway voice. "Queen!"

Ellery called: "Here!" several times in a loud but weary voice, and resumed his cigaret.

Soon they heard someone thrashing toward them through the woods. In a few minutes Dr. Varrow appeared on the dead run.

"Queen," he panted. "It—*is*—blood! Human blood!" Seeing Gramaton he stopped, as if abashed.

Ellery nodded.

"Blood," repeated the Angers in a loathing voice. "And Borcca's missing. And you found his cufflink on that hideous trail." She shivered.

"Someone stabbed him to death in the studio last night," whispered Miss Eames, "and in the struggle his blood got on the portrait."

"And then either threw his body out the window," said the actress, barely audible, "or he fell out during the fight. And then, whoever it was—came down and dragged the body all the way through the woods to—to this horrible place, and . . ."

"We could probably," said Dr. Varrow thickly, "find the body ourselves, right here in the lake."

Gramaton said very slowly: "We ought to send for the police."

They all looked at Ellery, stricken by the word. But Ellery continued to smoke without saying anything.

"I don't suppose," faltered Miss Eames finally, "you can hope to *conceal* a—murder, can you?"

Gramaton began to trudge back in the direction of his house.

"Oh, just a moment," Ellery said, flinging his cigaret into

the lake. Gramaton stopped, without turning around. "Gramaton, you're a fool."

"What do you mean?" growled the artist. But he still did not turn around.

"Are you the nice chap you seem to be," demanded Ellery, "or are you what your wife and ex-wife and friends seem to think you are—a homicidal maniac?"

Gramaton wheeled then, his ugly face crimson. "All right!" he yelled. "I killed him!"

"No," cried Mimi, half-rising from her stone. "Mark, no!"

"Pshaw," said Ellery, "there's no need to be so vehement, Gramaton. A child could see you're protecting your wife— or think you are." Gramaton sank onto a boulder. "That," continued Ellery equably, "gives you a character. You don't know what to believe about your wife, but you're willing to confess to a murder you think she committed—just the same."

"I killed him, I say," said Gramaton sullenly.

"Killed whom, Gramaton?"

They all looked at him then. "Mr. Queen," cried Mimi. "No!"

"It's no use, Mrs. Gramaton," said Ellery. "All this would have been avoided if you'd been sensible enough to trust your husband in the first place. That's what husbands, poor saps, are for."

"But Borcca—" began Dr. Varrow.

"Ah, yes, Borcca. Yes, indeed, we must discuss Mr. Borcca. But first we must discuss our hostess's charming back."

"My back?" said Mimi faintly.

"What about my wife's back?" shouted Gramaton.

"Everything, or nearly," smiled Ellery, lighting another cigaret. "Smoke? You need one badly. . . . You see, your wife's back is not only beautiful, Gramaton; it's eloquent, too.

"I've been in Natchitauk over a week; I've had the pleasure of observing it on several precious occasions; it's always been bared to the world, as beautiful things should be; and in fact Mrs. Gramaton told me herself that you were so proud of it you selected her clothes—with an eye, I suppose, to keeping it constantly on exhibition."

Miss Eames made a muffled noise, and Mimi looked sick.

"This morning," drawled Ellery, "Mrs. Gramaton suddenly appears garbed in a heavy, all-concealing gown; she wears a long, all-concealing coat; she announces she will no longer pose for your mural, in which her nude back is the central motif. These despite the facts: first, that it is an extremely hot day; second, that up to late last night I myself saw her back bare and beautiful as ever; third, that she is well aware what it must mean to you to be denied suddenly, and without explanation, the inspiration of her charms in such an ambitious artistic undertaking as the New Arts mural. Yet," said Ellery, "she suddenly covers her back and refuses to pose. Why?"

Gramaton looked at his wife, his brow contorted.

"Shall I tell you why, Mrs. Gramaton?" said Ellery gently. "Because obviously you are *concealing* your back. Because obviously something happened between the time I left you last night and breakfast this morning that *forced* you to conceal your back. Because obviously something happened to your back last night which you don't want your husband to see, and which he would have to see if as usual you posed for him this morning. Am I right?"

Mimi Gramaton's lips moved, but she said nothing. Gramaton and the others stared at Ellery, bewildered.

"Of course I am," smiled Ellery, "Well, I said to myself, what could have happened to your back last night? Was there any clue? There certainly was—the portrait of the fourth Lord Gramaton!"

"The portrait?" repeated Miss Eames, wrinkling her nose.

"For, mark you, last night Lord Gramaton's breast bled

THE ADVENTURE OF

again. Ah, what a story! I left you in the studio, and
the noble lord bled, and this morning you concealed your
back. . . . Surely it makes sense? The bleeding picture
might have been a bad joke; it might have been—forgive
me—a supernatural phenomenon; but at least it *was* blood—
human blood, Dr. Varrow has established. Well, human
blood has to flow, and that means a wound. Whose wound?
Lord Gramaton's? Pshaw! Blood is blood, and canvas
doesn't wound easily. *Your* blood, Mrs. Gramaton, and *your*
wound, to be sure; otherwise why were you afraid to display
your back?"

"Oh Lord," said Gramaton. "Mimi—darling—" Mimi
began to weep and Gramaton buried his ugly face in his
hands.

"It was easy to reconstruct what must have happened. It was
in the studio; there are signs there of a tussle. You were attacked—with the palette-knife, of course; we found it thrown
away. You backed against the portrait, the wound in your
back streaming blood: Lord Gramaton was set flush with the
floor, and was lifesize, so your back-wound smeared Lord
Gramaton's breast in just the right place, happily for the
ghost-story. I assume you fainted, and Jeff—he was outside
when I left, so he must have been attracted by the sounds of
the struggle—found you, carried you to your room, and
treated your wound and kept his mouth shut like the loyal
soul he is, because you begged him to." Mimi nodded, sobbing.

"Mimi!" Gramaton sprang to her.

"But—Borcca," muttered Dr. Varrow. "I don't see——"

Ellery flicked ashes. "It's wonderful what the imagination is," he grinned. "Blood—Borcca missing—plenty of
motive for murder—the trail of a human body through the
woods . . . murder! How very illogical, and how very
human."

He puffed. "I saw, of course, that Borcca must have been
the attacker: the man threatened to kill Mrs. Gramaton yes-

terday in my hearing, and he was plainly insane with jealousy and a deep thwarted passion. What happened to Borcca? Ah, the open window. It had been shut when I saw it the night before. Now it was open. Below, in the pansy bed, the plain sign of a fallen body, two deep trenches in the soil showing where his feet must have landed. . . . In short, panicky, a coward, perhaps thinking he had committed murder, hearing Jeff lumbering upstairs, Borcca jumped out of Gramaton's window in a blind impulse to escape—and fell two stories."

"But how can you know he jumped?" frowned the Angers. "How do you know—Jeff, say, didn't catch and kill him and throw his dead body out and then drag it . . ."

"No," smiled Ellery. "The dragging marks stretched out a considerable distance through these woods. In one place, as you saw, it led under some brambles so thick that I couldn't have gone through it except on my belly; yet the trail went right through, didn't it? If Borcca was dead, and his body was being dragged, how did the murderer get the body through those brambles? In fact, why should he want to? Surely he wouldn't crawl himself at that point, hauling the body after him. It would have been easier to go by an unobstructed path nearby, as we did.

"So," said Ellery, rising and beginning to pick his way across the rocky neck, "it was evident that Borcca had *not* been dragged, *that Borcca had dragged himself,* crawling on his stomach. Therefore he was alive, and no murder had been committed at all, you see."

Slowly they began to follow. Gramaton had his arm about Mimi, humbly, his big chin on his breast.

"But why should he crawl all that distance?" demanded Dr. Varrow. "He might crawl *to* the woods to escape being seen, but once in the woods, at night, surely he didn't have to . . ."

"Exactly; he didn't have to," said Ellery. "But he crawled nevertheless. Then he *must* have had to . . . He had jumped two stories. He had landed feet first, and from the turning-in of the toemarks in the pansy bed his feet had twisted inward in landing. So, I said to myself, he must have broken his ankles. You see?"

He stopped. They stopped. Ellery had led them to the end of the path on the eastward part of the island. They could see the abandoned shack through the trees.

"A man with two broken feet—both were broken, because the trail showed two parallel shoe-marks dragging, indicating that he could not use even one leg for pushing—cannot swim, without foot leverage he can hardly be conceived as rowing, and there is neither a motorboat nor a bridge on this island. I felt sure," he said in a low voice, "that he was therefore still on the island."

Gramaton growled deep in his throat, like a bloodhound.

"And in view of Jeff's inability to find our Mr. Borcca this morning, it also seemed probable that he had taken refuge in that shack." Ellery looked into Gramaton's gray eyes. "For more than twelve hours the creature has been cowering in there, in intense pain, thinking himself a murderer, waiting to be routed out for the capital punishment he believes he's earned. I imagine he's been punished enough, don't you Gramaton?"

The big man's eyes blinked. Then, without a word, he said: "Mimi?" in a low voice, and she looked up at him and took his arm and he turned her carefully around and began to walk her back to the western end of the island.

Offshore, resting on his oars like a watchful Buddha, sat Jeff.

"You may as well go back, too," said Ellery gently to the two women. He waved his arm at Jeff. "Dr. Varrow and I have a nasty job to—finish."

A Unique Group of
**ELLERY QUEEN
SPORTS MYSTERIES**

**MAN BITES DOG
LONG SHOT
MIND OVER MATTER
TROJAN HORSE**

MAN BITES DOG

MAN BITES DOG

MAN BITES DOG

Anyone observing the tigerish pacings, the gnawings of lip, the contortions of brow, and the fierce melancholy which characterized the conduct of Mr. Ellery Queen, the noted sleuth, during those early October days in Hollywood, would have said reverently that the great man's intellect was once more locked in titanic struggle with the forces of evil.

"Paula," Mr. Queen said to Paula Paris, "I am going mad."

"I hope," said Miss Paris tenderly, "it's love."

Mr. Queen paced, swathed in yards of thought. Queenly Miss Paris observed him with melting eyes. When he had first encountered her, during his investigation of the double murder of Blythe Stuart and Jack Royle, the famous motion picture stars,* Miss Paris had been in the grip of a morbid psychology. She had been in deathly terror of crowds. "Crowd phobia," the doctors called it. Mr. Queen had cured her by the curious method of making love to her. And now she was infected by the cure.

"Is it?" asked Miss Paris, her heart in her eyes.

"Eh?" said Mr. Queen. "What? Oh, no. I mean—it's the World Series." He looked savage. "Don't you realize what's happening? The New York Giants and the New York Yankees are waging mortal combat to determine the baseball championship of the world, and I'm three thousand miles away!"

"Oh," said Miss Paris. Then she said cleverly: "You poor darling."

"Never missed a New York series before," wailed Mr. Queen. "Driving me cuckoo. And what a battle! Great-

* Related in *The Four of Hearts*, by Ellery Queen. Frederick A. Stokes Company, 1938.

est series ever played. Moore and DiMaggio have done miracles in the outfield. Giants have pulled a triple play. Goofy
Gomez struck out fourteen men to win the first game.
Hubbell's pitched a one-hit shutout. And today Dickey
came up in the ninth inning with the bases loaded, two out,
and the Yanks three runs behind, and slammed a homer over
the right-field stands!"

"Is that good?" asked Miss Paris.

"Good!" howled Mr. Queen. "It merely sent the series into
a seventh game."

"Poor darling," said Miss Paris again, and she picked up her
telephone. When she set it down she said: "Weather's
threatening in the East. Tomorrow the New York Weather
Bureau expects heavy rains."

Mr. Queen stared wildly. "You mean——"

"I mean that you're taking tonight's plane for the East.
And you'll see your beloved seventh game day after tomorrow."

"Paula, you're a genius!" Then Mr. Queen's face fell.
"But the studio, tickets . . . *Bigre!* I'll tell the studio I'm
down with elephantiasis, and I'll wire dad to snare a box.
With his pull at City Hall, he ought to—Paula, I don't know
what I'd do . . ."

"You might," suggested Miss Paris, "kiss me . . . good-
bye."

Mr. Queen did so, absently. Then he started. "Not at
all! You're coming with me!"

"That's what I had in mind," said Miss Paris contentedly.

And so Wednesday found Miss Paris and Mr. Queen at the
Polo Grounds, ensconced in a field box behind the Yankees'
dugout.

Mr. Queen glowed, he revelled, he was radiant. While
Inspector Queen, with the suspiciousness of all fathers, engaged Paula in exploratory conversation, Ellery filled his lap
and Paula's with peanut hulls, consumed frankfurters and

soda pop immoderately, made hypercritical comments on the appearance of the various athletes, derided the Yankees, extolled the Giants, evolved complicated fifty-cent bets with Detective-Sergeant Velie, of the Inspector's staff, and leaped to his feet screaming with fifty thousand other maniacs as the news came that Carl Hubbell, the beloved Meal Ticket of the Giants, would oppose Señor El Goofy Gomez, the ace of the Yankee staff, on the mound.

"Will the Yanks murder that apple today!" predicted the Sergeant, who was an incurable Yankee worshiper. "And will Goofy mow 'em down!"

"Four bits," said Mr. Queen coldly, "say the Yanks don't score three earned runs off Carl."

"It's a pleasure!"

"I'll take a piece of that, Sergeant," chuckled a handsome man to the front of them, in a rail seat. "Hi, Inspector. Swell day for it, eh?"

"Jimmy Connor!" exclaimed Inspector Queen. "The old Song-and-Dance Man in person. Say, Jimmy, you never met my son Ellery, did you? Excuse me. Miss Paris, this is the famous Jimmy Connor, God's gift to Broadway."

"Glad to meet you, Miss Paris," smiled the Song-and-Dance Man, sniffing at his orchidaceous lapel. "Read your *Seeing Stars* column, every day. Meet Judy Starr."

Miss Paris smiled, and the woman beside Jimmy Connor smiled back, and just then three Yankee players strolled over to the box and began to jeer at Connor for having had to take seats behind the hated Yankee dugout.

Judy Starr was sitting oddly still. She was the famous Judy Starr who had been discovered by Florenz Ziegfeld—a second Marilyn Miller, the critics called her; dainty and pretty, with a perky profile and great honey-colored eyes, who had sung and danced her way into the heart of New York. Her day of fame was almost over now. Perhaps, thought Paula, staring at Judy's profile, that explained the pinch of her little mouth, the fine lines about her tragic eyes, the singing tension of her figure.

Perhaps. But Paula was not sure. There was immediacy, a defense against a palpable and present danger, in Judy Starr's tautness. Paula looked about. And at once her eyes narrowed.

Across the rail of the box, in the box at their left, sat a very tall, leather-skinned, silent and intent man. The man, too, was staring out at the field, in an attitude curiously like that of Judy Starr, whom he could have touched by extending his big, ropy, muscular hand across the rail. And on the man's other side there sat a woman whom Paula recognized instantly. Lotus Verne, the motion picture actress!

Lotus Verne was a gorgeous, full-blown redhead with deep mercury-colored eyes who had come out of Northern Italy Ludovica Vernicchi, changed her name, and flashed across the Hollywood skies in a picture called *Woman of Bali*, a color-film in which loving care had been lavished on the display possibilities of her dark, full, dangerous body. With fame, she had developed a passion for press-agentry, borzois in pairs, and tall brown men with muscles. She was arrayed in sun-yellow, and she stood out among the women in the field boxes like a butterfly in a mass of grubs. By contrast little Judy Starr, in her flame-colored outfit, looked almost old and dowdy.

Paula nudged Ellery, who was critically watching the Yankees at batting practice. "Ellery," she said softly, "who is that big, brown, attractive man in the next box?"

Lotus Verne said something to the brown man, and suddenly Judy Starr said something to the Song-and-Dance Man; and then the two women exchanged the kind of glance women use when there is no knife handy.

Ellery said absently: "Who? Oh! That's Big Bill Tree."

"Tree?" repeated Paula. "Big Bill Tree?"

"Greatest left-handed pitcher major-league baseball ever saw," said Mr. Queen, staring reverently at the brown man.

"Six feet three inches of bull-whip and muscle, with a temper as sudden as the hook on his curve ball and a change of pace that fooled the greatest sluggers of baseball for fifteen years. What a man!"

"Yes, isn't he?" smiled Miss Paris.

"Now what does that mean?" demanded Mr. Queen.

"It takes greatness to escort a lady like Lotus Verne to a ball game," said Paula, "to find your wife sitting within spitting distance in the next box, and to carry it off as well as your muscular friend Mr. Tree is doing."

"That's right," said Mr. Queen softly. "Judy Starr *is* Mrs. Bill Tree."

He groaned as Joe DiMaggio hit a ball to the clubhouse clock.

"Funny," said Miss Paris, her clever eyes inspecting in turn the four people before her: Lotus Verne, the Hollywood siren; Big Bill Tree, the ex-baseball pitcher; Judy Starr, Tree's wife; and Jimmy Connor, the Song-and-Dance Man, Mrs. Tree's escort. Two couples, two boxes . . . and no sign of recognition. "Funny," murmured Miss Paris. "From the way Tree courted Judy you'd have thought the marriage would outlast eternity. He snatched her from under Jimmy Connor's nose one night at the Winter Garden, drove her up to Greenwich at eighty miles an hour, and married her before she could catch her breath."

"Yes," said Mr. Queen politely. "Come on, you Giants!" he yelled, as the Giants trotted out for batting practice.

"And then something happened," continued Miss Paris reflectively. "Tree went to Hollywood to make a baseball picture, met Lotus Verne, and the wench took the overgrown country boy the way the overgrown country boy had taken Judy Starr. What a fall was there, my baseball-minded friend."

"What a wallop!" cried Mr. Queen enthusiastically, as Mel Ott hit one that bounced off the right-field fence.

"And Big Bill yammered for a divorce, and Judy refused to

give it to him because she loved him, I suppose," said Paula softly—"and now this. How interesting."

Big Bill Tree twisted in his seat a little; and Judy Starr was still and pale, staring out of her tragic, honey-colored eyes at the Yankee bat-boy and giving him unwarranted delusions of grandeur. Jimmy Connor continued to exchange sarcastic greetings with Yankee players, but his eyes kept shifting back to Judy's face. And beautiful Lotus Verne's arm crept about Tree's shoulders.

"I don't like it," murmured Miss Paris a little later.

"You don't like it?" said Mr. Queen. "Why, the game hasn't even started."

"I don't mean your game, silly. I mean the quadrangular situation in front of us."

"Look, darling," said Mr. Queen. "I flew three thousand miles to see a ball game. There's only one angle that interests me—the view from this box of the greatest li'l ol' baseball tussle within the memory of gaffers. I yearn, I strain, I hunger to see it. Play with your quadrangle, but leave me to my baseball."

"I've always been psychic," said Miss Paris, paying no attention. "This is—bad. Something's going to happen."

Mr. Queen grinned. "I know what. The deluge. See what's coming."

Someone in the grandstand had recognized the celebrities, and a sea of people was rushing down on the two boxes. They thronged the aisle behind the boxes, waving pencils and papers, and pleading. Big Bill Tree and Lotus Verne ignored their pleas for autographs; but Judy Starr with a curious eagerness signed paper after paper with the yellow pencils thrust at her by people leaning over the rail. Good-naturedly Jimmy Connor scrawled his signature, too.

"Little Judy," sighed Miss Paris, setting her natural straw straight as an autograph-hunter knocked it over her eyes, "is flustered and unhappy. Moistening the tip of your pencil with your tongue is scarcely a mark of poise. Seated next to her Lotus-bound husband, she hardly knows what she's doing, poor thing."

"Neither do I," growled Mr. Queen, fending off an octopus which turned out to be eight pleading arms offering score-cards.

Big Bill sneezed, groped for a handkerchief, and held it to his nose, which was red and swollen. "Hey, Mac," he called irritably to a red-coated usher. "Do somethin' about this mob, huh?" He sneezed again. "Damn this hay-fever!"

"The touch of earth," said Miss Paris. "But definitely attractive."

"Should 'a' seen Big Bill the day he pitched that World Series final against the Tigers," chuckled Sergeant Velie. "He was sure attractive that day. Pitched a no-hit shutout!"

Inspector Queen said: "Ever hear the story behind that final game, Miss Paris? The night before, a gambler named Sure Shot McCoy, who represented a betting syndicate, called on Big Bill and laid down fifty grand in spot cash in return for Bill's promise to throw the next day's game. Bill took the money, told his manager the whole story, donated the bribe to a fund for sick ball players, and the next day shut out the Tigers without a hit."

"Byronic, too," murmured Miss Paris.

"So then Sure Shot, badly bent," grinned the Inspector, "called on Bill for the payoff. Bill knocked him down two flights of stairs."

"Wasn't that dangerous?"

"I guess," smiled the Inspector, "you could say so. That's why you see that plug-ugly with the smashed nose sitting over there right behind Tree's box. He's Mr. Terrible Turk, late of Cicero, and since that night Big Bill's shadow. You don't see Mr. Turk's right hand, because Mr. Turk's right hand is holding on to an automatic under his jacket. You'll notice, too, that Mr. Turk hasn't for a second taken his eyes

off that pasty-cheeked customer eight rows up, whose name
is Sure Shot McCoy."

Paula stared. "But what a silly thing for Tree to do!"

"Well, yes," drawled Inspector Queen, "seeing that when
he popped Mr. McCoy Big Bill snapped two of the carpal
bones of his pitching wrist and wrote finis to his baseball
career."

Big Bill Tree hauled himself to his feet, whispered something to the Verne woman, who smiled coyly, and left his
box. His bodyguard, Turk, jumped up; but the big man
shook his head, waved aside a crowd of people, and vaulted
up the concrete steps toward the rear of the grandstand.

And then Judy Starr said something bitter and hot and
desperate across the rail to the woman her husband had
brought to the Polo Grounds. Lotus Verne's mercurial eyes
glittered, and she replied in a careless, insulting voice that
made Bill Tree's wife sit up stiffly. Jimmy Connor began to
tell the one about Walter Winchell and the Seven Dwarfs
. . . loudly and fast.

The Verne woman began to paint her rich lips with short,
vicious strokes of her orange lipstick; and Judy Starr's flame
kid glove tightened on the rail between them.

And after a while Big Bill returned and sat down again.
Judy said something to Jimmy Connor, and the Song-and-
Dance Man slid over one seat to his right, and Judy slipped
into Connor's seat; so that between her and her husband there
was now not only the box rail but an empty chair as well.

Lotus Verne put her arm about Tree's shoulders again.

Tree's wife fumbled inside her flame suède bag. She said
suddenly: "Jimmy, buy me a frankfurter."

Connor ordered a dozen. Big Bill scowled. He jumped up
and ordered some, too. Connor tossed the vendor two one-
dollar bills and waved him away.

A new sea deluged the two boxes, and Tree turned round,
annoyed. "All right, all right, Mac," he growled at the red-

coat struggling with the pressing mob. "We don't want a
riot here. I'll take six. Just six. Let's have 'em."

There was a rush that almost upset the attendant. The
rail behind the boxes was a solid line of fluttering hands, arms,
and scorecards.

"Mr. Tree—said—six!" panted the usher; and he grabbed
a pencil and card from one of the outstretched hands and gave
them to Tree. The overflow of pleaders spread to the next
box. Judy Starr smiled her best professional smile and reached
for a pencil and card. A group of players on the field, seeing
what was happening, ran over to the field rail and handed
her scorecards, too, so that she had to set her half-consumed
frankfurter down on the empty seat beside her. Big Bill set
his frankfurter down on the same empty seat; he licked the
pencil long and absently and began to inscribe his name in
the stiff, laborious hand of a man unused to writing.

The attendant howled: "That's six, now! Mr. Tree said
just six, so that's all!" as if God Himself had said six; and the
crowd groaned, and Big Bill waved his immense paw and
reached over to the empty seat in the other box to lay hold
of his half-eaten frankfurter. But his wife's hand got there
first and fumbled round; and it came up with Tree's frankfurter. The big brown man almost spoke to her then; but
he did not, and he picked up the remaining frankfurter,
stuffed it into his mouth, and chewed away, but not as if
he enjoyed its taste.

Mr. Ellery Queen was looking at the four people before
him with a puzzled, worried expression. Then he caught Miss
Paula Paris's amused glance and blushed angrily.

The groundkeepers had just left the field and the senior
umpire was dusting off the plate to the roar of the crowd
when Lotus Verne, who thought a double play was something
by Eugene O'Neill, flashed a strange look at Big Bill Tree.

"Bill! Don't you feel well?"

The big ex-pitcher, a sickly blue beneath his tanned skin,

put his hand to his eyes and shook his head as if to clear it.

"It's the hot dog," snapped Lotus. "No more for you!"

Tree blinked and began to say something, but just then Carl Hubbell completed his warming-up, Crosetti marched to the plate, Harry Danning tossed the ball to his second-baseman, who flipped it to Hubbell and trotted back to his position yipping like a terrier.

The voice of the crowd exploded in one ear-splitting burst. And then silence.

And Crosetti swung at the first ball Hubbell pitched and smashed it far over Joe Moore's head for a triple.

Jimmy Connor gasped as if someone had thrust a knife into his heart. But Detective-Sergeant Velie was bellowing: "Wha'd I tell you? It's gonna be a massacree!"

"What is everyone shouting for?" asked Paula.

Mr. Queen nibbled his nails as Danning strolled halfway to the pitcher's box. But Hubbell pulled his long pants up, grinning. Red Rolfe was waving a huge bat at the plate. Danning trotted back. Manager Bill Terry had one foot up on the edge of the Giant dugout, his chin on his fist, looking anxious. The infield came in to cut off the run.

Again fifty thousand people made no single little sound.

And Hubbell struck out Rolfe, DiMaggio, and Gehrig.

Mr. Queen shrieked his joy with the thousands as the Giants came whooping in. Jimmy Connor did an Indian war-dance in the box. Sergeant Velie looked aggrieved. Señor Gomez took his warm-up pitches, the umpire used his whiskbroom on the plate again, and Jo-Jo Moore, the Thin Man, ambled up with his war club.

He walked. Bartell fanned. But Jeep Ripple singled off Flash Gordon's shins on the first pitch; and there were Moore on third and Ripple on first, one out, and Little Mel Ott at bat.

Big Bill Tree got half out of his seat, looking surprised, and then dropped to the concrete floor of the box as if somebody had slammed him behind the ear with a fast ball.

Lotus screamed. Judy, Bill's wife, turned like a shot, shaking. People in the vicinity jumped up. Three red-coated attendants hurried down, preceded by the hard-looking Mr. Turk. The bench-warmers stuck their heads over the edge of the Yankee dugout to stare.

"Fainted," growled Turk, on his knees beside the prostrate athlete.

"Loosen his collar," moaned Lotus Verne. "He's so p-pale!"

"Have to git him outa here."

"Yes. Oh, yes!"

The attendants and Turk lugged the big man off, long arms dangling in the oddest way. Lotus stumbled along beside him, biting her lips nervously.

"I think," began Judy in a quivering voice, rising.

But Jimmy Connor put his hand on her arm, and she sank back.

And in the next box Mr. Ellery Queen, on his feet from the instant Tree collapsed, kept looking after the forlorn procession, puzzled, mad about something; until somebody in the stands squawked: "SIDDOWN!" and he sat down.

"Oh, I knew something would happen," whispered Paula.

"Nonsense!" said Mr. Queen shortly. "Fainted, that's all."

Inspector Queen said: "There's Sure Shot McCoy not far off. I wonder if——"

"Too many hot dogs," snapped his son. "What's the matter with you people? Can't I see my ball game in peace?" And he howled: "Come o-o-on, Mel!"

Ott lifted his right leg into the sky and swung. The ball whistled into right field, a long long fly, Selkirk racing madly back after it. He caught it by leaping four feet into the air with his back against the barrier. Moore was off for the plate like a streak and beat the throw to Bill Dickey by inches.

"Yip-ee!" Thus Mr. Queen.

The Giants trotted out to their positions at the end of the first inning leading one to nothing.

Up in the press box the working gentlemen of the press

tore into their chores, recalling Carl Hubbell's similar feat in the All-Star game when he struck out the five greatest batters of the American League in succession; praising Twinkletoes Selkirk for his circus catch; and incidentally noting that Big Bill Tree, famous ex-hurler of the National League, had fainted in a field box during the first inning. Joe Williams of the *World-Telegram* said it was excitement, Hype Igoe opined that it was a touch of sun—Big Bill never wore a hat —and Frank Graham of the *Sun* guessed it was too many frankfurters.

Paula Paris said quietly: "I should think, with your detective instincts, Mr. Queen, you would seriously question the 'fainting' of Mr. Tree."

Mr. Queen squirmed and finally mumbled: "It's coming to a pretty pass when a man's instincts aren't his own. Velie, go see what really happened to him."

"I wanna watch the game," howled Velie. "Why don't you go yourself, maestro?"

"And possibly," said Mr. Queen, "you ought to go too, dad. I have a hunch it may lie in your jurisdiction."

Inspector Queen regarded his son for some time. Then he rose and sighed: "Come along, Thomas."

Sergeant Velie growled something about some people always spoiling other people's fun and why the hell did he ever have to become a cop; but he got up and obediently followed the Inspector.

Mr. Queen nibbled his fingernails and avoided Miss Paris's accusing eyes.

The second inning was uneventful. Neither side scored.

As the Giants took the field again, an usher came running down the concrete steps and whispered into Jim Connor's ear. The Song-and-Dance Man blinked. He rose slowly. "Excuse me, Judy."

Judy grasped the rail. "It's Bill. Jimmy, tell me."

"Now, Judy——"

"Something's happened to Bill!" Her voice shrilled, and then broke. She jumped up. "I'm going with you."

Connor smiled as if he had just lost a bet, and then he took Judy's arm and hurried her away.

Paula Paris stared after them, breathing hard.

Mr. Queen beckoned the redcoat. "What's the trouble?" he demanded.

"Mr. Tree passed out. Some young doc in the crowd tried to pull him out of it up at the office, but he couldn't, and he's startin' to look worried——"

"I knew it!" cried Paula as the man darted away. "Ellery Queen, are you going to sit here and do *nothing*?"

But Mr. Queen defiantly set his jaw. Nobody was going to jockey him out of seeing this battle of giants; no, ma'am!

There were two men out when Frank Crosetti stepped up to the plate for his second time at bat and, with the count two all, plastered a wicked single over Ott's head.

And, of course, Sergeant Velie took just that moment to amble down and say, his eyes on the field: "Better come along, Master Mind. The old man wouldst have a word with thou. Ah, I see Frankie's on first. Smack it, Red!"

Mr. Queen watched Rolfe take a ball. "Well?" he said shortly. Paula's lips were parted.

"Big Bill's just kicked the bucket. What happened in the second inning?"

"He's . . . *dead*?" gasped Paula.

Mr. Queen rose involuntarily. Then he sat down again. "Damn it," he roared, "it isn't fair. I won't go!"

"Suit yourself. Attaboy, Rolfe!" bellowed the Sergeant as Rolfe singled sharply past Bartell and Crosetti pulled up at second base. "Far's I'm concerned, it's open and shut. The little woman did it with her own little hands."

"Judy *Starr*?" said Miss Paris.

"Bill's wife?" said Mr. Queen. "What are you talking about?"

"That's right, little Judy. She poisoned his hot dog."
Velie chuckled. "Man bites dog, and—zowie."

"Has she confessed?" snapped Mr. Queen.

"Naw. But you know dames. She gave Bill the business,
all right. C'mon, Joe! And I gotta go. What a life."

Mr. Queen did not look at Miss Paris. He bit his lip.
"Here, Velie, wait a minute."

DiMaggio hit a long fly that Leiber caught without moving in his tracks, and the Yankees were retired without a
score.

"Ah," said Mr. Queen. "Good old Hubbell." And as
the Giants trotted in, he took a fat roll of bills from his
pocket, climbed onto his seat, and began waving greenbacks
at the spectators in the reserved seats behind the box. Sergeant Velie and Miss Paris stared at him in amazement.

"I'll give five bucks," yelled Mr. Queen, waving the money,
"for every autograph Bill Tree signed before the game! In
this box right here! Five bucks, gentlemen! Come and get
it!"

"You nuts?" gasped the Sergeant.

The mob gaped, and then began to laugh, and after a few
moments a pair of sheepish-looking men came down, and then
two more, and finally a fifth. An attendant ran over to find
out what was the matter.

"Are you the usher who handled the crowd around Bill
Tree's box before the game, when he was giving autographs?"
demanded Mr. Queen.

"Yes, sir. But, look, we can't allow——"

"Take a gander at these five men . . . You, bud? Yes,
that's Tree's handwriting. Here's your fin. Next!" and
Mr. Queen went down the line, handing out five-dollar bills
with abandon in return for five dirty scorecards with Tree's
scrawl on them.

"Anybody else?" he called out, waving his roll of bills.

But nobody else appeared, although there was ungentle

badinage from the stands. Sergeant Velie stood there shaking his big head. Miss Paris looked intensely curious.

"Who didn't come down?" rapped Mr. Queen.

"Huh?" said the usher, his mouth open.

"There were six autographs. Only five people turned up. Who was the sixth man? Speak up!"

"Oh." The redcoat scratched his ear. "Say, it wasn't a man. It was a kid."

"A *boy*?"

"Yeah, a little squirt in knee-pants."

Mr. Queen looked unhappy. Velie growled: "Sometimes I think society's takin' an awful chance lettin' you run around loose," and the two men left the box. Miss Paris, bright-eyed, followed.

"Have to clear this mess up in a hurry," muttered Mr. Queen. "Maybe we'll still be able to catch the late innings."

Sergeant Velie led the way to an office, before which a policeman was lounging. He opened the door, and inside they found the Inspector pacing. Turk, the thug, was standing with a scowl over a long still thing on a couch covered with newspapers. Jimmy Connor sat between the two women; and none of the three so much as stirred a foot. They were all pale and breathing heavily.

"This is Dr. Fielding," said Inspector Queen, indicating an elderly white-haired man standing quietly by a window. "He was Tree's physician. He happened to be in the park watching the game when the rumor reached his ears that Tree had collapsed. So he hurried up here to see what he could do."

Ellery went to the couch and pulled the newspaper off Bill Tree's still head. Paula crossed swiftly to Judy Starr and said: "I'm horribly sorry, Mrs. Tree," but the woman, her eyes closed, did not move. After a while Ellery dropped the newspaper back into place and said irritably: "Well, well, let's have it."

"A young doctor," said the Inspector, "got here before Dr.

Fielding did, and treated Tree for fainting. I guess it was his fault——"

"Not at all," said Dr. Fielding sharply. "The early picture was compatible with fainting, from what he told me. He tried the usual restorative methods—even injected caffeine and picrotoxin. But there was no convulsion, and he didn't happen to catch that odor of bitter almonds."

"Prussic!" said Ellery. "Taken orally?"

"Yes. HCN—hydrocyanic acid, or prussic, as you prefer. I suspected it at once because—well," said Dr. Fielding in a grim voice, "because of something that occurred in my office only the other day."

"What was that?"

"I had a two-ounce bottle of hydrocyanic acid on my desk —I sometimes use it in minute quantities as a cardiac stimulant. Mrs. Tree," the doctor's glance flickered over the silent woman, "happened to be in my office, resting in preparation for a metabolism test. I left her alone. By a coincidence, Bill Tree dropped in the same morning for a physical check-up. I saw another patient in another room, returned, gave Mrs. Tree her test, saw her out, and came back with Tree. It was then I noticed the bottle, which had been plainly marked DANGER—POISON, was missing from my desk. I thought I had mislaid it, but now . . ."

"I didn't take it," said Judy Starr in a lifeless voice, still not opening her eyes. "I never even saw it."

The Song-and-Dance Man took her limp hand and gently stroked it.

"No hypo marks on the body," said Dr. Fielding dryly. "And I am told that fifteen to thirty minutes before Tree collapsed he ate a frankfurter under . . . peculiar conditions."

"I didn't!" screamed Judy. "I didn't do it!" She pressed her face, sobbing, against Connor's orchid.

Lotus Verne quivered. "She made him pick up her frankfurter. I saw it. They both laid their frankfurters down on that empty seat, and she picked up his. So he had to pick up hers. She poisoned her own frankfurter and then saw to it that he ate it by mistake. Poisoner!" She glared hate at Judy.

"Wench," said Miss Paris *sotto voce*, glaring hate at Lotus.

"In other words," put in Ellery impatiently, "Miss Starr is convicted on the usual two counts, motive and opportunity. Motive—her jealousy of Miss Verne and her hatred—an assumption—of Bill Tree, her husband. And opportunity both to lay hands on the poison in your office, Doctor, and to sprinkle some on her frankfurter, contriving to exchange hers for his while they were both autographing scorecards."

"She hated him," snarled Lotus. "And me for having taken him from her!"

"Be quiet, you," said Mr. Queen. He opened the corridor door and said to the policeman outside: "Look, McGillicuddy, or whatever your name is, go tell the announcer to make a speech over the loud-speaker system. By the way, what's the score now?"

"Still one to skunk," said the officer. "Them boys Hubbell an' Gomez are hot, what I mean."

"The announcer is to ask the little boy who got Bill Tree's autograph just before the game to come to this office. If he does, he'll receive a ball, bat, pitcher's glove, and an autographed picture of Tree in uniform to hang over his itsy-bitsy bed. Scram!"

"Yes, *sir*," said the officer.

"King Carl pitching his heart out," grumbled Mr. Queen, shutting the door, "and me strangulated by this blamed thing. Well, dad, do you think, too, that Judy Starr dosed that frankfurter?"

"What else can I think?" said the Inspector absently. His ears were cocked for the faint crowd-shouts from the park.

"Judy Starr," replied his son, "didn't poison her husband any more than I did."

Judy looked up slowly, her mouth muscles twitching. Paula said, gladly: "You wonderful man!"

"She didn't?" said the Inspector, looking alert.

"The frankfurter theory," snapped Mr. Queen, "is too screwy for words. For Judy to have poisoned her husband, she had to unscrew the cap of a bottle and douse her hot dog on the spot with the hydrocyanic acid. Yet Jimmy Connor was seated by her side, and in the only period in which she could possibly have poisoned the frankfurter a group of Yankee ball players was *standing before her* across the field rail getting her autograph. Were they all accomplices? And how could she have known Big Bill would lay his hot dog on that empty seat? The whole thing is absurd."

A roar from the stands made him continue hastily: "There was one plausible theory that fitted the facts. When I heard that Tree had died of poisoning, I recalled that at the time he was autographing the six scorecards, *he had thoroughly licked the end of a pencil* which had been handed to him with one of the cards. It was possible, then, that the pencil he licked had been poisoned. So I offered to buy the six autographs."

Paula regarded him tenderly, and Velie said: "I'll be a so-and-so if he didn't."

"I didn't expect the poisoner to come forward, but I knew the innocent ones would. Five claimed the money. The sixth, the missing one, the usher informed me, had been a small boy."

"A kid poisoned Bill?" growled Turk, speaking for the first time. "You're crazy from the heat."

"In spades," added the Inspector.

"Then why didn't the boy come forward?" put in Paula quickly. "Go on, darling!"

"He didn't come forward, not because he was guilty but because he wouldn't sell Bill Tree's autograph for anything. No, obviously a hero-worshiping boy wouldn't try to poison the great Bill Tree. Then, just as obviously, he didn't realize what he was doing. Consequently, he must have been an innocent tool. The question was—and still is—of whom?"

"Sure Shot," said the Inspector slowly.

Lotus Verne sprang to her feet, her eyes glittering. "Perhaps Judy Starr didn't poison that frankfurter, but if she didn't then she hired that boy to give Bill——"

Mr. Queen said disdainfully: "Miss Starr didn't leave the box once." Someone knocked on the corridor door and he opened it. For the first time he smiled. When he shut the door they saw that his arm was about the shoulders of a boy with brown hair and quick clever eyes. The boy was clutching a scorecard tightly.

"They say over the announcer," mumbled the boy, "that I'll get a autographed pi'ture of Big Bill Tree if . . ." He stopped, abashed at their strangely glinting eyes.

"And you'll certainly get it, too," said Mr. Queen heartily. "What's your name, sonny?"

"Fenimore Feigenspan," replied the boy, edging toward the door. "Gran' Concourse, Bronx. Here's the scorecard. How about the pi'ture?"

"Let's see that, Fenimore," said Mr. Queen. "When did Bill Tree give you this autograph?"

"Before the game. He said he'd on'y give six——"

"Where's the pencil you handed him, Fenimore?"

The boy looked suspicious, but he dug into a bulging pocket and brought forth one of the ordinary yellow pencils sold at the park with scorecards. Ellery took it from him gingerly, and Dr. Fielding took it from Ellery, and sniffed its tip. He nodded, and for the first time a look of peace came over Judy Starr's still face and she dropped her head tiredly to Connor's shoulder.

Mr. Queen ruffled Fenimore Feigenspan's hair. "That's swell, Fenimore. Somebody gave you that pencil while the Giants were at batting practice, isn't that so?"

"Yeah." The boy stared at him.

"Who was it?" asked Mr. Queen lightly.

"I dunno. A big guy with a coat an' a turned-down hat an' a mustache, an' big black sun-glasses. I couldn't see his face good. Where's my pi'ture? I wanna see the game!"

"Just where was it that this man gave you the pencil?"

"In the—" Fenimore paused, glancing at the ladies with embarrassment. Then he muttered: "Well, I hadda go, an' this guy says—in there—he's ashamed to ask her for her autograph, so would I do it for him——"

"What? What's that?" exclaimed Mr. Queen. "Did you say 'her'?"

"Sure," said Fenimore. "The dame, he says, wearin' the red hat an' red dress an' red gloves in the field box near the Yanks' dugout, he says. He even took me outside an' pointed down to where she was sittin'. Say!" cried Fenimore, goggling. "That's her! That's the dame!" and he levelled a grimy forefinger at Judy Starr.

Judy shivered and felt blindly for the Song-and-Dance Man's hand.

"Let me get this straight, Fenimore," said Mr. Queen softly. "This man with the sun-glasses asked you to get this lady's autograph for him, and gave you the pencil and scorecard to get it with?"

"Yeah, an' two bucks too, sayin' he'd meet me after the game to pick up the card, but——"

"But you didn't get the lady's autograph for him, did you? You went down to get it, and hung around waiting for your chance, but then you spied Big Bill Tree, your hero, in the next box and forgot all about the lady, didn't you?"

The boy shrank back. "I didn't mean to, honest, Mister. I'll give the two bucks back!"

"And seeing Big Bill there, your hero, you went right over to get *his* autograph for *yourself*, didn't you?" Fenimore nodded, frightened. "You gave the usher the pencil and scorecard this man with the sun-glasses had handed you,

and the usher turned the pencil and scorecard over to Bill
Tree in the box—wasn't that the way it happened?"

"Y-yes, sir, an' . . ." Fenimore twisted out of Ellery's
grasp, "an' so I—I gotta go." And before anyone could stop
him he was indeed gone, racing down the corridor like the
wind.

The policeman outside shouted, but Ellery said: "Let him
go, officer," and shut the door. Then he opened it again and
said: "How's she stand now?"

"Dunno exactly, sir. Somethin' happened out there just
now. I think the Yanks scored."

"Damn," groaned Mr. Queen, and he shut the door again.

"So it was Mrs. Tree who was on the spot, not Bill,"
scowled the Inspector. "I'm sorry, Judy Starr . . . Big man
with a coat and hat and mustache and sun-glasses. Some
description!"

"Sounds like a phony to me," said Sergeant Velie.

"If it was a disguise, he dumped it somewhere," said the
Inspector thoughtfully. "Thomas, have a look in the Men's
Room behind the section where we were sitting. And
Thomas," he added in a whisper, "find out what the score is."
Velie grinned and hurried out. Inspector Queen frowned.
"Quite a job finding a killer in a crowd of fifty thousand
people."

"Maybe," said his son suddenly, "maybe it's not such a
job after all. . . . What was used to kill? Hydrocyanic acid.
Who was intended to be killed? Bill Tree's wife. Any connection between anyone in the case and hydrocyanic acid?
Yes—Dr. Fielding 'lost' a bottle of it under suspicious circumstances. Which were? That Bill Tree's wife could have
taken that bottle . . . *or Bill Tree himself.*"

"Bill Tree!" gasped Paula.

"Bill?" whispered Judy Starr.

"Quite! Dr. Fielding didn't miss the bottle until *after* he
had shown you, Miss Starr, out of his office. He then returned to his office with your husband. Bill could have

slipped the bottle into his pocket as he stepped into the room."

"Yes, he could have," muttered Dr. Fielding.

"I don't see," said Mr. Queen, "how we can arrive at any other conclusion. We know his wife was intended to be the victim today, so obviously she didn't steal the poison. The only other person who had opportunity to steal it was Bill himself."

The Verne woman sprang up. "I don't believe it! It's a frame-up to protect *her*, now that Bill can't defend himself!"

"Ah, but didn't he have motive to kill Judy?" asked Mr. Queen. "Yes, indeed; she wouldn't give him the divorce he craved so that he could marry *you*. I think, Miss Verne, you would be wiser to keep the peace. . . . Bill had opportunity to steal the bottle of poison in Dr. Fielding's office. He also had opportunity to hire Fenimore today, for he was the *only* one of the whole group who left those two boxes during the period when the poisoner must have searched for someone to offer Judy the poisoned pencil.

"All of which fits for what Bill had to do—get to where he had cached his disguise, probably yesterday; look for a likely tool; find Fenimore, give him his instructions and the pencil; get rid of the disguise again; and return to his box. And didn't Bill know better than anyone his wife's habit of moistening a pencil with her tongue—a habit she probably acquired from *him*?"

"Poor Bill," murmured Judy Starr brokenly.

"Women," remarked Miss Paris, "are *fools*."

"There were other striking ironies," replied Mr. Queen. "For if Bill hadn't been suffering from a hay-fever attack, he would have smelled the odor of bitter almonds when his own poisoned pencil was handed to him and stopped in time to save his worthless life. For that matter, if he hadn't been Fenimore Feigenspan's hero, Fenimore would not have handed him his own poisoned pencil in the first place.

"No," said Mr. Queen gladly, "putting it all together, I'm

satisfied that Mr. Big Bill Tree, in trying to murder his wife, very neatly murdered himself instead."

"That's all very well for *you*," said the Inspector disconsolately. "But *I* need proof."

"I've told you how it happened," said his son airily, making for the door. "Can any man do more? Coming, Paula?"

But Paula was already at a telephone, speaking guardedly to the New York office of the syndicate for which she worked, and paying no more attention to him than if he had been a worm.

"What's the score? What's been going on?" Ellery demanded of the world at large as he regained his box seat. "Three to three! What the devil's got into Hubbell, anyway? How'd the Yanks score? What inning is it?"

"Last of the ninth," shrieked somebody. "The Yanks got three runs in the eighth on a walk, a double, and DiMag's homer! Danning homered in the sixth with Ott on base! Shut up!"

Bartell singled over Gordon's head. Mr. Queen cheered.

Sergeant Velie tumbled into the next seat. "Well, we got it," he puffed. "Found the whole outfit in the Men's Room —coat, hat, fake mustache, glasses and all. What's the score?"

"Three-three. Sacrifice, Jeep!" shouted Mr. Queen.

"There was a rain-check in the coat pocket from the sixth game, with Big Bill's box number on it. So there's the old man's proof. Chalk up another win for you."

"Who cares? . . . *Zowie!*"

Jeep Ripple sacrificed Bartell successfully to second.

"Lucky stiff," howled a Yankee fan nearby. "That's the breaks. See the breaks they get? See?"

"And another thing," said the Sergeant, watching Mel Ott stride to the plate. "Seein' as how all Big Bill did was cross himself up, and no harm done except to his own carcass, and seein' as how organized baseball could get along without a murder, and seein' as how thousands of kids like Fenimore Feigenspan worship the ground he walked on——"

"Sew it up, Mel!" bellowed Mr. Queen.

"—and seein' as how none of the newspaper guys know what happened, except that Bill passed out of the picture after a faint, and seein' as everybody's only too glad to shut their traps——"

Mr. Queen awoke suddenly to the serious matters of life. "What's that? What did you say?"

"Strike him out, Goofy!" roared the Sergeant to Señor Gomez, who did not hear. "As I was sayin', it ain't cricket, and the old man would be broke out of the force if the big cheese heard about it . . ."

Someone puffed up behind them, and they turned to see Inspector Queen, red-faced as if after a hard run, scrambling into the box with the assistance of Miss Paula Paris, who looked cool, serene, and star-eyed as ever.

"Dad!" said Mr. Queen, staring. "With a murder on your hands, how can you——"

"Murder?" panted Inspector Queen. "What murder?" And he winked at Miss Paris, who winked back.

"But Paula was telephoning the story——"

"Didn't you hear?" said Paula in a coo, setting her straw straight and slipping into the seat beside Ellery's. "I fixed it all up with your dad. Tonight all the world will know is that Mr. Bill Tree died of heart failure."

They all chuckled then—all but Mr. Queen, whose mouth was open.

"So now," said Paula, "your dad can see the finish of your precious game just as well as *you*, you selfish oaf!"

But Mr. Queen was already fiercely rapt in contemplation of Mel Ott's bat as it swung back and Señor Gomez's ball as it left the Señor's hand to streak toward the plate.

LONG SHOT

LONG SHOT

LONG SHOT

"One moment, dear. My favorite fly's just walked into the parlor," cried Paula Paris into her ashes-of-roses telephone. "Oh, Ellery, do sit down! . . . No, dear, you're fishing. This one's a grim hombre with silv'ry eyes, and I have an option on him. Call me tomorrow about the Garbo excitement. And I'll expect your flash the moment Crawford springs her new *coiffure* on palpitating Miss America."

And, the serious business of her Hollywood gossip column concluded, Miss Paris hung up and turned her lips pursily towards Mr. Queen. Mr. Queen had cured Miss Paris of homophobia, or morbid fear of crowds, by the brilliant counter-psychology of making love to her. Alas for the best-laid plans! The patient had promptly succumbed to the cure and, what was worse, in succumbing had infected the physician, too.

"I do believe," murmured the lovely patient, "that I need an extended treatment, Doctor Queen."

So the poor fellow absently gave Miss Paris an extended treatment, after which he rubbed the lipstick from his mouth.

"No oomph," said Miss Paris critically, holding him off and surveying his gloomy countenance. "Ellery Queen, you're in a mess again."

"Hollywood," mumbled Mr. Queen. "The land God forgot. No logic. Disorderly creation. The abiding place of chaos. Paula, your Hollywood is driving me c-double-o-ditto!"

"You poor imposed-upon Wimpie," crooned Miss Paris, drawing him onto her spacious maple settee. "Tell Paula all about the nasty old place."

So, with Miss Paris's soft arms about him, Mr. Queen unburdened himself. It seemed that Magna Studios ("The

Movies Magnificent"), to whom his soul was chartered, had ordered him as one of its staff writers to concoct a horse-racing plot with a fresh patina. A mystery, of course, since Mr. Queen was supposed to know something about crime.

"With fifty writers on the lot who spend all their time —and money—following the ponies," complained Mr. Queen bitterly, "of course they have to pick on the one serf in their thrall who doesn't know a fetlock from a wither. Paula, I'm a sunk scrivener."

"You don't know *anything* about racing?"

"I'm not interested in racing. I've never even *seen* a race," said Mr. Queen doggedly.

"Imagine that!" said Paula, awed. And she was silent. After a while Mr. Queen twisted in her embrace and said in accusing despair: "Paula, you're thinking of something."

She kissed him and sprang from the settee. "The wrong tense, darling. I've *thought* of something!"

Paula told him all about old John Scott as they drove out into the green and yellow ranch country.

Scott was a vast, shapeless Caledonian with a face as craggy as his native heaths and a disposition not less dour. His inner landscape was bleak except where horses breathed and browsed; and this vulnerable spot had proved his undoing, for he had made two fortunes breeding thoroughbreds and had lost both by racing and betting on them.

"Old John's never stood for any of the crooked dodges of the racing game," said Paula. "He fired Weed Williams, the best jockey he ever had, and had him blackballed by every decent track in the country, so that Williams became a saddle-maker or something, just because of a peccadillo another owner would have winked at. And yet—the inconsistent old coot!—a few years later he gave Williams's son a job, and Whitey's going to ride *Danger*, John's best horse, in the Handicap next Saturday."

"You mean the $100,000 Santa Anita Handicap everybody's in a dither about out here?"

"Yes. Anyway, old John's got a scrunchy little ranch, *Danger*, his daughter Kathryn, and practically nothing else except a stable of also-rans and breeding disappointments."

"So far," remarked Mr. Queen, "it sounds like the beginning of a Class B movie."

"Except," sighed Paula, "that it's not entertaining. John's really on a spot. If Whitey doesn't ride *Danger* to a win in the Handicap, it's the end of the road for John Scott. . . . Speaking about roads, here we are."

They turned into a dirt road and ploughed dustily towards a ramshackle ranch-house. The road was pitted, the fences dilapidated, the grassland patchy with neglect.

"With all his troubles," grinned Ellery, "I fancy he won't take kindly to this quest for Racing in Five Easy Lessons."

"Meeting a full-grown man who knows nothing about racing may give the old gentleman a laugh. Lord knows he needs one."

A Mexican cook directed them to Scott's private track, and they found him leaning his weight upon a sagging rail, his small buried eyes puckered on a cloud of dust eddying along the track at the far turn. His thick fingers clutched a stop-watch.

A man in high-heeled boots sat on the rail two yards away, a shotgun in his lap pointing carelessly at the head of a too well-dressed gentleman with a foreign air who was talking to the back of Scott's shaggy head. The well-dressed man sat in a glistening roadster beside a hard-faced chauffeur.

"You got my proposition, John?" said the well-dressed man, with a toothy smile. "You got it?"

"Get the hell off my ranch, Santelli," said John Scott, without turning his head.

"Sure," said Santelli, still smiling. "You think my proposition over, hey, or maybe somethin' happen to your nag,. hey?"

They saw the old man quiver, but he did not turn; and Santelli nodded curtly to his driver. The big roadster roared away.

The dust-cloud on the track rolled towards them and they saw a small, taut figure in sweater and cap perched atop a gigantic stallion, black-coated and lustrous with sweat. The horse was bounding along like a huge cat, his neck arched. He thundered magnificently by.

"2:02⅖," they heard Scott mutter to his stop-watch. "*Rosemont's* ten-furlong time for the Handicap in '37. Not bad . . . Whitey!" he bellowed to the jockey, who had pulled the black stallion up. "Rub him down good!"

The jockey grinned and pranced *Danger* towards the adjacent stables.

The man with the shotgun drawled: "You got more company, John."

The old man whirled, frowning deeply; his craggy face broke into a thousand wrinkles and he engulfed Paula's slim hand in his two paws. "Paula! It's fine to see ye. Who's this?" he demanded, fastening his cold keen eyes on Ellery.

"Mr. Ellery Queen. But how is Katie? And *Danger?*"

"You saw him." Scott gazed after the dancing horse. "Fit as a fiddle. He'll carry the handicap weight of a hundred twenty pounds Saturday an' never feel it. Did it just now with the leads on him. Paula, did ye see that murderin' scalawag?"

"The fashion-plate who just drove away?"

"That was Santelli, and ye heard what he said might happen to *Danger*." The old man stared bitterly down the road.

"Santelli!" Paula's serene face was shocked.

"Bill, go look after the stallion." The man with the shotgun slipped off the rail and waddled towards the stable. "Just made me an offer for my stable. Hell, the dirty thievin' bookie owns the biggest stable west o' the Rockies—what's he want with my picayune outfit?"

"He owns *Broomstick*, the Handicap favorite, doesn't he?"

asked Paula quietly. "And *Danger* is figured strongly in the running, isn't he?"

"Quoted five to one now, but track odds'll shorten his price. *Broomstick's* two to five," growled Scott.

"It's very simple, then. By buying your horse, Santelli can control the race, owning the two best horses."

"Lassie, lassie," sighed Scott. "I'm an old mon, an' I know these thieves. Handicap purse is $100,000. And Santelli just offered me $100,000 for my stable!" Paula whistled. "It don't wash. My whole shebang ain't worth it. *Danger's* no cinch to win. Is Santelli buyin' up all the other horses in the race, too?—the big outfits? I tell ye it's somethin' else, and it's rotten." Then he shook his heavy shoulders straight. "But here I am gabbin' about my troubles. What brings ye out here, lassie?"

"Mr. Queen here, who's a—well, a friend of mine," said Paula, coloring, "has to think up a horse-racing plot for a movie, and I thought you could help him. He doesn't know a thing about racing."

Scott stared at Mr. Queen, who coughed apologetically. "Well, sir, I don't know but that ye're not a lucky mon. Ye're welcome to the run o' the place. Go over an' talk to Whitey; he knows the racket backwards. I'll be with ye in a few minutes."

The old man lumbered off, and Paula and Ellery sauntered towards the stables.

"Who is this ogre Santelli?" asked Ellery with a frown.

"A gambler and bookmaker with a national hook-up." Paula shivered a little. "Poor John. I don't like it, Ellery."

They turned a corner of the big stable and almost bumped into a young man and a young woman in the lee of the wall, clutching each other desperately and kissing as if they were about to be torn apart for eternity.

"Pardon *us*," said Paula, pulling Ellery back.

The young lady, her eyes crystal with tears, blinked at her. "Is—is that Paula Paris?" she sniffled.

"The same, Kathryn," smiled Paula. "Mr. Queen, Miss Scott. What on earth's the matter?"

"Everything," cried Miss Scott tragically. "Oh, Paula, we're in the most awful trouble!"

Her amorous companion backed bashfully off. He was a slender young man clad in grimy, odoriferous overalls. He wore spectacles floury with the chaff of oats, and there was a grease smudge on one emotional nostril.

"Miss Paris—Mr. Queen. This is Hank Halliday, my—my boy-friend," sobbed Kathryn.

"I see the whole plot," said Paula sympathetically. "Papa doesn't approve of Katie's taking up with a stablehand, the snob! and it's tragedy all around."

"Hank *isn't* a stablehand," cried Kathryn, dashing the tears from her cheeks, which were rosy with indignation. "He's a college graduate who——"

"Kate," said the odoriferous young man with dignity, "let me explain, please. Miss Paris, I have a character deficiency. I am a physical coward."

"Heavens, so am I!" said Paula.

"But a man, you see . . . I am particularly afraid of animals. Horses, specifically." Mr. Halliday shuddered. "I took this—this filthy job to conquer my unreasonable fear." Mr. Halliday's sensitive chin hardened. "I have not yet conquered it, but when I do I shall find myself a real job. And then," he said firmly, embracing Miss Scott's trembling shoulders, "I shall marry Kathryn, papa or no papa."

"Oh, I hate him for being so mean!" sobbed Katie.

"And I——" began Mr. Halliday somberly.

"Hankus-Pankus!" yelled a voice from the stable. "What the hell you paid for, anyway? Come clean up this mess before I slough you one!"

"Yes, Mr. Williams," said Hankus-Pankus hastily, and he hurried away with an apologetic half-bow. His lady-love ran sobbing off towards the ranch-house.

Mr. Queen and Miss Paris regarded each other. Then Mr.

Queen said: "I'm getting a plot, b'gosh, but it's the wrong one."

"Poor kids," sighed Paula. "Well, talk to Whitey Williams and see if the divine spark ignites."

During the next several days Mr. Queen ambled about the Scott ranch, talking to Jockey Williams, to the bespectacled Mr. Halliday—who, he discovered, knew as little about racing as he and cared even less—to a continuously tearful Kathryn, to the guard named Bill—who slept in the stable near *Danger* with one hand on his shotgun—and to old John himself. He learned much about jockeys, touts, racing procedure, gear, handicaps, purses, forfeits, stewards, the ways of bookmakers, famous races and horses and owners and tracks; but the divine spark perversely refused to ignite.

So, on Friday at dusk, when he found himself unaccountably ignored at the Scott ranch, he glumly drove up into the Hollywood hills for a laving in the waters of Gilead.

He found Paula in her garden soothing two anguished young people. Katie Scott was still weeping and Mr. Halliday, the self-confessed craven, for once dressed in an odorless garment, was awkwardly pawing her golden hair.

"More tragedy?" said Mr. Queen. "I should have known. I've just come from your father's ranch, and there's a pall over it."

"Well, there should be!" cried Kathryn. "I told my father where *he* gets off. Treating Hank that way! I'll never speak to him as long as I live! He's—he's *unnatural!*"

"Now Katie," said Mr. Halliday reprovingly, "that's no way to speak of your own father."

"Hank Halliday, if you had one spark of manhood——!"

Mr. Halliday stiffened as if his beloved had jabbed him with the end of a live wire.

"I didn't mean that, Hankus," sobbed Kathryn, throwing herself into his arms. "I know you can't help being a coward. But when he knocked you down and you didn't even——"

Mr. Halliday worked the left side of his jaw thoughtfully. "You know, Mr. Queen, something happened to me when Mr. Scott struck me. For an instant I felt a strange—er—lust. I really believe if I'd had a revolver—and if I knew how to handle one—I might easily have committed murder then. I saw—I believe that's the phrase—red."

"Hank!" cried Katie in horror.

Hank sighed, the homicidal light dying out of his faded blue eyes.

"Old John," explained Paula, winking at Ellery, "found these two cuddling again in the stable, and I suppose he thought it was setting a bad example for *Danger*, whose mind should be on the race tomorrow; so he fired Hank, and Katie blew up and told John off, and she's left his home forever."

"To discharge me is his privilege," said Mr. Halliday coldly, "but now I owe him no loyalty whatever. I shall *not* bet on *Danger* to win the Handicap!"

"I hope the big brute loses," sobbed Katie.

"Now Kate," said Paula firmly, "I've heard enough of this nonsense. I'm going to speak to you like a Dutch aunt."

Katie sobbed on.

"Mr. Halliday," said Mr. Queen formally, "I believe this is our cue to seek a slight libation."

"Kathryn!"

"Hank!"

Mr. Queen and Miss Paris tore the lovers apart.

It was a little after ten o'clock when Miss Scott, no longer weeping but facially still tear-ravaged, crept out of Miss Paris's white frame house and got into her dusty little car.

As she turned her key in the ignition lock and stepped on the starter, a harsh bass voice from the shadows of the back seat said: "Don't yell. Don't make a sound. Turn your car around and keep going till I tell you to stop."

"Eek!" screeched Miss Scott.

A big leathery hand clamped over her trembling mouth. After a few moments the car moved away.

Mr. Queen called for Miss Paris the next day and they settled down to a snail's pace, heading for Arcadia eastward, near which lay the beautiful Santa Anita race-course.

"What happened to Lachrymose Katie last night?" demanded Mr. Queen.

"Oh, I got her to go back to the ranch. She left me a little after ten, a very miserable little girl. What did you do with Hankus-Pankus?"

"I oiled him thoroughly and then took him home. He'd hired a room in a Hollywood boarding-house. He cried on my shoulder all the way. It seems old John also kicked him in the seat of his pants, and he's been brooding murderously over it."

"Poor Hankus. The only honest male I've ever met."

"I'm afraid of horses, too," said Mr. Queen hurriedly.

"Oh, you! You're detestable. You haven't kissed me once today."

Only the cooling balm of Miss Paris's lips, applied at various points along U.S. Route 66, kept Mr. Queen's temper from boiling over. The roads were sluggish with traffic. At the track it was even worse. It seemed as though every last soul in Southern California had converged upon Santa Anita at once, in every manner of conveyance, from the dusty Model T's of dirt farmers to the shiny metal monsters of the movie stars. The magnificent stands seethed with noisy thousands, a wriggling mosaic of color and movement. The sky was blue, the sun warm, zephyrs blew, and the track was fast. A race was being run, and the sleek animals were small and fleet and sharply focused in the clear light.

"What a marvelous day for the Handicap!" cried Paula, dragging Ellery along. "Oh, there's Bing, and Al Jolson, and

Bob Burns! . . . Hello! . . . And Joan and Clark and Carole . . ."

Despite Miss Paris's overenthusiastic trail-breaking, Mr. Queen arrived at the track stalls in one piece. They found old John Scott watching with the intentness of a Red Indian as a stablehand kneaded *Danger's* velvety forelegs. There was a stony set to Scott's gnarled face that made Paula cry: "John! Is anything wrong with *Danger?*"

"*Danger's* all right," said the old man curtly. "It's Kate. We had a blow-up over that Halliday boy an' she ran out on me."

"Nonsense, John. I sent her back home last night myself."

"She was at your place? She didn't come home."

"She didn't?" Paula's little nose wrinkled.

"I guess," growled Scott, "she's run off with that Halliday coward. He's not a mon, the lily-livered——"

"We can't all be heroes, John. He's a good boy, and he loves Katie."

The old man stared stubbornly at his stallion, and after a moment they left and made their way towards their box.

"Funny," said Paula in a scared voice. "She couldn't have run off with Hank; he was with you. And I'd swear she meant to go back to the ranch last night."

"Now, Paula," said Mr. Queen gently. "She's all right." But his eyes were thoughtful and a little perturbed.

Their box was not far from the paddock. During the preliminary races, Paula kept searching the sea of faces with her binoculars.

"Well, well," said Mr. Queen suddenly, and Paula became conscious of a rolling thunder from the stands about them.

"What's the matter? What's happened?"

"*Broomstick*, the favorite, has been scratched," said Mr. Queen dryly.

"*Broomstick?* Santelli's horse?" Paula stared at him, paling. "But why? Ellery, there's something in this——"

"It seems he's pulled a tendon and can't run."

"Do you think," whispered Paula, "that Santelli had anything to do with Katie's . . . not getting . . . home?"

"Possible," muttered Ellery. "But I can't seem to fit the blinking thing——"

"Here they come!"

The shout shook the stands. A line of regal animals began to emerge from the paddock. Paula and Ellery rose with the other restless thousands, and craned. The Handicap contestants were parading to the post!

There was *High Tor*, who had gone lame in the stretch at the Derby two years before and had not run a race since. This was to be his come-back; the insiders held him in a contempt which the public apparently shared, for he was quoted at 50 to 1. There was little *Fighting Billy*. There was *Equator*, prancing sedately along with Buzz Hickey up. There was *Danger*! Glossy black, gigantic, imperial, *Danger* was nervous. Whitey Williams was having a difficult time controlling him and a stablehand was struggling at his bit.

Old John Scott, his big shapeless body unmistakable even at this distance, lumbered from the paddock towards his dancing stallion, apparently to soothe him.

Paula gasped. Ellery said quickly: "What is it?"

"There's Hank Halliday in the crowd. Up there! Right above the spot where *Danger's* passing. About fifty feet from John Scott. And Kathryn's not with him!"

Ellery took the glasses from her and located Halliday.

Paula sank into her chair. "Ellery, I've the queerest feeling. There's something wrong. See how pale he is . . ."

The powerful glasses brought Halliday to within a few inches of Ellery's eyes. The boy's glasses were steamed over; he was shaking, as if he had a chill; and yet Ellery could see the globules of perspiration on his cheeks.

And then Mr. Queen stiffened very abruptly.

John Scott had just reached the head of *Danger*; his thick arm was coming up to pull the stallion's head down. And in that instant Mr. Hankus-Pankus Halliday fumbled in his clothes; and in the next his hand appeared clasping a snub-nosed automatic. Mr. Queen very nearly cried out. For, the short barrel wavering, the automatic in Mr. Halliday's trembling hands pointed in the general direction of John Scott, there was an explosion, and a puff of smoke blew out of the muzzle.

Miss Paris leaped to her feet, and Miss Paris did cry out, "Why, the crazy young fool!" said Mr. Queen dazedly.

Frightened by the shot, which had gone wild, *Danger* reared. The other horses began to kick and dance. In a moment the place below boiled with panic-stricken thoroughbreds. Scott, clinging to *Danger's* head, half-turned in an immense astonishment and looked inquiringly upwards. Whitey struggled desperately to control the frantic stallion.

And then Mr. Halliday shot again. And again. And a fourth time. And at some instant, in the spaces between those shots, the rearing horse got between John Scott and the automatic in Mr. Halliday's shaking hand.

Danger's four feet left the turf. Then, whinnying in agony, flanks heaving, he toppled over on his side.

"Oh, gosh; oh, *gosh*," said Paula biting her handkerchief.

"Let's go!" shouted Mr. Queen, and he plunged for the spot.

By the time they reached the place where Mr. Halliday had fearfully discharged his automatic, the bespectacled youth had disappeared. The people who had stood about him were still too stunned to move. Elsewhere, the stands were in pandemonium.

In the confusion, Ellery and Paula managed to slip through the inadequate track-police cordon hastily thrown about the fallen *Danger* and his milling rivals. They found old John on his knees beside the black stallion, his big hands steadily stroking the glossy, veined neck. Whitey, pale and bewildered-looking, had stripped off the tiny saddle, and the track veterinary was examining a bullet-wound in *Danger's* side, near the shoulder. A group of track officials conferred excitedly nearby.

"He saved my life," said old John in a low voice to no one in particular. "He saved my life."

The veterinary looked up. "Sorry, Mr. Scott," he said grimly. "*Danger* won't run this race."

"No. I suppose not." Scott licked his leathery lips. "Is it —mon, is it serious?"

"Can't tell till I dig out the bullet. We'll have to get him out of here and into the hospital right away."

An official said: "Tough luck, Scott. You may be sure we'll do our best to find the scoundrel who shot your horse."

The old man's lips twisted. He climbed to his feet and looked down at the heaving flanks of his fallen thoroughbred. Whitey Williams trudged away with *Danger's* gear, head hanging.

A moment later the loud-speaker system proclaimed that *Danger*, Number 5, had been scratched, and that the Handicap would be run immediately the other contestants could be quieted and lined up at the stall-barrier.

"All right, folks, clear out," said a track policeman as a hospital van rushed up, followed by a hoisting truck.

"What are you doing about the man who shot this horse?" demanded Mr. Queen, not moving.

"Ellery," whispered Paula nervously, tugging at his arm.

"We'll get him; got a good description. Move on, please."

"Well," said Mr. Queen slowly, "I know who he is, do you see."

"Ellery!"

"I saw him and recognized him."

They were ushered into the Steward's office just as the announcement was made that *High Tor*, at 50 to 1, had won the Santa Anita Handicap, purse $100,000, by two and a half lengths . . . almost as long a shot, in one sense, as the shot which had laid poor *Danger* low, commented Mr. Queen to Miss Paris, *sotto voce*.

"Halliday?" said John Scott with heavy contempt. "That yellow-livered pup try to shoot me?"

"I couldn't possibly be mistaken, Mr. Scott," said Ellery.

"I saw him, too, John," sighed Paula.

"Who is this Halliday?" demanded the chief of the track police.

Scott told him in monosyllables, relating their quarrel of the day before. "I knocked him down an' kicked him. I guess the only way he could get back at me was with a gun. An' *Danger* took the rap, poor beastie." For the first time his voice shook.

"Well, we'll get him; he can't have left the park," said the police chief grimly. "I've got it sealed tighter than a drum."

"Did you know," murmured Mr. Queen, "that Mr. Scott's daughter Kathryn has been missing since last night?"

Old John flushed slowly. "You think—my Kate had somethin' to do——"

"Don't be silly, John!" said Paula.

"At any rate," said Mr. Queen dryly, "her disappearance and the attack here today can't be a coincidence. I'd advise you to start a search for Miss Scott immediately. And, by the way, send for *Danger's* gear. I'd like to examine it."

"Say, who the devil are you?" growled the chief.

Mr. Queen told him negligently. The chief looked properly awed. He telephoned to various police headquarters, and he sent for *Danger's* gear.

Whitey Williams, still in his silks, carried the high small racing saddle in and dumped it on the floor.

"John, I'm awful sorry about what happened," he said in a low voice.

"It ain't your fault, Whitey." The big shoulders drooped.

"Ah, Williams, thank you," said Mr. Queen briskly. "This *is* the saddle *Danger* was wearing a few minutes ago?"

"Yes, sir."

"Exactly as it was when you stripped it off him after the shots?"

"Yes, sir."

"Has anyone had an opportunity to tamper with it?"

"No. sir. I been with it ever since, and no one's come near it but me."

Mr. Queen nodded and knelt to examine the empty-pocketed saddle. Observing the scorched hole in the flap, his brow puckered in perplexity.

· "By the way, Whitey," he asked, "how much do you weigh?"

"Hundred and seven."

Mr. Queen frowned. He rose, dusted his knees delicately, and beckoned the chief of police. They conferred in undertones. The policeman looked baffled, shrugged, and hurried out.

When he returned, a certain familiar-appearing gentleman in too-perfect clothes and a foreign air accompanied him. The gentleman looked sad.

"I hear some crackpot took a couple o' shots at you, John," he said sorrowfully, "an' got your nag instead. Tough luck."

There was a somewhat quizzical humor behind this ambiguous statement which brought old John's head up in a flash of belligerence.

"You dirty, thievin'——"

"Mr. Santelli," greeted Mr. Queen. "When did you know that *Broomstick* would have to be scratched?"

"*Broomstick?*" Mr. Santelli looked mildly surprised at this irrelevant question. "Why, last week."

"So that's why you offered to buy Scott's stable—to get control of *Danger?*"

"Sure." Mr. Santelli smiled genially. "He was hot. With my nag out, he looked like a cinch."

"Mr. Santelli, you're what is colloquially known as a cock-eyed liar." Mr. Santelli ceased smiling. "You wanted to buy *Danger* not to see him win, but to see him lose!"

Mr. Santelli looked unhappy. "Who is this," he appealed to the police chief, "Mister Wacky himself?"

"In my embryonic way," said Mr. Queen, "I have been making a few inquiries in the last several days and my information has it that your bookmaking organization covered a lot of *Danger* money when *Danger* was five to one."

"Say, you got somethin' there," said Mr. Santelli, suddenly deciding to be candid.

"You covered about two hundred thousand dollars, didn't you?"

"Wow," said Mr. Santelli. "This guy's got idears, ain't he?"

"So," smiled Mr. Queen, "if *Danger* won the Handicap you stood to drop a very frigid million dollars, did you not?"

"But it's my old friend John some guy tried to rub out," pointed out Mr. Santelli gently. "Go peddle your papers somewheres else, Mister Wack."

John Scott looked bewilderedly from the gambler to Mr. Queen. His jaw-muscles were bunched and jerky.

At this moment a special officer deposited among them Mr. Hankus-Pankus Halliday, his spectacles awry on his nose and his collar ripped away from his prominent Adam's-apple.

John Scott sprang towards him, but Ellery caught his flailing arms in time to prevent a slaughter.

"Murderer! Scalawag! Horse-killer!" roared old John. "What did ye do with my lassie?"

Mr. Halliday said gravely: "Mr. Scott, you have my sympathy."

The old man's mouth flew open. Mr. Halliday folded his scrawny arms with dignity, glaring at the policeman who had brought him in. "There was no necessity to manhandle me. I'm quite ready to face the—er—music. But I shall not answer any questions."

"No gat on him, Chief," said the policeman by his side.

"What did you do with the automatic?" demanded the chief. No answer. "You admit you had it in for Mr. Scott and tried to kill him?" No answer. "Where is Miss Scott?"

"You see," said Mr. Halliday stonily, "how useless it is."

"Hankus-Pankus," murmured Mr. Queen, "you are superb. You don't know where Kathryn is, do you?"

Hankus-Pankus instantly looked alarmed. "Oh, I say, Mr. Queen. Don't make me talk. Please!"

"But you're expecting her to join you here, aren't you?" Hankus paled. The policeman said: "He's a nut. He didn't even try to make a getaway. He didn't even fight back."

"Hank! Darling! Father!" cried Katie Scott; and, straggle-haired and dusty-faced, she flew into the office and flung herself upon Mr. Halliday's thin bosom.

"Katie!" screamed Paula, flying to the girl and embracing her; and in a moment all three, Paula and Kathryn and Hankus, were weeping in concert, while old John's jaw dropped even lower and all but Mr. Queen, who was smiling, stood rooted to their bits of Space in timeless stupefaction.

Then Miss Scott ran to her father and clung to him, and old John's shoulders lifted a little, even though the expression of bewilderment persisted; and she burrowed her head into her father's deep, broad chest.

In the midst of this incredible scene the track veterinary bustled in and said: "Good news, Mr. Scott. I've extracted the bullet and, while the wound is deep, I give you my word *Danger* will be as good as ever when it's healed." And he bustled out.

And Mr. Queen, his smile broadening, said: "Well, well, a pretty comedy of errors."

"Comedy!" growled old John over his daughter's golden curls. "D'ye call a murderous attempt on my life a comedy?" And he glared fiercely at Mr. Hank Halliday, who was at the moment borrowing a handkerchief from the policeman with which to wipe his eyes.

"My dear Mr. Scott," replied Mr. Queen, "there has been no attempt on your life. The shots were not fired at you.

From the very first *Danger*, and *Danger* only, was intended
to be the victim of the shooting."

"What's this?" cried Paula.

"No, no, Whitey," said Mr. Queen, smiling still more
broadly. "The door, I promise you, is well guarded."

The jockey snarled: "Yah, he's off his nut. Next thing
you'll say *I* plugged the nag. How could I be on *Danger's*
back and at the same time fifty feet away in the grandstand?
A million guys saw this screwball fire those shots!"

"A difficulty," replied Mr. Queen, bowing, "I shall be delighted to resolve. *Danger*, ladies and gentlemen, was handi-
capped officially to carry one hundred and twenty pounds in
the Santa Anita Handicap. This means that when his jockey,
carrying the gear, stepped upon the scales in the weighing-
out ceremony just before the race, the combined weight of
jockey and gear had to come to exactly one hundred and
twenty pounds; or Mr. Whitey Williams would never have
been allowed by the track officials to mount his horse."

"What's that got to do with it?" demanded the chief, eyeing Mr. Whitey Williams in a hard, unfeeling way.

"Everything. For Mr. Williams told us only a few minutes
ago that he weighs only a hundred and seven pounds. Consequently the racing saddle *Danger* wore when he was shot
must have contained various lead weights which, combined
with the weight of the saddle, made up the difference between
a hundred and seven pounds, Mr. Williams's weight, and a
hundred twenty pounds, the handicap weight. Is that
correct?"

"Sure. Anybody knows that."

"Yes, yes, elementary, in Mr. Holmes's imperishable phrase.
Nevertheless," continued Mr. Queen, walking over and prod-
ding with his toe the saddle Whitey Williams had fetched to
the office, "when I examined this saddle *there were no lead
weights in its pockets*. And Mr. Williams assured me no one
had tampered with the saddle since he had removed it from
Danger's back. But this was impossible, since without the

lead weights Mr. Williams and the saddle would have weighed out at less than a hundred and twenty pounds on the scales.

"And so I knew," said Mr. Queen, "that Williams had weighed out with a different saddle, that when he was shot *Danger* was wearing a different saddle, that the saddle Williams lugged away from the wounded horse was a different saddle; that he secreted it somewhere on the premises and fetched here on our request a *second* saddle—this one on the floor—which he had prepared beforehand with a bullet-hole nicely placed in the proper spot. And the reason he did this was that obviously there was something in that first saddle he didn't want anyone to see. And what could that have been but a special pocket containing an automatic, which in the confusion following Mr. Halliday's first, signal shot Mr. Williams calmly discharged into *Danger's* body by simply stooping over as he struggled with the frightened horse, putting his hand into the pocket, and firing while Mr. Halliday was discharging his three other futile shots fifty feet away? Mr. Halliday, you see, couldn't be trusted to hit *Danger* from such a distance, because Mr. Halliday is a stranger to firearms; he might even hit Mr. Williams instead, if he hit anything. That's why I believe Mr. Halliday was using blank cartridges and threw the automatic away."

The jockey's voice was strident, panicky. "You're crazy! Special saddle. Who ever heard——"

Mr. Queen, still smiling, went to the door, opened it, and said: "Ah, you've found it, I see. Let's have it. In *Danger's* stall? Clumsy, clumsy."

He returned with a racing saddle; and Whitey cursed and then grew still. Mr. Queen and the police chief and John Scott examined the saddle and, surely enough, there was a special pocket stitched into the flap, above the iron hoop, and in the pocket there was a snub-nosed automatic. And the bullet-hole piercing the special pocket had the scorched speckled appearance of powder-burns.

"But where," muttered the chief, "does Halliday figure?
I don't get him a-tall."

"Very few people would," said Mr. Queen, "because Mr.
Halliday is, in his modest way, unique among bipeds."

"Huh?"

"Why, he was Whitey's accomplice—weren't you,
Hankus?"

Hankus gulped and said: "Yes. I mean no. I mean——"

"But I'm sure Hank wouldn't—" Katie began to cry.

"You see," said Mr. Queen briskly, "Whitey wanted a set-
up whereby he would be the last person in California to be
suspected of having shot *Danger*. The quarrel between John
Scott and Hank gave him a ready-made instrument. If he
could make Hank seem to do the shooting, with Hank's obvious motive against Mr. Scott, then nobody would suspect
his own part in the affair.

"But to bend Hank to his will he had to have a hold on
Hank. What was Mr. Halliday's Achilles heel? Why, his
passion for Katie Scott. So last night Whitey's father, Weed
Williams, I imagine—wasn't he the jockey you chased from
the American turf many years ago, Mr. Scott, and who became a saddle-maker?—kidnaped Katie Scott, and then communicated with Hankus-Pankus and told him just what to
do today if he ever expected to see his beloved alive again.
And Hankus-Pankus took the gun they provided him with,
and listened very carefully, and agreed to do everything they
told him to do, and promised he would not breathe a word
of the truth afterward, even if he had to go to jail for his
crime, because if he did, you see, something terrible would
happen to the incomparable Katie."

Mr. Halliday gulped, his Adam's-apple bobbing violently.

"An' all the time this skunk," growled John Scott, glaring
at the cowering jockey, "an' his weasel of a father, they sat
back an' laughed at a brave mon, because they were havin'
their piddling revenge on me, ruining me!" Old John
shambled like a bear towards Mr. Halliday. "An' I am a

shamed mon today, Hank Halliday. For that was the bravest thing I ever did hear of. An' even if I've lost my chance for the Handicap purse, through no fault of yours, and I'm a ruined maggot, here's my hand."

Mr. Halliday took it absently, meanwhile fumbling with his other hand in his pocket. "By the way," he said, "who did win the Handicap, if I may ask? I was so busy, you see——"

"*High Tor*," said somebody in the babble.

"Really? Then I must cash this ticket," said Mr. Halliday with a note of faint interest.

"Two thousand dollars!" gasped Paula, goggling at the ticket. "He bet two thousand dollars on *High Tor* at fifty to one!"

"Yes, a little nest-egg my mother left me," said Mr. Halliday. He seemed embarrassed. "I'm sorry, Mr. Scott. You made me angry when you—er—kicked me in the pants, so I didn't bet it on *Danger*. And *High Tor* was such a beautiful name."

"Oh, Hank," sobbed Katie, beginning to strangle him.

"So now, Mr. Scott," said Hankus-Pankus with dignity, "may I marry Katie and set you up in the racing business again?"

"Happy days!" bellowed old John, seizing his future son-in-law in a rib-cracking embrace.

"Happy days," muttered Mr. Queen, seizing Miss Paris and heading her for the nearest bar.

Heigh, *Danger*!

MIND OVER MATTER

MIND OVER MATTER

Paula Paris found Inspector Richard Queen of the Homicide Squad inconsolable when she arrived in New York. She understood how he felt, for she had flown in from Hollywood expressly to cover the heavyweight fight between Champion Mike Brown and Challenger Jim Coyle, who were signed to box fifteen rounds at the Stadium that night for the championship of the world.

"You poor dear," said Paula. "And how about you, Master Mind? Aren't you disappointed, too, that you can't buy a ticket to the fight?" she asked Mr. Ellery Queen.

"I'm a jinx," said the great man gloomily. "If I went, something catastrophic would be sure to happen. So why should I want to go?"

"I thought witnessing catastrophes was why people *go to* fights."

"Oh, I don't mean anything gentle like a knockout. Something grimmer."

"He's afraid somebody will knock somebody off," said the Inspector.

"Well, doesn't somebody always?" demanded his son.

"Don't pay any attention to him, Paula," said the Inspector impatiently. "Look, you're a newspaperwoman. Can you get me a ticket?"

"You may as well get me one, too," groaned Mr. Queen.

So Miss Paris smiled and telephoned Phil Maguire, the famous sports editor, and spoke so persuasively to Mr. Maguire that he picked them up that evening in his cranky little sports roadster and they all drove uptown to the Stadium together to see the brawl.

"How do you figure the fight, Maguire?" asked Inspector Queen respectfully.

"On this howdedo," said Maguire, "Maguire doesn't care to be quoted."

"Seems to me the champ ought to take this boy Coyle."

Maguire shrugged. "Phil's sour on the champion," laughed Paula. "Phil and Mike Brown haven't been cuddly since Mike won the title."

"Nothing personal, y'understand," said Phil Maguire. "Only, remember Kid Berès? The Cuban boy. This was in the days when Ollie Stearn was finagling Mike Brown into the heavy sugar. So this fight was a fix, see, and Mike knew it was a fix, and the Kid knew it was a fix, and everybody knew it was a fix and that Kid Berès was supposed to lay down in the sixth round. Well, just the same Mike went out there and sloughed into the Kid and half-killed him. Just for the hell of it. The Kid spent a month in the hospital and when he came out he was only half a man." And Maguire smiled his crooked smile and pressed his horn gently at an old man crossing the street. Then he started, and said: "I guess I just don't like the champ."

"Speaking of fixes . . . " began Mr. Queen.

"Were we?" asked Maguire innocently.

"If it's on the level," predicted Mr. Queen gloomily, "Coyle will murder the champion. Wipe the ring up with him. That big fellow wants the title."

"Oh, sure."

"Damn it," grinned the Inspector, "who's going to win tonight?"

Maguire grinned back. "Well, you know the odds. Three to one on the champ."

When they drove into the parking lot across the street from the Stadium, Maguire grunted: "Speak of the devil." He had backed the little roadster into a space beside a huge twelve-cylinder limousine the color of bright blood.

"Now what's that supposed to mean?" asked Paula Paris.

"This red locomotive next to Lizzie," Maguire chuckled. "It's the champ's. Or rather, it belongs to his manager, Ollie

Stearn. Ollie lets Mike use it. Mike's car's gone down the river."

"I thought the champion was wealthy," said Mr. Queen.

"Not any more. All tangled up in litigation. Dozens of judgments wrapped around his ugly ears."

"He ought to be hunk after tonight," said the Inspector wistfully. "Pulling down more than a half a million bucks for his end!"

"He won't collect a red cent of it," said the newspaperman. "His loving wife—you know Ivy, the ex-strip tease doll with the curves and detours?—Ivy and Mike's creditors will grab it all off. Come on."

Mr. Queen assisted Miss Paris from the roadster and tossed his camel's-hair topcoat carelessly into the back seat.

"Don't leave your coat there, Ellery," protested Paula. "Some one's sure to steal it."

"Let 'em. It's an old rag. Don't know what I brought it for, anyway, in this heat."

"Come on, come on," said Phil Maguire eagerly.

From the press section at ringside the stands were one heaving mass of growling humanity. Two bantamweights were fencing in the ring.

"What's the trouble?" demanded Mr. Queen alertly.

"Crowd came out to see heavy artillery, not popguns," explained Maguire. "Take a look at the card."

"Six prelims," muttered Inspector Queen. "And all good boys, too. So what are these muggs beefing about?"

"Bantams, welters, lightweights, and one middleweight bout to wind up."

"So what?"

"So the card's too light. The fans came here to see two big guys slaughter each other. They don't want to be annoyed by a bunch of gnats—even good gnats. . . . Hi, Happy."

"Who's that?" asked Miss Paris curiously.

"Happy Day," the Inspector answered for Maguire. "Makes his living off bets. One of the biggest plungers in town."

Happy Day was visible a few rows off, an expensive Panama resting on a fold of neck-fat. He had a puffed face the color of cold rice pudding, and his eyes were two raisins. He nodded at Maguire and turned back to watch the ring.

"Normally, Happy's face is like a raw steak," said Maguire. "He's worried about something."

"Perhaps," remarked Mr. Queen darkly, "the gentleman smells a mouse."

Maguire glanced at the great man sidewise, and then smiled. "And there's Mrs. Champ herself. Ivy Brown. Some stuff, hey, men?"

The woman prowled down the aisle on the arm of a weazened, wrinkled little man who chewed nervously on a long green cold cigar. The champion's wife was a full-blown animal with a face like a Florentine cameo. The little man handed her into a seat, bowed elaborately, and hurried off.

"Isn't the little guy Ollie Stearn, Brown's manager?" asked the Inspector.

"Yes," said Maguire. "Notice the act? Ivy and Mike Brown haven't lived together for a couple of years, and Ollie thinks it's lousy publicity. So he pays a lot of attention in public to the champ's wife. What d'ye think of her, Paula? The woman's angle is always refreshing."

"This may sound feline," murmured Miss Paris, "but she's an overdressed harpie with the instincts of a she-wolf who never learned to apply make-up properly. Cheap—very cheap."

"Expensive—very expensive. Mike's wanted a divorce for a long time, but Ivy keeps rolling in the hay—and Mike's made plenty of hay in his time. Say, I gotta go to work."

Maguire bent over his typewriter.

The night deepened, the crowd rumbled, and Mr. Ellery Queen, the celebrated sleuth, felt uncomfortable. Specifically, his six-foot body was taut as a violin-string. It was a familiar but always menacing phenomenon. It meant that there was murder in the air.

The challenger appeared first. He was met by a roar, like the roar of a river at flood-tide bursting its dam.

Miss Paris gasped with admiration. "Isn't he the one!"

Jim Coyle was the one—an almost handsome giant six feet and a half tall, with preposterously broad shoulders, long smooth muscles, and a bronze skin. He rubbed his unshaven cheeks and grinned boyishly at the frantic fans.

His manager, Barney Hawks, followed him into the ring. Hawks was a big man, but beside his fighter he appeared puny.

"Hercules in trunks," breathed Miss Paris. "Did you ever see such a body, Ellery!"

"The question more properly is," said Mr. Queen jealously, "can he keep that body off the floor? That's the question, my girl."

"Plenty fast for a big man," said Maguire. "Faster than you'd think, considering all that bulk. Maybe not as fast as Mike Brown, but Jim's got height and reach in his favor, and he's strong as a bull. The way Firpo was."

"Here comes the champ!" exclaimed Inspector Queen.

A large ugly man shuffled down the aisle and vaulted into the ring. His manager—the little weazened, wrinkled man —followed him and stood bouncing up and down on the canvas, still chewing the unlit cigar.

"*Boo-oo-oo!*"

"They're booing the champion!" cried Paula. "Phil, why?"

"Because they hate his guts," smiled Maguire. "They hate his guts because he's an ornery, brutal, crooked slob with the kick of a mule and the soul of a pretzel. That's why, darlin'."

Brown stood six feet two inches, anatomically a gorilla, with a broad hairy chest, long arms, humped shoulders, and

large flat feet. His features were smashed, cruel. He paid
no attention to the hostile crowd, to his taller, bigger, younger
opponent. He seemed detached, indrawn, a subhuman fighting machine.

But Mr. Queen, whose peculiar genius it was to notice
minutiae, saw Brown's powerful mandibles working ever so
slightly beneath his leathery cheeks.

And again Mr. Queen's body tightened.

When the gong clamored for the start of the third round,
the champion's left eye was a purple slit, his lips were cracked
and bloody, and his simian chest rose and fell in gasps.

Thirty seconds later he was cornered, a beaten animal,
above their heads. They could see the ragged splotches over
his kidneys, blooming above his trunks like crimson flowers.

Brown crouched, covering up, protecting his chin. Big Jim
Coyle streaked forward. The giant's gloves sank into Brown's
body. The champion fell forward and pinioned the long
bronze merciless arms.

The referee broke them. Brown grabbed Coyle again.
They danced.

The crowd began singing *The Blue Danube*, and the
referee stepped between the two fighters again and spoke
sharply to Brown.

"The dirty double-crosser," smiled Phil Maguire.

"Who? What d'ye mean?" asked Inspector Queen,
puzzled.

"Watch the payoff."

The champion raised his battered face and lashed out feebly
at Coyle with his soggy left glove. The giant laughed and
stepped in.

The champion went down.

"Pretty as a picture," said Maguire admiringly.

At the count of nine, with the bay of the crowd in his
flattened ears, Mike Brown staggered to his feet. The bulk
of Coyle slipped in, shadowy, and pumped twelve solid, lethal

gloves into Brown's body. The champion's knees broke. A whistling six-inch uppercut to the point of the jaw sent him toppling to the canvas.

This time he remained there.

"But he made it look kosher," drawled Maguire.

The Stadium howled with glee and the satiation of blood-lust. Paula looked sickish. A few rows away Happy Day jumped up, stared wildly about, and then began shoving through the crowd.

"Happy isn't happy any more," sang Maguire.

The ring was boiling with police, handlers, officials. Jim Coyle was half-drowned in a wave of shouting people; he was laughing like a boy. In the champion's corner Ollie Stearn worked slowly over the twitching torso of the uncon-scious man.

"Yes, sir," said Phil Maguire, rising and stretching, "that was as pretty a dive as I've seen, brother, and I've seen some beauts in my day."

"See here, Maguire," said Mr. Queen, nettled. "I have eyes, too. What makes you so cocksure Brown just tossed his title away?"

"You may be Einstein on Centre Street," grinned Maguire, "but here you're just another palooka, Mr. Queen."

"Seems to me," argued the Inspector in the bedlam, "Brown took an awful lot of punishment."

"Oh, sure," said Maguire mockingly. "Look, you boobs. Mike Brown has as sweet a right hand as the game has ever seen. Did you notice him use his right on Coyle tonight—even once?"

"Well," admitted Mr. Queen, "no."

"Of course not. Not a single blow. And he had a dozen openings, especially in the second round. And Jimmy Coyle still carries his guard too low. But what did Mike do? Put his deadly right into cold storage, kept jabbing away with that silly left of his—it couldn't put Paula away!—covering

up, clinching, and taking one hell of a beating . . . Sure, he
made it look good. But your ex-champ took a dive just the
same!"

They were helping the gorilla from the ring. He looked
surly and tired. A small group followed him, laughing. Little
Ollie Stearn kept pushing people aside fretfully. Mr. Queen
spied Brown's wife, the curved Ivy, pale and furious, hurrying after them.

"It appears," sighed Mr. Queen, "that I was in error."

"What?" asked Paula.

"Hmm. Nothing."

"Look," said Maguire. "I've got to see a man about a man,
but I'll meet you folks in Coyle's dressing-room and we'll kick
a few gongs around. Jim's promised to help a few of the
boys warm up some hot spots."

"Oh, I'd love it!" cried Paula. "How do we get in, Phil?"

"What have you got a cop with you for? Show her,
Inspector."

Maguire's slight figure slouched off. The great man's scalp
prickled suddenly. He frowned and took Paula's arm.

The new champion's dressing-room was full of smoke,
people, and din. Young Coyle lay on a training table like
Gulliver in Lilliput, being rubbed down. He was answering
questions good-humoredly, grinning at cameras, flexing his
shoulder-muscles. Barney Hawks was running about with
his collar loosened handing out cigars like a new father.

The crowd was so dense it overflowed into the adjoining
shower-room. There were empty bottles on the floor and
near the shower-room window, pushed into a corner, five
men were shooting craps with enormous sobriety.

The Inspector spoke to Barney Hawks, and Coyle's manager introduced them to the champion, who took one look at
Paula and said: "Hey, Barney, how about a little privacy?"

"Sure, sure. You're the champ now, Jimmy-boy!"

"Come on, you guys, you got enough pictures to last you a

lifetime. What did he say your name is, beautiful? Paris? That's a hell of a name."

"Isn't yours Couzzi?" asked Paula coolly.

"Socko," laughed the boy. "Come on, clear out, guys. This lady and I got some sparring to do. Hey, lay off the liniment, Louie. He didn't hardly touch me."

Coyle slipped off the rubbing table, and Barney Hawks began shooing men out of the shower-room, and finally Coyle grabbed some towels, winked at Paula, and went in, shutting the door. They heard the cheerful hiss of the shower.

Five minutes later Phil Maguire strolled in. He was perspiring and a little wobbly.

"Heil, Hitler," he shouted. "Where's the champ?"

"Here I am," said Coyle, opening the shower-room door and rubbing his bare chest with a towel. There was another towel draped around his loins. "Hya, Phil-boy. Be dressed in a shake. Say, this doll your Mamie? If she ain't, I'm staking out my claim."

"Come on, come on, champ. We got a date with Fifty-second Street."

"Sure! How about you, Barney? You joining us?"

"Go ahead and play," said his manager in a fatherly tone. "Me, I got money business with the management." He danced into the shower-room, emerged with a hat and a camel's-hair coat over his arm, kissed his hand affectionately at Coyle, and lumbered out.

"You're not going to stay in here while he dresses?" said Mr. Queen petulantly to Miss Paris. "Come on—you can wait for your hero in the hall."

"Yes, sir," said Miss Paris submissively.

Coyle guffawed. "Don't worry, fella. I ain't going to do you out of nothing. There's plenty of broads."

Mr. Queen piloted Miss Paris firmly from the room. "Let's meet them at the car," he said in a curt tone.

Miss Paris murmured: "Yes, *sir*."

They walked in silence to the end of the corridor and

turned a corner into an alley which led out of the Stadium and into the street. As they walked down the alley Mr. Queen could see through the shower-room window into the dressing-room: Maguire had produced a bottle and he, Coyle, and the Inspector were raising glasses. Coyle in his athletic underwear was—well . . .

Mr. Queen hurried Miss Paris out of the alley and across the street to the parking lot. Cars were slowly driving out. But the big red limousine belonging to Ollie Stearn still stood beside Maguire's roadster.

"Ellery," said Paula softly, "you're such a fool."

"Now, Paula, I don't care to discuss——"

"What do you think I'm referring to? It's your topcoat, silly. Didn't I warn you someone would steal it?"

Mr. Queen glanced into the roadster. His coat was gone. "Oh, that. I was going to throw it away, anyway. Now look, Paula, if you think for one instant that I could be jealous of some oversized . . . Paula! What's the matter?"

Paula's cheeks were gray in the brilliant arc-light. She was pointing a shaky forefinger at the blood-red limousine.

"In—in there . . . Isn't that—Mike Brown?"

Mr. Queen glanced quickly into the rear of the limousine. Then he said: "Get into Maguire's car, Paula, and look the other way."

Paula crept into the roadster, shaking.

Ellery opened the rear door of Stearn's car.

Mike Brown tumbled out of the car to his feet, and lay still.

And after a moment the Inspector, Maguire, and Coyle strolled up, chuckling over something Maguire was relating in a thick voice.

Maguire stopped. "Say. Who's that?"

Coyle said abruptly: "Isn't that Mike Brown?"

The Inspector said: "Out of the way, Jim." He knelt beside Ellery.

And Mr. Queen raised his head. "Yes, it's Mike Brown. Someone's used him for a pin-cushion."

Phil Maguire yelped and ran for a telephone. Paula Paris crawled out of Maguire's roadster and blundered after him, remembering her profession.

"Is he . . . is he—" began Jim Coyle, gulping.

"The long count," said the Inspector grimly. "Say, is that girl gone? Here, help me turn him over."

They turned him over. He lay staring up into the blinding arc-light. He was completely dressed; his fedora was still jammed about his ears and a gray tweed topcoat was wrapped about his body, still buttoned. He had been stabbed ten times in the abdomen and chest, through his topcoat. There had been a great deal of bleeding; his coat was sticky and wet with it.

"Body's warm," said the Inspector. "This happened just a few minutes ago." He rose from the dust and stared unseeingly at the crowd which had gathered.

"Maybe," began the champion, licking his lips, "maybe——"

"Maybe what, Jim?" asked the Inspector, looking at him.

"Nothing, nothing."

"Why don't you go home? Don't let this spoil your night, kid."

Coyle set his jaw. "I'll stick around."

The Inspector blew a police whistle.

Police came, and Phil Maguire and Paula Paris returned, and Ollie Stearn and others appeared from across the street, and the crowd thickened, and Mr. Ellery Queen crawled into the tonneau of Stearn's car.

The rear of the red limousine was a shambles. Blood stained the mohair cushions, the floor-rug, which was wrinkled and scuffed. A large coat-button with a scrap of fabric still clinging to it lay on one of the cushions, beside a crumpled camel's-hair coat.

Mr. Queen seized the coat. The button had been torn from it. The front of the coat, like the front of the murdered man's coat, was badly bloodstained. But the stains had a pattern. Mr. Queen laid the coat on the seat, front up, and slipped the buttons through the button-holes. Then the bloodstains met. When he unbuttoned the coat and separated the two sides of the coat the stains separated, too, and on the side where the buttons were the blood traced a straight edge an inch outside the line of buttons.

The Inspector poked his head in. "What's that thing?"

"The murderer's coat."

"Let's see that!"

"It won't tell you anything about its wearer. Fairly cheap coat, label's been ripped out—no identifying marks. Do you see what must have happened in here, dad?"

"What?"

"The murder occurred, of course, in this car. Either Brown and his killer got into the car simultaneously, or Brown was here first and then his murderer came, or the murderer was skulking in here, waiting for Brown to come. In any event, the murderer wore this coat."

"How do you know that?"

"Because there's every sign of a fierce struggle, so fierce Brown managed to tear off one of the coat-buttons of his assailant's coat. In the course of the struggle Brown was stabbed many times. His blood flowed freely. It got all over not only his own coat but the murderer's as well. From the position of the bloodstains the murderer's coat must have been buttoned at the time of the struggle, which means he wore it."

The Inspector nodded. "Left it behind because he didn't want to be seen in a bloody coat. Ripped out all identifying marks."

From behind the Inspector came Paula's tremulous voice. "Could that be *your* camel's-hair coat, Ellery?"

Mr. Queen looked at her in an odd way. "No, Paula."

"What's this?" demanded the Inspector.

"Ellery left his topcoat behind in Phil's car before the fight," Paula explained. "I told him somebody would steal it, and somebody did. And now there's a camel's-hair coat—in this car."

"It isn't mine," said Mr. Queen patiently. "Mine has certain distinguishing characteristics which don't exist in this one—a cigaret burn at the second buttonhole, a hole in the right pocket."

The Inspector shrugged and went away.

"Then your coat's being stolen has nothing to do with it?" Paula shivered. "Ellery, I could use a cigaret."

Mr. Queen obliged. "On the contrary. The theft of my coat has everything to do with it."

"But I don't understand. You just said——"

Mr. Queen held a match to Miss Paris's cigaret and stared intently at the body of Mike Brown.

Ollie Stearn's chauffeur, a hard-looking customer, twisted his cap and said: "Mike tells me after the fight he won't need me. Tells me he'll pick me up on the Grand Concourse. Said he'd drive himself."

"Yes?"

"I was kind of—curious. I had a hot dog at the stand there and I—watched. I seen Mike come over and climb into the back——"

"Was he alone?" demanded the Inspector.

"Yeah. Just got in and sat there. A couple of drunks come along then and I couldn't see good. Only seemed to me somebody else come over and got into the car after Mike."

"Who? Who was it? Did you see?"

The chauffeur shook his head. "I couldn't see good. I don't know. After a while I thought it ain't my business. so

I walks away. But when I heard police sirens I come back."

"The one who came after Mike Brown got in," said Mr. Queen with a certain eagerness. "That person was wearing a coat, eh?"

"I guess so. Yeah."

"You didn't witness anything else that occurred?" persisted Mr. Queen.

"Nope."

"Doesn't matter, really," muttered the great man. "Line's clear. Clear as the sun. Must be that——"

"What are you mumbling about?" demanded Miss Paris in his ear.

Mr. Queen started. "Was I mumbling?" He shook his head.

Then a man from Headquarters came up with a dudish little fellow with frightened eyes who babbled he didn't know nothing, nothing, he didn't know nothing; and the Inspector said: "Come on, Oetjens. You were heard shooting off your mouth in that gin-mill. What's the dope?"

And the little fellow said shrilly: "I don't want no trouble, no trouble. I only said——"

"Yes?"

"Mike Brown looked me up this morning," muttered Oetjens, "and he says to me, he says, 'Hymie,' he says, 'Happy Day knows you, Happy Day takes a lot of your bets,' he says, 'so go lay fifty grand with Happy on Coyle to win by a K.O.,' Mike says. 'You lay that fifty grand for *me*, get it?' he says. And he says, 'If you shoot your trap off to Happy or anyone else that you bet fifty grand for me on Coyle,' he says, 'I'll rip your heart out and break your hands and give you the thumb,' he says, and a lot more, so I laid the fifty grand on Coyle to win by a K.O. and Happy took the bet at twelve to five, he wouldn't give no more."

Jim Coyle growled: "I'll break your neck, damn you."

"Wait a minute, Jim——"

"He's saying Brown took a dive!" cried the champion. "I

licked Brown fair and square. I beat the hell out of him fair and square!"

"You thought you beat the hell out of him fair and square," muttered Phil Maguire. "But he took a dive, Jim. Didn't I tell you, Inspector? Laying off that right of his——"

"It's a lie! Where's my manager? Where's Barney? They ain't going to hold up the purse on this fight!" roared Coyle. "I won it fair—I won the title fair!"

"Take it easy, Jim," said the Inspector. "Everybody knows you were in there leveling tonight. Look here, Hymie, did Brown give you the cash to bet for him?"

"He was busted," Oetjens cringed. "I just laid the bet on the cuff. The payoff don't come till the next day. So I knew it was okay, because with Mike himself betting on Coyle the fight was in the bag——"

"I'll cripple you, you tinhorn!" yelled young Coyle.

"Take it easy, Jim," soothed Inspector Queen. "So you laid the fifty grand on the cuff, Hymie, and Happy covered the bet at twelve to five, and you knew it would come out all right because Mike was going to take a dive, and then you'd collect a hundred and twenty thousand dollars and give it to Mike, is that it?"

"Yeah, yeah. But that's all, I swear——"

"When did you see Happy last, Hymie?"

Oetjens looked scared and began to back away. His police escort had to shake him a little. But he shook his head stubbornly.

"Now it couldn't be," asked the Inspector softly, "that somehow Happy got wind that you'd laid that fifty grand, not for yourself, but for Mike Brown, could it? It couldn't be that Happy found out it was a dive, or suspected it?" The Inspector said sharply to a detective: "Find Happy Day."

"I'm right here," said a bass voice from the crowd; and the fat gambler waded through and said hotly to Inspector Queen: "So I'm the sucker, hey? I'm supposed to take the rap, hey?"

"Did you know Mike Brown was set to take a dive?"

"No!"

Phil Maguire chuckled.

And little Ollie Stearn, pale as his dead fighter, shouted: "Happy done it, Inspector! He found out, and he waited till after the fight, and when he saw Mike laying down he came out here and gave him the business! That's the way it was!"

"You lousy rat," said the gambler. "How do I know you didn't do it yourself? He wasn't taking no dive you couldn't find out about! Maybe you stuck him up because of that fancy doll of his. Don't tell *me*. I know all about you and that Ivy broad. I know——"

"Gentlemen, gentlemen," said the Inspector with a satisfied smile, when there was a shriek and Ivy Brown elbowed her way through the jam and flung herself on the dead body of her husband for the benefit of the press.

And as the photographers joyously went to work, and Happy Day and Ollie Stearn eyed each other with hate, and the crowd milled around, the Inspector said happily to his son: "Not too tough. Not too tough. A wrap-up. It's Happy Day, all right, and all I've got to do is find——"

The great man smiled and said: "You're riding a dead nag."

"Eh?"

"You're wasting your time."

The Inspector ceased to look happy. "What am I supposed to be doing, then? You tell me. You know it all."

"Of course I do, and of course I shall," said Mr. Queen. "What are you to do? Find my coat."

"Say, what *is* this about your damn' coat?" growled the Inspector.

"Find my coat, and perhaps I'll find your murderer."

It was a peculiar sort of case. First there had been the ride to the Stadium, and the conversation about how Phil Maguire didn't like Mike Brown, and then there was the ringside gossip, the preliminaries, the main event, the champion's knockout, and all the rest of—all unimportant, all stodgy little details . . . until Mr. Queen and Miss Paris strolled across the parking lot and found two things—or rather, lost one thing—Mr. Queen's coat—and found another—Mike Brown's body; and so there was an important murder-case, all nice and shiny.

And immediately the great man began nosing about and muttering about his coat, as if an old and shabby topcoat being stolen could possibly be more important than Mike Brown lying there in the gravel of the parking space full of punctures, like an abandoned tire, and Mike's wife, full of more curves and detours than the Storm King highway, sobbing on his chest and calling upon Heaven and the New York press to witness how dearly she had loved him, poor dead gorilla.

So it appeared that Mike Brown had had a secret rendez-vous with someone after the fight, because he had got rid of Ollie Stearn's chauffeur, and the appointment must have been for the interior of Ollie Stearn's red limousine. And who-ever he was, he came, and got in with Mike, and there was a struggle, and he stabbed Mike almost a dozen times with something long and sharp, and then fled, leaving his camel's-hair coat behind, because with blood all over its front it would have given him away.

That brought up the matter of the weapon, and everybody began nosing about, including Mr. Queen, because it was a cinch the murderer might have dropped it in his flight. And, sure enough, a radio-car man found it in the dirt under a parked car—a long, evil-looking stiletto with no distinguish-ing marks whatever and no fingerprints except the finger-prints of the radio-car man. But Mr. Queen persisted in nosing even after that discovery, and finally the Inspector asked him peevishly: "What are you looking for now?"

"My coat," explained Mr. Queen. "Do you see anyone with my coat?"

But there was hardly a man in the crowd with a coat. It was a warm night.

So finally Mr. Queen gave up his queer search and said: "I don't know what you good people are going to do, but, as for me, I'm going back to the Stadium."

"For heaven's sake, what for?" cried Paula.

"To see if I can find my coat," said Mr. Queen patiently.

"I told you you should have taken it with you!"

"Oh, no," said Mr. Queen. "I'm glad I didn't. I'm glad I left it behind in Maguire's car. I'm glad it was stolen."

"But why, you exasperating idiot?"

"Because now," replied Mr. Queen with a cryptic smile, "I have to go looking for it."

And while the morgue wagon carted Mike Brown's carcass off, Mr. Queen trudged back across the dusty parking lot and into the alley which led to the Stadium dressing-rooms. And the Inspector, with a baffled look, herded everyone— with special loving care and attention for Mr. Happy Day and Mr. Ollie Stearn and Mrs. Ivy Brown—after his son. He didn't know what else to do.

And finally they were assembled in Jim Coyle's dressing-room, and Ivy was weeping into more cameras, and Mr. Queen was glumly contemplating Miss Paris's red straw hat, that looked like a pot, and there was a noise at the door and they saw Barney Hawks, the new champion's manager, standing on the threshold in the company of several officials and promoters.

"What ho," said Barney Hawks with a puzzled glance about. "You still here, champ? What goes on?"

"Plenty goes on," said the champ savagely. "Barney, did you know Brown took a dive tonight?"

"What? What's this?" said Barney Hawks, looking around virtuously. "Who says so, the dirty liar? My boy won that title on the up and up, gentlemen! He beat Brown fair and square."

"Brown threw the fight?" asked one of the men with Hawks, a member of the Boxing Commission. "Is there any evidence of that?"

"The hell with that," said the Inspector politely. "Barney, Mike Brown is dead."

Hawks began to laugh, then he stopped laughing and sputtered: "What's this? What's this? What's the gageroo? Brown dead?"

Jim Coyle waved his huge paw tiredly. "Somebody bumped him off tonight, Barney. In Stearn's car across the street."

"Well, I'm a bum, I'm a bum," breathed his manager, staring. "So Mike got his, hey? Well, well. Tough. Loses his title and his life. Who done it, boys?"

"Maybe you didn't know my boy was dead!" shrilled Ollie Stearn. "Yeah, you put on a swell act, Barney! Maybe you fixed it with Mike so he'd take a dive so your boy could win the title! Maybe you——"

"There's been another crime committed here tonight," said a mild voice, and they all looked wonderingly around to find Mr. Ellery Queen advancing toward Mr. Hawks.

"Hey?" said Coyle's manager, staring stupidly at him.

"My coat was stolen."

"Hey?" Hawks kept gaping.

"And, unless my eyes deceive me, as the phrase goes," continued the great man, stopping before Barney Hawks, "I've found it again."

"Hey?"

"On your arm." And Mr. Queen gently removed from Mr. Hawks's arm a shabby camel's-hair topcoat, and unfolded it, and examined it. "Yes. My very own."

Barney Hawks turned green in the silence.

Something sharpened in Mr. Queen's silver eyes, and he bent over the camel's-hair coat again. He spread out the sleeves and examined the armhole seams. They had burst.

As had the seam at the back of the coat. He looked up and at Mr. Hawks reproachfully.

"The least you might have done," he said, "is to have returned my property in the same condition in which I left it."

"Your coat?" said Barney Hawks damply. Then he shouted: "What the hell is this? That's my coat! My camel's-hair coat!"

"No," Mr. Queen dissented respectfully, "I can prove this to be mine. You see, it has a telltale cigaret burn at the second buttonhole, and a hole in the right-hand pocket."

"But—I found it where I left it! It was here all the time! I took it out of here after the fight and went up to the office to talk to these gentlemen and I've been—" The manager stopped, and his complexion faded from green to white. "Then where's my coat?" he asked slowly.

"Will you try this on?" asked Mr. Queen with the deference of a clothing salesman, and he took from a detective the bloodstained coat they had found abandoned in Ollie Stearn's car.

Mr. Queen held the coat up before Hawks; and Hawks said thickly: "All right. It's my coat. I guess it's my coat, if you say so. So what?"

"So," replied Mr. Queen, "someone knew Mike Brown was broke, that he owed his shirt, that not even his lion's share of the purse tonight would suffice to pay his debts. Someone persuaded Mike Brown to throw the fight tonight, offering to pay him a large sum of money, I suppose, for taking the dive. That money no one would know about. That money would not have to be turned over to the clutches of Mike Brown's loving wife and creditors. That money would be Mike Brown's own. So Mike Brown said yes, realizing that he could make more money, too, by placing a large bet with Happy Day through the medium of Mr. Oetjens. And with this double nest-egg he could jeer at the unfriendly world.

"And probably Brown and his tempter conspired to meet in Stearn's car immediately after the fight for the pay-off, for Brown would be insistent about that. So Brown sent the chauffeur away, and sat in the car, and the tempter came to keep the appointment—armed not with the pay-off money but with a sharp stiletto. And by using the stiletto he saved himself a tidy sum—the sum he'd promised Brown—and also made sure Mike Brown would never be able to tell the wicked story to the wicked world."

Barney Hawks licked his dry lips. "Don't look at me, Mister. You got nothing on Barney Hawks. I don't know nothing about this."

And Mr. Queen said, paying no attention whatever to Mr. Hawks: "A pretty problem, friends. You see, the tempter came to the scene of the crime in a camel's-hair coat, and he had to leave the coat behind because it was bloodstained and would have given him away. Also, in the car next to the murder-car lay, quite defenseless, my own poor camel's-hair coat, its only virtue the fact that it was stained with no man's blood.

"We found a coat abandoned in Stearn's car and my coat, in the next car, stolen. Coincidence? Hardly. The murderer certainly took my coat to replace the coat he was forced to leave behind."

Mr. Queen paused to refresh himself with a cigaret, glancing whimsically at Miss Paris, who was staring at him with a soul-satisfying worship. Mind over matter, thought Mr. Queen, remembering with special satisfaction how Miss Paris had stared at Jim Coyle's muscles. Yes, sir, mind over matter.

"Well?" said Inspector Queen. "Suppose this bird did take your coat? What of it?"

"But that's exactly the point," mourned Mr. Queen. "He took my poor, shabby, worthless coat. Why?"

"Why?" echoed the Inspector blankly.

"Yes, why? Everything in this world is activated by a reason. Why did he take my coat?"

"Well, I—I suppose to wear it."

"Very good," applauded Mr. Queen, playing up to Miss Paris. "Precisely. If he took it he had a reason, and since its only function under the circumstances could have been its wearability, so to speak, he took it to wear it." He paused, then murmured: "But why should he want to wear it?"

The Inspector looked angry. "See here, Ellery—" he began.

"No, dad, no," said Mr. Queen gently. "I'm talking with a purpose. There's a point. *The* point. You might say he had to wear it because he'd got blood on his suit *under* the coat and required a coat to hide the bloodstained suit. Or mightn't you?"

"Well, sure," said Phil Maguire eagerly. "That's it."

"You may be an Einstein in your sports department, Mr. Maguire, but here you're just a palooka. No," said Mr. Queen, shaking his head sadly, "that's not it. He couldn't possibly have got blood on his suit. The coat shows that at the time he attacked Brown he was wearing it *buttoned*. If the topcoat was buttoned, his suit didn't catch any of Brown's blood."

"He certainly didn't need a coat because of the weather," muttered Inspector Queen.

"True. It's been warm all evening. You see," smiled Mr. Queen, "what a cute little thing it is. He'd left his own coat behind, its labels and other identifying marks taken out, unworried about its being found—otherwise he would have hidden it or thrown it away. Such being the case, you would say he'd simply make his escape in the clothes he was wearing *beneath* the coat. But he didn't. He stole another coat, my coat, for his escape." Mr. Queen coughed gently. "So surely it's obvious that if he stole my coat for his escape, he *needed* my coat for his escape? That if he escaped without my coat he would be *noticed*?"

"I don't get it," said the Inspector. "He'd be noticed? But if he was wearing ordinary clothing——"

"Then obviously he wouldn't need my coat," nodded Mr. Queen.

"Or—say! If he was wearing a uniform of some kind— say he was a Stadium attendant——"

"Then still obviously he wouldn't need my coat. A uniform would be a perfect guarantee that he'd pass in the crowds unnoticed." Mr. Queen shook his head. "No, there's only one answer to this problem. I saw it at once, of course." He noted the Inspector's expression and continued hastily: "And that was: If the murderer had been wearing clothes— *any* normal body-covering—beneath the bloodstained coat, he could have made his escape in those clothes. But since he didn't, it can only mean that he *wasn't* wearing clothes, you see, and that's why he needed a coat not only to come to the scene of the crime, but to escape from it as well."

There was another silence, and finally Paula said: "Wasn't wearing clothes? A . . . naked man? Why, that's like something out of Poe!"

"No," smiled Mr. Queen, "merely something out of the Stadium. You see, we had a classification of gentlemen in the vicinity tonight who wore no—or nearly no—clothing. In a word, the gladiators. Or, if you choose, the pugilists. . . . Wait!" he said swiftly. "This is an extraordinary case, chiefly because I solved the hardest part of it almost the instant I knew there was a murder. For the instant I discovered that Brown had been stabbed, and that my coat had been stolen by a murderer who left his own behind, I knew that the murderer could have been *only one of thirteen men* . . . the thirteen living prizefighters left after Brown was killed. For you'll recall there were fourteen fighters in the Stadium tonight—twelve distributed among six preliminary bouts, and two in the main bout.

"Which of the thirteen living fighters had killed Brown? That was my problem from the beginning. And so I had to find my coat, because it was the only concrete connection I could discern between the murderer and his crime. And now I've found my coat, and now I know which of the thirteen murdered Brown."

Barney Hawks was speechless, his jaws agape.

"I'm a tall, fairly broad man. In fact, I'm six feet tall," said the great man. "And yet the murderer, in wearing my coat to make his escape, burst its seams at the armholes and back! That meant he was a big man, a much bigger man than I, much bigger and broader.

"Which of the thirteen fighters on the card tonight were bigger and broader than I? Ah, but it's been a very light card—bantamweights, welterweights, lightweights, middleweights! Therefore none of the twelve preliminary fighters could have murdered Brown. Therefore only one fighter was left—a man six and a half feet tall, extremely broad-shouldered and broad-backed, a man who had every motive—the greatest motive—to induce Mike Brown to throw the fight tonight!"

And this time the silence was ghastly with meaning. It was broken by Jim Coyle's lazy laugh. "If you mean me, you must be off your nut. Why, I was in that shower-room taking a shower at the time Mike was bumped off!"

"Yes, I mean you, Mr. Jim Coyle Stiletto-Wielding Couzzi," said Mr. Queen clearly, "and the shower-room was the cleverest part of your scheme. You went into the shower-room in full view of all of us, with towels, shut the door, turned on the shower, slipped a pair of trousers over your bare and manly legs, grabbed Barney Hawks's camel's-hair coat and hat which were hanging on a peg in there, and then ducked out the shower-room window into the alley. From there it was a matter of seconds to the street and the parking lot across the street. Of course, when you stained Hawks's coat during the commission of your crime, you couldn't risk coming back in it. And you had to have a coat—a buttoned coat—to cover your nakedness for the return trip. So you stole mine, for which I'm very grateful, because otherwise—Grab him, will you? My right isn't very good," said Mr. Queen, employing a dainty and beautiful bit of footwork to escape Coyle's sudden homicidal lunge in his direction.

And while Coyle went down under an avalanche of flailing arms and legs, Mr. Queen murmured apologetically to Miss Paris: "After all, darling, he *is* the heavyweight champion of the world."

TROJAN HORSE

TROJAN HORSE

"Whom," demanded Miss Paula Paris across the groaning board, "do you like, Mr. Queen?"

Mr. Queen instantly mumbled: "You," out of a mouthful of Vermont turkey, chestnut stuffing, and cranberry sauce.

"I didn't mean that, silly," said Miss Paris, nevertheless pleased. "However, now that you've brought the subject up—will you say such pretty things when we're married?"

Mr. Ellery Queen paled and, choking, set down his weapons. When he had first encountered the lovely Miss Paris, Hollywood's reigning goddess of gossip, Miss Paris had been suffering from homophobia, or morbid fear of man; she had been so terrified of crowds that she had not for years set foot outside her virginal white frame house in the Hollywood hills. Mr. Queen, stirred by a nameless emotion, determined to cure the lady of her psychological affliction. The therapy, he conceived, must be both shocking and compensatory; and so he made love to her.

And lo! although Miss Paris recovered, to his horror Mr. Queen found that the cure may sometimes present a worse problem than the affliction. For the patient promptly fell in love with her healer; and the healer did not himself escape certain excruciating emotional consequences.

His precious liberty faced with this alluring menace, Mr. Queen now choked over the luscious Christmas dinner which Miss Paris had cunningly cooked with her own slim hands and served *en tête-à-tête* in her cosy maple and chintz dining-room.

"Oh, relax," pouted Miss Paris. "I was joking. What makes you think I'd marry a creature who studies cut throats and chases thieves for the enjoyment of it?"

"Horrible fate for a woman," Mr. Queen hastened to agree. "Besides, I'm not good enough for you."

"Darned tootin' you're not! But you haven't answered my question. Do you think Carolina will lick USC next Sunday?"

"Oh, the Rose Bowl game," said Mr. Queen, discovering his appetite miraculously. "More turkey, please! . . . Well, if Ostermoor lives up to his reputation, the Spartans should breeze in."

"Really?" murmured Miss Paris. "Aren't you forgetting that Roddy Crockett is the whole Trojan backfield?"

"Southern California Trojans, Carolina Spartans," said Mr. Queen thoughtfully, munching. "Spartans versus Trojans . . . Sort of modern gridiron Siege of Troy."

"Ellery Queen, that's plagiarism or—or something! You read it in my column."

"Is there a Helen for the lads to battle over?" grinned Mr. Queen.

"You're so romantic, Queenikins. The only female involved is a very pretty, rich, and sensible co-ed named Joan Wing, and she isn't the kidnaped love of any of the Spartans."

"Curses," said Mr. Queen, reaching for the brandied plum pudding. "For a moment I thought I had something."

"But there's a Priam of a sort, because Roddy Crockett is engaged to Joan Wing, and Joanie's father, Pop Wing, is just about the noblest Trojan of them all."

"Maybe you know what you're talking about, beautiful," said Mr. Queen, "but I don't."

"You're positively the worst-informed man in California! Pop Wing is USC's most enthusiastic alumnus, isn't he?"

"Is he?"

"You mean you've never heard of Pop Wing?" asked Paula incredulously.

"Not guilty," said Mr. Queen. "More plum pudding, please."

"The Perennial Alumnus? The Boy Who Never Grew Up?"

"Thank you," said Mr. Queen. "I beg your pardon."

"The Ghost of Exposition Park and the L.A. Coliseum, who holds a life seat for all USC football games? The unofficial trainer, rubber, water-boy, pep-talker, Alibi Ike, booster, and pigskin patron-in-chief to the Trojan eleven? Percy Squires 'Pop' Wing, Southern California '04, the man who sleeps, eats, and breathes only for Trojan victories and who married and, failing a son, created a daughter for the sole purpose of snaring USC's best fullback in years?"

"Peace, peace; I yield," moaned Mr. Queen, "before the crushing brutality of the characterization. I now know Percy Squires Wing as I hope never to know anyone again."

"Sorry!" said Paula, rising briskly. "Because directly after you've filled your bottomless tummy with plum pudding we're going Christmas calling on the great man."

"No!" said Mr. Queen with a shudder.

"You want to see the Rose Bowl game, don't you?"

"Who doesn't? But I haven't been able to snag a brace of tickets for love or money."

"Poor Queenie," purred Miss Paris, putting her arms about him. "You're *so* helpless. Come on watch me wheedle Pop Wing out of two seats for the game!"

The lord of the château whose towers rose from a magnificently preposterous parklike estate in Inglewood proved to be a flatbellied youngster of middle age, almost as broad as he was tall, with a small bald head set upon small ruddy cheeks, so that at first glance Mr. Queen thought he was viewing a Catawba grape lying on a boulder.

They came upon the millionaire seated on his hams in the center of a vast lawn, arguing fiercely with a young man who by his size—which was herculean—and his shape—which was cuneiform—and his coloring—which was coppery—could only be of the order *footballis*, and therefore Mr. Wing's future son-in-law and the New Year's Day hope of the Trojans.

They were manipulating wickets, mallets, and croquet balls in illustration of a complex polemic which apparently concerned the surest method of frustrating the sinister quarter-back of the Carolina eleven, Ostermoor.

A young lady with red hair and a saucy nose sat cross-legged on the grass nearby, her soft blue eyes fixed on the brown face of the young man with that naked worshipfulness young ladies permit themselves to exhibit in public only when their young men have formally yielded. This, concluded Mr. Queen without difficulty, must be the daughter of the great man and Mr. Roddy Crockett's fiancée, Joan Wing.

Mr. Wing hissed a warning to Roddy at the sight of Mr. Queen's unfamiliar visage, and for a moment Mr. Queen felt uncomfortably like a spy caught sneaking into the enemy's camp. But Miss Paris hastily vouched for his devotion to the cause of Troy, and for some time there were Christmas greet-ings and introductions, in the course of which Mr. Queen made the acquaintance of two persons whom he recognized instantly as the hybrid genus *house-guest perennialis*. One was a bearded gentleman with high cheek-bones and a Musco-vite manner (pre-Soviet) entitled the Grand Duke Ostrov; the other was a thin, dark, whiplike female with inscrutable black eyes who went by the mildly astonishing name of Madame Mephisto.

These two barely nodded to Miss Paris and Mr. Queen; they were listening to each word which dropped from the lips of Mr. Percy Squires Wing, their host, with the adoration of novitiates at the feet of their patron saint.

The noble Trojan's ruddiness of complexion, Mr. Queen pondered, came either from habitual exposure to the outdoors or from high blood-pressure; a conclusion which he discov-ered very soon was accurate on both counts, since Pop Wing revealed himself without urging as an Izaak Walton, a golfer, a Nimrod, a mountain-climber, a polo-player, and a racing yachtsman; and he was as squirmy and excitable as a small boy.

The small-boy analogy struck Mr. Queen with greater force when the Perennial Alumnus dragged Mr. Queen off to inspect what he alarmingly called "my trophy room." Mr. Queen's fears were vindicated; for in a huge vaulted chamber presided over by a desiccated, gloomy, and monosyllabic old gentleman introduced fantastically as "Gabby" Huntswood, he found himself inspecting as heterogeneous and remarkable an assemblage of junk as ever existed outside a small boy's dream of Paradise.

Postage stamp albums, American college banners, mounted wild-animal heads, a formidable collection of match-boxes, cigar bands, stuffed fish, World War trench helmets of all nations . . . all were there; and Pop Wing beamed as he exhibited these priceless treasures, scurrying from one collection to another and fondling them with such ingenuous pleasure that Mr. Queen sighed for his own lost youth.

"Aren't these objects too—er—valuable to be left lying around this way, Mr. Wing?" he inquired politely.

"Hell, no. Gabby's more jealous of their safety than I am!" shouted the great man. "Hey, Gabby?"

"Yes, sir," said Gabby; and he frowned suspiciously at Mr. Queen.

"Why, Gabby made me install a burglar-alarm system. Can't see it, but this room's as safe as a vault."

"Safer," said Gabby, glowering at Mr. Queen.

"Think I'm crazy, Queen?"

"No, no," said Mr. Queen, who meant to say "Yes, yes."

"Lots of people do," chuckled Pop Wing. "Let 'em. Between 1904 and 1924 I just about vegetated. But something drove me on. Know what?"

Mr. Queen's famous powers of deduction were unequal to the task.

"The knowledge that I was making enough money to retire a young man and kick the world in the pants. And I did! Retired at forty-two and started doing all the things I'd never had time or money to do when I was a shaver. Collecting things. Keeps me young! Come here, Queen, and

!ook at my *prize* collection." And he pulled Mr. Queen over to a gigantic glass case and pointed gleefully, an elder Penrod gloating over a marbles haul.

From his host's proud tone Mr. Queen expected to gaze upon nothing less than a collection of the royal crowns of Europe. Instead, he saw a vast number of scuffed, streaked, and muddy footballs, each carefully laid upon an ebony rest, and on each a legend lettered in gold leaf. One that caught his eye read: "Rose Bowl, 1930. USC 47-Pitt 14." The others bore similar inscriptions.

"Wouldn't part with 'em for a million dollars," confided the great man. "Why, the balls in this case represent every Trojan victroy for the past fifteen years!"

"Incredible!" exclaimed Mr. Queen.

"Yes, sir, right after every game they win the team presents old Pop Wing with the pigskin. What a collection!" And the millionaire gazed worshipfully at the unlovely oblate spheroids.

"They must think the world of you at USC."

"Well, I've sort of been of service to my Alma Mater," said Pop Wing modestly, "especially in football. Wing Athletic Scholarship, you know; Wing Dorm for 'Varsity athletes; and so on. I've scouted prep schools for years, personally; turned up some mighty fine 'Varsity material. Coach is a good friend of mine. I guess," and he drew a happy breath, "I can have just about what I damn well ask for at the old school!"

"Including football tickets?" said Mr. Queen quickly, seizing his opportunity. "Must be marvelous to have that kind of drag. I've been trying for days to get tickets for the game."

The great man surveyed him. "What was your college?"

"Harvard," said Mr. Queen apologetically. "But I yield to no man in my ardent admiration of the Trojans. Darn it, I did want to watch Roddy Crockett mop up those Spartan upstarts."

"You did, huh?" said Pop Wing. "Say, how about you and Miss Paris being my guests at the Rose Bowl Sunday?"

"Couldn't think of it—" began Mr. Queen mendaciously, already savoring the joy of having beaten Miss Paris, so to speak, to the turnstiles.

"Won't hear another word." Mr. Wing embraced Mr. Queen. "Say, long as you'll be with us, I'll let you in on a little secret."

"Secret?" wondered Mr. Queen.

"Rod and Joan," whispered the millionaire, "are going to be married right after the Trojans win next Sunday!"

"Congratulations. He seems like a fine boy."

"None better. Hasn't got a cent, you understand—worked his way through—but he's graduating in January and . . . shucks! he's the greatest fullback the old school ever turned out. We'll find something for him to do. Yes, sir, Roddy's last game . . ." The great man sighed. Then he brightened. "Anyway, I've got a hundred thousand dollar surprise for my Joanie that ought to make her go right out and raise another triple-threat man for the Trojans!"

"A—how much of a surprise?" asked Mr. Queen feebly.

But the great man looked mysterious. "Let's go back and finish cooking that boy Ostermoor's goose!"

New Year's Day was warm and sunny; and Mr. Queen felt strangely as he prepared to pick up Paula Paris and escort her to the Wing estate, from which their party was to proceed to the Pasadena stadium. In his quaint Eastern fashion, he was accustomed to don a mountain of sweater, scarf, and overcoat when he went to a football game; and here he was *en route* in a sports jacket!

"California, thy name is Iconoclast," muttered Mr. Queen, and he drove through already agitated Hollywood streets to Miss Paris's house.

"Heavens," said Paula, "you can't barge in on Pop Wing that way."

"What way?"

"Minus the Trojan colors. We've got to keep on the old darlin's good side, at least until we're safely in the stadium. Here!" And with a few deft twists of two lady's handkerchiefs Paula manufactured a breast-pocket kerchief for him in cardinal and gold.

"I see you've done yourself up pretty brown," said Mr. Queen, not unadmiringly; for Paula's figure was the secret envy of many better-advertised Hollywood ladies, and it was clad devastatingly in a cardinal-and-gold creation that was a cross between a suit and a dirndl, to Mr. Queen's inexperienced eye, and it was topped off with a perky, feathery hat perched nervously on her blue-black hair, concealing one bright eye.

"Wait till you see Joan," said Miss Paris, rewarding him with a kiss. "She's been calling me all week about *her* clothes problem. It's not every day a girl's called on to buy an outfit that goes equally well with a football game and a wedding." And as Mr. Queen drove off towards Inglewood she added thoughtfully: "I wonder what that awful creature will wear. Probably a turban and seven veils."

"What creature?"

"Madame Mephisto. Only her real name is Suzie Lucadamo, and she quit a dumpy little magic and mind-reading vaudeville act to set herself up in Seattle as a seeress—you know, we positively guarantee to pierce the veil of the Unknown? Pop met her in Seattle in November during the USC-Washington game. She wangled a Christmas-week invitation out of him for the purpose, I suppose, of looking over the rich Hollywood sucker-field without cost to herself."

"You seem to know a lot about her."

Paula smiled. "Joan Wing told me some—Joanie doesn't like the old gal nohow—and I dug out the rest . . . well, you know, darling, I know everything about *everybody*."

"Then tell me," said Mr. Queen. "Who exactly is the Grand Duke Ostrov?"

"Why?"

"Because," replied Mr. Queen grimly, "I don't like His Highness, and I do like—heaven help me!—Pop Wing and his juvenile amusements."

"Joan tells me Pop likes you, too, the fool! I guess in his adolescent way he's impressed by a real, live detective. Show him your G-man badge, darling." Mr. Queen glared, but Miss Paris's gaze was dreamy. "Pop may find it handy having you around today, at that."

"What d'ye mean?" asked Mr. Queen sharply.

"Didn't he tell you he had a surprise for Joan? He's told everyone in Los Angeles, although no one knows what it is but your humble correspondent."

"And Roddy, I'll bet. He did say something about a 'hundred thousand dollar surprise.' What's the point?"

"The point is," murmured Miss Paris, "that it's a set of perfectly matched star sapphires."

Mr. Queen was silent. Then he said: "You think Ostrov——"

"The Grand Duke," said Miss Paris, "is even phonier than Madame Suzie Lucadamo Mephisto. *His* name is Louie Batterson, and he hails from the Bronx. Everybody knows it but Pop Wing." Paula sighed. "But you know Hollywood —live and let live; you may need a sucker yourself some day. Batterson's a high-class deadbeat. He's pulled some awfully aromatic stunts in his time. I'm hoping he lays off our nostrils this sunny day."

"This," mumbled Mr. Queen, "is going to be one heck of a football game, I can see that."

Bedlam was a cloister compared with the domain of the Wings. The interior of the house was noisy with decorators, caterers, cooks, and waiters; and with a start Mr. Queen recalled that this was to be the wedding day of Joan Wing and Roddy Crockett.

They found their party assembled in one of the formal

gardens—which, Mr. Queen swore to Miss Paris, outshone Fontainebleau—and apparently Miss Wing had solved her dressmaking problem, for while Mr. Queen could find no word to describe what she was wearing, Mr. Roddy Crockett could, and the word was "sockeroo."

Paula went into more technical raptures, and Miss Wing clung to her gridiron hero, who looked a little pale; and then the pride of Troy went loping off to the wars, leaping into his roadster and waving farewell with their cries of good cheer in his manly, young, and slightly mashed ears.

Pop Wing ran down the driveway after the roadster, bellowing: "Don't forget that Ostermoor defense, Roddy!"

And Roddy vanished in a trail of dusty glory; the noblest Trojan of them all came back shaking his head and muttering: "It ought to be a pipe!"; flunkies appeared bearing mounds of canapés and cocktails; the Grand Duke, regally Cossack in a long Russian coat gathered at the waist, amused the company with feats of legerdemain—his long soft hands were very fluent—and Madame Mephisto, minus the seven veils but, as predicted, wearing the turban, went into a trance and murmured that she could see a "glorious Trojan vic-to-ree"—all the while Joan Wing sat smiling dreamily into her cocktail and Pop Wing pranced up and down vowing that he had never been cooler or more confident in his life.

And then they were in one of Wing's huge seven-passenger limousines—Pop, Joan, the Grand Duke, Madame, Gabby, Miss Paris, and Mr. Queen—bound for Pasadena and the fateful game.

And Pop said suddenly: "Joanie, I've got a surprise for you."

And Joan dutifully looked surprised, her breath coming a little faster; and Pop drew out of the right-hand pocket of his jacket a long leather case, and opened it, and said with a chuckle: "Wasn't going to show it to you till tonight, but Roddy told me before he left that you look so beautiful I ought to give you a preview as a reward. From me to you, Joanie. Like 'em?"

Joan gasped: "*Like* them!" and there were exclamations of "Oh!" and "Ah!", and they saw lying upon black velvet eleven superb sapphires, their stars winking royally—a football team of perfectly matched gems.

"Oh, *Pop!*" moaned Joan, and she flung her arms about him and wept on his shoulder, while he looked pleased and blustery, and puffed and closed the case and returned it to the pocket from which he had taken it.

"Formal opening tonight. Then you can decide whether you want to make a necklace out of 'em or a bracelet or what." And Pop stroked Joan's hair while she sniffled against him; and Mr. Queen, watching the Grand Duke Ostrov, *né* Batterson, and Madame Mephisto, *née* Lucadamo, thought they were very clever to have concealed so quickly those startling expressions of avarice.

Surrounded by his guests, Pop strode directly to the Trojans' dressing-room, waving aside officials and police and student athletic underlings as if he owned the Rose Bowl and all the multitudinous souls besieging it.

The young man at the door said: "Hi, Pop," respectfully, and admitted them under the envious stares of the less fortunate mortals outside.

"Isn't he grand?" whispered Paula, her eyes like stars; but before Mr. Queen could reply there were cries of: "Hey! Femmes!" and "Here's Pop!" and the Coach came over, wickedly straight-arming Mr. Roddy Crockett, who was lacing his doeskin pants, aside, and said with a wink: "All right, Pop. Give it to 'em."

And Pop, very pale now, shucked his coat and flung it on a rubbing table; and the boys crowded round, very quiet suddenly; and Mr. Queen found himself pinned between a mountainous tackle and a behemoth of a guard who growled down at him: "Hey, you, stop squirming. Don't you see Pop's gonna make a speech?"

And Pop said, in a very low voice: "Listen, gang. The last time I made a dressing-room spiel was in '33. It was on a January first, too, and it was the day USC played Pitt in the Rose Bowl. That day we licked 'em thirty-three to nothing."

Somebody shouted: "Yay!" but Pop held up his hand.

"I made three January first speeches before that. One was in '32, before we knocked Tulane over by a score of twenty-one to twelve. One was in 1930, the day we beat the Panthers forty-seven to fourteen. And the first in '23, when we took Penn State by fourteen to three. And that was the first time in the history of Rose Bowl that we represented the Pacific Coast Conference in the inter-sectional classic. There's just one thing I want you men to bear in mind when you dash out there in a few minutes in front of half of California."

The room was very still.

"I want you to remember that the Trojans have played in four Rose Bowl games. And I want you to remember that the Trojans have *won* four Rose Bowl games," said Pop.

And he stood high above them, looking down into their intent young faces; and then he jumped to the floor, breathing heavily.

Hell broke loose. Boys pounded him on the back; Roddy Crockett seized Joan and pulled her behind a locker; Mr. Queen found himself pinned to the door, hat over his eyes, by the elbow of the Trojan center, like a butterfly to a wall; and the Coach stood grinning at Pop, who grinned back, but tremulously.

"All right, men," said the Coach. "Pop?" Pop Wing grinned and shook them all off, and Roddy helped him into his coat, and after a while Mr. Queen, considerably the worse for wear, found himself seated in Pop's box directly above the fifty-yard line.

And then, as the two teams dashed into the Bowl across

the brilliant turf, to the roar of massed thousands, Pop Wing
uttered a faint cry.

"What's the matter?" asked Joan quickly, seizing his arm.
"Aren't you feeling well, Pop?"

"The sapphires," said Pop Wing in a hoarse voice, his hand
in his pocket. "They're gone."

Kick-off! Twenty-two figures raced to converge in a tum-
bling mass, and the stands thundered, the USC section fluttering madly with flags . . . and then there was a groan that
rent the blue skies, and deadly, despairing silence.

For the Trojans' safety man caught the ball, started forward, slipped, the ball popped out of his hands, the Carolina
right end fell on it—and there was the jumping, gleeful
Spartan team on the Trojans' 9-yard line, Carolina's ball,
first down, and four plays for a touchdown.

And Gabby, who had not heard Pop Wing's exclamation,
was on his feet shrieking: "But they can't *do* that! Oh,
heavens—Come *on*, USC! Hold that line!"

Pop glanced at Mr. Huntswood with bloodshot surprise, as
if a three-thousand-year-old mummy had suddenly come to
life; and then he muttered: "Gone. Somebody's—picked my
pocket."

"*What!*" whispered Gabby; and he fell back, staring at
his employer with horror.

"But thees ees fantastic," the Grand Duke exclaimed.

Mr. Queen said quietly: "Are you positive, Mr. Wing?"

Pop's eyes were on the field, automatically analyzing the
play; but they were filled with pain. "Yes, I'm sure. Some
pickpocket in the crowd . . ."

"No," said Mr. Queen.

"Ellery, what do you mean?" cried Paula.

"From the moment we left Mr. Wing's car until we entered the Trojan dressing-room we surrounded him completely. From the moment we left the Trojan dressing-
room until we sat down in this box, we surrounded him

completely. No, our pickpocket is one of this group, I'm afraid."

Madame Mephisto shrilled: "How dare you! Aren't you forgetting that it was Mr. Crockett who helped Mr. Wing on with his coat in that dressing-room?"

"You—" began Pop in a growl, starting to rise.

Joan put her hand on his arm and squeezed, smiling at him. "Never mind her, Pop."

Carolina gained two yards on a plunge through center. Pop shaded his eyes with his hand, staring at the opposing lines.

"Meester Queen," said the Grand Duke coldly, "that ees an insult. I demand we all be—how you say?—searched."

Pop waved his hand wearily. "Forget it. I came to watch a football game." But he no longer looked like a small boy.

"His Highness's suggestion," murmured Mr. Queen, "is an excellent one. The ladies may search one another; the men may do the same. Suppose we all leave here together— in a body—and retire to the rest rooms?"

"Hold 'em," muttered Pop, as if he had not heard. Carolina gained 2 yards more on an off-tackle play. 5 yards to go in two downs. They could see Roddy Crockett slapping one of his linesmen on the back.

The lines met, and buckled. No gain.

"D'ye see Roddy go through that hole?" muttered Pop.

Joan rose and, rather imperiously, motioned Madame and Paula to precede her. Pop did not stir. Mr. Queen motioned to the men. The Grand Duke and Gabby rose. They all went quickly away.

And still Pop did not move. Until Ostermoor rifled a flat pass into the end zone, and a Carolina end came up out of the ground and snagged the ball. And then it was Carolina 6, USC 0, the big clock indicating that barely a minute of the first quarter's playing time had elapsed.

"Block that kick!"

Roddy plunged through the Spartan line and blocked it. The Carolina boys trotted back to their own territory, grinning.

"Hmph," said Pop to the empty seats in his box; and then he sat still and simply waited, an old man.

The first quarter rolled along. The Trojans could not get out of their territory. Passes fell incomplete. The Spartan line held like iron.

"Well, we're back," said Paula Paris. The great man looked up slowly. "We didn't find them."

A moment later Mr. Queen returned, herding his two companions. Mr. Queen said nothing at all; he merely shook his head, and the Grand Duke Ostrov looked grandly contemptuous, and Madame Mephisto tossed her turbaned head angrily. Joan was very pale; her eyes crept down the field to Roddy, and Paula saw that they were filled with tears.

Mr. Queen said abruptly: "Will you excuse me, please?" and left again with swift strides.

The first quarter ended with the score still 6 to 0 against USC and the Trojans unable to extricate themselves from the menace of their goal post . . . pinned back with inhuman regularity by the sharp-shooting Mr. Ostermoor. There is no defense against a deadly accurate kick.

When Mr. Queen returned, he wiped his slightly moist brow and said pleasantly: "By the way, Your Highness, it all comes back to me now. In a former incarnation—I believe in that life your name was Batterson, and you were the flower of an ancient Bronx family—weren't you mixed up in a jewel robbery?"

"Jewel robbery!" gasped Joan, and for some reason she looked relieved. Pop's eyes fixed coldly on the Grand Duke's suddenly oscillating beard.

"Yes," continued Mr. Queen, "I seem to recall that the

fence tried to involve you, Your Highness, saying you were the go-between, but the jury wouldn't believe a fence's word, and so you went free. You were quite charming on the stand, I recall—had the courtroom in stitches."

"It's a damn lie," said the Grand Duke thickly, without the trace of an accent. His teeth gleamed wolfishly at Mr. Queen from its thicket.

"You thieving four-flusher—" began Pop Wing, half-rising from his seat.

"Not yet, Mr. Wing," said Mr. Queen.

"I have never been so insulted—" began Madame Mephisto.

"And you," said Mr. Queen with a little bow, "would be wise to hold your tongue, Madame Lucadamo."

Paula nudged him in fierce mute inquiry, but he shook his head. He looked perplexed.

No one said anything until, near the end of the second quarter, Roddy Crockett broke loose for a 44-yard gain, and on the next play the ball came to rest on Carolina's 26-yard line.

Then Pop Wing was on his feet, cheering lustily, and even Gabby Huntswood was yelling in his cracked, unoiled voice: "Come on, Trojans!"

"Attaboy, Gabby," said Pop with the ghost of a grin. "First time I've ever seen you excited about a football game."

Three plays netted the Trojans 11 yards more: first down on Carolina's 15-yard line! The half was nearly over. Pop was hoarse, the theft apparently forgotten. He groaned as USC lost ground, Ostermoor breaking up two plays. Then, with the ball on Carolina's 22-yard line, with time for only one more play before the whistle ending the half, the Trojan quarterback called for a kick formation and Roddy booted the ball straight and true between the uprights of the Spartans' goal.

The whistle blew. Carolina 6, USC 3.

Pop sank back, mopping his face. "Have to do better. That damn Ostermoor! What's the matter with Roddy?"

During the rest period Mr. Queen, who had scarcely watched the struggle, murmured: "By the way, Madame, I've heard a good deal about your unique gift of divination. We can't seem to find the sapphires by natural means; how about the supernatural?"

Madame Mephisto glared at him. "This is no time for jokes!"

"A true gift needs no special conditions," smiled Mr. Queen.

"The atmosphere—scarcely propitious——"

"Come, come, Madame! You wouldn't overlook an opportunity to restore your host's hundred thousand dollar loss?"

Pop began to inspect Madame with suddenly keen curiosity.

Madame closed her eyes, her long fingers at her temples. "I see," she murmured, "I see a long jewel-case . . . yes, it is closed, closed . . . but it is dark, very dark . . . it is in a, yes, a dark place . . ." She sighed and dropped her hands, her dark lids rising. "I'm sorry. I can see no more."

"It's in a dark place, all right," said Mr. Queen dryly. "It's in my pocket." And to their astonishment he took from his pocket the great man's jewel-case.

Mr. Queen snapped it open. "Only," he remarked sadly, "it's empty. I found it in a corner of the Trojans' dressing-room."

Joan shrank back, squeezing a tiny football charm so hard it collapsed. The millionaire gazed stonily at the parading bands blaring around the field.

"You see," said Mr. Queen, "the thief hid the sapphires somewhere and dropped the case in the dressing-room. And we were all there. The question is: Where did the thief cache them?"

"Pardon me," said the Grand Duke. "Eet seems to me the theft must have occurred in Meester Wing's car, after he returned the jewel-case to his pocket. So perhaps the jewels are hidden in the car."

"I have already," said Mr. Queen, "searched the car."

"Then in the Trojan dressing-room!" cried Paula.

"No, I've also searched there—floor to ceiling, lockers, cabinets, clothes, everything. The sapphires aren't there."

"The thief wouldn't have been so foolish as to drop them in an aisle on the way to this box," said Paula thoughtfully. "Perhaps he had an accomplice——"

"To have an accomplice," said Mr. Queen wearily, "you must know you are going to commit a crime. To know that you must know there will be a crime to commit. Nobody but Mr. Wing knew that he intended to take the sapphires with him today—is that correct, Mr. Wing?"

"Yes," said Pop. "Except Rod—Yes. No one."

"Wait!" cried Joan passionately. "I know what you're all thinking. You think Roddy had—had something to do with this. I can see it—yes, even you, Pop! But don't you see how silly it is? Why should Rod steal something that will belong to him, anyway? I *won't* have you thinking Roddy's a—a thief!"

"I did not," said Pop feebly.

"Then we're agreed the crime was unpremeditated and that no accomplice could have been provided for," said Mr. Queen. "Incidentally, the sapphires are not in this box. I've looked."

"But it's ridiculous!" cried Joan. "Oh, I don't care about losing the jewels, beautiful as they are; Pop can afford the loss; it's just that it's such a mean, dirty thing to do. Its very cleverness makes it dirty."

"Criminals," drawled Mr. Queen, "are not notoriously fastidious, so long as they achieve their criminal ends. The point is that the thief has hidden those gems somewhere— the place is the very essence of his crime, for upon its simplicity and later accessibility depends the success of his theft. So it's obvious that the thief's hidden the sapphires where no one would spot them easily, where they're unlikely to be found even by accident, yet where he can safely retrieve them at his leisure."

"But heavens," said Paula, exasperated, "they're not in the car, they're not in the dressing-room, they're not on any of us, they're not in this box, there's no accomplice . . . it's impossible!"

"No," muttered Mr. Queen. "Not impossible. It was done. But how? How?"

The Trojans came out fighting. They carried the pig-skin slowly but surely down the field toward the Spartans' goal line. But on the 21-yard stripe the attack stalled. The diabolical Mr. Ostermoor, all over the field, intercepted a forward pass on third down with 8 yards to go, ran the ball back 51 yards, and USC was frustrated again.

The fourth quarter began with no change in the score; a feeling that was palpable settled over the crowd, a feeling that they were viewing the first Trojan defeat in its Rose Bowl history. Injuries and exhaustion had taken their toll of the Trojan team; they seemed dispirited, beaten.

"When's he going to open up?" muttered Pop. "That trick!" And his voice rose to a roar. "Roddy! Come on!"

The Trojans drove suddenly with the desperation of a last strength. Carolina gave ground, but stubbornly. Both teams tried a kicking duel, but Ostermoor and Roddy were so evenly matched that neither side gained much through the interchange.

Then the Trojans began to take chances. A long pass— successful. Another!

"Roddy's going to town!"

Pop Wing, sapphires forgotten, bellowed hoarsely; Gabby shrieked encouragement; Joan danced up and down; the Grand Duke and Madame looked politely interested; even Paula felt the mass excitement stir her blood.

But Mr. Queen sat frowning in his seat, thinking and thinking as if cerebration were a new function to him.

The Trojans clawed closer and closer to the Carolina goal line, the Spartans fighting back furiously but giving ground, unable to regain possession of the ball.

First down on Carolina's 19-yard line, with seconds to go!

"Roddy, the kick! The kick!" shouted Pop.

The Spartans held on the first plunge. They gave a yard on the second. On the third—the inexorable hand of the big clock jerked towards the hour mark—the Spartans' left tackle smashed through USC's line and smeared the play for a 6-yard loss. Fourth down, seconds to go, and the ball on Carolina's 24-yard line!

"If they don't go over next play," screamed Pop, "the game's lost. It'll be Carolina's ball and they'll freeze it . . . *Roddy!*" he thundered. *"The kick play!"*

And, as if Roddy could hear that despairing voice, the ball snapped back, the Trojan quarterback snatched it, held it ready for Roddy's toe, his right hand between the ball and the turf . . . Roddy darted up as if to kick, but as he reached the ball he scooped it from his quarterback's hands and raced for the Carolina goal line.

"It worked!" bellowed Pop. "They expected a place kick to tie—and it worked! *Make it, Roddy!*"

USC spread out, blocking like demons. The Carolina team was caught completely by surprise. Roddy wove and slithered through the bewildered Spartan line and crossed the goal just as the final whistle blew.

"We win! We win!" cackled Gabby, doing a war dance.

"Yowie!" howled Pop, kissing Joan, kissing Paula, almost kissing Madame.

Mr. Queen looked up. The frown had vanished from his brow. He seemed serene, happy.

"Who won?" asked Mr. Queen genially.

But no one answered. Struggling in a mass of worshipers, Roddy was running up the field to the 50-yard line; he dashed up to the box and thrust something into Pop Wing's hands, surrounded by almost the entire Trojan squad.

"Here it is, Pop," panted Roddy. "The old pigskin. Another one for your collection, and a honey! Joan!"

"Oh, Roddy."

"My boy," began Pop, overcome by emotion; but then he stopped and hugged the dirty ball to his breast.

Roddy grinned and, kissing Joan, yelled: "Remind me that I've got a date to marry you tonight!" and ran off towards the Trojan dressing-room followed by a howling mob.

"Ahem!" coughed Mr. Queen. "Mr. Wing, I think we're ready to settle your little difficulty."

"Huh?" said Pop, gazing with love at the filthy ball. "Oh." His shoulders sagged. "I suppose," he said wearily, "we'll have to notify the police——"

"I should think," said Mr. Queen, "that that isn't necessary, at least just yet. May I relate a parable? It seems that the ancient city of Troy was being besieged by the Greeks, and holding out very nicely, too; so nicely that the Greeks, who were very smart people, saw that only guile would get them into the city. And so somebody among the Greeks conceived a brilliant plan, based upon a very special sort of guile; and the essence of this guile was that the Trojans should be made to do the very thing the Greeks had been unable to do themselves. You will recall that in this the Greeks were successful, since the Trojans, overcome by curiosity and the fact that the Greeks had sailed away, hauled the wooden horse with their own hands into the city and, lo! that night, when all Troy slept, the Greeks hidden within the horse crept out, and you know the rest. Very clever, the Greeks. May I have that football, Mr. Wing?"

Pop said dazedly: "Huh?"

Mr. Queen, smiling, took it from him, deflated it by opening the valve, unlaced the leather thongs, shook the limp pigskin over Pop's cupped hands . . . and out plopped the eleven sapphires.

"You see," murmured Mr. Queen, as they stared speechless

at the gems in Pop Wing's shaking hands, "the thief stole the jewel-case from Pop's coat pocket while Pop was haranguing his beloved team in the Trojan dressing-room before the game. The coat was lying on a rubbing table and there was such a mob that no one noticed the thief sneak over to the table, take the case out of Pop's coat, drop it in a corner after removing the sapphires, and edge his way to the table where the football to be used in the Rose Bowl game was lying, still uninflated. He loosened the laces surreptitiously, pushed the sapphires into the space between the pigskin wall and the rubber bladder, tied the laces, and left the ball apparently as he had found it.

"Think of it! All the time we were watching the game, the eleven sapphires were in this football. For one hour this spheroid has been kicked, passed, carried, fought over, sat on, smothered, grabbed, scuffed, muddied—with a king's ransom in it!"

"But how did you know they were hidden in the ball," gasped Paula, "and who's the thief, you wonderful man?"

Mr. Queen lit a cigaret modestly. "With all the obvious hiding places eliminated, you see, I said to myself: 'One of us is a thief, and the hiding place must be accessible to the thief after this game.' And I remembered a parable and a fact. The parable I've told you, and the fact was that after every winning Trojan game the ball is presented to Mr. Percy Squires Wing."

"But you can't think—" began Pop, bewildered.

"Obviously you didn't steal your own gems," smiled Mr. Queen. "So, you see, the thief had to be someone who could take equal advantage with you of the fact that the winning ball is presented to you. Someone who saw that there are two ways of stealing gems: to go to the gems, or to make the gems come to you.

"And so I knew that the thief was the man who, against all precedent and his taciturn nature, has been volubly imploring the Trojan team to win this football game; the man who knew that if the Trojans won the game the ball would immediately be presented to Pop Wing, and who gambled upon the Trojans; the man who saw that, with the ball given immediately to Pop Wing, he and he exclusively, custodian of Pop's wonderful and multifarious treasures, could retrieve the sapphires safely unobserved—grab the old coot, Your Highness!—Mr. Gabby Huntswood."

Donna
Lovell 684-8324
2447 Bush St